GOTHIC

TIME
TRAVEL
SHORT STORIES

ANTHOLOGY OF NEW & CLASSIC TALES

Foreword by David Wittenberg

FLAME TREE PUBLISHING

FANTASY

This is a FLAME TREE Book

Publisher & Creative Director: Nick Wells
Project Editor: Laura Bulbeck
Editorial Board: Gillian Whitaker, Josie Mitchell, Catherine Taylor

Publisher's Note: Due to the historical nature of the classic text, we're aware that there may be some language used which has the potential to cause offence to the modern reader. However, wishing overall to preserve the integrity of the text, rather than imposing contemporary sensibilities, we have left it unaltered.

FLAME TREE PUBLISHING
6 Melbray Mews, Fulham,
London SW6 3NS, United Kingdom
www.flametreepublishing.com

First published 20\7

Copyright © 2017 Flame Tree Publishing Ltd

Stories by modern authors are subject to international copyright law,
and are licensed for publication in this volume.

17 19 21 20 18
1 3 5 7 9 10 8 6 4 2

ISBN: 978-1-78664-463-3

The cover image is created by Flame Tree Studio
based on artwork by Slava Gerj and Gabor Ruszkai.

A copy of the CIP data for this book is available from the British Library.

Printed and bound in Turkey

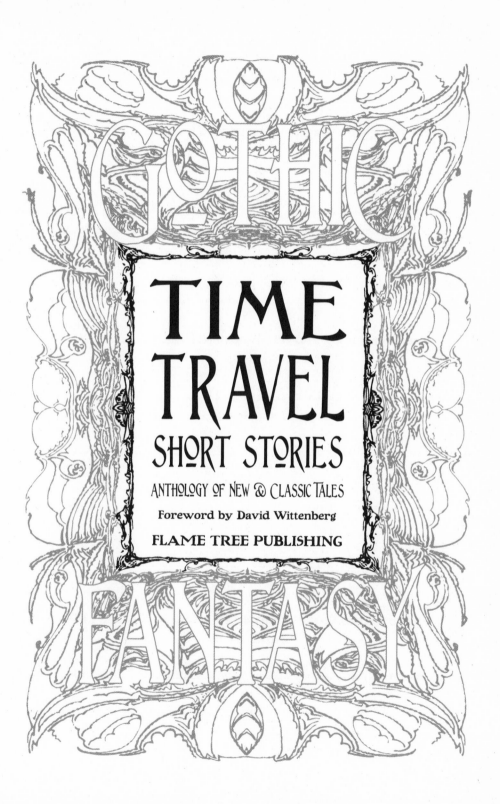

TIME
TRAVEL

SHORT STORIES

ANTHOLOGY OF NEW & CLASSIC TALES

Foreword by David Wittenberg

FLAME TREE PUBLISHING

GOTHIC

FANTASY

Contents

GOTHIC FANTASY

Foreword: Time Travel Short Stories

IT MAY SURPRISE readers to know that the sorts of spectacular time travel plots one typically encounters in contemporary science fiction, full of multiplied time lines, paradoxes, revisions of history and butterfly effects, are a late innovation of the genre. In its earliest forms, time-travel fiction was nearly always a subsidiary feature or motif of other types of literature. Sometimes, as in Charles Dickens's *A Christmas Carol* or Washington Irving's 'Rip Van Winkle', it was a catalyst for personal reflection or self-criticism – in other stories, such as L. Maria Child's 'Hilda Silfverling' or Mark Twain's *A Connecticut Yankee in King Arthur's Court*, time travel was a means to construct a fable with a credible political edge.

When the genre of utopian romance burgeoned in the second half of the nineteenth century, providing time travel with its first real heyday, time travel narrative still functioned chiefly as a tool for political prognostication. By the 1880s, and especially following the success of Edward Bellamy's *Looking Backward*, utopian writers were increasingly anxious to depict social progress in as scientific and realistic a way as possible. Time travel was a convenient means for doing just that – after all, a centuries-long coma gets your narrator more plausibly to a future that represents the direct outgrowth of *this* social present than any fantastical dream-vision or accidentally discovered subterranean kingdom. Even the most famous prototype of science-fictional time travel, H.G. Wells's *The Time Machine*, is primarily a story about politics, with Wells using his machine to show us the future evolution and eventual disintegration of British culture and class society.

It was not until the 1930s, well after the language of relativity and quantum physics had become entrenched in the popular imagination, that time travel fiction became a standalone literary type. Only then did authors begin regularly to play with time itself in their stories, giving free rein to the causal loops, historical reversals, retro-eradications of characters and events, and paradoxical multiplications of plot lines that are now standard fodder for the genre. Much literary richness was gained with this proliferation of narrative experimentation in later time travel fiction. Arguably, no other type of popular literature has been so free to contemplate and manipulate the very structures of storytelling, history and causality, or even to engage directly with the philosophy of space and time.

But with these new developments in science fiction time travel, a great deal was also lost. By the 1930s, the sociopolitical emphasis so integral to older time travel narrative, when its devices still served as means for utopian or existential speculation, was gone save for remnants and echoes. Looking back through the classic time travel stories in this anthology, the reader can perhaps appreciate the very direct engagement of these early authors with politics both present and future, and their simultaneous aspirations toward scientific social theory and persuasive literary realism.

There are sporadic moments that anticipate later time travel fiction in its more obviously science-fictional mode, for instance the fourth-dimensional navigation of Wells's time machine, the hints of reverse causality in Edward Page Mitchell's 'The Clock That Went Backward', and the comical pseudo-physics of Copernicus Droop in Harold Steele Mackaye's *The Panchronicon*. But the most genuine pleasure of reading these classic stories may be in observing their deeply ethical conviction that the purpose of time travelling is to help us draw clear-eyed, realistic portraits of society, industry, progress and conflict – a conviction that, like utopianism and realism themselves, eventually gave way to the more narratively complex but less politically self-reflective time travel of twentieth- and twenty-first-century science fiction.

David Wittenberg

Publisher's Note

STORIES OF TRAVELLING through time bring us ancient and future civilizations, terrifying visions, dreamlike utopias and cautionary tales. Time travel comes in a variety of forms, and within this volume you'll find it all: from the time machines of Edward Page Mitchell and H.G. Wells, to cross-time communication in Rudyard Kipling's 'Wireless' or cryopreservation in L. Maria Child's 'Hilda Silfverling'. As our collection of books grows, so too does the task of finding new classic fiction. In order to create what we believe to be a truly good stand-alone Time Travel collection, we have included a small number of classic stories which appear in some of our other anthologies – these were tales we felt it would be detrimental to leave out, and we wanted to make sure there's a great mix of classic fiction on offer. In this same spirit, there were novels we felt we had to include and so we offer extracts here, with a link at the end to download the full novel for free.

Every year the response to our call for submissions seems to grow and grow, giving us a rich universe of stories to choose from, but making our job all the more difficult in narrowing down the final selection. We've loved delving into so many realms of possibility, and ultimately chose a selection of stories we hope sit comfortably alongside each other and with the classic selection, to provide a fantastic *Time Travel* book for all to enjoy.

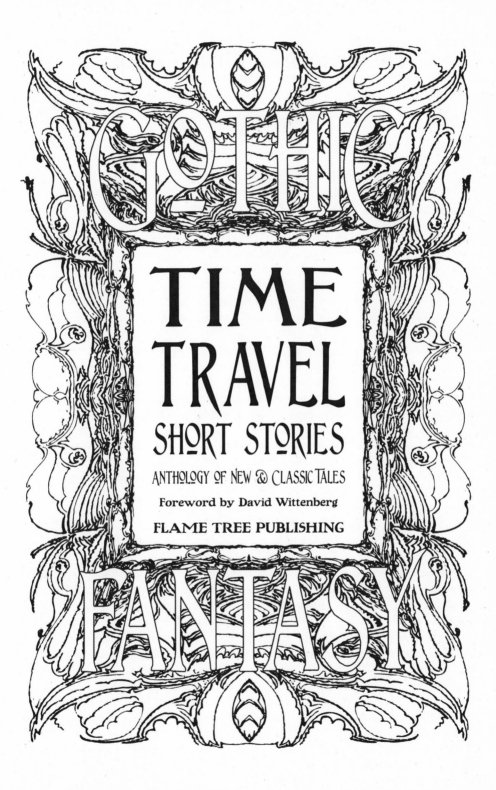

GOTHIC

TIME TRAVEL

SHORT STORIES

ANTHOLOGY OF NEW & CLASSIC TALES

Foreword by David Wittenberg

FLAME TREE PUBLISHING

FANTASY

Tourmalin's Time Cheques

F. Anstey

The Prologue

MR. PETER TOURMALIN was sitting, or rather lying, in a steamer-chair, on the first-class saloon-deck of the P. and O. ship *Boomerang*, which had not been many days as yet on the voyage home from Sydney. He had been trying to read; but it was a hot morning, and the curry, of which he had partaken freely at breakfast, had made him feel a little heavy and disinclined for mental exertion just then, particularly as Buckle's *History of Civilization*, the first volume of which he had brought up from the ship's library, is not exactly light literature at any time.

He wanted distraction of some sort, but he could not summon up sufficient energy to rise and pace the deck, as his only acquaintance on board, a Mr. Perkins, was doing with a breezy vigor which Tourmalin found himself feebly resenting.

Another alternative was open to him, it is true: not far away were other deck-chairs, in which some of the lady passengers were reading, writing, and chatting more or less languidly. There were not very many on board – for it was autumn, a time at which homewardbound vessels are not apt to be crowded – but even in that small group there were one or two with whom it might have seemed possible to pass a little time in a pleasant and profitable manner. For instance, there was that tall, graceful girl in the navy-blue skirt, and the striped cotton blouse confined at her slender waist by a leathern belt. (Tourmalin, it should be mentioned, was in the habit of noticing the details of feminine costume.) She had regular features, gray eyes which lighted up whenever she spoke, and an expression of singular nobility and sweetness; her fair hair was fastened up in loose gleaming masses under her highly becoming straw hat.

Peter watched her surreptitiously, from time to time, from behind the third page of Buckle. She was attempting to read a novel; but her attention, like his own, wandered occasionally, and he even fancied that he surprised her now and then in the act of glancing at himself with a certain interest.

Near her was another girl, not quite so tall, and darker, but scarcely less pleasing in appearance. She wore a cool-looking pink frock, and her luxuriant bronze tresses were set off by a simple white flannel cap. She held some embroidery in her listless fingers, but was principally occupied in gazing out to sea with a wistful and almost melancholy expression. Her eyes were soft and brown, and her features piquantly irregular; giving Peter, who considered himself no mean judge of female character, the impression of a highly emotional and enthusiastic temperament. He thought he saw signs that she also honoured him by her notice.

Peter was a flat-headed little man, with weak eyes and flaxen hair; but even flat-headed little men may indulge these fancies at times, without grossly deceiving themselves.

He knew, as one does learn such things on board ship, that the name of the first young lady was Tyrrell, and that she was the daughter of a judge who had been spending the Long Vacation in a voyage to recruit his health. Of the other, he knew no more than that she was a Miss Davenport.

At present, however, he had no personal acquaintance with either of them, and, in fact, as has already been said, knew nobody on board to speak to, except the energetic Mr. Perkins, a cheery man with a large fund of general information, who was going home on some business connected with a banking house in Melbourne.

And yet it is not difficult to make acquaintances on board ship, if a man cares to do so; accident or design will provide opportunities in plenty, and two or three days at sea are equivalent to at least as many weeks on shore. And Peter being quite aware of these facts, and by no means indifferent to the society of the other sex, which, indeed he considered more interesting than that of his own, it would seem that he must have had some strong reason for having kept studiously apart from the social life on board the *Boomerang*.

He had a reason, and it was this: he was an engaged man, and on his probation. A bachelor, still under thirty, of desultory habits which unfitted him to shine in any profession, he had a competency – that refuge of the incompetent – which made him independent.

Some months previously he had had the good fortune to meet with a lady somewhat his junior in years, but endowed with charms of mind and character which excited his admiration and reverence. He recognized that she supplied the qualities in which he felt himself deficient; he was weary of the rather purposeless life he had led. He wanted a wife who would regulate and organize his existence; and Miss Sophia Pinceney, with her decision and her thoroughness, was eminently the person to do it. So it was not long before he took courage and proposed to her.

Miss Pinceney, though she had been highly educated, and possessed a considerable fortune of her own, was by no means inclined to look unfavourably upon such a suitor. He might not be quite her intellectual equal, but he was anxious to improve his mind. He was amiable and amenable, and altogether likely, under careful guidance, to prove an excellent husband.

But she was prudent, and reason told her that the suddenness of Peter's passion was no guarantee of its enduring qualities. She had heard and seen too much of a rather catholic susceptibility in his nature, to feel it safe to incur so grave a risk as marriage until she had certain proof that his attachment to her was robust enough to bear the severest test; and to that test she was determined to submit him.

She consented to an engagement on one condition, that he was to take a long voyage. If he returned in the same mind, she would be sufficiently sure of his constancy to marry him as soon as he wished: if he did not, her misgivings would be amply justified. There was very little sentiment about Sophia; she took a practical and philosophical view of the marriage union, as became a disciple of Ibsen.

"I like you, Peter," she told him frankly; "you have many qualities that endear you to me, but I don't feel that I can depend upon you at present. And from what I know of you, I fear it is only too probable that absence and the attractive society of a passenger-ship may lead you to discover that you have mistaken the depth of the feeling you entertain for me."

"But look here, Sophia," he had expostulated; "if you're afraid of that, why do you make me go?"

"Because," she had replied, with her admirable common sense, "because, if my fears should prove to be unhappily only too well-founded, I shall, at least, have made the discovery before it is too late."

And, in spite of all his protests, Peter had to go. Sophia sought to reconcile him to this necessity by pointing out the advantages of travel, the enlarging effect it would have upon his mind, and the opportunities a long sea-voyage afforded for regular and uninterrupted study on the lines she had already mapped out for him; but despite these consolations, he went away in low spirits. When the moment came for parting, even the strong-minded Sophia was seized with a kind of compunction.

"Something tells me, Peter," she said, "that the ordeal will prove too much for you: in spite of your good resolutions, you will sooner or later be drawn into some flirtation which will make you forget me. I know you so well, Peter!"

"I wish you could show a little more confidence in me," he had answered in a wounded tone. "Since I met you, Sophia, I have ceased to be the butterfly I was. But as you seem to doubt me, it may relieve your mind if I promise faithfully that, while I am away from you, I will never, under any inducement, allow myself to overstep the limits of the most ordinary civility toward any woman with whom I may be brought in contact. I swear it, Sophia! Are you satisfied now?"

Perhaps he had a secret prevision that a time might come when this oath would prove a salutary restraint upon his straying fancy, and it certainly had an immediate and most reassuring effect upon Sophia.

Tourmalin had gone out to Australia, had seen something of the country during his stay in the colony, and was now, as we have seen, on his return; and during the whole time his oath, to his great credit, had been literally and faithfully kept.

During the voyage out, he had been too persistently unwell to be inclined to dally with sentiment; but in his subsequent wanderings, he had avoided, or rather escaped, all intercourse with any Colonial ladies who might by any possibility affect his allegiance to Sophia, whose image consequently still held undisputed possession of his heart.

In case he should feel himself wavering at any time, he had been careful to provide himself with a talisman in the shape of a photograph, the mere sight of which would be instantly effectual. But somehow, since he had been on board the *Boomerang*, the occasions on which he had been driven to refer to this photograph had been growing more and more frequent; while, at the same time, he had a tormenting consciousness that it took an increasingly longer time to work.

He brought it out now, and studied it attentively. It was the likeness of a girl without any great pretensions to beauty, with dark hair rolled neatly back from a massive brow that shone with intellectuality; penetrating eyes, whose keenness was generally tempered by folding glasses; a large, firm mouth, and a square chin; altogether, the face of a young woman who would stand no trifling.

He put it back respectfully in his pocket; but the impulse to go across and drop, in an accidental fashion, into a vacant seat near one of those two girls was still unconquered. He was feeling so dull; he had got such a very little way into the *History of Civilization*, a work which he was reading rather for Sophia's satisfaction than his own, and there was such a lot more of it! Might he not allow himself a brief holiday, and beguile the long weary morning with a little cheerful conversation? It was most unlikely, strict etiquette being by general consent suspended on board ship, that either young lady would resent a hazarded remark at all events, he could but try.

But then his oath – his rash and voluntary oath to Sophia – what of that? He had not, it was true, debarred himself from ordinary civility; but could he be sure of keeping always within those bounds if the acquaintanceship was once established? He had reasons for doubting this very seriously. And, besides, had not Sophia more than hinted in her last letter that, as a reward for his fidelity, she might join the ship at Gibraltar with her mother, and so put an earlier end to his term of probation? He could not be too careful. After holding out so long, it would be madness to relax his precautions now. No, he would resist these Sirens, like a modern Ulysses; though, in the latter's case, the Sirens were not actually on board, and, even then, the hero had to be lashed to the mast. But Tourmalin felt confident, notwithstanding, that he would prove at least as obdurate as the wily Greek.

He was not a strong-minded man; but he had one quality which is almost as valuable a safeguard against temptation as strength of mind – namely, timidity.

His love for his betrothed was chastened by a considerable dash of awe, and he was resolved not to compromise himself in her eyes just for the sake of a little temporary distraction.

At this point of his deliberations he looked at his watch: it was close upon twelve; only one hour to be got through before tiffin. Why, an hour was nothing; he could surely contrive to kill it over Buckle! A little courage, a little concentration, and he would certainly attain to an interest in 'the laws which govern human actions.'

The ship's bells were just striking; he counted the strokes: one, two, three, four, five – and no more! There must be some mistake; it could not possibly be only halfpast ten. Why, it was hours since breakfast!

"Looking at your watch, eh?" said his friend Perkins, as he reached Peter's chair for about the hundredth time. "Ah! You're fast, I see. Haven't altered your watch yet? They've put the ship's clock back again this morning; nearly half an hour it was this time – it was rather less yesterday and the day before: we shall go on gaining so much extra time a day, I suppose, till we get to Gib."

"You don't mean to tell me that!" exclaimed Peter, with a half-suppressed groan. If the time had seemed tedious and interminable enough before, how much more so was it now! How infinitely greater would the effort be to fix his thoughts resolutely on Buckle, and ignore the very existence of his distracting neighbors, now that it was to be daily prolonged in this exasperating manner!

"You don't seem to appreciate the arrangement?" remarked the Manager, as he allowed himself to drop cautiously – for he was a bulky man – into a hammock-chair beside Tourmalin.

"Appreciate it!" said Peter, with strong disgust. "Aren't there enough half-hours, and confoundedly long ones, too, in the day as it is, without having extra ones forced on you like this? And giving it to us in the daytime, too! They might at least put the clock back at night, when it wouldn't so much matter. I do think it's very bad management, I must say!"

His companion began a long explanation about the meridian, and sun's time, and ship's time, and Greenwich time, to which Peter gave but a very intermittent attention, so stupefied did he feel at this unwelcome discovery.

"It's a curious thing to think of," the other was saying thoughtfully, "that a man by simply making a voyage like this, should make a clear gain of several hours which he would never have had at all if he had stayed at home!"

"I would much rather be without them," said Peter. "I find it quite difficult enough to spend the time as it is; and how on earth I can spend any more, I don't know!"

"Why spend it, then?" asked his friend quietly.

"What else am I to do with it?"

"What else? See here, my friend; when you have an amount of spare cash that you've no immediate use for, you don't let it lie idle at home, do you? You pay it in to your credit at a bank, and let it remain on deposit till you *do* want it – eh? Well, then, why not treat your spare time as you would your spare cash. Do you see what I mean?"

"Not altogether," confessed Peter, considerably puzzled.

"It's simple enough nowadays. For instance, the establishment I have the honour to be connected with – the Anglo-Australian Joint Stock Time Bank, Limited – confines itself, as you are doubtless aware, almost entirely to that class of business."

"Ah!" said Peter, no more enlightened than before, "does it indeed? Would you mind explaining what particular class of business it carries on? I don't quite understand."

"Bless my soul, sir!" said the Manager, rather irritably, you must be uncommonly ignorant of financial matters not to have heard of this before! However, I will try to make it clear to you. I dare say you have heard that 'Time is money?' Very well, all our operations are conducted on that principle. We are prepared to make advances, on good security of course, of time to almost any amount; and we are simply overwhelmed with applications for loans. Business men, as you may know, are perpetually pressed for time, and will consent to almost anything to obtain it. Our transactions in time, sir, are immense. Why, the amount of Time passing through our books annually during the last ten years, averages – ah! About sixty centuries! That's pretty well, I think, sir?"

He was so perfectly business-like and serious that Peter almost forgot to see anything preposterous in what he said.

"It sounds magnificent," he said politely; "only you see, I don't want to borrow any time myself. I've too much on my hands already."

"Just so," said the Manager; "but if you will kindly hear me out, I am coming to that. Lending time is only one side of our business; we are also ready to accept the charge of any spare time that customers may be willing to deposit with us, and, with our experience and facilities, I need hardly say that we are able to employ it to the best advantage. Now, say, for example, that you wish to open an account with us. "Well, we'll take these spare half-hours of yours that are only an encumbrance to you at present, and if you choose to allow them to remain on deposit, they will carry interest at five per cent, per month; that is, five minutes on every hour and three quarters roughly, for each month, until you withdraw them. In that way alone, by merely leaving your time with us for six months you will gain – now, let me see – over three additional hours in compound interest on your original capital of ten hours or so. And no previous notice required before withdrawal! Let me tell you, sir, you will not find many banks do business on such terms as that!"

"No," said Peter, who could not follow all this arithmetic, "so I should imagine. Only, I don't quite see, if you will pardon my saying so, what particular advantage I should gain if I did open an account of this sort."

"You don't? You surprise me, you really do! Here are you, with these additional hours lying idle on your hands; you didn't expect 'em, and don't want 'em. But how do you know that you *mayn't* be glad of 'em at some time or other? Just think how grateful you might be hereafter, if you could get back a single one of these half-hours which you find so tedious now. Half an hour on board a fine ship like this, splendid weather, bracing sea air, perfect rest, pleasant company, and so on – why, you'd be willing to pay any money for it! Well, bank your extra time; and you can draw every individual hour in quarters, halves, or wholes, when you please and *as* you please. *That's* the advantage of it, sir!"

"I think I see," said Peter; "only how am I to make the deposit in the first instance?"

"That's easily arranged. The captain can't compel you to accept the time now by merely putting back the hands of the clock, can he? So all *you* have to do is to abstain from altering your watch so long as you are on board, and to fill up a little form; after which I shall be happy to supply you with a book of Time Cheques, which you can fill up and present whenever you wish to spend a given number of minutes in the pleasantest possible of ways."

"But where am I to present these cheques?" inquired Peter.

"Oh!" said the Manager, "there will be no difficulty whatever about that. Any clock will cash it for you – provided, of course, that it hasn't stopped. You merely have to slip your cheque underneath or behind it, and you will at once be paid whatever amount of time the cheque is drawn for. I can show you one of our forms if you like?"

Here he brought out a bulky leather case, from which he extracted a printed document, which he handed to Peter.

Peter, however, being naturally cautious, felt a hesitation which he scarcely liked to confess.

"You see," he said, "the fact is, I should like to know first…I've never been engaged in a – a transaction of tins kind before; and, well what 1 mean is, do I incur any risk of – er – a supernatural character?…It isn't like that business of Faust's, eh, don't you know?"

The Manager took back the paper with an abruptness which showed that his temper was ruined by this suspicion.

"My good sir!" he said, with a short offended laugh, "don't, on any account, imagine that *I* care two pins whether you become a depositor or not. I dare say our house will continue to exist without your account. As for liability, ours is a limited concern; and, besides, a deposit would not constitute you a shareholder. If you meant anything more – well, I have still to learn that there's anything diabolical about *me*, sir! I simply thought I was doing you a good turn by making the suggestion; and, besides, as a business man, I never neglect any opportunity, however small. But it's entirely as you please, I'm sure."

There was nothing in the least demoniacal, even in his annoyance, and Peter was moved to contrition and apology.

"I – I really beg your pardon!" he said. "I do hope I haven't offended you; and, if you will allow me, I shall consider it a personal favour to be allowed to open an account with your bank. It would certainly be a great convenience to draw some of this superfluous time at some future day, instead of wasting it now. Where do I sign the form?"

The Manager was appeased; and produced the form once more, indicating the place for the signature, and even providing a stylograph-pen for the purpose. It was still somewhat of a relief to Peter's mind to find that the ink it contained was of the ordinary black hue.

"And now, about cheques," said his friend, after the signature had been obtained. "How many, do you think you would require? I should say that, as the deposit is rather small, you will find fifty more than sufficient? We shall debit you with fifty seconds to cover the cheque-book. And we always recommend 'bearer' cheques as, on the whole, more convenient."

Peter said he would have fifty bearer cheques, and was accordingly given an oblong gray-green book, which, except that it was a trifle smaller, was in nowise different, outwardly, from an ordinary cheque-book. Still, his curiosity was not completely satisfied.

"There is just one question more," he said. "When I draw this time, where will it be spent?"

"Why, naturally, on board this ship," explained the Manager. "You see that the time you will get must necessarily be the extra time to which you are entitled by virtue of your passage, and which you *would* have spent as it accrued if you had not chosen to deposit it with us. By the way, when you are filling up cheques, we much prefer not to be called upon to honour drafts for less than fifteen minutes; as much more as you like, but not less. Well, then, we may consider that settled. I am extremely glad to have had the opportunity of obliging you; and I think I can promise that you will have no reason to repent of having made such a use of your time. I'll wish you good-by for the present, sir!"

The Manager resumed his hygienic tramp round the deck, leaving Peter with the chequebook in his hand. He was no longer surprised: now that he was more familiar with the idea, it seemed a perfectly natural and matter-of-fact arrangement; he only wondered that he had never thought of so obvious a plan before. And it was an immense relief to know that he had got rid of his extra hours for the present, at all events, and that he could now postpone them to a period at which they would be a boon rather than a burden.

And very soon he put the cheque-book away, and forgot all about it.

Chapter I
Tourmalin's First Cheque, And How He Took It

PETER TOURMALIN'S probation was at an end, and, what was more, he had come through the ordeal triumphantly. How he managed this, he scarcely knew; no doubt he was aided by the consciousness that the extra hours which he felt himself most liable to mis-spend had been placed beyond his disposal. At all events, when he met Sophia again, he had been able to convince her that her doubts of his constancy, even under the most trying conditions, were entirely undeserved. Now he was receiving his recompense: his engagement to Sophia was no longer conditional, but a recognized and irrevocable fact. It is superfluous to say that he was happy. Sophia had set herself to repair the deficiencies in his education and culture; she took him to scientific lectures and classical concerts, and made him read standard authors without skipping. He felt himself daily acquiring balance and seriousness, and an accurate habit of thought, and all the other qualities which Sophia wished him to cultivate.

Still, there were moments when he felt the need of halting and recovering his wind, so to speak, in the steep and toilsome climb to her superior mental level – times when he felt that his overtaxed brain absolutely required relaxation of some sort.

He felt this particularly one dreary morning, late in November, as he sat in his London chambers, staring with lack-lustre eyes at the letter he had that day received from his betrothed. For, although they met nearly every day, she never allowed one to pass without a letter – no fond and foolish effusion, be it understood, but a kind of epistolary examination paper, to test the progress he was making. This one contained some searching questions on Buckle's *History of Civilization*, which he was expected to answer by return of post. He was not supposed to look at the book, though he had; and even then he felt himself scarcely better fitted to floor the tremendous posers devised by Sophia's unwearying care.

The day before, he had had 'search-questions' in English poetry from Chaucer to Mr. Lewis Morris, which had thinned and whitened his hair; but this was, if possible, even worse.

He wished now that he had got up his Buckle more thoroughly during his voyage on the *Boomerang* and, with the name, his arrangement with the manager suddenly rose to his recollection. What had he done with that book of Time Cheques? If he could only get away, if but for a quarter of an hour – away from those sombre rooms, with their outlook on dingy house-tops and a murky, rhubarb-colored sky – if he could really exchange all that for the sunniness and warmth and delicious idleness which had once seemed so tedious, what a rest it would be! And would he not return after such an interlude with all his faculties invigorated, and better able to cope with the task he now found almost insuperable?

The first thing was to find the cheque-book, which did not take him long; though when he had found it, something made him pause before filling up a cheque. What if he had been made a fool of – if the Anglo-Australian Time Cheque Bank never existed, or had suspended payment? But that was easily settled by presenting a cheque. Why should he not, just by way of experiment? His balance was intact as yet; he was never likely to need a little ready time more than he did just then. He would draw the minimum amount, fifteen minutes, and see how the system worked.

So, although he had little real confidence that anything would happen at all, he drew a cheque, and slipped it behind the frivolous and rather incorrect little ormolu clock upon his chimney-piece.

The result was instantaneous, and altogether beyond his expectations! The four walls of his room assumed the transparency of gauze for a second, before fading entirely away; the olive fog changed to translucent blue; there was a briny breath in the air, and he himself was leaning upon the rail at the forward end of the hurricane-deck of the *Boomerang*, which was riding with a slow and stately rise and fall over the heaving swell.

That was surprising enough; but more surprising still was the discovery that he was apparently engaged in close and confidential conversation with a lovely person in whom he distinctly recognized Miss Tyrrell.

"Yes, I forgive you, Mr. Tourmalin," she was saying, with an evident effort to suppress a certain agitation; but indeed, indeed, you must never speak to me like that again!"

Now, as Peter was certainly not conscious of ever having spoken to her at all in his life, this was naturally a startling and even embarassing beginning.

But he had presence of mind enough to take in the position of affairs, and adapt himself to them. This was one of the quarters of an hour he *would* have had, and it was clear that in some portion or other of his spare time he would have made Miss Tyrrell's acquaintance in some way. Of course he ought to have been paid that particular time first; but he could easily see from her manner, and the almost tender friendliness which shone in her moistened eyes, that at this period they had advanced considerably beyond mere acquaintanceship. There had been some little mistake probably; the cheques had been wrongly numbered perhaps, or else they were honoured without regard to chronological sequence, which was most confusing.

Still, he had nothing to do but conceal his ignorance as well as he could, and pick up the loose threads as he went along. He was able, at all events, to assure her that he would not, if he could help it, incur her displeasure by speaking to her 'like that' in future.

"Thanks," she said. "I know it was only a temporary forgetfulness; and – and if what you suspect should prove to be really true – why, then, Mr. Tourmalin, then, of course, you may come and tell me so."

"I will," he said. "I shall make a point of it. Only," he thought to himself, "she will have to tell me first *what* I'm to tell her."

"And in the mean time," she said, "let us go on as before, as if you had never brought yourself to confide your sad story to me."

So he had told a sad story, had he? he thought, much bewildered; for, as he had no story belonging to him of that character, he was afraid he must have invented one, while, of course, he could not ask for information.

"Yes," he said, with great presence of mind, "forget my unhappy story – let it never be mentioned between us again. We will go on as before – *exactly* as before."

"It is our only course," she agreed. "And now," she added, with a cheerfulness that struck him as a little forced, "suppose we talk of something else."

Peter considered this a good suggestion, provided it was a subject he knew a little more about; which, unhappily, it was not.

"You never answered my question," she reminded him.

He would have liked, as Ministers say in the House, 'previous notice of that question,' but he could hardly say so in so many words.

"No," he said. "Forgive me if I say that it is a – a painful subject to me."

"I understand that," she said gently (it was more than *he* did); "but tell me only this: was it *that* that made you behave as you did? You are sure you had no *other* reason?"

["If I said I had," thought Peter, "she will ask me what it was."] "I will be as frank as possible, Miss Tyrrell," he replied. "I had *no* other reason. What other reason *could* I have had?"

"I half fancied – but I ought to have seen from the first that, whatever it was, it was not that. And now you have made everything quite clear."

"I am glad you find it so," said Peter, with a touch of envy.

"But I might have gone on misunderstanding and misjudging, putting you down as proud and cold and unsociable, or prejudiced, but for the accident which brought us together, in spite of your determination that we should remain total strangers."

It was an *accident* which had made them acquainted, then. He would draw the cheque which contained that episode of his extra time sooner or later; but it was distinctly inconvenient not to have at least *some* idea of what had happened.

"A fortunate accident for me, at all events," he said with a judicious recourse to compliment.

"It might have been a very unfortunate one for poor papa," she said, "but for you. I do believe he would have been quite inconsolable."

Peter felt an agreeable shock. Had he really been fortunate enough to distinguish himself by rescuing the Judge's fair daughter from some deadly peril? It looked very like it. He had often suspected himself of a latent heroism which had never had an opportunity of being displayed. This opportunity must have occurred, and he have proved equal to the occasion, in one of those extra hours!

"I can quite imagine that he would be inconsolable indeed!" he said gallantly. "Fortunately, I was privileged to prevent such a calamity."

"Tell me again exactly *how* you did it," she said. "I never quite understood."

Peter again took refuge in a discreet vagueness.

"Oh," he replied, modestly, "there is not much to tell. I saw the – er – danger, and knew there wasn't a moment to lose; and then I sprang forward, and – well, you know the rest as well as I do!"

"You only just caught him as he was going up the rigging, didn't you?" she asked.

So it was the Judge he had saved not his daughter! Peter felt a natural disappointment. But he saw the state of the case now: a powerful judicial intellect over-strained, melancholia, suicidal impulses – it was all very sad; but happily he had succeeded in saving this man to his country.

"I – ventured to detain him," he said, considerately, "seeing that he was – er – rather excited."

"But weren't you afraid he would bite you?"

"No," said Peter, pained at this revelation of the Judge's condition, "that possibility did *not* occur to me. In fact I am sure that – er – though the strongest intellects are occasionally subject to attacks of this sort, he would never so far forgot himself as to – er – bite a complete stranger."

"Ah!" she said, "you don't know what a savage old creature he can be sometimes. He never ought to be let loose; I'm sure he's dangerous!"

"Oh! But think, Miss Tyrrell," remonstrated Peter, unmistakably shocked at this unfilial attitude toward a distinguished parent; "if he was – er – dangerous, he would not be upon the Bench now, surely!"

She glanced over her shoulder with evident apprehension.

"How you frightened me!" she said. "I thought he was really there! But I hope they'll shut him up in future, so that he won't be able to do any more mischief. You didn't tell me how you got hold of him. Was it by his chain or his tail?"

Peter did not know; and, besides, it was as difficult for him to picture himself in the act of seizing a hypochondriacal judge by his watch-chain or coat-tail, as it was for him to comprehend the utter want of feeling that could prompt such a question from the sufferer's own daughter.

"I hope," he said, with a gravity which he intended as a rebuke – "I hope I treated him with all the respect and consideration possible under the – er – circumstances...I am sorry that that remark appears to amuse you!"

For Miss Tyrrell was actually laughing, with a merriment in which there was nothing forced.

"How can I help it?" she said, as soon as she could speak. "It is too funny to hear you talking of being regretful and considerate to a horrid monkey!"

"A *monkey*!" he repeated involuntarily.

So it was a monkey that was under restraint and not a Judge of her Majesty's Supreme Court of Judicature; a discovery which left him as much in the dark as to what particular service he had rendered as ever, and made him tremble to think what he might have said. But apparently, by singular good fortune, he had not committed himself beyond recovery; for Miss Tyrrell only said:

"I thought you were speaking of the monkey, the little wretch that came up behind papa and snatched away all his notes – the notes he had made for the great case he tried last term, and has to deliver judgment upon when the Courts sit again. Surely he told you how important they were, and how awkward it would have been if the monkey had escaped with them, and torn them into pieces or dropped them into the sea? – as he probably would have done but for you!"

"Oh, ah, yes!" said Peter, feeling slightly crest-fallen, for he had hoped he had performed a more dashing deed than catching a loose monkey. "I believe your father Sir John?" he hazarded..."Sir William, of course, thank you...did mention the fact. But it really was such a trifling thing to do."

"Papa didn't think so," she said. "He declares he can never be grateful enough to you. And, whatever it was," she added softly, and even shyly, "I, at least, can never think lightly of a service which has – has made us what we are to one another."

What they were to one another! And what was *that*? A dreadful uncertainty seized upon Peter. Was it possible that, in some way he did not understand, he was engaged to this very charming girl, who was almost a stranger to him? The mere idea froze his blood; for if that was so, how did it affect his position toward Sophia? At all hazards, he must know the worst at once!

"Tell me," he said with trembling accents, "I know you have told me already, but tell me once more precisely what we are to one another at present. It would be so much more satisfactory to my mind," he added, in a deprecatory tone, "to have that clearly understood."

"I thought I had made it quite clear already," she said, with the least suspicion of coldness, "that we can be nothing more to one another than friends."

The relief was almost too much for him. What a dear, good, sensible girl she was! How perfectly she appreciated the facts!

"*Friends*!" he cried. "Is that *all*? Do you really mean we are nothing more than friends?"

He caught her hand, in the fervor of his gratitude, and she allowed it to remain in his grasp; which in the altered state of things, he found rather pleasant than otherwise.

"Ah!" she murmured, "don't ask me for more than I have said – more than I can ever say, perhaps! Let us be content with remaining friends – dear friends, if you like – but no more!"

"I will," said Peter promptly, "I will be content. Dear friends, by all means; but no more!"

"No," she assented; "unless a time should come when –"

"Yes," said Peter, encouragingly, as she hesitated. "You were about to say, a time when –?"

Her lips moved, a faint flush stole into her cheeks; she was about to complete her sentence, when her hand seemed to melt away in his own, and he stood, grasping the empty air, by his own mantelpiece. The upper deck, the heaving bows, the blue seaboard, Miss Tyrrell herself, all had vanished; and in their stead were the familiar surroundings of his chamber, the grimy London housefronts, and Sophia's list of questions lying still unanswered upon his writing-table! His fifteen minutes had come to an end; the cheque was nowhere to be seen. The minute-hand of his clock had not moved since he last saw it; but this last circumstance, as he saw on reflection, was only natural, for otherwise the Time Deposit would have conferred no real advantage, as he would never have regained the hours he had temporarily foregone.

For some time Peter sat perfectly still, with his head between his hands, occupied in a mental review of this his initial experience of the cheque-book system. It was as different as possible from the spell of perfect rest he had anticipated; but had it been unpleasant on that account? In spite of an element of mystification at starting, which was inevitable, he was obliged to admit to himself that he had enjoyed this little adventure more than perhaps he should have done. With all his attachment to Sophia, he could hardly be insensible to the privilege of suddenly finding himself the friend – and more than that, the dear friend – of so delightful a girl as this Miss Tyrrell.

There was a strange charm, a peculiar and quite platonic tenderness about an intimacy of this peculiar and unprecedented nature, which increased at every fresh recollection of it. It increased so rapidly indeed, that almost unconsciously he drew the cheque-book toward him, and began to fill up another cheque with a view to an immediate return to the *Boomerang*.

But when he had torn the cheque out, he hesitated. It was all quite harmless: the most severe moralist could not convict him of even the most shadowy infidelity toward his finacée, if he chose to go back and follow up a purely retrospective episode like this – an episode which interested and fascinated him so strongly – only, what would Sophia say to it? Instinctively he felt that the situation, innocent as it was, would fail to commend itself to her. He had no intention of informing her, it was true; but he knew that he was a poor dissembler – he might easily betray himself in some unguarded moment, and then – No! It was vexing, no doubt; but upon the whole, it was wiser and better to renounce those additional hours on board the *Boomerang* altogether – to allow this past, that never had, but only might have been, to remain unsummoned and unknown forever. Otherwise, who could tell that, by gradual assaults, even such an affection as he had for Sophia might not be eventually undermined.

But this fear, as he saw the next moment, was almost too extravagant to be seriously taken into account. He felt nothing, and never could feel anything, but warm and sincere friendship for Miss Tyrrell; and it was satisfactory to know that she was in no danger of mistaking his sentiments. Still, of course there was always a certain risk, particularly when he was necessarily in ignorance of all that had preceded and followed the only colloquy they had had as yet. At last he decided upon a compromise: he would not cash that second cheque for the present, at all events; he would reserve it for an emergency, and only use it if he was absolutely driven to do so as a mental tonic. Perhaps Sophia would not compel him to such a necessity again; he hoped – at least he *thought* – she would not.

So he put the unpresented cheque in an inner pocket, and set to work with desperate energy at his examination-paper; although his recent change must have proved less stimulating to his jaded faculties than he had hoped, since Sophia, after reading his answers, made the cutting remark that she scarcely knew which he had more completely failed to apprehend – the purport of his author, or that of the very simple questions she had set him.

Peter could not help thinking, rather ruefully, that Miss Tyrrell would never have been capable of such severity as that; but, then, Miss Tyrrell was not his *fiancée*, only a very dear friend, whom he would, most probably, never meet again.

Chapter II
The Second Cheque

THE KNOWLEDGE that one has a remedy within reach is often as effectual as the remedy itself, if not more so; which may account for the fact that, although a considerable number of weeks had elapsed since Peter Tourmalin had drawn his second cheque on the Anglo-Australian Joint Stock Time Bank, that cheque still remained unpresented.

The day fixed for his wedding with Sophia was drawing near; the flat in the Marylebone Road, which was to be the scene of their joint felicity, had to be furnished, and this occupied most of his time. Sophia took the entire business upon herself, for she had scientific theories on the subject of decoration and color harmonies which Peter could only accept with admiring awe; but, nevertheless, she required him to be constantly at hand, so that she could consult him after her own mind had been irrevocably made up.

One February afternoon he was wandering rather disconsolately about the labyrinthine passages of one of the monster upholstery establishments in the Tottenham Court Road, his chief object being to evade the courtesies of the numerous assistants as they anxiously inquired what they might have the pleasure of showing him. He and Sophia had been there since midday; and she had sat in judgment upon carpets which were brought out, plunging like unbroken colts, by panting foremen, and unrolled before her in a blinding riot of colour. Peter had only to express the mildest commendation of any carpet to seal that carpet's doom instantly; so that he soon abstained from personal interference.

Now Sophia was in the ironmongery department, choosing kitchen utensils, and his opinion being naturally of no value on such matters, he was free to roam wherever he pleased within the limits of the building. He felt tired and rather faint, for he had had no lunch; and presently he came to a series of show-rooms fitted up as rooms in various styles: there was one inviting-looking interior, with an elaborate chimneypiece which had cosy cushioned nooks on either side of the fireplace, and into one of these corners he sank with heartfelt gratitude; for it was a comfortable seat, and he had not sat down for hours. But as his weariness wore away, he felt the want of something to occupy his mind, and searched in his pockets to see if he had any letters there – even notes of congratulation upon his approaching marriage would be better than nothing in his present reduced condition. But he had left all his correspondence at his chambers. The only document he came upon was the identical time cheque he had drawn long ago: it was creased and rumpled; but none the less negotiable, if he could find a clock. And on the built-up chimneypiece there was a clock, a small *faience* affair surmounted by a Japanese monster in peacock-blue. Moreover, by some chance, this clock was actually going – he could hear it ticking as he sat there. Should he present his cheque or not; he was feeling a little aggrieved at Sophia's treatment of him, she had snubbed him so unmercifully over the carpets; it was pleasant to think that, if he chose, he could transport himself that very instant to the society of a sweet and appreciative companion from whom snubbing was the last thing to be apprehended.

Yes; Sophia's treatment quite justified him in making an exception to the rule he had laid down for himself – he *would* present that cheque. And he rose softly from his seat and pushed the cheque under the little timepiece....

As before, his draft was honoured immediately; he found himself on a steamer-chair in a sheltered passage between two of the deck-cabins. It was night, and he could not clearly distinguish any objects around him for some little time, owing to the darkness; but from a glimmer of white drapery that was faintly visible close by, he easily inferred that there was another chair adjoining his, which could only be occupied by Miss Tyrrell. He could just hear the ship's band playing a waltz at the further end of the ship; it was one of the evenings when there had been dancing, and he and Miss Tyrrell were sitting out together.

All this he realized instantly, and not without a thrill of interest and expectation, which, however, the first words she uttered were sufficient to reduce to the most prosaic perplexity.

"What have I said?" she was moaning, in a voice hardly recognizable from emotion and the fleecy wrap in which her face was muffled – "Oh! What *have* I said?"

Peter was naturally powerless to afford her any information on this point, even if she really required it; he made a rapid mental note to the effect that their intimacy had evidently made great progress since their last interview.

"I'm afraid," he said, deciding that candour was his only course, "I can't exactly tell you what you did say; for, as a matter of fact, I didn't quite catch it."

"Ah! You say that to spare me," she murmured; "you *must* have heard; but, promise me you will forget it?"

"Willingly," said Peter, with the greatest readiness to oblige; "I will consider it forgotten."

"If I could but hope that!" she said. "And, yet," she added recklessly, "why should I care what I say?"

"To be sure," agreed Tourmalin at random, "why *should* you, you know?"

"You must have seen from the first that I was very far from being happy?"

"I must confess," said Peter, with the air of a man whom nothing escaped, "that I did observe that."

"And you were right! Was it unnatural that I should be nothing but grateful to the chance which first brought us together?"

"Not at all," said Peter, delighted to feel himself on solid ground again; "indeed, if I may speak for myself, I have even greater reason to feel grateful to that monkey."

"To *what* monkey?" she exclaimed.

"Why, naturally, my dear Miss Tyrrell, to the animal which was the unconscious instrument in making us acquainted. You surely can not have forgotten already that it *was* a monkey?"

She half rose with an impetuous movement, the mantilla fell from her face, and even in the faint starlight, he could perceive that, beautiful as that face undoubtedly was, it was as certainly not the face of Miss Tyrrell!

"*You* seem to have forgotten a great deal," she retorted, with a suppressed sob in her voice, "or you would at least remember that my name is Davenport. Why you should choose to call me Miss Tyrrell, whom I don't even know by sight, I can't conceive!"

Here was a discovery, and a startling one! It appeared that he had not merely one, but two dear friends on board this P. and O. steamer; and the second seemed, if possible, even dearer than the first! He must have made the very most of those extra hours!

There was one comfort, however, Miss Davenport did not, contrary to his impression, know Miss Tyrrell; so that they need not necessarily clash – still, it was undeniably awkward. He had to get out of his mistake as well as he could, which was but lamely.

"Why, of course" he protested, "I know you are Miss Davenport. Most stupid of me to address you as Miss Tyrrell! The – the only explanation I can offer is, that before I had the pleasure of speaking to you, I was under the impression that your proper name was *Tyrrell*, and so it slipped out again just then from habit."

This – though the literal, if not the moral, truth – did not seem to satisfy her entirely.

"That may be so," she said, curtly; "still it does not explain why you should address me as *Miss* Anybody, after asking and receiving permission, only last night, to call me by my Christian name!"

Obviously their relations were even closer than he had imagined. He had no idea they had got as far as Christian names already, any more than he had of what hers might happen to be.

There was a painful want of method in the manner this Time Bank conducted its business, as he could not help remarking to himself; however, Peter, perhaps, from the very timidity in his character, developed unexpected adroitness in a situation of some difficulty.

"So you did!" he said. "You allowed me to call you by your – er – Christian name; but I value such a privilege too highly to use it – er – indiscriminately."

"You are very strange tonight!" she said, with a plaintive and almost childish quiver of the lip. "First you call me 'Miss Tyrrell' and then 'Miss Davenport,' and then you will have it that we were introduced by a monkey! As if I should ever allow a monkey to introduce *anybody* to me! Is saving a girl's life such an ordinary event with you, that you forget all about such a trifle?"

This last sentence compensated Peter for all that had gone before. Here was a person whose life he really *had* saved; and his heart warmed to her from that moment. Rescuing a girl from imminent bodily peril was a more heroic achievement than capturing the most mischievous of monkeys; and, besides, he felt it was far more in his style. So it was in his best manner he replied to her question:

"It would be strange, indeed," he said reproachfully, "If I could ever forget that I was the humble means of preserving you from – from a watery grave" – (he risked the epithet, concluding that on a voyage it could hardly be any other description of grave; and she did not challenge it, so he continued) – "a watery grave; but I *had* hoped you would appreciate the motive which restrained me from – er – seeming to dwell upon such a circumstance."

This appeal, unprincipled as it was, subdued her instantly.

"Oh, forgive me!" she said, putting out her hand with the prettiest penitence. "I might have known you better than that. I didn't mean it. Please say you forgive me, and – and call me Maud again!"

Relief at being supplied with a missing clue made Peter reckless; indeed, it is to be feared that demoralization had already set in; he took the hand she gave him, and it did not occur to him to let it go immediately.

"Maud, then," he said obediently; "I forgive you, Maud."

It was a prettier name to pronounce than Sophia.

"How curious it is," she was saying, dreamily, as she nestled comfortably in her chair beside him, "that, up to the very moment when you rushed forward that day, I scarcely gave your existence a thought! And now – how little we ever know what is going to happen to us, do we?"

["Or what *has* happened, for that matter!" he thought.] This time he would not commit himself to details until he could learn more about the precise nature of his dauntless act, which he at once proceeded to do.

"I should very much like to know," he suggested, "what your sensations were at that critical moment."

"My sensations? I hardly know," she said, "I remember leaning over the bulwarks, is it?" (Peter said it *was* bulwarks) – "the bulwarks, watching a sailor in a little balcony below, who was doing something with a long line –"

"Heaving the lead," said Peter; "so he was – go on!"

He was intensely excited; it was all plain enough: she had lost her balance and fallen overboard; he had plunged in, and gallantly kept her above water till help arrived. He had always known he was capable of this sort of thing; now he had proved it.

"– When all at once," she continued, "I felt myself roughly dragged back by somebody – that was you! I was rather angry for the moment, for it did seem quite a liberty for a total stranger to take, – when, that very instant, I saw the line with a great heavy lump of lead at the end of it whirled round exactly where my head had been, and then I knew that I owed my life to your presence of mind!"

Peter was more than disappointed – he was positively disgusted at this exceedingly tame conclusion; it *did* seem hard that, even under conditions when any act of daring might have been possible to him, he could do nothing more brilliant than this. It was really worse than the monkey business!

"I'm afraid you make too much of the very little I did," he said.

"Do I? Perhaps that is because if you had not done it, we should never come to know one another as we do!" (So far, it was a very one-sided sort of knowledge, Peter thought.) "And yet," she added, with a long-drawn sigh, "I sometimes think that we should both be happier if we never *had* known one another; if you had stood aside, and the lead had struck me and I had died!"

"No, no!" said Peter, unfeignedly alarmed at this morbid reflection, "you mustn't take such a gloomy view of it as all that, you know!"

"Why not?" she said, in a sombre tone. "It is gloomy – *how* gloomy I know better than you!" ("She might well do that," thought Tourmalin.) "Why did I not see that I was slowly, imperceptibly drifting – drifting?"

"Well," said Peter, with a levity he was far from feeling, "if the drifting was imperceptible, you naturally *wouldn't* see it, you know!"

"You might have spared a joke at such a time as this!" she cried, indignantly.

"I – I wasn't aware there was a close time for jokes," he said, humbly; "not that it was much of a joke!"

"Indeed it was not," she replied. "But oh, Peter, *now* we have both drifted!"

"Have we?" he exclaimed, blankly. "I – I mean – *haven't* we!"

"I was so blind – so willfully, foolishly blind! I told myself we were friends!"

"Surely we are?" he said, retaking possession of her hand; he had entirely forgotten Sophia in the ironmongery department, at Tottenham Court Road. "I – I understood we were on that footing?"

"No," she said, "let us have no subterfuges any more – we must look facts in the face. After what we have both said tonight, we can no longer deceive ourselves by words... Peter," she broke off suddenly, "I am going to ask you a question, and on your answer my fate – and yours too, perhaps – will depend! Tell me truthfully..." Her voice failed her for the moment, as she bent over toward him, and clutched his arm tightly in her excitement; her eyes shone with a wild, intense eagerness for his reply...."Would you –" she repeated...

"Would you have the bottle-jack all brass, or japanned? The brass ones are a shilling more."

Peter gave a violent start, for the voice in which this most incongruous and irrelevant question was put was that of Sophia!

Miss Davenport with her hysterical appeal, the steamer-chairs, and the starlight, all had fled, and he stood, supporting himself limply by the arm of the chimney-nook in the upholsterer's showroom, staring at Sophia, who stood there, sedate and practical, inviting his attention to a couple of bottle-jacks which an assistant was displaying with an obsequious smile: the transition was rather an abrupt one.

"Oh, I think the brass one is very nice," he stammered, feebly enough.

"Then that settles it," remarked Sophia; "we'll take the *japanned* one, please," she said to the assistant.

"Aren't you feeling well, Peter dear?" she asked presently, in an undertone. "You look so odd!"

"Quite well," he said; "I – ah! – was thinking of something else for the moment, and you startled me, that's all."

"You had such a far-away expression in your eyes," said Sophia, "and you did jump so when I spoke to you; you should really try to conquer that tendency to let yourself wander, Peter."

"I will, my love," he said; and he meant it, for he had let himself wander farther than he quite intended.

Chapter III
The Third Cheque

AS THE READER may imagine, this second experience had an effect upon Peter that was rather deterrent than encouraging.

It was a painful piece of self-revelation to find that, had he chosen to avail himself of the extra hours on board the *Boomerang* as they occurred, he would have so employed them as to place himself in relations of considerable ambiguity toward two distinct young ladies. How far he was committed to either, or both, he could not tell; but he had an uneasy suspicion that neither of them would have been quite so emotional had he conducted himself with the same prudence that had marked his behaviour throughout the time which he *was* able to account for.

And yet his conscience acquitted him of any actual default; if he had ever really had any passages at all approaching the sentimental with either Miss Tyrrell or Miss Davenport, his mind could hardly be so utterly blank on the subject as it certainly was. No; at the worst, his failings were only potential peccadilloes, the kind of weaknesses he might have given way to if he had not wisely postponed the hours in which the occasions were afforded.

He had had a warning, a practical moral lesson which had merely arrived, as such things often do, rather after date.

But, so far as it was possible to profit by it, he would: at least, he would abstain from making any further inroads upon the balance of extra time which still remained to his credit at the bank; he would draw no further cheques; he would return to that P. and O. steamer no more. For an engaged man whose wedding day was approaching by leaps and bounds, it was – however innocent – too disturbing and exciting a form of distraction to be quite safely indulged in.

The resolution cost him something, nevertheless. Peter was not a man who had hitherto been spoiled by feminine adoration. Sophia was fond of him, but she never affected to place him upon any sort of pinnacle; on the contrary, she looked down upon him protectingly and indulgently from a moral and intellectual pedestal of her own. He had not objected to this, in fact he rather liked it, but it was less gratifying and stimulating to his self-esteem than the romantic and idealizing sentiments which he had seemingly inspired in two exceedingly bewitching young persons with whom he felt so much in sympathy. It was an agreeable return from the bread-and-butter of engaged life to the *petits fours* of semi-flirtation. After all, Peter was but human, and a man is seldom esteemed for being otherwise. He could not help a natural regret at having to abandon experiences which, judging from the fragmentary samples he had obtained, promised so much and such varied interest. That the interest was not consecutive, only made it the more amusing – it was a living puzzle-picture, the pieces of which he could fit together as he received them. It was tantalizing to look at his cheque-book and feel that upon its leaves the rest of the story was written, but that he must never seek to decipher it: it became so tantalizing, that he locked the cheque-book up at last.

But already some of the edge had worn off his resolution, and he had begun to see only the more seductive side of interviews which at the time, had not been free from difficulty and embarrassment. Having put himself beyond the reach of temptation, he naturally began to cast about for some excuse for again exposing himself to it.

It was the eve of his wedding-day; he was in his chambers for the last time and alone, for he would not see Sophia again until he met her in bridal array at the church door, and he had no bachelor friends whom he cared to invite to help him to keep up his spirits.

Peter was horribly restless and nervous; he needed a sedative of some kind, and even trying on his wedding garments failed to soothe him, as he felt almost certain there was a wrinkle between the shoulders, and it was too late to have it altered.

The idea of one more visit to the *Boomerang* – one more interview, the last, with one or other of his amiable and fascinating friends – it did not matter very much which – presented itself in a more and more attractive light. If it did nothing else, it would provide him with something to think about for the rest of the evening.

Was it courteous, was it even right, to drop his friends without the slightest apology or explanation? Ought he not, as a gentleman and a man of honour, to go back and bid them 'Good-bye?' Peter, after carefully considering the point, discovered that it was clearly his duty to perform this trifling act of civility.

As soon as he had settled that, he got out his cheque-book from the dispatch-box, in which he had placed it for his own security, and, sitting down just as he was, drew another fifteen minutes, and cashed them, like the first, at the ormolu clock....

This time he found himself sitting on a cushioned bench in the music-room of the *Boomerang*. It was shortly after sunset, as he could tell from the bar of dusky crimson against the violet sea, which, framed in the ports opposite, rose and sank with each roll of the ship. There was a swell on, and she rolled more than he could have wished.

As he expected, he was not alone; but, as he had *not* expected, his companion was neither Miss Tyrrell nor Miss Davenport, but a grim and portly matron, who was eyeing him with a look of strong disfavour, which made Peter wish he had not come. "What," he wondered, "was he in for now?" His uneasiness was increased as he glanced down upon his trousers, which, being new and of a delicate lavender tint, reminded him that in his impatience he had come away in his wedding garments. He feared that he must present rather an odd appearance on board ship in this festal attire; but there he would have to stay for the next quarter of an hour, and he must make the best of it.

"I repeat, Mr. Tourmalin," said the matron, "you are doubtless not unprepared for the fact that I have requested a few minutes' private conversation with you?"

"Pardon me," said Peter, quaking already at this alarming opening, "but I am very much unprepared." ("Surely," he thought, "this could not be *another* dear friend? No, that was too absurd – he must have drawn the line *somewhere*!")

"Then permit me to enlighten you," she said raspingly. "I sent for you at a time when we are least likely to be interrupted, to demand an explanation from you upon a very delicate and painful matter which has recently come to my knowledge."

"*Oh!*" said Peter – and nothing more. He guessed her purpose at once; she was going to ask him his intentions with regard to her daughter! He could have wished for some indication as to whether she was Lady Tyrrell or Mrs. Davenport; but, as he had none at present, "Oh" seemed the safest remark to make.

"Life on board a large passenger-ship, Mr. Tourmalin," she went on to observe, "though relaxed in some respects, is still not without decencies which a gentleman is bound to respect."

"Quite so," said Peter, unable to discover the bearings which lay in the application of this particular observation.

"You *say* 'Quite so'; but what has your *behaviour* been, sir?"

"That," said Peter, "is exactly what I should like to know myself!"

"A true gentleman would have considered the responsibility he incurred by giving currency to idle and malicious gossip!"

His apprehensions were correct then: it *was* one of the young ladies' mothers – but *which*?

"I can only assure you, madam," he began, "that if unhappily I have – er – been the means of furnishing gossip, it has been entirely unintentional."

She seemed so much mollified by this, that he proceeded with more confidence:

"As to anything I may have said to your daughter –" when she almost bounded from her seat with fury.

"My *daughter*, sir! Do you mean to sit there and tell me that you had the audacity to so much as hint of such a thing to my daughter, of all people?"

"So – so much depends on who your daughter is!" said Peter, completely losing his head.

"You dared to strike this cruel and unmanly blow at the self-respect of a sensitive girl – to poison her defenseless ears with your false, dastardly insinuations – and you can actually admit it?"

"I don't know whether I can admit it or not yet," he replied. "And – and you do put things so very strongly! It is like this: if you are referring to any conversation I may have had with Miss Tyrrell –"

"*Miss Tyrrell*? You have told her *too*!" exclaimed this terrible old matron, thereby demonstrating that, at least, she was not Lady Tyrrell.

"I – I *should* have said Miss Davenport," said Peter, correcting himself precipitately.

"Miss Davenport as well? Upon my word! And pray, sir, may I ask how many other ladies on board this ship are in possession of your amiable confidences?"

He raised his hands in utter despair.

"I can't say," he groaned. "I don't really know what I may have said, or whom I may have said it to! I – I seem to have done so much in my spare time, but I never meant anything!"

"It may be so," she said; "indeed, you hardly seem to me accountable for your actions, or you would not appear in such a ridiculous costume as that, with a sprig of orange-blossom in jour button-hole and a high hat, too!"

"I quite feel," said Peter, blushing, "that such a costume must strike you as inappropriate; but – but I happened to be trying them on, and – rather than keep you waiting –"

"Well, well, sir, never mind your costume – the question is, if you are genuinely anxious to repair the wrong you have done, what course do you propose to take?"

"I will be perfectly frank with you, madam," said Peter: "I am not in a position to repair any wrong I have done – if I *have* done any wrong (which I don't admit) – by taking any course whatever!"

"You are *not*!" she cried. "And you tell me so to my face?"

After all, reflected Peter, why should he be afraid of this old lady? In a few more minutes he would be many hundreds of miles away, and he would take very good care not to come back again. He felt master of the situation, and determined to brazen it out.

"I do, madam!" he said, crossing his legs in an easy fashion. "Look at it from a reasonable point of view. There is safety in numbers; and if I have been so unfortunate as to give several young ladies here an entirely erroneous impression, I must leave it to you to undeceive them as considerately but distinctly as you can. For me to make any selection would only create ill-feeling among the rest; and their own good sense will show them that I am forbidden by the laws of my country, which I am the last person to set at defiance – that I am forbidden (even if I were free in other respects, which I am not) to marry them all!"

"The only possible explanation of your conduct is, that you are not in your right mind!" she said. "Who in the world spoke or dreamed of your marrying any one of them? Certainly not *I*!"

"Oh!" said Peter, hopelessly fogged once more. "I thought I might unintentionally have given them grounds for some such expectation. I'm very glad I was mistaken. You see, you must really make allowances for my utter ignorance."

"If this idiotic behaviour is not a mere feint, sir, I can make allowances for much; but, surely, you are at least sufficiently in your proper senses to see how abominably you have behaved?"

"Have I?" said Peter, submissively. "I don't wish to contradict you, if you say so, I'm sure. And, as I have some reason to believe that my stay on board this ship will not last very much longer, I should like before I go to express my very sincere regret."

"There is an easy way of proving your sincerity, sir, if you choose to avail yourself of it," she said. "I find it very difficult to believe, from the evident feebleness of your intellect, that you can be the person chiefly responsible for this scandal. Am I correct in my supposition?"

"You are, madam," said Peter. "I should never have got myself into such a tangle as this, if I had not been talked over by Mr. Perkins. I don't know if I can succeed in making myself clear, for the whole business is rather complicated; but I can try to explain it, if you will only have a little patience."

"You have said quite enough," she said. "I know all I wish, to know now. So it was Mr. Perkins who has been using you as his instrument, was it?"

"Certainly," said Peter; "but for him, nothing of this would have happened."

"You will have no objection to repeating that statement, should I call upon you to do so?"

"No," said Peter, who observed with pleasure that her wrath against himself was almost entirely moderated; "but you will have to call soon, or I shall have gone. I – I don't know if I shall have another opportunity of meeting Mr. Perkins; but if I did, I should certainly tell him that I do not consider he has treated me quite fairly. He has put me in what I may call a false position, in several false positions; and if I had had the knowledge I have now, I should have had nothing to do with him from the first. He entirely misled me over this business!"

"Very well, sir," she said; "you have shown a more gentlemanly spirit, on the whole, than I expected. I am glad to find that your evil has been wrought more by want of thought than heart. It will be for you to complete your reparation when the proper time arrives. In the mean time, let this be a warning to you, sir, never to –"...

But here Peter made the sudden discovery that he was no longer in the music-room of the *Boomerang*, but at home in his old easy-chair by his bachelor fireside.

"Phew!" he muttered to himself, "that was a bad quarter of an hour while it lasted! What an old she-dragon it was! But she's right – it *is* a warning to me. I mustn't – I really must *not* draw any more of these confounded time cheques. I've made that ship too hot to hold me already! I'd better remain forever in contented ignorance of how I spent that extra time, than to go on getting into one mess after another like this! It was a wonder I got out of this one as well as I did; but evidently that old woman knew what Perkins is, and saw *I* wasn't to blame. Now she'll explain the whole affair to all those girls (whoever they may be), and pitch into Perkins and serve him right! *I'm* out of it, at any rate; and now, thank goodness, after tomorrow I shall have nothing to do but live contentedly and happily with dearest Sophia! I'd better burn this beastly cheque-book – I shall never want it again!"

It would have been well for Peter if he had burned that cheque-book; but when it came to the point, he could not bring himself to destroy it. After all, it was an interesting souvenir of some very curious, if not unique, experiences; and, as such, he decided to preserve it.

Chapter IV
The Fourth Cheque

PETER TOURMALIN enjoyed his honeymoon extremely, in a calm, sober, and rational manner. Sophia discouraged rapture; but, on the other hand, no one was better fitted to inspire and sustain an intelligent interest in the wonders of Geology; and, catching her scientific enthusiasm, Peter spent many happy hours with her along the cliffs, searching for fossil remains. In fact, the only cloud that threatened to mar their felicity at all was an unfortunate tendency on his part to confuse a trilobite with a graptolite, a blunder for which Sophia had no tolerance. He was hazy about his periods, too, until she sent up to town for Lyell's great work on the subject as a birthday surprise for him, and he read it aloud to her on the sands. Altogether, it was a peaceful, happy time.

And never once in the whole course of his honeymoon did he seriously entertain the possibility of making any further use of his book of blank Time Cheques. If he had contemplated it, no harm would have been done, however, as the book was lying among his neglected papers at his former chambers.

He felt no poignant regret when the month came to an end, and they returned to town to take possession of their Marylebone flat: for what was it but shifting the scene of their happiness? And after this had taken place, Peter was still too much occupied to have leisure for idle and mischievous thoughts. Marrying Sophia was, indeed, like loving Sir Richard Steele's fair lady, 'a liberal education;' and Peter enjoyed the undivided benefit of her rare talent for instruction.

He had been giving his attention to Astronomy of late, an unguarded remark of his having betrayed to Sophia the extreme crudity of his ideas respecting that science, and she had insisted upon his getting a popular primer, with diagrams, and mastering it as a preliminary to deeper study.

One evening he was in the smaller room of the two that, divided by an arch, served for study and drawing-room combined; and he was busily engaged in working out a simple practical illustration, by the aid of one of the aforesaid diagrams. The experiment required a lamp, a ball of cotton, and an orange transfixed by a knitting-needle, and it had something to do with the succession of the seasons, solar and lunar eclipses, and the varying lengths of day and night on different portions of our globe, though he was not very clear what.

"Don't you find you understand the inclination of the moon's orbit to the plane of the ecliptic better now?" said Sophia, as she came through the arch.

"I think I shall, as soon as I can get the moon to keep steadier," he said, with more hope than he felt; "and it's rather hard to remember whereabouts I am supposed to be on this orange."

"I must get you something to make that clearer," she said; "and you haven't tilted the orange nearly enough. But leave it for a moment; I've brought you in this packet of letters and things the people at your old rooms have just sent down. I wish, while I am away – I shall be back in a minute – you would just run over them, and tell me if there are any papers you want kept, or if they may all be burned."

While she was gone, he undid the string which fastened the packet, and found, at the bottom of a mass of bills and documents of no value, the small oblong cheque-book which he had vowed never to see again. Somehow, as his eyes rested on its green cover, the old longing came upon him for a complete change of air and scene. He felt as if he *must* get away from that orange: there were no lamps but electric lights, and no oranges, on board the *Boomerang.*

But then, his last visit had not turned out a success: what if he were to find he had drawn another quarter of an hour with that irate matron of the music-room?

However, he had left her, as he remembered, in a comparatively pacific mood. She understood him better now; and besides, thanks to the highly erratic system (if there was any system) on which the payments were made, the chances were immensely against his coming across the same old lady twice running. He thought he would risk that. It was much more likely that he would meet Miss Tyrrell or Miss Davenport, or it might even be another person to whom he was unconsciously allied by the bond of dear friendship. The only question was, how far he could trust himself in such companionship. But here he felt himself guilty of a self-distrust that was unworthy of him. If, on the two previous occasions, he could not call to mind that he had entertained any deeper sentiment for either young lady than a cordial and sympathetic interest, was it likely that, now he was a married man, he would be more susceptible? He was as devoted to his Sophia as ever, but the wear and tear of several successive evenings spent in elementary Astronomy were telling upon his constitution. Such high thinking did not agree with him; he wanted a plainer mental diet for a change. Fifteen minutes spent in the society of someone with a mind rather less cultivated than his wife's would be very restful. Then, when he came back, he would give his whole mind to the orange again.

In short, all Peter's good resolutions were thrown overboard once more, and he wrote out a cheque for the usual amount in desperate fear lest Sophia might return before he could get it honoured. He felt a certain compunction, even then, in presenting it to the severe and intensely respectable black marble timepiece which recorded the flying hours of his domestic bliss. He almost doubted whether it would countenance so irregular a proceeding; but, although it was on the verge of striking nine, it cashed the cheque without hesitation....

It was midday: Peter was sitting on a folding seat, protected from the scorching sun by the awning which was stretched above and along the exposed side of the deck; and, to his great satisfaction, he found Miss Tyrrell reclining in a deck chair between himself and the railing, and a pleasant picture of fresh and graceful girlhood she presented.

As usual, he was not in time for the beginning of the conversation, for she was evidently commenting upon something he had said.

"How delightful it sounds," she was saying, "and what a free, unfettered kind of life yours must be, Mr. Tourmalin, from your description!"

Now, this was awkward; because he must have been giving her an airy description of his existence as the bachelor and butterfly he had ceased to be. He answered guardedly, awaiting his opportunity to lead up to a disclosure of the change in his circumstances since they had last met.

"It is pleasant enough," he said. "A little dull at times, perhaps," he added, thinking of the orange.

She laughed.

"Oh, you mustn't expect me to pity you!" she said. "I don't believe you need ever be dull, unless you choose. There must always be friends who are glad to see you."

"I am glad to think," said Peter, "that, when I do feel dull, I have at least one friend – one dear friend – from whom I may count upon a welcome!"

He accompanied this speech with such a look, that she could not well pretend to mistake his meaning; and the next moment he regretted it, for he saw he had gone too far.

"That is a very pretty speech," she said, with a faint flush; "but isn't it a little premature, Mr. Tourmalin, considering that we have scarcely known one another two days!"

For the moment, Peter had forgotten the want of consecutiveness in these eccentric Time-Cheques. This interview should by rights have preceded the first he had had with her. He felt annoyed with himself, and still more with the unbusiness-like behaviour of the Bank.

"I – I was anticipating, perhaps," he said. "But I assure you that we shall certainly *be* friends – I may even go so far as to say, dear friends – sooner or later. You see if I am not right!"

Miss Tyrrell smiled.

"Are you sure," she said, with her eyes demurely lowered – are you sure that there is nobody who might object to our being on quite such intimate terms as that?"

Peter started. Could she possibly have guessed, and how much did she know?

"There could be nothing for anybody to object to," he said. "Are you – er – referring to any person in particular?"

She still kept her eyes down, but then she was occupied just at the moment in removing a loose splinter of bamboo from the arm of her chair.

"You mustn't think me curious or – or indiscreet, if I tell you," she said; "but before I knew you to speak to, I – I couldn't help noticing how often, as you sat on deck, you used to pull something out of your pocket and look at it."

"My watch?" suggested Peter, feeling uncomfortable.

"No, not your watch; it looked more like – well, like a photograph."

"It may have been a photograph, now you mention it," he admitted. "Well, Miss Tyrrell?"

"Well," she said, "I often amuse myself by making up stories about people I meet – quite strangers, I mean. And, do you know, I made up my mind that that photograph was the portrait of someone – some lady you are engaged to. I should so much like to know if I was right or not?"

Here was Peter's opportunity of revealing his real status, and preventing all chance of future misunderstanding. It was not too late; but still it might be best and kindest to break the news gradually.

"You were partly right and partly wrong," he said: "that was the portrait of a lady I was – er – *once* engaged to."

Unless Peter was very much mistaken, there was a new light in her face, an added brightness in her soft gray eyes as she raised them for an instant before resuming her labours upon the wicker-chair.

"Then you mean," she said softly, "that the engagement is broken off?"

Peter began to recognize that explanation was a less simple affair than it had seemed. If he said that he was no longer engaged but *married* to the original of that photograph, she would naturally want to know why he had just led her to believe, as he must have done, that he was still a careless and unattached bachelor; she would ask *when* and *where* he was married; and how could he give a straightforward and satisfactory answer to such questions?

And then another side of the case struck him. As a matter of fact he was undeniably married; but would he be strictly correct in describing himself as being so *in this particular interview*? It belonged properly to the time he had made the voyage home, and he was certainly not married *then*.

In the difficulty he was in he thought it best to go on telling the truth until it became absolutely impossible, and then fall back on invention.

"The fact is, Miss Tyrrell," he said, "that I can't be absolutely certain whether the engagement is ended or not at this precise moment."

Her face was alive with the sweetest sympathy.

"Poor Mr. Tourmalin!" she said, "how horribly anxious you must be to get back and know!"

"Ah!" said Peter, "yes, I – I shall know when I get home, I suppose."

And he sighed; for the orange recurred once more to his reluctant memory.

"Don't tell me if it pains you too much," she said gently. "I only ask because I do feel so sorry for you. Do you think that, when you do get home, you will find her married?"

"I have every reason for believing so," he said.

"That will be a terrible blow for you, of course?"

"A blow?" said Peter, forgetting himself. "Good gracious me, no! Why *should* it be? I – I mean, I shall be prepared for it, don't you know?"

"Then it's not so bad, after all?" she said.

"It's not at all bad!" said Peter, with a vague intention of loyalty to Sophia. "I like it!"

"I think I understand," she said slowly: "you will not be sorry to find she has married; but she may tell you that she never had the least intention of letting you go so easily?"

"Yes," said Peter, "she may tell me that, certainly –" ("if she finds out where I've been," he added, mentally.)

"And," she continued, "what would you do then?"

"I suppose," he said – "I suppose I should have to do whatever she wished."

"Yes!" she agreed warmly, "you *will* do that, even if it costs you something, won't you? Because it will be the only right, the only honourable course to take – you will be the happier for it in the end, Mr. Tourmalin, I am sure you will!"

After all, it seemed to him that she must understand about the Time Cheques – or, why should she urge him to give them up if Sophia demanded such a sacrifice?

"No, I shall not," he said; "I shall miss these times terribly. You don't know what they are to me, or you wouldn't speak like that!"

"Mr. Tourmalin!" she cried, "I – I must not listen to you! You can't possibly mean what you seem to mean. It is wrong – wrong to me, and wrong to her – to say things that – that, for all you know, you are not free to say! Don't let me think badly of you!"

Peter was absolutely horrified! What had he said to agitate her like that? He had merely meant to express the pleasure he found in these brief and stolen visits to the *Boomerang* and she had misconstrued him like this! At all hazards, he must explain now, if it took him days to make it clear.

"My dear Miss Tyrrell," he protested earnestly, "you quite misunderstood me – you did indeed! Pray be calm, and I will endeavor to make my position a little clearer than I'm afraid I have done. The worst of it is," he added, "that the whole thing has got into such a muddle that, for the life of me, I can't exactly make out what my position is at the present moment!"

"You can if you will only recollect that you are this mourning-pin," said a familiar voice; and, with the abruptness characteristic of the Time Cheque system, he was back in his study, staring at the ground glass globe of the lamp and the transfixed orange. The clock behind him was striking nine, and Sophia was offering him a pin with a big black head.

"Oh! Am I the mourning-pin?" he repeated, helplessly.

"Really, Peter," said Sophia, "I think the pin just at this moment, has the more intelligent expression of the two. Do try to look a little less idiotic! Now, see; you stick the pin into the orange to represent your point of view, and then keep on twirling it slowly round."

So Peter twirled the orange slowly round for the remainder of the evening, though his thoughts were far away with Miss Tyrrell. He was wondering what she could have thought of him, and, worse still, what she would think if she could see him as he was employed at that moment?

"I tell you what we must do, Peter – when you get a little more advanced," said Sophia, enthusiastically, that evening, "we must see if we can't pick up a small secondhand orrery somewhere – it would be so nice to have one!"

"Oh, delightful!" he said absently.

He was not very clear as to what an orrery was, unless it was the dusty machine that was worked with handles at sundry Assembly room lectures he had attended in early youth. But of one thing he felt grimly certain – that it was something which would render it necessary to draw more Time Cheques!

Chapter V
Periodic Drawings

WHETHER it was natural sin on Peter's part, or an excusable spirit of revolt against the oppression of an orrery which Sophia succeeded in picking up a great bargain at an auction somewhere, his drafts on the Anglo-Australian Time Bank did not end with the one recorded in the preceding chapter. And, which was more discreditable still, he no longer pretended to himself that he meant to stop until his balance was completely exhausted. His only care now was to economize, to regulate his expenditure by spreading his drawings over as long a period as possible. "With this object he made a careful calculation, and found there were still several hours to his credit; whereupon, lest he should yield to the temptation of drawing too much at any one time, he made out a number of cheques for fifteen minutes apiece, and limited himself to one a week – an allowance which, even under the severest provocation, he rarely permitted himself to exceed.

These weekly excursions, short as they were, were a source of the greatest comfort to him, especially now that he had thrown off any idea of moral responsibility.

By degrees he possessed himself of most of the back-numbers, if they may be so termed, of his dual romance. At one time, he found himself being presented by the grateful Sir William to his daughter; and now that he knew what service he had rendered the Judge, he was less at sea than he would certainly have been otherwise. Another time, he discovered himself in the act of dragging Miss Davenport unceremoniously back from the bulwarks; but here again his memory furnished him with the proper excuse for conduct which, considering that he was not supposed to be acquainted with her, he might have found it difficult to account for satisfactorily. So, after all, there did seem to be a sort of method in the operation of the Time Cheques, arbitrary as it appeared.

One fact that went far to reconcile him to his own conscience was the circumstance that, though the relations he stood in toward both young ladies varied at each interview with the most bewildering uncertainty, so that one week he would be upon the closest and most confidential terms, and the next be thrown back into the conventional formality of a first introduction – these relations never again approached the dangerous level of sentiment which had so alarmed him.

He flattered himself that the judicious attitude he was adopting to both was correcting the false impressions which might have – and for that matter actually had – been given.

He was always pleased to see them again, whichever one it was; they were simply charming friends – frank, natural, unaffected girls – and not too clever. Sometimes, indeed, he recognized, and did his best to discourage, symptoms of a dawning tenderness on their part which it was not in his power to reciprocate.

Peter was in no danger of losing his heart to either; possibly the attractions of each served as a conductor to protect him from the influence of the other. He enjoyed their society, their evident appreciation of all he said and did, but that was all; and as they recognized that there could be no closer bond than that of cordial friendship between them, he was relieved of all misgivings.

Surely it was a blameless and legitimate manner, even for a married man, of spending the idle moments which belonged properly to the days of his bachelorhood! Still, he did not confide this harmless secret of his to Sophia; he might tell her when it was all over, but not so long as her disapproval could affect his plans. And he had an instinct that such a story as he had to tell would fail to appeal to a person of her accurately logical habit of mind.

So, on one occasion when he discovered that he had lost one of the loose cheques he now carried constantly about with him, it was with a feeling very like panic that he reflected that he might have dropped it about the house, where its unusual form would inevitably provoke Sophia's curiosity; and he was much reassured when he was able to conclude, from the fact that she made no reference to it, that he must have lost it out of doors.

It must have been some time after this before his serenity again met with a slight shock: he was walking up and down the deck with Miss Davenport – it happened to be one of the days when he knew her very well indeed.

"Sometimes," she was saying, "I feel as if I *must* speak to somebody!"

"You know where you will always find a very willing listener!" he said, with a kind of fatherly floweriness that he felt sat well upon him.

"I didn't mean you," she said – "to some girl of my own age, I meant."

"Oh!" said Peter, "well, that's a very natural feeling, I'm sure. I can quite understand it!"

"Then you wouldn't mind – you wouldn't be angry if I did?" she said, looking up at him with her great childishly serious eyes.

"My dear child," said Peter, getting more fatherly every moment, "how could I possibly object to your speaking to any lady on board if you want to?"

He would have liked to make one or two exceptions perhaps; but he thought he had better not.

"I am so glad," she said, "because I did – this very morning. I did so want someone to advise me – to tell me what a girl ought to do, what she would do herself in my place."

"Ah!" said Peter, sympathetically, "it is – er – a difficult position for you, no doubt."

"And for you, too!" she said quickly; "remember that."

"And for me, *too*, of course," said Peter, assenting, as he always did now from habit, to anything he did not understand at the moment. "My position might be described as one of – er – difficulty, certainly. And so you asked advice about yours, eh?"

"I couldn't very well help myself," she said. "There was a girl, a little older than I am, perhaps, sitting next to me on deck, and she mentioned your name, and somehow – I hardly know how it came about – but she seemed so kind, and so interested in it all, that – that I believe I told her everything…You aren't *angry* with me, are you, Peter?"

She had been making a *confidante* of Miss Tyrrell! It was awkward, extremely awkward and annoying, if, as he began to fear, her confidences were of a tender character.

"I – I am not exactly angry," he said; "but I do think you might be more careful whom you speak to. What did you tell her?"

"*All!*" she said, with the same little quiver in her underlip he had noticed before.

"That is no answer," said Peter (it certainly was none for him). "Tell me *what* you said?"

"I – I told her about you, and about me…and – and about *him!*"

"Oh!" said Peter, "about me, and you, and him? Well, and – and how did she *take* it?"

"She didn't say very much; she turned very pale. It was rather rough at the time, and I don't think she can be a very good sailor; for before I had even finished she got up and went below, and I haven't seen her since."

"But you told her about 'him'?" he persisted; "and when you say 'him,' I presume you refer to –?"

Here he paused expectantly.

"Of course!" she answered, with a touch of impatience. "Whom else should I be *likely* to refer to?"

"It's excessively absurd!" said Peter, driven to candour at last. "I – I remember perfectly that you did mention all the circumstances at the time; but I've a shocking memory for names, and, just for the minute, I – I find it difficult to recall where 'he' comes in exactly. Curious, isn't it?"

"Curious?" she said, passionately; "it's *abominable!*"

"It is," agreed Peter; "I quite admit that I *ought* to know – only, I *don't.*"

"This is cruel, unmanly!" she said, brokenly. "How *could* you forget – how can you insult me by *pretending* that you could forget such a thing as that? It is odious of you to make a – a joke of it all, when you know perfectly well that –"

"My – my dear young lady!" he declared, as she left her speech unfinished, "I am as far from any disposition to be jocular as ever I was in my life. Let me beg you to be a little more explicit. We seem to have got into a trifling misunderstanding, which, I am sure, a little patience will easily put right…."

"Put right?" said Sophia, behind him. "I was not aware, Peter, that the clock was out of order. What is the matter with it?"

He almost staggered back from the chimneypiece, upon which he had found himself leaning in an attitude of earnest persuasion.

"I – I was only thinking, my love," he said, "that it wanted regulating."

"If it does," said Sophia, "you are hardly the proper person to do it Peter. The less you meddle with it the better, I should think!"

"Perhaps so, my dear Sophia, perhaps so!" said Peter, sitting down with the utmost docility. He had narrowly escaped exciting suspicion. It was fortunate that there was nothing compromising in the few words she had overheard, but he must not allow himself to be caught so near the clock again.

He was not a little disturbed by the tenor of this last interview. It was bad enough that in some way he seemed to have seriously displeased Miss Davenport; but, besides that, he could not contemplate without uneasiness the probable effect which her confidences, whatever their exact purport, might have upon Miss Tyrrell. For hitherto he had seen no necessity to mention to one young lady that he was even distantly acquainted with the other.

As he never by any chance drew them both together, there seemed no object in volunteering such information.

But this only made him more apprehensive of a scene when his next turn with Miss Tyrrell arrived. Perhaps, he thought, it would be wiser to keep away from the *Boomerang* for a week or two, and give them all time to calm down a little.

However, he had the moral, or rather the immoral, courage to present a check as usual at the end of the next week, with results that were even less in accordance with his anticipations than before.

It came about in this way. He was comfortably seated by the fireplace opposite Sophia in a cosy, domesticated fashion, and was reading to her aloud; for he had been let off the orrery that evening. The book he was reading by Sophia's particular request was Ibsen's *Doll's House*, and it was not the fault of the subject (which interested her deeply), but of Peter's elocution, which was poor, that, on glancing from the text, he found that she had sunk into a profound and peaceful slumber.

It was a chance he had been waiting for all day. He was rather tired of Nora, with her innocence and her macaroons, her tarantella and her taradiddles, her forgery and her fancy dress, and he had the cheque by him in readiness; so he stole on tiptoe to the mantelpiece, slipped the paper under the clock, and was just in time to sink back into his easy-chair before it turned out to be one of the revolving-seats in the dining-saloon on the *Boomerang*.

There was a tumbler of whisky-and-seltzer on the table in front of him, and he was sitting in close confabulation with his former acquaintance, Mr. Perkins, the bank manager. "That's precisely what I don't know, sir, and what I'm determined to find out!" were the first words he heard from the latter gentleman, who looked flushed and angry. "But it's a scandalous thing, isn't it?"

"Very," said Peter, rather bored and deeply disappointed; for the manager was but an indifferent substitute for the companion he had been counting upon. "Oh, very!"

"Have you happened to hear anything said about it yourself?" inquired his friend.

"Not a word!" said Peter, with the veracity he always endeavored to maintain on these occasions.

"To go and shift a statement of that kind on to my shoulders like that, it's like the fellow's confounded impudence!"

For the moment Peter felt a twinge; could the other be referring to anything he had said himself in the music-room? But the manager was evidently not angry with *him*, so it must be some other fellow. Only Peter decided not to allude to the faulty working of the time cheques, as he had half intended to do. Perkins was not in the mood for remonstrances just then.

"Most impudent, I must say," he replied. "By the way," he added carelessly, "what was the statement exactly?"

"Why, God bless my soul, sir!" cried the manager, with unnecessary vehemence, "haven't I been telling you the whole story? Didn't you just ask me who the fellow was who has brought me into this business?"

"So I did," said Peter, "and – and who *was* he?"

"Your attention seems very wandering this evening! Why, I told you the old woman wouldn't give me his name". Peter's alarm returned at this allusion to an old woman; what old woman could it be but the terrible matron whom he had encountered in the music-room? However, it was fortunate that she had not mentioned any names; if Perkins knew that he had put all the blame of his entanglements upon the manager's broad shoulders, he would certainly consider it an ungrateful return for what was intended as a kindness.

"So you said before," he remarked; "some old women are so obstinate!"

"Obstinate? That's the first sensible remark you've made for a long while!" said his candid friend. "I should think she was obstinate! "Why, I talked myself hoarse trying to make that old harridan believe that I was as innocent as an unborn babe of any responsibility for this precious scandal – that I'd never so much as heard it breathed till she told me of it; but it wasn't any good, sir; she would have it that I was the originator!"

("So you were!" thought Peter, though he prudently refrained from saying so.)

"She's going to kick up the dooce's own delight as soon as she meets her brother; and all I could get her to say was that then, and not till then, she would give me an opportunity of having it out with the cowardly villain, whoever he may be, that has dared to lay all this gossip at *my* door!"

Peter did not quarrel with this arrangement of the old lady's, for he would certainly not be on board the *Boomerang* when she arrived at Plymouth.

"Ah!" he said, with as much interest as he could display in a subject that did not concern him, "he'll find that unpleasant, I dare say."

"I think he will!" said Mr. Perkins, emphatically. "Unless he retracts his infamous calumny. I – I'll kick him from one end of the ship to the other!"

Involuntarily Peter's eyes sought his friend's boots, which, as he sat in a corner seat with his feet extended, were much in evidence; they were strong, suitable boots, stouter than those generally worn on a sea-voyage, and Peter could not repress a slight shudder.

"From one end of the ship to the other," he repeated; "that – that's rather a long way!"

"Quite long enough for him, though not nearly long enough for me!" said the Manager. "I'll teach him to mix me up in these squabbles, when I find him, sir – when I find him! Here, steward, bring some more of these dry biscuits; you'll have some more, won't you?"

But Peter was not in the vein for dry biscuits at that moment, and the Manager continued:

"By-the-by, *you* might help me in this if you only will. I want to find out if I can before we reach Gib, who this fellow is, but the less I talk about the affair the better."

"Oh! Yes," said Peter. "I – I wouldn't talk about it at all, if I were you."

"No. I dare say you're right – can't be too careful with an old cat like that. Well, what I want you to do is to try and find out – quietly, you know – who this infernal fellow is!"

"Well, I daresay I could do that," said Peter.

"No one would think a mild, innocent-looking little chap like you had any particular motive for asking: you might ask some of the men in the smoking-room, and pick up some clue or other."

"So I might," said Peter, "good idea!"

"Or, I'll tell you what – you might pump the old lady for me, eh?"

"I don't think I quite care about pumping the old lady," said Peter, "but anything else I'll do with pleasure."

"Thanks," said the Manager, "that's a good fellow. I knew I could depend upon you!"

"You can," replied Peter, "though, I fancy," he added, soothingly – "indeed, I am sure you will find that the old woman has made a good deal out of nothing at all...."

"*What* old woman, Peter?" asked Sophia with drowsy asperity. "Not Mrs. Linden, surely!"

Mrs. Linden! "Was that the name of the old she-dragon of the music-room? Why, of course not; he was in his arm-chair by his own fire, reading Ibsen to his wife!

"I don't know, indeed, my love – it *may* be Mrs. Linden," he answered cautiously.

"Nonsense!" said Sophia, crossly. "She's not meant to be old in the play, and *who* says 'the old woman has made a good deal out of nothing?' Helmer, or Doctor Rank, or Krogstad, or who? You do read so badly, it's quite impossible to make out!"

"*No* one says it, my dear Sophia; at least, it's not in my edition of the text. You – you must have imagined it, I think!"

"I certainly thought I heard you read it out," she replied; "but your voice is so monotonous, that it's just possible I dropped off for a minute or two."

"I dropped off myself about the same time," he confessed hypocritically.

"You wouldn't drop off, or allow me to drop off either, Peter," said Sophia, who was now thoroughly awake again, "if you felt a more intelligent interest in the tremendous problem Ibsen has set in this play. I don't believe you realize in the least what the lesson is that he means to teach; now *do* you, Peter?"

"Well, I'm not sure that I do altogether, my love," he admitted.

"I thought as much! What Ibsen insists upon is, the absolute necessity of one-ness between man and wife, Peter. They must belong to each other, complete each other – they must be Twin Souls. Are *you* a Twin Soul, Peter?"

"Upon my word, my dear, I can't say!" he replied, in some perplexity. In the present very divided state of his sympathies, he could not help thinking that his Soul was more like a Triplet.

"But think," persisted Sophia, earnestly: "have you shared all your Past with me? Is there nothing you have kept back – no feelings, no experiences, which you confine to your own bosom? When you left me to take that voyage, you promised that nothing should induce you to be more than civil to any woman, however young and attractive, with whom Fate might bring you in contact. I want you to tell me, Peter, whether, when you were returning home on board the *Boomerang*, you kept that promise or not?"

Fortunately for him, she put her question in a form which made it easy to give a satisfactory and a truthful answer.

"When I was returning home on board the *Boomerang*" he said, "I did not, to the best of my recollection and belief, exchange two words with any female whatever, attractive or otherwise – until," he added, with a timely recollection that she had come on board at Gibraltar – "until I met you. You pain me with these suspicions, Sophia – you do, indeed!"

"I believe you, Peter," she said, moved by his sincerity, which, paradoxical as it may sound, was quite real; for his intentions had been so excellent throughout, that he felt injured by her doubts. "You have never told me a falsehood yet; but for some time I have been tormented by a fancy that you were concealing something from me. I can hardly say what gave me such an impression – a glance, a tone, trifles which, I am glad to think now, had not the importance I invested them with. Ah, Peter, never treat me as Helmer did Nora! Never shut me out from the serious side of your life, and think to make amends by calling me your 'little lark,' or your 'squirrel;' you must not look upon me as a mere doll!"

"My *dear* Sophia!" he exclaimed, "I should never think of addressing you as either a squirrel or a lark; and any one less like a doll in every respect I never met!"

"I hope you will always think so, Peter," she said; "for I tell you frankly, that if I once discovered that you had ceased to trust me, that you lived in a world apart into which I was not admitted, that very moment, Peter, I should act just as Nora did – I should leave you; for our marriage would have ceased to be one in any true sense of the word!"

The mere idea of being abandoned by Sophia made him shiver. What a risk he had been running, after all! Was it worth while to peril his domestic happiness for the sake of a few more conversations with two young ladies, whose remarks were mostly enigmatic, and for whom he was conscious in his heart of hearts of not caring two straws?

"Sophia," he said plaintively, "don't talk of leaving me! What should I do without you? Who would teach me Astronomy and things? You know I don't care for anybody but you! Why will you dwell on such unpleasant subjects?"

"I was wrong, Peter," she confessed – "indeed, I doubt you no longer. It was all my morbid imagination that led me to do you such injustice. Forgive me, and let us say no more about it!"

"I do forgive you," was his generous reply to this appeal, which, coming from Sophia, was a very handsome apology, "and we *will* say no more about it."

And, upon the whole, Peter thought he had got out of a particularly tight place with more credit than he had any reason to expect – a conclusion in which the reader, however much he or she may disapprove of his conduct on moral grounds, will probably be inclined to agree with him.

Chapter VI
Foil And Counterfoil

IT WOULD BE more satisfactory to an author's feelings, especially when he is aware that he will be held accountable by an indignant public for the slightest deviation on his hero's part from the narrow path of ideal rectitude – it would be more satisfactory to be able to record that this latest warning had a permanent effect upon Peter Tourmalin's rather shifty disposition.

But an author, even of a modest performance such as this, can not but feel himself in a position of grave responsibility. He must relate such facts as he has been able to collect, without suppression on the one side or distortion on the other. It is a duty he can not and dare not evade, under penalty of forfeiting the confidence of his readers.

Peter Tourmalin *did* draw more Time Cheques, he *did* go back to the *Boomerang*, and it would be useless to assert the contrary. We may be able to rehabilitate him to some extent before this story concludes; at present, we can only follow his career with pain and disapproval.

Some allowances must be made for the peculiar nature of the case. To a person of Peter's natural inclination to the study of psychology, there was a strong fascination in watching the gradual unfolding and revelation of two characters so opposite and so interesting as those of Miss Tyrrell and Miss Davenport. That was the point of view he took himself, and it is difficult to say that such a plea is wholly without plausibility.

Then, too, he was intensely curious to know how it would all end, and he might ascertain that in the very next quarter of an hour he drew; there was absolutely no telling.

As for Sophia's threat, that soon lost all terrors for him. She would abandon him, no doubt, if she ever knew; but who was going to tell her, and how could she possibly discover the truth unaided, especially now that her awakening suspicions had been lulled? His secret was perfectly safe, and he could unravel the tangled thread of the history of his remaining extra hours on board the *Boomerang* without any other hindrance than that of his own scruples – which practically amounted to no hindrance at all.

So Peter continued to be the slave of his clock and his cheque-book, from the counterfoils of which he was disagreeably surprised to discover that he had drawn more frequently, and in consequence had an even smaller balance left to his credit than he had supposed.

However, he consoled himself by concluding that one or two cheques had probably been mislaid, and were still unpresented, while he was entitled to some additional time in respect of compound interest; so that he need not stint himself at present. Fifteen minutes a week was not an extravagant allowance; and sooner or later, even with the utmost economy, a day would come when his balance would be exhausted, and his cheques returned from the clock marked 'No effects – refer to drawer,' or some equivalent intimation.

But that day was still distant, and in the mean time he went on drawing with a light heart.

It was a Saturday evening, the day on which Peter generally presented his weekly cheque; but, although it was nearly half-past ten, he had had no opportunity of doing so as yet. He was in the drawing-room, and Sophia was reading aloud to him this time, an article on 'Bi-metalism' from one of the reviews; for she had been an ardent bi-metalist from early girlhood, and she naturally wished to win Peter from his Laodicean apathy on so momentous a subject. He listened with surface resignation, although inwardly he was in a fever of impatience to get back upon the *Boomerang*, where Miss Davenport had been more interesting than usual on his last visit. But he could hardly rise and slip a cheque under the clock before Sophia's very eyes without inventing some decent pretext for such an action, and bi-metalism had reduced him to a mental condition which was no longer fertile in expedients.

Suddenly Sophia stopped reading and remarked: "If I remember right, Professor Dibbs has stated the argument more correctly in his little book on *Currency*. It would be interesting to compare the two; I'll get it."

As Professor Dibbs's work was apparently on a shelf in the study, Sophia took the lamp into the further room.

"Now's my time!" thought Peter, as he brought out the cheque from his waistcoat pocket. "I mayn't get such another chance this evening."

Even if Sophia could lay her hand on the volume at once, he would have had his quarter of an hour and be comfortably back long before she could pass the arch which separated the two rooms; for, as we have seen, this instantaneous action was one of the chief recommendations of the Time Cheques.

So he cashed his cheque, and was at once transported to the secluded passage between the deck-cabins, the identical place where he had first conversed with Miss Davenport. He was on the same steamer-chair, too, and she was at his side; the wind carried the faint strains of a set of 'Lancers' to them; from all of which circumstances he drew the inference that he was going to be favoured with the sequel to the conversation that had been so incongruously broken in upon by Sophia's question respecting the comparative merits of bottle-jacks in the Tottenham Court Road warehouse. This was so far satisfactory, indicating as it did that he was at last, after so much trying back, to make some real progress.

"What I want to know first," Miss Davenport was saying, "is whether you are capable of facing danger for my sake?"

"I thought," he remonstrated mildly, "that I had already given proof of that!"

"The danger you faced then threatened only me. But, supposing you had to meet a danger to yourself, could you be firm and cool? Much will depend on that."

"I – I think," he answered frankly, "that perhaps you had better not count upon me. I have never been a man to court danger; it might find me equal to it if it came – or it might not."

He did not mean to give it the opportunity.

"Then we are lost, that is all!" she said, with gloomy conviction. "Lost, both of us!"

Peter certainly intended to be lost if the moment of trial ever arrived. Even now he was resolving, for about the twentieth time that this positively should be his very last cheque; for he by no means liked the manner in which the situation seemed to be developing.

But, seeing that the danger, whatever it might be, was still far enough off, he thought, very sensibly, that it would be a pity to cloud this last interview by any confession of pusillanimity. Knowing that he would return no more, he could surely afford to treat with contempt any consequences his imprudence might have entailed.

So he laughed, as he said: "You mustn't conclude that I'm a coward because I don't care to boast. On the contrary, I believe I am not exactly deficient in physical courage."

"You are not?" she cried, relieved. "Then – then you would not be afraid to face a desperate man?"

"Not a dozen desperate men, if it comes to that!" said Peter, supported by the certainty that it would not come to so much as half a desperate man.

"Then I can tell you *now* what I have scarcely dared to think of before. Peter, you will have to reckon with Alfred!"

"Well, I'm not much alarmed at anything *Alfred* may do!" said Peter, wondering who the deuce Alfred was.

"He will come on board; he will demand an explanation; he will insist on seeing you!" she cried.

"*Let* him!" said Peter.

"You are brave – braver even than I thought; but, ah! Peter, you don't know what Alfred is!"

Peter did not even know who Alfred was, but he was unmoved.

"You leave Alfred to me," he said, confidently, "I'll settle *him*!"

"But I must tell you all. I – I led you to believe that Alfred would raise no objections; that he would quietly accept facts which it is useless to contend against. He will do nothing of the sort! He is a man of violent passions – fierce and relentless when wronged. In the first burst of fury at meeting you, when he comes on board, he is capable of some terrible vengeance, which nothing but perfect coolness on your part – perhaps not even that – will be able to avert. And I – I have brought this upon you!"

"Don't cry," said Peter. "You see, I'm perfectly calm. *I* don't mind it. If Alfred considers himself wronged by me – though, what I have ever done to give him any reason for revenging himself by personal violence, I must say I can't conceive –"

She stopped him.

"Ah! You have given him cause enough!" she cried. "What is the use of taking that tone to me?"

"I want to see Alfred's point of view, that's all," said Peter. "What does he complain of?"

"*What does he complain of?* You ask me that, when – Peter," she broke off suddenly, "there is somebody round the corner listening to us – a woman, I'm sure of it. I heard the rustle of a dress.…Go and see if there is not!"

Go and see, and find himself face to face with Miss Tyrrell, who might faint or go into hysterics. Peter knew better than that.

"It's merely your fancy," he said, soothingly. "Who can be there? They are all at the other end of the ship, dancing. Go on telling me about Alfred. I don't yet understand how I have managed to offend him."

"Are you really so dull," she said, with a slight touch of temper, "that you can't see that a man who thought he was going to meet the woman he was engaged to, and finds she has learned to care for – for somebody else, is likely, even if he was the mildest man in the world – which Alfred is far from being – to betray some annoyance?"

"No, I see that," said Peter; "but – but he can't blame me. *I* couldn't help it!"

He said this, although her last speech had opened his eyes considerably. He knew now who Alfred was, and also that, in some moment of madness which was in one of the quarters of an hour he had not yet drawn, he must have placed himself in the position of Alfred's rival.

"What was he to do? He could not, without brutality, tell this poor girl that he had not the smallest intention of depriving Alfred of her affections; it was better, and easier too, to humor her for the short time that remained.

"Alfred will not take that as an excuse," she said. "It is true we could neither of us help what has happened, but that will not alter the fact that he is quite capable of shooting us both the instant he comes on deck. Alfred is like that!"

"Well," said Peter, unable to abstain from a little more of such very cheap heroism, "I do not fear death – with you!"

"Say that once more," she said; which Peter very obligingly did. "Oh, Peter, how I admire you now! How little I knew you were capable of going so calmly to your doom! You give me courage. I feel that I, too, can face death; only not *that* death – it is so horrid to be shot!"

"It would be unpleasant," said Peter, placidly, "but soon over."

"No," she said, "I couldn't bear it. I can see him pointing his revolver – for he always carries one, even at a picnic – first at *your* head, then mine! No, Peter; since we must die, I prefer at least to do so without bloodshed!"

"So do I," he agreed, "very much."

"You do?" she cried. "Then, oh, Peter! Why should we wait any longer for a fate that is inevitable? Let us do it now, together!"

"Do *what*?" said Peter.

"Slip over the side together; it would be quite easy, no one will see us. Let us plunge arm-in-arm into the merciful sea! A little struggle – a moment's battle for breath – then all will be over!"

"Yes, I suppose it *would* be over then"; he said; "but we should have to swallow such a lot of salt water first!"

He reflected that, even if he emerged from the agonies of drowning, to find himself bi-metalizing with Sophia, the experience would be none the less unpleasant while it lasted. There really must be some limit to his complaisance, and he set it at suicide.

"No," he said; "I have always held that to escape a difficulty by putting an end to one's own life, is a cowardly proceeding."

"I *am* a coward," she said; "but oh, Peter, be a coward with me for once!"

"Ask me anything else!" he said firmly, "but not stoop to cowardice. There is really no necessity for it, you see," he added, feeling that he had better speak out plainly. "I have no doubt that Alfred will listen to reason; and when he is told that, although, as is excusable enough with two natures that have much in common, we – we have found a mutual pleasure in each other's society – there has been nothing on either side inconsistent with the – the most ordinary friendship; when he hears that...Where are you going?" for she was rising from her chair.

"Where am I going?" she replied, with an unsteady laugh. "Why, overboard, if you care to know!"

"But you mustn't!" he cried, scarcely knowing what he said. "The – the captain wouldn't like it. There's a penalty, I'm sure, for leaving the ship while it's in motion I've seen it on a notice!"

"There is a penalty for having believed in you," she replied bitterly, "and I am going to pay it!"

She broke away and rushed out upon the deck into the starlight, with Peter in pursuit. Here was a nice result of his philandering, he thought bitterly. And yet, what had he done? How could he help the consequences of follies committed in time he had not even spent yet? However, what he had to do now was to prevent Miss Davenport from leaping overboard at any cost. He would even promise to jump over with her, if that would soothe her, and of course he could appoint some time next day – say, after breakfast – for the performance.

He ran down the shadowy deck until he overtook a flying female form, whose hand he seized as she crouched against the bulwarks.

"Miss Davenport, if you will only just..." he began, when, without warning, he found himself back upon his own hearth-rug, holding Sophia firmly by the wrist!

He felt confused, as well he might, but he tried to pass it off.

"Did you find *Dibbs on Currency*, my dear?" he inquired, with a ghastly smile, as he dropped her hand.

"I did not," said Sophia, gravely; "I was otherwise engaged. Peter, what have you been doing?"

"What have I been doing?" he said. "Why, it's not a minute since you went into the study to get that book; look at the clock and see!"

"Don't appeal to the clock, Peter – answer my question. How have you been occupied?"

"I've been waiting for you to finish that article on bi-metalism," he had the hardihood to say. "Deuced well-written article it is, too; so clear!"

"I don't refer to what you were doing here," said Sophia. "What were you doing on board the *Boomerang*?"

"It – it's so long ago that I really forget," he said. "I – I read Buckle on deck, and I talked with a man named Perkins – nice fellow he was – manager of a bank out in Australia."

"It's useless to prevaricate, Peter!" she said. "What I want to know is, who was that girl, and why should she attempt to destroy herself?"

He could hardly believe his ears.

"Girl!" he stammered. "How do you know that any girl attempted anything of that sort?"

"How do I know, Peter?" said Sophia. "I will tell you how I know. *I was on board the Boomerang too!*"

At this awful piece of intelligence, Peter dropped into his arm-chair, speechless and quaking. What would come next he could not tell; but anything seemed possible, and even probable, after that!

Chapter VII
The Culminating Cheque

"BEFORE I say anything else," said Sophia, who was still standing upon the hearth-rug, gazing down upon the wretched Peter as he sat huddled up in his chair, "you would probably like to know how I came to follow you to that ship. It is a long story, but I will tell you if you wish to hear?"

Peter's lips moved without producing any articulate sounds, and Sophia proceeded:

"Some weeks ago," she said, "one afternoon when you had gone out for a walk, I found what seemed to be a loose cheque on the carpet. I knew how carelessly you leave things about, and I picked it up and found that, though it was like a cheque in other respects, it was rather curiously worded. I could not understand it at all, but it seemed to have something to do with the ship you came home from Australia in; so, intending to ask you for an explanation when you came in, I thought in the mean time I would put it in some safe place where I should be sure to see it, and I put it behind the clock; and then – oh, Peter –!"

Peter understood. The cheques were all payable to 'self or bearer.' Sophia had innocently presented one, and it had been paid. If he had only taken 'order' cheques, this would not have happened, but it was too late now! He continued to imitate the tactics of that eminent strategist, Brer Rabbit; in other words, he 'lay low and said nuffin,' while Sophia continued:

"Then, without in the least knowing how I came there, I found I was on a big steamer, and as I walked along, perfectly bewildered, I saw the name *Boomerang* painted on some fire-buckets, and of course I knew then that that was your ship. I fancied that perhaps, in some way, you might be on board too, and would explain how this had happened to me. At all events, I decided to find out if you were; and, seeing a girl reading on deck, I took a chair near her, and after a few introductory remarks I mentioned your name. The effect upon her was such as to convince me that she felt more than an ordinary interest in you. By degrees I drew from her the whole story of her relations with you: she even asked me – *me* – for advice!"

So Miss Davenport's *confidante* had not been Miss Tyrrell after all – but Sophia! If he had only known that before!

"I could not speak to her," continued Sophia, "I felt stifled, stupefied by what I had heard! I could bear no more; and so I rose and left her, and walked down some stairs, and somehow found myself back in our own room again! I was more bewildered than ever. I looked for the cheque, but there was nothing, and soon I was forced to believe that the whole thing was imaginary. Still, I was not wholly satisfied. You may remember how I questioned you one evening when you were reading the *Doll's House* to me; well, your answers quite reassured me for the time. I told myself that my suspicions were too wildly improbable not to have been a delusion.

I was even afraid that my brain must be slightly affected, for I had always prided myself upon having my imagination under thorough control. But by degrees, Peter – by degrees – I began to doubt again whether it was really nothing but fancy on my part. I noticed that your manner was suspiciously odd at times. I discovered that there was one drawer in your secretary that you kept carefully locked. I caught your eye wandering toward the clock from time to time. *What* I suspected I hardly know; but I felt certain that I should find the explanation of that mystery in the locked drawer. I tried key after key, until I found one that fitted. Oh, I am not at all ashamed of it! Had I not a *right* to know? There were no letters, nothing but a cheque-book; but that cheque-book proved to me that, after all, I had imagined nothing: all the cheques were the same as the one I found on the carpet! I tore one out and kept it by me, and from that time I watched you closely. I saw how restless and impatient you were this evening, and I was certain that you were intending to use a cheque from that book. You were bent on getting back to the *Boomerang*, and I was equally determined that, if I could help it, you should not go alone. Only I could not be quite sure how you managed to get there, and at last I hit upon a little device for finding out. There is no such person as Professor Dibbs, Peter; I invented him to put you off your guard. As I passed into the other room with the lamp, I saw you, reflected in the mirror over the study chimneypiece, rise and go to the drawing-room mantelpiece: you had a slip of paper in your hand – a cheque, of course. I had the cheque I tore out hidden in the waistband of my dress; and so, as soon as I saw you slip your cheque behind the clock in the drawing-room, I put my cheque behind the one in the study. I was on the deck at once, and it was dark, but I could hear your voice and another's – round a corner. I held my breath and listened. What I heard, you know!"

Peter shrank up in his chair, utterly confounded by this last vagary on the part of the Time Cheques. He certainly would not have supposed that the mere presentation even of a 'bearer' cheque by Sophia would entitle her to the same fifteen minutes he was receiving himself. He could only account for it by the fact that the two cheques were cashed simultaneously at two separate clocks; but even this explanation was not wholly satisfactory.

He found his voice at last: "Well," he said, "now that you know all, what are you going to do about it, Sophia? I would rather know the worst!"

"I will tell you that in good time," she replied; "but, first of all, I want you to tell me exactly how you came to have these cheques, and what use you made of them on previous occasions?"

So, slightly reassured by her manner, which was composed, Peter gave her a plain, unvarnished account of the way in which he had been led to deposit his extra time, and the whole story of his interviews with Miss Davenport. He did not mention any others, because he felt that the affair was quite complicated enough without dragging in extraneous and irrelevant matter.

"I may have been imprudent," he concluded; "but I do assure you, Sophia, that in all the quarters of an hour I have had as yet, I never once behaved to that young lady in any capacity but that of a friend. I only went on drawing the cheques because I wanted a little change of air and scene now and then. You have no idea how it picked me up!"

"I saw in what society it set you down, Peter," was Sophia's chilling answer.

"You – you mustn't think she is *always* like that," he urged. "It took me quite by surprise – it was a most painful position for me. I think, Sophia, your own sense of fairness will acknowledge that, considering the awkwardness of my situation, I – I behaved as well as could be expected. You do admit that, don't you?"

Sophia was silent for a minute or so before she spoke again.

"I must have time to think, Peter," she said: "it is all so strange, so contrary to all my experience, that I can hardly see things as yet in their proper light. But I may tell you at once that, from what I was able to observe, and from all you have just told me, I am inclined to think that you are free from actual culpability in the matter. It was quite clear that that very forward girl was the principal throughout, and that you were nothing more than an unwilling and most embarrassed accessory."

This was so much more lenient a view than he had dared to expect that Peter recovered his ordinary equanimity.

"That was all," he said. "I am very glad you saw it, my dear. I was perfectly helpless!"

"And then," said Sophia, "I was more than pleased by your firm refusal to commit suicide. What you said was so very sound and true, Peter."

"I hope so, said Peter, with much complacency. "Yes, I was pretty firm with her! By the way," he added, "you – you didn't happen to see whether she really did jump overboard, I suppose?"

"I came away just at the crisis," she said. "I thought you would tell *me*!"

"*I* came away, too," said Peter. "It doesn't matter, of course; but still I should have rather liked to know whether she meant it or not."

"How can you speak of it so heartlessly, Peter? She may have been trying to frighten you; she is just the kind of girl who would. But she may have been in earnest after all!"

"You see, Sophia," said Peter, "it doesn't matter whether she was or not – it isn't as if it had ever really happened."

"Not really happened? But I was *there*; I heard, I saw it – nothing could be more real!"

"At any rate," he said, "it only happens when I use those cheques; and she can't possibly carry out her rash intention until I draw another – which I promise you faithfully I will never do. If you doubt me, I will burn the book now before your eyes!"

"With these words he went to the drawer and took out the cheque-book.

"No," said Sophia, "you must not do that, Peter. There is much about this Time Bank that I don't pretend to understand, that I can not account for by any known natural law; but I may not disbelieve my own eyes and ears! These events that have happened in the extra time you chose to defer till now are just as real as any other events. You *have* made this girl's acquaintance; you have – I don't say through any fault of your own, but still you *have* – caused her to transfer her affections from the man she was engaged to, and, being a creature of ill-regulated mind and no strength of character, she has resolved to put an end to her life rather than meet his just indignation. She is now on the very point of accomplishing this folly. Well, badly as she has behaved, you can not possibly leave the wretched girl there! You must go back at once, restrain her by main force, and not leave her until you have argued her into a rational frame of mind."

Peter was by no means anxious to go back at first.

"It's not at all necessary," he said; "and besides, I don't know if you're aware of it, but with the way these cheques are worked, it's ten chances to one against my hitting off the right fifteen minutes! Still," he added, with an afterthought, "I can try, of course, if you insist upon it. I can take my chance with another fifteen minutes, but that must be the last. I am sick and tired of this *Boomerang* business, I am indeed!"

Shameful as it is to state, he had altered his mind from a sudden recollection that he would not mind seeing Miss Tyrrell for just once more. He had not drawn her for several weeks.

"No," said Sophia, thoughtfully; "I see your objection – fifteen minutes is not enough, unless you could be sure of getting the successors to the last. But I have an idea, Peter – if you draw out the whole balance of your time, you can't possibly help getting the right fifteen minutes somewhere or other. I think that's logical?"

"Oh, devilish logical!" muttered Peter to himself, who had reasons, which he could not divulge to her, for strongly disapproving of such a plan.

"The fact is, my dear," he said, "it – it's rather late this evening to go away for any time!"

"You forget," she said, "that, however long you are away, you will come back at exactly the same time you start. But you have some other reason, Peter – you had better tell me!"

"Well," he owned, "I might come across someone I'd rather not meet."

"You are thinking of the man that girl said she had been engaged to – Alfred, wasn't it?"

Peter had forgotten Alfred for the moment; and besides, he was not likely to turn up till the *Boomerang* got to Plymouth, and he knew his extra hours stopped before that. Still, Alfred did very well as an excuse.

"Ah!" he said, "Alfred. You heard what she said about him? A violent character – with a revolver, Sophia!"

"But you told her you were not afraid of him. I felt so proud of you when you said it. And think, you may be able to bring them together – to heal the breach between them!"

"He's more likely to make a breach in me that won't heal!" said Peter.

"Still, as you said yourself, it isn't as if it was all actually existing. What does it matter, even if he should shoot you?"

"I don't see any advantage in exposing myself to any such unpleasant experiences, even if they are only temporary," he said.

"It is not a question of advantage, Peter," rejoined Sophia; "it is a simple duty, and I'm surprised that you don't see it as such. Whatever the consequences of your conduct may be, you can not evade them like this; you have chosen to begin, and you must go on! I am quite clear about that. Let me see" – (here she took the cheque-book, and made some rapid calculations from the counterfoils) – "yes, you have two hours and three-quarters at least still standing to your credit; and then there's the compound interest. I will tear out all these small cheques and burn them." Which she did as she spoke. "And now, Peter, sit down and fill up one of the blank ones at the end for the whole amount."

"Do you know, Sophia," said Peter, "it occurs to me that this is just one of those matters which can only be satisfactorily arranged by – er – a woman's tact. Suppose I make the cheque payable to *you* now – eh?"

"You mean, that you want me to go instead of you?" she asked.

"Well," said Peter, "if it wouldn't be bothering you, my dear, I think perhaps it *would* be –"

"Don't say another word," she interrupted, "or I shall begin to *despise* you, Peter! If I thought you meant it seriously, I would go upstairs, put on my bonnet, and go back to mamma forever. I could not bear to be the wife of a coward!"

"Oh, I'll go!" said Peter, in much alarm. "I said what I did out of consideration, not cowardice. But wouldn't tomorrow do just as well, Sophia? It is late to turn out!"

"Tomorrow will *not* do as well," she said: "fill up that cheque tonight or you will lose me forever!"

"There!" said Peter, as he scrawled off the cheque. "Are you satisfied *now*, Sophia?"

"I shall be when I see you present it."

"Er – yes," he said; "oh! I mean to present it – presently. I – I think I'll take a small glass of brandy before I go, my dear, to keep the cold out."

"As you will certainly be in a summer, if not tropical, temperature the next moment," she said, "I should advise you to take nothing of the kind."

"I say," he suggested, "suppose I find she has jumped overboard – what shall I do then?"

"Do! Can you possibly ask? You will jump after her, of course!"

"It's easy to say 'of course'," he said; "but I never *could* swim more than twenty strokes!"

"Swim those twenty then, and let come what will; you will be back all the sooner. But don't stand there talking about it, Peter – go!"

"I'm going," he said meekly. "You'll sit up for me, Sophia, if – if I'm late, won't you?"

"Don't be absurd!" she said. "You know perfectly well that, as I said before, you won't be away a second."

"It won't be a second for you," he said, "but it will be several hours for *me*; and goodness only knows what I may have to go through in the time! However," he added, with an attempt to be cheerful, "it may all pass off quite pleasantly – don't you think it may, Sophia?"

"How can I tell? You will only find out by going."

"I'm going, my dear – I'm going at once!…You'll give me just one kiss before I start, won't you?"

"I will give you no kiss till you come back and I hear what you have done," said Sophia.

"Very well," he retorted; "you may be sorry you refused when it's too late! I may never come back at all, for anything I can tell!"

And, little as he knew it, he spoke with an almost prophetic anticipation of what was to come. Never again was he destined to stand on that hearth-rug!

But he dared not linger longer, as he could see from her expression that she would suffer no further trifling; and he slipped his last cheque under the clock – with consequences that must be reserved for the next chapter.

Chapter VIII
Paid In His Own Coin

PETER FOUND HIMSELF below this time, in the broad passage, furnished with seats and tables for writing, and which divided the passengers' cabins. Above, he heard a confused stir and bustle of excitement, the trampling of feet, the creaking and rattle of chains, orders shouted in English and Hindustani. From the absence of all vibration, in the vessel, it was evident that she had been brought to. *Why?*

Peter guessed the cause only too easily: the unhappy Miss Davenport had indeed succeeded in carrying out her rash design. She had jumped overboard, and the captain had stopped the engines and lowered a boat in the hope of picking her up before she sank! And he himself – why was he skulking below like this? He had only too much reason to fear that he must have been a witness of the fatal leap; and, instead of plunging overboard to the rescue as a hero ought, had rushed down here ignominiously.

Had he been observed? "Was his connection with the tragedy suspected? Could he venture up on deck and inform himself? He tried, but his nerve failed him, and he sank into one of the chairs in a state of almost unbearable suspense.

Just at this moment, he saw the skirts of a muslin gown appear at the head of the broad companion which led to the dining-saloon. Someone, a girl evidently, was descending. Presently, he saw her fully revealed – it was Miss Tyrrell.

Perhaps he had never been so glad to see her before. She was a friend, a dear friend. She, at least, would sympathize with him, would understand that it was not his fault if he had been too late to avert a catastrophe.

She was coming to him. Her eyes were friendly and pitiful as they sought his. She, at least, did not turn from him!

"How pale, how terribly pale you look!" she said. "You must nerve yourself to see her – it can not be long now!"

"Has she been brought on board yet?" he gasped. "Is – is there any hope?"

"We shall know very soon. It is possible you may find that all is at an end."

"All! You think so? But – but no one will say it was *my* fault, will they? I – I was ready to make any sacrifice only somehow, when the moment comes, I am apt to lose my presence of mind."

"Yes, I know," she said feelingly; "you are not quite yourself yet, but I know you would make the sacrifice if your duty demanded it. But she may have taken advantage of your absence to free herself and you from all obligation, may she not?"

This suggestion comforted Peter.

"She *must* have done!" he said. "Yes, of course. I could not be expected to prevent it, if I wasn't there; and I wasn't, when it came to the poieynt. But, Miss Tyrrell, do you think that it is really all over? She – she may come round after all!"

"She may – but of course, if it is true that she is engaged to another, she can have no possible claim on *you*."

What a sensible right-minded way this girl had of looking at things! thought Peter, not for the first time.

"Why, of course she can't!" he cried. "And it *is* true. She is engaged – to a fellow of the name of Alfred."

"You know that as a fact?" she exclaimed.

"I know it from her own lips, and I need not say that I should be the last person to wish to – er – upset so desirable an arrangement."

"Why – *why* didn't you tell me all this before?" she inquired.

"I – I didn't think it would interest you," he replied.

Here, to Peter's utter astonishment, she covered her face with her hands.

"Not interest me!" she murmured at last. "Oh, how *could* you – how could you keep this from me? Can't you see – can't you guess what a difference it has made in my feelings?"

It might be very dull of him, but he could *not* perceive why the fact of Miss Davenport's engagement to Alfred should affect Miss Tyrrell so strangely as this!

"I may call you 'Peter' now," she said. "Oh, Peter, *how* happy you have made me! Why did you keep silence so long? It was too quixotic! Don't you understand even yet?"

"No," said Peter, blankly, "I'm afraid I don't."

"Then, if you are really so diffident, I – I must tell you that if you were to ask a certain question once more, I might – I don't say I should, but I might – meet it with a different answer!"

"Good Heavens!" he ejaculated, involuntarily.

"But you must not ask me yet – not just yet. I must have time to consider. I must tell papa before I decide anything. You *will* wait a little longer, won't you, Peter?"

"Yes," he said, feeling limp, "I'll wait. I'd rather!"

She smiled radiantly upon him, and then fled lightly up the companion, leaving him with fresh cause for uneasiness. He could no longer doubt that, for some reason, she expected him to propose to her, which it seemed he had already, in one of those confounded extra minutes, been unprincipled enough to do! Now she had gone to inform her father, the judge, and he would have the disagreeable task of disabusing them before long!

At this point he started, believing that he was visited by an apparition; for a cabin-door opened, and Miss Davenport came out and stood before him.

But she was so obviously flesh and blood – and so dry – that he soon saw that all his anxiety on her account had been superfluous.

"Then you – you didn't jump overboard after all?" he faltered, divided between relief and annoyance at having been made to come back, as it were, on false pretenses.

"You know who prevented me, and by what arguments!" she said, in a low strained voice.

"*Do* I?" he said, helplessly.

"Who should, if you do not? Did not you implore me not to leave you, and declare that, if I would only have courage and wait, we should be happy even yet? And I *did* wait. For what, I ask you, Peter Tourmalin – for *what*?"

"It's really no use asking *me*," he said, "for I've no idea!"

"I waited – to discover that all this time you have had a secret understanding with another; that you are about to transfer your fickle affections to – to that fair girl! Don't deny it, Peter! I was listening. I see it all – all!"

"I wish to goodness *I* did!" he said. "I never was in such a muddle as this in my life. I can only assure you that if that young lady really imagines that I am, or can be, anything more to her than a friend, she is entirely mistaken. I was just about to go up and explain as much to her father!"

"You are not deceiving me?" she asked, earnestly. "You are *sure*?"

"I will swear it, if you wish!" he replied.

"No," she said, relenting visibly, "your word is enough. I do believe you, and I am almost happy again. So long as you do not desert me, even Alfred loses half his terrors!"

"Exactly," he said; "and now, if you will excuse me, I'll just run up on deck and settle this other business."

He went up to the hurricane-deck, and found the ship had anchored. In front was a huge barren rock, with lines of forts, walls, and telegraph poles; and at its base a small white town huddled. They had arrived at Gibraltar, which accounted for the absence of motion.

As he stood there, taking this in, he was accosted by Sir William Tyrrell, who thrust his arm through Peter's in a friendly manner.

"My dear boy," said the Judge, heartily, "Violet has just told me the good news. I can only say that I am delighted – most delighted! I have always felt a warm interest in you, ever since that affair of –"

"Of the monkey," said Peter. "I am very glad to hear it, Sir William; but – but I ought to tell you that I am afraid Miss Tyrrell was – a little premature. She misinterpreted a remark of mine, which, in point of fact, referred to somebody else altogether."

"Then you have no more reason than before for assuming that your *finacée* has thrown you over. Am I to understand that?"

"No more reason than before," admitted Peter.

"And your uncertainty still continues? Very unsatisfactory, I must say! I do think, my dear fellow, that, in your position, you should have been more careful to refrain from betraying any interest in Violet until you knew that you were free to speak. As it is, you may have cast a shadow upon her young life that it may take years to dispel!"

Peter's heart sank into his boots for very shame at this gentle and almost paternal reproof.

"Yes," continued the worthy judge, "Violet is a high-minded girl, scrupulously sensitive on points of honour; and, unless the young lady you are under a semi-engagement to should release you of her own free will, I know my daughter too well to doubt that she will counsel you to fulfill your contract and renounce all hope so far as she is concerned."

Peter felt a little easier.

"I – I am prepared to do that," he said.

"Well, I don't say myself that I go quite so far as she does; but strictly, no doubt, a promise is a promise, and should be kept at all hazards. You have done all that a man can honourably do to put himself right. You have written to this young lady, so I understand, informing her of the change in your sentiments, and offering, nevertheless, to redeem your promise if she insisted upon it. I think that was the general purport of your letter."

Here was one more evil fruit of his extra time! What would Sophia think, or say, or do, if such a letter as that ever came to her knowledge? Fortunately, that at least was impossible!

"You have some grounds," the judge went on, "for assuming that the lady has already treated the contract as non-existent – a person called Alfred, I think my daughter said?"

"No, that was a mistake," explained Peter. "Alfred is engaged to quite a different person."

"Well, in any case, it is quite possible that you may obtain your release when you meet her; and your suspense will soon be over now. Miss – er – Pincher, is it? – will probably be on board the ship before many minutes. I see the boats are putting out from the harbour already."

"*What*!" cried Peter, with the terrible conviction darting through his mind that Sir William spoke the bare truth.

Sophia had said something about meeting him at Gibraltar; but if she had done so during the real voyage, how could he have the meeting all over again, with this ghastly variation? If he could only remember whether she had come out, or not! It was singular, incomprehensible! But his memory was a blank on such a vital fact as this!

"Would you like to have my field-glass for a moment?" said Sir William, considerately.

Peter took them, and the next moment the binocular fell from his nerveless hands. He had seen only too clearly the familiar form of Sophia seated in the peaked stern of a small craft which a Spanish boatman was 'scissoring' through the waves toward the *Boomerang*.

"Come, courage!" said the Judge kindly, as he picked up his glass and wiped the lenses. "Don't be nervous, my boy. You don't know what she may have to say to you yet, you know!"

"No, I don't!" he groaned. "I – I think I ought to go down to the gangway and meet her," he added, tremulously – not that he had any intention of doing so, but he wanted to be alone.

Before the Judge could even express his approbation of Peter's course, Tourmalin was down on the saloon-deck seeking a quiet spot wherein to collect his thoughts.

Before he could find the quiet spot, however, he almost ran into the arms of the matron from Melbourne, whom he had not seen since the episode of the music-room.

"A word with you, Mr. Tourmalin!" she said.

"I – I really can't stop now," stammered Peter. "I – I'm expecting friends!"

"I, too," she said, "am expecting a relation, and it is for that reason that I wish to speak to you now. My brother, who has been staying at Gibraltar on account of his health, will be as determined as I am to trace and punish the infamous calumny upon the name and career of our honoured parent."

"I dare say, madam," said Peter – "I dare say. Very creditable to you both – but I really can't stop just now!"

"You appear to forget, sir, that, unless you can satisfactorily establish your innocence, my brother will certainly treat you as the person primarily responsible for an atrocious slander!"

"A slander – upon your father!…*Me*?" said the indignant Peter. "Why, I never *heard* of the gentleman!"

"Denial will not serve you now," she said. "I have not only your own admissions in the music-room, but the evidence of more than one trustworthy witness, to prove that you circulated a report that my dear father – one of the most honoured and respected citizens of Melbourne – began his Colonial career as – as a transported convict!"

After all, as the hapless Peter instantly saw, he *might* have said so, for anything he knew, in one of those still unexhausted extra quarters of an hour!

"If I said so, I was misinformed," he said.

"Just so; and in our conversation on the subject, you mentioned the name of the person who used you as his mouthpiece to disseminate his malicious venom. What I wish to know now is, whether you are prepared or not to repeat that statement?"

Peter recollected now that he had used expressions implicating Mr. Perkins although merely as the origin of totally different complications.

"I can't positively go so far as that," he said. "I – I made the statement generally."

"As you please," she said. "I can merely say that my brother, whom I expect momentarily, is, although an invalid in some respects, a powerful and determined man; and unless you repeat in his presence the sole excuse you have to offer, he will certainly horsewhip you in the presence of the other passengers. That is all, sir!"

"Thank you – it's quite enough!" murmured Peter, thinking that Alfred himself could hardly be much more formidable; and he slipped down the companion to the cabin saloon, where he found Miss Davenport anxiously expecting him.

"He is here," she whispered. "I have just seen him through the port-hole."

"What – the old lady's brother!" he replied.

"He has *no* sister who is an old lady. I mean Alfred."

"*Alfred*?" he almost yelped. "Alfred *here*!"

"Of course he is here. Is not his battalion stationed at Gibraltar? You knew it, we were to meet him here!"

"I didn't, indeed – or I should never have come!" he protested.

"Don't let us waste words now. He is here; he will demand an explanation from you. He has his pistol with him – I could tell by the bulge under his coat. We must both face him; and the question is, what are you going to say?"

Peter thrust his hands through his carefully parted hair:

"Say!" he repeated. "I shall tell him the simple, straightforward truth. I shall frankly admit that we have walked, and sat, and talked together; but I shall assure him, as I can honestly, that during the whole course of our acquaintance I have never once regarded you in any other light but that of a friend."

"And you suppose that, knowing how I have changed, he will believe that!" she cried. "He will fire long before you can finish one of those fine sentences!"

"In that case," suggested Peter, "why tell him anything at all? Why not spare him, poor fellow, at all events for the time? It will only upset him just now. Let him suppose that we are strangers to one another; and you can break the truth to him gently when you reach England, you know. I'm sure that's *much* the more sensible plan!"

She broke into strange mirthless laughter.

"Your prudence comes too late," she said. "You forget that the truth was broken to him some days ago, in the letter I wrote from Brindisi."

"You wrote and broke it to him at Brindisi!" cried Peter. "What induced you to do *that*?"

"Why, *you*!" she retorted. "You insisted that it was due to him; and though I knew better than you what the effect would be, I dared not tell you the whole truth. I wanted to end the engagement, too; and I scarcely cared then what consequences might follow. Now they are upon us, and it is useless to try to escape them. Since we must die, let us go up on deck and get it over!"

"One moment," he said; "Alfred can wait a little. I – I must go to my cabin first, and put on a clean collar."

And with this rather flimsy pretext, he again made his escape. He made up his mind what to do as he rushed toward his cabin. He could hardly have been anything like an hour on board the *Boomerang* as yet; he had to get through at least another three before he could hope for deliverance. His only chance was to barricade himself inside his cabin, and steadfastly refuse to come out, upon any consideration whatever, until he was released by the natural expiration of time.

He sped down the passage, and found, to his horror, that he had forgotten the number of his berth. However, he knew where it ought to be, and darted into an open door, which he fastened securely with hook and bolt, and sank breathless on one of the lower berths.

"You seem in a hurry, my friend!" said a voice opposite; and Peter's eyes, unused at first to the comparative dimness, perceived that a big man was sitting on the opposite berth, engaged in putting on a pair of spiked cricket-shoes. He had bolted himself inside the cabin with Mr. Perkins!

Chapter IX
Compound Interest

THE BANK MANAGER looked across at Peter with an amused smile; he seemed quite friendly. Whether he was in Peter's cabin, or Peter in his, did not appear; and perhaps it was not of much consequence either way. If the cabin belonged to Mr. Perkins, he did not, at all events, appear to resent the intrusion.

"You seem rather put out about something," he said again, as Peter was still too short of breath for words.

"Oh, no," panted Peter, "it's nothing. There was so much bustle going on above that I thought I'd come in here for a little quiet; that's all."

"Well," said the manager, "I'm glad you looked in; for, as it happens, you're the very man I wanted to see. I dare say you're wondering why I'm putting on these things?"

Peter nodded his head, which was all he felt equal to.

"Why, I've just been having a talk with that old she-griffin from Melbourne. Perhaps you don't know that her brother is coming on board directly?"

"O yes, I *do*!" said Peter.

"Well, it seems she means to denounce me to him as the slanderer of her father. She may, if she chooses; my conscience is perfectly clear on that score. No one can bring anything of the sort home to me; and I've no doubt I shall soon satisfy him that I'm as innocent as an unborn babe. Still, I want you, as a respectable man and the only real friend I have on board, to come with me and be my witness that you never heard such a rumor from my lips; and besides, sir, we shall have an opportunity at last of seeing the unutterable scamp who has had the barefaced impudence to say I told him this precious story! She's going to produce him, sir; and if he dares to stand me out to my face well, *he'll* know why I've put on these shoes! Come along; I can't let you off."

Peter dared not refuse, for fear of attracting his friend's suspicions. He could only trust to slipping away in the confusion; and so, unfastening the cabin-door, the manager caught the unresisting Tourmalin tightly by the arm, and hurried him along the central passage and up the companion.

Even Miss Davenport would have been a welcome diversion at that moment; but she was not there to intercept him, and he reached the upper deck more dead than alive.

"Where's that old vixen *now*?" exclaimed the Manager, dropping Peter's arm." Here, just stay where you are a minute, till I find her and her confounded brother!"

He bustled off, leaving Tourmalin by the davits, quite incapable of action of any kind in the presence of this new and awful dilemma. He had been spreading a cruel and unjustifiable slander against an irreproachable colonial magnate, whose son was now at hand to demand reparation with a horsewhip. He could only propitiate him by denouncing Perkins as his informant, and if he did that he would be kicked from one end of the ship to the other with a spiked boot! This was Nemesis indeed, and it was Sophia who had insisted upon his exposing himself to it. "What a fool he was not to fly back to that cabin while he could!

He turned to flee, and as he did so a hand was passed softly through his arm.

"Not *that* way, Peter!" said Miss Tyrrell's voice.

A wild, faint hope came to him that he might be going to receive one of the back quarters of an hour. The caprices of the Time Cheques were such that it was quite possible he would be thrown back into an earlier interview. Little as he felt inclined for any social intercourse just then, he felt that it would afford him a brief interlude – would at least give him breathing-time before his troubles began again.

"I will go wherever you choose," he said; "I am in your hands."

"I came," she said, "to take you to her. She is asking for you."

"She?" said Peter. "For heaven's sake, *who*?"

"Why, Miss Pinceney, of course. I knew who it was directly I saw her face. Peter, is it true, as papa tells me, that I misunderstood you just now – that she is *not* engaged to Alfred?"

"Alfred? No!" he replied. "If she is engaged to any one at all, I have strong grounds for supposing it's to me!"

"Then we must submit, that is all," said Miss Tyrrell. "But we do not know her decision yet; there is still hope!"

"Yes," he said, "there is hope still. Let us go to her; make haste!"

He meant what he said. Sophia could at least extricate him from a portion of his difficulties. Miss Tyrrell – magnanimous and unselfish girl that she was, in spite of her talent for misapprehension – was ready to resign him to a prior claim, if one was made. And Sophia was bound to claim him; for if the engagement between them had been broken off, he could not now be her husband, as he was. Even Time Cheques must recognize accomplished facts.

He followed her across the ship, turning down the very passage in which he had sat through more than one cheque with Miss Davenport; and on the opposite side he found Sophia standing, with her usual composure, waiting for his arrival.

She was so identically the same Sophia that he had left so lately, that he felt reassured. She, at least, could not be the dupe of all this. She had come – how, he did not trouble himself to think – but she had come with the benevolent intention of saving him!

"How do you do, my love?" he began. "I – I thought I should see you here."

"You only see me here, Peter," she replied, in a voice that trembled slightly, in spite of her efforts to command it, "because I felt very strongly that it was my duty to put an end at the earliest moment to a situation which has become impossible!"

"I'm sure," said Peter, "it is quite time it *was* put an end to – it couldn't go on like this much longer."

"It shall not, if I can help it," she said. "Miss Tyrrell, pray don't go away; what I have to say concerns you too."

"No; don't go away, Miss Tyrrell," added Peter, who felt the most perfect confidence in Sophia's superior wisdom, and was now persuaded that somehow it was all going to be explained. "Sir William, will you kindly step this way too? Sir William Tyrrell – Miss Pinceney. Miss Pinceney has something to tell you which will make my position thoroughly clear."

"I have only to say," she said, "that your honourable and straightforward conduct, Peter, has touched me to the very heart. I feel that I am the only person to blame, for it was I who insisted upon you subjecting yourself to this test."

"It was," said Peter. "I told you something would happen – and it has!"

"I would never hold you to a union from which all love on your side had fled; do not think so, Peter. And now that I see my – my rival, I confess that I could expect no other result. So, dear Miss Tyrrell, I resign him to you freely – yes, cheerfully – for, by your womanly self-abnegation you have proved yourself the worthier. Take her, Peter; you have my full consent!"

"My dear young lady," said the Judge, deeply affected, "this is most noble of you! Allow me to shake you by the hand."

"I can't thank you, dear, *dear*, Miss Pinceney!" sobbed his daughter. "Peter, tell her for me how we shall both bless and love her all our lives for this!"

Peter's brain reeled. Was *this* Sophia's notion of getting him out of a difficulty?

As he gazed distractedly around, his eyes became fixed and glazed with a new terror. A stalwart stranger, with a bushy red beard, was coming toward him, with a stout riding-whip in his right hand. By his side walked the Manager, from whose face all vestige of friendliness had vanished.

"As soon as you have quite finished your conversation with these ladies," said the Manager, with iron politeness, "this gentleman would be glad of a few moments with you; after which I shall request your attention to a little personal affair of my own. Don't let us *hurry* you, you know!"

"I – I won't," returned Peter, flurriedly; "but I'm rather busy just now: a little later, I – I shall be delighted."

As he stood there, he was aware that they had withdrawn to a bench some distance away, where they conferred with the elderly lady from Melbourne. He could feel their angry glare upon him, and it contributed to rob him of the little self-possession he had left.

"Sophia," he faltered piteously, "I say this is too bad – it is, really! You *can't* mean to leave me in such a hole as this – do let's get home at once!"

Before she could make any reply to an appeal which seemed to astonish her considerably, a thin, bilious-looking man, with a face twitching with nervous excitement, a heavy black mustache, and haggard eyes, in which a red fire smoldered, appeared at the gangway and joined the group.

"I beg your pardon," he said, lifting his hat; "forgive me if I interrupt you, but my business is urgent – most urgent! Perhaps you could kindly inform me if there is a – a gentleman" (the word cost him a manifest struggle to pronounce) "a gentleman on board of the name of Tourmalin? I have a little matter of business" (here his right hand stole to his breast-pocket) "to transact with him," he explained, with a sinister smile that caused Peter to give suddenly at the knees.

"It's that infernal Alfred!" he thought. "Now I *am* done for!"

"Why," said Miss Tyrrell, who was clinging affectionately to Peter's arm, "*this* is Mr. Tourmalin! You can speak to him now – here, if you choose. We have no secrets from one another – have we, Peter?"

"I have lately learned," said the gloomy man, "that a certain Mr. Tourmalin has stolen from me the affection of one who was all heaven and earth to me!"

"Then it *must* be another Mr. Tourmalin," said Miss Tyrrell, "not this one; because – surely you do not need to be told that you have no rivalry to fear from him?" she broke off, with a blush of charming embarrassment.

Alfred's scowl distinctly relaxed, and Peter felt that, after all, this unfortunate misunderstanding on Miss Tyrrell's part might prove serviceable to him. Since Sophia, for reasons of her own, refused to assist him, he must accept any other help that offered itself.

"The best proof I can give you of my innocence," he said, "is to mention that I have the honour to be engaged to this lady."

He heard a stifled shriek from behind him as he made this assertion, and the next moment Miss Davenport, who must have come up in time to catch the last words, had burst into the center of the group.

"It is not true!" she cried. "Alfred, you must not believe him!"

"Not *true*?" exclaimed Alfred, Sophia, Miss Tyrrell, and Sir William, in the same breath.

"No!" said Miss Davenport; "at least, if he has really engaged himself, it is within the last few minutes, and with the chivalrous intention of shielding me! Peter, I will not be shielded by such means. Our love is too precious to be publicly denied. I can not suffer it; I will acknowledge it, though it costs me my life! You," she added, turning to Sophia – "you can prove that I speak the truth. It was to you that I confided, that day we met on deck, the story of our fatal attachment."

"I really think you must be mistaken," said Sophia coldly. "If you confided such a story to anybody, it could not have been to me; for, until a few minutes ago, I had never set foot upon this ship."

How Sophia could stand there and, remembering, as she must do, her recent appropriation of the Time Cheque, tell such a downright fib as this, passed Peter's comprehension. But, as her statement was in his favour so far as it went, he knew better than to contradict it.

"Whether it was you or not," insisted Miss Davenport, "it is he and no one else who rendered my engagement to Alfred utterly repugnant to me! Can you look at him now, and doubt me longer?"

"So, Peter," said Sophia severely, "you could not even be faithful to your unfaithfulness!"

Miss Tyrrell made no comment, but she dropped his arm as if it had scorched her fingers, whereupon Miss Davenport clung to it in her stead, to Peter's infinite dismay and confusion.

"He *is* faithful!" she cried. "It is only a mistaken sense of honour that made him apparently false. Yes, Alfred, what I wrote to you, and the postscript he added, is the simple truth. We can not command our own hearts. Such love as I once had for you is dead – it died on the fatal day which brought him across my path. We met – we love; deal with us as you will! I would rather, ever so much rather, die with him than lose him now!"

Alfred was already beginning to fumble fiercely in his breast-pocket. Peter felt the time had arrived for plain speaking; he could not submit to be butchered under a ridiculous misapprehension of this kind.

"Listen to me!" he said eagerly, "before you do anything rash, or you may bitterly regret it afterward. I do assure you that I am the victim – we are *all* the victims of a series of unfortunate cheques – I should say, mistakes. It's absurd to make me responsible for the irregular proceedings of a nonsensical Bank. If I had spent my time as I ought to have done at the time, instead of putting it out on deposit I should never have dreamed of employing it in any kind of philandering!"

"That," said Sophia, "is undeniable; but you spent it as you ought *not* to have done!"

"Such a speech comes ill from you," he said, reproachfully, "after having expressly condoned the past; and, however I may have appeared to philander, I can conscientiously declare that my sentiments toward both of these young ladies – *both*, you understand – have been restricted to a respectful and – and merely friendly esteem....Don't shoot, Alfred!...I thought that was quite understood on all sides. Only have a little more patience,

Alfred, and I will undertake to convince even you that I could not for a moment have contemplated depriving you of the hand of this extremely charming and attractive lady, who will *not* let go my arm....I – I am a married man!"

"Married!" shrieked Miss Davenport, cowering back.

"Married!" exclaimed Miss Tyrrell, as she hid her face upon her father's shoulder.

"Married!" shouted the Judge. "By heavens, sir, you shall account to me for this!"

"Married!" cried Sophia, "Oh, Peter, I was *not* prepared for this! When? Where?"

"*When? Where?*" he echoed. "You were not prepared for it? Perhaps you will ask me next who my wife is!"

"I shall not indeed," said Sophia, "for I have no longer the slightest curiosity on such a subject!"

Peter collapsed upon the nearest bench.

"Sophia?" he cried hoarsely, "Why keep this up any longer? Surely it is gone far enough – you *can't* pretend you don't know!"

But while he spoke the words, he saw suddenly that his attempt to force her hand was hopeless: she was quite sincere in her surprise; she was the Sophia of *six months ago*, and no amount of explanation could ever make her comprehend what had happened since that time!

And here Alfred broke his silence.

"What you have just confessed," he said, "removes my last scruple. I might, for all I can tell, have stayed my hand and spared your life upon your promise to make Maud happy; for, in spite of her treatment of me, her happiness is still my first consideration. But now you have declared that impossible, why, as soon as I can get this revolver out of my pocket – for it has stuck in the confounded lining – I will shoot you like a rabbit!"

"Sir William," cried Peter, "I appeal to you! You are the representative of Law and Order here. He is threatening a breach of the Peace – the *Queen's* Peace! I call upon you to interfere!"

"I am no advocate," said Sir William, with judicial calm, "for taking the law into one's own hands. I even express a hope that this gentleman will not carry out his avowed intention, at least until I have had time to withdraw, and I must not be understood to approve his action in any way. At the same time, I am distinctly of opinion that he has received sufficient provocation to excuse even such extreme measures, and that the fate he threatens will, if summary, at least be richly deserved."

"I think so too," said Sophia, "though it would be painful to be compelled to witness it!"

"Terrible!" agreed Miss Tyrrell. "Let us hide our eyes, dear!"

"Stay, Alfred!" Miss Davenport implored, "Have some pity! Think – with all your faults, you are a keen sportsman – you would not shoot even a rabbit sitting! Give Mr. Tourmalin a start of a few seconds – let him have a run before you fire!"

All this time Alfred was still fumbling for and execrating the obstinate weapon.

"I decline to run!" Peter cried from his seat; he knew too well that he could not stir a limb." Shoot me sitting, or not at all, but don't keep me waiting any longer!"

His prayer seemed likely to be granted, for Alfred had at last succeeded in extricating the revolver; but before he could take aim, the Bank Manager and the Melbourne man ran in and interposed.

"Hold on one minute, sir," they said; "we, too, have business with the gentleman on the seat there, and you will admit that it must be concluded before yours, if it is to be settled at all. We must really ask you to postpone your little affair until we have finished. We will not keep you waiting any longer than we can help."

The Judge, with an ostentatious indifference, had strolled away to the smoking-room, probably to avoid being called upon to decide so nice a point as this disputed precedence; his daughter, Miss Davenport, and Sophia, had turned their backs, and, stopping their ears, were begging to be told when all was over.

Alfred was struggling to free his pistol-arm, which was firmly held by the other two men, and all three were talking at once in hot and argumentative support of their claims. As for Peter, he sat and looked on, glued to his seat by terror: if he had any preference among the disputants, he rather hoped that Alfred would be the person to gain his point.

All at once he saw Sophia turn round and, with her fingers still pressed to her ears, make energetic contortions of her lips, evidently for his benefit. After one or two repetitions, he made out the words she was voicelessly framing.

"*Run for it!*" he interpreted. "*Quick...while you can!*"

With his habitual respect for her advice, he rose and, finding that the power of motion had suddenly returned, he *did* run for it; he slipped quietly round the corner and down the passage to the other side of the ship, where he hoped to reach the saloon-entrance, and eventually regain his cabin.

Unhappily for him, the grim lady from Melbourne had noted his flight and anticipated its object. Long before he got to the open doors, he saw her step out and bar the way; she had an open sunshade in her hand, which she was preparing to use as a butterfly net.

He turned and fled abruptly in the opposite direction, intending to cross the bridge which led aft to the second-class saloon deck, where he might find cover; but as he saw, on turning the corner, the Manager had already occupied the passage, Peter turned again and doubled back across the ship, making for the forecastle; but he was too late, for the Melbourne man was there before him, and cut off all hope of retreat in that quarter.

There was only one thing left now; he must take to the rigging, and accordingly the next moment, scarcely knowing how he came there, he was clambering up the shrouds for dear life!

Higher and higher he climbed, slipping and stumbling, and catching his unaccustomed feet in the ratlins at every step; and all the way he had a dismal conviction that as yet he had not nearly exhausted the cheque he had drawn. He must have at least another couple of hours to get through, not to mention the compound interest, which the bank seemed characteristically enough to be paying first.

Still, if he could only stay quietly up aloft till his time was up, he might escape the worst yet. Surely it was a sufficient penalty for his folly to have embroiled himself with every creature he knew; to have been chivied about the deck of an ocean steamer by three violent men, each thirsting for his blood; and to be reduced to mount the rigging like an escaped monkey!

A few more steps and he was safe at last! Just above was a huge yard, flattened on the upper surface, with a partially furled sail, behind which he could crouch unseen; his hands were almost upon it, when a bronzed and bearded face appeared above the canvas – it was one of the English crew.

"Beg your pardon, sir," said the man, civilly enough, "but I shall 'ave fur to trouble you to go down agin, please. Capt'in's strick orders, sir. Passengers ain't allowed to amuse theirselves climbing the rigging!"

"My good man!" said Peter, between his pants, "do I *look* as if I was amusing myself? I am pursued, I tell you. As an honest, goodhearted British seaman – which I am sure you are – I entreat you to give me a hand up, and hide me; it – it may be life or death for me!"

The man wavered; the desperate plight Peter was in seemed to arouse his compassion, as it well might.

"I *could* 'ide yer, I suppose, come to that," he said slowly; "but it's too late to think o' that now. Look below, sir!"

Peter glanced down between his feet, and saw two swarthy Lascars climbing the rigging like cats. Lower still, he had a bird's-eye view of the deck, about which his enemies were posted in readiness for his arrival: the Manager exhibiting his spiked boots to Sir William, who shook his head in mild deprecation; the old lady shaking her sunshade in angry denunciation, while her brother flourished his horsewhip; and Alfred stood covering him with his revolver, prepared to pick him off the instant he came within range!

And Peter hung there by his hands – for his feet had slipped out of the ratlins – as helpless a target as any innocent bottle in a shooting gallery, and the Lascars were getting nearer and nearer!

He could see their bilious eyeballs, and their teeth gleaming in their dusky faces. He felt a bony hand reaching for his ankles, and then a dizziness came over him; his grip upon the coarse, tarry cordage relaxed, and, shutting his eyes, he fell – down – down – down. Would the fall never come to an end? Would he never arrive?…

Chapter X
Denouement

AT LAST! The shock was over; and he feebly opened his eyes once more, to find that he was undoubtedly on the deck; and, yes, the Bank Manager was standing over him with a kind of triumphant grin!

"Mercy!" Peter murmured faintly. "You – you surely wouldn't kick a man when he's down!"

"My dear sir!" protested the Manager, "why should I wish to kick you in any position?"

He must be fatally injured, if even the Manager had relented!

"Is – is Alfred there?" asked Tourmalin, anxiously. "Keep him away, if you can!"

"Certainly!" said Mr. Perkins. "Who *is* Alfred?"

"Why, the man with the revolver. I thought you knew!"

"Come, come," said the Manager, "there's no man of that kind here, I assure you. Pull yourself together, sir; you're on board the *Boomerang* now!"

"I know," said Peter, dolefully, – "I know I am!"

He shut his eyes resignedly. He was about to receive some other portion of his time-balance. If he could only hope that no fresh complications would arise! Would he meet Miss Tyrrell or Miss Davenport next, he wondered, and how would they behave?

"Haven't you had sleep enough yet?" said the Manager. "You're not more than half awake even now!"

"Sleep?" exclaimed Tourmalin, sitting up and rubbing his eyes. "Why, you don't mean to tell me I've been dreaming all this time?"

"I don't know about dreaming; but I can answer for your snoring. Why, you almost drowned the ship's band! I knew what would happen when you *would* have two helpings of curry at breakfast. Worst thing to take in the world, especially if you don't walk it off!

"Why, you've been the joke of the whole ship for the last half-hour. I wish you could have seen yourself, with your head hanging over the arm of your chair and your mouth wide open! I thought at last it was only kind to wake you up. Those two young ladies over there have been in fits of laughter!"

Peter picked up Buckle, which was lying face downward on the deck. His own face was very red, possibly from stooping, as he inquired: "Er – *which* two young ladies?"

"Can't tell you their names; but those two uncommonly nice-looking girls – one in white and navy-blue, and the darker one in pink. Dear me, I thought they would have died!"

Even now they seemed to have the greatest difficulty in controlling their countenances, for happening just then to look round and catch Peter's glance of confused and still somnolent suspicion, they buried their faces in their handkerchiefs once more, in agonies of suppressed mirth.

And these were the two whom his dreaming fancies had pictured as tenderly, desperately, madly devoted to him! The reality was decidedly disenchanting: they were very ordinary girls, he saw, after all.

"Well," said Mr. Perkins, "it's not far off tiffin time now; so, you see, you managed to get through your extra time after all!"

"Yes," said Peter, with a little natural embarrassment; "but I think, do you know, that, on reflection, I – I *won't* deposit the extra hours after all! If you will kindly take back the – the cheque-book," he added, feeling in his pockets, "and give me the form I signed, we will consider the arrangement canceled – eh?"

"It's my belief," said the Manager, "that your head isn't quite clear yet; for, hang me if I know what you're talking about! Deposit? Cheque-book? Form? What is it all about?"

Peter coloured more furiously than before.

"It was the curry," he said. "I wasn't quite sure whether – but it's really too absurd to explain. I am wide-awake now, at all events!"

He was awake now, and knew that no time-bargain of this monstrous kind had ever been actually effected, and all the wild events which seemed to have taken whole months to accomplish themselves, were the work of a single hour's indigestion! He was still a bachelor; still engaged to Sophia: he had still to make the acquaintance of Miss Tyrrell and Miss Davenport, and endure the ordeal of remaining for some weeks to come – to say nothing of the extra hours – exposed to the peril of their fascinations!

But whatever happened now, it could not be said, at least, that he had not received abundant warning of the consequences which might ensue from any yielding, however blameless or defensible, on his part.

And Peter Tourmalin resolved that henceforth Buckle should monopolize his attention.

The Epilogue

THERE ARE ALWAYS a few inquiring persons who, at the conclusion of any story, insist upon being told 'what happened after that.' And if such a question is ever justified, it is so in the case of a narrative that, as in the present instance, ends almost at the precise moment at which it began.

So it is not impossible that some readers may be sufficiently interested to wish to know the particular effect produced upon Peter Tourmalin's subsequent conduct by a vision more than usually complicated and connected.

Did he receive it, for example, as a solemnly prophetic warning, and forswear all female society while on the *Boomerang*? Or was he rather prompted to prove its fallibility by actual experience?

As to the motives which guided him, we are unable to speak with confidence, and they must be left to be accounted for by the reader's knowledge of human nature in general, and Peter's, so far as it has been self-revealed by his unconscious imagination in these pages, in particular.

But the author is in a position to state with certainty that, when Sophia and her mother met the ship, as they duly did at Gibraltar, nothing on Peter's part gave them the slightest ground for suspecting that he was on terms of even the most distant acquaintanceship with either Miss Tyrrell or Miss Davenport, and that the fact of his being far advanced in the third volume of Buckle's *History of Civilization* seemed to guarantee that he had employed his spare time on board the vessel both wisely and well.

Nor did he get into any difficulties by circulating gossip concerning any matron from Melbourne, owing to the circumstance that there was no lady passenger who at all answered the description. She, like much else in his experiences, was purely a creation of the curry.

Lastly, it may be added that Peter is now married to his Sophia, and is far happier than even he could have expected. She tempers her intellectuality out of consideration for his mental barrenness; and as yet he has never found her society in the least oppressive, nor has his errant fancy wandered back in any perfidious sense to the time he spent, when freed from her supervision, on board the *Boomerang*.

The Meaning that You Choose

Bo Balder

I
Gluttony

ON MISS HEE'S first day as a trainee TEPO (Time Escape Prevention Officer), her teacher was a man. That was *aju* scary in itself. He seemed old, although looking back on it he was probably only middle-aged.

He shooed her to a waiting set of chairs, in front of a scratched and dented old screen. "I don't believe in explaining things beforehand. Just watch and tell me what you see."

Miss Hee sat down in the chair, made from a plastic so ancient it had started to crumble. The hive elders hadn't wanted her to enter Time Branch, because they were always underfunded and understaffed. But she just loved history. This seemed like a great opportunity to see it firsthand.

Mr. Mukerjee fiddled with a yellowed remote. Escape Prevention 101 Day 1, read the file he clicked on.

A summer's day in the past, just after dawn, showing a hayfield in grey morning light. The camera zoomed in on one plant. The seed heads looked thick and pale. Late August?

Mr. Mukerjee lifted his eyebrows at Miss Hee.

"Ripe wheat," she said meekly. "Anywhere between 8000 B.C. and 2200 Common Time."

There was no way to be any more precise except if you were a botanist specializing in the evolution of wheat. She thought she was doing well.

He nodded.

Footsteps and voices sounded off-camera. The view didn't change. Probably a fixed location feed.

People dressed in rough homespun came filing in, the women with kirtled up skirts and loose linen blouses, the men bare-chested. The men started swinging their tools, tall poles with a long curved blade at the bottom.

"Scything. The women follow the men and tie up the sheaves of wheat," Miss Hee said. "Between 600 and 1800 A.D., Europe."

"Not wrong, but I want more."

She leaned forward, as if that would help resolve the low quality of the feed. She tried to gauge skin tone, skull shape and hair and eye color. To her hive elders' bafflement, she'd specialized in North-Western European history, focal point 800 A.D. She could tell the difference between a Saxon and a Jute, a Frisian or a Tubantian, a Frank and a Merovingian. The clothes, the dyes, imports from the East, the rise of knitted items, all these things were supposed to help her distinguish between 700 A.D. and 800 A.D., Denmark or Holland or Germany, not that those countries had existed in those days.

But reality is stubborn. These people could be Frisians or Jutes. The time span was a 1000 years, she just couldn't narrow it down. Peasants were hard. They'd never had the money for the kind of items that would distinguish them, their hair looked dark because it was dirty, their faces were disfigured by disease and violence.

The scythes. Those were probably a clue. She just couldn't remember if there had been a revolution in scything science in that era. The plow, year 500. Harvesting combines in the 20th century. But *chincha*, scythes?

"Scythe. Introduction into Europe in the 13th century or thereabouts." Miss Hee was startled to hear herself speak. Sometimes she knew things she didn't know she knew.

One of the women started humming a song. Most people joined in. It sounded a bit rough and discordant, the way people sing who have no access to professional music or recordings.

The song changed. Hey, that tune was actually cheerful. A tall women smiled and hummed along while she bound sheaves. Her head scarf had slipped down on her shoulders.

Mr. Mukerjee froze the frame.

"Well?"

"I don't know," she stammered. "Maybe the grips on the snaith indicate..."

"Not the scythe, Miss Hee, the music! Recognize the tune?"

She blanked.

He whistled it. Then, impatient at her utter lack of comprehension, he clicked over to a music app and voila, the identical song blasted forth in a clunky old fashioned arrangement.

"Yellow Submarine, by the Beatles," she read out loud. "Oh! Oh! That's a song that's newer than that scene. So there's a time traveler in there!"

Mr. Mukerjee sighed. "Exactly. An agent followed the suspect into the field, whistled the song and waited for the suspect to join in unthinkingly."

"Tricky!" she said. *Cheating*, she thought.

"People can't help themselves, it's been proven over and over. Music gets in under their guard, they start smiling or tapping their feet or whistling along, and their rational brain just cannot stop them doing that. So even if they've ditched all their implants, are wearing the right clothes and blending in with all their might, we catch them anyways."

He clicked the feed back into motion. The woman who'd started the song fished a Traveler link from her pocket, hooked arms with the unsuspecting time escapee and they were gone before either the hayers or Miss Hee could blink.

"I think of it as Gluttony," Mr. Mukerjee said. "Using up resources that aren't theirs. The inability to stop consuming."

II
Pride

MISS HEE swallowed and pulled her veil tighter over her face. Why, oh why had she chosen West-Europe to specialize in? She must have been mad. No one with her face could walk around in the millennia of its history without elaborate precautions and disguises.

This was an annoying period where veils weren't acceptable and Asian faces not yet common. And London *circa* 1910 also happened to be one of the most popular time travel locations in the history of Escapees. Miss Hee couldn't understand it. Who'd want to go live where the color of your skin made you an outsider? On the verge of a terrible war?

She opened the huge doors a crack and slid inside. The greenish gloom of gaslight cast flickering shadows over the tiled walls. The classroom full of children scheduled for TB tests was already waiting, impatient or resigned parents checking their thick mechanical timepieces.

It was the hobble skirts. She always underestimated the time it took her to walk from the Underground station to the school.

She sat down, opened her list and called out the first name. The little boy was pushed forward by his parents, but then she had to wait while his forearm was bared. Jacket, wrist buttons, little shirtsleeves that needed rolling up, woolen underlayers to be peeled off.

Miss Hee stood and asked parents to prepare their children to speed up the procedure. Her voice always made her self-conscious. The light was too bright for her veil to hide her much. Oh, how she hated walking around in whiteface.

As she scratched the little boy's elbow crease, she unobtrusively checked the mother's face. No make-up. Still, there was something about the woman.

"Return Wednesday or Thursday evening. I will have to check the results."

"Can't we just check ourselves, miss?" the mother asked. Her accent seemed authentic. "If there's no reaction, he's not been exposed, right?"

Did she know just a little too much about medicine for an ordinary mum? Also, if the boy had been inoculated in another time, he might show a false positive. The mother wouldn't want to risk that. She was tall and lean, not in an impoverished way but in a sporty way. Check.

Miss Hee shook her head and slid the homing beacon into the little boy's wool undershirt. "Regulations, madam. Otherwise I cannot declare him healthy."

As the mother walked off, fussing with the little boy, Miss Hee reflected on the sin of Pride. Somewhere in this woman's basement or attic they would find sports equipment. As Mr. Mukerjee had shown her, people just couldn't stop themselves adhering to the standards of beauty of their home time. And the mother wasn't afraid enough of TB, as if she deep down knew it could be treated by antibiotics. That put her as an early Escapee, because new resistant TB was something that Miss Hee knew very well how to fear.

III
Lust

THE WOMEN WALKED. Even after two months, Miss Hee was still exhausted after each day of trailing behind the army proper, enveloped in their dust cloud, treading in the butter churn of manure and mud left behind by their horses. Would she ever get used to it? Not just to the walking, although her outwardly period-correct boots concealed the best in boot technology her age possessed, but to the way the women were treated.

They walked, they carried the tents and the possessions, and still they were supposed to cook dinner, be ready for their service as wives, look good, be cheerful and in their nonexistent spare moments bear and look after the children. All so the men could conquer Asia in peace, following Genghis Kahn westwards. Tüley, her mistress Tantsetseg's husband, talked of nothing but horses and arrow practice. Tantsetseg herself lived in permanent deep cover in this time. Miss Hee didn't even know her real name. How did she stand it?

TEPO's good undercover practice kept them from discussing their situation directly, of course, but Tantsetseg refused to acknowledge even the subtlest hint. Her conversation ranged from soup to men to babies to the war, even while the hot lava of emotions seething underneath scorched Miss Hee. Miss Hee felt very lonely while she churned milk (no butter ever resulted from it), brewed tea (undrinkable) and inexpertly felted Tüley's boot inlays. She suspected Tantsetseg stayed up late to fix her mistakes. Tüley's coming in and slurping his soup became the highlight of her day.

Genghis Khan's army was supposed to be a hotspot for Escapees. But she hadn't studied West-European history for nothing. Why put her here, in a situation where she wouldn't spot an Escapee unless he whipped out a Vone and started texting? Maybe the powers that be were punishing her for choosing another culture to study instead of her own. What would Mr. Mukerjee have done in this situation? She kept her head down and did what she was told. TEPO always had good reason for their actions.

It was very easy to be here, in other ways. She looked enough like a Mongol woman that no one looked at her twice. The press of people around her all day, albeit tall and robust ones, resembled the business of her home hive enough that it comforted her – as long as she didn't look up into the blue, empty sky above. She got over the fear of not wearing a face mask, although not over the smell. Her nose kept warning her about dome spills and toxic chemicals, even if her brain knew it was just steppe dust and warrior pee.

One searing summer day the men came in late, limping but triumphant. Tüley brought Miss Hee a sackful of clinking metal dishes, shining a dull yellow. Gold? She'd only ever seen fakes, but the real thing looked no different. She accepted it demurely, as a Chinese slave ought to. From the corners of her eyes, she saw the edge of Tantsetseg's embroidered sleeve twitch. She'd done something wrong.

Tüley stood and fiddled with his hands a bit. Miss Hee knew better now than to meet his eye or do anything than hold her utter stillness. Eventually he left.

"What?" Miss Hee whispered.

"You accepted his gift. He's now courting you," Tantsetseg muttered while slamming down clots of cream to be dried. The cream didn't deserve to be handled so roughly.

"I thought I was a slave. How can he court me?" Miss Hee asked, dutifully pushing her felting wool around, knowing it would never properly felt.

"He shouldn't. He should just buy you, or even just use you since you're my property."

"So?"

"You're causing a stir. Just what we don't need."

"Are you under suspicion?"

"No!" Tantsetseg stood and pushed the bucket of to be creamed milk away so hard some of it sloshed on the carpet. "You finish the cream. I need to check the goats."

Did this mean Tüley was the Escapee and her mistress was in trouble for not having noticed? That was just too confusing.

Miss Hee ate all the dollops of cream she scooped out of the milk. It was delicious, full, rich, tasting of the wildflowers the goats ate. She just wanted to indulge herself for once. Just this once.

After fifteen scoops she went outside to be sick. The human stomach was no longer suited to a protein and fat content that high.

The next morning she was transferred back to headquarters without the slightest warning. She stood, reeling, blinking, still in her Mongol outfit, and received orders for 19th century Florence.

She'd never know what churned inside Tantsetseg, never know the touch of her lips. Never even know why she was sent out there in the first place. That was the job.

Months later, Miss Hee heard that both Tüley and Tantsetseg had been arrested. One for escaping, the other for aiding and abetting the misuse of resources in and out of time. No thanks to her, though. So few males were born....She never would have thought to look for a male Escapee.

IV
Despair

MISS HEE couldn't believe it. It was unmistakably Mr. Mukerjee sitting there in the dusty courtyard, scantily dressed in some kind of loin cloth. First, it hard to believe that he of all people had deserted, had Escaped. Or well, tried to. And the second hardest thing to believe, was that he of all people had gone to this pivotal time period. Sitting under a tree with the Buddha, for God's sake. As if he wouldn't be found there.

She paused the image and rubbed her nose. He must have known he would be found fast. So he'd calculated that in. Didn't care.

Why? She sagged back in the uncomfortable chair. And wasn't thinking about why exactly what she'd always counseled her own students not to do? She'd learnt that from Mr. Mukerjee.

But she had to know.

She stood up. She'd go herself instead of sending one of the first-years. It would be fun to go out into the field again. Something in her gut twinged. No, higher up. Her heart knew that she ought to follow her own maxims if she didn't want to get hurt. *Stay aloof from people in the past, stay aloof from the Escapees. They'll pull you in, subvert you, make you feel sorry for them. Pretend they're not real. You're real, and the people in your own timeline. The rest are just actors, or might well be. Concentrate on punishing the sinners.*

As she walked through the office on her way to Wardrobe and Make-up, she admitted it to herself. That advice had never worked and it never would. People, in whatever timeline, were real. They breathed, they sweated, they had feelings. As did the Escapee Prevention officers.

Her skin was darkened to average Indian Continent levels 500 B.C., her wig coiled and her clothes wrapped. Mr. Mukerjee'd been like an auntie to her in the beginning, when she'd felt so lonely without her hive-mates. And now she had to bring him in for punishment.

That wasn't her department, but it wasn't as if she didn't know what would happen to him. Food theft cost you a hand, illegal pregnancy and Escaping your head. It was only fair to punish those who used up more than their share of resources. Only fair.

Still, when it was someone you knew, it was harder. Keeping her professional detachment used up energy Miss Hee didn't have to spare. She rubbed her stomach. Rations had been cut again, even at her level, and she was hungry. It always took a while before you got used to it again.

Clothed, coiffed, adorned and scented appropriately, Miss Hee stepped into the past.

It was hot there, pleasantly so. The European reaches where Miss Hee had long worked, and still occasionally went into the field, had been fairly chilly before global warming. She always got stiff shoulders and tension headaches from the cold.

She pulled a slip of her garment over her head, as she saw other women do, and knelt down in the shade of a banyan tree, a dozen yards or so where Mr. Mukerjee sat in a pose she vowed to look up as soon as she got back. Cross-legged, one hand open in his lap, the other touching the ground.

Miss Hee'd found herself delaying the arrest. She'd wanted him to have a few moments of inner peace, or whatever it was he'd been searching for.

After half an hour or so, her loins aching from the unfamiliar position, she stood up and crouched down next to and a little bit behind Mr. Mukerjee.

"*Sa Bum Nim*," she said softly. "It is time for you to leave."

Mr. Mukerjee's left hand twitched. "Already?"

"I can no longer postpone it. I'm sorry."

She inclined her head. He wouldn't be able to see it, but that didn't matter. The bow was for herself. He'd taught her everything she knew.

She hadn't planned on it, but she spoke. "What teaching would you like for me to take away from this situation?"

"You know I always make you answer that question yourself," he said. She was almost sure she heard a smile in his voice.

Miss Hee shifted to a more comfortable position. "What made my venerated teacher become a criminal? What sin?"

She pretended to look him over. "Not Gluttony. Not Pride." He was neither fat nor overly groomed, nor had he taken books or music to enjoy. Mentally she ticked off the other sins. Envy. Pride. Sloth. Wrath.

She swallowed. "Despair. You saw that whatever we did, no matter how many criminals we punished, the world did not become a better place. So you gave in to despair and Escaped. How did your act make the world better?"

"Oh, my child, you see too well. A person who despairs only seeks to please himself, to alleviate his own pain. Of that I am doubtless guilty. Take me home."

Miss Hee's eyes swam. She couldn't see which button she should press, but it didn't matter. It was big as well as red.

V
Lovingkindness

MISS HEE kept her head down and walked through the TEPO corridors to TT unit 17. Sneaking through the building at night wasn't good for her inner peace.

But inner peace, however nice, wasn't her goal. Mr. Mukerjee had showed her that road led nowhere. She'd allowed his teaching to mislead her. She should have paid attention to his subtext, not his words. Her job was to ask the questions he had warned her away from. Why did people Escape? What could be their goal if not to satisfy their own personality defects? Why go to the past when the past often wasn't that great? Apart from all the wannabe saviors, usually men, who tried assassinating Genghis Kahn, Napoleon, Hitler, Yun Fat, and other assorted tyrants, why go to war zones, why starve yourself playing a peasant?

As she set the timer settings by hand, from calculations she'd made secretly at home, noted down on her own skin, she remembered finding the bones of an Escapee into prehistory. She must have died within hours of her arrival, her clothes hadn't even smudged. Life had always been dangerous. The past was not paradise, as the romantics would have it. Nothing romantic about starvation, violence, suppression of women, and early death by horrible disease or childbirth.

Life's task, for every human being, was to give meaning to the present. Her present. Visiting the past had helped her to find that meaning. Growing up in a hive had sharpened her vision. Less than one per cent of her whole hive generation had been permitted to give birth. One niece for hundred-and-twenty aunties. Raised on strict rationing, they were all tiny and scrawny. Only one in a hundred nieces of that generation in all the hives would be selected for procreation. Would that be enough to shrink down humanity to a manageable size? And would it be in time? No one knew.

She had finally realized what the Escapees were doing. Why they often didn't seem to mind, didn't seem surprised to be caught. They weren't escaping for themselves. They were doing their bit for their present, the future of mankind. Acting for the world. Trying, one person at the time, one recycling act at a time, to prevent the future from happening. One more tree planted in a forest. One less snack consumed. Choosing to see the future as a function of the present.

She stepped into the booth, remote in hand, and pressed the button for Champs Elysées, Paris, 2016.

She scuttled through the street, cleaving close to the buildings. Bicycles raced by her, people carrying sticks of bread. Many people, but still not enough to be like home. The exhaust and industrial scents comforted her a little, but the un-domed skies had never lost their frightening aspect. Although she met many small Asian women, guilt and fear urged her inner crocodile to cower and start and never feel any peace, not even in conformity, the greatest solace of her childhood.

There it was, the Anti-Global Warning demonstration. The big square in front of the Parliament building was hemmed in by rows of heavily armed police. Anticipating violence. But the people streaming in from all sides weren't here to do violence. They were here to remind the world leaders at the Climate Conference of their responsibilities.

She was only one of many tiny Asian females. She smiled at all of them, just in case one, or all of them, were also from the future. And then she smiled at everyone who wasn't Asian or female. At humanity.

At everyone who was doing their bit. Dropping their penny in the sea, just in case it might help. Just like the future had happened one felled tree at a time, one baby at a time. The woods can spare one more tree. One more child won't make a difference. That's what people in the past had thought. And they had been wrong.

Miss Hee lifted her banner and made her own meaning, knowing she would be apprehended and not caring. She'd made her choice.

Looking Backward
Chapters I–III
Edward Bellamy

Author's Preface

Historical Section Shawmut College, Boston,
December 26, 2000

LIVING AS WE DO in the closing year of the twentieth century, enjoying the blessings of a social order at once so simple and logical that it seems but the triumph of common sense, it is no doubt difficult for those whose studies have not been largely historical to realize that the present organization of society is, in its completeness, less than a century old. No historical fact is, however, better established than that till nearly the end of the nineteenth century it was the general belief that the ancient industrial system, with all its shocking social consequences, was destined to last, with possibly a little patching, to the end of time. How strange and well nigh incredible does it seem that so prodigious a moral and material transformation as has taken place since then could have been accomplished in so brief an interval! The readiness with which men accustom themselves, as matters of course, to improvements in their condition, which, when anticipated, seemed to leave nothing more to be desired, could not be more strikingly illustrated. What reflection could be better calculated to moderate the enthusiasm of reformers who count for their reward on the lively gratitude of future ages!

The object of this volume is to assist persons who, while desiring to gain a more definite idea of the social contrasts between the nineteenth and twentieth centuries, are daunted by the formal aspect of the histories which treat the subject. Warned by a teacher's experience that learning is accounted a weariness to the flesh, the author has sought to alleviate the instructive quality of the book by casting it in the form of a romantic narrative, which he would be glad to fancy not wholly devoid of interest on its own account.

The reader, to whom modern social institutions and their underlying principles are matters of course, may at times find Dr. Leete's explanations of them rather trite – but it must be remembered that to Dr. Leete's guest they were not matters of course, and that this book is written for the express purpose of inducing the reader to forget for the nonce that they are so to him. One word more. The almost universal theme of the writers and orators who have celebrated this bimillennial epoch has been the future rather than the past, not the advance that has been made, but the progress that shall be made, ever onward and upward, till the race shall achieve its ineffable destiny. This is well, wholly well, but it seems to me that nowhere can we find more solid ground for daring anticipations of human development during the next one thousand years, than by 'Looking Backward' upon the progress of the last one hundred.

That this volume may be so fortunate as to find readers whose interest in the subject shall incline them to overlook the deficiencies of the treatment is the hope in which the author steps aside and leaves Mr. Julian West to speak for himself.

Chapter I

I FIRST SAW the light in the city of Boston in the year 1857. "What!" you say, "eighteen fifty-seven? That is an odd slip. He means nineteen fifty-seven, of course." I beg pardon, but there is no mistake. It was about four in the afternoon of December the 26th, one day after Christmas, in the year 1857, not 1957, that I first breathed the east wind of Boston, which, I assure the reader, was at that remote period marked by the same penetrating quality characterizing it in the present year of grace, 2000.

These statements seem so absurd on their face, especially when I add that I am a young man apparently of about thirty years of age, that no person can be blamed for refusing to read another word of what promises to be a mere imposition upon his credulity. Nevertheless I earnestly assure the reader that no imposition is intended, and will undertake, if he shall follow me a few pages, to entirely convince him of this. If I may, then, provisionally assume, with the pledge of justifying the assumption, that I know better than the reader when I was born, I will go on with my narrative. As every schoolboy knows, in the latter part of the nineteenth century the civilization of today, or anything like it, did not exist, although the elements which were to develop it were already in ferment. Nothing had, however, occurred to modify the immemorial division of society into the four classes, or nations, as they may be more fitly called, since the differences between them were far greater than those between any nations nowadays, of the rich and the poor, the educated and the ignorant. I myself was rich and also educated, and possessed, therefore, all the elements of happiness enjoyed by the most fortunate in that age. Living in luxury, and occupied only with the pursuit of the pleasures and refinements of life, I derived the means of my support from the labor of others, rendering no sort of service in return. My parents and grand-parents had lived in the same way, and I expected that my descendants, if I had any, would enjoy a like easy existence.

But how could I live without service to the world? you ask. Why should the world have supported in utter idleness one who was able to render service? The answer is that my great-grandfather had accumulated a sum of money on which his descendants had ever since lived. The sum, you will naturally infer, must have been very large not to have been exhausted in supporting three generations in idleness. This, however, was not the fact. The sum had been originally by no means large. It was, in fact, much larger now that three generations had been supported upon it in idleness, than it was at first. This mystery of use without consumption, of warmth without combustion, seems like magic, but was merely an ingenious application of the art now happily lost but carried to great perfection by your ancestors, of shifting the burden of one's support on the shoulders of others. The man who had accomplished this, and it was the end all sought, was said to live on the income of his investments. To explain at this point how the ancient methods of industry made this possible would delay us too much. I shall only stop now to say that interest on investments was a species of tax in perpetuity upon the product of those engaged in industry which a person possessing or inheriting money was able to levy. It must not be supposed that an arrangement which seems so unnatural and preposterous according to modern notions was never criticized by your ancestors. It had been the effort of lawgivers and prophets from the earliest ages to abolish interest, or at least to limit it to the smallest possible rate. All these efforts had, however, failed, as they necessarily must so long as the ancient social organizations prevailed. At the time of which I write, the latter part of the nineteenth century, governments had generally given up trying to regulate the subject at all.

By way of attempting to give the reader some general impression of the way people lived together in those days, and especially of the relations of the rich and poor to one another, perhaps I cannot do better than to compare society as it then was to a prodigious coach which the masses of humanity were harnessed to and dragged toilsomely along a very hilly and sandy road. The driver was hunger, and permitted no lagging, though the pace was necessarily very slow. Despite the difficulty of drawing the coach at all along so hard a road, the top was covered with passengers who never got down, even at the steepest ascents. These seats on top were very breezy and comfortable. Well up out of the dust, their occupants could enjoy the scenery at their leisure, or critically discuss the merits of the straining team. Naturally such places were in great demand and the competition for them was keen, everyone seeking as the first end in life to secure a seat on the coach for himself and to leave it to his child after him. By the rule of the coach a man could leave his seat to whom he wished, but on the other hand there were many accidents by which it might at any time be wholly lost. For all that they were so easy, the seats were very insecure, and at every sudden jolt of the coach persons were slipping out of them and falling to the ground, where they were instantly compelled to take hold of the rope and help to drag the coach on which they had before ridden so pleasantly. It was naturally regarded as a terrible misfortune to lose one's seat, and the apprehension that this might happen to them or their friends was a constant cloud upon the happiness of those who rode.

But did they think only of themselves? you ask. Was not their very luxury rendered intolerable to them by comparison with the lot of their brothers and sisters in the harness, and the knowledge that their own weight added to their toil? Had they no compassion for fellow beings from whom fortune only distinguished them? Oh, yes; commiseration was frequently expressed by those who rode for those who had to pull the coach, especially when the vehicle came to a bad place in the road, as it was constantly doing, or to a particularly steep hill. At such times, the desperate straining of the team, their agonized leaping and plunging under the pitiless lashing of hunger, the many who fainted at the rope and were trampled in the mire, made a very distressing spectacle, which often called forth highly creditable displays of feeling on the top of the coach. At such times the passengers would call down encouragingly to the toilers of the rope, exhorting them to patience, and holding out hopes of possible compensation in another world for the hardness of their lot, while others contributed to buy salves and liniments for the crippled and injured. It was agreed that it was a great pity that the coach should be so hard to pull, and there was a sense of general relief when the specially bad piece of road was gotten over. This relief was not, indeed, wholly on account of the team, for there was always some danger at these bad places of a general overturn in which all would lose their seats.

It must in truth be admitted that the main effect of the spectacle of the misery of the toilers at the rope was to enhance the passengers' sense of the value of their seats upon the coach, and to cause them to hold on to them more desperately than before. If the passengers could only have felt assured that neither they nor their friends would ever fall from the top, it is probable that, beyond contributing to the funds for liniments and bandages, they would have troubled themselves extremely little about those who dragged the coach.

I am well aware that this will appear to the men and women of the twentieth century an incredible inhumanity, but there are two facts, both very curious, which partly explain it. In the first place, it was firmly and sincerely believed that there was no other way in which Society could get along, except the many pulled at the rope and the few rode, and not only this, but that no very radical improvement even was possible, either in the harness, the coach, the roadway, or the distribution of the toil. It had always been as it was, and it always would be so. It was a pity, but it could not be helped, and philosophy forbade wasting compassion on what was beyond remedy.

The other fact is yet more curious, consisting in a singular hallucination which those on the top of the coach generally shared, that they were not exactly like their brothers and sisters who pulled at the rope, but of finer clay, in some way belonging to a higher order of beings who might justly expect to be drawn. This seems unaccountable, but, as I once rode on this very coach and shared that very hallucination, I ought to be believed. The strangest thing about the hallucination was that those who had but just climbed up from the ground, before they had outgrown the marks of the rope upon their hands, began to fall under its influence. As for those whose parents and grandparents before them had been so fortunate as to keep their seats on the top, the conviction they cherished of the essential difference between their sort of humanity and the common article was absolute. The effect of such a delusion in moderating fellow feeling for the sufferings of the mass of men into a distant and philosophical compassion is obvious. To it I refer as the only extenuation I can offer for the indifference which, at the period I write of, marked my own attitude toward the misery of my brothers.

In 1887 I came to my thirtieth year. Although still unmarried, I was engaged to wed Edith Bartlett. She, like myself, rode on the top of the coach. That is to say, not to encumber ourselves further with an illustration which has, I hope, served its purpose of giving the reader some general impression of how we lived then, her family was wealthy. In that age, when money alone commanded all that was agreeable and refined in life, it was enough for a woman to be rich to have suitors; but Edith Bartlett was beautiful and graceful also.

My lady readers, I am aware, will protest at this. "Handsome she might have been," I hear them saying, "but graceful never, in the costumes which were the fashion at that period, when the head covering was a dizzy structure a foot tall, and the almost incredible extension of the skirt behind by means of artificial contrivances more thoroughly dehumanized the form than any former device of dressmakers. Fancy any one graceful in such a costume!" The point is certainly well taken, and I can only reply that while the ladies of the twentieth century are lovely demonstrations of the effect of appropriate drapery in accenting feminine graces, my recollection of their great-grandmothers enables me to maintain that no deformity of costume can wholly disguise them.

Our marriage only waited on the completion of the house which I was building for our occupancy in one of the most desirable parts of the city, that is to say, a part chiefly inhabited by the rich. For it must be understood that the comparative desirability of different parts of Boston for residence depended then, not on natural features, but on the character of the neighboring population. Each class or nation lived by itself, in quarters of its own. A rich man living among the poor, an educated man among the uneducated, was like one living in isolation among a jealous and alien race. When the house had been begun, its completion by the winter of 1886 had been expected. The spring of the following year found it, however, yet incomplete, and my marriage still a thing of the future. The cause of a delay calculated to be particularly exasperating to an ardent lover was a series of strikes, that is to say, concerted refusals to work on the part of the brick-layers, masons, carpenters, painters, plumbers, and other trades concerned in house building. What the specific causes of these strikes were I do not remember. Strikes had become so common at that period that people had ceased to inquire into their particular grounds. In one department of industry or another, they had been nearly incessant ever since the great business crisis of 1873. In fact it had come to be the exceptional thing to see any class of laborers pursue their avocation steadily for more than a few months at a time.

The reader who observes the dates alluded to will of course recognize in these disturbances of industry the first and incoherent phase of the great movement which ended in the establishment of the modern industrial system with all its social consequences. This is all so plain in the retrospect that a child can understand it, but not being prophets, we of that day had no clear idea what was happening to us. What we did see was that industrially the country was in a very queer way. The relation between the workingman and the employer, between labor and capital, appeared in some unaccountable manner to have become dislocated. The working classes had quite suddenly and very generally become infected with a profound discontent with their condition, and an idea that it could be greatly bettered if they only knew how to go about it. On every side, with one accord, they preferred demands for higher pay, shorter hours, better dwellings, better educational advantages, and a share in the refinements and luxuries of life, demands which it was impossible to see the way to granting unless the world were to become a great deal richer than it then was. Though they knew something of what they wanted, they knew nothing of how to accomplish it, and the eager enthusiasm with which they thronged about any one who seemed likely to give them any light on the subject lent sudden reputation to many would-be leaders, some of whom had little enough light to give. However chimerical the aspirations of the laboring classes might be deemed, the devotion with which they supported one another in the strikes, which were their chief weapon, and the sacrifices which they underwent to carry them out left no doubt of their dead earnestness.

As to the final outcome of the labor troubles, which was the phrase by which the movement I have described was most commonly referred to, the opinions of the people of my class differed according to individual temperament. The sanguine argued very forcibly that it was in the very nature of things impossible that the new hopes of the workingmen could be satisfied, simply because the world had not the wherewithal to satisfy them. It was only because the masses worked very hard and lived on short commons that the race did not starve outright, and no considerable improvement in their condition was possible while the world, as a whole, remained so poor. It was not the capitalists whom the laboring men were contending with, these maintained, but the iron-bound environment of humanity, and it was merely a question of the thickness of their skulls when they would discover the fact and make up their minds to endure what they could not cure.

The less sanguine admitted all this. Of course the workingmen's aspirations were impossible of fulfillment for natural reasons, but there were grounds to fear that they would not discover this fact until they had made a sad mess of society. They had the votes and the power to do so if they pleased, and their leaders meant they should. Some of these desponding observers went so far as to predict an impending social cataclysm. Humanity, they argued, having climbed to the top round of the ladder of civilization, was about to take a header into chaos, after which it would doubtless pick itself up, turn round, and begin to climb again. Repeated experiences of this sort in historic and prehistoric times possibly accounted for the puzzling bumps on the human cranium. Human history, like all great movements, was cyclical, and returned to the point of beginning. The idea of indefinite progress in a right line was a chimera of the imagination, with no analogue in nature. The parabola of a comet was perhaps a yet better illustration of the career of humanity. Tending upward and sunward from the aphelion of barbarism, the race attained the perihelion of civilization only to plunge downward once more to its nether goal in the regions of chaos.

This, of course, was an extreme opinion, but I remember serious men among my acquaintances who, in discussing the signs of the times, adopted a very similar tone. It was no doubt the common opinion of thoughtful men that society was approaching a critical period which might result in great changes. The labor troubles, their causes, course, and cure, took lead of all other topics in the public prints, and in serious conversation.

The nervous tension of the public mind could not have been more strikingly illustrated than it was by the alarm resulting from the talk of a small band of men who called themselves anarchists, and proposed to terrify the American people into adopting their ideas by threats of violence, as if a mighty nation which had but just put down a rebellion of half its own numbers, in order to maintain its political system, were likely to adopt a new social system out of fear.

As one of the wealthy, with a large stake in the existing order of things, I naturally shared the apprehensions of my class. The particular grievance I had against the working classes at the time of which I write, on account of the effect of their strikes in postponing my wedded bliss, no doubt lent a special animosity to my feeling toward them.

Chapter II

THE THIRTIETH DAY of May, 1887, fell on a Monday. It was one of the annual holidays of the nation in the latter third of the nineteenth century, being set apart under the name of Decoration Day, for doing honor to the memory of the soldiers of the North who took part in the war for the preservation of the union of the States. The survivors of the war, escorted by military and civic processions and bands of music, were wont on this occasion to visit the cemeteries and lay wreaths of flowers upon the graves of their dead comrades, the ceremony being a very solemn and touching one. The eldest brother of Edith Bartlett had fallen in the war, and on Decoration Day the family was in the habit of making a visit to Mount Auburn, where he lay.

I had asked permission to make one of the party, and, on our return to the city at nightfall, remained to dine with the family of my betrothed. In the drawing-room, after dinner, I picked up an evening paper and read of a fresh strike in the building trades, which would probably still further delay the completion of my unlucky house. I remember distinctly how exasperated I was at this, and the objurgations, as forcible as the presence of the ladies permitted, which I lavished upon workmen in general, and these strikers in particular. I had abundant sympathy from those about me, and the remarks made in the desultory conversation which followed, upon the unprincipled conduct of the labor agitators, were calculated to make those gentlemen's ears tingle. It was agreed that affairs were going from bad to worse very fast, and that there was no telling what we should come to soon. "The worst of it," I remember Mrs. Bartlett's saying, "is that the working classes all over the world seem to be going crazy at once. In Europe it is far worse even than here. I'm sure I should not dare to live there at all. I asked Mr. Bartlett the other day where we should emigrate to if all the terrible things took place which those socialists threaten. He said he did not know any place now where society could be called stable except Greenland, Patagonia, and the Chinese Empire."

"Those Chinamen knew what they were about," somebody added, "when they refused to let in our western civilization. They knew what it would lead to better than we did. They saw it was nothing but dynamite in disguise."

After this, I remember drawing Edith apart and trying to persuade her that it would be better to be married at once without waiting for the completion of the house, spending the time in travel till our home was ready for us. She was remarkably handsome that evening, the mourning costume that she wore in recognition of the day setting off to great advantage the purity of her complexion. I can see her even now with my mind's eye just as she looked that night. When I took my leave she followed me into the hall and I kissed her good-by as usual. There was no circumstance out of the common to distinguish this parting from previous occasions when we had bade each other goodbye for a night or a day. There was absolutely no premonition in my mind, or I am sure in hers, that this was more than an ordinary separation.

Ah, well!

The hour at which I had left my betrothed was a rather early one for a lover, but the fact was no reflection on my devotion. I was a confirmed sufferer from insomnia, and although otherwise perfectly well had been completely fagged out that day, from having slept scarcely at all the two previous nights. Edith knew this and had insisted on sending me home by nine o'clock, with strict orders to go to bed at once.

The house in which I lived had been occupied by three generations of the family of which I was the only living representative in the direct line. It was a large, ancient wooden mansion, very elegant in an old-fashioned way within, but situated in a quarter that had long since become undesirable for residence, from its invasion by tenement houses and manufactories. It was not a house to which I could think of bringing a bride, much less so dainty a one as Edith Bartlett. I had advertised it for sale, and meanwhile merely used it for sleeping purposes, dining at my club. One servant, a faithful colored man by the name of Sawyer, lived with me and attended to my few wants. One feature of the house I expected to miss greatly when I should leave it, and this was the sleeping chamber which I had built under the foundations. I could not have slept in the city at all, with its never ceasing nightly noises, if I had been obliged to use an upstairs chamber. But to this subterranean room no murmur from the upper world ever penetrated. When I had entered it and closed the door, I was surrounded by the silence of the tomb. In order to prevent the dampness of the subsoil from penetrating the chamber, the walls had been laid in hydraulic cement and were very thick, and the floor was likewise protected. In order that the room might serve also as a vault equally proof against violence and flames, for the storage of valuables, I had roofed it with stone slabs hermetically sealed, and the outer door was of iron with a thick coating of asbestos. A small pipe, communicating with a wind-mill on the top of the house, insured the renewal of air.

It might seem that the tenant of such a chamber ought to be able to command slumber, but it was rare that I slept well, even there, two nights in succession. So accustomed was I to wakefulness that I minded little the loss of one night's rest. A second night, however, spent in my reading chair instead of my bed, tired me out, and I never allowed myself to go longer than that without slumber, from fear of nervous disorder. From this statement it will be inferred that I had at my command some artificial means for inducing sleep in the last resort, and so in fact I had. If after two sleepless nights I found myself on the approach of the third without sensations of drowsiness, I called in Dr. Pillsbury.

He was a doctor by courtesy only, what was called in those days an 'irregular' or 'quack' doctor. He called himself a 'Professor of Animal Magnetism.' I had come across him in the course of some amateur investigations into the phenomena of animal magnetism. I don't think he knew anything about medicine, but he was certainly a remarkable mesmerist. It was for the purpose of being put to sleep by his manipulations that I used to send for him when I found a third night of sleeplessness impending. Let my nervous excitement or mental preoccupation be however great, Dr. Pillsbury never failed, after a short time, to leave me in a deep slumber, which continued till I was aroused by a reversal of the mesmerizing process. The process for awaking the sleeper was much simpler than that for putting him to sleep, and for convenience I had made Dr. Pillsbury teach Sawyer how to do it.

My faithful servant alone knew for what purpose Dr. Pillsbury visited me, or that he did so at all. Of course, when Edith became my wife I should have to tell her my secrets. I had not hitherto told her this, because there was unquestionably a slight risk in the mesmeric sleep, and I knew she would set her face against my practice. The risk, of course, was that it might become too profound and pass into a trance beyond the mesmerizer's power to break, ending in death. Repeated experiments had fully convinced me that the risk was next to nothing if reasonable precautions were exercised, and of this I hoped, though doubtingly, to convince Edith. I went directly home after leaving her, and at once sent Sawyer to fetch Dr. Pillsbury. Meanwhile I sought my subterranean sleeping chamber, and exchanging my costume for a comfortable dressing-gown, sat down to read the letters by the evening mail which Sawyer had laid on my reading table.

One of them was from the builder of my new house, and confirmed what I had inferred from the newspaper item. The new strikes, he said, had postponed indefinitely the completion of the contract, as neither masters nor workmen would concede the point at issue without a long struggle. Caligula wished that the Roman people had but one neck that he might cut it off, and as I read this letter I am afraid that for a moment I was capable of wishing the same thing concerning the laboring classes of America. The return of Sawyer with the doctor interrupted my gloomy meditations.

It appeared that he had with difficulty been able to secure his services, as he was preparing to leave the city that very night. The doctor explained that since he had seen me last he had learned of a fine professional opening in a distant city, and decided to take prompt advantage of it. On my asking, in some panic, what I was to do for someone to put me to sleep, he gave me the names of several mesmerizers in Boston who, he averred, had quite as great powers as he.

Somewhat relieved on this point, I instructed Sawyer to rouse me at nine o'clock next morning, and, lying down on the bed in my dressing-gown, assumed a comfortable attitude, and surrendered myself to the manipulations of the mesmerizer. Owing, perhaps, to my unusually nervous state, I was slower than common in losing consciousness, but at length a delicious drowsiness stole over me.

Chapter III

"HE IS GOING to open his eyes. He had better see but one of us at first."

"Promise me, then, that you will not tell him."

The first voice was a man's, the second a woman's, and both spoke in whispers.

"I will see how he seems," replied the man.

"No, no, promise me," persisted the other.

"Let her have her way," whispered a third voice, also a woman.

"Well, well, I promise, then," answered the man. "Quick, go! He is coming out of it."

There was a rustle of garments and I opened my eyes. A fine looking man of perhaps sixty was bending over me, an expression of much benevolence mingled with great curiosity upon his features. He was an utter stranger. I raised myself on an elbow and looked around. The room was empty. I certainly had never been in it before, or one furnished like it. I looked back at my companion. He smiled.

"How do you feel?" he inquired.

"Where am I?" I demanded.

"You are in my house," was the reply.

"How came I here?"

"We will talk about that when you are stronger. Meanwhile, I beg you will feel no anxiety. You are among friends and in good hands. How do you feel?"

"A bit queerly," I replied, "but I am well, I suppose. Will you tell me how I came to be indebted to your hospitality? What has happened to me? How came I here? It was in my own house that I went to sleep."

"There will be time enough for explanations later," my unknown host replied, with a reassuring smile. "It will be better to avoid agitating talk until you are a little more yourself. Will you oblige me by taking a couple of swallows of this mixture? It will do you good. I am a physician."

I repelled the glass with my hand and sat up on the couch, although with an effort, for my head was strangely light.

"I insist upon knowing at once where I am and what you have been doing with me," I said.

"My dear sir," responded my companion, "let me beg that you will not agitate yourself. I would rather you did not insist upon explanations so soon, but if you do, I will try to satisfy you, provided you will first take this draught, which will strengthen you somewhat."

I thereupon drank what he offered me. Then he said, "It is not so simple a matter as you evidently suppose to tell you how you came here. You can tell me quite as much on that point as I can tell you. You have just been roused from a deep sleep, or, more properly, trance. So much I can tell you. You say you were in your own house when you fell into that sleep. May I ask you when that was?"

"When?" I replied, "When? Why, last evening, of course, at about ten o'clock. I left my man Sawyer orders to call me at nine o'clock. What has become of Sawyer?"

"I can't precisely tell you that," replied my companion, regarding me with a curious expression, "but I am sure that he is excusable for not being here. And now can you tell me a little more explicitly when it was that you fell into that sleep, the date, I mean?"

"Why, last night, of course; I said so, didn't I? That is, unless I have overslept an entire day. Great heavens! That cannot be possible; and yet I have an odd sensation of having slept a long time. It was Decoration Day that I went to sleep."

"Decoration Day?"

"Yes, Monday, the 30th."

"Pardon me, the 30th of what?"

"Why, of this month, of course, unless I have slept into June, but that can't be."

"This month is September."

"September! You don't mean that I've slept since May! God in heaven! Why, it is incredible."

"We shall see," replied my companion; "you say that it was May 30th when you went to sleep?"

"Yes."

"May I ask of what year?"

I stared blankly at him, incapable of speech, for some moments.

"Of what year?" I feebly echoed at last.

"Yes, of what year, if you please? After you have told me that I shall be able to tell you how long you have slept."

"It was the year 1887," I said.

My companion insisted that I should take another draught from the glass, and felt my pulse.

"My dear sir," he said, "your manner indicates that you are a man of culture, which I am aware was by no means the matter of course in your day it now is. No doubt, then, you have yourself made the observation that nothing in this world can be truly said to be more wonderful than anything else. The causes of all phenomena are equally adequate, and the results equally matters of course. That you should be startled by what I shall tell you is to be expected; but I am confident that you will not permit it to affect your equanimity unduly. Your appearance is that of a young man of barely thirty, and your bodily condition seems not greatly different from that of one just roused from a somewhat too long and profound sleep, and yet this is the tenth day of September in the year 2000, and you have slept exactly one hundred and thirteen years, three months, and eleven days."

Feeling partially dazed, I drank a cup of some sort of broth at my companion's suggestion, and, immediately afterward becoming very drowsy, went off into a deep sleep.

When I awoke it was broad daylight in the room, which had been lighted artificially when I was awake before. My mysterious host was sitting near. He was not looking at me when I opened my eyes, and I had a good opportunity to study him and meditate upon my extraordinary situation, before he observed that I was awake. My giddiness was all gone, and my mind perfectly clear. The story that I had been asleep one hundred and thirteen years, which, in my former weak and bewildered condition, I had accepted without question, recurred to me now only to be rejected as a preposterous attempt at an imposture, the motive of which it was impossible remotely to surmise.

Something extraordinary had certainly happened to account for my waking up in this strange house with this unknown companion, but my fancy was utterly impotent to suggest more than the wildest guess as to what that something might have been. Could it be that I was the victim of some sort of conspiracy? It looked so, certainly; and yet, if human lineaments ever gave true evidence, it was certain that this man by my side, with a face so refined and ingenuous, was no party to any scheme of crime or outrage. Then it occurred to me to question if I might not be the butt of some elaborate practical joke on the part of friends who had somehow learned the secret of my underground chamber and taken this means of impressing me with the peril of mesmeric experiments. There were great difficulties in the way of this theory; Sawyer would never have betrayed me, nor had I any friends at all likely to undertake such an enterprise; nevertheless the supposition that I was the victim of a practical joke seemed on the whole the only one tenable. Half expecting to catch a glimpse of some familiar face grinning from behind a chair or curtain, I looked carefully about the room. When my eyes next rested on my companion, he was looking at me.

"You have had a fine nap of twelve hours," he said briskly, "and I can see that it has done you good. You look much better. Your color is good and your eyes are bright. How do you feel?"

"I never felt better," I said, sitting up.

"You remember your first waking, no doubt," he pursued, "and your surprise when I told you how long you had been asleep?"

"You said, I believe, that I had slept one hundred and thirteen years."

"Exactly."

"You will admit," I said, with an ironical smile, "that the story was rather an improbable one."

"Extraordinary, I admit," he responded, "but given the proper conditions, not improbable nor inconsistent with what we know of the trance state. When complete, as in your case, the vital functions are absolutely suspended, and there is no waste of the tissues. No limit can be set to the possible duration of a trance when the external conditions protect the body from physical injury. This trance of yours is indeed the longest of which there is any positive record, but there is no known reason wherefore, had you not been discovered and had the chamber in which we found you continued intact, you might not have remained in a state of suspended animation till, at the end of indefinite ages, the gradual refrigeration of the earth had destroyed the bodily tissues and set the spirit free."

I had to admit that, if I were indeed the victim of a practical joke, its authors had chosen an admirable agent for carrying out their imposition. The impressive and even eloquent manner of this man would have lent dignity to an argument that the moon was made of cheese. The smile with which I had regarded him as he advanced his trance hypothesis did not appear to confuse him in the slightest degree.

"Perhaps," I said, "you will go on and favour me with some particulars as to the circumstances under which you discovered this chamber of which you speak, and its contents. I enjoy good fiction."

"In this case," was the grave reply, "no fiction could be so strange as the truth. You must know that these many years I have been cherishing the idea of building a laboratory in the large garden beside this house, for the purpose of chemical experiments for which I have a taste. Last Thursday the excavation for the cellar was at last begun. It was completed by that night, and Friday the masons were to have come. Thursday night we had a tremendous deluge of rain, and Friday morning I found my cellar a frog-pond and the walls quite washed down. My daughter, who had come out to view the disaster with me, called my attention to a corner of masonry laid bare by the crumbling away of one of the walls. I cleared a little earth from it, and, finding that it seemed part of a large mass, determined to investigate it. The workmen I sent for unearthed an oblong vault some eight feet below the surface, and set in the corner of what had evidently been the foundation walls of an ancient house. A layer of ashes and charcoal on the top of the vault showed that the house above had perished by fire. The vault itself was perfectly intact, the cement being as good as when first applied. It had a door, but this we could not force, and found entrance by removing one of the flagstones which formed the roof. The air which came up was stagnant but pure, dry and not cold. Descending with a lantern, I found myself in an apartment fitted up as a bedroom in the style of the nineteenth century. On the bed lay a young man. That he was dead and must have been dead a century was of course to be taken for granted; but the extraordinary state of preservation of the body struck me and the medical colleagues whom I had summoned with amazement. That the art of such embalming as this had ever been known we should not have believed, yet here seemed conclusive testimony that our immediate ancestors had possessed it. My medical colleagues, whose curiosity was highly excited, were at once for undertaking experiments to test the nature of the process employed, but I withheld them. My motive in so doing, at least the only motive I now need speak of, was the recollection of something I once had read about the extent to which your contemporaries had cultivated the subject of animal magnetism. It had occurred to me as just conceivable that you might be in a trance, and that the secret of your bodily integrity after so long a time was not the craft of an embalmer, but life. So extremely fanciful did this idea seem, even to me, that I did not risk the ridicule of my fellow physicians by mentioning it, but gave some other reason for postponing their experiments. No sooner, however, had they left me, than I set on foot a systematic attempt at resuscitation, of which you know the result."

Had its theme been yet more incredible, the circumstantiality of this narrative, as well as the impressive manner and personality of the narrator, might have staggered a listener, and I had begun to feel very strangely, when, as he closed, I chanced to catch a glimpse of my reflection in a mirror hanging on the wall of the room. I rose and went up to it. The face I saw was the face to a hair and a line and not a day older than the one I had looked at as I tied my cravat before going to Edith that Decoration Day, which, as this man would have me believe, was celebrated one hundred and thirteen years before. At this, the colossal character of the fraud which was being attempted on me, came over me afresh. Indignation mastered my mind as I realized the outrageous liberty that had been taken.

"You are probably surprised," said my companion, "to see that, although you are a century older than when you lay down to sleep in that underground chamber, your appearance is unchanged. That should not amaze you. It is by virtue of the total arrest of the vital functions that you have survived this great period of time. If your body could have undergone any change during your trance, it would long ago have suffered dissolution."

"Sir," I replied, turning to him, "what your motive can be in reciting to me with a serious face this remarkable farrago, I am utterly unable to guess; but you are surely yourself too intelligent to suppose that anybody but an imbecile could be deceived by it. Spare me any more of this elaborate nonsense and once for all tell me whether you refuse to give me an intelligible account of where I am and how I came here. If so, I shall proceed to ascertain my whereabouts for myself, whoever may hinder."

"You do not, then, believe that this is the year 2000?"

"Do you really think it necessary to ask me that?" I returned.

"Very well," replied my extraordinary host. "Since I cannot convince you, you shall convince yourself. Are you strong enough to follow me upstairs?"

"I am as strong as I ever was," I replied angrily, "as I may have to prove if this jest is carried much farther."

"I beg, sir," was my companion's response, "that you will not allow yourself to be too fully persuaded that you are the victim of a trick, lest the reaction, when you are convinced of the truth of my statements, should be too great."

The tone of concern, mingled with commiseration, with which he said this, and the entire absence of any sign of resentment at my hot words, strangely daunted me, and I followed him from the room with an extraordinary mixture of emotions. He led the way up two flights of stairs and then up a shorter one, which landed us upon a belvedere on the house-top. "Be pleased to look around you," he said, as we reached the platform, "and tell me if this is the Boston of the nineteenth century."

At my feet lay a great city. Miles of broad streets, shaded by trees and lined with fine buildings, for the most part not in continuous blocks but set in larger or smaller inclosures, stretched in every direction. Every quarter contained large open squares filled with trees, among which statues glistened and fountains flashed in the late afternoon sun. Public buildings of a colossal size and an architectural grandeur unparalleled in my day raised their stately piles on every side. Surely I had never seen this city nor one comparable to it before. Raising my eyes at last towards the horizon, I looked westward. That blue ribbon winding away to the sunset, was it not the sinuous Charles? I looked east; Boston harbor stretched before me within its headlands, not one of its green islets missing.

I knew then that I had been told the truth concerning the prodigious thing which had befallen me.

<hr />

**The complete and unabridged text is available
online, from** *flametreepublishing.com/extras*

The Gap in the Curtain
Part I: Whitsuntide at Flambard

John Buchan

"Si la conscience qui sommeille dans l'instinct se réveillait, s'il s'intériorisait en connaissance au lieu de s'extérioriser en action, si nous savions l'interroger et s'il pouvait répondre, il nous livrerait les secrets de la vie."
Bergson, *L'Evolution Créatrice*

"But no!" cried Mr Mantalini. "It is a demn'd horrid dream. It is not reality. No!"
Nicholas Nickleby

I

AS I TOOK my place at the dinner-table I realised that I was not the only tired mortal in Lady Flambard's Whitsuntide party. Mayot, who sat opposite me, had dark pouches under his eyes and that unwholesome high complexion which in a certain type of physique means that the arteries are working badly. I knew that he had been having a heavy time in the House of Commons over the Committee stage of his Factory Bill. Charles Ottery, who generally keeps himself fit with fives and tennis, and has still the figure of an athletic schoolboy, seemed nervous and out of sorts, and scarcely listened to his companion's chatter. Our hostess had her midseason look; her small delicate features were as sharp as a pin, and her blue eyes were drained of colour. But it was Arnold Tavanger farther down the table who held my attention. His heavy, sagacious face was a dead mask of exhaustion. He looked done to the world, and likely to fall asleep over his soup.

It was a comfort to me to see others in the same case, for I was feeling pretty near the end of my tether. Ever since Easter I had been overworked out of all reason. There was a batch of important Dominion appeals before the Judicial Committee, in every one of which I was engaged, and I had some heavy cases in the Commercial Court. Of the two juniors who did most of my 'devilling' one had a big patent-law action of his own, and the other was in a nursing-home with appendicitis. To make matters worse, I was chairman of a Royal Commission which was about to issue its findings, and had had to rewrite most of the report with my own hand, and I had been sitting as a one-man Commission in a troublesome dispute in the shipbuilding trade. Also I was expected to be pretty regularly in the House of Commons to deal with the legal side of Mayot's precious Bill, and the sittings had often stretched far into the next morning.

There is something about a barrister's spells of overwork which makes them different in kind from those of other callings. His duties are specific as to time and place. He must be in court at a certain hour. He must be ready to put, or to reply to, an argument when he is called upon; he can postpone or rearrange his work only within the narrowest limits. He is a cog in an inexorable machine, and must revolve with the rest of it. For myself I usually enter upon a period of extreme busyness with a certain lift of spirit, for there is a sporting interest in not being able to see your way through your work. But presently this goes, and I get into a mood of nervous irritation. It is easy enough to be a carthorse, and it is easy enough to be a racehorse, but it is difficult to be a carthorse which is constantly being asked to take Grand National fences. One has to rise to hazards, but with each the take-off gets worse and the energy feebler. So at the close of such a spell I am in a wretched condition of soul and body – weary, but without power to rest, and with a mind so stale that it sees no light or colour in anything. Even the end of the drudgery brings no stimulus. I feel that my form has been getting steadily poorer, and that virtue has gone out of me which I may never recapture.

I had been in two minds about accepting Sally Flambard's invitation. She is my very good friend, but her parties are rather like a table d'hôte. Her interests are multitudinous, and all are reflected in her hospitality, so that a procession goes through her house which looks like a rehearsal for the Judgement Day. Politics, religion, philanthropy, letters, science, art and the most brainless fashion – she takes them all to her capacious heart. She is an innocent lion-hunter, too, and any man or woman who figures for the moment in the Press will be a guest at Flambard. And she drives her team, for all are put through their paces. Sally makes her guests work for their entertainment. In her own way she is a kind of genius, and what Americans call a wonderful 'mixer.' Everyone has got to testify, and I have seen her make a bishop discourse on Church union, and a mathematician on hyper-space to an audience which heard of the topics for the first time. The talk is apt to be a little like a magazine page in a popular newspaper – very good fun, if you are feeling up to it, but not quite the thing for a rest-cure.

It was my memory of Flambard itself that decided me. The place is set amid the greenest and quietest country on earth. The park is immense, and in early June is filled with a glory of flowers and blossoming trees. I could borrow one of Evelyn's horses and ride all day through the relics of ancient forests, or up on to the cool, windy spaces of the Downs. There was good dry-fly fishing in the little Arm, which runs through a shallow vale to the young Thames. At Whitsuntide you can recover an earlier England. The flood of greenery hides modern blemishes which are revealed by the bareness of winter, and an upland water-meadow is today just as it met the eye of the monks when they caught their Friday's trout, or of the corsleted knights as they rode out to the King's wars. It is the kind of scene that comforts me most, for there, as some poet says, 'old Leisure sits knee-deep in grass.' Also the house is large enough for peace. It is mostly Restoration period, with some doubtful Georgian additions, but there is a Tudor wing, the remnant of the old house, which the great Earl of Essex once used as a hunting lodge. Sally used to give me a room at the top of the Essex wing, with a wide prospect north into the Cotswold dales. The hall and the drawing-rooms and the great terrace might be as full of 'turns' as a music-hall stage, but somewhere in the house fatigue could find sanctuary.

I had arrived just in time to dress for dinner, and had spoken to none of my fellow-guests, so my inspection of the table had a speculative interest. It was a large party, and I saw a good many faces that I knew. There were the Nantleys, my best of friends, and their daughter Pamela, who was in her first season...There was old Folliot, the bore of creation, with his little grey imperial, and his smirk, and his tired eyes. He was retailing some ancient scandal to Mrs Lamington, who was listening with one ear and devoting the other to what Lady Altrincham was saying across the table. George Lamington a little farther down was arguing with his host about the Ascot entries – his puffy red face had that sudden shrewdness which it acquires when George's mind is on horses…There was a man opposite him of whom I could only catch the profile – a dark head with fine-drawn features. I heard his voice, a pleasant voice, with full deep tones like a tragic actor's, and, as he turned, I had an impression of a face full of swift, nervous strength…There was a good deal of youth in the party, four girls besides Pamela Brune, and several boys with sleek hair and fresh voices. One of them I knew, Reggie Daker, who was a friend of my nephew's.

I was on Sally's left hand, and as she was busy with Mayot, and the lady on my left was deep in a controversy with her neighbour over some book, I was free to look about me. Suddenly I got a queer impression. A dividing line seemed to zigzag in and out among us, separating the vital from the devitalised. There was a steady cackle of talk, but I felt that there were silent spaces in it. Most of the people were cheerful, eupeptic souls who were enjoying life. The Nantleys, for example, sedate country gentlefolk, whose days were an ordered routine of pleasant cares…Pamela Brune? I was not so sure of her, for a young girl's first season is a trying business, like a boy's first half at school…Old Folliot, beyond doubt – he was perfectly happy as long as he was in a great house with somebody to listen to his archaic gossip… Evelyn Flambard and George Lamington and the boys who were talking Ascot and next winter's hunting plans…Lady Altrincham, sixty but with the air of thirty, who lives for her complexion and her famous pearls…But I realised that there were people here who were as much at odds with life as myself – Mayot and Tavanger and Charles Ottery, and perhaps the dark fellow who sat opposite George Lamington.

Sally turned to me, hiding a yawn with her small hand. Her head on its slim neck was as erect as a bird's, and her body had a darting, bird-like poise, but I could see that the poise required some effort to maintain it. She patted my sleeve in her friendly way.

"I am so glad you came," she said. "I know you want a rest." She screwed up her eyes and peered at me. "You look as if you hadn't been in bed for a month!"

"I'm nearly all out," I said. "You must let me moon about by myself, please, for I'm no sort of company for anybody."

"You shall do exactly as you like. I'm pretty tired also, and I'm giving a ball next week, and there's Ascot looming ahead. Happily we're having quite a small party – and a very quiet one."

"Is this the lot?" I asked, looking down the table. I knew her habit of letting guests appear in relays during a weekend till the result was a mob.

"Practically. You know all the people?"

"Most of them. Who's the dark fellow opposite George Lamington?"

Her face brightened into interest. "That's my new discovery. A country neighbour, no less – but a new breed altogether. His name is Goodeve – Sir Robert Goodeve. He has just succeeded to the place and title."

Of course I knew Goodeve, that wonderful moated house in the lap of the Downs, but I had never met one of the race. I had had a notion that it had died out. The Goodeves are one of those families about which genealogists write monographs, a specimen of that unennobled gentry which is the oldest stock in England. They had been going on in their undistinguished way since Edward the Confessor.

"Tell me about him," I said.

"I can't tell you much. You can see what he looks like. Did you ever know a face so lit up from behind?…He was the son of a parson in Northumberland, poor as a church mouse, so he had to educate himself. Local grammar school, some provincial university, and then with scholarships and tutoring he fought his way to Oxford. There he was rather a swell, and made friends with young Marburg, old Isaac's son, who got him a place in his father's business. The War broke out, and he served for four years, while Marburgs kept his job open. After that they moved him a good deal about the world, and he was several years in their New York house. It is really a romance, for at thirty-five he had made money, and now at thirty-eight he has inherited Goodeve and a good deal more…Yes, he's a bachelor. Not rich as the big fortunes go, but rich enough. The thing about him is that he has got his jumping-off ground reasonably young, and is now about to leap. Quite modest, but perfectly confident, and terribly ambitious. He is taking up politics, and I back him to make you all sit up. I think he's the most impressive mortal I have ever met. Bored stiff with women – as stony-hearted as you, Ned. He's a sort of ascetic, vowed to a cause."

"His own career?" I asked.

"No. No. He's not a bit of an egotist. There's a pent-up force that's got to come out. He's a fanatic about some new kind of Empire development, and I know people who think him a second Rhodes. I want you to make friends with him and tell me what you think, for in your fish-like way you have good judgement."

Sally yawned again, and I respected more than ever the courage of women who can go on till they drop and keep smiling. She turned away in response to a question of Mayot's, and I exchanged banalities with the lady on my other side. Presently I found myself free again to look round the table. I was right: we were the oddest mixture of the fresh and the blasé, the care-free and the care-worn. To look at Tavanger's hollow eyes and hear in one's ear the babble of high young voices made a contrast which was almost indecent…I had a feeling as if we were all on a vast, comfortable raft in some unknown sea, and that, while some were dancing to jazz music, others were crowding silently at the edge, staring into the brume ahead. Staring anxiously, too, for in that mist there might be fearful as well as wonderful things…I found myself studying George Lamington's face, and felt a childish dislike of him. His life was so padded and cosseted and bovine. He had just inherited another quarter of a million from an uncle, and he had not the imagination of a rabbit in the use of money. Why does wealth make dull people so much duller? I had always rather liked George, but now I felt him intolerable. I must have been very tired, for I was getting as full of silly prejudices as a minor poet.

Sally was speaking again, as she collected eyes.

"Don't be afraid. This is going to be a very peaceful party."

"Will you promise me," I said, "that I won't come down tomorrow and find half a dozen new faces at breakfast?"

"Honest Injun," she replied. "They are all here except one, and he arrives tonight."

When the women had gone Evelyn Flambard brought his port to my side. Having exhausted horses during dinner, he regaled me with the Englishman's other main topic, politics. Evelyn despaired of the republic. He had grievances against the Budget, the new rating law, and the Government's agricultural policy. He was alarmed about the condition of India, where he had served in his old Hussar days, and about Egypt, where he had large investments. His views on America were calculated to make a serious breach between the two sections of the Anglo-Saxon race. But if he feared the Government he despised the Opposition, though for politeness' sake he added that his strictures did not apply to me. There was no honest Toryism left, so his plaint ran; there was not a pin to choose between the parties; they were all out to rob struggling virtue – meaning himself and other comfortable squires. He nodded down the table towards Goodeve. "Look at that chap," he whispered darkly. "I mean to say, he don't care a straw what he says or does, and he'll have Tommy Twiston's seat, which is reckoned the safest in England. He as good as told George Lamington this afternoon that he'd like to see a Soviet Government in power for a week in England under strict control, for it was the only way to deal with men like him. Hang it all, there's nothing wrong with old George except that he's a bit fussy, if you see what I mean."

I said that I rather agreed with Goodeve, and that set Evelyn pouring out his woes to the man on the other side. Reggie Daker had come up next me, his eye heavy with confidences. I had acted as a sort of father-confessor to Reggie ever since he came down from the University, but I hadn't much credit by my disciple. He was infinitely friendly, modest, and good-humoured, but as hard to hold as a knotless thread. Usually he talked to me about his career, and I had grown very tired of finding him jobs, which he either shied off or couldn't hold for a week. Now it seemed that this was not his trouble. He had found his niche at last, and it was dealing in rare books. Reggie considered that a lad like himself, with a fine taste and a large acquaintance, could make a lot of money by digging out rarities from obscure manor-houses and selling them to American collectors. He had taken up the study very seriously, he told me, and he actually managed to get a few phrases of bibliophile's jargon into his simple tale. He felt that he had found his life's work, and was quite happy about it.

The trouble was Pamela Brune. It appeared that he was deeply in love, and that she was toying with his young heart. "There's a strong lot of entries," he explained, "and Charles Ottery has been the favourite up till now. But she seems a bit off Charles, and…and… anyhow, I'm going to try my luck. I wangled an invitation here for that very purpose. I say, you know – you're her godfather, aren't you? If you could put in a kind word…"

But my unreceptive eye must have warned Reggie that I was stony soil. He had another glass of port, and sighed.

I intended to go to bed as soon as I decently could. I was not sleepy, but I was seeing things with the confusion of a drowsy man. As I followed my host across the hall, where someone had started a gramophone, I seemed more than ever to be in a phantasmal world. The drawing-room, with the delicate fluted pilasters in its panelling and the Sir Joshuas and Romneys between them, swam in a green dusk, which was partly the afterglow through the uncurtained windows and partly the shading of the electric lamps. A four at bridge had been made up, and the young people were drifting back towards the music. Lady Nantley beckoned me from a sofa. I could see her eyes appraising my face and disapproving of it, but she was too tactful to tell me that I looked ill.

"I heard that you were to be here, Ned," she said, "and I was very glad. Your god-daughter is rather a handful just now, and I wanted your advice."

"What's wrong?" I asked. "She's looking uncommonly pretty." I caught a glimpse of Pamela patting her hair as she passed a mirror, slim and swift as a dryad.

"She's uncommonly perverse. You know that she has been having an affair with Charles Ottery ever since Christmas at Wirlesdon. I love Charles, and Tom and I were delighted. Everything most suitable – the right age, enough money, chance of a career, the same friends. There's no doubt that Charles adores her, and till the other day I thought that she was coming to adore Charles. But now she has suddenly gone off at a tangent, and has taken to snubbing and neglecting him. She says that he's too good for her, and that his perfections choke her – doesn't want to play second fiddle to an Admirable Crichton – wants to shape her own life – all the rubbish that young people talk nowadays."

Mollie's charming eyes were full of real distress, and she put an appealing hand on my arm.

"She likes you, Ned, and believes in you. Couldn't you put a little sense into her head?"

I wanted to say that I was feeling like a ghost from another sphere, and that it was no good asking a tenuous spectre to meddle with the affairs of warm flesh and blood. But I was spared the trouble of answering by the appearance of Lady Flambard.

"Forgive me, Mollie dear," she said, "but I must carry him off. I'll bring him back to you presently."

She led me to a young man who was standing near the door. "Bob," she said, "this is Sir Edward Leithen. I've been longing for you two to meet."

"So have I," said the other, and we shook hands. Now that I saw Goodeve fairly, I was even more impressed than by his profile as seen at dinner. He was a finely made man, and looked younger than his thirty-eight years. He was very dark, but not in the least swarthy; there were lights in his hair which suggested that he might have been a blond child, and his skin was a clear brown, as if the blood ran strongly and cleanly under it. What I liked about him was his smile, which was at once engaging and natural, and a little shy. It took away any arrogance that might have lurked in the tight mouth and straight brows.

"I came here to meet you, sir," he said. "I'm a candidate for public life, and I wanted to see a man who interests me more than anybody else in the game. I hope you don't mind my saying that…What about going into the garden? There's a moon of sorts, and the nightingales will soon begin. If they're like the ones at Goodeve, eleven's their hour."

We went through the hall to the terrace, which lay empty and quiet in a great dazzle of moonlight. It was only about a fortnight till midsummer, a season when in fine weather in southern England it is never quite dark. Now, with a moon nearing the full, the place was bright enough to read print. The stone balustrade and urns were white as snow, and the two stairways that led to the sunk garden were a frosty green like tiny glaciers.

We threaded the maze of plots and lily-ponds and came out on a farther lawn, which ran down to the little river. That bit of the Arm is no good for fishing, for it has been trimmed into a shallow babbling stretch of ornamental water, but it is a delicious thing in the landscape. There was no sound except the lapse of the stream, and the occasional squattering flight of a moorhen. But as we reached the brink a nightingale began in the next thicket.

Goodeve had scarcely spoken a word. He was sniffing the night scents, which were a wonderful blend of early roses, new-mown hay, and dewy turf. When we reached the Arm, we turned and looked back at the house. It seemed suddenly to have gone small, set in a great alley-way of green between olive woods, an alley-way which swept from the high downs to the river meadows. Far beyond it we could see the bare top of Stobarrow. But it looked as perfect as a piece of carved ivory – and ancient, ancient as a boulder left millenniums ago by a melting ice-cap.

"Pretty good," said my companion at last. "At Flambard you can walk steadily back into the past. Every chapter is written plain to be read."

"At Goodeve, too," I said.

"At Goodeve, too. You know the place? It is the first home I have had since I was a child, for I have been knocking about for years in lodgings and tents. I'm still a little afraid of it. It's a place that wants to master you. I'm sometimes tempted to give myself up to it and spend my days listening to its stories and feeling my way back through the corridors of time. But I know that that would be ruin."

"Why?"

"Because you cannot walk backward. It is too easy, and the road leads nowhere. A man must keep his eyes to the front and resist the pull of his ancestors. They're the devil, those ancestors, always trying to get you back into their own rut."

"I wish mine would pull harder," I said. "I've been badly overworked lately, and I feel at this moment like a waif, with nothing behind me and nothing before."

He regarded me curiously. "I thought you looked a little done up. Well, that's the penalty of being a swell. You'll lie fallow for a day or two and the power will return. There can't be much looking backward in your life."

"Nor looking forward. I seem to live between high blank walls. I never get a prospect."

"Oh, but you are wrong," he said seriously. "All your time is spent in trying to guess what is going to happen – what view the Courts will take of a case, what kind of argument will hit the prospective mood of the House. It is the same in law and politics and business and everything practical. Success depends on seeing just a little more into the future than other people."

I remembered my odd feeling at dinner of the raft on the misty sea, and the anxious peering faces at the edge.

"Maybe," I said. "But just at the moment I'm inclined to envy the people who live happily in the present. Our host, for example, and the boys and girls who are now dancing." In the stillness the faint echo of music drifted to us from the house.

"I don't envy them a bit," he said. "They have no real sporting interest. Trying to see something solid in the mist is the whole fun of life, and most of its poetry."

"Anyhow, thank Heaven, we can't see very far. It would be awful to look down an avenue of time as clear as this strip of lawn, and see the future as unmistakable as Flambard."

"Perhaps. But sometimes I would give a good deal for one moment of prevision."

After that, as we strolled back, we talked about commonplace things – the prospects of a not very secure Government, common friends, the ways of our hostess, whom he loved, and the abilities of Mayot, which – along with me – he doubted. As we entered the house again we found the far end of the hall brightly lit, since the lamps had been turned on in the porch. The butler was ushering in a guest who had just arrived, and Sally had hastened from the drawing-room to greet him.

The newcomer was one of the biggest men I have ever seen, and one of the leanest. A suit of grey flannel hung loose upon his gigantic bones. He reminded me of Nansen, except that he was dark instead of fair. His forehead rose to a peak, on which sat one solitary lock, for the rest of his head was bald. His eyes were large and almost colourless, mere pits of light beneath shaggy brows. He was bowing over Sally's hand in a foreign way, and the movement made him cough.

"May I present Sir Edward Leithen?" said Sally. "Sir Robert Goodeve...Professor Moe."

The big man gave me a big hand, which felt hot and damp. His eyes regarded me with a hungry interest. I had an impression of power – immense power, and also an immense fragility.

II

I DID NOT have a good night; I rarely do when I have been overworking. I started a chapter of *Barchester Towers*, dropped off in the middle, and woke in two hours, restless and unrefreshed. Then I must have lain awake till the little chill before dawn which generally sends me to sleep. The window was wide open, and all the minute sounds of a summer night floated through it, but they did not soothe me. I had one of those fits of dissatisfaction which often assail the sleepless. I felt that I was making very little of my life. I earned a large income, and had a considerable position in the public eye, but I was living, so to speak, from hand to mouth. I had long lost any ordinary ambitions, and had ceased to plan out my career ahead, as I used to do when I was a young man. There were many things in public life on which I was keen, but it was only an intellectual keenness; I had no ardour in their pursuit. I felt as if my existence were utterly shapeless.

It was borne in on me that Goodeve was right. What were his words? – "Trying to see something solid in the mist is the whole fun of life, and most of its poetry." Success, he had argued, depended upon looking a little farther into the future than other people. No doubt; but then I didn't want success – not in the ordinary way. He had still his spurs to win, whereas I had won mine, and I didn't like the fit of them. Yet all the same I wanted some plan and policy in my life, for I couldn't go on living in the mud of the present. My mind needed prospect and horizon. I had often made this reflection before in moments of disillusionment, but now it came upon me with the force of a revelation. I told myself that I was beginning to be cured of my weariness, for I was growing discontented, and discontent is a proof of vitality…As I fell asleep I was thinking of Goodeve and realising how much I liked him. His company might prove the tonic I required.

I rose early and went for a walk along the Arm to look for a possible trout. The May-fly season was over, but there were one or two good fish rising beyond a clump of reeds where the stream entered the wood. Then I breakfasted alone with Evelyn, for Flambard is not an early house. His horses were mostly at grass, but he lent me a cob of Sally's. I changed into breeches, cut a few sandwiches, and set out for the high Downs. I fancied that a long lonely day on the hills would do me as much good as anything.

It was a quiet dim morning which promised a day of heat. I rode through a mile of woods full of nesting pheasants, then over a broomy common, and then by way of a steep lane on to the turf of the Downs. I found myself on the track where Evelyn exercised his race-horses, for he trained at home, so I gave my beast its head, and had that most delectable of experiences, a gallop over perfect turf. This brought me well up on the side of Stobarrow, and by the time I reached its summit the haze was clearing, and I was looking over the Arm and the young Thames to the blue lift of Cotswold.

I spent the whole day on the uplands. I ate my sandwiches in a clump of thorns, and had a mug of rough cider at an alehouse. I rode down long waterless combes, and ascended other tops besides Stobarrow. For an hour I lay on a patch of thyme, drowsy with the heat and the aromatic scents. I smoked a pipe with an old shepherd, and heard slow tales of sheep and dogs and storms and forgotten fox-hunts. In the end I drugged myself into a sort of animal peace. Thank God, I could still get back when I pleased to the ancient world of pastoral.

But when on my return I came over the brink of Stobarrow I realised that I had gained little. The pastoral world was not mine; my world was down below in the valley where men and women were fretting and puzzling…I no longer thought of them as on a raft looking at misty seas, but rather as spectators on a ridge, trying to guess what lay beyond the next hill. Tavanger and Mayot and Goodeve – they were all at it. A futile game, maybe, but inevitable, since what lay beyond the hill was life and death to them. I must recapture the mood for this guessing game, for it was the mainspring of effort, and therefore of happiness.

I got back about six, had a bath, and changed into flannels. Sally gave me a cup of tea at a table in the hall which carried food for a multitude, but did not look as if it had been much patronised. Evelyn and the Lamingtons had gone to see the Wallingdon training stables; the young people had had tea in the tennis-court pavilion; Mayot had motored to Cirencester to meet a friend, and Tavanger had gone to Goodeve to look at the pictures, in which subject he was a noted connoisseur; Charles Ottery had disappeared after luncheon, and she had sent the Professor to bed till dinner.

Sally's face wore something between a smile and a frown.

"Reggie Daker is in bed, too. He was determined to try Sir Vidas over the jumps in the park, though Evelyn warned him that the horse was short of exercise and was sure to give trouble. The jumps haven't been mended for months, and the take-off at some of them is shocking. Well, Sir Vidas came down all right, and Reggie fell on his head and nearly cracked his skull. He was concussed, and unconscious for a quarter of an hour. Dr Micklem sewed him up, and he is now in bed, covered with bandages, and not allowed to speak or be spoken to till tomorrow. It's hard luck on poor Reggie, but it will keep him for a little from making a fool of himself about Pamela Brune. He hasn't a chance there, you know, and he is such a tactless old donkey that he is spoiling the field for Charles Ottery."

But it was not Reggie's misfortunes that made my hostess frown. Presently I learned the reason.

"I'm very glad of the chance of a quiet talk with you," she said. "I want to speak to you about Professor Moe. You saw him when he arrived last night. What did you think of him?"

"He seemed a formidable personage," I replied. "He looked very ill."

"He *is* very ill. I had no notion how ill he was. He makes light of it, but there must be something mortally wrong with his lungs or his heart. He seems to be always in a fever, and now and then he simply gasps for breath. He says he has been like that for years, but I can't believe it. It's a tragedy, for he is one of the greatest minds in the world."

"I never heard of him before."

"You wouldn't. You're not a scientist. He's a most wonderful mathematician and physicist – rather in the Einstein way. He has upset every scientific law, but you can't understand just how unless you're a great scientist yourself. Our own people hush their voices when they mention him."

"How did you come across him?"

"I met him last year in Berlin. You know I've a flair for clever people, and they seem to like me, though I don't follow a word they say. I saw that he was to be in London to read a paper to some society, so I thought I'd ask him to Flambard to show him what English country life was like. Rather to my surprise he accepted – I think London tired him and he wanted a rest."

"You're worried about him? Are you afraid that he'll die on your hands?"

"No-o," she answered. "He's very ill, but I don't think he'll die just yet. What worries me is to know how to help him. You see, he took me into his confidence this morning. He accepted my invitation because he wanted the quiet of the country to finish a piece of work. A tremendous piece of work – the work of his life...He wants something more. He wants our help. It seems that some experiment is necessary before he can be quite sure of his ground."

"What sort of experiment?"

"With human beings – the right kind of human beings. You mustn't laugh at me, Ned, for I can't explain what he told me, though I thought I understood when he was speaking...It has something to do with a new theory of Time. He thinks that Time is not a straight line, but full of coils and kinks. He says that the Future is here with us now, if we only knew how to look for it. And he believes he has found a way of enabling one to know what is going to happen a long time ahead."

I laughed. "Useful for Evelyn and George. They'll be able to back all the Ascot winners." But Sally did not laugh.

"You must be serious. The Professor is a genius, and I believe every word he says. He wants help, he told me. Not people like Evelyn and George. He has very clear ideas about the kind of man he needs. He wants Mr Mayot and Mr Tavanger and perhaps Charles Ottery, though he's not quite sure about Charles. Above all, he wants you and Bob Goodeve. He saw you last night, and took a tremendous fancy to you both."

I forbore to laugh only out of deference to Sally's gravity. It seemed a reduction to the absurd of Goodeve's talk the night before and my reflections on the Downs. I had decided that I must be more forward-looking, and here was a wild foreigner who believed that he had found the exact technique of the business.

"I don't like it," I said. "The man is probably mad."

"Oh, no, he isn't. He is brilliantly sane. You have only to talk to him to realise that. Even when I couldn't follow him I could see that he was not talking nonsense. But the point is that he wants to put it all before you. He is certain that he can make a convert of you."

"But I don't know the first thing about science. I have often got up a technical subject for a case, and then washed it out of my mind. I've never been instructed in the first principles. I don't understand the language."

"That is just why Professor Moe wants you. He says he wants a fresh mind, and a mind trained like yours to weigh evidence. It wasn't your *beaux yeux*, Ned, that he fell for, but your reputation as a lawyer."

"I don't mind listening to what he has got to say. But look here, Sally, I don't like this experiment business. What does he propose?"

"Nothing in the least unpleasant. It only means one or two people preparing themselves for an experience, which he says he can give them, by getting into a particular frame of mind. He's not sure if he can bring it off, you know. The experiment is to be the final proof of his discovery. He was emphatic that there was no danger and no unpleasantness, whether it was successful or not...But he was very particular about the people he wanted. He was looking at us all this morning with the queerest appraising eyes. He wants you and Bob especially, and Mr Mayot and Mr Tavanger, and possibly Charles. Oh, yes, and he thinks he may want me. But nobody else. He was perfectly clear about that."

I must say that this rather impressed me. He had chosen exactly those whom I had selected at dinner the previous night as the care-full as opposed to the care-free. He wanted people whose physical vitality was low, and who were living on the edge of their nerves, and he had picked them unerringly out of Sally's house-party.

"All right," I said. "I'll have a talk to him after dinner. But I want you to be guided by me, and if I think the thing fishy to call it off. If the man is as clever as you say, he may scare somebody into imbecility."

Before I dressed I rang up Landor, and was lucky enough to find him still in London. Landor, besides being a patent-law barrister pretty near the top of his branch, is a Fellow of the Royal Society, and a devotee of those dim regions where physics, metaphysics, and mathematics jostle each other. He has published and presented me with several works which I found totally incomprehensible.

When I asked him about Professor Moe he replied with a respectful gurgle. "You don't mean to say you've got him at Flambard? What astounding luck! I thought he had gone back to Stockholm. There are scores of people who would walk twenty miles barefoot to get a word with him."

Landor confirmed all that Sally had said about the Professor's standing. He had been given the Nobel Prize years ago, and was undoubtedly the greatest mathematician alive. But recently he had soared into a world where it was not easy to keep abreast of him. Landor confessed that he had only got glimmerings of meaning from the paper he had read two days before to the Newton Club. "I can see the road he is travelling," he said, "but I can't quite grasp the stages." And he quoted Wordsworth's line about "Voyaging through strange seas of thought alone."

"He's the real thing," I asked, "and not a charlatan?"

I could hear Landor's cackle at the other end of the line.

"You might as well ask a conscript to vouch for Napoleon's abilities as ask me to give a certificate of respectability to August Moe."

"You're sure he's quite sane?

"Absolutely. He's only mad in so far as all genius is mad. He is reputed to be a very good fellow and very simple. Did you know that he once wrote a book on Hans Andersen? But he looked to me a pretty sick man. There's a lot of hereditary phthisis in his race."

Dinner that evening was a pleasanter meal for me. I had more of an appetite, there was a less leaden air about my companions in fatigue, the sunburnt boys and girls were in good form, and Reggie Daker's woebegone countenance was safe on its pillow. Charles Ottery, who sat next to Pamela Brune, seemed to be in a better humour, and Mrs Lamington was really amusing about the Wallingdon stables and old Wallingdon's stable-talk. I had been moved farther down the table, and had a good view of Professor Moe, who sat next to our hostess. His was an extraordinary face – the hollow cheeks and the high cheekbones, the pale eyes, the broad high brow, and the bald head rising to a peak like Sir Walter Scott's. The expression was very gentle, like a musing child, but now and then he seemed to kindle, and an odd gleam appeared in his colourless pits of eyes. For all his size he looked terribly flimsy. Something had fretted his body to a decay.

He came up to me as soon as we left the dining-room. He spoke excellent English, but his voice made me uneasy – it seemed to come with difficulty from a long way down in his big frame. There was a vague, sad kindliness about his manner, but there was a sense of purpose too. He went straight to the point.

"Some time you are going to give me your attention, Sir Edward, and I in return will give you my confidence. Her ladyship has so informed me. She insists, that gracious one, that I must go to bed, for I am still weary. Shall our talk be tomorrow after breakfast? In the garden, please, if the sun still shines."

III

I FIND IT almost impossible to give the gist of the conversation which filled the next forenoon. We sat in wicker chairs on the flags of the Dutch garden in a grilling sun, for heat seemed to be the one physical comfort for which the Professor craved. I shall always associate the glare of a June sky with a frantic effort on my part to grasp the ultimate imponderables of human thought.

The Professor was merciful to my weakness. He had a great writing-pad on his knee, and would fain have illustrated his argument with diagrams, but he desisted when he found that they meant little to me and really impeded his exposition. Most scientists use a kind of shorthand – formulas and equations which have as exact a meaning for them as an ordinary noun has for the ordinary man. But there was no chance for this shorthand with me. He had to begin from the very beginning, taking nothing for granted. I realised his difficulty. It was as if I had had to argue an intricate case, not before a learned judge, but before an intelligent ignoramus, to whom each technical legal term had to be laboriously explained.

There was another difficulty, which applied not to me only, but to the most intelligent auditor in the world. Suppose you are trying to expound to a man who has been stone-deaf from birth the meaning of sound. You can show him the physical effects of it, the brain and sense reactions, but the *fact* of sound you cannot bring home to him by any diagram or calculation. It is something for him without sensory vividness, altogether outside his realised universe. It was the same with the Professor's exposition of strange new dimensions, the discovery of which depended on logical processes. I could not grasp them imaginatively, and, not having lived as he had done with the arguments, I could not comprehend them intellectually.

But here – very crudely and roughly – is the kind of thing he tried to tell me.

He began by observing that in the blind instinct of man there was something which the normal intellect lacked – a prevision of future happenings, for which reason gave no warrant. We all of us had occasionally dim anticipations of coming events, lurking somewhere in our nerves. A man walking in the dark was aware subconsciously of a peril and subconsciously braced himself to meet it. He quoted the sentences from Bergson which I have put at the head of the chapter. His aim was to rationalise and systematise this anticipatory instinct.

Then he presented me with a theory of Time, for he had an orderly mind, and desired to put first things first. Here he pretty well bogged me at the start. He did not call Time a fourth dimension, but I gathered that it amounted to that, or rather that it involved many new dimensions. There seemed to be a number of worlds of presentation travelling in Time, and each was contained within a world one dimension larger. The self was composed of various observers, the normal one being confined to a small field of sensory phenomena, observed or remembered. But this field was included in a larger field and, to the observer in the latter, future events were visible as well as past and present.

In sleep, he went on, where the attention was not absorbed, as it was in waking life, with the smaller field of phenomena, the larger field might come inside the pale of consciousness. People had often been correctly forewarned in dreams. We all now and then were amazed at the familiarity with which we regarded a novel experience, as if we recognised it as something which had happened before. The universe was extended in Time, and the dreamer, with nothing to rivet his attention to the narrow waking field, ranged about, and might light on images which belonged to the future as well as to the past. The sleeper was constantly crossing the arbitrary frontier which our mortal limitations had erected.

At this point I began to see light. I was prepared to assent to the conclusion that in dreams we occasionally dip into the future, though I was unable to follow most of the Professor's proofs. But now came the real question. Was it possible to attain to this form of prevision otherwise than in sleep? Could the observer in the narrow world turn himself by any effort of will into the profounder observer in the world of ampler dimensions? Could the anticipating power of the dreamer be systematised and controlled, and be made available to man in his waking life?

It could, said the Professor. Such was the result of the researches to which he had dedicated the last ten years of his life. It was as a crowning proof that he wished an experiment at Flambard.

I think that he realised how little I had grasped of his exposition of the fundamentals of his theory. He undertook it, I fancy, out of his scrupulous honesty; he felt bound to put me in possession of the whole argument, whether I understood it or not. But, now that he had got down to something concrete which I could follow, his manner became feverishly earnest. He patted my knee with a large lean hand, and kept thrusting his gaunt face close to mine. His writing-pad fell into the lily-pond, but he did not notice it.

He needed several people for his experiment – the more the better, for he wanted a variety of temperaments, and he said something, too, about the advantage of a communal psychical effort…But they must be the right kind of people – people with highly developed nervous systems – not men too deeply sunk in matter. (I thought of Evelyn and the Lamingtons and old Folliot.) He deprecated exuberant physical health or abounding vitality, since such endowments meant that their possessors would be padlocked to the narrower sensory world. He ran over his selection again, dwelling on each, summing each up with what seemed to me astounding shrewdness, considering that he had met them for the first time two days before. He wanted the hungry and the forward-looking. Tavanger and Mayot. "They will never be content," he said, "and their hunger is of the spirit, though maybe an earthy spirit…" Myself. He turned his hollow eyes on me, but was too polite to particularise what my kind of hunger might be…Charles Ottery. "He is unhappy, and that means that his hold on the present is loose…" Sally Flambard. "That gracious lady lives always *sur la branche* – is it not so? She is like a bird, and has no heavy flesh to clog her. Assuredly she must be one." Rather to my surprise he added Reggie Daker. Reggie's recent concussion, for some reason which I did not follow, made him a suitable object…Above all, there was Goodeve. He repeated his name with satisfaction, but offered no comment.

I asked him what form his experiment would take.

"A little training. No more. A little ascesis, partly of the body, but mainly of the mind. It must be disciplined to see what it shall see."

Then, speaking very slowly, and drawing words apparently from as deep a cavern as that from which he drew his breath, he explained his plan.

There must be a certain physical preparation. I am as unlearned in medical science as in philosophy, but I gathered that recently there had been some remarkable advances made in the study of the brain and its subsidiary organs. Very likely I am writing nonsense, for the Professor at this point forgot about tempering the wind to the shorn lamb, and poured forth a flood of technicalities. But I understood him to say that, just as the cortex of the brain was the seat of the intellectual activities, so the subcortical region above the spinal cord was the home of the instinctive faculties. He used a lot of jargon, which, not being an anatomist, I could not follow, but he was obliging enough to draw me a diagram in his pocket-book, the writing-pad being in the lily-pond.

In particular there was a thing which he called an 'intercalated cell,' and which had a very special importance in his scheme. Just as the faculty of sight, he said, had for its supreme function the creation of an extended world, a world of space perception, so the instinct which had its seat in this cell specialised in time-perception…I had been reading lately about telegnosis, and mentioned that word, but he shook his head impatiently. The faculty he spoke of had nothing to do with telegnosis. "You have not understood my exposition," he said. "But no matter. It is enough if you understand my purpose."

It was desirable to stimulate the functioning of this cell. That could only be done in a small degree. A certain diet was necessary, for he had discovered that the cell was temporarily atrophied by the wrong foods. Also there was a drug, which acted upon it directly.

At this I protested, but he was quick to reassure me. "On my honour," he cried, "it is the mildest drug. Its bodily effect is as innocuous as a glass of tonic water. But I have proved experimentally that it lulls the other faculties, and very slightly stimulates this one of which I speak."

Then he revealed his main purpose.

"I am still groping at the edge of mysteries," he said. "My theory I am assured is true, but in practice I can only go a very little way. Some day, when I am ashes, men will look at the future as easily as today they look out of a window at a garden. At present I must be content to exemplify my doctrine by small trivial things. I cannot enable you to gaze at a segment of life at some future date, and watch human beings going about their business. The most I hope for is to show you some simple matter of sense-perception as it will be at that date. Therefore I need some object which I am assured will be still in existence, and which I am also assured will have changed from what it now is. Name to me such an object."

I suggested, rather foolishly, the position of the planets in the sky.

"That will not do, for now we can predict that position with perfect certainty."

"A young tree?"

"The visible evidence of change would be too minute. I cannot promise to open up the future very far ahead. A year – two years maybe – no more."

"A building which we all know, and which is now going up?"

Again he shook his head. "You may be familiar with the type of the completed structure, and carry the picture of it in your memory…There is only one familiar object, which continues and likewise changes. You cannot guess? Why, a journal. A daily or weekly paper."

He leaned towards me and laid a hand on each of my knees.

"Today is the sixth of June. Four days from now, if you and the others consent, I will enable you to see for one instant of time – no longer – a newspaper of the tenth day of June next year."

He lay back in his chair and had a violent fit of coughing, while I digested this startling announcement…He was right on one point – a newspaper was the only thing for his experiment; that at any rate I saw clearly. I own to having been tremendously impressed by his talk, but I was not quite convinced; the thing appeared to be clean out of nature and reason. You see, I had no such stimulus to belief as a scientist would have had who had followed his proofs…Still, it seemed harmless. Probably it would end in nothing – the ritual prepared, and the mystics left gaping at each other…No. That could scarcely happen, I decided; the mystagogue was too impressive.

The Professor had recovered himself, and was watching me under drooped eyelids. All the eagerness had gone out of his face, but that face had the brooding power and the ageless wisdom of the Sphinx. If he were allowed to make the experiment something must happen.

Lady Flambard had promised to abide by my decision…There could be no risk, I told myself. A little carefulness in diet, which would do everybody good. The drug? I would have to watch that. The Professor seemed to read my thoughts, for he broke in:

"You are worrying about the drug? It is of small consequence. If you insist, it can be omitted."

I asked how he proposed to prepare the subjects of his experiment. Quite simply, he replied. A newspaper – *The Times*, for example – would be made to play a large part in our thoughts…I observed that it already played a large part in the thoughts of educated Englishmen, and he smiled – the first time I had seen him smile. There was an air of satisfaction about him, as if he knew what my answer would be.

"I see no objection to what you propose," I said at last. "I warn you that I am still a bit of a sceptic. But I am willing, if you can persuade the others."

He smiled again. "With the others there will be no difficulty. Our gracious hostess is already an enthusiast. Before luncheon I will speak to Mr Tavanger and Mr Mayot – and to Mr Ottery when he returns. I shall not speak to them as I have spoken to you."

"Why?" I asked.

"Because they are longing for such a revelation as I propose, whereas you care not at all. But I would beg of you to say a word on my behalf to Sir Robert Goodeve. His co-operation I especially seek."

He raised with difficulty his huge frame from the wicker chair, blinking his eyes in the hot sun, and leaning on a sundial as if he were giddy. I offered my arm, which he took, and together we went under the striped awning, which shaded one part of the terrace, into the coolness of the great hall.

You know the kind of banality with which, out of shyness, one often winds up a difficult conversation. I was moved to observe, as I left him, that in four days I hoped to be introduced to a new world. He made no answer. "To enter, waking, into the world of sleep," I added fatuously.

Then he said a thing which rather solemnised me.

"Not only the world of sleep," he said. "It is the world to which we penetrate after death."

As I watched his great back slowly mounting the staircase, I had a sudden feeling that into the peace of Flambard something fateful and tremendous had broken.

IV

I DO NOT KNOW what Professor Moe said to Tavanger and Mayot. I knew both men, but not intimately, for they were a little too much of the unabashed careerist for my taste, and I wondered how, in spite of his confidence, he was going to interest their most practical minds.

After luncheon I wanted to be alone, so I took my rod and went down to the Arm, beyond the stretch where it ran among water-meadows.

It was a still, bright afternoon, with a slight haze to temper the glare of the sun. The place was delicious, full of the scents of mint and meadowsweet, yellow flag-irises glowing by the water's edge, and the first dog-roses beginning to star the hedges. There was not much of a rise, but I caught a few trout under the size limit, and stalked and lost a big fellow in the mill pool. But I got no good of the summer peace, and my mind was very little on fishing, for the talk of the morning made a merry-go-round in my head.

I had moments of considering the whole business a farce, and wondering if I had not made a fool of myself in consenting to it. But I could not continue long in that mood. The Professor's ardent face would come before me like a reproachful schoolmaster's, and under those compelling eyes of his I was forced back into something which was acquiescence, if not conviction. There was a shadow of anxiety at the back of my mind. The man was an extraordinary force, with elemental powers of brain and will; was it wise to let such an influence loose on commonplace people who happened to be at the moment a little loose from their moorings? I was not afraid of myself, but what about the high-strung Sally, and the concussed Reggie, and Charles Ottery in the throes of an emotional crisis? I kept telling myself that there was no danger, that nothing could happen…And then I discovered, to my amazement, that, if that forecast proved true, I should be disappointed. I wanted something to happen. Nay, I believed at the bottom of my heart that something would happen.

In the smoking-room, before dinner, I found Charles Ottery and Reggie Daker – a rather pale and subdued Reggie, with a bandage round his head and a black eye. They were talking on the window seat, and when I entered they suddenly stopped. When they saw who it was, Charles called to me to join them.

"I hear you're in this business, Ned," he said. "I got the surprise of my life when the Professor told me that you had consented. It's a new line of country for a staid old bird like you."

"The man's a genius," I replied. "I see no harm in helping him in his experiment. Did you understand his argument?"

"I didn't try. He didn't argue much, but one could see that he had any quantity of scientific stuff behind him. He hopes to make us dream while we're awake, and I thought it such a sporting proposition that I couldn't refuse. It must all be kept deadly secret, of course. We have to get into the right atmosphere, and tune our minds to the proper pitch, and it would never do to rope in a born idiot like George Lamington. He'd guy it from the start."

"You were convinced by the Professor?" I asked.

"I won't say convinced. I was interested. It's an amusing game anyhow, and I want to be amused."

Charles spoke with a lightness which seemed to me to be assumed. He had obviously been far more impressed than he cared to admit. I could see that, since Pamela was giving him a difficult time, he longed for something to distract him, something which was associated with that world of new emotions in which he was living.

The lady's other suitor made no concealment. Reggie was honestly excited. He was flattered, perhaps, by being made one of the circle, and may have attributed his choice to his new role as an authority on books. At last he was being taken seriously. Also his recent concussion may have predisposed him to some research into the mysteries of mind, for as he explained, he could not remember one blessed thing that happened between putting Sir Vidas at a fence which he cleared with a yard to spare, and finding himself in bed with clouts on his head. He was insistent on the need of confidence in the experiment. "What I mean to say is, we've got to help the old boy out. If we don't believe the thing will come off, then it won't – if you see what I mean."

He dropped his voice as Evelyn Flambard and his terriers came noisily into the room.

As I was going upstairs to dress, I found Goodeve's hand on my shoulder.

"I hear you're on in this piece," he whispered jovially, as if the whole thing was a good joke.

"And you?" I whispered back.

"Oh, I'm on. I rather like these psychical adventures. I'm a hopeless subject, you know, and calculated to break up any séance. I haven't got enough soul – too solidly tied to earth. But I never mind offering myself as a victim."

He laughed and passed into his bedroom, leaving me wondering how the Professor had so signally failed with the man who was his special choice. He had obtained Goodeve's consent, so there was no need of pressure from me, but clearly he had not made any sort of convert of him.

At dinner we all tried to behave as if nothing special was afoot, and I think we succeeded. George Lamington had never had so good an audience for his dreary tales. He was full of racing reminiscences, the point of which was the preternatural cunning with which he had outwitted sundry rivals who had tried to beguile him. I never knew anyone whose talk was so choked with adipose tissue, but he generally managed to wallow towards some kind of point, which he and Evelyn found dramatic...During most of the meal I talked to his wife. She could be intelligent enough when she chose, and had a vigorous interest in foreign affairs, for she was an Ambassador's daughter. When I first knew her she had affected a foreign accent, and professed to be more at home in Paris and Vienna than in London. Now she was English of the English, and her former tastes appeared only in intermittent attempts to get George appointed to a Dominion Governorship, where he would most certainly have been a failure. For the present, however, the drums and trumpets did not sound for her. The recent addition to the Lamington fortunes had plunged her deep in the upholstery of life. She was full of plans for doing up their place in Suffolk, and, as I am as ignorant as a coal-heaver about bric-à-brac, I could only listen respectfully. She had the mannerism of the very rich, whose grievance is not against the price of things, but the inadequacy of the supply.

The Professor's health appeared to have improved, or it may have been satisfaction with his initial success, for he was almost loquacious. He seemed to have acute hearing, for he would catch fragments of conversation far down the table, and send his great voice booming towards the speaker in some innocent interrogation. As I have said, his English was excellent, but his knowledge of English life seemed to be on the level of a South Sea islander. He was very inquisitive, and asked questions about racing and horses which gave Evelyn a chance to display his humour. Among the younger people he was a great success. Pamela Brune, who sat next to him, lost in his company her slight air of petulance and discontent, and became once again the delightful child I had known. I was obliged to admit that the Flambard party had improved since yesterday, for certain of its members seemed to have shaken off their listlessness.

While youth was dancing or skylarking on the terrace, and the rest were set solidly to bridge, we met in the upper chamber in the Essex wing, which had been given me as a sitting-room. At first, while we waited for the Professor, we were a little self-conscious. Tavanger and Mayot, especially, looked rather like embarrassed elders at a children's party. But I noticed that no one – not even Reggie Daker – tried to be funny about the business.

The Professor's coming turned us into a most practical assembly. Without a word of further explanation he gave us our marching orders. He appeared to assume that we were all ready to surrender ourselves to his directions.

The paper chosen was *The Times*. For the next three days we were to keep our minds glued to that news-sheet, and he was very explicit about the way in which we were to do it.

First of all, we were to have it as much as possible before our eyes, so that its physical form became as familiar to each of us as our razors and cigarette cases. We started, of course, with a considerable degree of knowledge, for we were all accustomed to look at it every morning. I remember wondering why the Professor had fixed so short a time as three days for this intensive contemplation, till he went on to give his further orders.

This ocular familiarity was only the beginning. Each of us must concentrate on one particular part to which his special interest was pledged – Tavanger on the first City page, for example, Mayot on the leader page, myself on the Law Reports – any part we pleased. Of such pages we had to acquire the most intimate knowledge, so that by shutting our eyes we could reconstruct the make-up in every detail. The physical make-up, that is to say; there was no necessity for any memorising of contents.

Then came something more difficult. Each of us had to perform a number of exercises in concentration and anticipation. We knew the kind of things which were happening, and within limits the kind of topic which would be the staple of the next day's issue. Well, we had to try to forecast some of the contents of the next day's issue, which we had not seen. And not merely in a general sense. We had to empty our minds of everything but the one topic, and endeavour to make as full as possible a picture of part of the exact contents of *The Times* next morning – to see it not as a concept but as a percept – the very words and lines and headings.

For example. Suppose that I took the Law Reports pages. There were some cases the decisions on which were being given by the House of Lords today, and would be published tomorrow. I could guess the members of the tribunal who would deliver judgement, and could make a fair shot at what that judgement would be. Well, I was to try so to forecast these coming pages that I could picture the column of type, and, knowing the judges' idiosyncrasies, see before my eyes the very sentences in which their wisdom would be enshrined…Tavanger, let us say, took the first City page. Tomorrow he knew there would be a report of a company meeting in which he was interested. He must try to get a picture of the paragraph in which the City Editor commented on the meeting…If Mayot chose the leader page, he must try to guess correctly what would be the subject of the first or second leader, and, from his knowledge of *The Times* policy and the style of its leader-writers, envisage some of the very sentences, and possibly the headings.

It seemed to me an incredibly difficult game, and I did not believe that, for myself, I would get any results at all. I have never been much good at guessing. But I could see the general lay-out. Everything would depend upon the adequacy of the knowledge we started with. To make an ocular picture which would have any exactitude, I must be familiar with the Lord Chancellor's mannerisms, Tavanger with the mentality and the style of the City Editor, and Mayot with the policy of the paper and the verbal felicities of its leader-writers… Some of us found the prescription difficult, and Reggie Daker groaned audibly.

But there was more to follow. We were also to try to fling our minds farther forward – not for a day, but for a year. Each morning at seven – I do not know why he fixed that hour – we were to engage in a more difficult kind of concentration – by using such special knowledge as we possessed to help us to forecast the kind of development in the world which June of next year would show. And always we had to aim at seeing our forecasts not in vague concepts, but in concrete black and white in the appropriate corner of *The Times*.

I am bound to say that, when I heard this, I felt that we had been let in for a most futile quest. We had our days mapped out in a minute programme – certain hours for each kind of concentration. We would meet the Professor in my sitting-room at stated times…I think that he felt the atmosphere sceptical, for on this last point his manner lost its briskness and he became very solemn.

"It is difficult," he said, "but you must have faith. And I myself will help you. Time – all time – is with us *now*, but we are confined to narrow fields of presentation. With my help you will enlarge these fields. If you will give me honestly all your powers, I can supplement them."

Lastly he spoke of the necessary régime. Too much exercise was forbidden, for it was desirable that our health should be rather an absence of ailments than a positive, aggressive well-being. There were to be no cold baths. We might smoke, but alcohol was strictly forbidden – not much of a hardship, for we were an abstemious lot. As to diet, we had to behave like convalescents – no meat, not even fish – nothing which, in the Professor's words, 'possessed automobility.' We were allowed weak tea, but not coffee. Milk, cheese, fruit, eggs and cereals were to be our staples.

It all reminded me rather eerily of the ritual food which used to be given to human beings set apart for sacrifice to the gods.

"Our gracious hostess has so arranged it that the others will not be curious," said the Professor, and Sally nodded a mystified head.

I went to bed feeling that I should probably get a liver attack from lack of exercise, if I did not starve from lack of food. Next morning I found a *Times* on the tray which brought my morning tea. Sally must have sent ten miles to a main-line station to get it.

V

IT IS DIFFICULT to write the consecutive story of the next three days. I kept a diary, but on consulting it, I find only a bare record of my hours of meditation on that confounded newspaper, and of our conferences with the Professor. I began in a mood which was less one of scepticism than of despair. I simply did not believe that I could get one step forward in this preposterous business. But I was determined to play the game to the best of my capacity, for Moe's talk last night had brought me fairly under his spell.

I did as I had been told. I emptied my mind of every purpose except the one. I read the arguments in the case – it was an appeal by an insurance company – and then sat down to forecast what the report of the judgement would be, as given by *The Times* next day. Of the substance of the judgement I had not much doubt, and I was pretty certain that it would be delivered by the Lord Chancellor, with the rest of the Court concurring. I knew Boland's style, having listened often enough to his pronouncements, and it would have been easy enough to forecast the kind of thing he would say, using some of his pet phrases. But my job was to forecast what *The Times* reporters would make him say – a very different matter. I collected a set of old copies of the paper and tried to get into their spirit. Then I made a number of jottings, but I found myself slipping into the manner of the official Law Reports, which was not what I wanted. I remember looking at my notes with disfavour, and reflecting that this guessing game was nothing but a deduction from existing knowledge. If I had made a close study of *The Times* reports, I should probably get a good deal right, but since I had only a superficial knowledge I would get little. Moe's grandiose theories about Time had nothing to do with it. It was not a question of casting the mind forward into a new field of presentation, but simply of a good memory from which one made the right deductions.

After my first attempt I went for a walk, and tried to fix my mind on something different. I had been making a new rock-garden at Borrowby, and I examined minutely Sally's collection of Tibetan alpines. On my return the butler handed me a note. The Professor had decided to have conferences with each of us separately, and my hour was three in the afternoon.

Before that hour I had two other bouts of contemplation. I wrestled honourably with the incurably evasive, and filled several sheets of foolscap with notes. Then I revised them, striking out phrases which were natural enough to Boland, but unsuitable for a newspaper summary. The business seemed more ridiculous than ever. I was simply chewing the cud of memories – very vague, inexact memories.

The Professor received me in Sally's boudoir. Now, the odd thing was that in his presence I had no self-consciousness. If anyone had told me that I should have been unburdening my mind in a ridiculous game to a queer foreigner, with the freedom of a novice in the confessional, I should have declared it impossible. But there it was. He sat before me with his gaunt face and bottomless pits of eyes, very grave and gentle, and without being asked I told him what I had been doing.

"That is a beginning," he said, "only a beginning. But your mind is too active as yet to *perceive*. You are still in the bonds of ratiocination. Your past knowledge is only the jumping-off stage from which your mind must leap. Suffer yourself to be more quiescent, my friend. Do not torture your memory. It is a deep well from which the reason can only draw little buckets of water."

I told him that I had been making notes, and he approved. "But do not shape them as you would shape a logical argument. Let them be raw material out of which a picture builds itself. Your business is perception, not conception, and perception comes in flashes." And then he quoted what Napoleon had once said, how after long pondering he had his vision of a battle plan in a blinding flash of white light.

He said a great deal more which I do not remember very clearly. But one thing I have firm in my recollection – the compelling personality of the man. There must have been some strange hypnotic force about him, for as he spoke I experienced suddenly a new confidence and an odd excitement. He seemed to wake unexpected powers in me, and I felt my mind to be less a machine clamped to a solid concrete base, than an aeroplane which might rise and soar into space. Another queer thing – I felt slightly giddy as I left him. Unquestionably he was going to make good his promise and supplement our efforts, for an influence radiated from him, more masterful than any I have ever known in a fellow mortal. It was only after we had parted that the reaction came, and I felt a faint sense of antagonism, almost of fear.

In my last effort before dinner I struggled to follow his advice. I tried to picture next day's *Times*. The judgement, from its importance, would occupy a column at least; I saw that column and its heading, and it seemed to me to be split up into three paragraphs. I saw some of the phrases out of my notes, and one or two new ones. There was one especially, quite in Boland's manner, which seemed to be repeated more than once – something like this: "It is a legal commonplace that a contract of insurance is one *uberrimae fidei*, which is vitiated by any nondisclosure, however innocent, of material facts." I scribbled this down, and found, when I re-read it, that I had written *uberrimi*, and deplored my declining scholarship.

At dinner our group were as glum as owls. I did not know how the Professor had handled the others, but I assumed that his methods had been the same as with me, and certainly he had produced an effect. We all seemed to have something on our minds, and came in for a good deal of chaff, the more as we refrained from so many dishes. Reggie Daker escaped, for he was a convalescent, but Evelyn had a good deal to say about Goodeve's abstinence. Goodeve was supposed to be entering for a tennis contest which the young people had got up, while George Lamington started the legend that I was reducing my weight for the next Bar point-to-point. Happily this interest in our diet diverted their attention from our manners, which must have been strange. All seven of us were stricken with aphasia, and for myself I felt that I was looking on at a movie-show.

The Professor gathered us together in my sitting-room a little before midnight. As I looked at the others I had an impression of a kindergarten. Compared with him we all seemed ridiculously young, crude, and ignorant. Mayot's alert intelligence was only the callow vivacity of a child; Tavanger's heavy face was merely lumpish; even Goodeve looked the bright schoolboy. As for Sally and Reggie and Charles Ottery, something had happened to them which drained the personality from their faces, and made them seem slight and wispish. Moe himself brooded over us like a vital Buddha. I had an uneasy sense of looking at a man who lived most of his time in another world than ours.

He did not instruct us; he talked, and his talk was like a fierce cordial. Looking back at what I can remember of it, it does not seem to make any kind of sense, but it had an overwhelming effect on his hearers. It was as if he were drawing aside curtain after curtain, and, though we could not see into the land beyond the curtains, we were convinced of its existence. As I have said, I cannot make sense of my recollection of it, but while I was listening it seemed to be quite simple and intelligible...

He spoke of the instinct which gave perceptions, and of its immense power as compared to our petty reason which turned percepts into concepts. He spoke of what he called the 'eye of the mind,' and said the very phrase pointed to some intuition in the ordinary being of a gift which civilisation had atrophied...Then Reggie Daker became important. The Professor elicited from the coy Reggie that in his childhood he had been in the habit of seeing abstract things in a concrete form. For Reggie the different days of the week had each a special shape, and each of the Ten Commandments a special colour. Monday was a square and Saturday an oval, and Sunday a circle with a segment bitten out; the Third Commandment was dark blue, and the Tenth a pale green with spots. Reggie had thought of Sin as a substance like black salt, and the Soul as something in the shape of a kidney bean...

It all sounds the wildest nonsense, but the Professor made out of Reggie's confidences a wonderful thing. His images might seem ridiculous, but they showed perception struggling to regain its rightful place. He had some theory of the relation between the concrete vision and the abstract thought, which he linked somehow or other to his doctrine of Time. In the retrospect I cannot remember his argument, but he convinced me absolutely...He had a lot to say about the old astrologers and magic-makers who worked with physical charms and geometrical figures, and he was clear that they had had a knowledge of mysteries on which the door had long been locked. Also he talked about certain savage beliefs in ancient Greece and in modern Africa – which he said were profundity and not foolishness...He spoke, too, about the world of dreams, and how its fantasy had often a deeper reality than waking life. "We are children on the seashore," he said, "watching the jetsam of the waves, and every fragment of jetsam is a clue to a land beyond the waters which is our true home."

Not for a moment did any of us think him mad. We sat like beggars, hungrily picking up crumbs from a feast. Of one thing I was presently convinced. Moe had cast a stronger spell over the others than over myself. I found my mind trying feebly to question some of his sayings, to link them with the ordinary world of thought; but it was plain that the rest accepted everything as inspired and infallible gospel.

I dare say I was tired, for I slept more soundly than I had done for weeks. I was called at seven, and set myself, according to instructions, to a long-range forecast – what would be likely to happen on June tenth a year ahead. It sounds a futile job, and so I found it. My head soon grew dizzy with speculations, some of them quite outside the legal sphere which I had marked out as my own. But I found one curious thing. I had lost the hopelessness which had accompanied my contemplations of the previous day. I *believed* now that I could make something of the task. Also I found my imagination far more lively. I convinced myself that in a year's time there would be a new Lord Chancellor and a new Lord of Appeal. I beheld them sitting in the Lords, but the figure on the Woolsack was so blurred that I could not recognise it. But I saw the new Lord clearly, and his face was the face of young Molsom, who had only taken silk two years ago. Molsom's appointment was incredible, but, as often as the picture of the scarlet benches of the Upper House came before me, there was Molsom, with his dapper little figure and his big nose and his arms folded after his habit. I realised that I was beginning to use the 'mind's eye,' to see things, and not merely to think them.

The Times was brought to my bedside at eight, and I opened it eagerly. There was the judgement in my case, delivered, as I had expected, by Boland. It ran not to a whole column, but to less than three-quarters; but I had been right on one point – it was broken up into three paragraphs. The substance of the judgement was much as I had foreseen, but I had not been lucky in guessing the wording, and Boland had referred to only two of the cases I had marked down for him...

But there was one amazing thing. He had used the sentence about *uberrimae fidei* – very much in the form I had anticipated. More – far more. *The Times* had that rare thing, a misprint: it had *uberrimi*, the very blunder I had made myself in my anticipatory jottings.

This made me feel solemn. My other correct anticipations might be set down to deductions from past knowledge. But here was an indubitable instance of anticipatory perception.

From that hour I date my complete conversion. I was as docile now as Sally, and I stopped trying to reason. For I understood that, behind all the régime and the exercises, there was the tremendous fact of Professor Moe himself. If we were to look into the future it must be largely through his eyes. By the sheer power of intellect he had won a gift, and by some superabundant force of personality he was able to communicate in part that gift to others.

I am not going to attempt to write in detail the story of the next two days, because external detail matters little; the true history was being made in the heads of the seven of us. I went obediently through the prescribed ritual. I pored over *The Times* as if my salvation depended upon it. I laboured to foresee the next day's issue, and I let my mind race into the next year. I felt my imagination becoming more fecund and more vivid, and my confidence growing hourly. And always I felt behind me some mighty impetus driving me on and holding me up. I was in the charge of a Moses, like the puzzled Israelites stumbling in the desert.

I spent the intervals with a rod beside the Arm, and there I first became conscious of certain physical symptoms. An almost morbid nervous alertness was accompanied by a good deal of bodily lassitude. This could not be due merely to the diet and lack of exercise, for I had often been sedentary for a week on end and lived chiefly on bread and cheese. Rather it seemed that I was using my nervous energy so lavishly in one direction that I had little left for the ordinary purposes of life...Another thing. My sight is very good, especially for long distances, and in dry-fly fishing I never need to use a glass to spot a fish. Well, in the little fishing I did that day, I found my eyes as good as ever, but I noted one remarkable defect. I saw the trout perfectly clearly, but I could not put a fly neatly over him. There was nothing wrong with my casting; the trouble was in my eye, which had somehow lost its liaison with the rest of my body. The fly fell on the water as lightly as thistledown, but it was many inches away from the fish's nose.

That day the Professor made us fix our minds principally on the lay-out of June tenth, next year. He wanted to have that date orientated for us with relation to other recurrent events – the Derby, Ascot, the third reading of the Budget, the conference of Empire Journalists and so forth. Also he provided us with sheets of blank paper, the size of *The Times*, which were to be, so to speak, the screen on which the magic lantern of our prevision cast its picture. He was very careful, almost fussy, about this business. The sheets had nothing printed on them, but they had to be exactly right in size, and he rejected the first lot that Sally provided.

But I cannot say that I paid much attention to these or any other details. I was in a mood of utter obedience, simply doing what I was told to do to the best of my power. I was in the grip of a power which I had no desire to question, and which by some strong magic was breaking down walls for me and giving me a new and marvellous freedom. For there was no doubt about it – I could now set my mind at will racing into the future, and placing before me panoramas which might or might not be true, but which had all the concrete sharpness of reality. There were moments when I seemed almost to feel one sphere of presentation give place to another, as the driver of a car changes gear.

Dinner that night – Sally had sent the Professor to bed after tea – was as lively as the meal of the previous evening had been dull – lively, that is, for the rest of the party, not for us seven. For we seven suddenly developed a remarkable capacity for making sport for the populace, by a kind of mental light-heartedness, similar to my clumsiness with the trout. Our minds seemed to have jolted out of focus. There is a species of bêtise, which I believe at Cambridge is named after some don, and which consists in missing completely the point of a metaphor or a joke, in setting the heavy heel of literalness on some trivial flower of fancy. It is a fault to which the Scots are supposed to be prone, and it is the staple of most of the tales against that nation. The classic instance is Charles Lamb's story of how he was once present at a dinner given in honour of Burns, at which a nephew of the poet was to be present. As the company waited on the arrival of the guest, Lamb remarked that he wished the uncle were coming instead of the nephew: upon which several solemn Scotsmen arose to inform him that that was impossible, because Burns was dead.

That night we seven became unconscious Caledonians. Reggie Daker began it, by asking a ridiculous question about a story of Evelyn's. At first Evelyn looked wrathful, suspecting irony, and then, realising Reggie's guilelessness, he turned the laugh against that innocent. The extraordinary thing was that we all did it. Sally was the worst, and Charles Ottery a good second. Even Mayot fell into the trick – Mayot, who had a reputation for a quick and caustic wit. George Lamington was talking politics. "A Bengali Cabinet in England," George began, and was interrupted by Mayot with, "But, hang it, man, there's no Bengali Cabinet in England!" The fact that I noted our behaviour would seem to prove that I was not so deeply under the spell as the others.

We made sport, as I have said, for the company, and some of them enjoyed the pleasant sense of superiority which comes when people who have a reputation for brains make fools of themselves. Yet the mirth struck me as a little uneasy. There was a sense somewhere that all was not well, that odd things were going on beneath the surface. Pamela Brune, I remember, let her eyes rest on Charles Ottery as she left the room, and in those eyes I read bewilderment, almost pain.

Next morning we began the drug. There were in all three doses – the first with morning tea, the second at three in the afternoon, and the third after dinner. For myself I felt no particular effects, but I can testify that that day, the last day of our preparation, my mood changed.

For the first time I found some dregs of fear in my mind. My confidence in Moe was in no way abated, but I began to feel that we were moving on the edge of things, not mysterious only but terrible. My first cause for uneasiness was the Professor himself. When I met him that morning I was staggered by his looks. His colour was like white wax, and the gauntness of his face was such that it seemed that not only flesh had gone but muscle and blood, so that there remained only dead skin stretched tight over dead bone. His eyes were alive, and no longer placid pools, but it was a sick life, and coughing shook him as an autumn wind shakes the rafters of a ruined barn. He professed to be well enough, but I realised that his experiment was draining his scanty strength. The virtue was going out of him into us, and I wondered if before the appointed time the dynamo might not fail us.

My other anxiety was Goodeve. He had begun by being the most sceptical of the lot of us, but I noticed that at each conference with Moe he grew more silent, his face more strained, and his eyes more unquiet. There was now something positively furtive in them, as if he were in dread of some menace springing out at him from ambush. He hung upon the Professor's words with dog-like devotion, very odd in a personality so substantial and well defined. By tacit consent none of us ever spoke of the experiment, as if we felt that any communication among ourselves might weaken the strong effluence from our leader's mind, so I could not put out any feelers. But the sight of Goodeve at luncheon increased my lurking fear that we were getting very near the edge of some indefinable danger.

I felt very drowsy all day, and dozed in a garden chair between the exercises. I usually dream a good deal of nights, but now I slept like a log – which may have been due to nervous fatigue, or more likely to the switching of the dream-world over into the waking hours. The strangest thing about the whole experience was that I never felt one moment of boredom. I was doing something infinitely monotonous, and yet my powers bent themselves to it as readily as if every moment were a new excitement. That, too, rather frightened me. If this stimulus was so potent for a flat nature like mine, what must be its power over more mercurial souls?

I must record what happened at tea. Nearly all the guests were there, and a cheerful party of young people had come over from a neighbouring house. Now Sally had a much-loved terrier, a Dandie Dinmont called Andrew, who had been on a visit to the vet and had only returned that afternoon. Andrew appeared when tea was beginning, and was received by his mistress with every kind of endearment. But Andrew would not go near her; he fled, knocking over a table, and took refuge between Evelyn's legs, and nothing would draw him from his sanctuary. He used to be a friend of mine, but he met my advances with a snap and the most dismal howling. There he stood, pressed against Evelyn's shins, his teeth bared, his big head lowered and bristling. He seemed to have no objection to the others, only to Sally and me. Then Mayot came in with Tavanger, and again Andrew wailed to the skies. Charles Ottery and Reggie received the same greeting; Goodeve, too, who sat down next to Evelyn, and thereby drove Andrew yelping to a corner. After that he recovered a little and accepted a bit of bread and butter from Pamela Brune, by whose side he had ensconced himself. I was deeply interested in the whole performance, for it was not humanity that Andrew disliked, but that section of it which was engaged in the experiment. I was pondering on this marvel, when there came a howl like nothing on earth, and I saw Andrew streaking out of the drawing-room, slithering over rugs and barging into stools, with Evelyn after him. I also saw that Moe had just entered by another door, looking like a death-in-life.

The Professor sat himself by me, and drank his tea thirstily. The tiny cup seemed almost too great a weight for the mighty hand to raise. He turned to me with the ghost of a smile.

"That dog pays tribute to our success," he said. "The animal has instinct and the man reason, and on those terms they live together. Let a man attain instinct and the animal will flee from him. I have noted it before."

Some neighbours came to dinner, so we made a big party, and the silent conclave passed unnoticed, though Sally's partner must have wondered what had become of her famous sparkle, for she was the palest and mutest of spectres. I felt myself an observer set at a distance not only from the ordinary members of the party but from our coterie – which proves that I must have been less under Moe's spell than my companions. For example, I could not only watch with complete detachment the behaviour of the cheerful young people, and listen to George Lamington's talk of his new Lancia, but I could observe from without Sally's absent-mindedness and stammered apologies, and Goodeve's look of unhappy expectation, and Charles Ottery's air of one struggling with something on the edge of memory, and Tavanger's dry lips – the man drank pints of water. One thing I noticed. They clearly hated those outside our group. Sally would shrug her shoulders as if unbearably tried, and Mayot looked murderously now and then at Evelyn, and Charles Ottery, who sat next to Pamela Brune, regarded her with hard eyes. I was conscious of something of the same sort myself, for most of my fellows had come to look to me like chattering mannikins. They bored me, but I did not feel for them the overwhelming distaste which was only too apparent in the other members of the group. Their attitude was the opposite of Miranda's cry –

> "O brave new world
> That has such people in't."

I doubt if they thought the world brave, and for certain they had no illusion about its inhabitants.

It was a very hot night, and I went out beyond the terrace to sniff the fragrance of Sally's rock garden. As I sat dangling my legs over the parapet I felt a hand on my arm, and turned to find Pamela Brune.

"Come for a walk, Uncle Ned," she said. "I want to talk to you."

She slipped her arm through mine, and we went down the long alley between yews at the end of the Dutch garden. I felt her arm tremble, and when she spoke it was in a voice which she strove to make composed.

"What has happened to you all?" she asked. "I thought this Whitsuntide was going to be such fun, and it began well – and now everybody is behaving so oddly, Sally hasn't smiled for two days, and Reggie is more half-witted than ever, and you look most of the time as if you were dropping off to sleep."

"I am pretty tired," I replied.

"Oh yes, I know," she said impatiently. "There are excuses for you – and for Sally perhaps, for she has been overdoing it badly…But there is a perfect epidemic of bad manners abroad. Tonight at dinner I could have boxed Charles Ottery's ears. He was horribly rude."

"You haven't been very kind to him," I said lamely.

She withdrew her hand.

"What do you mean? I have always been civil…and he has been very, very unkind to me…I hate him. I'll never speak to him again."

Pamela fled from me down the shadowed alley like a nymph surprised by Pan, and I knew that she fled that I might not see her tears.

Later that night we had our last conference with Moe, for next morning at seven in my sitting-room we were to meet for the final adventure. It was a short conference, and all he seemed to do was to tighten the cords with which he had bound us. I felt his influence more sharply than ever, but I was not in such perfect thraldom as the others, for with a little fragment of my mind I could still observe and think objectively…

I observed the death-mask of the Professor. That is the only word by which to describe his face. Every drop of blood seemed to have fled from it, and in his deep pits of eyes there was no glimmer of life. It was a mask of death, but it was also a mask of peace. In that I think lay its compelling power. There was no shadow of unrest or strife or doubt in it. It had been purged of human weakness as it had been drained of blood. I remembered "grey-haired Saturn, quiet as a stone."

I thought – what did I think? I kept trying as a desperate duty to make my mind function a little on its own account. I cast it back over the doings of the past days, but I could not find a focus…I was aware that somehow I had acquired new and strange gifts. I had become an adept at prospecting the immediate future, for, though I made many blunders, I had had an amazing percentage of successes. But the Professor did not set much store apparently by this particular expertise, and my main task had been long-range forecasts a year ahead. These, of course, could not be verified, but I had managed to create a segment of a future world as shot with colour and as diversified with incident as the world of sense around me…

About that there were some puzzles which I could not solve. In guessing the contents of the next day's *Times* I had a mass of concrete experience to build on, but I had not that experience to help me in constructing what might happen across the space of a year, with all a year's unaccountable chances…Then I reflected that the power of short-range forecasts had come in only a small degree from the exercise of my reason upon past experience. That was but a dim light: it was the daemonic power of the Professor's mind which had given me those illuminations. Could the strong wings of that spirit carry seven humdrum folk over the barriers of sense and habit into a new far world of presentation?

That was my last thought before I fell asleep, and I remember that I felt a sudden horror. We were feeding like parasites upon something on which lay the shadow of dissolution.

VI

I WAS UP and dressed long before seven. The drug, or the diet, or the exercises, or all combined, made me sleepy during the day, but singularly alert at first waking. Alert in body, that is – the feeling that I could run a mile in record time, the desire for something to task my bodily strength. But my brain these last mornings had not been alert. It had seemed a passive stage over which a pageant moved, a pageant of which I had not the direction…But this morning the pageant had stopped, the stage was empty, or rather it was brooded over by a vast vague disquiet.

It was a perfect midsummer morning, with that faint haze in the distance which means a hot noon. The park under my window lay drenched and silvered with dew. The hawthorns seemed to be bowed over the grasses under their weight of blossom. The birds were chattering in the ivy, and two larks were singing. Just under me, beyond the ha-ha, a foal was standing on tottering legs beside its mother, lifting its delicate nozzle to sniff the air. The Arm, where the sun caught it, was a silver crescent, and there was a little slow drift of amethyst smoke from the head keeper's cottage in a clump of firs. The scene was embodied, deep, primordial peace, and though, as I have said, my ordinary perception had become a little dulled, the glory of the June morning smote me like a blow.

It wakened a thousand memories, and memories of late had been rare things with me…I thought of other such dawns, when I had tiptoed through wet meadows to be at the morning rise – water lilies, and buckbean, and arrowhead, and the big trout feeding; dawn in the Alps, when, perched on some rock pinnacle below the last ridge of my peak, I had eaten breakfast and watched the world heave itself out of dusk into burning colour; a hundred hours when I had thanked God that I was alive…A sudden longing woke in me, as if these things were slipping away. These joys were all inside the curtain of sense and present perception, and now I was feeling for the gap in the curtain, and losing them. What mattered the world beyond the gap? Why should we reach after that which God had hidden?…

Fear, distaste, regret chased each other through my mind. Something had weakened this morning. Had the *mystica catena* snapped?…And then I heard a movement in my sitting-room, and turned away from the window. My mind might be in revolt, but my will was docile.

We sat in a semicircle round the Professor. It was a small room with linen-fold panelling, a carved chimney-piece, and one picture – a French hunting scene. The morning sun was looking into it, so the blinds were half-lowered. We sat in a twilight, except in one corner, where the floor showed a broad shaft of light. I was next to Sally at the left-hand edge of the circle. That is all I remember about the scene, except that each of us had a copy of *The Times* – not the blank paper we had had before, but that morning's *Times*, the issue for the tenth of June in that year of grace.

I must have slipped partly out of the spell, for I could use my eyes and get some message from them. I dare say I could have understood one of *The Times* leaders. But I realised that the others were different. They could not have made sense of one word. To them it was blank white paper, an empty slate on which something was about to be written. They had the air of dull, but obedient pupils, with their eyes chained to their master.

The Professor wore a dressing-gown, and sat in the writing-table chair – deathly white, but stirred into intense life. He sat upright, with his hands on his knees, and his eyes, even in the gloom, seemed to be probing and kneading our souls…I felt the spell, and consciously struggled against it. His voice helped my resistance. It was weak and cracked, without the fierce vitality of his face.

"For three minutes you will turn your eyes inward – into the darkness of the mind which I have taught you to make. Then – I will give the sign – you will look at the paper. There you will see words written, but only for one second. Bend all your powers to remember them."

But my thoughts were not in the darkness of the mind. I looked at the paper and saw that I could read the date and the beginning of an advertisement. I had broken loose; I was a rebel, and was glad of it. And then I looked at Moe, and saw there something which sent a chill to my heart.

The man was dying – dying visibly. With my eyes I saw the body shrink and the jaw loosen as the vital energy ebbed. Now I knew how we might bridge the gap of Time. His personality had lifted us out of our world, and, by a supreme effort of brain and will, his departing soul might carry us into a new one – for an instant only, before that soul passed into a timeless eternity.

I could see all this, because I had shaken myself free from his spell, yet I felt the surge of his spirit like a wind in my face. I heard the word "Now," croaked with what must have been his last breath. I saw his huge form crumple and slip slowly to the floor. But the eyes of the others did not see this; they were on *The Times* pages.

All but Sally. The strain had become more than she could bear. With a small cry she tilted against my shoulder, and for the few seconds before the others returned to ordinary consciousness and realised that Moe was dead, she lay swooning in my arms.

In that fateful moment, while the soul of a genius was quitting the body, five men, staring at what had become the simulacrum of a *Times* not to be printed for twelve months, read certain things.

Mayot had a vision of the leader page, and read two sentences of comment on a speech by the Prime Minister. In one sentence the Prime Minister was named, and the name was not that of him who then held the office.

Tavanger, on the first City page, had a glimpse of a note on the formation of a great combine, by the Anatilla Corporation, of the michelite-producing interests of the world.

Reggie Daker, on the Court page, saw an account of the departure of an archaeological expedition to Yucatan, and his name appeared as one of the members.

Goodeve and Charles Ottery – the one on the page opposite the leaders and the other on the first page of the paper – read the announcement of their own deaths.

The complete and unabridged text is available online, from *flametreepublishing.com/extras*

Shaping Things to Come

Dominick Cancilla

HERBERT NEVER KNEW if he was alone. He kept windows and doors barred, trapping the day's heat in a room full of stale air but providing no protection where intruders were concerned. Although it was late afternoon, he lay in near darkness atop sweat-soaked sheets and listened for any hint of a Hound's approach.

Because his cabin was well away from the city, there were no passersby or motorcars to disturb him. For that reason, any sound could be significant.

The trees rustled outside his window, sending worry crawling up the back of his neck. A simple summer breeze, or someone attempting to reach his roof and chimney? The soft roar of the kiln in the corner made it even more difficult to separate innocuous noise from subtle alarm, but it was a necessary evil.

Herbert half wished that one of them would appear, as one might wish for the other boot to drop. The constant worry was far worse than the eventual materialization. It clawed at his mind, kept him jumping at shadows, ate at his sleep.

Herbert hadn't been able to rest without first reaching the point of exhaustion since before the first Hound. Knowing that it was in some odd, unquantifiable measure his fault only made things that much worse. And having grown dependent on them pushed him to within a hair's breadth of madness.

Across the room, the clock struck three. Its chimes had once recalled more innocent days, but at present they only reminded him of the time. All the other possessions Herbert's parents' double suicide had made his had long ago found their way to a pawn shop or private sale, to snipping a few links from his great chain of debt. He made a silent promise that the clock would follow shortly.

Just as the last echo of three o'clock was fading from his aching head, a short, sharp puff of air washed over Herbert. He sat up quickly and fumbled to light the lamp on the table beside him.

He had first felt that breeze in his mother's kitchen when he was a lad of eleven, just before a barely dressed woman had appeared from nowhere and started asking Mama very personal questions as if it were the most natural thing in the world. The woman – she had asked to be called simply 'the biographer' – came whenever she pleased all through Herbert's youth, eventually scraping raw his parents' nerves along with his own. She would show up at meal times, when they had company – even while he was in the privy. It was not unusual to be awakened in the middle of the night by the feel of her sitting upon the mattress beside him. This first Hound was always in a great hurry, and offended in her self-importance if everything was not dropped so that her inquiries could be tended to.

Herbert had finally stopped her when he was sixteen, but by that time he was friendless and his family was too far gone to be saved.

The lamp sputtered to life, spreading light and shadow through Herbert's room. The furniture and bare walls hadn't changed in the fifteen years he had lived in the cabin. He liked the monotony of them, having learned to loathe anything new or surprising. But surprises were something he could not easily avoid.

The Hound appeared like clockwork twelve and a half seconds after the heralding burst of air. It was a man this time – tall, lean, muscular, tanned white, and grinning like an idiot. He wore no mask, which made him pre-2240, and wore a gray dress, which put him after 2053. The belt of lights around his waist indicated he had not reached the twenty-second century. His stiff hat further narrowed the possibilities. Herbert guessed 2080 or there abouts. There should be no trouble understanding the man's speech, though it may be a bit odd. The intruder had no visible translation device so the aging tomes beneath his arm were likely in English – a great convenience.

"Mr. Wells?" said the Hound, apparently oblivious to the rudeness of appearing in a man's room uninvited. "My name is Tiberius, and come to visit from year 2088," he paused for effect, "in the twenty-first century!"

Over the years, Herbert had noticed that the further in the future a Hound came from, the less time he would stay. A quick mental calculation, based on decades of careful record keeping, revealed that this particular intruder's stay would last some 125 minutes – a decent amount of time, and probably enough for Herbert to wring something useful from the distasteful encounter.

Since contacting people in the past was apparently a crime, everyone who came back to harass Herbert did so covertly, and they all assumed they were the only ones who had. Because he hated the smug bastards with passion unbounded, it disgusted Herbert to play along with their conceited fantasies, but it seemed the only way to get what he wanted. He got up from the bed, wide-eyed in mock wonder.

"My goodness, a time traveler!" Herbert said with long-practiced surprise. "Why, this is the most fantastic moment of my experience! Are you aware that I've written a story on that very subject?" It was a blatant lie of course. Herbert hadn't put two words of fiction together in his life. The state of his nerves made it impossible for him to concentrate on creative writing or anything of the sort. How could he craft sentence and plot knowing that at any moment one of the Hounds might appear to demand his attention? And besides, his tastes ran more toward social and political works than romances of science.

But claiming authorship of the time travel novel never failed to thrill the annoying bastards. He wondered how they would feel if they knew that his manuscript of it sat in a trunk beneath the bed, and that he blamed it so thoroughly for his present situation that he intended never to publish it unless his financial situation became somehow even more unbearable.

"Truth!" the Hound said, still grinning like a loon in response to Herbert's question. "That's why I came, Mr. Wells. *The Time Machine* has been my favored read since I hatched!" Since the man was pre-24th century, Herbert knew that the reference to hatching was just a turn of phrase. "Because of the way tech works, time is limited." He let out a cough-short laugh, as if he'd made a joke. "I'll get to facts. I'm a 'pendous fan, and I request you sign these for me." He held out his stack of books.

They always had a stack of books.

"Certainly, my boy, certainly. Just put them on the desk and I'll be right with you." Herbert pointed to the aging roll-top across the room, behind the Hound.

"Without problems!" The fool followed Herbert's direction like an automaton.

"Could you find my fountain pen in the desk as well, please? And tell me more about how this time travel business works while you're at it. Is it similar to the concept I used in my book?" The Hound's resulting chatter gave Herbert opportunity to retrieve the pistol from beneath his pillow, and noise to cover any telltale sound he might make.

"Happily!" the Hound said, rolling the desk open with some effort after taking a moment to puzzle out how it worked. "It's basically a projectile system, firing along fourteen space-time axes. At the apex of flight, the traveler enters norm space for a limited time and," blah blah blah. Herbert paid no attention to a speech he'd heard a hundred times before, but concentrated on padding silently across the room.

The uninvited guest babbled on, comparing the reality of time travel to Herbert's book and a movie some pal of his had made. Herbert put the pistol to the base of the Hound's skull and pulled the trigger.

Ever since he discovered that people from the 24th century and beyond were bulletproof, Herbert had experienced a brief moment of unbearable tension each time he fired his pistol into a Hound. So it was with a great deal of relief that Herbert saw the Hound's head explode and his body crumble to the bare floor like a stricken marionette.

Ignoring the spreading mess, Herbert dropped the gun on the desk and dragged the body toward the kiln. He could hardly wait to see what books the Hound had brought, and as such made quick work of the disposal. The bullet had passed clear through and so did not need to be removed, another convenience.

The first few times he'd killed Hounds, Herbert had worried that some kind of temporal police would show up to place him in irons. Certainly someone would notice if time travelers kept returning as freshly murdered corpses. Erasing evidence of the crime with fire was an early solution, and it seemed to work. But if the lack of intervention by authorities was due to his efforts or because for some reason authorities were unable to detect in what time the victim had been slain, he did not know. In fact, for all he knew these criminals had kept their trips so secret that they were not discovered even after their disappearance. It hardly mattered, so long as the reality of the situation kept working in his favor.

So with no legal ramifications and no mess (the bodies disappeared down to the last platelet when their time ran out), Herbert had become quite the confident assassin.

It was a mystery to Herbert why a bullet lodged in a body returned to the future along with the corpse – just as, he assumed, the ink from his signature in a book did – but nothing brought from the future could be left in the past. Of course, if future objects could be left behind, Herbert would have little excuse for killing the Hounds, and that would be a shame indeed.

After getting the lantern, Herbert took a seat at his desk and pulled the Hound's books toward him. *The Shape of Things to Come*, *The Time Machine* (of course), and *Great SF Short Stories*. A good selection. He opened the third book first, since it was rare for a Hound to bring anything with stories by authors other than Wells in it.

The book's table of contents listed three of his short stories – 'The Man Who Could Work Miracles,' 'The Crystal Egg,' and 'I, Robot' (a story for which Herbert learned he'd gotten credit for creating the word 'robotics'). All of them were stories he had already published. After giving the matter careful thought, he chose 'There Will

Come Soft Rains,' by one Ray Bradbury, both because he'd encountered the author's name in conversation with Hounds and because the story was short enough for him to get through in the time he had before the book vanished.

When he first got the idea of copying from the books that were brought to him, Herbert had been fool enough to try and ask the Hounds for permission. Most had been rudely indignant that 'such a great man' would even consider such a thing, and all informed him that doing so might disrupt the time stream irreparably. They were, to a one, hypocrites.

Herbert's attempts at becoming a draper or pharmacist had come to nothing, and his prospects for eroding his mountain of debt would be bleak indeed without what he took from the Hounds. Fortunately, Herbert had been able to sell every story he'd copied, and a magazine would soon be serializing the novel about Martians that he'd painstakingly duplicated over the years. It brought in enough to keep him barely fed without having to resort to an outside job where his nervousness would bring odd looks, and in a few more years his debt would finally be gone.

The story he'd selected from the anthology turned out to be quite good, if a little flowery. With luck, it would keep the few critics who had noted Herbert praising his ability to write in varied styles. Indeed, the story was good enough that he would be proud to have written it.

This was the first time Herbert had copied a story that had another author's name attached. At least as far as he could recall. Once he copied and published it under his own name it would be his story so far as history was concerned, and the Hound's book he now held would have an alternate table of contents. But would he remember that the story had once been credited to another author? Herbert didn't know and, at the moment, he was really too busy to give it much thought.

It took Herbert some three quarters of an hour to copy the story, writing with the great speed of pen he'd cultivated.

When the hurry of work was past, Herbert set pen aside with a relieved sigh. Exhaustion rose up in him like cool water filling a bath. He was momentarily tempted by thoughts of trying to sleep and had just gotten up from his chair when what calm he had gathered was stolen by a knock on the door.

Who could it be at four in the afternoon at such a remote location? A traveler in need? An officer of the law? A rabid creditor? No matter who it was, it was trouble.

The stench from the kiln would still be there for ten or fifteen minutes at least. There was some blood on his hands and clothing, and bloody footprints ran here and there on the floor. If he let anyone into the cabin, all would be lost. Because lantern light was certainly leaking beneath the door, he could not pretend to be away from home.

"Who is it?" he called, madly trying to think of a way to stall until the evidence of his crime had departed.

"Mr. Wells?" a woman's voice responded from outside. The way her words sounded, as if they were passing through a long tube, brought him instant relief. It was a tell-tale characteristic of a 23rd-century environmental suit. "I'm designate Node 23 and I'm from the future. Would you be pleased to put your name in my anthology of *The Martian Chronicles*?"

Herbert allowed himself a sly grin. The title sounded promising – he wondered if it could be a sequel to his first Martian book.

"Just a minute," he said, picking up the pistol. "I'll be right there."

No longer interested in wasting time, Herbert hurried to the door. He raised the gun to about chest level before lifting the latch and turning the knob. It was going to be a very productive afternoon.

Hilda Silfverling
A Fantasy

L. Maria Child

Thou hast nor youth nor age;
But, as it were, an after dinner's sleep,
Dreaming on both.
Measure for Measure

HILDA GYLLENLOF was the daughter of a poor Swedish clergyman. Her mother died before she had counted five summers. The good father did his best to supply the loss of maternal tenderness; nor were kind neighbors wanting, with friendly words, and many a small gift for the pretty little one. But at the age of thirteen, Hilda lost her father also, just as she was receiving rapidly from his affectionate teachings as much culture as his own education and means afforded. The unfortunate girl had no other resource than to go to distant relatives, who were poor, and could not well conceal that the destitute orphan was a burden. At the end of a year, Hilda, in sadness and weariness of spirit, went to Stockholm, to avail herself of an opportunity to earn her living by her needle, and some light services about the house.

She was then in the first blush of maidenhood, with a clear innocent look, and exceedingly fair complexion. Her beauty soon attracted the attention of Magnus Andersen, mate of a Danish vessel then lying at the wharves of Stockholm. He could not be otherwise than fascinated with her budding loveliness; and alone as she was in the world, she was naturally prone to listen to the first words of warm affection she had heard since her father's death. What followed is the old story, which will continue to be told as long as there are human passions and human laws. To do the young man justice, though selfish, he was not deliberately unkind; for he did not mean to be treacherous to the friendless young creature who trusted him. He sailed from Sweden with the honest intention to return and make her his wife; but he was lost in a storm at sea, and the earth saw him no more.

Hilda never heard the sad tidings; but, for another cause, her heart was soon oppressed with shame and sorrow. If she had had a mother's bosom on which to lean her aching head, and confess all her faults and all her grief, much misery might have been saved. But there was none to whom she dared to speak of her anxiety and shame. Her extreme melancholy attracted the attention of a poor old woman, to whom she sometimes carried clothes for washing. The good Virika, after manifesting her sympathy in various ways, at last ventured to ask outright why one so young was so very sad. The poor child threw herself on the friendly bosom, and confessed all her wretchedness. After that, they had frequent confidential conversations; and the kind-hearted peasant did her utmost to console and cheer the desolate orphan. She said she must soon return to her native village in the Norwegian valley of Westfjordalen; and as she was alone in the world, and wanted some-thing to love, she would gladly take the babe, and adopt it for her own.

Poor Hilda, thankful for any chance to keep her disgrace a secret, gratefully accepted the offer. When the babe was ten days old, she allowed the good Virika to carry it away; though not without bitter tears, and the oft-repeated promise that her little one might be reclaimed, whenever Magnus returned and fulfilled his promise of marriage.

But though these arrangements were managed with great caution, the young mother did not escape suspicion. It chanced, very unfortunately, that soon after Virika's departure, an infant was found in the water, strangled with a sash very like one Hilda had been accustomed to wear. A train of circumstantial evidence seemed to connect the child with her, and she was arrested. For some time, she contented herself with assertions of innocence, and obstinately refused to tell anything more. But at last, having the fear of death before her eyes, she acknowledged that she had given birth to a daughter, which had been carried away by Virika Gjetter, to her native place, in the parish of Tind, in the Valley of Westfjordalen. Inquiries were accordingly made in Norway, but the answer obtained was that Virika had not been heard of in her native valley, for many years. Through weary months, Hilda lingered in prison, waiting in vain for favourable testimony; and at last, on strong circumstantial evidence she was condemned to die.

It chanced there was at that time a very learned chemist in Stockholm; a man whose thoughts were all gas, and his hours marked only by combinations and explosions. He had discovered a process of artificial cold, by which he could suspend animation in living creatures, and restore it at any prescribed time. He had in one apartment of his laboratory a bear that had been in a torpid state five years, a wolf two years, and so on. This of course excited a good deal of attention in the scientific world. A metaphysician suggested how extremely interesting it would be to put a human being asleep thus, and watch the reunion of soul and body, after the lapse of a hundred years. The chemist was half wild with the magnificence of this idea; and he forthwith petitioned that Hilda, instead of being beheaded, might be delivered to him, to be frozen for a century. He urged that her extreme youth demanded pity; that his mode of execution would be a very gentle one, and, being so strictly private, would be far less painful to the poor young creature than exposure to the public gaze.

On the day of execution, the chaplain came to pray with her, but found himself rather embarrassed in using the customary form. He could not well allude to her going in a few hours to meet her final judge; for the chemist said she would come back in a hundred years, and where her soul would be meantime was more than theology could teach. Under these novel circumstances, the old nursery prayer seemed to be the only appropriate one for her to repeat:

> *Now I lay me down to sleep,*
> *I pray the Lord my soul to keep:*
> *If I should die before I wake,*
> *I pray the Lord my soul to take.*

The subject of this curious experiment was conveyed in a close carriage from the prison to the laboratory. A shudder ran through soul and body, as she entered the apartment assigned her. It was built entirely of stone, and rendered intensely cold by an artificial process. The light was dim and spectral, being admitted from above through a small circle of blue glass. Around the sides of the room, were tiers of massive stone shelves, on which reposed various objects in a torpid state. A huge bear lay on his back, with paws crossed on his breast, as devoutly as some pious knight of the fourteenth century. There was in fact no inconsiderable resemblance in the proceedings by which both these characters gained their worldly possessions; they were equally based on the maxim that 'might makes right.' It is true, the Christian obtained a better name, inasmuch as he paid a tithe of his gettings to the holy church, which the bear never had the grace to do. But then it must be remembered that the bear had no soul to save, and the Christian knight would have been very unlikely to pay fees to the ferryman, if he likewise had had nothing to send over.

The two public functionaries, who had attended the prisoner, to make sure that justice was not defrauded of its due, soon begged leave to retire, complaining of the unearthly cold. The pale face of the maiden became still paler, as she saw them depart. She seized the arm of the old chemist, and said, imploringly, "You will not go away, too, and leave me with these dreadful creatures?"

He replied, not without some touch of compassion in his tones, "You will be sound asleep, my dear, and will not know whether I am here or not. Drink this; it will soon make you drowsy."

"But what if that great bear should wake up?" asked she, trembling.

"Never fear. He cannot wake up," was the brief reply.

"And what if I should wake up, all alone here?"

"Don't disturb yourself," said he, "I tell you that you will not wake up. Come, my dear, drink quick; for I am getting chilly myself."

The poor girl cast another despairing glance round the tomb-like apartment, and did as she was requested. "And now," said the chemist, "let us shake hands, and say farewell; for you will never see me again."

"Why, won't you come to wake me up?" inquired the prisoner; not reflecting on all the peculiar circumstances of her condition.

"My great-grandson may," replied he, with a smile. "Adieu, my dear. It is a great deal pleasanter than being beheaded. You will fall asleep as easily as a babe in his cradle."

She gazed in his face, with a bewildered drowsy look, and big tears rolled down her cheeks. "Just step up here, my poor child," said he; and he offered her his hand.

"Oh, don't lay me so near the crocodile!" she exclaimed. "If he *should* wake up!"

"You wouldn't know it, if he did," rejoined the patient chemist; "but never mind. Step up to this other shelf, if you like it better."

He handed her up very politely, gathered her garments about her feet, crossed her arms below her breast, and told her to be perfectly still. He then covered his face with a mask, let some gasses escape from an apparatus in the centre of the room, and immediately went out, locking the door after him.

The next day, the public functionaries looked in, and expressed themselves well satisfied to find the maiden lying as rigid and motionless as the bear, the wolf, and the snake. On the edge of the shelf where she lay was pasted an inscription: "Put to sleep for infanticide, Feb. 10, 1740, by order of the king. To be wakened Feb. 10, 1840."

The earth whirled round on its axis, carrying with it the Alps and the Andes, the bear, the crocodile, and the maiden. Summer and winter came and went; America took place among the nations; Bonaparte played out his great game, with kingdoms for pawns; and still the Swedish damsel slept on her stone shelf with the bear and the crocodile.

When ninety-five years had passed, the bear, having fulfilled his prescribed century, was waked according to agreement. The curious flocked round him, to see him eat, and hear whether he could growl as well as other bears. Not liking such close observation, he broke his chain one night, and made off for the hills. How he seemed to his comrades, and what mistakes he make in his recollections, there were never any means of ascertaining. But bears, being more strictly conservative than men, happily escape the influence of French revolutions, German philosophy, Fourier theories, and reforms of all sorts; therefore Bruin doubtless found less change in *his* fellow citizens, than an old knight or viking might have done, had he chanced to sleep so long.

At last, came the maiden's turn to be resuscitated. The populace had forgotten her and her story long ago; but a select scientific few were present at the ceremony, by special invitation. The old chemist and his children all "slept the sleep that knows no waking." But carefully written orders had been transmitted from generation to generation; and the duty finally devolved on a great grandson, himself a chemist of no mean reputation.

Life returned very slowly; at first by almost imperceptible degrees, then by a visible shivering through the nerves. When the eyes opened, it was as if by the movement of pulleys, and there was something painfully strange in their marble gaze. But the lamp within the inner shrine lighted up, and gradually shone through them, giving assurance of the presence of a soul. As consciousness returned, she looked in the faces round her, as if seeking for someone; for her first dim recollection was of the old chemist. For several days, there was a general sluggishness of soul and body; an overpowering inertia, which made all exertion difficult, and prevented memory from rushing back in too tumultuous a tide.

For some time, she was very quiet and patient; but the numbers who came to look at her, their perpetual questions how things seemed to her, what was the state of her appetite and her memory, made her restless and irritable. Still worse was it when she went into the street. Her numerous visitors pointed her out to others, who ran to doors and windows to stare at her, and this soon attracted the attention of boys and lads. To escape such annoyances, she one day walked into a little shop, bearing the name of a woman she had formerly known. It was now kept by her grand-daughter, an aged woman, who was evidently as afraid of Hilda, as if she had been a witch or a ghost.

This state of things became perfectly unendurable. After a few weeks, the forlorn being made her escape from the city, at dawn of day, and with money which had been given her by charitable people, she obtained a passage to her native village, under the new name of Hilda Silfverling. But to stand, in the bloom of sixteen, among well-remembered hills and streams, and not recognise a single human face, or know a single human voice, this was the most mournful of all; far worse than loneliness in a foreign land; sadder than sunshine on a ruined city. And all these suffocating emotions must be crowded back on her own heart; for if she revealed them to any one, she would assuredly be considered insane or bewitched.

As the thought became familiar to her that even the little children she had known were all dead long ago, her eyes assumed an indescribably perplexed and mournful expression, which gave to them an appearance of supernatural depth. She was seized with an inexpressible longing to go where no one had ever heard of her, and among scenes she had never looked upon. Her thoughts often reverted fondly to old Virika Gjetter, and the babe for whose sake she had suffered so much; and her heart yearned for Norway. But then she was chilled by the remembrance that even if her child had lived to the usual age of mortals, she must have been long since dead; and if she had left descendants, what would they know of *her?* Overwhelmed by the complete desolation of her lot on earth, she wept bitterly.

But she was never utterly hopeless; for in the midst of her anguish, something prophetic seemed to beckon through the clouds, and call her into Norway.

In Stockholm, there was a white-haired old clergyman, who had been peculiarly kind, when he came to see her, after her centennial slumber. She resolved to go to him, to tell him how oppressively dreary was her restored existence, and how earnestly she desired to go, under a new name, to some secluded village in Norway, where none would be likely to learn her history, and where there would be nothing to remind her of the gloomy past. The good old man entered at once into her feelings, and approved her plan. He had been in that country himself, and had staid a few days at the house of a kind old man, named Eystein Hansen. He furnished Hilda with means for the journey, and gave her an affectionate letter of introduction, in which he described her as a Swedish orphan, who had suffered much, and would be glad to earn her living in any honest way that could be pointed out to her.

It was the middle of June when Hilda arrived at the house of Eystein Hanson. He was a stout, clumsy, red-visaged old man, with wide mouth, and big nose, hooked like an eagle's beak; but there was a right friendly expression in his large eyes, and when he had read the letter, he greeted the young stranger with such cordiality, she felt at once that she had found a father. She must come in his boat, he said, and he would take her at once to his island-home, where his good woman would give her a hearty welcome. She always loved the friendless; and especially would she love the Swedish orphan, because her last and youngest daughter had died the year before. On his way to the boat, the worthy man introduced her to several people, and when he told her story, old men and young maidens took her by the hand, and spoke as if they thought Heaven had sent them a daughter and a sister. The good Brenda received her with open arms, as her husband had said she would. She was an old weather-beaten woman, but there was a whole heart full of sunshine in her honest eyes.

And this new home looked so pleasant under the light of the summer sky! The house was embowered in the shrubbery of a small island, in the midst of a fiord, the steep shores of which were thickly covered with pine, fir, and juniper, down to the water's edge.

The fiord went twisting and turning about, from promontory to promontory, as if the Nereides, dancing up from the sea, had sportively chased each other into nooks and corners, now hiding away behind some bold projection of rock, and now peeping out suddenly, with a broad sunny smile. Directly in front of the island, the fiord expanded into a broad bay, on the shores of which was a little primitive romantic-looking village. Here and there a sloop was at anchor, and picturesque little boats tacked off and on from cape to cape, their white sails glancing in the sun. A range of lofty blue mountains closed in the distance. One giant, higher than all the rest, went up perpendicularly into the clouds, wearing a perpetual crown of glittering snow. As the maiden gazed on this sublime and beautiful scenery, a new and warmer tide seemed to flow through her stagnant heart. Ah, how happy might life be here among these mountain homes, with a people of such patriarchal simplicity, so brave and free, so hospitable, frank and hearty!

The house of Eystein Hansen was built of pine logs, neatly white-washed. The roof was covered with grass, and bore a crop of large bushes. A vine, tangled among these, fell in heavy festoons that waved at every touch of the wind. The door was painted with flowers in gay colours, and surmounted with fantastic carving. The interior of the dwelling was ornamented with many little grotesque images, boxes, bowls, ladles, etc., curiously carved in the close-grained and beautifully white wood of the Norwegian fir. This was a common amusement with the peasantry, and Eystein being a great favourite among them, received many such presents during his frequent visits in the surrounding parishes.

But nothing so much attracted Hilda's attention as a kind of long trumpet, made of two hollow half cylinders of wood, bound tightly together with birch bark. The only instrument of the kind she had ever seen was in the possession of Virika Gjetter, who called it a *luhr*, and said it was used to call the cows home in her native village, in Upper Tellemarken. She showed how it was used, and Hilda, having a quick ear, soon learned to play upon it with considerable facility.

And here in her new home, this rude instrument reappeared; forming the only visible link between her present life and that dreamy past! With strange feelings, she took up the pipe, and began to play one of the old tunes. At first, the tones flitted like phantoms in and out of her brain; but at last, they all came back, and took their places rank and file. Old Brenda said it was a pleasant tune, and asked her to play it again; but to Hilda it seemed awfully solemn, like a voice warbling from the grave. She would learn other tunes to please the good mother, she said; but this she would play no more; it made her too sad, for she had heard it in her youth.

"Thy youth!" said Brenda, smiling." One sees well that must have been a long time ago. To hear thee talk, one might suppose thou wert an old autumn leaf, just ready to drop from the bough, like myself."

Hilda blushed, and said she felt old, because she had had much trouble.

"Poor child," responded the good Brenda: "I hope thou hast had thy share."

"I feel as if nothing could trouble me here," replied Hilda, with a grateful smile; "all seems so kind and peaceful." She breathed a few notes through the *luhr*, as she laid it away on the shelf where she had found it. "But, my good mother," said she, "how clear and soft are these tones! The pipe I used to hear was far more harsh."

"The wood is very old," rejoined Brenda: "They say it is more than a hundred years. Alerik Thorild gave it to me, to call my good man when he is out in the boat. Ah, he was such a Berserker [1] of a boy! And in truth he was not much more sober when he was here three years ago. But no matter what he did; none could never help loving him."

"And who is Alerik?" asked the maiden.

Brenda pointed to an old house, seen in the distance, on the declivity of one of the opposite hills. It overlooked the broad bright bay, with its picturesque little islands, and was sheltered in the rear by a noble pine forest. A waterfall came down from the hillside, glancing in and out among the trees; and when the sun kissed it as he went away, it lighted up with a smile of rainbows.

"That house," said Brenda, "was built by Alerik's grandfather. He was the richest man in the village. But his only son was away among the wars for a long time, and the old place has been going to decay. But they say Alerik is coming back to live among us; and he will soon give it a different look. He has been away to Germany and Paris, and other outlandish parts, for a long time. Ah! The rogue! There was no mischief he didn't think of. He was always tying cats together under the windows, and barking in the middle of the night, till he set all the dogs in the neighbourhood a howling. But as long as it was Alerik that did it, it was all well enough: for everybody loved him, and he always made one believe just what he liked. If he wanted to make thee think thy hair was as black as Noeck's [2] mane, he *would* make thee think so."

Hilda smiled as she glanced at her flaxen hair, with here and there a gleam of paly gold, where the sun touched it. "I think it would be hard to prove *this* was black," said she.

"Nevertheless," rejoined Brenda, "If Alerik undertook it, he would do it. He always has his say, and does what he will. One may as well give in to him first as last."

This account of the unknown youth carried with it that species of fascination, which the idea of uncommon power always has over the human heart. The secluded maiden seldom touched the *luhr* without thinking of the giver; and not unfrequently she found herself conjecturing when this wonderful Alerik would come home.

Meanwhile, constant but not excessive labour, the mountain air, the quiet life, and the kindly hearts around her, restored to Hilda more than her original loveliness. In her large blue eyes, the inward-looking sadness of experience now mingled in strange beauty with the out-looking clearness of youth. Her fair complexion was tinged with the glow of health, and her motions had the airy buoyancy of the mountain breeze. When she went to the mainland, to attend church, or rustic festival, the hearts of young and old greeted her like a May blossom. Thus with calm cheerfulness her hours went by, making no noise in their flight, and leaving no impress. But here was an unsatisfied want! She sighed for hours that did leave a mark behind them. She thought of the Danish youth, who had first spoken to her of love; and plaintively came the tones from her *luhr*, as she gazed on the opposite hills, and wondered whether the Alerik they talked of so much, was indeed so very superior to other young men.

Father Hansen often came home at twilight with a boat full of juniper boughs, to be strewed over the floors, that they might diffuse a balmy odour, inviting to sleep. One evening, when Hilda saw him coming with his verdant load, she hastened down to the water's edge to take an armful of the fragrant boughs. She had scarcely appeared in sight, before he called out, "I do believe Alerik has come! I heard the organ up in the old house. Somebody was playing on it like a Northeast storm; and surely, said I, that must be Alerik."

"Is there an organ there?" asked the damsel, in surprise.

"Yes, he built it himself, when he was here three years ago. He can make anything he chooses. An organ, or a basket cut from a cherry stone, is all one to him."

When Hilda returned to the cottage, she of course repeated the news to Brenda, who exclaimed joyfully, "Ah, then we shall see him soon! If he does not come before, we shall certainly see him at the weddings in the church tomorrow."

"And plenty of tricks we shall have now," said Father Hansen, shaking his head with a good-natured smile." There will be no telling which end of the world is uppermost, while he is here."

"Oh yes, there will, my friend," answered Brenda, laughing; "for it will certainly be whichever end Alerik stands on. The handsome little Berserker! How I should like to see him!"

The next day there was a sound of lively music on the waters; for two young couples from neighbouring islands were coming up the fiord, to be married at the church in the opposite village. Their boats were ornamented with gay little banners, friends and neighbours accompanied them, playing on musical instruments, and the rowers had their hats decorated with garlands. As the rustic band floated thus gayly over the bright waters, they were joined by Father Hansen, with Brenda and Hilda in his boat. Friendly villagers had already decked the simple little church with ever-greens and flowers, in honour of the bridal train. As they entered, Father Hansen observed that two young men stood at the door with clarinets in their hands. But he thought no more of it, till, according to immemorial custom, he, as clergy man's assistant, began to sing the first lines of the hymn that was given out. The very first note he sounded, up struck the clarinets at the door. The louder they played, the louder the old man bawled; but the instruments gained the victory. When he essayed to give out the lines of the next verse, the merciless clarinets brayed louder than before. His stentorian voice had become vociferous and rough, from thirty years of halloing across the water, and singing of psalms in four village churches. He exerted it to the utmost, till the perspiration poured down his rubicund visage; but it was of no use. His rivals had strong lungs, and they played on clarinets in F. If the whole village had screamed fire, to the shrill accompaniment of rail-road whistles, they would have over-topped them all.

Father Hansen was vexed at heart, and it was plain enough that he was so. The congregation held down their heads with suppressed laughter all except one tall vigorous young man, who sat up very serious and dignified, as if he were reverently listening to some new manifestation of musical genius. When the people left church, Hilda saw this young stranger approaching toward them, as fast as numerous hand-shakings by the way would permit. She had time to observe him closely. His noble figure, his vigorous agile motions, his expressive countenance, hazel eyes with strongly marked brows, and abundant brown hair, tossed aside with a careless grace, left no doubt in her mind that this was the famous Alerik Thorild; but what made her heart beat more wildly was his strong resemblance to Magnus the Dane. He went up to Brenda and kissed her, and threw his arms about Father Hansen's neck, with expressions of joyful recognition. The kind old man, vexed as he was, received these affectionate demonstrations with great friendliness. "Ah, Alerik," said he, after the first salutations were over, "that was not kind of thee."

"Me! What!" exclaimed the young man, with well-feigned astonishment.

"To put up those confounded clarinets to drown my voice," rejoined he bluntly. "When a man has led the singing thirty years in four parishes, I can assure thee it is not a pleasant joke to be treated in that style. I know the young men are tired of my voice, and think they could do things in better fashion, as young fools always do; but I may thank thee for putting it into their heads to bring those cursed clarinets."

"Oh, dear Father Hansen," replied the young man, in the most coaxing tones, and with the most caressing manner, "you *couldn't* think I would do such a thing!"

"On the contrary, it is just the thing I think thou couldst do," answered the old man: "Thou need not think to cheat me out of my eye-teeth, this time. Thou has often enough made me believe the moon was made of green cheese. But I know thy tricks. I shall be on my guard now; and mind thee, I am not going to be bamboozled by thee again."

Alerik smiled mischievously; for he, in common with all the villagers, knew it was the easiest thing in the world to gull the simple-hearted old man. "Well, come, Father Hansen," said he, "shake hands and be friends. When you come over to the village, tomorrow, we will drink a mug of ale together, at the Wolf's Head."

"Oh yes, and be played some trick for his pains," said Brenda.

"No, no," answered Alerik, with great gravity; "he is on his guard now, and I cannot bamboozle him again." With a friendly nod and smile, he bounded off, to greet someone whom he recognised. Hilda had stepped back to hide herself from observation. She was a little afraid of the handsome Berserker; and his resemblance to the Magnus of her youthful recollections made her sad.

The next afternoon, Alerik met his old friend, and reminded him of the agreement to drink ale at the Wolf's Head. On the way, he invited several young companions. The ale was excellent, and Alerik told stories and sag songs, which filled the little tavern with roars of laughter. In one of the intervals of merriment, he turned suddenly to the honest old man, and said, "Father Hansen, among the many things I have learned and done in foreign countries, did I ever tell you I had made a league with the devil, and am shot-proof?"

"One might easily believe thou hadst made a league with the devil, before thou wert born," replied Eystein, with a grin at his own wit; "but as for being shot-proof, that is another affair."

"Try and see," rejoined Alerik. "These friends are witnesses that I tell you it is perfectly safe to try. Come, I will stand here; fire your pistols, and you will soon see that the Evil One will keep the bargain he made with me."

"Be done with thy nonsense, Alerik," rejoined his old friend.

"Ah, I see how it is," replied Alerik, turning towards the young men. "Father Hansen used to be a famous shot. Nobody was more expert in the bear or the wolf-hunt than he; but old eyes grow dim, and old hands will tremble. No wonder he does not like to have us see how much he fails."

This was attacking honest Eystein Hansen on his weak side. He was proud of his strength and skill in shooting, and he did not like to admit that he was growing old. "I not hit a mark!" exclaimed he, with indignation: "When did I ever miss a thing I aimed at?"

"Never, when you were young," answered one of the company; "but it is no wonder you are afraid to try now."

"Afraid!" exclaimed the old hunter, impatiently. "Who the devil said I was afraid?"

Alerik shrugged his shoulders, and replied carelessly, "It is natural enough that these young men should think so, when they see you refuse to aim at me, though I assure you that I am shot proof, and that I will stand perfectly still."

"But art thou really shot-proof?" inquired the guileless old man. "The devil has helped thee to do so many strange things, that one never know what he will help thee to do next."

"Really, Father Hansen, I speak in earnest. Take up your pistol and try, and you will soon see with your own eyes that I am shot-proof." Eystein looked round upon the company like one perplexed. His wits, never very bright, were somewhat muddled by the ale. "What shall I do with this wild fellow?" inquired he. "You see he *will* be shot."

"Try him, try him," was the general response. "He has assured you he is shot-proof; what more do you need?"

The old man hesitated awhile, but after some further parley, took up his pistol and examined it. "Before we proceed to business," said Alerik, "Let me tell you that if you do *not* shoot me, you shall have a gallon of the best ale you ever drank in your life. Come and taste it, Father Hansen, and satisfy yourself that it is good."

While they were discussing the merits of the ale, one of the young men took the ball from the pistol. "I am ready now," said Alerik: "Here I stand. Now don't lose your name for a good marksman."

The old man fired, and Alerik fell back with a deadly groan. Poor Eystein stood like a stone image of terror. His arms adhered rigidly to his sides, his jaw dropped, and his great eyes seemed starting from their sockets. "Oh, Father Hansen, how *could* you do it!" exclaimed the young men.

The poor horrified dupe stared at them wildly, and gasping and stammering replied, "Why he said he was shot-proof; and you all told me to do it."

"Oh yes," said they; "but we supposed you would have sense enough to know it was all in fun. But don't take it too much to heart. You will probably forfeit your life; for the government will of course consider it a poor excuse, when you tell them that you fired at a man merely to oblige him, and because he said he was shot-proof. But don't be too much cast down, Father Hansen. We must all meet death in some way; and if worst comes to worst, it will be a great comfort to you and your good Brenda that you did not intend to commit murder."

The poor old man gazed at them with an expression of such extreme suffering, that they became alarmed, and said, "Cheer up, cheer up. Come, you must drink something to make you feel better." They took him by the shoulders, but as they led him out, he continued to look back wistfully on the body.

The instant he left the apartment, Alerik sprang up and darted out of the opposite door; and when Father Hansen entered the other room, there he sat, as composedly as possible, reading a paper, and smoking his pipe.

"There he is!" shrieked the old man, turning paler than ever.

"Who is there?" inquired the young men.

"Don't you see Alerik Thorild?" exclaimed he, point, with an expression of intense horror.

They turned to the landlord, and remarked, in a compassionate tone, "Poor Father Hansen has shot Alerik Thorild, whom he loved so well; and the dreadful accident has so affected his brain, that he imagines he sees him."

The old man pressed his broad hand hard against his forehead, and again groaned out, "Oh, don't you see him?"

The tones indicated such agony, that Alerik had not the heart to prolong the scene. He sprang on his feet, and exclaimed, "Now for your gallon of ale, Father Hansen! You see the devil did keep his bargain with me."

"And *are* you alive?" shouted the old man.

The mischievous fellow soon convinced him of that, by a slap on the shoulder, that made his bones ache.

Eystein Hansen capered like a dancing bear. He hugged Alerik, and jumped about, and clapped his hands, and was altogether beside himself. He drank unknown quantities of ale, and this time sang loud enough to drown a brace of clarinets in F.

The night was far advanced when he went on board his boat to return to his island home. He pulled the oars vigorously, and the boat shot swiftly across the moon-lighted waters. But on arriving at the customary landing, he could discover no vestige of his white-washed cottage. Not knowing that Alerik, in the full tide of his mischief, had sent men to paint the house with a dark brown wash, he thought he must have made a mistake in the landing; so he rowed round to the other side of the island, but with no better success. Ashamed to return to the mainland, to inquire for a house that had absconded, and a little suspicious that the ale had hung some cobwebs in his brain, he continued to row hither and thither, till his strong muscular arms fairly ached with exertion. But the moon was going down, and all the landscape settling into darkness; and he at last reluctantly concluded that it was best to go back to the village inn.

Alerik, who had expected this result much sooner, had waited there to receive him. When he had kept him knocking a sufficient time, he put his head out of the window, and inquired who was there.

"Eystein Hansen," was the disconsolate reply. "For the love of mercy let me come in and get a few minutes sleep, before morning. I have been rowing about the bay these four hours, and I can't find my house any where."

"This is a very bad sign," replied Alerik, solemnly. "Houses don't run away, except from drunken men. Ah, Father Hansen! Father Hansen! What *will* the minister say?"

He did not have a chance to persecute the weary old man much longer; for scarcely had he come under the shelter of the house, before he was snoring in a profound sleep.

Early the next day, Alerik sought his old friends in their brown-washed cottage. He found it not so easy to conciliate them as usual. They were really grieved; and Brenda even said she believed he wanted to be the death of her old man. But he had brought them presents, which he knew they would like particularly well; and he kissed their hands, and talked over his boyish days, till at last he made them laugh. "Ah now," said he, "you have forgiven me, my dear old friends. And you see, father, it was all your own fault. You put the mischief into me, by boasting before all those young men that I could never bamboozle you again."

"Ah thou incorrigible rogue!" answered the old man. "I believe thou hast indeed made a league with the devil; and he gives thee the power to make everyone love thee, do what thou wilt."

Alerik's smile seemed to express that he always had a pleasant consciousness of such power. The *luhr* lay on the table beside him, and as he took it up, he asked, "Who plays on this? Yesterday, when I was out in my boat, I heard very wild pretty little variations on some of my old favourite airs."

Brenda, instead of answering, called, "Hilda! Hilda!" and the young girl came from the next room, blushing as she entered. Alerik looked at her with evident surprise. "Surely, this is not your Gunilda?" said he.

"No," replied Brenda, "She is a Swedish orphan, whom the all-kind Father sent to take the place of our Gunilda, when she was called hence."

After some words of friendly greeting, the visitor asked Hilda if it was she who played so sweetly on the *luhr*. She answered timidly, without looking up. Her heart was throbbing; for the tones of his voice were like Magnus the Dane.

The acquaintance thus begun, was not likely to languish on the part of such an admirer of beauty as was Alerik Thorild. The more he saw of Hilda, during the long evenings of the following winter, the more he was charmed with her natural refinement of look, voice, and manner. There was, as we have said, a peculiarity in her beauty, which gave it a higher character than mere rustic loveliness. A deep, mystic, plaintive expression in her eyes; a sort of graceful bewilderment in her countenance, and at times in the carriage of her head, and the motions of her body; as if her spirit had lost its way, and was listening intently. It was not strange that he was charmed by her spiritual beauty, her simple untutored modesty. No wonder she was delighted with his frank strong exterior, his cordial caressing manner, his expressive eyes, now tender and earnest, and now sparkling with merriment, and his "smile most musical," because always so in harmony with the inward feeling, whether of sadness, fun, or tenderness. Then his moods were so bewitchingly various. Now powerful as the organ, now bright as the flute, now *naive* as the oboe. Brenda said everything he did seemed to be alive. He carved a wolf's head on her old man's cane, and she was always afraid it would bite her.

Brenda, in her simplicity, perhaps gave as good a description of genius as *could* be given, when she said everything it did seemed to be alive. Hilda thought it certainly was so with Alerik's music. Sometimes all went madly with it, as if fairies danced on the grass, and ugly gnomes came and made faces at them, and shrieked, and clutched at their garments; the fairies pelted them off with flowers, and then all died away to sleep in the moonlight. Sometimes, when he played on flute, or violin, the sounds came mournfully as the midnight wind through ruined towers; and they stirred up such sorrowful memories of the past, that Hilda pressed her hand upon her swelling heart, and said, "Oh, not such strains as that, dear Alerik." But when his soul overflowed with love and happiness oh, then how the music gushed and nestled!

> *"The lark could scarce get out his notes for joy,*
> *But shook his song together, as he neared*
> *His happy home, the ground."*

The old *luhr* was a great favourite with Alerik; not for its musical capabilities, but because it was entwined with the earliest recollections of his childhood. "Until I heard thee play upon it," said he, "I half repented having given it to the good Brenda. It has been in our family for several generations, and my nurse used to play upon it when I was in my cradle. They tell me my grandmother was a foundling. She was brought to my great-grandfather's house by an old peasant woman, on her way to the valley of Westfjordalen. She died there, leaving the babe and the *luhr* in my great-grandmother's keeping. They could never find out to whom the babe belonged; but she grew up very beautiful, and my grandfather married her."

"What was the old woman's name?" asked Hilda; and her voice was so deep and suppressed, that it made Alerik start.

"Virika Gjetter, they have always told me," he replied. "But my dearest one, what *is* the matter?"

Hilda, pale and fainting, made no answer. But when he placed her head upon his bosom, and kissed her forehead, and spoke soothingly, her glazed eyes softened, and she burst into tears. All his entreaties, however, could obtain no information at that time. "Go home now," she said, in tones of deep despondency. "Tomorrow I will tell thee all. I have had many unhappy hours; for I have long felt that I ought to tell thee all my past history; but I was afraid to do it, for I thought thou wouldst not love me any more; and that would be worse than death. But come tomorrow, and I will tell thee all."

"Well, dearest Hilda, I will wait," replied Alerik; "but what my grandmother, who died long before I was born, can have to do with my love for thee, is more than I can imagine."

The next day, when Hilda saw Alerik coming to claim the fulfillment of her promise, it seemed almost like her death-warrant. "He will not love me any more," thought she, "he will never again look at me so tenderly; and then what can I do, but die?"

With much embarrassment, and many delays, she at last began her strange story. He listened to the first part very attentively, and with a gathering frown; but as she went on, the muscles of his face relaxed into a smile; and when she ended by saying, with the most melancholy seriousness, "So thou seest, dear Alerik, we cannot be married; because it is very likely that I am thy great-grandmother" – he burst into immoderate peals of laughter.

When his mirth had somewhat subsided, he replied, "Likely as not thou art my great-grandmother, dear Hilda; and just as likely I was thy grandfather, in the first place. A great German scholar [3] teaches that our souls keep coming back again and again into new bodies. An old Greek philosopher is said to have come back for the fourth time, under the name of Pythagoras. If these things are so, how the deuce is a man ever to tell whether he marries his grandmother or not?"

"But dearest Alerik, I am not jesting," rejoined she. "What I have told thee is really true. They did put me to sleep for a hundred years."

"Oh, yes," answered he, laughing, "I remember reading about it in the Swedish papers; and I thought it a capital joke. I will tell thee how it is with thee, my precious one. The elves sometimes seize people, to carry them down into their subterranean caves; but if the mortals run away from them, they, out of spite, forever after fill their heads with gloomy insane notions. A man in Drontheim ran away from them, and thy made him believe he was an earthen coffee-pot. He sat curled up in a corner all the time, for fear somebody would break his nose off."

"Nay, now thou art joking, Alerik, but really" –

"No, I tell thee, as thou has told me, it was no joke at all," he replied. "The man himself told me he was a coffee-pot."

"But be serious, Alerik," said she, "and tell me, dost thou not believe that some learned men can put people to sleep for a hundred years?"

"I don't doubt some of my college professors could," rejoined he; "provided their tongues could hold out so long."

"But, Alerik, dost thou not think it possible that people may be alive, and yet not alive?"

"Of course I do," he replied; "the greater part of the world are in that condition."

"Oh, Alerik, what a tease thou art! I mean, is it not possible that there are people now living, or staying somewhere, who were moving about on this earth ages ago?"

"Nothing more likely," answered he; "for instance, who knows what people there may be under the ice-sea of Folgefond? They say the cocks are heard crowing down there, to this day. How a fowl of any feather got there is a curious question; and what kind of atmosphere he has to crow in, is another puzzle. Perhaps they are poor ghosts, without sense of shame, crowing over the recollections of sins committed in the human body. The ancient Egyptians thought the soul was obliged to live three thousand years, in a succession of different animals, before it could attain to the regions of the blest. I am pretty sure I have already been a lion and a nightingale. What I shall be next, the Egyptians know as well as I do. One of their sculptors made a stone image, half woman and half lioness. Doubtless his mother had been a lioness, and had transmitted to him some dim recollection of it. But I am glad, dearest, they sent thee back in the form of a lovely maiden; for if thou hadst come as a wolf, I might have shot thee; and I shouldn't like to shoot my – great-grandmother. Or if thou hadst come as a red herring, Father Hansen might have eaten thee in his soup; and then I should have had no Hilda Silfverling."

Hilda smiled, as she said, half reproachfully, "I see well that thou dost not believe one word I say."

"Oh yes, I do, dearest," rejoined he, very seriously. "I have no doubt the fairies carried thee off some summer's night and made thee verily believe thou hadst slept for a hundred years. They do the strangest things. Sometimes they change babies in the cradle; leave an imp, and carry off the human to the metal mines, where he hears only clink! clink! Then the fairies bring him back, and put him in some other cradle. When he grows up, how he does hurry skurry after the silver! He is obliged to work all his life, as if the devil drove him. The poor miser never knows what is the matter with him; but it is all because the gnomes brought him up in the mines, and he could never get the clink out of his head. A more poetic kind of fairies sometimes carry a babe to Aeolian caves, full of wild dreamy sounds; and when he is brought back to upper earth, ghosts of sweet echoes keep beating time in some corner of his brain, to something which *they* can hear, but which nobody else is the wiser for. I know that is true; for I was brought up in those caves myself."

Hilda remained silent for a few minutes, as he sat looking in her face with comic gravity. "Thou wilt do nothing but make fun of me," at last she said. "I do wish I could persuade thee to be serious. What I told thee was no fairy story. It really happened. I remember it as distinctly as I do our sail round the islands yesterday. I seem to see that great bear now, with his paws folded up, on the shelf opposite to me."

"He must have been a great bear to have staid there," replied Alerik, with eyes full of roguery. "If I had been in his skin, may I be shot if all the drugs and gasses in the world would have kept *me* there, with my paws folded on my breast."

Seeing a slight blush pass over her cheek, he added, more seriously, "After all, I ought to thank that wicked elf, whoever he was, for turning thee into a stone image; for otherwise thou wouldst have been in the world a hundred years too soon for me, and so I should have missed my life's best blossom."

Feeling her tears on his hand, he again started off into a vein of merriment. "Thy case was not so very peculiar," said he. "There was a Greek lady, name Niobe, who was changed to stone. The Greek gods changed women into trees, and fountains, and all manner of things. A man couldn't chop a walking-stick in those days, without danger of cutting off some lady's finger. The tree might be his great-grandmother; and she of course would take it very unkindly of him."

"All these things are like the stories of Odin and Frigga," rejoined Hilda. "They are not true, like the Christian religion. When I tell thee a true story, why dost thou always meet me with fairies and fictions?"

"But tell me, best Hilda," said he, "what the Christian religion has to do with penning up young maidens with bears and crocodiles? In its marriage ceremonies, I grant that it sometimes does things not very unlike that, only omitting the important part of freezing the maiden's heart. But since thou hast mentioned the Christian religion, I may as well give thee a bit of consolation from that quarter. I have read in my mother's big Bible, that a man must not marry his grandmother; but I do not remember that it said a single word against his marrying his *great*-grandmother."

Hilda laughed, in spite of herself. But after a pause, she looked at him earnestly, and said, "Dost thou indeed think there would be no harm in marrying, under these circumstances, if I were really thy great-grandmother? Is it thy earnest? Do be serious for once, dear Alerik!"

"Certainly there would be no harm," answered he. "Physicians have agreed that the body changes entirely once in seven years. That must be because the soul outgrows its clothes; which proves that the soul changes every seven years, also. Therefore, in the course of one hundred years, thou must have had fourteen complete changes of soul and body. It is therefore as plain as daylight, that if thou wert my great-grandmother when thou fell asleep, thou couldst not have been my great-grandmother when they waked thee up."

"Ah, Alerik," she replied, "It is as the good Brenda says, there is no use in talking with thee. One might as well try to twist a string that is not fastened at either end."

He looked up merrily in her face. The wind was playing with her ringlets, and freshened the colour on her cheeks. "I only wish I had a mirror to hold before thee," said he; "that thou couldst see how very like thou art to a – great-grandmother."

"Laugh at me as thou wilt," answered she; "but I assure thee I have strange thoughts about myself sometimes. Dost thou know," added she, almost in a whisper, "I am not always quite certain that I have not died, and am now in heaven?"

A ringing shout of laughter burst from the light-hearted lover. "Oh, I like that! I like that!" exclaimed he. "That is good! That a Swede coming to Norway does not know certainly whether she is in heaven or not."

"Do be serious, Alerik," said she imploringly. "Don't carry thy jests too far."

"Serious? I am serious. If Norway is not heaven, one sees plainly enough that it must have been the scaling place, where the old giants got up to heaven; for they have left their ladders standing. Where else wilt thou find clusters of mountains running up perpendicularly thousands of feet right into the sky? If thou wast to see some of them, thou couldst tell whether Norway is a good climbing place into heaven."

"Ah, dearest Alerik, thou hast taught me that already," she replied, with a glance full of affection; "so a truce with thy joking. Truly one never knows how to take thee. Thy talk sets everything *in* the world, and *above* it, dancing together in the strangest fashion."

"Because they all do dance together," rejoined the perverse man.

"Oh, be done! Be done, Alerik!" she said, putting her hand playfully over his mouth. "Thou wilt tie my poor brain all up into knots."

He seized her hand and kissed it, then busied himself with braiding the wild spring flowers into a garland for her fair hair. As she gazed on him earnestly, her eyes beaming with love and happiness, he drew her to his breast, and exclaimed fervently, "Oh, thou art beautiful as an angel; and here or elsewhere, with thee by my side, it seemeth heaven."

They spoke no more for a long time. The birds now and then serenaded the silent lovers with little twittering gushes of song. The setting sun, as he went away over the hills, threw diamonds on the bay, and a rainbow ribbon across the distant waterfall. Their hearts were in harmony with the peaceful beauty of Nature. As he kissed her drowsy eyes, she murmured, "Oh, it was well worth a hundred years with bears and crocodiles, to fall asleep thus on thy heart."

* * *

The next autumn, a year and a half after Hilda's arrival in Norway, there was another procession of boats, with banners, music and garlands. The little church was again decorated with evergreens; but no clarinet players stood at the door to annoy good Father Hansen. The worthy man had in fact taken the hint, though somewhat reluctantly, and had good-naturedly ceased to disturb modern ears with his clamorous vociferation of the hymns. He and his kind-hearted Brenda were happy beyond measure at Hilda's good fortune. But when she told her husband anything he did not choose to believe, they could never rightly make out what he meant by looking at her so slyly, and saying, "Pooh! Pooh! Tell that to my great-grandmother."

Footnote 1. A warrior famous in the Northern Sagas for his stormy and untamable character.
Footnote 2. An elfish spirit, which, according to popular tradition in Norway, appears in the form of a coal-black horse.
Footnote 3. Lessing.

The Shape of My Name

Nino Cipri

THE YEAR 2076 smells like antiseptic gauze and the lavender diffuser that Dara set up in my room. It has the bitter aftertaste of pills: probiotics and microphages and PPMOs. It feels like the itch of healing, the ache that's settled on my pubic bone. It has the sound of a new name that's fresh and yet familiar on my lips.

The future feels lighter than the past. I think I know why you chose it over me, Mama.

* * *

My bedroom has changed in the hundred-plus years that passed since I slept there as a child. The floorboards have been carpeted over, torn up, replaced. The walls are thick with new layers of paint. The windows have been upgraded, the closet expanded. The oak tree that stood outside my window is gone, felled by a storm twenty years ago, I'm told. But the house still stands, and our family still lives here, with all our attendant ghosts. You and I are haunting each other, I think.

I picture you standing in the kitchen downstairs, over a century ago. I imagine that you're staring out through the little window above the sink, your eyes traveling down the path that leads from the backdoor and splits at the creek; one trail leads to the pond, and the other leads to the shelter and the anachronopede, with its rows of capsules and blinking lights.

Maybe it's the afternoon you left us. June 22, 1963: storm clouds gathering in the west, the wind picking up, the air growing heavy with the threat of rain. And you're staring out the window, gazing across the dewy fields at the forking path, trying to decide which one you'll take.

My bedroom is just above the kitchen, and my window has that same view, a little expanded: I can see clear down to the pond where Dad and I used to sit on his weeks off from the oil fields. It's spring, and the cattails are only hip-high. I can just make out the silhouette of a great blue heron walking along among the reeds and rushes.

You and I, we're twenty feet and more than a hundred years apart.

* * *

You went into labor not knowing my name, which I know now is unprecedented among our family: you knew Dad's name before you laid eyes on him, the time and date of my birth, the hospital where he would drive you when you went into labor. But my name? My sex? Conspicuously absent on Uncle Dante's gilt-edged book where all these happy details were recorded in advance.

Dad told me later that you thought I'd be a stillbirth. He didn't know about the record book, about the blank space where a name should go. But he told me that nothing he said while you were pregnant could convince you that I'd come into the world alive. You thought I'd slip out of you strangled and blue, already decaying.

Instead, I started screaming before they pulled me all the way out.

Dad said that even when the nurse placed me in your arms, you thought you were hallucinating. "I had to tell her, over and over: Miriam, you're not dreaming, our daughter is alive."

I bit my lip when he told me that, locked the words 'your son' out of sight. I regret that now; maybe I could have explained myself to him. I should have tried, at least.

You didn't name me for nearly a week.

* * *

1954 tastes like Kellogg's Rice Krispies in fresh milk, delivered earlier that morning. It smells like woodsmoke, cedar chips, Dad's Kamel cigarettes mixed with the perpetual smell of diesel in his clothes. It feels like the worn velvet nap of the couch in our living room, which I loved to run my fingers across.

I was four years old. I woke up in the middle of the night after a loud crash of lightning. The branches of the oak tree outside my window were thrashing in the wind and the rain.

I crept out of bed, dragging my blanket with me. I slipped out of the door and into the hallway, heading for your and Dad's bedroom. I stopped when I heard voices coming from the parlor downstairs: I recognized your sharp tones, but there was also a man's voice, not Dad's baritone but something closer to a tenor.

The door creaked when I pushed it open, and the voices fell silent. I paused, and then you yanked open the door.

The curlers in your hair had come undone, descending down towards your shoulders. I watched one tumble out of your hair and onto the floor like a stunned beetle. I only caught a glimpse of the man standing in the corner; he had thin, hunched shoulders and dark hair, wet and plastered to his skull. He was wearing one of Dad's old robes, with the initials monogrammed on the pocket. It was much too big for him.

You snatched me up, not very gently, and carried me up to the bedroom you shared with Dad.

"Tom," you hissed. You dropped me on the bed before Dad was fully awake, and shook his shoulder. He sat up, blinking at me, and looked to you for an explanation.

"There's a visitor," you said, voice strained.

Dad looked at the clock, pulling it closer to him to get a proper look. "Now? Who is it?"

Your jaw was clenched, and so were your hands. "I'm handling it. I just need you to watch –"

You said my name in a way I'd never heard it before, as if each syllable were a hard, steel ball dropping from your lips. It frightened me, and I started to cry. Silently, though, since I didn't want you to notice me. I didn't want you to look at me with eyes like that.

You turned on your heel and left the room, clicking the door shut behind you and locking it.

Dad patted me on the back, his wide hand nearly covering the expanse of my skinny shoulders. "It's all right, kid," he said. "Nothing to be scared of. Why don't you lie down and I'll read you something, huh?"

In the morning, there was no sign a visitor had been there at all. You and Dad assured me that I must have dreamed the whole thing.

I know now that you were lying, of course. I think I knew it even then.

* * *

I had two childhoods.

One happened between Dad's ten-day hitches in the White County oil fields. That childhood smells like his tobacco, wool coats, wet grass. It sounds like the opening theme songs to all our favorite TV shows. It tastes like the peanut-butter sandwiches that you'd pack for us on our walks, which we'd eat down by the pond, the same one I can just barely see from my window here. In the summer, we'd sit at the edge of the water, dipping our toes into the mud. Sometimes, Dad told me stories, or asked me to fill him in on the episodes of *Gunsmoke* and *Science Fiction Theater* he'd missed, and we'd chat while watching for birds. The herons have always been my favorite. They moved so slow, it always felt like a treat to spot one as it stepped cautiously through the shallow water. Sometimes, we'd catch sight of one flying overhead, its wide wings fighting against gravity.

And then there was the childhood with you, and with Dara, the childhood that happened when Dad was away. I remember the first morning I came downstairs and she was eating pancakes off of your fancy china, the plates that were decorated with delicate paintings of evening primrose.

"Hi there. I'm Dara," she said.

When I looked at you, shy and unsure, you told me, "She's a cousin. She'll be dropping in when your father is working. Just to keep us company."

Dara didn't really look much like you, I thought; not the way that Dad's cousins and uncles all resembled each other. But I could see a few similarities between the two of you; hazel eyes, long fingers, and something I didn't have the words to describe for a long time: a certain discomfort, the sense that you held yourselves slightly apart from the rest of us. It had made you a figure of gossip in town, though I didn't know that until high school, when the same was said of me.

"What should I call you?" Dara asked me.

You jumped in and told her to call me by my name, the one you'd chosen for me, after the week of indecision following my birth. How can I ever make you understand how much I disliked that name? It felt like it belonged to a sister I'd never known, whose legacy I could never fulfill or surpass or even forget. Dara must have caught the face that I made, because later, when you were out in the garden, she asked me, "Do you have another name? That you want me to call you instead?"

When I shrugged, she said, "It doesn't have to be a forever-name. Just one for the day. You can introduce yourself differently every time you see me."

And so every morning when I woke up and saw Dara sitting at the table, I gave her a different name: Doc, Buck, George, Charlie. Names that my heroes had, from television and comics and the matinees in town. They weren't my name, but they were better than the one I had. I liked the way they sounded, the shape of them rolling around my mouth.

You just looked on, lips pursed in a frown, and told Dara you wished she'd quit indulging my silly little games.

The two of you sat around our kitchen table and – if I was quiet and didn't draw any attention to myself – talked in a strange code about *jumps* and *fastenings* and *capsules,* dropping names of people I never knew. More of your cousins, I figured.

You told our neighbors that all of your family was spread out, and disinclined to make the long trip to visit. When Dara took me in, she made up a tale about a long-lost cousin whose parents had kicked him out for being trans. Funny, the way the truth seeps into lies.

* * *

I went to see Uncle Dante in 1927. I wanted to see what he had in that book of his about me, and about you and Dara.

1927 tastes like the chicken broth and brown bread he fed me, after I showed up at his door. It smelled like the musty blanket he hung around my shoulders, like kerosene lamps and woodsmoke. It sounds like the scratchy records he played on his phonograph: Duke Ellington and Al Jolson, the Gershwin brothers and Gene Austin.

"Your mother dropped in back in '24," he said, settling down in an armchair in front of the fireplace. It was the same fireplace that had been in our parlor, though Dad had sealed off the chimney in 1958, saying it let in too many drafts. "She was very adamant that your name be written down in the records. She seemed…upset." He let the last word hang on its own, lonely, obviously understated.

"That's not my name," I told him. "It's the one she gave me, but it was never mine."

I had to explain to him then – he'd been to the future, and so it didn't seem so far-fetched, my transition. I simplified it for him: didn't go into HRT or mastectomies, the phalloplasty I'd scheduled a century and a half in the future. I skipped the introduction to gender theory, Susan Stryker, *Stone Butch Blues*, all the things that Dara gave me to read when I asked for books about people like me.

"My aunt Lucia was of a similar disposition," he told me. "Once her last child was grown, she gave up on dresses entirely. Wore a suit to church for her last twelve years, which gave her a reputation for eccentricity."

I clamped my mouth shut and nodded, still feeling ill and shaky from the jump. The smell of Uncle Dante's cigar burned in my nostrils. I wished we could have had the conversation outside, on the porch; the parlor seemed too familiar, too laden with the ghost of your presence.

"What name should I put instead?" he asked, pulling the book down from the mantle: the gilt-edged journal where he recorded our family's births, marriages, and deaths.

"It's blank when I'm born," I told him. He paused in the act of sharpening his pencil – he knew better than to write the future in ink. "Just erase it. White it out if you need to."

He sat back in his chair, and combed his fingers through his beard. "That's unprecedented."

"Not anymore," I said.

* * *

1963 feels like a menstrual cramp, like the ache in my legs as my bones stretched, like the twinges in my nipples as my breasts developed. It smells like Secret roll-on deodorant and the menthol cigarettes you had taken up smoking. It tastes like the peach cobbler I burned in Home-Ec class, which the teacher forced me to eat. It sounds like Sam Cooke's album *Night Beat*, which Dara, during one of her visits, had told me to buy.

And it looks like you, jumpier than I'd ever seen you, so twitchy that even Dad commented on it before he left for his hitch in the oil fields.

"Will you be all right?" he asked after dinner.

I was listening to the two of you talk from the kitchen doorway. I'd come in to ask Dad if he was going to watch *Gunsmoke* with me, which would be starting in a few minutes, and caught the two of you with your heads together by the sink.

You leaned forward, bracing your hands on the edge of the sink, looking for all the world as if you couldn't hold yourself up, as if gravity was working just a little bit harder on you than it was for everyone else. I wondered for a second if you were going to tell him about Dara. I'd grown up keeping her a secret with you, though the omission had begun to weigh heavier on me. I loved Dad, and I loved Dara; being unable to reconcile the two of them seemed trickier each passing week.

Instead you said nothing. You relaxed your shoulders, and you smiled for him, and kissed his cheek. You said the two of us would be fine, not to worry about his girls.

And the very next day, you pulled me out of bed and showed me our family's time machine, in the old tornado shelter with the lock I'd never been able to pick.

* * *

I know more about the machine now, after talking with Uncle Dante, reading the records that he kept. The mysterious man, Moses Stone, that built it in 1905, when Grandma Emmeline's parents leased out a parcel of land. He called it the anachronopede, which probably sounded marvelous in 1905, but even Uncle Dante was rolling his eyes at the name twenty years later. I know that Stone took Emmeline on trips to the future when she was seventeen, and then abandoned her after a few years, and nobody's been able to find him since then. I know that the machine is keyed to something in Emmeline's matrilineal DNA, some recessive gene.

I wonder if that man, Stone, built the anachronopede as an experiment. An experiment needs parameters, right? So build a machine that only certain people in one family can use. We can't go back before 1905, when the machine was completed, and we can't go past August 3, 2321. What happens that day? The only way to find out is to go as far forward as possible, and then wait. Maroon yourself in time. Exile yourself as far forward as you can, where none of us can reach you.

I'm sure you were lonely, waiting for me to grow up so you could travel again. You were exiled when you married Dad in 1947, in that feverish period just after the war. It must have been so romantic at first: I've seen the letters he wrote during the years he courted you. And you'd grown up seeing his name written next to yours, and the date that you'd marry him. When did you start feeling trapped, I wonder? You were caught in a weird net of fate and love and the future and the past. You loved Dad, but your love kept you hostage. You loved me, but you knew that someday, I'd transform myself into someone you didn't recognize.

* * *

At first, when you took me underground, to see the anachronopede, I thought you and Dad had built a fallout shelter. But there were no beds or boxes of canned food. And built into the rocky wall were rows of doors that looked like the one on our icebox. Round light bulbs lay just above the doors, nearly all of them red, though one or two were slowly blinking between orange and yellow.

Nearly all the doors were shut, except for two, near the end, which hung ajar.

"Those two capsules are for us, you and me," you said. "Nobody else can use them."

I stared at them. "What are they for?"

I'd heard you and Dara speak in code for nearly all of my life, jumps and capsules and fastenings. I'd imagined all sorts of things. Aliens and spaceships and doorways to another dimension, all the sort of things I'd seen Truman Bradley introduce on *Science Fiction Theater*.

"Traveling," you said.

"In time or in space?"

You seemed surprised. I'm not sure why. Dad collected pulp magazines, and you'd given me books by H.G. Wells and Jules Verne for Christmas in years past. The Justice League had gone into the future. I'd seen *The Fly* last year during a half-price matinee. You know how it was back then: such things weren't considered impossible, so much as inevitable. The future was a country we all wanted so badly to visit.

"In time," you said.

I immediately started peppering you with questions: how far into the future had you gone? When were you born? Had you seen dinosaurs? Had you met King Arthur? What about jetpacks? Was Dara from the future?

You held a hand to your mouth, watching as I danced around the small cavern, firing off questions like bullets being sprayed from a tommy gun.

"Maybe you are too young," you said, staring at the two empty capsules in the wall.

"I'm not!" I insisted. "Can't we go somewhere? Just a – just a quick jump?"

I added in the last part because I wanted you to know I'd been listening, when you and Dara had talked in code at the kitchen table. I'd been waiting for you include me in the conversation.

"Tomorrow," you decided. "We'll leave tomorrow."

* * *

The first thing I learned about time travel was that you couldn't eat anything before you did it. And you could only take a few sips of water: no juice or milk. The second thing I learned was that it was the most painful thing in the world, at least for me.

"Your grandmother Emmeline called it the fastening," you told me. "She said it felt like being a button squeezed through a too-narrow slit in a piece of fabric. It affects everyone differently."

"How's it affect you?"

You twisted your wedding ring around on your finger. "I haven't done it since before you were born."

You made me go to the bathroom twice before we walked back on that path, taking the fork that led to the shelter where the capsules were. The grass was still wet with dew, and there was a chill in the air. Up above, thin, wispy clouds were scratched onto the sky, but out west, I could see dark clouds gathering. There'd be storms later.

But what did I care about later? I was going into a time machine.

I asked you, "Where are we going?"

You replied, "To visit Dara. Just a quick trip."

There was something cold in your voice. I recognized the tone: the same you used when trying to talk me into wearing the new dress you'd bought me for church, or telling me to stop tearing through the house and play quietly for once.

In the shelter, you helped me undress, though it made me feel hotly embarrassed and strange to be naked in front of you again. I'd grown wary of my own body in the last few months, the way it was changing: I'd been dismayed by the way my nipples had grown tender, at the fatty flesh that had budded beneath them. It seemed like a betrayal.

I hunched my shoulders and covered my privates, though you barely glanced at my naked skin. You helped me lie down in the capsule, showed me how to pull the round mask over the bottom half of my face, attach the clip that went over my index finger. Finally, you lifted one of my arms up and wrapped a black cuff around the crook of my elbow. I noticed, watching you, that you had bitten all of your nails down to the quick, that the edges were jagged and tender-looking.

"You program your destination date in here, you see?" You tapped a square of black glass that lay on the ceiling of the capsule, and it lit up at the touch. Your fingers flew across the screen, typing directly onto it, rearranging colored orbs that seemed to attach themselves to your finger as soon as you touched them.

"You'll learn how to do this on your own eventually," you said. The screen, accepting whatever you'd done to it, blinked out and went black again.

I breathed through my mask, which covered my nose and face. A whisper of air blew against my skin, a rubbery, stale, lemony scent.

"Don't be scared," you said. "I'll be there when you wake up. I'm sending myself back a little earlier, so I'll be there to help you out of the capsule."

You kissed me on the forehead and shut the door. I was left alone in the dark as the walls around me started to hum.

Calling it 'the fastening' does it a disservice. It's much more painful than that. Granny Emmeline is far tougher than I'll ever be, if she thought it was just like forcing a button into place.

For me, it felt like being crushed in a vice that was lined with broken glass and nails. I understood, afterwards, why you had forbidden me from eating or drinking for twenty-four hours. I would have vomited in the mask, shat myself inside the capsule. I came back to myself in the dark, wild with terror and the phantom remains of that awful pain.

The door opened. The light needled into my eyes, and I screamed, trying to cover them. The various cuffs and wires attached to my arms tugged my hands back down, which made me panic even more.

Hands reached in and pushed me down, and eventually, I registered your voice in my ear, though not what you were saying. I stopped flailing long enough for all the straps and cuffs to be undone, and then I was lifted out of the capsule. You held me in your arms, rocking and soothing me, rubbing my back as I cried hysterically onto your shoulder.

I was insensible for a few minutes. When my sobs died away to hiccups, I realized that we weren't alone in the shelter. Dara was with us as well, and she had thrown a blanket over my shoulders.

"Jesus, Miriam," she said, over and over. "What the hell were you thinking?"

I found out later that I was the youngest person in my family to ever make a jump. Traditionally, they made their first jumps on their seventeenth birthday. I was nearly five years shy of that.

You smoothed back a lock of my hair, and I saw that all your fingernails had lost their ragged edge. Instead, they were rounded and smooth, topped with little crescents of white.

* * *

Uncle Dante told me that it wasn't unusual for two members of the family to be lovers, especially if there were generational gaps between them. It helped to avoid romantic entanglements with people who were bound to linear lives, at least until they were ready to settle down for a number of years, raising children. Pregnancy didn't mix well with time travel. It was odder to do what you had done: settle down with someone who was, as Dara liked to put it, stuck in the slow lane of linear time.

Dara told me about the two of you, eventually; that you'd been lovers before you met Dad, before you settled down with him in 1947. And that when she started visiting us in 1955, she wasn't sleeping alone in the guest bedroom.

I'm not sure if I was madder at her or you at the time, though I've since forgiven her. Why wouldn't I? You've left both of us, and it's a big thing, to have that in common.

* * *

1981 is colored silver, beige, bright orange, deep brown. It feels like the afghan blanket Dara kept on my bed while I recovered from my first jump, some kind of cheap fake wool. It tastes like chicken soup and weak tea with honey and lime Jell-O.

And for a few days, at least, 1981 felt like a low-grade headache that never went away, muscle spasms that I couldn't always control, dry mouth, difficulty swallowing. It smelt like a lingering olfactory hallucination of frying onions. It sounded like a ringing in the ears.

"So you're the unnamed baby, huh?" Dara said, that first morning when I woke up. She was reading a book, and set it down next to her on the couch.

I was disoriented: you and Dara had placed me in the southeast bedroom, the same one I slept in all through childhood. (The same one I'm recovering in right now.) I'm not sure if you thought it would comfort me, to wake up to familiar surroundings. It was profoundly strange, to be in my own bedroom, but have it be so different: the striped wallpaper replaced with avocado green paint; a loveseat with floral upholstering where my dresser had been; all my posters of Buck Rogers and Superman replaced with framed paintings of unfamiliar artwork.

"Dara?" I said. She seemed different, colder. Her hair was shorter than the last time I'd seen her, and she wore a pair of thick-framed glasses.

She cocked her head. "That'd be me. Nice to meet you."

I blinked at her, still disoriented and foggy. "We met before," I said.

She raised her eyebrows, like she couldn't believe I was so dumb. "Not by my timeline."

Right. Time travel.

You rushed in then. You must have heard us talking. You crouched down next to me and stroked the hair back from my face.

"How are you feeling?" you asked.

I looked down at your fingernails, and saw again that they were smooth, no jagged edges, and a hint of white at the edges. Dara told me later that you'd arrived two days before me, just so you two could have some time to be together. After all, you'd only left her for 1947 a few days before. The two of you had a lot to talk about.

"Alright, I guess," I told you.

* * *

It felt like the worst family vacation for those first few days. Dara was distant with me and downright cold to you. I wanted to ask what had happened, but I thought that I'd get the cold shoulder if I did. I caught snippets of the arguments you had with Dara; always whispered in doorways, or downstairs in the kitchen, the words too faint for me to make out.

It got a little better once I was back on my feet, and able to walk around and explore. I was astonished by everything; the walnut trees on our property that I had known as saplings now towered over me. Dara's television was twice the size of ours, in color, and had over a dozen stations. Dara's car seemed tiny, and shaped like a snake's head, instead of the generous curves and lines of the cars I knew.

I think it charmed Dara out of her anger a bit, to see me so appreciative of all these futuristic wonders – which were all relics of the past for her – and the conversations between the three of us got a little bit easier. Dara told me a little bit more about where she'd come from – the late 21st century – and why she was in this time – studying with some poet that I'd never heard of. She showed me the woman's poetry, and though I couldn't make much of it out at the time, one line from one poem has always stuck with me. "I did not recognize the shape of my own name."

I pondered that, lying awake in my bedroom – the once and future bedroom that I'm writing this from now, that I slept in then, that I awoke in when I was a young child, frightened by a storm. The rest of that poem made little sense to me, a series of images that were threaded together by a string of line breaks.

But I know about names, and hearing the one that's been given to you, and not recognizing it. I was trying to stammer this out to Dara one night, after she'd read that poem to me. And she asked, plain as could be, "What would you rather be called instead?"

I thought about how I used to introduce myself after the heroes of the TV shows my father and I watched: Doc and George and Charlie. It had been a silly game, sure, but there'd been something more serious underneath it. I'd recognized something in the shape of those names, something I wanted for myself.

"I dunno. A boy's name," I said. "Like George in the Famous Five."

"Well, why do you want to be called by a boy's name?" Dara asked gently.

In the corner, where you'd been playing solitaire, you paused while laying down a card. Dara noticed too, and we both looked over at you. I cringed, wondering what you were about to say; you hated that I didn't like my name, took it as a personal insult somehow.

But you said nothing, just resumed playing, slapping the cards down a little more heavily than before.

* * *

I forgive you for drugging me to take me back to 1963. I know I screamed at you after we arrived and the drugs wore off, but I was also a little relieved. It was a sneaking sort of relief, and didn't do much to counterbalance the feelings of betrayal and rage, but I know I would have panicked the second you shoved me into one of those capsules.

You'd taken me to the future, after all. I'd seen the relative wonders of 1981: VHS tapes, the Flash Gordon movie, the Columbia Space Shuttle. I would have forgiven you so much for that tiny glimpse.

I don't forgive you for leaving me, though. I don't forgive you for the morning after, when I woke up in my old familiar bedroom and padded downstairs for a bowl of cereal, and found, instead, a note that bore two words in your handwriting: *I'm sorry*.

The note rested atop the gilt-edged book that Grandma Emmeline had started as a diary, and that Uncle Dante had turned into both a record and a set of instructions for future generations: the names, birth dates, and the locations for all the traveling members of our family; who lived in the house and when; and sometimes, how and when a person died. The book stays with the house; you must have kept it hidden in the attic.

I flipped through it until I found your name: Miriam Guthrie (nee Stone): born November 21, 1977, Harrisburg, IL. Next to it, you penciled in the following.

Jumped forward to June 22, 2321 CE, and will die in exile beyond reach of the anachronopede.

Two small words could never encompass everything you have to apologize for.

* * *

I wonder if you ever looked up Dad's obituary. I wonder if you were even able to, if the record for one small man's death even lasts that long.

When you left, you took my father's future with you. Did you realize that? He was stuck in the slow lane of linear time, and to Dad, the future he'd dreamed of must have receded into the distance, something he'd never be able to reach.

He lost his job in the fall of 1966, as the White County oil wells ran dry, and hanged himself in the garage six months later. Dara cut him down and called the ambulance; her visits became more regular after you left us, and she must have known the day he would die.

(I can't bring myself to ask her: couldn't she have arrived twenty minutes earlier and stopped him entirely? I don't want to know her answer.)

In that obituary, I'm first in the list of those who survived him, and it's the last time I used the name you gave me. During the funeral, I nodded, received the hugs and handshakes from Dad's cousins and friends, bowed my head when the priest instructed, prayed hard for his soul. When it was done, I walked alone to the pond where the two of us had sat together, watching birds and talking about the plots of silly television shows. I tried to remember everything that I could about him, trying to preserve his ghost against the vagaries of time: the smell of Kamel cigarettes and diesel on his clothes; the red-blonde stubble that dotted his jaw; the way his eyes brightened when they landed on you.

I wished so hard that you were there with me. I wanted so much to cry on your shoulder, to sob as hard and hysterically as I had when you took me to 1981. And I wanted to be able to slap you, hit you, to push you in the water and hold you beneath the surface. I could have killed you that day, Mama.

When I was finished, Dara took me back to the house. We cleaned it as best we could for the next family member who would live here: there always has to be a member of the Stone family here, to take care of the shelter, the anachronopede, and the travelers that come through.

Then she took me away, to 2073, the home she'd made more than a century away from you.

* * *

Today was the first day I was able to leave the house, to take cautious, wobbling steps to the outside world. Everything is still tender and bruised, though my body is healing faster than I ever thought possible. It feels strange to walk with a weight between my legs; I walk differently, with a wider stride, even though I'm still limping.

Dara and I walked down to the pond today. The frogs all hushed at our approach, but the blackbirds set up a racket. And off in the distance, a heron lifted a cautious foot and placed it down again. We watched it step carefully through the water, hesitantly. Its beak darted into the water and came back up with a wriggling fish, which it flipped into its mouth. I suppose it was satisfied with that, because it crouched down, spread its wings, and then jumped into the air, enormous wings fighting against gravity until it rose over the trees.

Three days before my surgery, I went back to you. The pain of it is always the same, like I'm being torn apart and placed back together with clumsy, inexpert fingers, but by now I've gotten used to it. I wanted you to see me as the man I've always known I am, that I slowly became. And I wanted to see if I could forgive you; if I could look at you and see anything besides my father's slow decay, my own broken and betrayed heart.

I knocked at the door, dizzy, ears ringing, shivering, soaked from the storm that was so much worse than I remembered. I was lucky that you or Dara had left a blanket in the shelter, so I didn't have to walk up to the front door naked; my flat, scarred chest at odds with my wide hips, the thatch of pubic hair with no flesh protruding from it. I'd been on hormones for a year, and this second puberty reminded me so much of my first one, with you in 1963: the acne and the awkwardness, the slow reveal of my future self.

You answered the door with your hair in curlers, just as I remembered, and fetched me one of Dad's old robes. I fingered the monogramming at the breast pocket, and I wished, so hard, that I could walk upstairs and see him.

"What the hell," you said. "I thought the whole family knew these years were off-limits while I'm linear."

You didn't quite recognize me, and you tilted your head. "Have we met before?"

I looked you in the eye, and my voice cracked when I told you I was your son.

Your hand went to your mouth. "I'll have a son?" you asked.

And I told you the truth: "You have one already."

Your hand went to your gut, as if you would be sick. You shook your head, so hard that your curlers started coming loose. That's when the door creaked open, just a crack. You flew over there and yanked it all the way open, snatching the child there up in your arms. I barely caught a glimpse of my own face looking back at me, as you carried my child-self up the stairs.

I left before I could introduce myself to you: my name is Heron, Mama. I haven't forgiven you yet, but maybe someday, I will. And when I do, I will travel back one last time, to that night you left me and Dad for the future. I'll tell you that your apology has finally been accepted, and will give you my blessing to live in exile, marooned in a future beyond all reach.

A Christmas Carol
Chapter IV

Charles Dickens

[Publisher's Note: At this point in the story, Ebenezer Scrooge has already been visited by the Ghost of Christmas Past and the Ghost of Christmas Present. Now comes the third and final spirit promised to visit him.]

Chapter IV
The Last of the Spirits

THE PHANTOM slowly, gravely, silently, approached. When it came near him, Scrooge bent down upon his knee; for in the very air through which this Spirit moved it seemed to scatter gloom and mystery.

It was shrouded in a deep black garment, which concealed its head, its face, its form, and left nothing of it visible save one outstretched hand. But for this it would have been difficult to detach its figure from the night, and separate it from the darkness by which it was surrounded.

He felt that it was tall and stately when it came beside him, and that its mysterious presence filled him with a solemn dread. He knew no more, for the Spirit neither spoke nor moved.

"I am in the presence of the Ghost of Christmas Yet To Come?" said Scrooge.

The Spirit answered not, but pointed onward with its hand.

"You are about to show me shadows of the things that have not happened, but will happen in the time before us," Scrooge pursued. "Is that so, Spirit?"

The upper portion of the garment was contracted for an instant in its folds, as if the Spirit had inclined its head. That was the only answer he received.

Although well used to ghostly company by this time, Scrooge feared the silent shape so much that his legs trembled beneath him, and he found that he could hardly stand when he prepared to follow it. The Spirit paused a moment, as observing his condition, and giving him time to recover.

But Scrooge was all the worse for this. It thrilled him with a vague uncertain horror, to know that behind the dusky shroud, there were ghostly eyes intently fixed upon him, while he, though he stretched his own to the utmost, could see nothing but a spectral hand and one great heap of black.

"Ghost of the Future!" he exclaimed, "I fear you more than any spectre I have seen. But as I know your purpose is to do me good, and as I hope to live to be another man from what I was, I am prepared to bear you company, and do it with a thankful heart. Will you not speak to me?"

It gave him no reply. The hand was pointed straight before them.

"Lead on!" said Scrooge. "Lead on! The night is waning fast, and it is precious time to me, I know. Lead on, Spirit!"

The Phantom moved away as it had come towards him. Scrooge followed in the shadow of its dress, which bore him up, he thought, and carried him along.

They scarcely seemed to enter the city; for the city rather seemed to spring up about them, and encompass them of its own act. But there they were, in the heart of it; on 'Change, amongst the merchants; who hurried up and down, and chinked the money in their pockets, and conversed in groups, and looked at their watches, and trifled thoughtfully with their great gold seals; and so forth, as Scrooge had seen them often.

The Spirit stopped beside one little knot of business men. Observing that the hand was pointed to them, Scrooge advanced to listen to their talk.

"No," said a great fat man with a monstrous chin, "I don't know much about it, either way. I only know he's dead."

"When did he die?" inquired another.

"Last night, I believe."

"Why, what was the matter with him?" asked a third, taking a vast quantity of snuff out of a very large snuff-box. "I thought he'd never die."

"God knows," said the first, with a yawn.

"What has he done with his money?" asked a red-faced gentleman with a pendulous excrescence on the end of his nose, that shook like the gills of a turkey-cock.

"I haven't heard," said the man with the large chin, yawning again. "Left it to his company, perhaps. He hasn't left it to *me*. That's all I know."

This pleasantry was received with a general laugh.

"It's likely to be a very cheap funeral," said the same speaker; "for upon my life I don't know of anybody to go to it. Suppose we make up a party and volunteer?"

"I don't mind going if a lunch is provided," observed the gentleman with the excrescence on his nose. "But I must be fed, if I make one."

Another laugh.

"Well, I am the most disinterested among you, after all," said the first speaker, "for I never wear black gloves, and I never eat lunch. But I'll offer to go, if anybody else will. When I come to think of it, I'm not at all sure that I wasn't his most particular friend; for we used to stop and speak whenever we met. Bye, bye!"

Speakers and listeners strolled away, and mixed with other groups. Scrooge knew the men, and looked towards the Spirit for an explanation.

The Phantom glided on into a street. Its finger pointed to two persons meeting. Scrooge listened again, thinking that the explanation might lie here.

He knew these men, also, perfectly. They were men of business: very wealthy, and of great importance. He had made a point always of standing well in their esteem: in a business point of view, that is; strictly in a business point of view.

"How are you?" said one.

"How are you?" returned the other.

"Well!" said the first. "Old Scratch has got his own at last, hey?"

"So I am told," returned the second. "Cold, isn't it?"

"Seasonable for Christmas time. You're not a skater, I suppose?"

"No. No. Something else to think of. Good morning!"

Not another word. That was their meeting, their conversation, and their parting.

Scrooge was at first inclined to be surprised that the Spirit should attach importance to conversations apparently so trivial; but feeling assured that they must have some hidden purpose, he set himself to consider what it was likely to be. They could scarcely be supposed to have any bearing on the death of Jacob, his old partner, for that was Past, and this Ghost's province was the Future. Nor could he think of any one immediately connected with himself, to whom he could apply them. But nothing doubting that to whomsoever they applied they had some latent moral for his own improvement, he resolved to treasure up every word he heard, and everything he saw; and especially to observe the shadow of himself when it appeared. For he had an expectation that the conduct of his future self would give him the clue he missed, and would render the solution of these riddles easy.

He looked about in that very place for his own image; but another man stood in his accustomed corner, and though the clock pointed to his usual time of day for being there, he saw no likeness of himself among the multitudes that poured in through the Porch. It gave him little surprise, however; for he had been revolving in his mind a change of life, and thought and hoped he saw his new-born resolutions carried out in this.

Quiet and dark, beside him stood the Phantom, with its outstretched hand. When he roused himself from his thoughtful quest, he fancied from the turn of the hand, and its situation in reference to himself, that the Unseen Eyes were looking at him keenly. It made him shudder, and feel very cold.

They left the busy scene, and went into an obscure part of the town, where Scrooge had never penetrated before, although he recognised its situation, and its bad repute. The ways were foul and narrow; the shops and houses wretched; the people half-naked, drunken, slipshod, ugly. Alleys and archways, like so many cesspools, disgorged their offences of smell, and dirt, and life, upon the straggling streets; and the whole quarter reeked with crime, with filth, and misery.

Far in this den of infamous resort, there was a low-browed, beetling shop, below a pent-house roof, where iron, old rags, bottles, bones, and greasy offal, were bought. Upon the floor within, were piled up heaps of rusty keys, nails, chains, hinges, files, scales, weights, and refuse iron of all kinds. Secrets that few would like to scrutinise were bred and hidden in mountains of unseemly rags, masses of corrupted fat, and sepulchres of bones. Sitting in among the wares he dealt in, by a charcoal stove, made of old bricks, was a grey-haired rascal, nearly seventy years of age; who had screened himself from the cold air without, by a frousy curtaining of miscellaneous tatters, hung upon a line; and smoked his pipe in all the luxury of calm retirement.

Scrooge and the Phantom came into the presence of this man, just as a woman with a heavy bundle slunk into the shop. But she had scarcely entered, when another woman, similarly laden, came in too; and she was closely followed by a man in faded black, who was no less startled by the sight of them, than they had been upon the recognition of each other. After a short period of blank astonishment, in which the old man with the pipe had joined them, they all three burst into a laugh.

"Let the charwoman alone to be the first!" cried she who had entered first. "Let the laundress alone to be the second; and let the undertaker's man alone to be the third. Look here, old Joe, here's a chance! If we haven't all three met here without meaning it!"

"You couldn't have met in a better place," said old Joe, removing his pipe from his mouth. "Come into the parlour. You were made free of it long ago, you know; and the other two an't strangers. Stop till I shut the door of the shop. Ah! How it skreeks!

There an't such a rusty bit of metal in the place as its own hinges, I believe; and I'm sure there's no such old bones here, as mine. Ha, ha! We're all suitable to our calling, we're well matched. Come into the parlour. Come into the parlour."

The parlour was the space behind the screen of rags. The old man raked the fire together with an old stair-rod, and having trimmed his smoky lamp (for it was night), with the stem of his pipe, put it in his mouth again.

While he did this, the woman who had already spoken threw her bundle on the floor, and sat down in a flaunting manner on a stool; crossing her elbows on her knees, and looking with a bold defiance at the other two.

"What odds then! What odds, Mrs. Dilber?" said the woman. "Every person has a right to take care of themselves. *He* always did."

"That's true, indeed!" said the laundress. "No man more so."

"Why then, don't stand staring as if you was afraid, woman; who's the wiser? We're not going to pick holes in each other's coats, I suppose?"

"No, indeed!" said Mrs. Dilber and the man together. "We should hope not."

"Very well, then!" cried the woman. "That's enough. Who's the worse for the loss of a few things like these? Not a dead man, I suppose."

"No, indeed," said Mrs. Dilber, laughing.

"If he wanted to keep 'em after he was dead, a wicked old screw," pursued the woman, "why wasn't he natural in his lifetime? If he had been, he'd have had somebody to look after him when he was struck with Death, instead of lying gasping out his last there, alone by himself."

"It's the truest word that ever was spoke," said Mrs. Dilber. "It's a judgment on him."

"I wish it was a little heavier judgment," replied the woman; "and it should have been, you may depend upon it, if I could have laid my hands on anything else. Open that bundle, old Joe, and let me know the value of it. Speak out plain. I'm not afraid to be the first, nor afraid for them to see it. We know pretty well that we were helping ourselves, before we met here, I believe. It's no sin. Open the bundle, Joe."

But the gallantry of her friends would not allow of this; and the man in faded black, mounting the breach first, produced *his* plunder. It was not extensive. A seal or two, a pencil-case, a pair of sleeve-buttons, and a brooch of no great value, were all. They were severally examined and appraised by old Joe, who chalked the sums he was disposed to give for each, upon the wall, and added them up into a total when he found there was nothing more to come.

"That's your account," said Joe, "and I wouldn't give another sixpence, if I was to be boiled for not doing it. Who's next?"

Mrs. Dilber was next. Sheets and towels, a little wearing apparel, two old-fashioned silver teaspoons, a pair of sugar-tongs, and a few boots. Her account was stated on the wall in the same manner.

"I always give too much to ladies. It's a weakness of mine, and that's the way I ruin myself," said old Joe. "That's your account. If you asked me for another penny, and made it an open question, I'd repent of being so liberal and knock off half-a-crown."

"And now undo *my* bundle, Joe," said the first woman.

Joe went down on his knees for the greater convenience of opening it, and having unfastened a great many knots, dragged out a large and heavy roll of some dark stuff.

"What do you call this?" said Joe. "Bed-curtains!"

"Ah!" returned the woman, laughing and leaning forward on her crossed arms. "Bed-curtains!"

"You don't mean to say you took 'em down, rings and all, with him lying there?" said Joe.

"Yes I do," replied the woman. "Why not?"

"You were born to make your fortune," said Joe, "and you'll certainly do it."

"I certainly shan't hold my hand, when I can get anything in it by reaching it out, for the sake of such a man as He was, I promise you, Joe," returned the woman coolly. "Don't drop that oil upon the blankets, now."

"His blankets?" asked Joe.

"Whose else's do you think?" replied the woman. "He isn't likely to take cold without 'em, I dare say."

"I hope he didn't die of anything catching? Eh?" said old Joe, stopping in his work, and looking up.

"Don't you be afraid of that," returned the woman. "I an't so fond of his company that I'd loiter about him for such things, if he did. Ah! you may look through that shirt till your eyes ache; but you won't find a hole in it, nor a threadbare place. It's the best he had, and a fine one too. They'd have wasted it, if it hadn't been for me."

"What do you call wasting of it?" asked old Joe.

"Putting it on him to be buried in, to be sure," replied the woman with a laugh. "Somebody was fool enough to do it, but I took it off again. If calico an't good enough for such a purpose, it isn't good enough for anything. It's quite as becoming to the body. He can't look uglier than he did in that one."

Scrooge listened to this dialogue in horror. As they sat grouped about their spoil, in the scanty light afforded by the old man's lamp, he viewed them with a detestation and disgust, which could hardly have been greater, though they had been obscene demons, marketing the corpse itself.

"Ha, ha!" laughed the same woman, when old Joe, producing a flannel bag with money in it, told out their several gains upon the ground. "This is the end of it, you see! He frightened everyone away from him when he was alive, to profit us when he was dead! Ha, ha, ha!"

"Spirit!" said Scrooge, shuddering from head to foot. "I see, I see. The case of this unhappy man might be my own. My life tends that way, now. Merciful Heaven, what is this!"

He recoiled in terror, for the scene had changed, and now he almost touched a bed: a bare, uncurtained bed: on which, beneath a ragged sheet, there lay a something covered up, which, though it was dumb, announced itself in awful language.

The room was very dark, too dark to be observed with any accuracy, though Scrooge glanced round it in obedience to a secret impulse, anxious to know what kind of room it was. A pale light, rising in the outer air, fell straight upon the bed; and on it, plundered and bereft, unwatched, unwept, uncared for, was the body of this man.

Scrooge glanced towards the Phantom. Its steady hand was pointed to the head. The cover was so carelessly adjusted that the slightest raising of it, the motion of a finger upon Scrooge's part, would have disclosed the face. He thought of it, felt how easy it would be to do, and longed to do it; but had no more power to withdraw the veil than to dismiss the spectre at his side.

Oh cold, cold, rigid, dreadful Death, set up thine altar here, and dress it with such terrors as thou hast at thy command: for this is thy dominion! But of the loved, revered, and honoured head, thou canst not turn one hair to thy dread purposes, or make one feature odious. It is not that the hand is heavy and will fall down when released; it is not that the heart and pulse are still; but that the hand was open, generous, and true; the heart brave, warm, and tender; and the pulse a man's. Strike, Shadow, strike! And see his good deeds springing from the wound, to sow the world with life immortal!

No voice pronounced these words in Scrooge's ears, and yet he heard them when he looked upon the bed. He thought, if this man could be raised up now, what would be his foremost thoughts? Avarice, hard-dealing, griping cares? They have brought him to a rich end, truly!

He lay, in the dark empty house, with not a man, a woman, or a child, to say that he was kind to me in this or that, and for the memory of one kind word I will be kind to him. A cat was tearing at the door, and there was a sound of gnawing rats beneath the hearth-stone. What *they* wanted in the room of death, and why they were so restless and disturbed, Scrooge did not dare to think.

"Spirit!" he said, "this is a fearful place. In leaving it, I shall not leave its lesson, trust me. Let us go!"

Still the Ghost pointed with an unmoved finger to the head.

"I understand you," Scrooge returned, "and I would do it, if I could. But I have not the power, Spirit. I have not the power."

Again it seemed to look upon him.

"If there is any person in the town, who feels emotion caused by this man's death," said Scrooge quite agonised, "show that person to me, Spirit, I beseech you!"

The Phantom spread its dark robe before him for a moment, like a wing; and withdrawing it, revealed a room by daylight, where a mother and her children were.

She was expecting someone, and with anxious eagerness; for she walked up and down the room; started at every sound; looked out from the window; glanced at the clock; tried, but in vain, to work with her needle; and could hardly bear the voices of the children in their play.

At length the long-expected knock was heard. She hurried to the door, and met her husband; a man whose face was careworn and depressed, though he was young. There was a remarkable expression in it now; a kind of serious delight of which he felt ashamed, and which he struggled to repress.

He sat down to the dinner that had been hoarding for him by the fire; and when she asked him faintly what news (which was not until after a long silence), he appeared embarrassed how to answer.

"Is it good?" she said, "or bad?" – to help him.

"Bad," he answered.

"We are quite ruined?"

"No. There is hope yet, Caroline."

"If *he* relents," she said, amazed, "there is! Nothing is past hope, if such a miracle has happened."

"He is past relenting," said her husband. "He is dead."

She was a mild and patient creature if her face spoke truth; but she was thankful in her soul to hear it, and she said so, with clasped hands. She prayed forgiveness the next moment, and was sorry; but the first was the emotion of her heart.

"What the half-drunken woman whom I told you of last night, said to me, when I tried to see him and obtain a week's delay; and what I thought was a mere excuse to avoid me; turns out to have been quite true. He was not only very ill, but dying, then."

"To whom will our debt be transferred?"

"I don't know. But before that time we shall be ready with the money; and even though we were not, it would be a bad fortune indeed to find so merciless a creditor in his successor. We may sleep tonight with light hearts, Caroline!"

Yes. Soften it as they would, their hearts were lighter. The children's faces, hushed and clustered round to hear what they so little understood, were brighter; and it was a happier house for this man's death! The only emotion that the Ghost could show him, caused by the event, was one of pleasure.

"Let me see some tenderness connected with a death," said Scrooge; "or that dark chamber, Spirit, which we left just now, will be for ever present to me."

The Ghost conducted him through several streets familiar to his feet; and as they went along, Scrooge looked here and there to find himself, but nowhere was he to be seen. They entered poor Bob Cratchit's house; the dwelling he had visited before; and found the mother and the children seated round the fire.

Quiet. Very quiet. The noisy little Cratchits were as still as statues in one corner, and sat looking up at Peter, who had a book before him. The mother and her daughters were engaged in sewing. But surely they were very quiet!

"'And He took a child, and set him in the midst of them.'"

Where had Scrooge heard those words? He had not dreamed them. The boy must have read them out, as he and the Spirit crossed the threshold. Why did he not go on?

The mother laid her work upon the table, and put her hand up to her face.

"The colour hurts my eyes," she said.

The colour? Ah, poor Tiny Tim!

"They're better now again," said Cratchit's wife. "It makes them weak by candle-light; and I wouldn't show weak eyes to your father when he comes home, for the world. It must be near his time."

"Past it rather," Peter answered, shutting up his book. "But I think he has walked a little slower than he used, these few last evenings, mother."

They were very quiet again. At last she said, and in a steady, cheerful voice, that only faltered once:

"I have known him walk with – I have known him walk with Tiny Tim upon his shoulder, very fast indeed."

"And so have I," cried Peter. "Often."

"And so have I," exclaimed another. So had all.

"But he was very light to carry," she resumed, intent upon her work, "and his father loved him so, that it was no trouble: no trouble. And there is your father at the door!"

She hurried out to meet him; and little Bob in his comforter – he had need of it, poor fellow – came in. His tea was ready for him on the hob, and they all tried who should help him to it most. Then the two young Cratchits got upon his knees and laid, each child a little cheek, against his face, as if they said, "Don't mind it, father. Don't be grieved!"

Bob was very cheerful with them, and spoke pleasantly to all the family. He looked at the work upon the table, and praised the industry and speed of Mrs. Cratchit and the girls. They would be done long before Sunday, he said.

"Sunday! You went today, then, Robert?" said his wife.

"Yes, my dear," returned Bob. "I wish you could have gone. It would have done you good to see how green a place it is. But you'll see it often. I promised him that I would walk there on a Sunday. My little, little child!" cried Bob. "My little child!"

He broke down all at once. He couldn't help it. If he could have helped it, he and his child would have been farther apart perhaps than they were.

He left the room, and went up-stairs into the room above, which was lighted cheerfully, and hung with Christmas. There was a chair set close beside the child, and there were signs of someone having been there, lately. Poor Bob sat down in it, and when he had thought a little and composed himself, he kissed the little face. He was reconciled to what had happened, and went down again quite happy.

They drew about the fire, and talked; the girls and mother working still. Bob told them of the extraordinary kindness of Mr. Scrooge's nephew, whom he had scarcely seen but once, and who, meeting him in the street that day, and seeing that he looked a little – "just a little down you know," said Bob, inquired what had happened to distress him. "On which," said Bob, "for he is the pleasantest-spoken gentleman you ever heard, I told him. 'I am heartily sorry for it, Mr. Cratchit,' he said, 'and heartily sorry for your good wife.' By the bye, how he ever knew *that*, I don't know."

"Knew what, my dear?"

"Why, that you were a good wife," replied Bob.

"Everybody knows that!" said Peter.

"Very well observed, my boy!" cried Bob. "I hope they do. 'Heartily sorry,' he said, 'for your good wife. If I can be of service to you in any way,' he said, giving me his card, 'that's where I live. Pray come to me.' Now, it wasn't," cried Bob, "for the sake of anything he might be able to do for us, so much as for his kind way, that this was quite delightful. It really seemed as if he had known our Tiny Tim, and felt with us."

"I'm sure he's a good soul!" said Mrs. Cratchit.

"You would be surer of it, my dear," returned Bob, "if you saw and spoke to him. I shouldn't be at all surprised – mark what I say! – if he got Peter a better situation."

"Only hear that, Peter," said Mrs. Cratchit.

"And then," cried one of the girls, "Peter will be keeping company with someone, and setting up for himself."

"Get along with you!" retorted Peter, grinning.

"It's just as likely as not," said Bob, "one of these days; though there's plenty of time for that, my dear. But however and whenever we part from one another, I am sure we shall none of us forget poor Tiny Tim – shall we – or this first parting that there was among us?"

"Never, father!" cried they all.

"And I know," said Bob, "I know, my dears, that when we recollect how patient and how mild he was; although he was a little, little child; we shall not quarrel easily among ourselves, and forget poor Tiny Tim in doing it."

"No, never, father!" they all cried again.

"I am very happy," said little Bob, "I am very happy!"

Mrs. Cratchit kissed him, his daughters kissed him, the two young Cratchits kissed him, and Peter and himself shook hands. Spirit of Tiny Tim, thy childish essence was from God!

"Spectre," said Scrooge, "something informs me that our parting moment is at hand. I know it, but I know not how. Tell me what man that was whom we saw lying dead?"

The Ghost of Christmas Yet To Come conveyed him, as before – though at a different time, he thought: indeed, there seemed no order in these latter visions, save that they were in the Future – into the resorts of business men, but showed him not himself. Indeed, the Spirit did not stay for anything, but went straight on, as to the end just now desired, until besought by Scrooge to tarry for a moment.

"This court," said Scrooge, "through which we hurry now, is where my place of occupation is, and has been for a length of time. I see the house. Let me behold what I shall be, in days to come!"

The Spirit stopped; the hand was pointed elsewhere.

"The house is yonder," Scrooge exclaimed. "Why do you point away?"

The inexorable finger underwent no change.

Scrooge hastened to the window of his office, and looked in. It was an office still, but not his. The furniture was not the same, and the figure in the chair was not himself. The Phantom pointed as before.

He joined it once again, and wondering why and whither he had gone, accompanied it until they reached an iron gate. He paused to look round before entering.

A churchyard. Here, then; the wretched man whose name he had now to learn, lay underneath the ground. It was a worthy place. Walled in by houses; overrun by grass and weeds, the growth of vegetation's death, not life; choked up with too much burying; fat with repleted appetite. A worthy place!

The Spirit stood among the graves, and pointed down to One. He advanced towards it trembling. The Phantom was exactly as it had been, but he dreaded that he saw new meaning in its solemn shape.

"Before I draw nearer to that stone to which you point," said Scrooge, "answer me one question. Are these the shadows of the things that Will be, or are they shadows of things that May be, only?"

Still the Ghost pointed downward to the grave by which it stood.

"Men's courses will foreshadow certain ends, to which, if persevered in, they must lead," said Scrooge. "But if the courses be departed from, the ends will change. Say it is thus with what you show me!"

The Spirit was immovable as ever.

Scrooge crept towards it, trembling as he went; and following the finger, read upon the stone of the neglected grave his own name, Ebenezer Scrooge.

"Am *I* that man who lay upon the bed?" he cried, upon his knees.

The finger pointed from the grave to him, and back again.

"No, Spirit! Oh no, no!"

The finger still was there.

"Spirit!" he cried, tight clutching at its robe, "hear me! I am not the man I was. I will not be the man I must have been but for this intercourse. Why show me this, if I am past all hope!"

For the first time the hand appeared to shake.

"Good Spirit," he pursued, as down upon the ground he fell before it: "Your nature intercedes for me, and pities me. Assure me that I yet may change these shadows you have shown me, by an altered life!"

The kind hand trembled.

"I will honour Christmas in my heart, and try to keep it all the year. I will live in the Past, the Present, and the Future. The Spirits of all Three shall strive within me. I will not shut out the lessons that they teach. Oh, tell me I may sponge away the writing on this stone!"

In his agony, he caught the spectral hand. It sought to free itself, but he was strong in his entreaty, and detained it. The Spirit, stronger yet, repulsed him.

Holding up his hands in a last prayer to have his fate reversed, he saw an alteration in the Phantom's hood and dress. It shrunk, collapsed, and dwindled down into a bedpost.

The complete and unabridged text is available online, from *flametreepublishing.com/extras*

Hostage

Kate Estabrooks

COLBY CLIMBED OUT of the manhole and ran. His boots slipped on the wet pavement, but he didn't slow. He could already hear the gurgling. The bakery was up ahead. Its fire escape was less than two hundred meters away. He pumped his legs harder. He'd make it.

One hundred meters. Fifty meters. Gurgling gave way to sloshing, then crashing water. A wave pool breaking its walls behind him. Five meters. Colby pushed another stride then jumped. His heart leapt as his hands wrapped around the iron rung. He'd done it.

A cold arm tightened around his knees. The cold spread upwards, pressing on his diaphragm. He tried to reach up and grab the ladder with his other hand, but the water (it wasn't really water, of course, but no one seemed to have a better name for it) yanked his elbow down.

The fluidic straightjacket tightened before swallowing Colby whole. The cold filled his nose and hit his brain like a thousand ice cream headaches. He had a split second to try to recall the last time he'd had ice cream – it was coffee ice cream, with Marie, two years ago, at that weathered gray picnic table. She'd come over to his bench because the one on her side was cracked down the middle – before his senses blurred.

* * *

Something hard and pointed was digging into his Colby's spine. He tried to shift his body and drift back into sleep. Each position was as uncomfortable as the last, and something equally sharp was poking around his mind.

The memory of the water wrapping around his chest rushed into focus. Colby bolted up flailing his arms to free himself. The trap that was no longer there. Actually, he was trapped. But this trap, at least, had room to breathe.

"That was an even dumber stunt than usual," said Ruben.

"Then why did you help me climb up there?"

"I'm a sucker for entertainment."

Colby's hands moved to his torso, then his legs, patting them down for signs of damage. Ruben was laughing.

"Don't worry, mate. It left you in one piece, same as always."

Colby looked at his cellmate. "I was so close this time," he said.

"I'm sure you were," Ruben stuck a twig in his molars and started to chew as he went on laughing, "I'm sure you were. Here," he shoved a canteen under Colby's nose, "you've been out for goin' on thirty six hours, now. You'd better drink before your muscles start cramping."

Ruben sauntered over to the opposite side of the cave where the other prisoners were huddled around the nutrition pond, dunking their canteens and chugging as much as they could. If they were quick enough, they'd get a chance to refill before the pond drained for another day.

Colby looked up at the grate on the ceiling, the only opening to the outside world, and took a gulp of the chalky slurry. All he could think about was coffee ice cream.

The water didn't only drag people in. Very occasionally, someone would be walking around minding their own business, too near the walls. The water would seep from the stone, then snap out like a tongue. Those people were gone before they had a chance to run. Consequently, the hostages spent as much time as possible near the center of the cell.

When the grate opened a few days later, Colby was surprised. It didn't feel like a month had passed since the last inspection. The guards rappelled to the floor, each with one hand on the rope, the other on their weapon. Colby always wondered what they thought their captives were going to do. Whip slurry-filled canteens at them?

Quite the contrary, everyone in the cell lined up dutifully. Sometimes, good behaviour meant a day of solid food. Colby stood back and waited until the others were in formation. He joined the end of the line.

The guard that reached Colby looked him over head to toe from behind the opaque visor covering his entire face. He said nothing. They rarely spoke, but Colby was expecting some form of discourse this time. If only to give him the reprimand he'd earned. A restriction on nutrition intake was the usual punishment for escape attempts.

Instead, the guard stood eye to eye with Colby for a long time. Colby found himself shifting his weight from one foot to the other.

The other guards began to make their exit. The one in front of Colby turned to go too. Then, he stopped with one hand on the rope that would lift him through the ceiling. His head turned back.

Colby barely had time to register movement before the guard had him by the shirt and was driving him backward with the full force of his body weight. The supposed stone felt like tepid velvet on Colby's back.

He tried to flail and kick. The guard's armour gave him limbs like tree trunks. Cold wrapped around Colby's neck. The suffocating oblivion returned.

This time, when he came to, Colby was sitting in a chair. The room was the same makeup as his previous cell. The same dirt and rock on the floor. The same walls. Only, from his place in the center, Colby could reach out and touch these walls. He chose not to, even when the restraining brackets holding him to the chair clicked and fell to the floor.

So this was to be his punishment then, isolation. Some of the older prisoners had mentioned this happening before. Colby hadn't believed them. None of the prisoners taken by the water since his arrival had ever come back.

He was wondering how long a typical sentence was when a hole opened in the wall and a bucket of nutrition slid out. He tried to recall what Jarvis and Spencer had said about isolation. A couple of days, maybe. He looked at the nutrition he'd been allotted. About a day's usual ration. Two days of isolation at half ration. *Ok, I can handle that.*

* * *

It was hard to measure the time, but Colby was pretty sure more than two days had passed. The toiletry station had appeared twenty-six times. It was on its usual schedule as far as he could tell. He'd always been ready to use it, but never too desperate.

The nutrition bucket had only been refilled once. Colby's throat was dry, and his legs were starting to feel wobbly when he stood. He looked at the remaining two inches of slurry and decided he could wait a little longer.

He put his mind on Marie. Where was she right now? What was she doing? It had been almost a year by his estimation. Where did she think he'd gone? He decided he didn't want to think about that.

* * *

Colby was slurping with relish from the second nutrition refill when the guard came. He looked up from his goopy hands, then around at the walls wondering how the cell was able to accommodate two bodies so comfortably.

The guard took the chair and leaned toward Colby, resting his forearms on his knees so casually Colby was almost surprised when he next words weren't 'How's it going?'

"You have a choice," the guard said, voice muffled only slightly by his helmet. "You can go back to your old cell, or stay here for the duration."

"What is the duration?"

Rather than reply, the guard gave Colby another minute or so to consider his situation. Then, he leaned in a little closer.

"The next time you try to escape will be the last time, one way or the other. Before you try again, consider carefully how much you've enjoyed having your own place." He swept his hand at the room. "Do you have an answer now, or do you need a couple of days to think it over?"

Colby opened his mouth, fully intending to say he was ready to go back to the group. Fully intending to wholeheartedly promise there would be no more escape attempts. But before the words came out, he looked at the place on the guard's visor where eyes should be. He remembered the first time he'd met a guard. *Were you one of them?* Probably not, he knew, but maybe. His chest burned at the thought.

* * *

Marie had said she would be home early that night, but she was late again. Colby tried not to read too much into it. When she finally walked in, he greeted her with a smile. He was faking the smile. At first. Then she pulled the bottle of wine out of her bag.

"Time to celebrate," she said.

"Celebrate what?"

Marie took two glasses from the cupboard and reached for the corkscrew. "We rested our case today, and Luke is taking the closing arguments. I stayed to help him prepare, but starting Monday it's back to shuffling paper nine to five for me. And that means more time for you, me," the cork popped, "and this."

The incredulity shouted through Colby's silence. Marie poured. A much more generous pour than civilized society would consider for a proper glass of wine.

"I mean it this time," she handed one of the glasses to Colby. He face melted into genuine pleasure.

* * *

The next memory Colby could conger was bolting up in bed as he realized someone was in the room with him. On instinct, his hand shot to Marie's side of the bed. She wasn't there. Only the two guards, abductors, were there in the dark with him. They'd taken him that night. They'd never given a reason.

The anger burned hotter. Colby stood and faced the guard in his cell, who rose with him rather than be caught at the lower vantage point.

"Fuck you," said Colby.

"I beg your pardon?" said the guard.

Colby glared into that cowardly visor. From this close, he could almost make out the shadows of a face.

"You've taken me from my home. You've separated me from my wife. What else do you think you can take from me? Send me back, leave me here. I don't give a shit." Colby was prepared to stand there for eternity. He'd be damned if he was going to turn away first.

Eternity turned out to be short. The guard's posture relaxed after no more than two seconds. A hand went to his hip. He sighed like he was late for a meeting and he'd hit his fourth red light in a row.

"I was afraid you were going to be one of those."

* * *

It was dark. They stood by the steps outside Colby's apartment, Colby and Jack. The guard had gone so far as to give his name. Though, 'Jack' was generic enough to leave Colby skeptical.

The water that wasn't really water had brought them here. Jack had conjured it with the baton on his belt. That explained some things. Every guard had one, but Colby had never seen one used on a prisoner, even by the guards who enjoyed their job a little too much.

There was a fine mist in the air left over from the rain that had fallen most of that day. Colby's last day with Marie.

"I remember this night just fine," said Colby.

"Really?" said Jack. "What time did you go to bed?"

"Around…well, I think it was –"

"Did you have a second glass of wine?"

"I –"

When did –"

"Ok, point taken…but after this I'll remember?"

"Like it was yesterday. Unfortunately."

"How do I know any of this is true? If you can take a person's memory in the first place, what's to say you can't give them new ones."

"Because it doesn't work like that."

"I'm supposed to take your word for it?"

"When the memories are back, you'll know they're real."

Marie's boots slapped the sidewalk. She jogged up the steps without a glance toward her audience. Colby's heart leapt at the sight of her pecan-brown hair swishing on the back of her coat.

"Do you see her?" asked Jack.

"Of course I see her."

"This will be easier on you if you keep one thing in mind."

"What?" Colby was barely breathing.

"This is only a remnant of a timeline. It is what it is. Once I immerse you, you'll experience it as you did before. You will have no control over it."

"Ok."

"I mean it, don't waste your energy."

"Got it."

"You ready?"

"Yes, yes definitely."

Jack touched the end of the baton to the back of Colby's neck."

* * *

Colby was shouting. He begged Marie to look for him, he was pretty sure he was being kept underground, there was a guard who called himself Jack. But all this went on in his head while he sipped his first, second, then third glass of wine.

Marie's feet were curled up against Colby's leg. They were watching a favorite movie. This being the third or fourth viewing, there was plenty of room to talk between more enthralling scenes.

"I might need to go in early on Tuesday," Marie slipped in as the distraction of a good action sequence was ramping up.

There is was. Colby set down his glass and turned to her. "A new case?"

"Just some paper work."

"Paperwork that can't wait until 9 a.m?"

"I want to get a jump on things."

Colby had wanted to believe her. The memory of trying to keep his cool as the conversation escalated was coming back one step ahead of the playback. The fight migrated from the couch, to the kitchen, to the stairs. He saw the shoe, his shoe, casually discarded at the top of the steps. And he remembered.

He tried to kick it out of the way, but instead turned back toward the kitchen, as he had the first time. In the same instant, Marie yelped.

Colby turned back in time to see she wouldn't be able to save her balance. He leapt toward her then. Just like before, his outstretched arm made contact and redirected her fall, but his fingers failed to find a hold on her sweater.

The sideways trajectory took her head to the base of the wrought-iron railing. The emergency vehicles came. The neighbours had overheard them arguing.

* * *

The water spit Colby out and left him double over, trying not to vomit, in the small cell with Jack.

"You see now?" said Jack.

Colby couldn't muster a reply.

"I can remove the harsher aspects of the memory again if you like. Exhibiting a certain level of emotional control is a prerequisite for release, and the guilt that comes with the memories has been shown to hinder rehabilitation. Generally, a full repression is most effective, but in some cases –

"Rehabilitation?" said Colby. "So this is...I'm in jail?"

"Yes," said Jack, as though he'd been asked if two plus two was four.

"It was an accident."

Jack almost smiled. "So you said at the trial."

"It was! She..." but the fight drained from Colby in an instant, displaced by the full presence of reality. Even if they let him out, Marie wouldn't be waiting for him.

* * *

Colby spent most of his subsequent days staring into space. If it weren't for Ruben, he probably would have forgotten to eat. Ruben asked him often about where he'd gone, what had happened, but Colby only said it didn't matter. When he said anything at all.

One day, after the nutrition pond had drained, Spencer sought Colby's company. He sat in a squat with his loose-skinned arms wrapped around pointy knees.

"I never had the heart to tell anyone either."

"Tell them what?" said Colby, not really caring."

"That it's their own damn fault they're in this place," said Spencer. "It was easier when you had righteous outrage to lean on, wasn't it?"

Colby shrugged.

Let 'em think it's for ransom, or politics, or whatever else they tell themselves," Spencer continued.

"How long have you known?" asked Colby.

"Must be almost thirty years now. Before that, I was a fighter like you. Now I know, a lifetime in this place won't begin to make up for what put me here."

"My wife fell down the stairs," said Colby. "They think I pushed her, but I didn't."

"Hmm," Spencer chewed on that one a moment. "If that's true, you should still be able to muster a little indignation to keep you going"

"What's the point? She's still dead."

Spencer studied Colby like he was an interesting specimen at the zoo.

"You do know you just traveled back in time, don't you?"

"In a manner of speaking, I guess. But my guard made it pretty clear I couldn't change anything, and he was right. Believe me I tried."

Spencer nodded thoughtfully. "Tell me about your arrest."

"Why?"

Spencer was quiet.

"It was at night," Colby finally said. "I was already in bed, and –"

"Your wife had just died from a fall down the stairs…but you were in bed?"

Colby thought about it again. "Yes, I…I remember checking to see if Marie was in bed too." Why had he done that? "But her side was empty…she was…"

"Go on," said Spencer.

Colby bolted to his feet, "Holy shit, she was at work! I remember thinking she was at work." A number of the other prisoners, Ruben included, glanced their way.

Spencer pulled him back down with one hand while putting the other to his lips, "Now you're getting to it."

"That was the night *before* she died," said Colby. "But the guards were there. Nothing had happened yet, why were that there?"

"Not guards, cops," said Spencer

"They didn't look like cops," said Colby.

"Special branch, for retro-preventable crime."

"Still, Marie died. I watched it happen."

"There's reason they call the timeline a remnant," said Spencer. "A leftover shadow from before they fixed things."

"You're telling me we're here for crimes that didn't really happen?"

Oh, they happened. And if they let us out they'll happen again. Or so the fancy machines tell them."

"She's out there…alive," Colby's breath caught, "and she must think I vanished for no reason."

"Better than the alternative," said Spencer.

"But I…" At Spencer's warning eyes, Colby brought his voice back down to a harsh whisper, "I didn't kill her in the first place."

"Doesn't matter," said Spencer.

"How can it not matter?"

"They run all kinds of scenarios in the time simulator before settling on a sentence. If you're still in here, then there's more than a good chance letting you out would result in the death of your wife."

"They're wrong, she fell down the stairs. I didn't even touch her…well, I mean, I touched her, but that's not why she fell."

Spencer got up, slapping him on the back, "Whatever you say."

* * *

The next time there was an inspection, Colby was able to pick out Jack easily despite the visor over his face. He kept eyes on him. Soon, Jack walked his way. Colby cast his eyes down as Jack made a show of giving him the usual once over.

Finally, as Colby had hoped, Jack leaned in closer, "Adjusting ok?" he asked in a low voice.

Colby let a few seconds of silence hang before lifting his eyes.

"Just fine," he said.

Colby had the baton in his hand before Jack could find the trigger of his gun.

* * *

Marie was fishing for her keys as she approached. Colby thought she would walk right into him, but she looked up just short of the apartment steps where he sat. She froze, hand still in her purse, and stared at him. Colby stood and reached his arms toward her. She took a step back.

"Whatever you were told, it's a lie," he said.

She leveled on him, "You mean about you pushing me down the stairs?"

Colby couldn't hide his surprise. "How do you…I thought that night didn't happen for you."

She pushed passed him, "I'm a lawyer, Colby. I know how these things work. Speaking of, this was a stupid place to come if you're looking to hide." She stuck the key in the lock. It was sticky.

"Do you really believe I'd do something like that? Not hide, I mean –"

Marie finally got the door open, but she didn't go inside. "I know what you mean."

"You could go see the remnant timeline with me" Colby said in a rush. "You could know for sure I didn't…you fell. I swear you fell."

"I'd have to experience it from my own point of view," she said.

"Oh," Colby thought for a few seconds. "What about one of the cops? The one who brought me to see it, he –"

"Jack wouldn't have been able to see anything but the anti-time bubble that brought you there," said Marie. "Remnants can only be experienced by those who lived them in the first place." She let a little smirk twitch her lips. "My job might be obsolete otherwise."

Colby sank back onto the steps. "I don't know how else to prove to you I'm not that guy." He looked around. "How long do you suppose before someone shows up to arrest me again?"

"I imagine they're on their way," said Marie.

Her words clicked. He turned and looked up at her, "How'd you know his name was Jack."

Marie sat down next to him. "I knew him in law school."

"That guy has a law degree?"

"I asked him to keep tabs on you, make sure you were ok."

"He has some interesting methods."

A few moments of silence passed between them.

I don't think you're that guy," Marie said.

"But you knew all this time I was in prison for your murder."

"I knew the simulations said if you and I share a timeline there's a seventy-one per cent chance you'll kill me in the next five years. Even if it is by mistake, what would you have me do?"

Fire lit up Colby's brain, but just as quickly it cooled. How could he argue he would never hurt her when he already had?

"You tripped over my shoe," he said. "I tried to grab you, but…"

She put a hand up to stop him. Then she rested it on his knee. "There is a thirty per cent chance they're wrong."

Colby considered that for a moment. "I was so sure when I came here," he said. "But knowing the numbers makes it different somehow."

"I know."

"I don't think I can take the chance."

"I'm not too keen on that myself," said Marie. "There are, however, always second opinions."

Colby turned questioning eyes on her.

"I can arrange to have the simulations run again," she said. "We'll go from there."

*　*　*

Jack looked through the one-way window where Colby and Marie were waiting for the results. One of the timeline techs came in and handed him a pad.

"With the stair incident averted, and the subject in the know, their odds are better for the next year," said the tech. "The guy is likely to be extra careful for a while."

"Until complacency sets in," said Jack.

"Right. Then the numbers all came out the same as before."

Jack rubbed his forehead with his fingertips. "Ok, I'll tell them. Have another officer ready to assist. But I'm guessing Colby won't put up a fight this time."

"There's something else you might want to consider," the tech said.

He leaned over the pad and started swiping though the individual simulation sets. "Seventy-one per cent chance of accidental death at the hands of Colby Watts within five years, until," he got to the set he wanted, "I add some extra inputs." He leaned back as Jack took in what was in front of him.

Jack squinted at the result, not sure he could believe what he was seeing. "You're telling me there's a ninety-eight per cent chance she won't be around long enough for it to matter."

"Right again."

"How did you get your hands on this information?" asked Jack.

"It's what I do."

Jack looked through the glass again, where Marie had her head leaned into nook of Colby's neck. Their hands were squeezed together. "Does she know?"

"Unlikely. It's all probabilities at this point. I doubt she has symptoms yet."

* * *

Colby almost fell off his chair getting up to greet Jack. He came in with a data pad and an expression so blank it must have been well practiced in the mirror. Jack's eyes slid from Colby to Marie, and back to Colby.

"Congratulations," he said. "With your knowledge of possible events, and the extra caution likely to result, there's now a greater than ninety per cent chance Marie's accidental death has been averted across timelines."

Marie erupted into nervous laughter, "Are you serious?" She reached for the data pad. Jack stepped back.

"The tech tells me you're both already in a murky area as far as knowing too much about possible future events. He's asked I don't disclose the details."

Marie's eyes narrowed at Jack, but she didn't push it. Colby was too dizzy to think of anything to say before Marie started pulling him to the door.

"Come on," she said. "I've got a great bottle of wine I've been saving. I can't think of a better night to open it."

Try, Try Again

K.L. Evangelista

I HAVE ALWAYS been ambitious. I work hard for what I want, and I don't give up.

I learnt that from my family. Our motto has always been 'If at first you don't succeed, try, try again.'

That's because we are a family of time travellers. We close our eyes, and concentrate, and with a *blink* we find ourselves back to an earlier moment of our lives.

I have developed a reputation for taking the motto to extremes.

* * *

"A *time traveller*?" the tall blond man sitting opposite Nina forgot himself, and stared at her incredulously. Until he suddenly remembered where he was and who he was talking to.

Tony wasn't sure where this story was going. Perhaps it was an allegory, or perhaps the President was exercising an elaborate joke at his expense. Either way, it was his job to shut up, listen and take notes.

Nina smiled crookedly, and continued her story.

* * *

"I want to be the President," I told my mother at age ten.

Her dark eyes smiled at me indulgently as she handed me a sandwich. "You can be anything you want to be, Nina," she said. And of course I believed her – why wouldn't I? There are no limits to our power.

When I was very young, before I developed my full abilities, I was only allowed to travel by holding the hand of an adult, and then only in very short time-steps. My mother spent a lot of time with my brother and me, explaining why she chose to reverse some things and not others. Later, she let us choose what to skip ourselves, and showed us the direct consequences of our actions. I didn't realise it then, but she was teaching us judgement, and a system of ethics.

My father knew all about our time-travelling powers, but he didn't have any himself. Dad was as American as they came; he used to play basketball in college. He *still* makes us stand for the National Anthem before every game on TV, and he cried when I was sworn in.

"Why do you want to be President, Nina?" He asked my ten year old self, shortly after I'd announced my intention to run.

"Because I want to make a difference," I'd explained. "Like Abraham Lincoln."

Dad nodded, and stretched out his long legs – he was forever trying to find a space for them under the tiny kitchen table. "Abraham Lincoln started out small. Why don't you start by helping out the kids at school."

And so I did. If a kid dropped their sandwich, I *blinked*, and caught it before it could faceplant in the dirt. If a bully tried to mess with another kid, I brought a teacher to the scene before it even begun. I even saved the gym teacher's life, once, by being prepared with a defibrillator just as his heart failed.

That one earned me a special commendation, and a proud smile from my mother. Helping others was what she had taught us to do.

It seemed like there was nothing that I couldn't fix – until the day I found the new girl, Suzie Wilson, sobbing in the library.

We all knew why Suzie startled at loud noises, and was so sad all the time. Her last school had been attacked by a gunman. She was the only survivor from her class.

* * *

"Ah…" said Tony with an enlightened sigh. He could see where *this* was going, at least. "The start of your gun control policies."

"Just so," acknowledged the President, with a graceful tilt of her head.

* * *

"Such a tragedy," I heard the adults murmur to each other, "If only something could be done."

I wasn't supposed to time travel further than a day. We had rules about that. But why were we given these powers, I asked myself, if it wasn't to make a difference?

I *blinked* back a month and rang 911. The operator didn't take me seriously, of course. I was only ten.

I didn't give up. I had the bit between my teeth, and just enough money to catch the bus to Suzie's school.

My mother met me at the front door. "Where are you going?" She asked. Her voice, which was usually as placid as a mountain lake, quivered with all the rage of an ocean storm. I shook my head, and cowered back. My mother had never hit me, but her expression in that moment terrified me to the core.

She had just come from identifying my dead body.

* * *

Tony shifted uncomfortably. The story had taken a dark turn. He could not believe this was a joke. The President was not known for her sense of humour.

* * *

In a calmer moment, my mother held me tightly, and explained that we had a duty of care to stop something terrible if we were close, but that we couldn't help everyone. "Like a doctor," she murmured, stroking my hair tenderly.

"But what about the family motto?" I asked tearfully. "If *you* came back with me…"

"No, Nina."

That was the first day that I met my grandfather. He lived only an hour from us, but to reach him we needed to be signed into a stark white building, and escorted through three locked doors. The sour faced orderlies led us to a small TV room. It smelled like urine and stale cigarette smoke. An old man in vivid red slippers sat on one of the stained couches. He gripped a newspaper tightly in his hand, but did not appear to be reading it – instead his eyes were staring fixedly into space. My mother kissed him gently on the cheek, but he didn't react or acknowledge our presence.

I had always assumed that my grandfather had died before I was born. I hadn't asked questions; like many children I was focussed on the present.

"Papa liked to read the paper," said my Mother. "He looked through their pages every day, so that he could travel back to right wrongs and avert tragedy. But it was too much for him. You can't save them all, Nina."

My grandfather's knuckles turned white, and the newspaper trembled. "You can't save them all," he echoed in a dry brittle voice.

And so we let the timeline run its course.

* * *

That lesson didn't dissuade me from a life of politics; if anything, it served to illustrate the limitations of an ordinary citizen. When school elections arrived I campaigned hard and got Vice President. "I don't know why I lost." I told my mother tearfully.

"Consider the critical point, and try, try again," she advised.

I nodded, dried my eyes and got back to it.

I redid my election speech a dozen times, and then another dozen times for good measure. It was somewhere in the middle of the third dozen that I realised I was wasting my time; the speech *wasn't* the critical point that had tipped the election.

I thought seriously for a long time, before I approached my mother with a proposition. "I'd like to go back and redo the school year."

She was reluctant to let me. "A whole year? Are you sure? Having the same conversations, doing the same classes…it won't be fun, Nina."

But I didn't need fun – I had a goal. I would not be dissuaded, and she relented.

* * *

Sometimes I enjoy the advantage that came of knowing exactly what happens next, but most of the time I want to scream at the predictability of it all. Have you ever been stuck at a family gathering, listening to your elder relatives tell the same stories that you've heard a hundred times before? You nod politely, and try to pretend to be engaged, but really you're just waiting for the moment when you can trade their tired old conversations for something new and exciting.

Repeating a large chunk of time is a little like that. But for me, the need for perfection outweighs my dislike of the tedium.

My brother hardly ever travels. He doesn't like repetition, of any sort. He once made me attend a college party, with the stated intention of meeting every girl there until he found 'the future Mrs. T'.

I did so under sufferance – and on my laptop. I was near the end of my degree, and still trying to figure out how to launch myself into a political career.

At the end of the night, Tiago found me in my corner. He held a surprised brunette by the hand. "Nina, this is Michelle. She takes second year chemistry. Time-skip me back to the beginning of the night and introduce us. Tell me to ask about the sour professor."

I *blinked*. The second time through, I watched wistfully as they experienced that first moment of connection together. He couldn't have time-skipped himself; if he wanted to stay with this girl, he could never skip this moment. You can't build that kind of genuine intimacy if you are too rehearsed. You can build respect, yes, but not intimacy.

I've always thought that is why I've never had any serious relationships.

"Couldn't have done it without you, sis," My brother said, as they left the party, his arm slung casually around Michelle's shoulder.

I watched after them for a moment – but only a moment. Because I'd realised that what I really needed to get into serious politics was a sponsor. Someone to introduce me to the right people.

* * *

I spent a year combing each state paper before I found my sponsor. Unfortunately she was 15 storeys high and about to jump.

"You don't need to jump." I said. The wind that howled around me was frigid, and I shivered in my thin cotton shirt.

"Yes, I do," the girl said, turning her mascara smudged eyes away.

I *blinked*.

"*Why* are you jumping?" I asked, my voice now muffled by the turtleneck of my wooden sweater.

"Because I've done something," her voice was raw, shaky, "Something terrible. It's killing me. I can't do this anymore."

"Guilt…" I surmised, wonderingly. For the first time, the waif looked at me, a glimmer of disbelief pushing through the despair.

"Don't you ever feel guilt?" She asked.

* * *

The President paused. Tony caught her eyes quickly flick to a photo frame on her desk, and away again. He shifted, and arched his neck casually to get a glimpse of the picture, but only succeeded in looking like an idiot.

"Well?" He prompted, "Don't you ever feel guilt?"

* * *

I remember the first time that told my mother I hated her. I must have been around six. I can't remember the cause, some perceived injustice no doubt.

What I can remember is the weight that settled almost immediately in my stomach, like a cancerous tumour. "I'm sorry, Mom…" I said.

She looked at me searchingly "*Are* you sorry, Nina?"

I nodded, and reached out to give her a hug.

She held me back at arm's length. "We don't waste time on guilt, Nina." She said, and let go. I *blinked*, and the words were unsaid. The tumour was gone.

* * *

"Don't you ever feel guilt?" The Governor's daughter asked in disbelief.

"Yes," I told her, "but if it is really that bad, I fix my mistake, and then the guilt goes away."

She hesitated on the edge, wavering. I waited in complete stillness, knowing from experience that if I moved at all she would jump.

Not long after that, the Governor called me into his office and told me he had found me a seat.

The campaign for the Massachusetts senate was difficult. I was inexperienced and working against the incumbent. It took several attempts before I had surrounded myself by the right team, and even longer until I discovered the heart of the state, and how the power flowed through it.

"How many times did you redo this year?" My brother asked at the victory party.

"This is my fifth."

"Goddamn your life is boring," he said, taking a swig of champagne.

* * *

I served my district well, making only minor mistakes that were easily remedied. After re-election, I started focussing my attention on Washington.

"You just can't put a foot wrong." One of my colleagues said at a party function – her tone equal parts admiring and envious.

However even with all my efforts and all the endless variations, I could not obtain a presidential nomination.

My key advisor explained that it was my gun control policies, and asked me to reconsider my stance. But I refused. I still exchanged Christmas cards with Suzie Wilson.

"I want to be the President one day," said a young boy at a school visit. He had vivid blood orange hair, and very determined grey eyes. I could not help but be reminded of myself at that age.

"Me too," I said, "My mother told me that if I work hard and never give up I can be anything I want to be. I'm still waiting to find out if she was right or not." The little boy laughed, but in the limousine on the way back to the office, I had to wonder – had I hit my limit? How many times could I try, before I conceded that what I was aiming for was impossible?

The phone rang, as if my advisor had sensed my doubts, "I think we can get you a nomination," he said. His tone was strained, though, not exuberant, as I would have expected.

"What is it?" I asked.

"The elementary school you just visited – it was shot to hell by some madman. Dozens of kids are dead. You need to turn around and get back your ass back there. Do what you can to help, and make a vow to prevent it from ever happening again. Be fierce."

Do what I can to help? I thought numbly. I spoke to the police and arranged to be the primary spokesman for parents and school teachers. I took the numbers of everyone I spoke to, and promised to personally provide them with updates. I arranged for tea, coffee and blankets for those waiting in the cold. I led a group prayer.

I met the parents of that little red headed boy. I held their hands, and wept with them. I made my vow.

* * *

Tony was growing disturbed. The President's dark eyes were serious. It seemed like...it seemed like she *believed* what she was saying.

He admired the President very much; everyone did. She was preternaturally calm under pressure and had the ability to quickly absorb and understand almost anything that was put in front of her. She was making great changes for the country.

He didn't want to believe that she might be losing her mind.

* * *

My mother visited my office the week after the shooting.

"Why am I still hearing about this shooting in the news?" she asked me bluntly.

"Because it is a horrible tragedy."

"Don't be a fool, Nina," she snapped. "You were there. You had security personnel *escorting* you to that school. You have a duty of care. Why haven't you stopped it?"

I took a deep shaky breath. "I could. I could stop it. But then what about the next one? And the one after that? Do I devote the rest of my life to becoming Batman, preventing every crime before it occurs? What about after I turn into Grandpa? Who will stop it then?"

"You are profiting from the death of children."

"I AM TRYING TO CHANGE THE WORLD." I shouted. But of course, that was too emotional, I seemed unstable.

I *blinked*.

"I am trying to change the world." I said calmly. "Please Mom. Don't interfere. I can do this."

* * *

The President reached towards the picture frame on the desk, and turned it down, flat against the table. Tony scribbled furiously, wishing he could get a look at that photo. He still wasn't sure what was going on – madness or whimsical autobiography – but he knew that he could spin a story out of it.

Tony's pen slowed, and then stopped entirely. *Could* he let this become a story? Really? When she was doing so much good? He looked up, and considered the woman in front of him. She had circles under her eyes, and he was reminded of the fact that no matter what else she was, she was human. "Madame President – why did you share your story with me today?" he asked.

Nina watched Tony wearily. "I suppose...I suppose I hoped that sharing my story with someone outside my immediate family would help, somehow. That it would unburden me." She smiled ironically, 'I've always found that the press are very good listeners."

Tony considered everything the President had told him. He *was* a good listener. "You mentioned President Lincoln earlier, ma'am," he said, "Perhaps one of his quotes, coined from the bible is relevant here: '*A house divided against itself cannot stand.*'"

Nina nodded. She stood up to escort him out.

Tony stood as well. He held her eyes as he deliberately placed his notes on her desk, leaving them behind.

At the door, Nina reached out impulsively and shook his hand. "Thank you, Tony." His hand was large, and very warm, and as he smiled at her with his bright blue eyes, she felt a moment of connection.

This was a kind man, Nina thought. This was a man she would like to get to know better. She *blinked*.

"Cancel the appointment with the reporter." Nina told her secretary, "And ring my mother instead."

* * *

It had been two years since Rosetta had visited her daughter at work. Now Nina's office was oval – such a strange concept and so much more oppressive than the regular kind of walls. Rosetta inspected the paintings, the seal in the carpet, the bust of Abraham Lincoln. She lingered for some time at the photo that stood in prominent position on Nina's desk.

It was of a young boy with bright red curly hair.

When Rosetta finally looked up, she could *see* the moment that her daughter's heart buckled from the pressure. Rosetta opened her arms and Nina practically fell into them, burying her head into her mother's shoulder.

When Nina's sobs subsided, Rosetta gently pushed her back a little so that she could see her face. Nina's eyes burned with a terrible anguish, and an even more terrible determination. *Exactly like her mother's eyes*, that is what the newspapers said during the campaign. But to Rosetta, they were more like her grandfather's eyes. He, too, always said he could save the world. But the world broke him first.

"We don't waste time on guilt," Rosetta murmured. She let go of Nina's hand and stepped away. She stared at her daughter, silently pleading with her to see sense.

Nina stood straight back and unblinking, determined to see this madness through.

Rosetta *blinked*.

* * *

"I want to be the President," Nina said at age ten.

Rosetta handed her daughter a sandwich and considered her words carefully. "Politics is a dirty business," she said at last. "If you want to make a difference you should think about becoming a doctor. There is nothing more noble than saving a life."

Nina nodded thoughtfully.

All for Bellkins

Tony Genova

NOBODY WAS INTERESTED in time travel once we achieved immortality. Well, immortality isn't the best word – someone could still die if their body suffered damage beyond repair. Cancer, heart disease, degenerative diseases – we solved those once we broke the cellular code. Time travel, however, was just too risky. There was no guarantee of success, and no way to know how the human body would handle it. There were too many variables to control for all of them. Why risk health and wellness to travel in time when there was a virtual guarantee of long life and prosperity going forward?

A small group of the brightest minds worked on it anyway. Once we determined you couldn't go forward in time, half of the group dropped out. I don't know what they were thinking – where would you go? Contrary to what some philosophers might say, the future didn't exist yet. You couldn't pinpoint it and figure out how to get there. Impossible.

Given 250 years to work on it, we knew we could figure out how to go backward. Most of us were in it for the scientific challenge. I lobbied a reclusive trillionaire for the funding and land to work on, and we built our research facility there. I was able to take control of the project. The others assumed it was for the glory. I let them assume.

First, we figured out how to send inanimate objects back in time. Then we sent a small cat. After that, a monkey. Once we figured out how to manipulate the timestream, it wasn't difficult to increase the scope. The brilliance of it was that anyone could have done this years ago if they looked at it the right way. Creating the bubble and manipulating the properties on the surface was the trick. Anything inside the bubble was subject to the same manipulation. Build a big enough bubble and anything could go back in time.

I insisted I be the first human test. It was my drive that had fueled this project, I should have the glory of being the first man to not be subject to the brutality of time's march. Of course, there was a catch. Isn't there always? Once you go back, there was no going forward except through the normal movement of time.

We designed the test to send me one minute back in time, to a secure location elsewhere in the facility. They didn't realize I had put an override deep in the code. I was going back 280 years. To them, I was a glory hound. They didn't suspect my true motivation.

I ended up exactly when I intended to. The where was tricky – too many variables, remember – but I got it close enough. I landed gently. We designed it to ease down using gravity, and it performed perfectly. I targeted what I knew to be an open area 50 miles outside of the city. It was the only way to be sure that my margin of error wasn't going to be deadly. I walked the ten miles to the nearest public transportation, which would take me into the city.

Our research group wasn't sure how to deal with the possibility of interacting with our past selves. I knew I wouldn't have time to waste, so in the years before leaving I changed my appearance enough that I didn't think I'd recognize myself. I was sure my past self wouldn't be looking for me, so I didn't worry about it much.

Once I got to the city, I went right to the park. I knew it well, and it looked exactly as I remembered. The swing set was there. The swing was there – third swing in. Now, I had to wait a week. I waited 280 years, I could wait another week.

It wasn't difficult to blend in, and I knew where I could stay and eat. It was a regional vacation week, and my parents were out of town. I knew how to get into to their condo, and I laid low. I even knew that Wednesday morning my past self would come by to check on the place. That week's timeline etched itself into my mind so many years ago.

The regional vacation week is what destroyed my life to begin with. All schools and most places of employment were off for the week. That was the only reason my wife and daughter were on that swing that day.

I figure I had three options. First, I could prevent my wife and daughter from ever getting on the swing. Second, I could stop the businessman from walking through the park, or at least delay him. Third, I could figure out who the shooter was and stop him before this ever got started.

Any of those options could solve everything. The problem with the third option is that the authorities never figured out who the shooter was. They were able to track the car via CCTV, but it didn't have proper registration and was only disguised to look like a self-driving model. Humans hadn't driven cars in decades. Someone figured out how to modify a car so a person could drive it, and make the people in the car disappear before they could be identified. It shouldn't have been possible, but with enough funding anything was.

I spent the week trying to call or otherwise communicate with the businessman. His people told me threats to his life were routine, and unless I had credible information they didn't want to talk to me. What could I give them that wasn't just hearsay at this point in time? I couldn't say I knew for sure he will be shot. Even if they did believe me, saying that makes me the obvious shooter. I couldn't come out and say that if he avoided that park, he would likely live long enough to live forever. People didn't understand the impact of immortality yet.

The only solution was to make sure Sandy and Bella didn't get on that swing.

I knew I wouldn't have listened to a crazy sounding stranger no matter what the story. I'd have to make my play at the park. That was the only way to be sure.

I got to the park two hours before the incident. The sun was shining in the clear blue sky, the same as in my memory. The fresh cut grass left a sweet scent. A scent that made me sick for 280 years.

I walked over to the swing, sat on it, and began to rock back and forth. Thirty feet to my right was the bench I'd be sitting on later today. Twenty feet in front of me was the metal fencing that would refuse to block the bullets. I felt like pure chance had destroyed my life, and I was only going to have one chance to bring it back.

I sat there for two hours. I knew the timeline better than I knew anything else in my life. In five minutes, I would walk in with my family via the entrance to my right.

I would sit on the bench, and Sandy and Bella would sit on this swing. Four minutes later, the businessman would walk in from the opposite entrance. He would stroll with his bodyguards directly through the park on his way to a lunch meeting. He would only make it to the swing set, and it would only take him a minute to get there.

At 11:30 I saw them – well, us – walk in. Bella was holding Sandy's hand. If I could keep them by the bench long enough, I'd have done my job.

As my past self sat down on the bench, I crouched down in front of Bella, holding a flower I picked from the other side of the park. My hair was cut and colored differently, and I had facial hair now. Even though I was roughly the same age, I had to hope neither Sandy nor my past self recognized me.

"Hi honey," I said, "this is for you." I handed her the flower. She looked at me with her deep brown eyes, eyes I hadn't seen in 280 years. Eyes I saw every night in my dreams. I saw her face light up.

She reached out for the flower, and when she took it she threw her arms around my neck. I began to sob.

Sandy reached for Bella's arm and tugged her away. "Bella, come with me," she said in that tone she used when she was deadly serious. I tried to hold on, but at the same time I felt someone grab my shirt and pull me up by the neck.

The person grabbed my shoulder and spun me around. It was me. I turned my head to the left. I could see the businessman and his bodyguards entering the park.

"What are you doing?" past me said.

"I'm sorry," I said, "I just thought...Bellkins...your daughter...she was – is – adorable."

He looked over at Sandy and Bella, who were walking over the swing set, and then back at me, He hadn't let go of my shoulder yet. I was still crying. His face sparked with a look of recognition. He let go of my shoulder and back off a step. "Wait a second, who are you?"

I heard tires screech nearby. I didn't remember that part. Self-driving cars don't screech their tires when accelerating. I turned and looked, the businessman was twenty feet from Sandy and Bella.

"I'm sorry, there's no time," I said and pushed my past self onto the bench. I ran over to the swing set.

"Sandy!" I heard from behind me.

As I got near the swing set, I could see the terror in Sandy's face. It broke my heart. I hesitated for a split second. Then I pulled Bella from her lap and pushed her off the swing backward.

I held Bella tight in my arms and began to run. I only made it two steps before someone tackled me. I began to lift myself up off the ground, but my past self was already pulling me up.

Shots rang out. A UZI. The bullets sounded like rapid hail on a roof, punctuated with the pings of those that hit the metal bars of the fence. I felt a number of rapid tugs on my side. Was Bella pulling at me? No, it wasn't Bella. I fell to the ground next to my past self. The gunfire hit him as well.

I couldn't move. Both Sandy and Bella were in my field of vision. Neither one had gotten up off the ground.

"Daddy! Daddy!" I heard Bella say. She jumped up and reached for her Dad. Sandy screamed my name and ran over, but she didn't run to me.

The last thing I saw was the businessman sitting up. He shook his head and looked around. He then opened his shirt and inspected his bulletproof vest.

My vision faded. "Daddy? Daddy, are you OK?" I heard Bella ask, though it sounded distant.

The last thing I felt was a small hand grabbing mine. A familiar hand.

Murder or a Duck

Beth Goder

GEORGE CALLED OUT, "Mrs. Whitman, you have a visitor."

Mrs. Whitman strode from her workroom, her white hair skipping out of its hairpins. She straightened her work skirt, massaged her bad knee, then hurried down the hall.

"George, what's happened to the lamp with the blue shade?"

"To which lamp are you referring?" George smoothed down a cravat embroidered with tiny trombones. Improper attire for a butler, but George had never been entirely proper.

Mrs. Whitman examined the sitting room in further depth. The blue lamp was gone, as were the doilies, thank goodness. An elegant table sat between the armchair and green sofa, which was infused with the stuffy smell of potpourri. Behind the sofa hung *The Roses of Wiltshire*, a painting that Mrs. Whitman had never cared for, despite its lush purples and pinks and reds. And the ficus was there, too, of course.

Mrs. Whitman pulled out a battered notebook. George's trombone cravat indicated she was in a timeline where he was courting Sonia. A good sign, indeed. Perhaps, after six hundred and two tries, she'd finally landed in a timeline where Mr. Whitman would return home safely.

Consulting her charts, she circled some continuities and crossed out others, referring often to an appendix at the back. The notebook was worn, its blue cover faded. And it was the twelfth one she'd had since starting the project.

George cleared his throat. Mrs. Whitman didn't even glance up. "You have a visitor," he said.

"George, I need to ask you a few questions."

George sighed, but made no comment.

"Has Mr. Whitman returned from his trip?" She always asked this question first, in the hope that George would direct her to the study, where she'd find Mr. Whitman reading a book or knitting socks.

"He's due back sometime today."

That was what George always said. Mrs. Whitman had been through it over and over again; she knew it was useless to organize a search until the evening, when everyone else would begin to worry.

Undeterred, Mrs. Whitman asked her control question. "Did you wear your navy suit anywhere this year?"

George raised an eyebrow, but said, "I wore my suit once to the Lacklustres' evening ball, and again at the horse show for troubled teens."

If the Lacklustres were holding a ball, then they hadn't gone bankrupt yet, which meant she was in a timeline where Winston Tuppers hadn't revealed Mr. Lacklustre's banking fraud. And the horse show for troubled teens never appeared without a corresponding tea party later in June. Mrs. Whitman flipped busily through her charts.

"Which tea cakes are they selling at the market on Quill Lane? Chocolate? Lavender? Orange and cream?" she asked.

"There is no market on Quill Lane. It was torn down last year," George said, a rare look of concern on his face. "Are you sure you're feeling quite all right?"

"Just one more question," said Mrs. Whitman, making a mark in her notebook. "Is it Sir Henry waiting in the foyer?"

"No," he said. "Mrs. Lane requests your attention."

Mrs. Whitman snapped the notebook closed. If Mrs. Lane was visiting, it could only mean one thing. She was either there to kill Mrs. Whitman or sell her a duck.

But if the market on Quill Lane was gone, perhaps she was truly in a new timeline. And if it was a new timeline, she needed to observe it, so she could cross it off her list.

"Shall I send Mrs. Lane in?" asked George.

Mrs. Whitman nodded, plopping down on the ugly green sofa. She flipped through her notebook, then sketched out a few calculations.

The convergence point, for once, was clear. To discover Mrs. Lane's intentions, she only needed to determine if the park on Stanton Street still existed. If the park was there, murder. If not, the duck.

Mrs. Whitman was double checking her maths when Mrs. Lane glided into the room. Impeccably dressed, as always, Mrs. Lane ran her hand along a blue and eggshell scarf, which hung upon a white dress of the latest fashion. She clutched a large handbag.

"Harriet, dear. So good to see you," Mrs. Lane said, smiling all the while.

Mrs. Whitman stuffed the notebook into a large pocket in her skirt. George guided Mrs. Lane to the armchair across from Mrs. Whitman. The two ladies exchanged pleasantries while George fetched the tea things.

Mrs. Whitman chose a lemon tart, then saw the jam pastries on the tray. She set down the tart, her appetite gone. Jam pastries had been Mr. Whitman's favorite. She pushed the thought out of her mind.

"Large bags must be in fashion," Mrs. Whitman said. "Shall I ask George to put yours in the coat room?"

"No need to bother. I'm quite comfortable with it here."

Mrs. Whitman gave an inward sigh. Several timelines back, Mrs. Lane had hidden cyanide in the purse, then dropped the poison daintily into Mrs. Whitman's tea. Mrs. Whitman clutched her teacup closer. She'd just have to make sure Mrs. Lane didn't have the opportunity.

"As much as I do love your company, Mildred, I suspect you've come here for some purpose," Mrs. Whitman said.

"Always business with you. Can't two friends just have a chat?" Mrs. Lane smiled a sharp smile.

"You must forgive me. At my age, I do tend to hurry along," said Mrs. Whitman, taking a sip of her tea. "Wonderful weather we've been having for picnicking. Have you been to the park on Stanton Street? I hear the tulips are all in bloom."

Mrs. Whitman leaned forward, hoping that the park wasn't there, and she was in for the duck after all.

"I'm not familiar with that park, but I'm never in that neighborhood, you know." Mrs. Lane nibbled her tart. "I did have the most delightful picnic at the park on Thindon Row."

Mrs. Lane launched into a description of the park, including which flowers were in bloom, and which walks offered the most shade, and how Miss Abba had organized a game of tennis without a net right on the grass. Mrs. Whitman was surprised that she didn't describe every petal on every flower.

Mrs. Whitman was plotting another way to find out about Stanton Street Park when George rushed into the room.

"Urgent phone call for you, madam," he said, cutting off Mrs. Lane mid-description. A most improper butler, indeed. Mrs. Whitman gave him a quick smile.

"I'll take it in the workroom," Mrs. Whitman said.

As Mrs. Whitman strode down the hall, she noted that the little end table by the bookcase was missing, and that a painting she had never seen before, some abstract nonsense with red squares, hung in the downstairs bathroom.

She went the long way around, so she wouldn't have to see the photographs of Mr. Whitman in the north hallway: that boating trip to Scotland, her thirty-fifth anniversary celebration, and worst of all, the dear portrait that Mrs. Whitman had taken herself, with Boris smiling up at her in his gentle way.

The workroom was as she'd left it. Gears from her latest Discrepancy Converter rested on a large, flat table, and the Quantum Stabilizer was whirring in the corner. A faint smell of oil hung in the air. She patted the Quantum Stabilizer fondly, then picked up the phone.

The phone call wasn't so urgent after all, just Mrs. Kempton from next door complaining about the state of the lawn.

"It's really quite overgrown," said Mrs. Kempton. "If you'll just let me give you the name of my gardener –"

"Mr. Whitman and I rather enjoy tending to the garden ourselves," said Mrs. Whitman. "But we've been quite busy these past few weeks. In fact, I have a visitor at this moment."

After ringing off, Mrs. Whitman strode into the hallway, where she found George waiting for her.

Mrs. Whitman looked at George in alarm. "George, if you're here, who's watching Mrs. Lane?"

"Watching Mrs. Lane?" George's brows knotted.

"Didn't I tell you never to let Mrs. Lane alone in the house, especially near the tea?"

"No, Mrs. Whitman. I don't believe you did."

Mucking about in multiple timelines did make it difficult to keep track of what she'd done in each one, although she wouldn't put it past George to simply forget such a thing.

"Nevermind that, now." Mrs. Whitman paused and peered down the hall. "I'm afraid I have a rather strange task for you."

"A strange task from you, madam?"

"None of your cheek, George." Mrs. Whitman straightened a hairpin. "Could you go down to Stanton Street and have a look about? Tell me if there might be a park along that walk?" Stanton Street was close enough. He shouldn't be gone more than half an hour. And then she'd know for sure. Murder or duck.

When George departed, Mrs. Whitman returned to the sitting room. Mrs. Lane sat with her hands folded in her lap, looking entirely proper even when alone. Her bag had moved several inches, and now rested directly in front of her feet.

"So sorry to keep you waiting," Mrs. Whitman said.

"I've been admiring your lovely decor," said Mrs. Lane. "You must tell me about the painting behind your sofa, with the marvelous little roses."

Mrs. Whitman described the history of *The Roses of Wiltshire*, which she had never liked much but which Mr. Whitman had bought at what he assured her was a bargain. And it did impress the neighbors. The thing was worth a fortune.

"I do so like the way the roses open up on the side, almost as if they were screaming," Mrs. Lane said, then took a sip of tea. "So lovely. Is it black tea? Perhaps Lapsang?"

Mrs. Whitman glanced at her teacup. Hadn't it been a few centimeters to the right of the sweets tray when she'd left the room?

"I believe it is," said Mrs. Whitman.

"You must not like it very much," said Mrs. Lane. "You've barely touched yours."

As the conversation progressed, Mrs. Whitman avoided her tea. Many times, she found herself fighting against the muscle memory of sixty-five years. It was almost as if her hand reached out on its own accord. As Mrs. Lane droned on about tulips and cross stitching and her niece's trick elbow, Mrs. Whitman found her hand wandering again and again toward her cup.

"Have I told you about the ride I took along South Mathilda Lane?" Mrs. Lane asked.

"I don't believe so," said Mrs. Whitman. She reached for her cup of tea, grasped the handle, then snatched back her hand so swiftly that she upset the sweets tray. A rain of scones and jam pastries fell to the ground.

"How clumsy of me," said Mrs. Whitman. "I'll just call to George." Then she remembered that she'd sent George out. But it had already been half an hour. Why hadn't he returned?

Mrs. Whitman bent to pick up a few of the sweets, then abandoned the rest, not wanting to put out her knee crawling about on the floor.

"What an awful mess, but it's past tea time, anyway," said Mrs. Lane, shoving the scattered sweets to the side with her foot. "And speaking of time, I suppose I should tell you why I've paid a visit. The Mallard Society is holding their annual charity auction, and they are seeking donations of several premium ducks to add to their auction list."

So it was the duck, after all. Mrs. Whitman smiled. "And what wonderful work the Mallard Society does. I'd be happy to help in any way I can."

"I'm so glad to hear it. It's for such a good cause," said Mrs. Lane, starting in upon a detailed description of the Mallard Society, how it was founded by Eunice T. Brotherford of Scotford on the Dale, the work they'd done in Pointips Row to clean up the river, and other highlights from the organization's illustrious fifty-two year history.

"Such a fascinating organization," said Mrs. Whitman, interrupting the story of how Sandra Pellings had chased a prized duck straight through Bell Park. "Put me down for five ducks."

"I'm surprised to find you so interested in the Mallard Society," said Mrs. Lane, her smile slipping a bit. "I thought your charity work was limited to the Targaine Art Society."

Mrs. Whitman froze. She couldn't have given that Society speech in this timeline. Mrs. Lane had tried to sell her a duck. The events were all wrong.

"My interests are wide ranging," Mrs. Whitman said, hoping she was wrong, hoping that Mrs. Lane would switch topics.

Mrs. Lane put down her teacup and took a breath. The look on her face was a little unbalanced. "I'm afraid I still haven't quite forgiven you for your little speech at the Art Society bicentennial celebration. It's caused me quite a lot of problems."

Mrs. Whitman cursed inwardly. She should never have made that joke about the *Dapper Violinist*.

"I assure you," said Mrs. Whitman, "I had no idea that the painting was not an original."

"Of course not," said Mrs. Lane, growing more agitated. "You simply implied it was a fraud in a room full of art critics and dealers." She picked up her bag and set it on her lap. "Do you know, I had a buyer all set up? But then he wanted to look into the provenance more closely."

Mrs. Lane reached into her bag. "I paid seven million pounds for the thing. *The Dapper Violinist*. He's not dapper at all, is he? Ghastly painting. All those swirls. All that pink. But I was promised that in a couple years, it would go for more. The buyer was offering eleven million."

"If I had known any of that," said Mrs. Whitman, "I would never have made that joke. But surely you must have heard it before, that *The Dapper Violinist* was too beautiful for Milliany Spark to have painted it. You've seen the other stuff she's done. So abstract. Brilliant, in its own way, I suppose. But not much to look at."

"Well, your one little remark cost me," Mrs. Lane said, fixing her gaze firmly on Mrs. Whitman. "It's not even the money that bothers me, although certainly one can never have too much. But yesterday I heard Mrs. Vallis telling Mr. Rall that I shouldn't be allowed back at the Society meetings. And then she made a joke about my taste in art. Mrs. Vallis." She said the name with particular venom. "And Mr. Rall laughed. I suppose you didn't anticipate any of that, either."

Mrs. Lane looked behind Mrs. Whitman, to the painting on the wall. "That painting, *The Roses of Wiltshire*, have you had it appraised, recently?"

"Why do you ask?" asked Mrs. Whitman.

"It must be worth quite a bit. The artist is well known, isn't he." Mrs. Lane smiled an entirely unpleasant smile. "I believe I'm going to take that painting. I already have a contact who will fence it for me."

"It's all yours," Mrs. Whitman said. "I've never liked the thing."

Mrs. Lane paused. She took a sip of tea with the hand that wasn't in the bag. "I don't believe that's enough, after all."

Mrs. Lane pulled a strange object from her bag, a transparent box filled with gears and springs, humming quietly. A mini Electron Calculation Converter, known among engineering circles as 'The Hieronymus Bosch,' perhaps for its triple geared structure, or perhaps for its complex and sometimes unintelligible inner workings. Although Mrs. Whitman recognized the machine, the design was unfamiliar.

This had certainly never happened before. What a strange timeline.

"You're always fiddling with things like this, aren't you?" asked Mrs. Lane. "So here's a gift for you. Perhaps you'd like to take a look?"

"Even from here, I can see that spring is set back at a dangerous angle."

"Oh, yes. That's the idea. But you needn't open it. I only need to undo this clasp, and point the machine in your direction to release a little piece of metal I've placed inside. It will be enough to put the thing in your hands, afterward." Mrs. Lane shook her head. "Done in by one of your machines. How tragic."

"Mildred," Mrs. Whitman said, "isn't this extreme? I assure you, I never meant you any harm."

"You know, I've never liked you, Harriet." Mrs. Lane clasped the machine in both hands. "Always with your eccentricities. Your bad manners. The inappropriate jokes. And we've all had to put up with it because of your important connections."

"You're one to talk," said Mrs. Whitman, the indignity of it all pushing past her fear. "Your grandmother was chairman of the Goldstone Bank."

"It's a shame that Mr. Whitman will suffer," said Mrs. Lane. "He's never been unkind to me."

"Boris?" Mrs. Whitman leaned forward and dug her hands into the sofa. "Then you've seen him? Recently?"

"He was walking through Lovedale Park just this morning." Mrs. Lane stared. "Why, you look as though I've said something strange."

Mrs. Whitman felt renewed vigor. She'd finally done it. After six hundred and two tries, she'd found a timeline with Mr. Whitman in it.

But now that she'd found him, Mrs. Whitman was soon to be expunged from this timeline, and perhaps, all timelines.

Mrs. Lane moved her hand to the machine's clasp. "Any last thing you'd like to say?"

Looking at the means of your immediate demise and keeping your mind enough to speak is no easy task. But Mrs. Whitman had faced many challenges in her life. She'd been the first person to row all the way to Charlestown in a kayak, she'd worked as a mechanical engineer at Vanton Prime and Gasket well past retirement age, and she'd once eaten twelve lemon tarts in one sitting, to win a bet. Worst of all, she'd weathered the disappearance of Mr. Whitman, never giving up hope that she would one day find him. Mrs. Whitman had never a little thing like fear get in the way of her goals.

Mustering all the grace that she could, Mrs. Whitman said, "You've never struck me as someone to do things improperly, Mrs. Lane."

Mrs. Lane kept her hand on the clasp, but held still. "Whatever do you mean?"

"Haven't you read *The Rules of Murder for Well Mannered Ladies*?" said Mrs. Whitman. Before Mrs. Lane could answer, Mrs. Whitman plunged on. "The first rule is that one must never attack while sitting. It's bad for the digestion."

"I don't care about your rules," Mrs. Lane said, but she took her finger off the clasp. "In any case, everyone will think your death the result of an unfortunate accident."

"You underestimate the deductive skills of the police. When they discover this was an act of ill intent, they'll report that you committed a crass murder, a common murder. The type of murder that you'd read about in those old three shilling newspapers."

"I'll be long gone by then," said Mrs. Lane. "It's no matter to me."

"Your reputation will be all that's left," said Mrs. Whitman. She stood up from the sofa, as if nothing at all was wrong, but slowly so as not to startle Mrs. Lane. "Now, I'm standing, and you'll stand, and then it will be proper. Like a duel."

Mrs. Lane rose and faced Mrs. Whitman. She repositioned the machine. "But now I might hit the painting."

"We'd best move, then," said Mrs. Whitman, working furiously not to glance down, even a little bit. "I'll just step this way." Mrs. Whitman held her hands out and moved slowly around the table.

As Mrs. Whitman shimmied to the left, Mrs. Lane shifted a corresponding amount. "Just a little more," Mrs. Whitman said.

Mrs. Lane set her foot down on a jam pastry, one of the ones that Mrs. Whitman had spilled earlier in the afternoon when she'd upset the sweets tray.

Several things happened at once. Mrs. Whitman ducked. Mrs. Lane slipped on the jammy pastry and crashed to the floor. Her hand threw open the clasp, and a jagged piece of metal discharged into the ugly green sofa.

The loudness of the sound stunned them both. Mrs. Whitman was the first to recover. Her bad knee ached as she scrambled up from the floor.

Mrs. Lane rose, her blue and eggshell scarf disarrayed, her carefully coiffed hair coming just the slightest bit undone. Her face looked a bit wild.

The two women faced each other. Finally, Mrs. Lane asked, "I don't suppose you'd be good enough to extend your original offer?" She pointed to *The Roses of Wiltshire*.

"You've just tried to murder me," said Mrs. Whitman.

Without another word, Mrs. Lane snatched the teapot. Mrs. Whitman tensed, ready to meet another attack, but Mrs. Lane flung the teapot at *The Roses of Wiltshire*, staining half the painting brown and tearing a hole in a corner of the canvas.

"Now no one will want to buy your painting either," said Mrs. Lane. But she didn't stop there. Mrs. Lane grabbed the butter knife and slashed at the canvas, tearing bits of roses out. Pink, purple, and red rained down in front of Mrs. Whitman.

She made no attempt to stop Mrs. Lane, but she moved to shield the ficus.

When the police burst in a moment later, that was how they found the situation. Mrs. Whitman poised in front of the ficus. A piece of metal embedded in the sofa. Mrs. Lane abusing a work of art. The tea things everywhere.

It took some time to get everything straightened out.

Mrs. Kempton, who had been nosing about in Mrs. Whitman's garden, had heard a mysterious noise and called the police. (Mrs. Whitman had to concede that nosy neighbors did have their uses, in some particular situations.)

Mrs. Lane denied any wrongdoing but was hard put to explain why she was destroying *The Roses of Wiltshire* or the presence of an odd and deadly machine covered in her fingerprints. With a few words from Mrs. Whitman, the situation became much clearer.

After the police had carted Mrs. Lane off, Mrs. Whitman sat down on the ruined sofa, gathering her thoughts.

The door closed with a bang. Wondering if the police had come back with more questions, Mrs. Whitman entered the foyer.

"Look who I found strolling in Avent Park with Sonia," said Mr. Whitman, pointing to a guilty-looking George.

"Boris!" Mrs. Whitman cried, throwing her arms around him.

"I must apologize for my tardiness," said George. "Only I hadn't seen Sonia for a week or more, and it seemed rude just to pass her by."

"And I'm sorry too, for not coming right in," said Mr. Whitman. "My train was early, and the weather was so pleasant that I had a bit of a walk."

"Never mind that now," said Mrs. Whitman, holding tight to her husband.

"My dear," said Mr. Whitman. "What's this? I've only been gone a couple of hours."

"But to me, it feels like years and years," she said.

Mr. Whitman kissed his wife on the cheek, then looked behind her into the sitting room and gasped. "What's happened to *The Roses of Wiltshire*? It's all stained and tattered. My word, is that a bit of metal impaled in the sofa?"

Mrs. Whitman released Mr. Whitman, but kept hold of his hand. "There's so much I need to tell you, my dear. But first, let's go to your study, and you can pick out a book, or knit a pair of socks, or do anything you like at all. And I'm going to be right there beside you."

And she led a puzzled Mr. Whitman down the hall, past the photographs of their thirty-fifth anniversary, never letting go of his hand.

Cattail Heart

Kate Heartfield

MY MOTHER told me, "You are my heart."

"I don't want to be a heart."

"I don't mean a heart like a lump of bloody meat. I mean a heart like the centre of a thing. Like the pith at the base of a cattail. If someone peeled all of me away bit by bit, what would be left would be you."

"I don't want to be a heart," I said.

I must have been about seven because she died soon after that. I wanted to lay cattails on her pale pine coffin before they put it in the ground.

Maybe my mother would have stopped the white people from taking me with the other children to the Indian Industrial School. My father was a good man but he wasn't as fierce as my mother.

For two long days we rode in a bumpy cart, the younger ones sniffling and us older ones sitting very tall and not looking at each other. When I got there they changed my name to Jane. They were going to make all us Indian children forget we were Indians. They were going to turn me into a proper farmer's wife.

For a long time, I thought the cart came for me because my mother died. I was just garbage after that. What does a dead woman need with a heart?

* * *

Miss Smith came to the school early in the summer of 1893. I had been at the school five years.

Every night of those five years, while I lay in bed pretending to be asleep, I wondered why I didn't just jump off that cart and run. It wouldn't have made any difference but I could have tried.

Sometimes I would shut my eyes up tight and picture myself jumping down off that cart and just running. All the other children watching, cheering me on.

As if I could remember it a way it didn't happen, just by trying hard enough.

On the night Miss Smith came, I rammed my fists hard into my eyes to stop myself from seeing. I wished I could stop myself from smelling because my hair and my hands stank like pig manure. The principal had smeared it on me, because I was bad, and told me I would be feeding the pigs for the next month.

"Because pigs like garbage and that's what you are," he said.

"Yes," I said.

The windows were open because of the heat. The peeps and croaks of frogs almost drowned out the whimpering in the bed next to mine, and the creaks of the floorboards under the teachers' feet.

Then a string of sharper sounds: the clop of hooves and the squeak of a cart wheel. Voices, outside. The big door opening and closing. Feet on stairs.

It was the new teacher, Miss Smith. I knew because the other teachers had been expecting her all day: The replacement for a mean old thing who had died of the same kind of fever that killed my mother. And a half-dozen students in the last month.

I didn't know anything about Miss Smith yet and I didn't dare to hope she would be any better than the rest.

I rolled over, burrowed my head under the thin pillow and told myself a wendigo story. For five years, every night, I told myself the wendigo stories my mother taught me. My mother and I both liked to be a little scared but not too scared.

Later I wondered whether that was what brought Miss Smith: me telling myself wendigo stories under the blanket.

But of course that was only a child's notion. Miss Smith brought herself. She came sniffing. She was curious.

* * *

She did not frighten me at first. In fact we all preferred Miss Smith to the other teachers, and not only because she was new and young. She was the least strict of any of them. She hardly ever strapped one of us and when she did she would go to the privy after and come out with a blotchy face. Even though she had long dark hair like me, her skin was papery with freckles on the nose and it held redness for a long time.

Half of every day except Sundays we sat in class and learned to read and write and do arithmetic. I was good at that part. Miss Smith smiled at me when I got my sums correct. She liked math best, she told me. I knew she meant she liked me best because I was good at it too.

The other half of the day, the girls scrubbed the floors, cooked the meals, washed the laundry and fed the animals. The boys did carpentry and worked in the print shop. I wanted to work in the print shop too so I did my chores badly and I got punished.

A few weeks after Miss Smith came, I was carrying the slop buckets out to the pigs when I felt someone watching me. I looked all around, just using my eyes so as not to let on that I knew I was being watched. I put my buckets down and knelt to scratch my ankle so I could twist my head around and look. No one.

I walked all the way to the sty and back, kicking my feet, taking my time, because it was safer outside than in, at that school.

Someone was watching me. I looked all around. Nobody but the chickens.

I was almost back to school when I stopped and did a full circle, turning around slowly, watching.

Miss Smith stood between the barn and the sty, staring straight at me. She was thin, like a little hungry tree standing against the sky.

That was when I first suspected she might be a wendigo.

In my mother's stories the wendigo was so thin its white bones were on the outside. It was so thin that you had to be looking at it face to face, or you might not see it at all. If you caught it off guard you might see a star on its forehead. I never saw a star on Miss Smith's forehead though.

A wendigo is thin because it is hungry. A wendigo began as human but became a monster when it ate humans for meat. It was cursed to starve and feed, to eat and eat the flesh of humans and never be satisfied, to curse itself again and again with each new crime.

"Remember," my mother said. "You can be born human and become a monster. You might not even know you've become a monster. It's easier than people think."

* * *

They taught us to fear, God and other things.

I saw my father once a year. He looked at me as if I were a stranger. He looked like someone was teaching him to fear too but I didn't know who it could be.

That summer when Miss Smith was at the school, she came one night with another teacher and took me out of the dormitory and they told me my father died. His heart just stopped. Hearts give out, they said. They get tired.

I nodded. Miss Smith cocked her head and watched me until the other teacher told me I could go back to the dormitory.

* * *

Miss Smith used to take me into Selkirk and even Winnipeg sometimes to help buy supplies. She would ask me questions, not about arithmetic but about other things: my parents, my home. When I did not know the answers or did not want to say, I said what she wanted to hear.

One day Miss Smith took me in a canoe to Selkirk for a treat, just the two of us. She gave me an apple and I gnawed it down to the core before I threw it in the river.

I paddled in the front. Miss Smith called out to me to switch sides.

She called out in Anishinaabemowin.

Miss Smith spoke our language badly. I paused for just a heartbeat and the water dripped off my paddle but then I thrust it in again and I didn't switch sides. I thought it was a trick. She asked me again but this time she spoke in English and I switched sides then just like she asked.

* * *

The next time we were in the canoe, a week or two later, she called out in my language again. It was hard to understand what she was trying to say but I think she was trying to tell me she was pulling the canoe over to the side. There was a little inlet there, thick with reeds where the air buzzed with insects.

It wasn't a trick, she said: I could speak the Ojibwe language if I wanted. I spoke English.

"Turn around to look at me, Jane," she said and I did, twisting around on my knees, resting my paddle carefully on the thwart so that it made the smallest possible noise.

"Look at these cattails," she said. She pulled one out. She had to use two hands because it was thick and slick with mud. Her long fingers got dirty.

"Look, did you know you can eat the inside?" she peeled away green strips from the base and threw all of it away except the smooth white heart. She held onto the gunwale and leaned forward, stretching out her arm to hand it to me but I did not take it.

My mother called me her heart.

Miss Smith sat back on her heels and chewed the cattail pith, looking at me all the time. She put her long white hand in front of her mouth and spit out little pale flecks. I guess there were some hard bits.

"Can you keep a secret, Jane?"

I just looked at her; my name wasn't even Jane. I had a lot of secrets already and I was only twelve.

"We're related, you and I are. We are part of the same family."

She looked like a white woman to me but I nodded anyway.

"I want you to know something. Because you always look so forlorn, little thing. I want you to know that one day, you will be a grandmother, and you will carry an eagle feather, and all of your children and grandchildren will have pride because of you. You will keep the language alive in the family. You will be the heart of the family, for years and years and even after you die, your great-great-grandchildren will know your name and..."

Her face was whiter than ever but her cheeks were red and she talked so fast she choked on her words and had to stop, shaking her head. She picked up her paddle again and pushed us out from the reeds and cattails.

Later on, when we could see the school near the shore, she said again, from behind me, "Look at you, a little strip of a girl, and one day, the heart of a great family. You will make change. You will force them to change. Everything depends on you."

I decided she was crazy. How could she know what I would be like as a grandmother?

And who wants to be a heart anyway?

* * *

I tried to avoid her as much as I could but you could not avoid anyone in that place. She kept asking for me to help her with errands but I pretended to be sick. Finally they threatened to beat me for malingering so I went with her to Winnipeg. It was autumn then, and little pinpricks of snow melted on our cheeks.

She drove the cart and I sat next to her, looking away, at the trees and farmhouses. I can still feel the rough wood of the side of the cart printing red lines in the palm of my right hand. It was not too far to the store where we were going so she talked even faster than she usually did.

She had a special machine, she told me. A time machine. It could take us to her time. I didn't know she had her own time.

"The late twenty-first century," she said, grinning. "How many years is 2067 into the future, Jane?"

"One hundred and seventy-four."

I should be dead by then. But I could visit, Miss Smith said, using her special machine. So long as I didn't talk to anyone because it was naughty what we were doing. And so long as I promised to come back.

"I can visit the twenty-first century?" I asked. I knew by then she wasn't going to punish me and she liked it when I asked her questions. "But why?"

"Oh, Jane, you'd love it. It's a wonderful place. So much better than what you're used to. The disease that killed your mother is gone, just gone. You can fly, up in the sky, in great big machines, any time you feel like it. You can find out anything you want to know just by asking machines that we have in our bodies. And you wouldn't have to go to a place like this. People understand, in my time, that these schools are evil places. You could go to a real school. You could do whatever you wanted."

"No, I mean why do you want me to go, Miss?"

"Oh," she said, and flicked the reins. It did not matter because that horse only went as fast as it wanted but I didn't tell her that.

Then she said, "Well, I guess because I owe you so much. Do you remember, Jane, when I told you that we are part of the same family?"

Of course I remembered. I wasn't stupid. I nodded.

"Well, you are my ancestor. Your children have children and they have children and… on down to my parents and me. That's why I came back. I wanted to see you in person, you understand?"

"Yes," I said, but I only understood the words, not her.

"But there's more than that. You were a strong woman in a difficult time. Your sacrifices and your strength are the reason I'm here today. So I want you to see that, to know that the world does get better, in large part because of people like you. It's only fair, isn't it, to know that what you do in this life, all this suffering, that it matters? That it has a purpose? That everything works out for the best in the end?"

I thought for a while.

"But what would happen if I went into the future, the time with the no disease and the machines and the good schools and all, but I didn't come back to this time?"

She smiled like she did when I got all the right answers on a test.

"Nobody's really tested that yet. This is all new, this time travel. I think, if you never came back in time to have your children, well, I would just cease to be at some point."

"Would I die if I tried to stay there?"

"Well, that's an interesting question, Jane. I think you would be fine. Because we need each other in different ways, don't we? I need you to be my ancestor. Always. But you only need me to come get you once. The me who exists as your descendant already exists for at least one cycle of time, and came back to get you at least once."

She must have thought I looked confused.

"You can understand, Jane. You're a bright girl."

"Yes." I did understand.

"Put it this way: my 2067, when I came from, that can't be changed. But if we travelled to 2067 together we would create a new 2067, by going back together. And I think that would be all right for both of us, so long as you eventually come back. If you stayed there past the age of nineteen, when you met your husband, well, that would take us – well, Jane, what date would that take us to?"

"To 2074."

"Right. Good girl. If you stayed that long, there would be no one here to bear my ancestors, so after that new 2074 there might suddenly be no me."

"Ah," I said.

"So obviously you have to come back before you turn nineteen, to start the family, to be the great woman you are going to be."

"Yes," I said.

"But I don't think a day's visit can hurt either of us."

"Yes."

When she said 'machine' I thought she meant something big for us to go in but she just jabbed her fingers at what looked to me like a little bar of black metal and the world changed around us. I felt something sucking on me and letting me go, like gravity was trying to eat me, like all the lines of the world were warping.

And just when I thought it was going to hollow me out from the inside, I blinked the tears out of my eyes and saw the world had changed.

* * *

She thought I was bright enough to answer her questions but not bright enough to make choices.

Sometimes, when I am in a happy mood, I think maybe Miss Smith expected me to run. Maybe she was even giving me a chance to do what I should have done when I was seven: just run.

Most of the time, I think she just assumed I would do what she said, like a good little Indian girl.

* * *

I ran away as soon as we got here. I haven't seen Miss Smith since. If she is looking for me she isn't very good at it.

I changed my name. I'm not Jane anymore. I lived on the sidewalks and in the alleys for a while and some of that was not much better than the residential school. Some of it was worse. But I found good people eventually, even a few people who speak my language and nobody gets in trouble for it now.

I'm nineteen now and in my second year at the University of Manitoba. I am taking math so I can work on time travel. I want to understand it better. Better than anyone.

I went to the archives and the library. I know everything that happens to Jane after 1893. She is like a character in a story to me. I know what happens to her three babies who live. I know how all seven of her dead babies die. I do want to have babies. I want to have three babies who live, not three babies who live and seven who die.

I won't graduate, though, if I go back in time to meet the man I'm supposed to marry, so I can become the heart of Miss Smith's family. So she can feed off of my strength and my sacrifices, gobble me right up and say thank you after.

Miss Smith might not have known she had a wendigo spirit but she had one all the same. She could only live by consuming me, the heart of the family. Feeding on hearts is a risky way to live. Hearts give out. They get tired.

* * *

I mark my twentieth birthday with my girlfriends. I cook Indian tacos and we walk down Corydon Avenue at midnight screeching with laughter. I tell them stories of the wendigo, stories my mother used to tell me because I liked to be scared when I was a little kid. I don't tell my girlfriends where I'm really from. I just say "the reserve" and they don't ask questions.

* * *

I go back to the archives and I look for my name. The only record of me now is from the Industrial School. They recorded my disappearance.

No dead babies for Jane, now, and no live ones either. Jane only lived for four years, between the time she didn't run away from the cart and the time she did run away from Miss Smith.

There are a few people I wish could have existed. My grandson – Jane's grandson – would have been a great drummer and singer. Jane's great-grand-daughter would have been a writer. She would have written about Jane. She would have been famous for her anger and her love. She would have been named Jane, after me.

I grieve a little for that woman I was supposed to be. And for others. Maybe I'm the wendigo now, I think sometimes, when I can't sleep. Maybe I'm eating people up, possible people, just so I can live.

I tell myself it doesn't matter to anyone that Miss Smith never existed. Lots of people never existed. Infinite people. She is one possibility that didn't become. A probability wave that collapsed.

She only lives now in my memory and if I squeeze my eyes shut and pretend hard enough, it's almost like she never existed at all. It's almost like neither of us did.

But still I feel something like grief for the wendigo woman. It is strange to think that those long white hands, that freckled nose, will never exist. She was kind to me in her way. She did not like to beat us and she let me come here, to her time, to visit. She admired me. She wanted me to be a grandmother, to show the world that all my suffering did not bow my head.

* * *

I am twenty years old. It is 2075 and I will be a grandmother one day. I do not need suffering to teach me how to hold my head.

Eternity and the Devil

Larry Hodges

EVER SINCE graduate school ten years ago, I'd been obsessed with solving 'GUT,' the Grand Unified Theory of physics. It would unify the four forces of physics – gravity, the electro-magnetic force, and the strong and weak nuclear forces – into one equation. Physicists since the time of Einstein had tried and failed. Solving this problem would be my contribution to humanity, and why I was still at the lab at MIT, scrawling equations on a blackboard at 2:30 a.m. despite another throbbing headache.

Unfortunately, I was getting nowhere. Depressed, I collapsed into a lounge chair. My work was at a standstill, with no progress in a year, not even a semblance of a breakthrough. With no papers to publish, no progress to report, my time at MIT was coming to an end. The department head had as much as told me so. Not a threat, just reality.

Depression overwhelmed me. I was licked.

"I would sell my soul to solve this problem," I muttered to myself. Except I wasn't the only listener, as the smiling Devil himself appeared in a flash of cigar smoke, with contract and pen in hand. The cigar smoke smelled of…well, sulfur and brimstone.

"Dr. Virgil Nordlinger, I believe we can do business," said the Devil, talking through a cigar in a Bronx accent – with perhaps a bit of British and Jamaican? He was an ordinary looking man in a gray business suit and black tie, short and chubby, perhaps 50 years old. He had a tie tack shaped like a tiny pitchfork and wore an old-fashioned derby hat. His piercing eyes stood out – one sky blue, the other bright gold.

"I have here the standard contract, personalized for you. You'll solve the Grand Unified Theory of physics, and get the standard 50 years of good, healthy life, followed by the standard eternity in Hell. Wha'da'ya say?"

"Uh," I began, rubbing my eyes. "You're supposed to be…?"

"Look, I know what you're thinking," said the Devil. "I'm used to people finding this hard to believe. Does this convince you?" There was another burst of cigar smoke, and the ordinary businessman was replaced by…the Devil.

He was seven feet tall and husky, and as popularly pictured – red, with ram-like horns and a pointy tail flicking back and forth. His eyes were still blue and gold.

In a deep, booming voice, the Devil said, "Now you believe. Of course, I can take on other appearances, but this seems to be the most convincing." Rolling his eyes, he added, "It's sort of a stereotype, don't you think?"

There was another burst of cigar smoke and he was back to his business persona. "Now, I'm a rather busy man. You ready to deal? Wha'da'ya say?"

Selling one's soul to the Devil isn't something you should consider lightly. But I'm an idealist, and solving GUT would really move mankind forward in understanding the universe. I was ready to sacrifice myself for the good of science and humanity. But why settle for the Devil's first offer?

"I think I'd like to have more than 50 years," I said. "And a few things besides GUT." I was about to outline other scientific breakthroughs I wanted, but the Devil interrupted.

"Sorry, very little of this is negotiable," he said. "You see, there are lots of others I do business with. There are only so many things I can give away and I have to spread them around. You get GUT, a major prize, but I have to keep other scientific discoveries for other deals. Otherwise, I wouldn't have anything to bargain with. And the 50 years – I got tired of negotiating that all the time, so I'm firm on that."

I talked him into adding a provision that would cure my migraines, and my name was soon on the contract. I signed with a blue ballpoint. The Devil, a lefty, extended an index finger, revealing a long, claw-like fingernail. He jabbed it into the palm of his other hand and signed in blood.

"It's a couple minutes before 3:00 a.m., February 27, 2010," said the Devil, tipping his hat at me – revealing two small growths coming out of the top of his forehead, where the Devil's horns had been. "I'll give you the extra two minutes and we'll call it 3:00 a.m. I will see you in 50 years!"

"*Wait a minute!*" We both turned to see the lab's secretary, Beatrice Summers, at the doorway. Had she been eavesdropping?

She and I were opposites in every way imaginable. I was tall but rather out of shape from deskwork; she was short and fit. I had dark brown hair; hers was sandy blond. I wore whatever was comfortable and cheapest; she wore designer clothing, which didn't hide the fact that she was about as plain-looking as one gets, nothing to look at. The odd looking mole on her chin didn't help. Other than the mole, I'd rarely noticed her.

"Sorry, but I've been listening. I want a deal too!" She hesitantly stepped into the room, eyes wide and staring at the Devil.

"No, you don't want to…" I began, but the Devil waved a hand and my mouth jammed shut.

"I believe we can do business," he said to Beatrice, as another contract appeared in his hand. They bargained briefly, and soon the Devil had another signed contract in hand. Beatrice would get 50 years of actress fame and a simple mole removal. In both transactions, he acted in a professional manner, other than shutting my mouth.

"Was that wise?" I asked her afterwards, when control of my mouth was returned and the Devil had left.

She looked back with excited eyes. "This is my dream," she said. "This is my shot and I'm taking it. Just as you are."

I tried to convince her that sacrificing oneself for the good of mankind is different than doing it for selfish reasons, but she disagreed, saying "Same result for both of us, right? Eternity, fire and brimstone?"

How long is eternity?

* * *

The years went by quickly, and the Devil followed both the letter and the spirit of the contract. I solved GUT, and we now have an almost complete understanding of how the universe works. The ramifications were stunning – everything from space travel to renewable energy. We solved food problems – grow it on the Moon, send to Earth with cheap energy. Pollution is a thing of the past. Even traffic and car accidents are gone – who needs a car when you can fly to work in a personal transporter powered by clean fusion power? All this because we now understood 'how things worked.'

After solving GUT, I moved on to temporal studies. I left MIT and switched coasts to join the research staff at Caltech in Pasadena, California. I progressed rapidly in those studies, as GUT gave us a new fundamental understanding of time itself. The prize money from both Nobels went to charity as I had no need of anything beyond my lab. I became pretty famous, and must admit I enjoyed that.

I followed Beatrice's career as she took over the box office as the number one actress in the world, with one blockbuster after another. Even as she aged, her appeal remained as she moved from glamorous roles in her youth to more mature ones later on. The Devil had done an incredible job on her. With a few subtle changes in her appearance, and newly-found acting skills that were the envy of her peers, she truly was the greatest in her profession.

Of course, what was 50 years of fame compared to an eternity of Hell? I too had sold my soul, but I had sacrificed myself for the good of others, a contribution that would last forever. I had come to accept my fate, although as the years went by I had a growing sense of uneasiness. I buried myself in my work, and the years went by far more quickly than I would have believed.

And then, out of the blue, the phone rang, on the 49th anniversary of our 'Deal.' It was Beatrice. Her voice was shaking. "Virgil? Is that you?" she asked.

"Beatrice?" I was caught off guard, but quickly recognized the voice. I'd just seen her in *Rising High*, another Oscar performance where she played the grandmotherly heroine who sacrificed her life to save her family. In the end, she'd bravely smiled as she met her fate, but a tear rolled down her cheek. Was such sacrifice worth it? If for the right reasons? "It's me."

"Virgil, it's been 49 years since we last saw each other." Technically, I'd seen her often on the big screen, but that's not what she meant.

"I know," I said. "One more year to go."

She asked if we could meet, and we arranged to do so the next day at a local restaurant. She'd fly in on her personal jet.

She showed up, bodyguards discreetly keeping their distance. She was in disguise – a wig and large hat pulled over her eyes. She joined me in a back table I'd reserved. In the dim light, no one would recognize her, so she removed the disguise. She was now about 70, but looked 50.

"It's been a long time," she said.

"Yes. A long time," I agreed. "And time is what we're running out of."

"What are we going to do?" she asked. But I had no answer for her.

Over steak and salads we discussed the past 49 years. "You know, after the first few years, you realize fame isn't really anything," she said. "It's just a lot of people who know you because of what you did. And I didn't really do anything. I didn't earn anything." Her eyes teared over.

"I didn't earn anything either," I said. "The Devil did it all."

"At least you did it for others," she said. "I did it all for myself. And now look what I've done to myself!" Now she was crying, her bowed head in one hand. I put my hand on her other hand. Both our palms were sweaty.

"Back then, I thought I did it for others," I said. "But now I realize that I did it for the same reason you did. For fame and fortune. I was driven back then, and when I failed, I grabbed at my only chance – just like you." And it was true – all these years I'd convinced myself I'd done it all for mankind. I had been fooling myself. I was no better than Beatrice.

I shook my head and continued. "He – Satan, the Devil, whatever, he just gave us what we wanted. Not help for mankind, not acting ability. Just fame and fortune, disguised as what we thought we wanted. We grabbed at it. We were both weak."

She looked up. "Is there any hope for us?"

I could lie, but what good was raising her hopes? There wasn't anything I could say but the truth. "No."

She nodded her head and squeezed my hand back. "I'm glad you can be honest with me. If we only have one year left, let's make the most of it."

We began seeing each other.

She retired from acting and bought a mansion in Pasadena to be near me. She wanted to move into my more humble home, but it just wasn't practical. We'd be mobbed by her fans. The mansion, with a security team, gave us security so we could live our final year in peace. So I moved in with her.

It was strictly platonic. Forty-nine years ago we had seemingly been opposites, but those differences now seemed minor. We were thrown together by our common experiences and our common future. We enjoyed each other's company. If we were going to spend eternity together in Hell, we might as well get started now.

As we moved into the final year, I put more and more hours into my temporal studies, trying to avoid thinking about the unavoidable. But that was impossible, and often I was grief-stricken. How could we have made such a deal?

They say a person in grief goes through five stages – denial, anger, bargaining, depression and acceptance. I went through all five. The Devil ignored me when I pleaded out loud for him to appear to renegotiate our deals, but thought I heard fleeting laughter coming from somewhere. That led to depression, and finally acceptance.

* * *

I made the breakthrough with six months to go. Until then, my temporal research had been theoretical. But recent work by myself and others led to another possibility: a working time machine. Others were working on it, but it was years away. I didn't have years.

With that in mind, I moved to a sixth stage – determination. I began work on the time machine, which I kept secret from all but Beatrice, working mostly nights when others weren't around.

I had been wrong to tell Beatrice there was no hope.

The last six months could only be described as hell on earth as I pushed myself to the brink of human endurance to complete the time machine. I had a firm deadline to meet. Despite my apparent advanced age, I had great energy. True to the deal with the Devil, I was in perfect health – I looked 85, but physically and mentally I was still 35.

I still made time for Beatrice, and she often visited me at the lab, but we both understood what my priority had to be. Seeing her gave me strength.

With just days to spare, the time machine was complete. It vaguely resembled an old-style Volkswagen, with a domed top. The ceiling and sides were mostly glass, so you could see in all directions. It had a door on each side and a storage area behind the two passenger seats. Beatrice had painted the non-glass outsides bright red – perhaps appropriate if we ended up in the burning fires of Hell?

I tested it, moving forward a few minutes at first, and then hours into the future. Time travel was essentially instantaneous, at least to the time traveler, so you could travel as far into the future as you wanted within seconds. The more you turned the time dial, the faster you moved through time. It was set exponentially, so time travel speed escalated rapidly as the dial turned. Digital readouts showed where you were in time and how fast you were moving through it.

One of the implications of GUT was that time only moved forward – you cannot go back, which explains why we aren't inundated with time travelers from the future, as Stephen Hawking had pointed out. So we couldn't go back and cancel the deal. But we could move forward as far as we wanted, at least to the end of time. From GUT and other discoveries, we knew the universe would continue to expand for another 97 billion years, and that time would essentially end at that point when the universe collapsed backwards to a single point, a singularity. The Devil said I'd be in Hell for eternity, but that could not be true since time would end in 97 billion years. So, if necessary, we'd travel to the end of time. Surely Hell and the Devil could not last to the end of time? If they did, how would the Devil find us in the vast expanse of time?

* * *

The appointed time approached: 3:00 a.m. on Feb. 27, 2060. We had to make sure to leave before that time. Shortly before midnight, I was prepared, with several months' supply of food and water for two and other supplies in the storage area. I had no family or even close friends – I'd devoted my life to science and the advancement of mankind – so I'd leave little behind other than the lab.

Beatrice also had no living relatives and was leaving her wealth to various charities. Not wanting to think about it, she'd put off making these arrangements until the last minute, and so spent her final night on this earth with lawyers. They charged her double-time for the late-night session, but we wouldn't need the money where we were going. She said she'd meet me at the lab at 2:00 a.m. How I wish I could go back and change that time!

At midnight, the Devil appeared in the lab, three hours early, dressed in his business suit. Sulfur & brimstone cigar smoke spread through the lab. "It's time," he said, with no preamble. No gloating, just very professional.

"It's only midnight," I pointed out. The Devil only raised his eyebrows and explained my mistake. What a blunder! I was in California – a different time zone from our deal of 50 years ago, at MIT, in Cambridge, Massachusetts, where it was now…3:00 a.m. The appointed hour.

"And so," the Devil concluded, "I believe I have fulfilled my end of the contract. It's time to go." As he spoke, I slowly approached the time machine – and quickly got inside, slamming the door, almost catching my billowing lab jacket. I started up the controls and reached to turn the dial. The Devil merely watched, chuckling.

"If you are done with your…toy…we really need to get going," he said. "And so…*I send you to Hell*!" he boomed. As he said this I turned the dial.

The time machine began to whir, and as I watched, the Devil began to fade from view. I was leaving him behind in time! Or…was I being sent to Hell? Had I been too slow in turning the dial?

The Devil must have realized what was happening, and with a growl, grabbed the time machine in his now rapidly disappearing arms. He was back to his full Devil persona, seven feet of spiteful red demon. But he was too late. Once started, nothing could move through the time distortion between the time machine and the outside world in either direction. As long as I was moving through time, I was safe from the Devil. But it also meant you couldn't see in or out while time traveling.

The lab faded out, and after moving two hours into the future where I hoped to pick up Beatrice, I brought the time machine to a halt…somewhere else. I could see that I was no longer in the lab, so the Devil had done something before I'd turned the dial. But where was I? And what had happened to poor Beatrice, who must have shown up at the lab after I'd left, hours late due to my blunder?

It took a moment to adjust to the dim light. I could hear screaming, and as my eyes adjusted I saw the source – and wanted to pluck my eyes out to stop what I saw.

There were rows and rows of people as far as the eye could see. They were spread out evenly in lines, in a grid, about one every ten feet, naked. Each had a foot tied to a stake in the solid rock ground. And what was happening to these people was…a nightmare. They were being burnt alive from flames that came out of the ground from the base of the stakes. They struggled and writhed, but the ropes held them firmly in the head-high flames that licked over their bodies.

The screaming was unending, a symphony of overwhelming agony and torture.

Overhead was a ceiling, perhaps 40 feet up, which looked to be made of luminescent rock, which cast a dim red glow.

The time machine had landed in a square made up by four of these stakes, but only three of them had people tied to them. The fourth stake was ominously empty, with just a rope tied to it, a bare stake in a sea of writhing bodies.

As I surveyed the human devastation, thinking it could not get worse, it did. One of those next to the time machine was none other than Beatrice. Like the others, she was screaming in agony, tied to a stake…her payment for 50 years of fame. She saw me through the window, and raised her arm toward me, pleading with her eyes. Flames licked over her body and she convulsed in agony, screaming horribly. Others that were nearby also saw the time machine and seemed to plead for help – but all were firmly tied to the stakes in the ground. Many tried to break free, but the ropes and stakes were impervious to their attempts as well as to the surrounding flames.

"Beatrice! Hold on – I'll save you!" I cried. I opened the door and started to get out. I was almost overwhelmed by the gust of hot air and the smell of sulfur and brimstone.

The Devil suddenly appeared and saw me. I jumped back into the time machine as he started to raise his arm and say something. I slammed the door closed and turned the dial again. He'd teleported me to Hell from my lab because I'd been too slow to turn the dial, and I wasn't going to give him another chance. The Devil faded away.

How far should I go? Once the time machine was moving through time, it took no power to continue moving since temporal momentum carried it – Newton's first law, applied to time. Moving a hundred years took the same power as moving five minutes because how fast you moved through time didn't affect power consumption, since temporal velocity is relative. Starting or stopping is what took power. I had enough battery power for perhaps a couple dozen starts and stops.

I needed to save Beatrice. I moved five hours into the future. Beatrice still stood next to the time machine, still screaming in agony, as were all the others. She looked up, and again stretched her arms at me, pleading. But again the Devil appeared in a puff of smoke, and before the smoke had dissipated I turned the time dial again.

I did a number of other stops, each hours or days apart. There didn't seem to be any change in the few seconds I had to look each time before the Devil appeared, forcing me to leave. Perhaps if I moved much farther into the future? I had no choice. I tried not to think about what Beatrice was going through.

I moved 10 years into the future. Everything still seemed the same. Beatrice and the others were in the same spot, still screaming in agony, covered in flames. *Had she and all the others been tortured, screaming and in agony, for 10 years?* I trembled at the thought. I had to save her, bring her into the time machine.

Again the Devil appeared, and feeling horrible, I left quickly, again leaving Beatrice and the rest to her fate. How many were being tortured and for how many years? Thousands? *Millions?*

I had to jump further into the future in hopes of getting away from the Devil and rescuing Beatrice. Somehow he could always sense my arrival.

I jumped one hundred years, one thousand years, one million years, and still no change. There was nothing I could do for her. Each time I noticed the empty stake still there, waiting, amid the tortured, screaming multitudes. A million years of torture…I couldn't imagine it. Each time the Devil appeared within seconds, and I had to leave.

I jumped millions, then billions of years into the future – still no change. I went 98 billion years in the future – a billion years after time itself should have ended with the universe now a singularity.

Apparently time and space are different in Hell. There was no change. Beatrice, and all the others as far as I could see, were still in agony, still being burnt alive unendingly for 98 billion years. The empty stake was still there, a vacancy waiting to be filled.

The Devil appeared and I took off again, tears streaking down my face at my powerlessness. *How long is eternity?*

* * *

I was nearly out of power from all the starts and stops. I would soon be stuck, either in Hell, unable to start, or traveling forward in time for all eternity, unable to stop as I slowly died from hunger or thirst. The latter would be infinitely preferable. And yet…perhaps there was a way….

I brought the time machine to a stop a trillion years in the future. I glanced at the power gauge – just enough, I hoped, for one more start. Outside, there was still no change. I waited.

Within seconds the raging Devil appeared. And now I found myself jammed inside my time machine with him.

* * *

"You've given me quite a run in this toy of yours. But your eternity in Hell begins *now!*" He motioned at the empty stake. "I've been holding a reservation for you, as I'm sure you've noticed. A trillion years – who would have thought! I'm impressed." He grinned.

"What happens now?" I asked, as if I didn't know. My lab coat was soaked with sweat, and not just from the heat.

He roared with laughter. "I miss conversing with you humans. Mankind died out a long time ago, and we haven't had any new arrivals in nearly a trillion years. It's been a long time since I had anyone sane to talk to!"

A trillion years must be a long time, even for the Devil, I thought. Or was it? "What are you going to do with me?" I asked.

The Devil roared with laughter. "You still don't get it!" he said. His hot, sulfurous breath filled the time machine, his face just inches from mine, his horns ripping into the time machine's roof.

"You understand eternity merely on a scientific level," he continued. "A trillion years is a trifle compared to eternity. Eternity goes on for trillions of years, then quadrillions, then quintillions. You can go a nonillion years, a secillion, a googol, even a googolplex – and even then, it's not a *fraction* of eternity." He smiled. *"Eternity is forever!"*

I began to tremble uncontrollably.

"I see you are beginning to understand," the Devil said. "As a physicist, one who studies time, you above all should understand what eternity is."

He stared into my eyes, his face just inches from mine, his hot breath overpowering me. I had to avert my eyes. "There's about ten billion of them – quite a collection, wouldn't you say? It's not a matter of who's good or evil, it's whoever I can work out a contract with. I collected them for eons before and after your time, one by one, each with their own deal. They've been tortured for a trillion years, and *it's not even the beginning for them*."

Ten billion for a trillion years, and I was about to join them. I gathered my courage. "Why do you do this?"

"Because I can and want to." He smiled broadly. "I find it interesting and, let's face it, amusing. You'll find all sorts here. Lots of dictators – Stalin was smart, got to live to an old age, and now realizes he wasn't so smart. Hitler was stupid, I got him on technicalities and brought him early. The place is full of politicians, artists, musicians, moms who wanted their kids to be successful, scientists like yourself, and lots and lots of professional athletes! Who needs steroids when they can have *Me*?"

Despite the situation, I had to grin inwardly at that. "What happens to me now?" I asked. "Do I get some personalized torture? Or does everyone just burn in Hell like these people?"

"You've only seen this section," the Devil said. "Actually, there are many others. There's this myth that 'evil-doers' will be punished in some way that matches what they did when alive. There's no connection – I just put 'em wherever I feel like it, and I keep it systematic so it's easier to run. There's the drowning section, the shark section, the electric section – thank you, Mr. Edison! And I think this section is fine for you. Which is why I've kept that reservation for you so long."

He again put his grinning face just inches from mine, his hot breath burning into me. "I've been doing this for a trillion years and eternity hasn't even *begun*. And so, now that you know just how long eternity truly is...*it's time for you to join them*!" He turned away and beckoned at the empty stake. Orange flames burst out of it. The rope tied to it leaped into the air, an animated snake waiting for its prey.

With the Devil looking away, I saw my chance and grabbed the time dial. I turned it, then quickly stepped out the door on the left. As the time machine faded from view, I saw the Devil try to leap out the open right door. However, with the time machine again moving through time, the time distortion made movement back and forth impossible. The Devil was too late, bouncing off the time distortion as if hitting a brick wall.

With that final leap forward, there was no more power. The time machine would move forward in time forever. *Bon Voyage!*

As the Devil faded into the future, the screaming faded away as well. The flames went out. The ropes fell away.

By the light of the luminescent rocks in the ceiling I saw people as far as the eye could see taking their first non-tortured breath in a trillion years.

A trillion years of burning hadn't left a physical mark on them, but their minds? As the people stumbled away from their stakes, their faces dribbled with drool, all I heard was incoherent mumbling.

Was I stranded in Hell with ten billion insane residents? Despair overwhelmed me and I fell to the ground, pounding my fist into the hard rock. Exhausted, I collapsed into a dreamless, hopeless sleep.

* * *

"Virgil?" I woke to the sound of my name, and opened my eyes. Beatrice was leaning over me. Behind her were dozens of others looking on. "Are you awake? Can you hear me?"

I sat up too quickly and almost knocked her over. I was overwhelmed. As I quickly discovered, she was sane!

Perhaps whatever it is that kept their bodies unchanged for a trillion years also kept their minds unchanged. It took a few hours, but nearly all of the billions were sane, the same physically and mentally as they had been when they first entered Hell.

Neither Beatrice nor any of the others have any memory of their trillion years of torture. I don't think Beatrice really believes me when I tell her how much time has passed and what she went through, but it's enough that she's here.

While they were tortured, the billions of humans here were essentially immortal, but now that that's over, we're all human again, with human frailties and human lifespans. I prefer that to the alternative.

We have a new frontier, one never imagined before. The Devil mentioned there were other sections, such as a drowning section and a shark section. That meant, at the least, water and seafood. Many of us are about to go search for these necessities, and to begin to explore this new land. Perhaps we'd settle it, and there would be future generations, a thriving civilization in Hell. I just don't know.

As to the Devil...

...*how long is eternity?*

Wireless

Rudyard Kipling

"IT'S A FUNNY THING, this Marconi business, isn't it?" said Mr. Shaynor, coughing heavily. "Nothing seems to make any difference, by what they tell me – storms, hills, or anything; but if that's true we shall know before morning."

"Of course it's true," I answered, stepping behind the counter. "Where's old Mr. Cashell?"

"He's had to go to bed on account of his influenza. He said you'd very likely drop in."

"Where's his nephew?"

"Inside, getting the things ready. He told me that the last time they experimented they put the pole on the roof of one of the big hotels here, and the batteries electrified all the water-supply, and" – he giggled – "the ladies got shocks when they took their baths."

"I never heard of that."

"The hotel wouldn't exactly advertise it, would it? Just now, by what Mr. Cashell tells me, they're trying to signal from here to Poole, and they're using stronger batteries than ever. But, you see, he being the guvnor's nephew and all that (and it will be in the papers too), it doesn't matter how they electrify things in this house. Are you going to watch?"

"Very much. I've never seen this game. Aren't you going to bed?"

"We don't close till ten on Saturdays. There's a good deal of influenza in town, too, and there'll be a dozen prescriptions coming in before morning. I generally sleep in the chair here. It's warmer than jumping out of bed every time. Bitter cold, isn't it?"

"Freezing hard. I'm sorry your cough's worse."

"Thank you. I don't mind cold so much. It's this wind that fair cuts me to pieces." He coughed again hard and hackingly, as an old lady came in for ammoniated quinine. "We've just run out of it in bottles, madam," said Mr. Shaynor, returning to the professional tone, "but if you will wait two minutes, I'll make it up for you, madam."

I had used the shop for some time, and my acquaintance with the proprietor had ripened into friendship. It was Mr. Cashell who revealed to me the purpose and power of Apothecaries' Hall what time a fellow-chemist had made an error in a prescription of mine, had lied to cover his sloth, and when error and lie were brought home to him had written vain letters.

"A disgrace to our profession," said the thin, mild-eyed man, hotly, after studying the evidence. "You couldn't do a better service to the profession than report him to Apothecaries' Hall."

I did so, not knowing what djinns I should evoke; and the result was such an apology as one might make who had spent a night on the rack. I conceived great respect for Apothecaries' Hall, and esteem for Mr. Cashell, a zealous craftsman who magnified his calling. Until Mr. Shaynor came down from the North his assistants had by no means agreed with Mr. Cashell. "They forget," said he, "that, first and foremost, the compounder is a medicine-man. On him depends the physician's reputation. He holds it literally in the hollow of his hand, Sir."

Mr. Shaynor's manners had not, perhaps, the polish of the grocery and Italian warehouse next door, but he knew and loved his dispensary work in every detail. For relaxation he seemed to go no farther afield than the romance of drugs – their discovery, preparation packing, and export – but it led him to the ends of the earth, and on this subject, and the Pharmaceutical Formulary, and Nicholas Culpepper, most confident of physicians, we met.

Little by little I grew to know something of his beginnings and his hopes – of his mother, who had been a school-teacher in one of the northern counties, and of his red-headed father, a small job-master at Kirby Moors, who died when he was a child; of the examinations he had passed and of their exceeding and increasing difficulty; of his dreams of a shop in London; of his hate for the price-cutting Co-operative stores; and, most interesting, of his mental attitude towards customers.

"There's a way you get into," he told me, "of serving them carefully, and I hope, politely, without stopping your own thinking. I've been reading Christie's *New Commercial Plants* all this autumn, and that needs keeping your mind on it, I can tell you. So long as it isn't a prescription, of course, I can carry as much as half a page of Christie in my head, and at the same time I could sell out all that window twice over, and not a penny wrong at the end. As to prescriptions, I think I could make up the general run of 'em in my sleep, almost."

For reasons of my own, I was deeply interested in Marconi experiments at their outset in England; and it was of a piece with Mr. Cashell's unvarying thoughtfulness that, when his nephew the electrician appropriated the house for a long-range installation, he should, as I have said, invite me to see the result.

The old lady went away with her medicine, and Mr. Shaynor and I stamped on the tiled floor behind the counter to keep ourselves warm. The shop, by the light of the many electrics, looked like a Paris-diamond mine, for Mr. Cashell believed in all the ritual of his craft. Three superb glass jars – red, green, and blue – of the sort that led Rosamund to parting with her shoes – blazed in the broad plate-glass windows, and there was a confused smell of orris, Kodak films, vulcanite, tooth-powder, sachets, and almond-cream in the air. Mr. Shaynor fed the dispensary stove, and we sucked cayenne-pepper jujubes and menthol lozenges. The brutal east wind had cleared the streets, and the few passers-by were muffled to their puckered eyes. In the Italian warehouse next door some gay feathered birds and game, hung upon hooks, sagged to the wind across the left edge of our window-frame.

"They ought to take these poultry in-all knocked about like that," said Mr. Shaynor. "Doesn't it make you feel fair perishing? See that old hare! The wind's nearly blowing the fur off him."

I saw the belly-fur of the dead beast blown apart in ridges and streaks as the wind caught it, showing bluish skin underneath. "Bitter cold," said Mr. Shaynor, shuddering. "Fancy going out on a night like this! Oh, here's young Mr. Cashell."

The door of the inner office behind the dispensary opened, and an energetic, spade-bearded man stepped forth, rubbing his hands.

"I want a bit of tin-foil, Shaynor," he said. "Good-evening. My uncle told me you might be coming." This to me, as I began the first of a hundred questions.

"I've everything in order," he replied. "We're only waiting until Poole calls us up. Excuse me a minute. You can come in whenever you like – but I'd better be with the instruments. Give me that tin-foil. Thanks."

While we were talking, a girl – evidently no customer – had come into the shop, and the face and bearing of Mr. Shaynor changed. She leaned confidently across the counter.

"But I can't," I heard him whisper uneasily – the flush on his cheek was dull red, and his eyes shone like a drugged moth's. "I can't. I tell you I'm alone in the place."

"No, you aren't. Who's *that*? Let him look after it for half an hour. A brisk walk will do you good. Ah, come now, John."

"But he isn't –"

"I don't care. I want you to; we'll only go round by St. Agnes. If you don't –"

He crossed to where I stood in the shadow of the dispensary counter, and began some sort of broken apology about a lady-friend.

"Yes," she interrupted. "You take the shop for half an hour – to oblige *me*, won't you?"

She had a singularly rich and promising voice that well matched her outline.

"All right," I said. "I'll do it – but you'd better wrap yourself up, Mr. Shaynor."

"Oh, a brisk walk ought to help me. We're only going round by the church." I heard him cough grievously as they went out together.

I refilled the stove, and, after reckless expenditure of Mr. Cashell's coal, drove some warmth into the shop. I explored many of the glass-knobbed drawers that lined the walls, tasted some disconcerting drugs, and, by the aid of a few cardamoms, ground ginger, chloric-ether, and dilute alcohol, manufactured a new and wildish drink, of which I bore a glassful to young Mr. Cashell, busy in the back office. He laughed shortly when I told him that Mr. Shaynor had stepped out – but a frail coil of wire held all his attention, and he had no word for me bewildered among the batteries and rods. The noise of the sea on the beach began to make itself heard as the traffic in the street ceased. Then briefly, but very lucidly, he gave me the names and uses of the mechanism that crowded the tables and the floor.

"When do you expect to get the message from Poole?" I demanded, sipping my liquor out of a graduated glass.

"About midnight, if everything is in order. We've got our installation-pole fixed to the roof of the house. I shouldn't advise you to turn on a tap or anything tonight. We've connected up with the plumbing, and all the water will be electrified." He repeated to me the history of the agitated ladies at the hotel at the time of the first installation.

"But what *is* it?" I asked. "Electricity is out of my beat altogether."

"Ah, if you knew *that* you'd know something nobody knows. It's just It – what we call Electricity, but the magic – the manifestations – the Hertzian waves – are all revealed by *this*. The coherer, we call it."

He picked up a glass tube not much thicker than a thermometer, in which, almost touching, were two tiny silver plugs, and between them an infinitesimal pinch of metallic dust. "That's all," he said, proudly, as though himself responsible for the wonder. "That is the thing that will reveal to us the Powers – whatever the Powers may be – at work – through space – a long distance away."

Just then Mr. Shaynor returned alone and stood coughing his heart out on the mat.

"Serves you right for being such a fool," said young Mr. Cashell, as annoyed as myself at the interruption. "Never mind – we've all the night before us to see wonders."

Shaynor clutched the counter, his handkerchief to his lips. When he brought it away I saw two bright red stains.

"I – I've got a bit of a rasped throat from smoking cigarettes," he panted. "I think I'll try a cubeb."

"Better take some of this. I've been compounding while you've been away." I handed him the brew.

"'Twon't make me drunk, will it? I'm almost a teetotaller. My word! That's grateful and comforting."

He sat down the empty glass to cough afresh.

"Brr! But it was cold out there! I shouldn't care to be lying in my grave a night like this. Don't *you* ever have a sore throat from smoking?" He pocketed the handkerchief after a furtive peep.

"Oh, yes, sometimes," I replied, wondering, while I spoke, into what agonies of terror I should fall if ever I saw those bright-red danger-signals under my nose. Young Mr. Cashell among the batteries coughed slightly to show that he was quite ready to continue his scientific explanations, but I was thinking still of the girl with the rich voice and the significantly cut mouth, at whose command I had taken charge of the shop. It flashed across me that she distantly resembled the seductive shape on a gold-framed toilet-water advertisement whose charms were unholily heightened by the glare from the red bottle in the window. Turning to make sure, I saw Mr. Shaynor's eyes bent in the same direction, and by instinct recognised that the flamboyant thing was to him a shrine. "What do you take for your – cough?" I asked.

"Well, I'm the wrong side of the counter to believe much in patent medicines. But there are asthma cigarettes and there are pastilles. To tell you the truth, if you don't object to the smell, which is very like incense, I believe, though I'm not a Roman Catholic, Blaudett's Cathedral Pastilles relieve me as much as anything."

"Let's try." I had never raided a chemist's shop before, so I was thorough. We unearthed the pastilles – brown, gummy cones of benzoin – and set them alight under the toilet-water advertisement, where they fumed in thin blue spirals.

"Of course," said Mr. Shaynor, to my question, "what one uses in the shop for one's self comes out of one's pocket. Why, stock-taking in our business is nearly the same as with jewellers – and I can't say more than that. But one gets them" – he pointed to the pastille-box – "at trade prices." Evidently the censing of the gay, seven-tinted wench with the teeth was an established ritual which cost something.

"And when do we shut up shop?"

"We stay like this all night. The gov. – old Mr. Cashell – doesn't believe in locks and shutters as compared with electric light. Besides it brings trade. I'll just sit here in the chair by the stove and write a letter, if you don't mind. Electricity isn't my prescription."

The energetic young Mr. Cashell snorted within, and Shaynor settled himself up in his chair over which he had thrown a staring red, black, and yellow Austrian jute blanket, rather like a table-cover. I cast about, amid patent medicine pamphlets, for something to read, but finding little, returned to the manufacture of the new drink. The Italian warehouse took down its game and went to bed. Across the street blank shutters flung back the gaslight in cold smears; the dried pavement seemed to rough up in goose-flesh under the scouring of the savage wind, and we could hear, long ere he passed, the policeman flapping his arms to keep himself warm. Within, the flavours of cardamoms and chloric-ether disputed those of the pastilles and a score of drugs and perfume and soap scents. Our electric lights, set low down in the windows before the tunbellied Rosamund jars, flung inward three monstrous daubs of red, blue, and green, that broke into kaleidoscopic lights on the facetted knobs of the drug-drawers, the cut-glass scent flagons, and the bulbs of the sparklet bottles. They flushed the white-tiled floor in gorgeous patches; splashed along the nickel-silver counter-rails, and turned the polished mahogany counter-panels to the likeness of intricate grained marbles – slabs of porphyry and malachite. Mr. Shaynor unlocked a drawer, and ere he began to write, took out a meagre bundle of letters. From my place by the stove, I could see the scalloped edges of the paper with a flaring monogram in the corner and could even smell the reek of chypre. At each page he turned toward the toilet-water lady of the advertisement and devoured her with over-luminous eyes. He had drawn the Austrian blanket over his shoulders, and among those warring lights he looked more than ever the incarnation of a drugged moth – a tiger-moth as I thought.

He put his letter into an envelope, stamped it with stiff mechanical movements, and dropped it in the drawer. Then I became aware of the silence of a great city asleep – the silence that underlaid the even voice of the breakers along the sea-front – a thick, tingling quiet of warm life stilled down for its appointed time, and unconsciously I moved about the glittering shop as one moves in a sick-room. Young Mr. Cashell was adjusting some wire that crackled from time to time with the tense, knuckle-stretching sound of the electric spark. Upstairs, where a door shut and opened swiftly, I could hear his uncle coughing abed.

"Here," I said, when the drink was properly warmed, "take some of this, Mr. Shaynor."

He jerked in his chair with a start and a wrench, and held out his hand for the glass. The mixture, of a rich port-wine colour, frothed at the top.

"It looks," he said, suddenly, "it looks – those bubbles – like a string of pearls winking at you – rather like the pearls round that young lady's neck." He turned again to the advertisement where the female in the dove-coloured corset had seen fit to put on all her pearls before she cleaned her teeth.

"Not bad, is it?" I said.

"Eh?"

He rolled his eyes heavily full on me, and, as I stared, I beheld all meaning and consciousness die out of the swiftly dilating pupils. His figure lost its stark rigidity, softened into the chair, and, chin on chest, hands dropped before him, he rested open-eyed, absolutely still.

"I'm afraid I've rather cooked Shaynor's goose," I said, bearing the fresh drink to young Mr. Cashell. "Perhaps it was the chloric-ether."

"Oh, he's all right." The spade-bearded man glanced at him pityingly. "Consumptives go off in those sort of doses very often. It's exhaustion…I don't wonder. I dare say the liquor will do him good. It's grand stuff," he finished his share appreciatively. "Well, as I was saying – before he interrupted – about this little coherer. The pinch of dust, you see, is nickel-filings. The Hertzian waves, you see, come out of space from the station that despatches 'em, and all these little particles are attracted together – cohere, we call it – for just so long as the current passes through them. Now, it's important to remember that the current is an induced current. There are a good many kinds of induction –"

"Yes, but what *is* induction?"

"That's rather hard to explain untechnically. But the long and the short of it is that when a current of electricity passes through a wire there's a lot of magnetism present round that wire; and if you put another wire parallel to, and within what we call its magnetic field – why then, the second wire will also become charged with electricity."

"On its own account?"

"On its own account."

"Then let's see if I've got it correctly. Miles off, at Poole, or wherever it is –"

"It will be anywhere in ten years."

"You've got a charged wire –"

"Charged with Hertzian waves which vibrate, say, two hundred and thirty million times a second." Mr. Cashell snaked his forefinger rapidly through the air.

"All right – a charged wire at Poole, giving out these waves into space. Then this wire of yours sticking out into space – on the roof of the house – in some mysterious way gets charged with those waves from Poole –"

"Or anywhere – it only happens to be Poole tonight."

"And those waves set the coherer at work, just like an ordinary telegraph-office ticker?"

"No! That's where so many people make the mistake. The Hertzian waves wouldn't be strong enough to work a great heavy Morse instrument like ours. They can only just make that dust cohere, and while it coheres (a little while for a dot and a longer while for a dash) the current from this battery – the home battery" – he laid his hand on the thing – "can get through to the Morse printing-machine to record the dot or dash. Let me make it clearer. Do you know anything about steam?"

"Very little. But go on."

"Well, the coherer is like a steam-valve. Any child can open a valve and start a steamer's engines, because a turn of the hand lets in the main steam, doesn't it? Now, this home battery here ready to print is the main steam. The coherer is the valve, always ready to be turned on. The Hertzian wave is the child's hand that turns it."

"I see. That's marvellous."

"Marvellous, isn't it? And, remember, we're only at the beginning. There's nothing we shan't be able to do in ten years. I want to live – my God, how I want to live, and see it develop!" He looked through the door at Shaynor breathing lightly in his chair. "Poor beast! And he wants to keep company with Fanny Brand."

"Fanny *who*?" I said, for the name struck an obscurely familiar chord in my brain – something connected with a stained handkerchief, and the word "arterial."

"Fanny Brand – the girl you kept shop for." He laughed, "That's all I know about her, and for the life of me I can't see what Shaynor sees in her, or she in him."

"*Can't* you see what he sees in her?" I insisted.

"Oh, yes, if *that's* what you mean. She's a great, big, fat lump of a girl, and so on. I suppose that's why he's so crazy after her. She isn't his sort. Well, it doesn't matter. My uncle says he's bound to die before the year's out. Your drink's given him a good sleep, at any rate." Young Mr. Cashell could not catch Mr. Shaynor's face, which was half turned to the advertisement.

I stoked the stove anew, for the room was growing cold, and lighted another pastille. Mr. Shaynor in his chair, never moving, looked through and over me with eyes as wide and lustreless as those of a dead hare.

"Poole's late," said young Mr. Cashell, when I stepped back. "I'll just send them a call."

He pressed a key in the semi-darkness, and with a rending crackle there leaped between two brass knobs a spark, streams of sparks, and sparks again.

"Grand, isn't it? *That's* the Power – our unknown Power – kicking and fighting to be let loose," said young Mr. Cashell. "There she goes – kick – kick – kick into space. I never get over the strangeness of it when I work a sending-machine – waves going into space, you know. T.R. is our call. Poole ought to answer with L.L.L."

We waited two, three, five minutes. In that silence, of which the boom of the tide was an orderly part, I caught the clear '*kiss – kiss – kiss*' of the halliards on the roof, as they were blown against the installation-pole.

"Poole is not ready. I'll stay here and call you when he is."

I returned to the shop, and set down my glass on a marble slab with a careless clink. As I did so, Shaynor rose to his feet, his eyes fixed once more on the advertisement, where the young woman bathed in the light from the red jar simpered pinkly over her pearls. His lips moved without cessation. I stepped nearer to listen. "And threw – and threw – and threw," he repeated, his face all sharp with some inexplicable agony.

I moved forward astonished. But it was then he found words – delivered roundly and clearly. These:

And threw warm gules on Madeleine's young breast.

The trouble passed off his countenance, and he returned lightly to his place, rubbing his hands.

It had never occurred to me, though we had many times discussed reading and prize-competitions as a diversion, that Mr. Shaynor ever read Keats, or could quote him at all appositely. There was, after all, a certain stained-glass effect of light on the high bosom of the highly-polished picture which might, by stretch of fancy, suggest, as a vile chromo recalls some incomparable canvas, the line he had spoken. Night, my drink, and solitude were evidently turning Mr. Shaynor into a poet. He sat down again and wrote swiftly on his villainous note-paper, his lips quivering.

I shut the door into the inner office and moved up behind him. He made no sign that he saw or heard. I looked over his shoulder, and read, amid half-formed words, sentences, and wild scratches:

– Very cold it was. Very cold
The hare – the hare – the hare –
The birds –

He raised his head sharply, and frowned toward the blank shutters of the poulterer's shop where they jutted out against our window. Then one clear line came:

The hare, in spite of fur, was very cold.

The head, moving machine-like, turned right to the advertisement where the Blaudett's Cathedral pastille reeked abominably. He grunted, and went on:

Incense in a censer –
Before her darling picture framed in gold –
Maiden's picture – angel's portrait –

"Hsh!" said Mr. Cashell guardedly from the inner office, as though in the presence of spirits. "There's something coming through from somewhere; but it isn't Poole." I heard the crackle of sparks as he depressed the keys of the transmitter. In my own brain, too, something crackled, or it might have been the hair on my head. Then I heard my own voice, in a harsh whisper: "Mr. Cashell, there is something coming through here, too. Leave me alone till I tell you."

"But I thought you'd come to see this wonderful thing – Sir," indignantly at the end.

"Leave me alone till I tell you. Be quiet."

I watched – I waited. Under the blue-veined hand – the dry hand of the consumptive – came away clear, without erasure:

And my weak spirit fails
To think how the dead must freeze –

He shivered as he wrote:

Beneath the churchyard mould.

Then he stopped, laid the pen down, and leaned back.

For an instant, that was half an eternity, the shop spun before me in a rainbow-tinted whirl, in and through which my own soul most dispassionately considered my own soul as that fought with an over-mastering fear. Then I smelt the strong smell of cigarettes from Mr. Shaynor's clothing, and heard, as though it had been the rending of trumpets, the rattle of his breathing. I was still in my place of observation, much as one would watch a rifle-shot at the butts, half-bent, hands on my knees, and head within a few inches of the black, red, and yellow blanket of his shoulder. I was whispering encouragement, evidently to my other self, sounding sentences, such as men pronounce in dreams.

"If he has read Keats, it proves nothing. If he hasn't – like causes *must* beget like effects. There is no escape from this law. *You* ought to be grateful that you know 'St. Agnes Eve' without the book; because, given the circumstances, such as Fanny Brand, who is the key of the enigma, and approximately represents the latitude and longitude of Fanny Brawne; allowing also for the bright red colour of the arterial blood upon the handkerchief, which was just what you were puzzling over in the shop just now; and counting the effect of the professional environment, here almost perfectly duplicated – the result is logical and inevitable. As inevitable as induction."

Still, the other half of my soul refused to be comforted. It was cowering in some minute and inadequate corner – at an immense distance.

Hereafter, I found myself one person again, my hands still gripping my knees, and my eyes glued on the page before Mr. Shaynor. As dreamers accept and explain the upheaval of landscapes and the resurrection of the dead, with excerpts from the evening hymn or the multiplication-table, so I had accepted the facts, whatever they might be, that I should witness, and had devised a theory, sane and plausible to my mind, that explained them all. Nay, I was even in advance of my facts, walking hurriedly before them, assured that they would fit my theory. And all that I now recall of that epoch-making theory are the lofty words: "If he has read Keats it's the chloric-ether. If he hasn't, it's the identical bacillus, or Hertzian wave of tuberculosis, *plus* Fanny Brand and the professional status which, in conjunction with the main-stream of subconscious thought common to all mankind, has thrown up temporarily an induced Keats."

Mr. Shaynor returned to his work, erasing and rewriting as before with swiftness. Two or three blank pages he tossed aside. Then he wrote, muttering:

The little smoke of a candle that goes out.

"No," he muttered. "Little smoke – little smoke – little smoke. What else?" He thrust his chin forward toward the advertisement, whereunder the last of the Blaudett's Cathedral pastilles fumed in its holder. "Ah!" Then with relief:

The little smoke that dies in moonlight cold.

Evidently he was snared by the rhymes of his first verse, for he wrote and rewrote 'gold – cold – mould' many times. Again he sought inspiration from the advertisement, and set down, without erasure, the line I had overheard:

And threw warm gules on Madeleine's young breast.

As I remembered the original it is 'fair' – a trite word – instead of 'young,' and I found myself nodding approval, though I admitted that the attempt to reproduce 'its little smoke in pallid moonlight died' was a failure.

Followed without a break ten or fifteen lines of bald prose – the naked soul's confession of its physical yearning for its beloved – unclean as we count uncleanliness; unwholesome, but human exceedingly; the raw material, so it seemed to me in that hour and in that place, whence Keats wove the twenty-sixth, seventh, and eighth stanzas of his poem. Shame I had none in overseeing this revelation; and my fear had gone with the smoke of the pastille.

"That's it," I murmured. "That's how it's blocked out. Go on! Ink it in, man. Ink it in!"

Mr. Shaynor returned to broken verse wherein 'loveliness' was made to rhyme with a desire to look upon 'her empty dress.' He picked up a fold of the gay, soft blanket, spread it over one hand, caressed it with infinite tenderness, thought, muttered, traced some snatches which I could not decipher, shut his eyes drowsily, shook his head, and dropped the stuff. Here I found myself at fault, for I could not then see (as I do now) in what manner a red, black, and yellow Austrian blanket coloured his dreams.

In a few minutes he laid aside his pen, and, chin on hand, considered the shop with thoughtful and intelligent eyes. He threw down the blanket, rose, passed along a line of drug-drawers, and read the names on the labels aloud. Returning, he took from his desk Christie's *New Commercial Plants* and the old Culpepper that I had given him, opened and laid them side by side with a clerky air, all trace of passion gone from his face, read first in one and then in the other, and paused with pen behind his ear.

"What wonder of Heaven's coming now?" I thought.

"Manna – manna – manna," he said at last, under wrinkled brows. "That's what I wanted. Good! Now then! Now then! Good! Good! Oh, by God, that's good!" His voice rose and he spoke rightly and fully without a falter:

> *Candied apple, quince and plum and gourd,*
> *And jellies smoother than the creamy curd,*
> *And lucent syrups tinct with cinnamon,*
> *Manna and dates in Argosy transferred*
> *From Fez; and spiced dainties, every one*
> *From silken Samarcand to cedared Lebanon.*

He repeated it once more, using 'blander' for 'smoother' in the second line; then wrote it down without erasure, but this time (my set eyes missed no stroke of any word) he substituted 'soother' for his atrocious second thought, so that it came away under his hand as it is written in the book – as it is written in the book.

A wind went shouting down the street, and on the heels of the wind followed a spurt and rattle of rain.

After a smiling pause – and good right had he to smile – he began anew, always tossing the last sheet over his shoulder:

> *The sharp rain falling on the window-pane,*
> *Rattling sleet – the wind-blown sleet.*

Then prose:

> *It is very cold of mornings when the wind brings rain and sleet with it. I heard*
> *the sleet on the window-pane outside, and thought of you, my darling. I am always*
> *thinking of you. I wish we could both run away like two lovers into the storm and*
> *get that little cottage by the sea which we are always thinking about, my own dear*
> *darling. We could sit and watch the sea beneath our windows. It would be a fairyland*
> *all of our own – a fairy sea – a fairy sea…*

He stopped, raised his head, and listened. The steady drone of the Channel along the sea-front that had borne us company so long leaped up a note to the sudden fuller surge that signals the change from ebb to flood. It beat in like the change of step throughout an army – this renewed pulse of the sea – and filled our ears till they, accepting it, marked it no longer.

> *A fairyland for you and me*
> *Across the foam – beyond…*
> *A magic foam, a perilous sea.*

He grunted again with effort and bit his underlip. My throat dried, but I dared not gulp to moisten it lest I should break the spell that was drawing him nearer and nearer to the high-water mark but two of the sons of Adam have reached. Remember that in all the millions permitted there are no more than five – five little lines – of which one can say: "These are the pure Magic. These are the clear Vision. The rest is only poetry." And Mr. Shaynor was playing hot and cold with two of them!

I vowed no unconscious thought of mine should influence the blindfold soul, and pinned myself desperately to the other three, repeating and re-repeating:

> *A savage spot as holy and enchanted*
> *As e'er beneath a waning moon was haunted*
> *By woman wailing for her demon lover.*

But though I believed my brain thus occupied, my every sense hung upon the writing under the dry, bony hand, all brown-fingered with chemicals and cigarette-smoke.

> *Our windows fronting on the dangerous foam,*

(he wrote, after long, irresolute snatches), and then:

> *Our open casements facing desolate seas*
> *Forlorn – forlorn –*

Here again his face grew peaked and anxious with that sense of loss I had first seen when the Power snatched him. But this time the agony was tenfold keener. As I watched it mounted like mercury in the tube. It lighted his face from within till I thought the visibly scourged soul must leap forth naked between his jaws, unable to endure. A drop of sweat trickled from my forehead down my nose and splashed on the back of my hand.

> *Our windows facing on the desolate seas*
> *And pearly foam of magic fairyland –*

"Not yet – not yet," he muttered, "wait a minute.
Please wait a minute. I shall get it then –"

> *Our magic windows fronting on the sea,*
> *The dangerous foam of desolate seas...*
> *For aye.*

"*Ouh*, my God!"

From head to heel he shook – shook from the marrow of his bones outwards – then leaped to his feet with raised arms, and slid the chair screeching across the tiled floor where it struck the drawers behind and fell with a jar. Mechanically, I stooped to recover it.

As I rose, Mr. Shaynor was stretching and yawning at leisure.

"I've had a bit of a doze," he said. "How did I come to knock the chair over? You look rather –"

"The chair startled me," I answered. "It was so sudden in this quiet."

Young Mr. Cashell behind his shut door was offendedly silent.

"I suppose I must have been dreaming," said Mr. Shaynor.

"I suppose you must," I said. "Talking of dreams – I – I noticed you writing – before –"

He flushed consciously.

"I meant to ask you if you've ever read anything written by a man called Keats."

"Oh! I haven't much time to read poetry, and I can't say that I remember the name exactly. Is he a popular writer?"

"Middling. I thought you might know him because he's the only poet who was ever a druggist. And he's rather what's called the lover's poet."

"Indeed. I must dip into him. What did he write about?"

"A lot of things. Here's a sample that may interest you."

Then and there, carefully, I repeated the verse he had twice spoken and once written not ten minutes ago.

"Ah. Anybody could see he was a druggist from that line about the tinctures and syrups. It's a fine tribute to our profession."

"I don't know," said young Mr. Cashell, with icy politeness, opening the door one half-inch, "if you still happen to be interested in our trifling experiments. But, should such be the case –"

I drew him aside, whispering, "Shaynor seemed going off into some sort of fit when I spoke to you just now. I thought, even at the risk of being rude, it wouldn't do to take you off your instruments just as the call was coming through. Don't you see?"

"Granted – granted as soon as asked," he said unbending. "I *did* think it a shade odd at the time. So that was why he knocked the chair down?"

"I hope I haven't missed anything," I said. "I'm afraid I can't say that, but you're just in time for the end of a rather curious performance. You can come in, too, Mr. Shaynor. Listen, while I read it off."

The Morse instrument was ticking furiously. Mr. Cashell interpreted:

"K.K.V. Can make nothing of your signals." A pause. *"M.M.V. M.M.V. Signals unintelligible. Purpose anchor Sandown Bay. Examine instruments tomorrow.*

"Do you know what that means? It's a couple of men-o'-war working Marconi signals off the Isle of Wight. They are trying to talk to each other. Neither can read the other's messages, but all their messages are being taken in by our receiver here. They've been going on for ever so long. I wish you could have heard it."

"How wonderful!" I said. "Do you mean we're overhearing Portsmouth ships trying to talk to each other – that we're eavesdropping across half South England?"

"Just that. Their transmitters are all right, but their receivers are out of order, so they only get a dot here and a dash there. Nothing clear."

"Why is that?"

"God knows – and Science will know tomorrow. Perhaps the induction is faulty; perhaps the receivers aren't tuned to receive just the number of vibrations per second that the transmitter sends. Only a word here and there. Just enough to tantalise."

Again the Morse sprang to life.

"That's one of 'em complaining now. Listen: *'Disheartening – most disheartening.'* It's quite pathetic. Have you ever seen a spiritualistic seance? It reminds me of that sometimes – odds and ends of messages coming out of nowhere – a word here and there – no good at all."

"But mediums are all impostors," said Mr. Shaynor, in the doorway, lighting an asthma-cigarette. "They only do it for the money they can make. I've seen 'em."

"Here's Poole, at last – clear as a bell. L.L.L. *Now* we shan't be long." Mr. Cashell rattled the keys merrily. "Anything you'd like to tell 'em?"

"No, I don't think so," I said. "I'll go home and get to bed. I'm feeling a little tired."

Before Adam
Chapters I–V
Jack London

Chapter I

PICTURES! Pictures! Pictures! Often, before I learned, did I wonder whence came the multitudes of pictures that thronged my dreams; for they were pictures the like of which I had never seen in real wake-a-day life. They tormented my childhood, making of my dreams a procession of nightmares and a little later convincing me that I was different from my kind, a creature unnatural and accursed.

In my days only did I attain any measure of happiness. My nights marked the reign of fear – and such fear! I make bold to state that no man of all the men who walk the earth with me ever suffer fear of like kind and degree. For my fear is the fear of long ago, the fear that was rampant in the Younger World, and in the youth of the Younger World. In short, the fear that reigned supreme in that period known as the Mid-Pleistocene.

What do I mean? I see explanation is necessary before I can tell you of the substance of my dreams. Otherwise, little could you know of the meaning of the things I know so well. As I write this, all the beings and happenings of that other world rise up before me in vast phantasmagoria, and I know that to you they would be rhymeless and reasonless.

What to you the friendship of Lop-Ear, the warm lure of the Swift One, the lust and the atavism of Red-Eye? A screaming incoherence and no more. And a screaming incoherence, likewise, the doings of the Fire People and the Tree People, and the gibbering councils of the horde. For you know not the peace of the cool caves in the cliffs, the circus of the drinking-places at the end of the day. You have never felt the bite of the morning wind in the tree-tops, nor is the taste of young bark sweet in your mouth.

It would be better, I dare say, for you to make your approach, as I made mine, through my childhood. As a boy I was very like other boys – in my waking hours. It was in my sleep that I was different. From my earliest recollection my sleep was a period of terror. Rarely were my dreams tinctured with happiness. As a rule, they were stuffed with fear – and with a fear so strange and alien that it had no ponderable quality. No fear that I experienced in my waking life resembled the fear that possessed me in my sleep. It was of a quality and kind that transcended all my experiences.

For instance, I was a city boy, a city child, rather, to whom the country was an unexplored domain. Yet I never dreamed of cities; nor did a house ever occur in any of my dreams. Nor, for that matter, did any of my human kind ever break through the wall of my sleep. I, who had seen trees only in parks and illustrated books, wandered in my sleep through interminable forests. And further, these dream trees were not a mere blur on my vision.

They were sharp and distinct. I was on terms of practised intimacy with them. I saw every branch and twig; I saw and knew every different leaf.

Well do I remember the first time in my waking life that I saw an oak tree. As I looked at the leaves and branches and gnarls, it came to me with distressing vividness that I had seen that same kind of tree many and countless times in my sleep. So I was not surprised, still later on in my life, to recognize instantly, the first time I saw them, trees such as the spruce, the yew, the birch, and the laurel. I had seen them all before, and was seeing them even then, every night, in my sleep.

This, as you have already discerned, violates the first law of dreaming, namely, that in one's dreams one sees only what he has seen in his waking life, or combinations of the things he has seen in his waking life. But all my dreams violated this law. In my dreams I never saw *anything* of which I had knowledge in my waking life. My dream life and my waking life were lives apart, with not one thing in common save myself. I was the connecting link that somehow lived both lives.

Early in my childhood I learned that nuts came from the grocer, berries from the fruit man; but before ever that knowledge was mine, in my dreams I picked nuts from trees, or gathered them and ate them from the ground underneath trees, and in the same way I ate berries from vines and bushes. This was beyond any experience of mine.

I shall never forget the first time I saw blueberries served on the table. I had never seen blueberries before, and yet, at the sight of them, there leaped up in my mind memories of dreams wherein I had wandered through swampy land eating my fill of them. My mother set before me a dish of the berries. I filled my spoon, but before I raised it to my mouth I knew just how they would taste. Nor was I disappointed. It was the same tang that I had tasted a thousand times in my sleep.

Snakes? Long before I had heard of the existence of snakes, I was tormented by them in my sleep. They lurked for me in the forest glades; leaped up, striking, under my feet; squirmed off through the dry grass or across naked patches of rock; or pursued me into the tree-tops, encircling the trunks with their great shining bodies, driving me higher and higher or farther and farther out on swaying and crackling branches, the ground a dizzy distance beneath me. Snakes! – with their forked tongues, their beady eyes and glittering scales, their hissing and their rattling – did I not already know them far too well on that day of my first circus when I saw the snake-charmer lift them up?

They were old friends of mine, enemies rather, that peopled my nights with fear.

Ah, those endless forests, and their horror-haunted gloom! For what eternities have I wandered through them, a timid, hunted creature, starting at the least sound, frightened of my own shadow, keyed-up, ever alert and vigilant, ready on the instant to dash away in mad flight for my life. For I was the prey of all manner of fierce life that dwelt in the forest, and it was in ecstasies of fear that I fled before the hunting monsters.

When I was five years old I went to my first circus. I came home from it sick – but not from peanuts and pink lemonade. Let me tell you. As we entered the animal tent, a hoarse roaring shook the air. I tore my hand loose from my father's and dashed wildly back through the entrance. I collided with people, fell down; and all the time I was screaming with terror. My father caught me and soothed me. He pointed to the crowd of people, all careless of the roaring, and cheered me with assurances of safety.

Nevertheless, it was in fear and trembling, and with much encouragement on his part, that I at last approached the lion's cage. Ah, I knew him on the instant. The beast! The terrible one! And on my inner vision flashed the memories of my dreams, – the midday sun shining on tall grass, the wild bull grazing quietly, the sudden parting of the grass before the swift rush of the tawny one, his leap to the bull's back, the crashing and the bellowing, and the crunch crunch of bones; or again, the cool quiet of the water-hole, the wild horse up to his knees and drinking softly, and then the tawny one – always the tawny one! – the leap, the screaming and the splashing of the horse, and the crunch crunch of bones; and yet again, the sombre twilight and the sad silence of the end of day, and then the great full-throated roar, sudden, like a trump of doom, and swift upon it the insane shrieking and chattering among the trees, and I, too, am trembling with fear and am one of the many shrieking and chattering among the trees.

At the sight of him, helpless, within the bars of his cage, I became enraged. I gritted my teeth at him, danced up and down, screaming an incoherent mockery and making antic faces. He responded, rushing against the bars and roaring back at me his impotent wrath. Ah, he knew me, too, and the sounds I made were the sounds of old time and intelligible to him.

My parents were frightened. "The child is ill," said my mother. "He is hysterical," said my father. I never told them, and they never knew. Already had I developed reticence concerning this quality of mine, this semi-disassociation of personality as I think I am justified in calling it.

I saw the snake-charmer, and no more of the circus did I see that night. I was taken home, nervous and overwrought, sick with the invasion of my real life by that other life of my dreams.

I have mentioned my reticence. Only once did I confide the strangeness of it all to another. He was a boy – my chum; and we were eight years old. From my dreams I reconstructed for him pictures of that vanished world in which I do believe I once lived. I told him of the terrors of that early time, of Lop-Ear and the pranks we played, of the gibbering councils, and of the Fire People and their squatting places.

He laughed at me, and jeered, and told me tales of ghosts and of the dead that walk at night. But mostly did he laugh at my feeble fancy. I told him more, and he laughed the harder. I swore in all earnestness that these things were so, and he began to look upon me queerly. Also, he gave amazing garblings of my tales to our playmates, until all began to look upon me queerly.

It was a bitter experience, but I learned my lesson. I was different from my kind. I was abnormal with something they could not understand, and the telling of which would cause only misunderstanding. When the stories of ghosts and goblins went around, I kept quiet. I smiled grimly to myself. I thought of my nights of fear, and knew that mine were the real things – real as life itself, not attenuated vapors and surmised shadows.

For me no terrors resided in the thought of bugaboos and wicked ogres. The fall through leafy branches and the dizzy heights; the snakes that struck at me as I dodged and leaped away in chattering flight; the wild dogs that hunted me across the open spaces to the timber – these were terrors concrete and actual, happenings and not imaginings, things of the living flesh and of sweat and blood. Ogres and bugaboos and I had been happy bed-fellows, compared with these terrors that made their bed with me throughout my childhood, and that still bed with me, now, as I write this, full of years.

Chapter II

I HAVE SAID that in my dreams I never saw a human being. Of this fact I became aware very early, and felt poignantly the lack of my own kind. As a very little child, even, I had a feeling, in the midst of the horror of my dreaming, that if I could find but one man, only one human, I should be saved from my dreaming, that I should be surrounded no more by haunting terrors. This thought obsessed me every night of my life for years – if only I could find that one human and be saved!

I must iterate that I had this thought in the midst of my dreaming, and I take it as an evidence of the merging of my two personalities, as evidence of a point of contact between the two disassociated parts of me. My dream personality lived in the long ago, before ever man, as we know him, came to be; and my other and wake-a-day personality projected itself, to the extent of the knowledge of man's existence, into the substance of my dreams.

Perhaps the psychologists of the book will find fault with my way of using the phrase, 'disassociation of personality.' I know their use of it, yet am compelled to use it in my own way in default of a better phrase. I take shelter behind the inadequacy of the English language. And now to the explanation of my use, or misuse, of the phrase.

It was not till I was a young man, at college, that I got any clue to the significance of my dreams, and to the cause of them. Up to that time they had been meaningless and without apparent causation. But at college I discovered evolution and psychology, and learned the explanation of various strange mental states and experiences. For instance, there was the falling-through-space dream – the commonest dream experience, one practically known, by first-hand experience, to all men.

This, my professor told me, was a racial memory. It dated back to our remote ancestors who lived in trees. With them, being tree-dwellers, the liability of falling was an ever-present menace. Many lost their lives that way; all of them experienced terrible falls, saving themselves by clutching branches as they fell toward the ground.

Now a terrible fall, averted in such fashion, was productive of shock. Such shock was productive of molecular changes in the cerebral cells. These molecular changes were transmitted to the cerebral cells of progeny, became, in short, racial memories. Thus, when you and I, asleep or dozing off to sleep, fall through space and awake to sickening consciousness just before we strike, we are merely remembering what happened to our arboreal ancestors, and which has been stamped by cerebral changes into the heredity of the race.

There is nothing strange in this, any more than there is anything strange in an instinct. An instinct is merely a habit that is stamped into the stuff of our heredity, that is all. It will be noted, in passing, that in this falling dream which is so familiar to you and me and all of us, we never strike bottom. To strike bottom would be destruction. Those of our arboreal ancestors who struck bottom died forthwith. True, the shock of their fall was communicated to the cerebral cells, but they died immediately, before they could have progeny. You and I are descended from those that did not strike bottom; that is why you and I, in our dreams, never strike bottom.

And now we come to disassociation of personality. We never have this sense of falling when we are wide awake. Our wake-a-day personality has no experience of it. Then – and here the argument is irresistible – it must be another and distinct personality that falls when we are asleep, and that has had experience of such falling – that has, in short, a memory of past-day race experiences, just as our wake-a-day personality has a memory of our wake-a-day experiences.

It was at this stage in my reasoning that I began to see the light. And quickly the light burst upon me with dazzling brightness, illuminating and explaining all that had been weird and uncanny and unnaturally impossible in my dream experiences. In my sleep it was not my wake-a-day personality that took charge of me; it was another and distinct personality, possessing a new and totally different fund of experiences, and, to the point of my dreaming, possessing memories of those totally different experiences.

What was this personality? When had it itself lived a wake-a-day life on this planet in order to collect this fund of strange experiences? These were questions that my dreams themselves answered. He lived in the long ago, when the world was young, in that period that we call the Mid-Pleistocene. He fell from the trees but did not strike bottom. He gibbered with fear at the roaring of the lions. He was pursued by beasts of prey, struck at by deadly snakes. He chattered with his kind in council, and he received rough usage at the hands of the Fire People in the day that he fled before them.

But, I hear you objecting, why is it that these racial memories are not ours as well, seeing that we have a vague other-personality that falls through space while we sleep?

And I may answer with another question. Why is a two-headed calf? And my own answer to this is that it is a freak. And so I answer your question. I have this other-personality and these complete racial memories because I am a freak.

But let me be more explicit.

The commonest race memory we have is the falling-through-space dream. This other-personality is very vague. About the only memory it has is that of falling. But many of us have sharper, more distinct other-personalities. Many of us have the flying dream, the pursuing-monster dream, color dreams, suffocation dreams, and the reptile and vermin dreams. In short, while this other-personality is vestigial in all of us, in some of us it is almost obliterated, while in others of us it is more pronounced. Some of us have stronger and completer race memories than others.

It is all a question of varying degree of possession of the other-personality. In myself, the degree of possession is enormous. My other-personality is almost equal in power with my own personality. And in this matter I am, as I said, a freak – a freak of heredity.

I do believe that it is the possession of this other-personality – but not so strong a one as mine – that has in some few others given rise to belief in personal reincarnation experiences. It is very plausible to such people, a most convincing hypothesis. When they have visions of scenes they have never seen in the flesh, memories of acts and events dating back in time, the simplest explanation is that they have lived before.

But they make the mistake of ignoring their own duality. They do not recognize their other-personality. They think it is their own personality, that they have only one personality; and from such a premise they can conclude only that they have lived previous lives.

But they are wrong. It is not reincarnation. I have visions of myself roaming through the forests of the Younger World; and yet it is not myself that I see but one that is only remotely a part of me, as my father and my grandfather are parts of me less remote. This other-self of mine is an ancestor, a progenitor of my progenitors in the early line of my race, himself the progeny of a line that long before his time developed fingers and toes and climbed up into the trees.

I must again, at the risk of boring, repeat that I am, in this one thing, to be considered a freak. Not alone do I possess racial memory to an enormous extent, but I possess the memories of one particular and far-removed progenitor. And yet, while this is most unusual, there is nothing over-remarkable about it.

Follow my reasoning. An instinct is a racial memory. Very good. Then you and I and all of us receive these memories from our fathers and mothers, as they received them from their fathers and mothers. Therefore there must be a medium whereby these memories are transmitted from generation to generation. This medium is what Weismann terms the 'germplasm.' It carries the memories of the whole evolution of the race. These memories are dim and confused, and many of them are lost. But some strains of germplasm carry an excessive freightage of memories – are, to be scientific, more atavistic than other strains; and such a strain is mine. I am a freak of heredity, an atavistic nightmare – call me what you will; but here I am, real and alive, eating three hearty meals a day, and what are you going to do about it?

And now, before I take up my tale, I want to anticipate the doubting Thomases of psychology, who are prone to scoff, and who would otherwise surely say that the coherence of my dreams is due to overstudy and the subconscious projection of my knowledge of evolution into my dreams. In the first place, I have never been a zealous student. I graduated last of my class. I cared more for athletics, and – there is no reason I should not confess it – more for billiards.

Further, I had no knowledge of evolution until I was at college, whereas in my childhood and youth I had already lived in my dreams all the details of that other, long-ago life. I will say, however, that these details were mixed and incoherent until I came to know the science of evolution. Evolution was the key. It gave the explanation, gave sanity to the pranks of this atavistic brain of mine that, modern and normal, harked back to a past so remote as to be contemporaneous with the raw beginnings of mankind.

For in this past I know of, man, as we today know him, did not exist. It was in the period of his becoming that I must have lived and had my being.

Chapter III

THE COMMONEST DREAM of my early childhood was something like this: It seemed that I was very small and that I lay curled up in a sort of nest of twigs and boughs. Sometimes I was lying on my back. In this position it seemed that I spent many hours, watching the play of sunlight on the foliage and the stirring of the leaves by the wind. Often the nest itself moved back and forth when the wind was strong.

But always, while so lying in the nest, I was mastered as of tremendous space beneath me. I never saw it, I never peered over the edge of the nest to see; but I *knew* and feared that space that lurked just beneath me and that ever threatened me like a maw of some all-devouring monster.

This dream, in which I was quiescent and which was more like a condition than an experience of action, I dreamed very often in my early childhood. But suddenly, there would rush into the very midst of it strange forms and ferocious happenings, the thunder and crashing of storm, or unfamiliar landscapes such as in my wake-a-day life I had never seen. The result was confusion and nightmare. I could comprehend nothing of it. There was no logic of sequence.

You see, I did not dream consecutively. One moment I was a wee babe of the Younger World lying in my tree nest; the next moment I was a grown man of the Younger World locked in combat with the hideous Red-Eye; and the next moment I was creeping carefully down to the water-hole in the heat of the day. Events, years apart in their occurrence in the Younger World, occurred with me within the space of several minutes, or seconds.

It was all a jumble, but this jumble I shall not inflict upon you. It was not until I was a young man and had dreamed many thousand times, that everything straightened out and became clear and plain. Then it was that I got the clue of time, and was able to piece together events and actions in their proper order. Thus was I able to reconstruct the vanished Younger World as it was at the time I lived in it – or at the time my other-self lived in it. The distinction does not matter; for I, too, the modern man, have gone back and lived that early life in the company of my other-self.

For your convenience, since this is to be no sociological screed, I shall frame together the different events into a comprehensive story. For there is a certain thread of continuity and happening that runs through all the dreams. There is my friendship with Lop-Ear, for instance. Also, there is the enmity of Red-Eye, and the love of the Swift One. Taking it all in all, a fairly coherent and interesting story I am sure you will agree.

I do not remember much of my mother. Possibly the earliest recollection I have of her – and certainly the sharpest – is the following: It seemed I was lying on the ground.

I was somewhat older than during the nest days, but still helpless. I rolled about in the dry leaves, playing with them and making crooning, rasping noises in my throat. The sun shone warmly and I was happy, and comfortable. I was in a little open space. Around me, on all sides, were bushes and fern-like growths, and overhead and all about were the trunks and branches of forest trees.

Suddenly I heard a sound. I sat upright and listened. I made no movement. The little noises died down in my throat, and I sat as one petrified. The sound drew closer. It was like the grunt of a pig. Then I began to hear the sounds caused by the moving of a body through the brush. Next I saw the ferns agitated by the passage of the body. Then the ferns parted, and I saw gleaming eyes, a long snout, and white tusks.

It was a wild boar. He peered at me curiously. He grunted once or twice and shifted his weight from one foreleg to the other, at the same time moving his head from side to side and swaying the ferns. Still I sat as one petrified, my eyes unblinking as I stared at him, fear eating at my heart.

It seemed that this movelessness and silence on my part was what was expected of me. I was not to cry out in the face of fear. It was a dictate of instinct. And so I sat there and waited for I knew not what. The boar thrust the ferns aside and stepped into the open. The curiosity went out of his eyes, and they gleamed cruelly. He tossed his head at me threateningly and advanced a step. This he did again, and yet again.

Then I screamed...or shrieked – I cannot describe it, but it was a shrill and terrible cry. And it seems that it, too, at this stage of the proceedings, was the thing expected of me. From not far away came an answering cry. My sounds seemed momentarily to disconcert the boar, and while he halted and shifted his weight with indecision, an apparition burst upon us.

She was like a large orangutan, my mother, or like a chimpanzee, and yet, in sharp and definite ways, quite different. She was heavier of build than they, and had less hair. Her arms were not so long, and her legs were stouter. She wore no clothes – only her natural hair. And I can tell you she was a fury when she was excited.

And like a fury she dashed upon the scene. She was gritting her teeth, making frightful grimaces, snarling, uttering sharp and continuous cries that sounded like "kh-ah! kh-ah!" So sudden and formidable was her appearance that the boar involuntarily bunched himself together on the defensive and bristled as she swerved toward him. Then she swerved toward me. She had quite taken the breath out of him. I knew just what to do in that moment of time she had gained. I leaped to meet her, catching her about the waist and holding on hand and foot – yes, by my feet; I could hold on by them as readily as by my hands. I could feel in my tense grip the pull of the hair as her skin and her muscles moved beneath with her efforts.

As I say, I leaped to meet her, and on the instant she leaped straight up into the air, catching an overhanging branch with her hands. The next instant, with clashing tusks, the boar drove past underneath. He had recovered from his surprise and sprung forward, emitting a squeal that was almost a trumpeting. At any rate it was a call, for it was followed by the rushing of bodies through the ferns and brush from all directions.

From every side wild hogs dashed into the open space – a score of them. But my mother swung over the top of a thick limb, a dozen feet from the ground, and, still holding on to her, we perched there in safety. She was very excited. She chattered and screamed, and scolded down at the bristling, tooth-gnashing circle that had gathered beneath. I, too, trembling, peered down at the angry beasts and did my best to imitate my mother's cries.

From the distance came similar cries, only pitched deeper, into a sort of roaring bass. These grew momentarily louder, and soon I saw him approaching, my father – at least, by all the evidence of the times, I am driven to conclude that he was my father.

He was not an extremely prepossessing father, as fathers go. He seemed half man, and half ape, and yet not ape, and not yet man. I fail to describe him. There is nothing like him today on the earth, under the earth, nor in the earth. He was a large man in his day, and he must have weighed all of a hundred and thirty pounds. His face was broad and flat, and the eyebrows over-hung the eyes. The eyes themselves were small, deep-set, and close together. He had practically no nose at all. It was squat and broad, apparently with-out any bridge, while the nostrils were like two holes in the face, opening outward instead of down.

The forehead slanted back from the eyes, and the hair began right at the eyes and ran up over the head. The head itself was preposterously small and was supported on an equally preposterous, thick, short neck.

There was an elemental economy about his body – as was there about all our bodies. The chest was deep, it is true, cavernously deep; but there were no full-swelling muscles, no wide-spreading shoulders, no clean-limbed straightness, no generous symmetry of outline. It represented strength, that body of my father's, strength without beauty; ferocious, primordial strength, made to clutch and gripe and rend and destroy.

His hips were thin; and the legs, lean and hairy, were crooked and stringy-muscled. In fact, my father's legs were more like arms. They were twisted and gnarly, and with scarcely the semblance of the full meaty calf such as graces your leg and mine. I remember he could not walk on the flat of his foot. This was because it was a prehensile foot, more like a hand than a foot. The great toe, instead of being in line with the other toes, opposed them, like a thumb, and its opposition to the other toes was what enabled him to get a grip with his foot. This was why he could not walk on the flat of his foot.

But his appearance was no more unusual than the manner of his coming, there to my mother and me as we perched above the angry wild pigs. He came through the trees, leaping from limb to limb and from tree to tree; and he came swiftly. I can see him now, in my wake-a-day life, as I write this, swinging along through the trees, a four-handed, hairy creature, howling with rage, pausing now and again to beat his chest with his clenched fist, leaping ten-and-fifteen-foot gaps, catching a branch with one hand and swinging on across another gap to catch with his other hand and go on, never hesitating, never at a loss as to how to proceed on his arboreal way.

And as I watched him I felt in my own being, in my very muscles themselves, the surge and thrill of desire to go leaping from bough to bough; and I felt also the guarantee of the latent power in that being and in those muscles of mine. And why not? Little boys watch their fathers swing axes and fell trees, and feel in themselves that some day they, too, will swing axes and fell trees. And so with me. The life that was in me was constituted to do what my father did, and it whispered to me secretly and ambitiously of aerial paths and forest flights.

At last my father joined us. He was extremely angry. I remember the out-thrust of his protruding underlip as he glared down at the wild pigs. He snarled something like a dog, and I remember that his eye-teeth were large, like fangs, and that they impressed me tremendously.

His conduct served only the more to infuriate the pigs. He broke off twigs and small branches and flung them down upon our enemies. He even hung by one hand, tantalizingly just beyond reach, and mocked them as they gnashed their tusks with impotent rage. Not content with this, he broke off a stout branch, and, holding on with one hand and foot, jabbed the infuriated beasts in the sides and whacked them across their noses. Needless to state, my mother and I enjoyed the sport.

But one tires of all good things, and in the end, my father, chuckling maliciously the while, led the way across the trees. Now it was that my ambitions ebbed away, and I became timid, holding tightly to my mother as she climbed and swung through space. I remember when the branch broke with her weight. She had made a wide leap, and with the snap of the wood I was overwhelmed with the sickening consciousness of falling through space, the pair of us. The forest and the sunshine on the rustling leaves vanished from my eyes. I had a fading glimpse of my father abruptly arresting his progress to look, and then all was blackness.

The next moment I was awake, in my sheeted bed, sweating, trembling, nauseated. The window was up, and a cool air was blowing through the room. The night-lamp was burning calmly. And because of this I take it that the wild pigs did not get us, that we never fetched bottom; else I should not be here now, a thousand centuries after, to remember the event.

And now put yourself in my place for a moment. Walk with me a bit in my tender childhood, bed with me a night and imagine yourself dreaming such incomprehensible horrors. Remember I was an inexperienced child. I had never seen a wild boar in my life. For that matter I had never seen a domesticated pig. The nearest approach to one that I had seen was breakfast bacon sizzling in its fat. And yet here, real as life, wild boars dashed through my dreams, and I, with fantastic parents, swung through the lofty tree-spaces.

Do you wonder that I was frightened and oppressed by my nightmare-ridden nights? I was accursed. And, worst of all, I was afraid to tell. I do not know why, except that I had a feeling of guilt, though I knew no better of what I was guilty. So it was, through long years, that I suffered in silence, until I came to man's estate and learned the why and wherefore of my dreams.

Chapter IV

THERE IS ONE puzzling thing about these prehistoric memories of mine. It is the vagueness of the time element. I lo not always know the order of events; or can I tell, between some events, whether one, two, or four or five years have elapsed. I can only roughly tell the passage of time by judging the changes in the appearance and pursuits of my fellows.

Also, I can apply the logic of events to the various happenings. For instance, there is no doubt whatever that my mother and I were treed by the wild pigs and fled and fell in the days before I made the acquaintance of Lop-Ear, who became what I may call my boyhood chum. And it is just as conclusive that between these two periods I must have left my mother.

I have no memory of my father than the one I have given. Never, in the years that followed, did he reappear. And from my knowledge of the times, the only explanation possible lies in that he perished shortly after the adventure with the wild pigs. That it must have been an untimely end, there is no discussion. He was in full vigor, and only sudden and violent death could have taken him off. But I know not the manner of his going – whether he was drowned in the river, or was swallowed by a snake, or went into the stomach of old Saber-Tooth, the tiger, is beyond my knowledge.

For know that I remember only the things I saw myself, with my own eyes, in those prehistoric days. If my mother knew my father's end, she never told me. For that matter I doubt if she had a vocabulary adequate to convey such information. Perhaps, all told, the Folk in that day had a vocabulary of thirty or forty sounds.

I call them *sounds*, rather than *words*, because sounds they were primarily. They had no fixed values, to be altered by adjectives and adverbs. These latter were tools of speech not yet invented. Instead of qualifying nouns or verbs by the use of adjectives and adverbs, we qualified sounds by intonation, by changes in quantity and pitch, by retarding and by accelerating. The length of time employed in the utterance of a particular sound shaded its meaning.

We had no conjugation. One judged the tense by the context. We talked only concrete things because we thought only concrete things. Also, we depended largely on pantomime. The simplest abstraction was practically beyond our thinking; and when one did happen to think one, he was hard put to communicate it to his fellows. There were no sounds for it. He was pressing beyond the limits of his vocabulary. If he invented sounds for it, his fellows did not understand the sounds. Then it was that he fell back on pantomime, illustrating the thought wherever possible and at the same time repeating the new sound over and over again.

Thus language grew. By the few sounds we possessed we were enabled to think a short distance beyond those sounds; then came the need for new sounds wherewith to express the new thought. Sometimes, however, we thought too long a distance in advance of our sounds, managed to achieve abstractions (dim ones I grant), which we failed utterly to make known to other folk. After all, language did not grow fast in that day.

Oh, believe me, we were amazingly simple. But we did know a lot that is not known today. We could twitch our ears, prick them up and flatten them down at will. And we could scratch between our shoulders with ease. We could throw stones with our feet. I have done it many a time. And for that matter, I could keep my knees straight, bend forward from the hips, and touch, not the tips of my fingers, but the points of my elbows, to the ground. And as for bird-nesting – well, I only wish the twentieth-century boy could see us. But we made no collections of eggs. We ate them.

I remember – but I out-run my story. First let me tell of Lop-Ear and our friendship. Very early in my life, I separated from my mother. Possibly this was because, after the death of my father, she took to herself a second husband. I have few recollections of him, and they are not of the best. He was a light fellow. There was no solidity to him. He was too voluble. His infernal chattering worries me even now as I think of it. His mind was too inconsequential to permit him to possess purpose. Monkeys in their cages always remind me of him. He was monkeyish. That is the best description I can give of him.

He hated me from the first. And I quickly learned to be afraid of him and his malicious pranks. Whenever he came in sight I crept close to my mother and clung to her. But I was growing older all the time, and it was inevitable that I should from time to time stray from her, and stray farther and farther. And these were the opportunities that the Chatterer waited for. (I may as well explain that we bore no names in those days; were not known by any name. For the sake of convenience I have myself given names to the various Folk I was more closely in contact with, and the 'Chatterer' is the most fitting description I can find for that precious stepfather of mine. As for me, I have named myself 'Big-Tooth.' My eye-teeth were pronouncedly large.)

But to return to the Chatterer. He persistently terrorized me. He was always pinching me and cuffing me, and on occasion he was not above biting me. Often my mother interfered, and the way she made his fur fly was a joy to see. But the result of all this was a beautiful and unending family quarrel, in which I was the bone of contention.

No, my home-life was not happy. I smile to myself as I write the phrase. Home-life! Home! I had no home in the modern sense of the term. My home was an association, not a habitation. I lived in my mother's care, not in a house. And my mother lived anywhere, so long as when night came she was above the ground.

My mother was old-fashioned. She still clung to her trees. It is true, the more progressive members of our horde lived in the caves above the river. But my mother was suspicious and unprogressive. The trees were good enough for her. Of course, we had one particular tree in which we usually roosted, though we often roosted in other trees when nightfall caught us. In a convenient fork was a sort of rude platform of twigs and branches and creeping things. It was more like a huge bird-nest than anything else, though it was a thousand times cruder in the weaving than any bird-nest. But it had one feature that I have never seen attached to any bird-nest, namely, a roof.

Oh, not a roof such as modern man makes! Nor a roof such as is made by the lowest aborigines of today. It was infinitely more clumsy than the clumsiest handiwork of man – of man as we know him. It was put together in a casual, helter-skelter sort of way. Above the fork of the tree whereon we rested was a pile of dead branches and brush. Four or five adjacent forks held what I may term the various ridge-poles. These were merely stout sticks an inch or so in diameter. On them rested the brush and branches. These seemed to have been tossed on almost aimlessly. There was no attempt at thatching. And I must confess that the roof leaked miserably in a heavy rain.

But the Chatterer. He made home-life a burden for both my mother and me – and by home-life I mean, not the leaky nest in the tree, but the group-life of the three of us. He was most malicious in his persecution of me. That was the one purpose to which he held steadfastly for longer than five minutes. Also, as time went by, my mother was less eager in her defence of me. I think, what of the continuous rows raised by the Chatterer, that I must have become a nuisance to her. At any rate, the situation went from bad to worse so rapidly that I should soon, of my own volition, have left home. But the satisfaction of performing so independent an act was denied me. Before I was ready to go, I was thrown out. And I mean this literally.

The opportunity came to the Chatterer one day when I was alone in the nest. My mother and the Chatterer had gone away together toward the blueberry swamp. He must have planned the whole thing, for I heard him returning alone through the forest, roaring with self-induced rage as he came. Like all the men of our horde, when they were angry or were trying to make themselves angry, he stopped now and again to hammer on his chest with his fist.

I realized the helplessness of my situation, and crouched trembling in the nest. The Chatterer came directly to the tree – I remember it was an oak tree – and began to climb up. And he never ceased for a moment from his infernal row. As I have said, our language was extremely meagre, and he must have strained it by the variety of ways in which he informed me of his undying hatred of me and of his intention there and then to have it out with me.

As he climbed to the fork, I fled out the great horizontal limb. He followed me, and out I went, farther and farther. At last I was out amongst the small twigs and leaves. The Chatterer was ever a coward, and greater always than any anger he ever worked up was his caution. He was afraid to follow me out amongst the leaves and twigs. For that matter, his greater weight would have crashed him through the foliage before he could have got to me.

But it was not necessary for him to reach me, and well he knew it, the scoundrel! With a malevolent expression on his face, his beady eyes gleaming with cruel intelligence, he began teetering. Teetering! – and with me out on the very edge of the bough, clutching at the twigs that broke continually with my weight. Twenty feet beneath me was the earth.

Wildly and more – wildly he teetered, grinning at me his gloating hatred. Then came the end. All four holds broke at the same time, and I fell, back-downward, looking up at him, my hands and feet still clutching the broken twigs. Luckily, there were no wild pigs under me, and my fall was broken by the tough and springy bushes.

Usually, my falls destroy my dreams, the nervous shock being sufficient to bridge the thousand centuries in an instant and hurl me wide awake into my little bed, where, perchance, I lie sweating and trembling and hear the cuckoo clock calling the hour in the hall. But this dream of my leaving home I have had many times, and never yet have I been awakened by it. Always do I crash, shrieking, down through the brush and fetch up with a bump on the ground.

Scratched and bruised and whimpering, I lay where I had fallen. Peering up through the bushes, I could see the Chatterer. He had set up a demoniacal chant of joy and was keeping time to it with his teetering. I quickly hushed my whimpering. I was no longer in the safety of the trees, and I knew the danger I ran of bringing upon myself the hunting animals by too audible an expression of my grief.

I remember, as my sobs died down, that I became interested in watching the strange light-effects produced by partially opening and closing my tear-wet eyelids. Then I began to investigate, and found that I was not so very badly damaged by my fall. I had lost some hair and hide, here and there; the sharp and jagged end of a broken branch had thrust fully an inch into my forearm; and my right hip, which had borne the brunt of my contact with the ground, was aching intolerably. But these, after all, were only petty hurts. No bones were broken, and in those days the flesh of man had finer healing qualities than it has today. Yet it was a severe fall, for I limped with my injured hip for fully a week afterward.

Next, as I lay in the bushes, there came upon me a feeling of desolation, a consciousness that I was homeless. I made up my mind never to return to my mother and the Chatterer. I would go far away through the terrible forest, and find some tree for myself in which to roost. As for food, I knew where to find it. For the last year at least I had not been beholden to my mother for food. All she had furnished me was protection and guidance.

I crawled softly out through the bushes. Once I looked back and saw the Chatterer still chanting and teetering. It was not a pleasant sight. I knew pretty well how to be cautious, and I was exceedingly careful on this my first journey in the world.

I gave no thought as to where I was going. I had but one purpose, and that was to go away beyond the reach of the Chatterer. I climbed into the trees and wandered on amongst them for hours, passing from tree to tree and never touching the ground. But I did not go in any particular direction, nor did I travel steadily. It was my nature, as it was the nature of all my folk, to be inconsequential. Besides, I was a mere child, and I stopped a great deal to play by the way.

The events that befell me on my leaving home are very vague in my mind. My dreams do not cover them. Much has my other-self forgotten, and particularly at this very period. Nor have I been able to frame up the various dreams so as to bridge the gap between my leaving the home-tree and my arrival at the caves.

I remember that several times I came to open spaces. These I crossed in great trepidation, descending to the ground and running at the top of my speed. I remember that there were days of rain and days of sunshine, so that I must have wandered alone for quite a time. I especially dream of my misery in the rain, and of my sufferings from hunger and how I appeased it. One very strong impression is of hunting little lizards on the rocky top of an open knoll. They ran under the rocks, and most of them escaped; but occasionally I turned over a stone and caught one. I was frightened away from this knoll by snakes. They did not pursue me. They were merely basking on flat rocks in the sun. But such was my inherited fear of them that I fled as fast as if they had been after me.

Then I gnawed bitter bark from young trees. I remember vaguely the eating of many green nuts, with soft shells and milky kernels. And I remember most distinctly suffering from a stomach-ache. It may have been caused by the green nuts, and maybe by the lizards. I do not know. But I do know that I was fortunate in not being devoured during the several hours I was knotted up on the ground with the colic.

Chapter V

MY VISION of the scene came abruptly, as I emerged from the forest. I found myself on the edge of a large clear space. On one side of this space rose up high bluffs. On the other side was the river. The earth bank ran steeply down to the water, but here and there, in several places, where at some time slides of earth had occurred, there were run-ways. These were the drinking-places of the Folk that lived in the caves.

And this was the main abiding-place of the Folk that I had chanced upon. This was, I may say, by stretching the word, the village. My mother and the Chatterer and I, and a few other simple bodies, were what might be termed suburban residents. We were part of the horde, though we lived a distance away from it. It was only a short distance, though it had taken me, what of my wandering, all of a week to arrive. Had I come directly, I could have covered the trip in an hour.

But to return. From the edge of the forest I saw the caves in the bluff, the open space, and the run-ways to the drinking-places. And in the open space I saw many of the Folk. I had been straying, alone and a child, for a week. During that time I had seen not one of my kind. I had lived in terror and desolation. And now, at the sight of my kind, I was overcome with gladness, and I ran wildly toward them.

Then it was that a strange thing happened. Someone of the Folk saw me and uttered a warning cry. On the instant, crying out with fear and panic, the Folk fled away. Leaping and scrambling over the rocks, they plunged into the mouths of the caves and disappeared...all but one, a little baby, that had been dropped in the excitement close to the base of the bluff. He was wailing dolefully. His mother dashed out; he sprang to meet her and held on tightly as she scrambled back into the cave.

I was all alone. The populous open space had of a sudden become deserted. I sat down forlornly and whimpered. I could not understand. Why had the Folk run away from me? In later time, when I came to know their ways, I was to learn. When they saw me dashing out of the forest at top speed they concluded that I was being pursued by some hunting animal. By my unceremonious approach I had stampeded them.

As I sat and watched the cave-mouths I became aware that the Folk were watching me. Soon they were thrusting their heads out. A little later they were calling back and forth to one another. In the hurry and confusion it had happened that all had not gained their own caves. Some of the young ones had sought refuge in other caves. The mothers did not call for them by name, because that was an invention we had not yet made. All were nameless. The mothers uttered querulous, anxious cries, which were recognized by the young ones. Thus, had my mother been there calling to me, I should have recognized her voice amongst the voices of a thousand mothers, and in the same way would she have recognized mine amongst a thousand.

This calling back and forth continued for some time, but they were too cautious to come out of their caves and descend to the ground. Finally one did come. He was destined to play a large part in my life, and for that matter he already played a large part in the lives of all the members of the horde. He it was whom I shall call Red-Eye in the pages of this history – so called because of his inflamed eyes, the lids being always red, and, by the peculiar effect they produced, seeming to advertise the terrible savagery of him. The color of his soul was red.

He was a monster in all ways. Physically he was a giant. He must have weighed one hundred and seventy pounds. He was the largest one of our kind I ever saw. Nor did I ever see one of the Fire People so large as he, nor one of the Tree People. Sometimes, when in the newspapers I happen upon descriptions of our modern bruisers and prizefighters, I wonder what chance the best of them would have had against him.

I am afraid not much of a chance. With one grip of his iron fingers and a pull, he could have plucked a muscle, say a biceps, by the roots, clear out of their bodies. A back-handed, loose blow of his fist could have smashed their skulls like egg-shells. With a sweep of his wicked feet (or hind-hands) he could have disembowelled them. A twist could have broken their necks, and I know that with a single crunch of his jaws he could have pierced, at the same moment, the great vein of the throat in front and the spinal marrow at the back.

He could spring twenty feet horizontally from a sitting position. He was abominably hairy. It was a matter of pride with us to be not very hairy. But he was covered with hair all over, on the inside of the arms as well as the outside, and even the ears themselves. The only places on him where the hair did not grow were the soles of his hands and feet and beneath his eyes. He was frightfully ugly, his ferocious grinning mouth and huge down-hanging under-lip being but in harmony with his terrible eyes.

This was Red-Eye. And right gingerly he crept out or his cave and descended to the ground. Ignoring me, he proceeded to reconnoitre. He bent forward from the hips as he walked; and so far forward did he bend, and so long were his arms, that with every step he touched the knuckles of his hands to the ground on either side of him. He was awkward in the semi-erect position of walking that he assumed, and he really touched his knuckles to the ground in order to balance himself. But oh, I tell you he could run on all-fours! Now this was something at which we were particularly awkward. Furthermore, it was a rare individual among us who balanced himself with his knuckles when walking. Such an individual was an atavism, and Red-Eye was an even greater atavism.

That is what he was – an atavism. We were in the process of changing our tree-life to life on the ground. For many generations we had been going through this change, and our bodies and carriage had likewise changed. But Red-Eye had reverted to the more primitive tree-dwelling type. Perforce, because he was born in our horde he stayed with us; but in actuality he was an atavism and his place was elsewhere.

Very circumspect and very alert, he moved here and there about the open space, peering through the vistas among the trees and trying to catch a glimpse of the hunting animal that all suspected had pursued me. And while he did this, taking no notice of me, the Folk crowded at the cave-mouths and watched.

At last he evidently decided that there was no danger lurking about. He was returning from the head of the run-way, from where he had taken a peep down at the drinking-place. His course brought him near, but still he did not notice me. He proceeded casually on his way until abreast of me, and then, without warning and with incredible swiftness, he smote me a buffet on the head. I was knocked backward fully a dozen feet before I fetched up against the ground, and I remember, half-stunned, even as the blow was struck, hearing the wild uproar of clucking and shrieking laughter that arose from the caves. It was a great joke – at least in that day; and right heartily the Folk appreciated it.

Thus was I received into the horde. Red-Eye paid no further attention to me, and I was at liberty to whimper and sob to my heart's content. Several of the women gathered curiously about me, and I recognized them. I had encountered them the preceding year when my mother had taken me to the hazelnut canyons.

But they quickly left me alone, being replaced by a dozen curious and teasing youngsters. They formed a circle around me, pointing their fingers, making faces, and poking and pinching me. I was frightened, and for a time I endured them, then anger got the best of me and I sprang tooth and nail upon the most audacious one of them – none other than Lop-Ear himself. I have so named him because he could prick up only one of his ears. The other ear always hung limp and without movement. Some accident had injured the muscles and deprived him of the use of it.

He closed with me, and we went at it for all the world like a couple of small boys fighting. We scratched and bit, pulled hair, clinched, and threw each other down. I remember I succeeded in getting on him what in my college days I learned was called a half-Nelson. This hold gave me the decided advantage. But I did not enjoy it long. He twisted up one leg, and with the foot (or hind-hand) made so savage an onslaught upon my abdomen as to threaten to disembowel me. I had to release him in order to save myself, and then we went at it again.

Lop-Ear was a year older than I, but I was several times angrier than he, and in the end he took to his heels. I chased him across the open and down a run-way to the river. But he was better acquainted with the locality and ran along the edge of the water and up another run-way. He cut diagonally across the open space and dashed into a wide-mouthed cave.

Before I knew it, I had plunged after him into the darkness. The next moment I was badly frightened. I had never been in a cave before. I began to whimper and cry out. Lop-Ear chattered mockingly at me, and, springing upon me unseen, tumbled me over. He did not risk a second encounter, however, and took himself off. I was between him and the entrance, and he did not pass me; yet he seemed to have gone away. I listened, but could get no clue as to where he was. This puzzled me, and when I regained the outside I sat down to watch.

He never came out of the entrance, of that I was certain; yet at the end of several minutes he chuckled at my elbow. Again I ran after him, and again he ran into the cave; but this time I stopped at the mouth. I dropped back a short distance and watched. He did not come out, yet, as before, he chuckled at my elbow and was chased by me a third time into the cave.

This performance was repeated several times. Then I followed him into the cave, where I searched vainly for him. I was curious. I could not understand how he eluded me. Always he went into the cave, never did he come out of it, yet always did he arrive there at my elbow and mock me. Thus did our fight transform itself into a game of hide and seek.

All afternoon, with occasional intervals, we kept it up, and a playful, friendly spirit arose between us. In the end, he did not run away from me, and we sat together with our arms around each other. A little later he disclosed the mystery of the wide-mouthed cave. Holding me by the hand he led me inside. It connected by a narrow crevice with another cave, and it was through this that we regained the open air.

We were now good friends. When the other young ones gathered around to tease, he joined with me in attacking them; and so viciously did we behave that before long I was let alone. Lop-Ear made me acquainted with the village. There was little that he could tell me of conditions and customs – he had not the necessary vocabulary; but by observing his actions I learned much, and also he showed me places and things.

He took me up the open space, between the caves and the river, and into the forest beyond, where, in a grassy place among the trees, we made a meal of stringy-rooted carrots. After that we had a good drink at the river and started up the run-way to the caves.

It was in the run-way that we came upon Red-Eye again. The first I knew, Lop-Ear had shrunk away to one side and was crouching low against the bank. Naturally and involuntarily, I imitated him. Then it was that I looked to see the cause of his fear. It was Red-Eye, swaggering down the centre of the run-way and scowling fiercely with his inflamed eyes. I noticed that all the youngsters shrank away from him as we had done, while the grown-ups regarded him with wary eyes when he drew near, and stepped aside to give him the centre of the path.

As twilight came on, the open space was deserted. The Folk were seeking the safety of the caves. Lop-Ear led the way to bed. High up the bluff we climbed, higher than all the other caves, to a tiny crevice that could not be seen from the ground. Into this Lop-Ear squeezed. I followed with difficulty, so narrow was the entrance, and found myself in a small rock-chamber. It was very low – not more than a couple of feet in height, and possibly three feet by four in width and length. Here, cuddled together in each other's arms, we slept out the night.

The complete and unabridged text is available online, from *flametreepublishing.com/extras*

The Panchronicon
Chapters I–V

Harold Steele MacKaye

Chapter I
The Theory of Copernicus Droop

THE TWO SISTERS were together in their garden.

Rebecca Wise, turned forty and growing slightly gray at the temples, was moving slowly from one of her precious plants to the next, leaning over each to pinch off a dead leaf or count the buds. It was the historic month of May, 1898, and May is the paradise of flower lovers.

Phoebe was eighteen years younger than her sister, and the beauty of the village. Indeed, many declared their belief that the whole State of New Hampshire did not contain her equal.

She was seated on the steps of the veranda that skirted the little white cottage, and the absent gaze of her frank blue eyes was directed through the gate at the foot of the little path bordered by white rose-bushes. In her lap was a bundle of papers yellowed by age and an ivory miniature, evidently taken from the carved wooden box at her side.

Presently Rebecca straightened her back with a slight grimace and looked toward her sister, holding her mold-covered hands and fingers spread away from her.

"Well," she inquired, "hev ye found anythin'?"

Phoebe brought her gaze back from infinity and replied:

"No, I ain't. Only that one letter where Isaac Burton writes her that the players have come to town."

"I don't see what good them letters'll do ye in the Shakespeare class, then."

Rebecca spoke listlessly – more interested in her garden than in her sister's search.

"I don't know," Phoebe rejoined, dreamily. "It's awful funny – but whenever I take out these old letters there comes over me the feelin' that I'm 'way off in a strange country – and I feel like somebody else."

Rebecca looked up anxiously from her work.

"Them sort o' philanderin' notions are foolish, Phoebe," she said, and flicked a caterpillar over the fence.

Phoebe gave herself a little shake and began to tie up the papers.

"That's so," she replied. "But they will come when I get these out, an' I got 'em out thinkin' the' might be somethin' about Shakespeare in 'em for our class."

She paused and looked wistfully at the letters again.

"Oh!" she cried, "how I do wonder if he was among those players at the Peacock Inn that day! You know 'players' is what they called play-actors in those days, and he was a play-actor, they say."

"Did he live very far back, then?" said Rebecca, wishing to appear interested, but really intent upon a new sprout at the foot of the lilac-bush.

"Yes, three hundred years ago. Three of these letters has a date in 1598 exactly."

There was a long silence, and at length Rebecca looked up from the ground to ascertain its cause. She frowned and drew her aching back stiffly straight again.

"Everlastin'ly lookin' at that pictur'!" she exclaimed. "I declare to goodness, Phoebe Wise, folks'll think you're vain as a pouter pigeon."

Phoebe laughed merrily, tossed the letters into the box and leaped to her feet. The miniature at which she had been gazing was still in her hands.

"Folks'll never see me lookin' at it, Rebecca – only you," she said.

Then with a coaxing tone and looking with appealing archness at her sister, she went on:

"Is it really like me, Rebecca? Honest true?"

The elder woman merely grunted and moved on to the next bed, and Phoebe, with another laugh, ran lightly into the house.

A few moments later she reappeared at the front door with consternation on her face.

"Land o' goodness, Rebecca!" she cried, "do you know what time it is? Near onto one o'clock, an' I've got to be at the Shakespeare class at half past. We'll have to dish up dinner right this minute, and I don't see how I can change my dress after it an' help with the dishes too."

She whisked into the house again, and Rebecca followed her as rapidly as possible.

She was very proud of her baby sister, proud of her having been 'clear through high school,' and proud of her eminence in the local literary society. There was certainly something inspiring in having a sister who was first corresponding secretary of the Women's Peltonville Association for the Study of Shakespearian History and Literature; and it was simply wonderful how much poetry she could repeat from the pages of her favorite author.

* * *

Peltonville Center, New Hampshire, was one of those groups of neatly kept houses surrounding a prettily shaded, triangular common which seem to be characteristic of New England. Standing two miles from the nearest railway station, this little settlement possessed its own combined store and post-office, from whose narrow veranda one might watch the rising generation playing Saturday base-ball on the grassy triangle.

The traditional old meeting-house stood on the opposite side of the common, facing the store. The good old days of brimstone theology were past, and the descendants of the godly Puritans who raised this steeple 'in the fear of the Lord,' being now deprived of their chief source of fear, found Sunday meetings a bore, and a village pastor an unnecessary luxury.

Indeed, there seemed little need of pastoral admonition in such a town as Peltonville Center. There was a grimly commonplace and universal goodness everywhere, and the village was only saved from unconsciousness of its own perfection by the individual shortcomings of one of its citizens. Fortunately for the general self-complacence, however, the necessary revealing contrast was found in him.

Copernicus Droop was overfond of the bottle, and in spite of the prohibition laws of his State, he proved himself a blessed example and warning by a too frequent and unmistakable intoxication in public. He was gentle and even apologetic in his cups, but he was clearly a 'slave of rum' and his mission was therefore fulfilled.

On this first of May, 1898, a number of idle young men sat in a row on the edge of the store veranda. Some were whittling, some making aimless marks in the dust with a stick. All leaned limply forward, with their elbows on their knees.

It was clearly not a Sunday, for the meeting-house was open, and from time to time, one or perhaps two young women together passed into the cool and silent room. The loungers at the store let none escape their notice, and the name of each damsel was passed down the line in an undertone as its owner entered the church.

A lantern-jawed young farmer at the end of the row slowly brushed the shavings from his clothes and remarked:

"Thet's the secon' meetin' of the Shekspeare class this month, ain't it?"

"Yep, an' there'll be two more afore the summer boarders comes up –"

The second speaker would have continued, but he was here interrupted by a third, who whispered loudly:

"Say, fellers, there goes Copernicus."

All eyes were raised and unanimously followed the shabby figure which had just emerged from behind the church and now started into the road leading away from the common toward the north.

"Walks pretty straight fer him, don't he?" snickered the first speaker.

"He's not ben tight fer two days."

"Bet ye a jack-knife he'll be spreein' it fer all he's wuth tomorrow."

Fortunately these comments did not reach the ears of their object, who, all unconscious of the interest which he inspired, made good his way at a fairly rapid pace.

Presently he stopped.

With muslin skirts swaying, hair rumpled, and fair young face flushed with exertion, Phoebe Wise was hurrying toward the common. She was almost running in her haste, for she was late and the Shakespeare class was a momentous institution.

"Oh, say, Cousin Phoebe," was the man's greeting, "can you tell me ef yer sister's to home?"

The young girl came to a sudden full stop in her surprise. This cousinly greeting from the village reprobate was as exciting and as inexplicable as it was unheard of.

"Why, Mr. Droop!" she exclaimed, "I – I – I s'pose so."

The truth was the truth, after all. But it was hard on Rebecca. What *could* this man want with her sister?

Droop nodded and passed on.

"Thank ye. Don't stop fer me," he said.

Phoebe moved forward slowly, watching Copernicus over her shoulder. She noted his steady steps and pale face and, reassured, resumed her flying progress with redoubled vigor. After all, Rebecca was forty-two years old and well able to take care of herself.

Meanwhile, Rebecca Wise, having carefully wrung out her dishcloth, poured out the water and swept the little sink, was slowly untying her kitchen apron, full of a thankful sense of the quiet hour before her wherein to knit and muse beside the front window of her little parlor.

In the centre of this room there stood a wide, round table, bearing a large kerosene-lamp and the week's mending. At the back and opposite the two windows stood the well-blacked, shiny, air-tight stove. Above this was a wooden mantel, painted to imitate marble, whereon were deposited two photographs, four curious Chinese shells, and a plaster cross to which there clung a very plaster young woman in scant attire, the whole being marked 'Rock of Ages' in gilt letters at the base.

Horse-hair furniture in all the glory of endless 'tidies' was arranged against walls bedight with a rainbow-like wilderness of morning-glories. The ceiling was of white plaster, and the floor was painted white and decked here and there with knitted rag-carpets, on whose Joseph's-coated surfaces Rebecca loved to gaze when in retrospective mood. In those humble floor-coverings her knowing eyes recognized her first clocked stockings and Phoebe's baby cloak. There was her brother Robert's wool tippet embalmed in loving loops with the remnants of his wife's best Sunday-go-to-meetin' ribbons. These two had long been dead, but their sister's loving eyes recreated them in rag-carpet dreams wherein she lived again those by-gone days.

Rebecca had just seated herself and was unrolling her work, when her eyes caught a glimpse of a man's form through the window. He had passed into her gate and was approaching the door. She leaned forward for a good look and then dropped back into her chair with a gasp of surprise.

"Copernicus Droop!" she exclaimed, "Did you ever!"

She sat in rigid astonishment until she heard his timid knock, followed by the sound of shoes vigorously wiped upon the door-mat.

"Well, come! Thet's a comfort!" she thought. "He won't muss the carpet" – and she rose to admit her visitor.

"Good mornin'," said Droop, timidly. "I seen Cousin Phoebe a-runnin' down the road, an' I sorter thought I'd run in an' see how you was."

"Come right in," said Rebecca, in non-committal tones. She shut the door and followed him into the parlor.

"Here, give me yer hat," she continued. "Set right there. How be ye?"

Droop obeyed. In a few moments the two were seated facing each other, and Rebecca's needles were already busy. There was an interval of awkward silence.

"Well, what did ye come fer?"

It was Rebecca who broke the spell. In her usual downright fashion, she came to the point at once. She thought it as well he should know that she was not deceived by his polite pretence of casual friendly interest.

Droop settled forward with elbows on his knees and brought his fingertips carefully and accurately together. He found this action amazingly promotive of verbal accuracy.

"Well, Cousin Rebecca," he began, slowly, "I'm lookin' fer a partner." He paused, considering how to proceed.

The spinster let her hands drop in speechless wonder. The audacity of the man! He – to her – a proposal! At her age! From him!

Fortunately the next few words disclosed her error, and she blushed for it as she lifted her work again, turning nearer the window as if for better light.

"Yes," Droop proceeded, "I've a little business plan, an' it needs capital an' a partner."

He waited, but there was no response.

"Capital an' a partner," he repeated, "an' intelligence an' ambition. So I come to you."

Rebecca turned toward him again, scarcely less surprised now than before.

"To me! D'ye mean to say ye've me in yer mind fer a partner – with capital?"

Droop nodded slowly and compressed his lips.

"Well, I want to know!" she exclaimed, helplessly.

"Oh, I know you ain't overly rich right now," said Droop, apologetically; "but it warn't no secret thet ye might hev hed Joe Chandler ef ye hadn't ben so shifty in yer mind an' fell betwixt two stools – an' Lord knows Joe Chandler was as rich as – as Peter Craigin down to Keene – pretty nigh."

Again Rebecca blushed, but this time in anger.

"See here, Copernicus Droop –" she began.

"Oh, I don't mean nothin' mean, now," he insisted, earnestly. "I'm jest leadin' up to the pint sorter natural like – breakin' the thing easy, ye know."

"What *air* you a-drivin' at?"

Droop shifted uneasily in his seat and ran his finger around inside of his collar before he replied:

"Ye see, it's sorter hard to explain. It's this way. I hev a mighty fine plan in my mind founded on a mixin' up of astronomical considerations with prior inventions –"

"Mister Droop!" exclaimed his hostess, gazing severely into his eyes, "ef you think I'll let you go to drinkin' rum till –"

"Honest to goodness, Miss Wise, I've not teched a drop!" cried Droop, leaping to his feet and leaning forward quickly. "You may smell my breath ef –"

A violent push sent him back to his chair.

"Thet'll do, Mr. Droop. I'll undertake to believe ye fer once, but I'll thank ye to speak plain English."

"I'll do my best," he sighed, plaintively. "I don't blame ye fer not takin' to it quick. I didn't myself at first. Well – here. Ye see – ye know –"

He paused and swallowed hard, gazing at the ceiling for inspiration. Then he burst out suddenly:

"Ye know the graphophone an' the kodak and the biograph an' all them things what ye can see down to Keene?"

Rebecca nodded slowly, with suspicion still in her eye.

"Well, the's a heap o' things ben invented since the Centennial of 1876. Don't you s'pose they've made hills o' money out o' them things – with patents an' all?"

"Of course."

"An' don't you s'pose that ef anybody in 1876 was to up an' bring out sech inventions all at once he'd be bigger than all the other inventors put together!"

Rebecca slowly pushed her needle through her hair, which was a sign of thoughtfulness.

"Wal, o' course," she said, at length, "ef anybody hed aben smart enough to've invented all them things in 1876 he'd aben a pretty big man, I guess."

Droop edged forward eagerly.

"An' s'posen' that you hed married Joe Chandler back in 1876, an' you was rich enough to back up an inventor like that, an' he come to you an' offered to give you half ef you'd up an' help him put 'em on the market, an' s'posen' –"

"What the land sake's the use o' s'posin'?" Rebecca cried, sharply. "This is 1898, an' I ain't married, thanks be to goodness!"

"Ah, but ye could be, ef we was in 1876! There, there – I know what you want to say – but 'taint so! What would ye say ef I was to tell ye that all ye've got to do is jest to get into a machine I've got an' I can take ye back to 1876 in next to no time! What would ye say –"

"I'd say ye was tighter'n a boiled owl, Copernicus Droop."

"But I ain't, I ain't!" he almost screamed. "I tell ye I hevn't teched liquor fer two days. I've reformed. Ef ye won't smell my breath –"

"Then you're plum crazy," she interrupted.

"No, nor crazy either," he insisted. "Why, the whole principle of it is so awful simple! Ef you'd ben to high school, now, an' knew astronomy an' all, you'd see right through it like nothin'."

"Well, then, you c'n explain it to them as hez ben to high school, an' that's sister Phoebe. Here she comes now."

She went at once to the door to admit the new-comer. Her visitor, watching the pretty younger sister as she stepped in, rosy and full of life, could not but remark the contrast between the two women.

"Twenty-two years makes a heap o' difference!" he muttered. "But Rebecca was jest as pretty herself, back in 1876."

"Look, Rebecca!" cried Phoebe, as she entered the door, "here's a new book Mrs. Bolton lent me today. All about Bacon writing Shakespeare's plays, an' how Bacon was a son of Queen Elizabeth. Do you s'pose he really did?"

"Oh, don't ask me, child!" was the nervous reply. "Mr. Droop's in the parlor."

Phoebe had forgotten her short interview with Droop, and she now snatched off her hat in surprise and followed her elder sister, nodding to their visitor as she entered.

"Set down, both o' ye," said Rebecca. "Now, then, Mr. Droop, perhaps you'll explain."

Rebecca was far more mystified and interested than she cared to admit. Her brusque manner was therefore much exaggerated – a dissimulation which troubled her conscience, which was decidedly of the tenderest New England brand.

Poor Copernicus experienced a sense of relief as he turned his eyes to those of the younger sister. She felt that Rebecca's manner was distinctly cold, and her own expression was the more cordial in compensation.

"Why, Miss Phoebe," he said, eagerly, "I've ben tellin' your sister about my plan to go back to the Centennial year – 1876, ye know."

"To – to what, Mr. Droop?"

Phoebe's polite cordiality gave place to amazed consternation. Droop raised a deprecating hand.

"Now don't you go to think I'm tight or gone crazy. You'll understand it, fer you've ben to high school. Now see! What is it makes the days go by – ain't it the daily revolution of the sun?"

Phoebe put on what her sister always called "that schoolmarm look" and replied:

"Why, it's the turning round of the earth on its axis once in –"

"Yes – yes – it's all one – all one," Droop broke in, eagerly. "To put it another way, it comes from the sun cuttin' meridians, don't it?"

Rebecca, who found this technical and figurative expression beyond her, paused in her knitting and looked anxiously at Phoebe, to see how she would take it. After a moment of thought, the young woman admitted her visitor's premises.

"Very good! An' you know's well's I do, Miss Phoebe, that ef a man travels round the world the same way's the sun, he ketches up on time a whole day when he gets all the way round. In other words, the folks that stays at home lives jest one day more than the feller that goes round the world that way. Am I right?"

"Of course."

Droop glanced triumphantly at Rebecca. This tremendous admission on her learned young sister's part stripped her of all pretended coldness. Her deep interest was evident now in her whole pose and expression.

"Now, then, jest follow me close," Droop continued, sitting far forward in his chair and pointing his speech with a thin forefinger on his open palm.

"Ef a feller was to whirl clear round the world an' cut all the meridians in the same direction as the sun, an' he made the whole trip around jest as quick as the sun did – time wouldn't change a mite fer him, would it?"

Phoebe gasped at the suggestion.

"Why, I should think – of course –"

She stopped and put her hand to her head in bewilderment.

"Et's a sure thing!" Droop exclaimed, earnestly. "You've said yerself that the folks who stayed to home would live one day longer than the fellow that went round. Now, ef that feller travelled round as fast as the sun, the stay-at-homes would only be one day older by the time he got back – ain't that a fact?"

Both sisters nodded.

"Well, an' the traveller would be one day younger than they'd be. An' ain't that jest no older at all than when he started?"

"My goodness! Mr. Droop!" Phoebe replied, feebly. "I never thought of that."

"Well, ain't it so?"

"Of course – leastways – why, it must be!"

"All right, then!"

Droop rose triumphantly to his feet, overcome by his feelings.

"Follow out that same reasonin' to the bitter end!" he cried, "an' what will happen ef that traveller whirls round, cuttin' meridians jest twice as fast as the sun – goin' the same way?"

He paused, but there was no reply.

"Why, as sure as shootin', I tell ye, that feller will get jest one day younger fer every two whirls round!"

There was a long and momentous silence. The tremendous suggestion had for the moment bereft both women of all reasoning faculty.

At length the younger sister ventured upon a practical objection.

"But how's he goin' to whirl round as fast as that, Mr. Droop?" she said.

Droop smiled indulgently.

"Et does sound outlandish, when ye think how big the world is. But what if ye go to the North Pole? Ain't all the twenty-four meridians jammed up close together round that part of the globe?"

"Thet's so," murmured Rebecca, "I've seen it many's the time on the map in Phoebe's geography book."

"Sure enough," Droop rejoined. "Then ain't it clear that ef a feller'll jest take a grip on the North Pole an' go whirlin' round it, he'll be cuttin' meridians as fast as a hay-chopper? Won't he see the sun gettin' left behind an' whirlin' the other way from what it does in nature? An' ef the sun goes the other way round, ain't it sure to unwind all the time thet it's ben a-rollin' up?"

Rebecca's ball of yarn fell from her lap at this, and, as she followed it with her eyes, she seemed to see a practical demonstration of Droop's marvellous theory.

Phoebe felt all the tremendous force of Droop's logic, and she flushed with excitement. One last practical objection was obvious, however.

"The thing must be all right, Mr. Droop," she said; "an' come to think of it, this must be the reason so many folks have tried to reach the North Pole. But it never *has* been reached yet, an' how are you agoin' to do it?"

"You think it never hez," Copernicus replied. "The fact is, though, that I've ben there."

"You!" Phoebe cried.

"And is there a pole there?" Rebecca asked, eagerly.

"The's a pole there, an' I've swung round it, too," Droop replied, sitting again with a new and delightful sense of no longer being unwelcome.

"Here's how 'twas. About a year ago there come to my back door a strange-lookin' man who'd hurt his foot some way. I took him in an' fixed him up – you know I studied for a doctor once – an' while he was bein' fixed up, he sorter took a fancy to me an' he begun to give me the story of his life. He said he was born in the year 2582, an' had ben takin' what he called a historical trip into the past ages. He went on at a great rate like that, an' I thought he was jest wanderin' in his mind with the fever, so I humored him. But he saw through me, an' he wouldn't take no but I should go down into Burnham's swamp with him to see how he'd done it.

"Well, down we went, and right spang in the thickest of the bushes an' muck we come across the queerest lookin' machine that ever ye see!

"Right there an' then he told me all the scientific talk about time an' astronomy thet I've told you, an' then he tuck me into the thing. Fust thing I knew he give a yank to a lever in the machinery an' there was a big jerk thet near threw me on the back o' my head. I looked out, an' there we was a-flyin' over the country through the air fer the North Pole!"

"There, now!" cried Rebecca, "didn't Si Wilkins' boy Sam say he seen a comet in broad daylight last June?"

"Thet was us," Droop admitted.

"And not a soul believed him," Phoebe remarked.

"Well," continued Droop, "to make a long story short, thet future-man whirled me a few times 'round the North Pole – unwound jest five weeks o' time, an' back we come to Peltonville a-hummin'!"

"And then?" cried the two women together.

"Ef you'll believe me, there we was back to the day he fust come – an' fust thing I knew, thet future-man was a-comin' up to my back door, same ez before, a-beggin' to hev his foot fixed. It was hard on him, but I was convinced fer keeps."

Copernicus shook his head sadly, with retrospective sadness.

"An' where is the future-man now?" Phoebe asked.

"Tuk cold on his lungs at the North Pole," said Droop, solemnly. "Hed pneumonia an' up'n died."

"But there warn't nobody round heerd of him except you," said Rebecca. "Who buried him?"

"Ah, thet's one o' the beauties o' the hull business. He'd showed me all the ropes on his machine – his Panchronicon, as he called it – an' so I up'n flew round the North Pole the opposite way as soon's he passed away, till I'd made up the five weeks we'd lost. Then when I got back it was five weeks after his funeral, an' I didn't hev to bother about it."

The two sisters looked at each other, quite overcome with admiration.

"My land!" Rebecca murmured, gathering up her yarn and knitting again. "Sence they've invented them X-rays an' took to picturin' folks' insides, I kin believe anythin'."

"You don't hev to take my word fer it," Droop exclaimed. "Ef you'll come right along with me this blessed minute, I'll show you the machine right now."

"I'd jest love to see it," said Rebecca, her coldness all forgotten, "but it's mos' too late fer this afternoon. There's the supper to get, you know, an' –"

"But the plan, Rebecca," Phoebe cried. "You've forgotten that I haven't heard Mr. Droop's plan."

"I wish't you'd call me 'Cousin Copernicus,'" said Droop, earnestly. "You know I've sworn off – quit drinkin' now."

Phoebe blushed at his novel proposal and insisted on the previous question.

"But what is the plan?" she said.

"Why, my idea is this, Cousin Phoebe. I want we should all go back to 1876 again. Thet's the year your sister could hev married Joe Chandler ef she'd wanted to."

Rebecca murmured something unintelligible, blushing furiously, with her eyes riveted to her knitting. Phoebe looked surprised.

"You know you could, Cousin Rebecca," Droop insisted. "Now what I say is, let's go back there. I'll invent the graphophone, the kodak, the vitascope, an' Milliken's cough syrup an' a lot of other big modern inventions. Rebecca'll marry Chandler, an' she an' her husband can back up my big inventions with capital. Why, Cousin Phoebe," he cried, with enthusiasm, "we'll all hev a million apiece!"

The sentimental side of Droop's plan first monopolized Phoebe's attention.

"Rebecca Wise!" she exclaimed, turning with mock severity to face her sister. "Why is it I've never heard tell about this love affair before now? Why, Joe Chandler's just a *fine* man. Is it you that broke his heart an' made him an old bachelor all his life?"

Rebecca must have dropped a stitch, for she turned toward the window again and brought her knitting very close to her face.

"What brought ye so early to home, Phoebe?" she said. "Warn't there no Shakespeare meetin' today?"

"No. Mis' Beecher was to lead, an' she's been taken sick, so I came right home. But you can't sneak out of answerin' me like that, Miss Slyboots," Phoebe continued, in high spirits.

Seating herself on the arm of her sister's chair, she put her arms about her neck and, bending over, whispered:

"Tell me honest, now, Rebecca, did Joe Chandler ever propose to you?"

"No, he never did!" the elder sister exclaimed, rising suddenly.

"Now, Mr. Droop," she continued, "your hull plan is jest too absurd to think of –"

Droop tried to expostulate, but she raised her voice, speaking more quickly.

"An' you come 'round again after supper an' we'll tell ye what we've decided," she concluded.

The humor of this reply was lost on Copernicus, but he moved toward the door with a sense of distinct encouragement.

"Remember the rumpus we'll make with all them inventions," Droop called back as he walked toward the gate, "think of the money we'll make!"

But Rebecca was thinking of something very different as she stood at the front door gazing with softened eyes at the pasture and woods beyond the road. She seemed to see a self-willed girl breaking her own heart and another's rather than acknowledge a silly error. She was wondering if that had really been Rebecca Wise. She felt again all the old bewitching heart-pangs, sweetened and mellowed by time, and she wondered if she were *now* really Rebecca Wise.

Chapter II
A Visit to the Panchronicon

AT PRECISELY eight o'clock that evening, a knock was again heard at the door of the Wise home, and Droop was admitted by the younger sister. She did not speak, and her face was invisible in the dark hall. The visitor turned to the right and entered the parlor, followed by his young hostess. Rebecca was sitting by the lamp, sewing. As she looked up and nodded, Droop saw that her features expressed only gloomy severity. He turned in consternation and caught sight for the first time of Phoebe's face. Her eyes and pretty nose were red and her mouth was drawn into a curve of plaintive rebellion.

"Set down, Mr. Droop. Give me yer hat," she said; and there was a suspicious catch in her voice.

The visitor seated himself by the centre-table beside the lamp and sat slowly rubbing his hands, the while he gazed mournfully from one to the other of the silent sisters. Phoebe sat on the long horse-hair "settle," and played moodily with the tassel hanging at its head.

There was a long pause. Each of the women seemed bent on forcing the other to break the silence.

Poor Droop felt that his plans were doomed, and he dared not urge either woman to speech, lest he hear the death-sentence of his hopes. Finally, however, the awkward silence became unbearable.

"Well?" he said, inquiringly, still rubbing his hands.

"Well," Rebecca exclaimed, "it seems it's not to be done," and she looked reproachfully at Phoebe.

The words fulfilled his fears, but the tone and glance produced a thrill of hope. It was evident that Rebecca at least favored his plans.

Turning now to the younger sister, Droop asked, in a melancholy tone:

"Don't you want to get rich, Cousin Phoebe?"

"Rich – me!" she replied, indignantly. "A mighty lot of riches it'll bring me, won't it? That's just what riles me so! You an' Rebecca just think of nothin' but your own selves. You never stop to think of me!"

Droop opened his eyes very wide indeed, and Rebecca said, earnestly:

"Phoebe, you know you ain't got any call to say sech a thing!"

"Oh, haven't I?" cried Phoebe, in broken accents. "Did either of you think what would happen to me if we all went back to 1876? Two years old! That's what I'd be! A little toddling baby, like Susan Mellick's Annie! Put to bed before supper – carried about in everybody's arms – fed on a bottle and – and perhaps – and perhaps getting *spanked*!"

With the last word, Phoebe burst into tears of mingled grief and mortification and rushed from the room.

The others dared not meet each other's guilty eyes. Droop gazed about the room in painful indecision. He could not bear to give up all hope, and yet – this unforeseen objection really seemed a very serious one. To leave the younger sister behind was out of the question. On the other hand, the consequences of the opposite course were – well, painful to her at least.

In his nervousness he unconsciously grasped a small object on the table upon which his left hand had been lying. It was a miniature daintily painted on ivory. He looked vacantly upon it; his mind at first quite absent from his eyes. But as he gazed, something familiar in the lovely face depicted there fixed his attention. Before long he was examining the picture with the greatest interest.

"Well, now!" he exclaimed, at length. "Ain't that pretty! Looks jest like her, too. When was that tuck, Miss Wise?"

"That ain't Phoebe," said Rebecca, dejectedly.

"Ain't Phoebe!" Droop cried, in amazement. "Why, it's the finest likeness – why – but – it *must* be yer sister!"

"Well, 'tain't. Thet pictur is jest three hundred years old."

"Three hundred –" he began – then very slowly, "Well, now, do tell!" he said.

"Phoebe's got the old letter that tells about it. The's a lot of 'em in that little carved-wood box there. They say it come over in the Mayflower."

Droop could not take his eyes from the picture. The likeness was perfect. Here was the pretty youthful oval of her face – the same playful blue eye – the sensitive red lips seeming about to sparkle into a smile – even the golden brown mist of hair that hid the delicately turned ear!

Then Droop suddenly remembered his plans, and with his hand he dropped the picture as his mind dismissed it. He rose and looked about for his hat.

"Ye wouldn't want to come back to '76 with me an' leave Cousin Phoebe behind, would ye?" he suggested, dismally.

"What!" cried Rebecca, giving vent to her pent-up feelings, "an' never see my sister again! Why, I'd hev to come livin' along up behind her, and, all I could do, I'd never catch up with her – never! You'd ought to be ashamed to stand there an' think o' sech a thing, Copernicus Droop!"

For some time he stood with bent head and shoulders, twirling his hat between his fingers. At length he straightened up suddenly and moved toward the door.

"Well," he said, "the' isn't any use you seem' the Panchronicon now, is the'?"

"What's it like, Mr. Droop?" Rebecca inquired.

He paused helpless before the very thought of description.

"Oh," he said, weakly, "et's like – et's a – why – oh, it's a machine!"

"Hez it got wings?"

"Not exactly wings," he began, then, more earnestly, "why don't ye come and see it, anyway! It can't do ye any harm to jest look at it!"

Rebecca dropped her hands into her lap and replied, with a hesitating manner:

"I'd like to fust rate – it must be an awful queer machine! But I don't get much time fer traipsin' 'round now days."

"Why can't ye come right along now?" Droop asked, eagerly. "It's dry as a bone underfoot down in the swamp now. The's ben no rain in a long time."

She pondered some time before replying. Her first impulse was to reject the proposal as preposterous. The hour seemed very ill chosen. Rebecca was not accustomed to leaving home for any purpose at night, and she was extremely conservative.

On the other hand, she felt that only under cover of the darkness could she consent to go anywhere in company with the village reprobate. Every tongue in the place would be set wagging were she seen walking with Copernicus Droop. She had not herself known how strong was the curiosity which his startling theories and incredible story had awakened in her. She looked up at her visitor with indecision in her eyes.

"I don't see how I could go now," she said. "Besides, it's mos' too dark to see the thing, ain't it?"

"Not a mite," he replied, confidently. "The's lights inside I can turn on, an' we'll see the hull thing better'n by daylight."

Then, as she still remained undecided, he continued, in an undertone:

"Cousin Phoebe's up in her room, ain't she? Ye might not get another chance so easy."

He had guessed instinctively that, under the circumstances, Rebecca preferred not revealing to Phoebe her own continued interest in the wonderful machine.

The suggestion was vital. Phoebe was in all probability sulking in her own bedroom, and in that event would not quit it for an hour. It seemed now or never.

Rebecca rolled up her knitting work and rose to her feet.

"Jest wait here a spell," she said, rapidly. "I won't be a minute!"

* * *

Shortly afterward, two swiftly moving, shadowy figures emerged from the little white gate and turned into a dark lane made more gloomy by overhanging maples. This was the shortest route to Burnham's swamp.

Copernicus was now more hopeful. He could not but feel that, if the elder sister came face to face with his marvellous machine, good must result for his plans. Rebecca walked with nervous haste, dreading Phoebe's possible discovery of this most unconventional conduct.

The night was moonless, and the two stumbled and groped their way down the lane at a pace whose slowness exasperated Rebecca.

"Ef I'd a-known!" she exclaimed, under her breath.

"We're 'most there, Cousin Rebecca," said Copernicus, with deprecating softness. "Here, give me holt o' yer hand while we climb over the wall. Here's Burnham's swamp right now."

Accepting the proffered aid, Rebecca found herself in the midst of a thicket of bushes, many of which were thorny and all of which seemed bent upon repelling nocturnal adventurers.

Droop, going ahead, did his best to draw aside the obstinate twigs, and Rebecca followed him with half-averted head, lifting her skirts and walking sidewise.

"'Mighty lucky, 'tain't wet weather!" she mumbled.

At that moment her guide stood still.

"There!" he exclaimed, in a low, half-awed voice.

Rebecca stopped and gazed about. A little to the right the dark gray of the sky was cut by a looming black mass of uncertain form.

It looked like the crouching phantom of some shapeless sea-monster. Rebecca half expected to see it dissolve like a wind-driven fog.

Their physical sight could distinguish nothing of the outer characteristics of this mysterious structure; but for this very reason, the imagination was the more active. Rebecca, with all her directness of nature and commonplace experience, felt in this unwonted presence that sense of awed mystery which she would have called a 'creepy feeling.'

What unknown and incomprehensible forces were locked within that formless mass? By what manner of race as yet unborn had its elements been brought together – no, no – *would* they be brought together? How assume a comfortable mental attitude toward this creation whose present existence so long antedated its own origin?

One sentiment, at least, Rebecca could entertain with hearty consistency. Curiosity asserted its supremacy over every other feeling.

"Can't we get into the thing, an' light a candle or suthin'?" she said.

"Of course we can," said Droop. "That's what I brought ye here fer. Take holt o' my hand an' lift yer feet, or you'll stumble."

Leading his companion by the hand, Copernicus approached the dark form, moving with great caution over the clumps of grassy turf. Presently he reached the side of the machine. Rebecca heard him strike it with his hand two or three times, as though groping for something. Then she was drawn forward again, and suddenly found herself entering an invisible doorway. She stumbled on the threshold and flung out her free hand for support. She clutched at a hand-rail that seemed to lead spirally upward.

Droop's voice came out of the blackness.

"Jest wait here a minute," he said. "I'll go up an' turn on the light."

She heard him climbing a short flight of stairs, and a few moments later a flood of light streamed from a doorway above her head, amply lighting the little hallway in which Rebecca was standing.

The hand-rail to which she was already clinging skirted the iron stairs leading to the light, and she started at once up this narrow spiral.

She was met at the door by Copernicus, who was smiling with a proud complacency.

"Wal, Cousin Rebecca," he said, with a sweeping gesture indicating their general surroundings, "what d'ye think o' this?"

They were standing at the head of a sort of companion-way in a roomy antechamber much resembling the general cabin of a luxurious old-time sailing-packet. The top of the stairs was placed between two windows in one side wall of the machine, through which there was just then entering a gentle breeze. Two similar openings faced these in the opposite side wall, and under each of the four windows there was a long wooden bench carrying a flat mattress cushion.

In the middle of the room, on a square deep-piled rug, stood a table covered with a red cloth and surrounded by three or four solid-looking upholstered chairs. Here were some books and papers, and directly over the table a handsome electric chandelier hung from the ceiling of dark-wood panels. This was the source of their present illumination.

"This here's the settin'-room," Droop explained. "An' these are the state-rooms – that's what he called 'em."

He walked toward two doors in one of the end walls and, opening one of them, turned the switch of the lamp within.

"'Lectric lights in it, like down to Keene," Rebecca remarked, approaching the cabin and peering in.

She saw a small bedroom comfortably furnished. The carpet was apparently new, and on the tastefully papered walls hung a number of small oil-paintings.

Droop opened the other door.

"They're both alike," he said.

Rebecca glanced into the second apartment, which was indeed the counterpart of its companion.

"Well, it wouldn't do no harm to sweep an' beat these carpets!" she exclaimed. Then, slipping her forefinger gingerly over the edge of a chair: "Look at that dust!" she said, severely, holding up her hand for inspection.

But Droop had bustled off to another part of the room.

"Here's lockers under these window-seats," he explained, with a dignified wave of the hand. "Here's books an' maps in this set o' shelves. Here's a small pianner that plays itself when you turn on the electricity –"

There was a stumbling crash and a suppressed cry at the foot of the stairs.

With his heart in his mouth, Droop leaped to the chandelier and turned out the lights; then rushed to the state-rooms and was about to turn their switches as well, when a familiar voice greeted their ears from below –

"Don't be scared – it's only Phoebe."

"What ever possessed –" began Rebecca, in a low tone.

But at that moment Phoebe's head appeared over the stair rail in the light shed from the two state-rooms.

"Won't you light up again, Mr. Droop?" she said, merrily, smiling the while into her sister's crestfallen face. "I heard you two leavin' the house, an' I just guessed what you'd be up to. So I followed you down here."

She dropped into one of the chairs beside the table just as Droop relighted the lamps.

With one slender hand resting upon the table, she looked up into Droop's face and went on:

"I was havin' a dreadful time, stumbling over stocks an' stones at every step, till suddenly there was quite a light struck my face, and first I knew I was lookin' right into your lighted windows. I guess we'll have a pleasant meetin' here of all the folks in town pretty soon – not to mention the skeeters, which are comin' right early this year!"

"Lands sakes!" cried Rebecca.

"There now!" exclaimed Copernicus, bustling toward the windows, "I must be a nateral born fool!"

Phoebe laughed in high spirits at thought of her prank, while Droop closed the tight iron shutters at each window, thus confining every ray of light.

Rebecca seated herself opposite Phoebe and looked severely straight before her with her hands folded in her lap. She was ashamed of her curiosity and much chagrined at being discovered in this unconventional situation by her younger sister.

Phoebe gazed about her and, having taken in the general aspect of the antechamber in which they were assembled, she explored the two state-rooms. Thence she returned for a more detailed survey. Droop followed her about explaining everything, but Rebecca remained unmoved.

"What's all those dials on the wall, Mr. Droop?" asked the younger sister.

"I wish't you'd call me Cousin Copernicus," said Droop, appealingly.

Phoebe ran up very close to a large steel dial-plate covered with figures.

"Now what the land is this for?" she exclaimed.

"Thet," said Droop, slowly, "is an indicator of height above ground and tells yer direction."

"And what d'ye do with this little handle?"

"Why, you set that for north or west or any other way, an' the hull machine keeps headed that way until ye change it."

"Oh, is that the rudder?"

"No, that is fer settin' jest one course fer a long ride – like's ef we was goin' north to the pole, ye know. The rudder's in here, 'long with the other machinery."

He walked to one of the two doors which faced the state-rooms.

Phoebe followed him and found herself in the presence of a bewildering array of controlling and guiding handles – gauges – test cocks – meters and indicators. She was quite overawed, and listened with a new respect for her distant relative as he explained the uses of the various instruments. It was evident that he had quite mastered the significance of each implement.

When Droop had completed his lecture, Phoebe found that she understood the uses of three of the levers. The rest was a mystery to her.

"This is the starting-lever," she said. "This steers, and this reverses. Is that it?"

"That's correct," said Droop, "an' if –

She cut him short by whisking out of the room.

"What drives the thing?" she asked, as he meekly followed her.

"Oh, the's power storage an' all kinds o' works down below stairs."

"An' what's this room for?" she asked, opening the door next the engine-room.

"Thet's the kitchen an' butler's pantry," said Droop. "It's mighty finely fitted up, I tell ye. That future-man was what ye call a conusure. My, but he could cook up fine victuals!"

Rebecca found this temptation stronger than her ill humor, and she rose with alacrity and followed her companions into the now brightly lighted kitchen.

Here the appointments were the completest possible, and, after she and Phoebe had mastered the theory of the electric range, they agreed that they had never seen such a satisfactory equipment.

Phoebe stood in the middle of the room and looked about her with kindling eyes. The novelty of this adventure had intoxicated her. Rebecca's enthusiasm was repeated threefold in the more youthful bosom of her sister.

"My!" she cried, "wouldn't it be lovely if we could make this our house down here for a while! What would the Mellicks an' the Tituses an' –"

"They'd take us for a lunatic asylum," Rebecca exclaimed, severely.

Phoebe considered a moment and then gravely replied:

"Yes, I s'pose they would."

Copernicus was pacing slowly up and down from range to china-closet and back, rubbing his hands slowly over each other.

"I wish't you'd try to see ef ye couldn't change yer mind, Cousin Phoebe," he said, earnestly. "Jest think of all there is in this extrordnery vessel – what with kitchen an' little cunnin' state-rooms – what with the hull machinery an' all – it's a sinful waste to leave it all to rot away down in this here swamp when we might all go back to the Centennial an' get rich as – as Solomon's temple!"

Phoebe led the way in silence to the outer room again, and Droop carefully extinguished the lights in the kitchen and engine-room.

As the three stood together under the main chandelier their faces were the exponents of three different moods.

Droop was wistful – anxious.

Rebecca looked grimly regretful.

In Phoebe's eyes there shone a cheerful light – but her expression was enigmatic.

"Now let's go home," she said, briskly. "I've got somethin' that I want to talk to Rebecca about. Can't you call in tomorrow mornin', Mr. Droop?"

"Don't ye believe ye might change yer mind?" he asked, mournfully.

"We'll be through with the breakfast an' have things set to rights by eight o'clock," said Phoebe.

Chapter III
A Nocturnal Evasion

PROMPTLY at the appointed time, Copernicus Droop might have been seen approaching the white cottage. Still nursing a faint hope, he walked with nervous rapidity, mumbling and gesticulating in his excitement. He attracted but little attention. His erratic movements were credited to his usual potations, and no one whom he passed even gave him a second glance.

Nearing the house he saw Phoebe leaning out of one of the second-story windows. She had been gazing westward toward Burnham's swamp, but she caught sight of Droop and nodded brightly to him. Then she drew in her head and pulled down the window.

Phoebe opened the door as Copernicus entered the garden gate, and it was at once apparent that her buoyant mood was still upon her, for she actually offered her hand to her visitor as he stood at the threshold wiping his feet.

"Good mornin'," she said. "I've ben tryin' to see if I could find the Panchronicon out of my window. It's just wonderful how well it's hidden in the bushes."

She led him to the parlor and offered him a seat.

"Where's Cousin Rebecca?" he said, as he carefully placed his hat on the floor beside his chair.

Phoebe seated herself opposite to her visitor with her back to the windows, so that her face was in shadow.

"Rebecca's upstairs," she replied.

Then, after a moment's pause: "She's packin' up," she said.

Droop straightened up excitedly.

"What – packin'!" he cried. "Hev ye decided ye'll go, then?"

"Well," said Phoebe, slowly, "we have an' – an' we haven't."

"What d'ye mean?"

"Why, Mr. Droop, it's just like this," she exclaimed, leaning forward confidentially. "Ye see, Rebecca an' I are both just plumb crazy to try that wonderful plan of cuttin' meridians at the

North Pole – an' we're wild fer a ride on that queer kind of a boat or whatever ye call it. At the same time, Rebecca has to acknowledge that it's askin' too much of me to go back to two years old an' live like a baby. For one thing, I wouldn't have a thing to wear."

"But ye might make some clothes before ye start," Droop suggested.

"Mr. Droop!" Phoebe exclaimed, severely, "what *do* you s'pose folks would say if Rebecca and I was to set to work makin' baby clothes – two old maids like us?"

Droop looked down in confusion and plucked at the edge of his coat.

"Phoebe Wise, you're only just tryin' to be smart fer argument!"

This sentence was delivered with a suddenness which was startling. Droop looked up with a jump to find Rebecca standing at the door with a pile of clean sheets on her arm.

She was gazing sternly at Phoebe, who appeared somewhat disconcerted.

"You know's well's I do," continued the elder sister, "that every one o' your baby clothes is folded an' put away as good as new in the attic."

Phoebe rallied quickly and repelled this attack with spirit.

"Well, I don't care. They'll stay right where they are, Rebecca," she answered, with irritation. "You know we settled it last night that I wasn't to be pestered about goin' back to 1876!"

"That's true," was the reply, "but don't you be givin' such fool reasons for it. It's really just because you're afraid o' bein' whipped an' put to bed – an' goodness knows, you deserve it!"

With this, Rebecca turned grimly and went into the garden to hang the sheets up for an airing.

There was a moment's awkward pause, and then Phoebe broke the silence.

"Our plan's this, Mr. Droop," she said, "an' I hope you'll agree. We want to have you take us to the North Pole and unwind about six years. That'll take us back before the World's Fair in Chicago, when I was eighteen years old, an' we can see fer ourselves how it feels to be livin' backward an' growin' younger instead of older every minute."

"But what's the good of that?" Droop asked, querulously. "I ain't goin' to do it jest fer fun. I'm growin' too old to waste time that way. My plan was to make money with all them inventions."

"Well, an' why can't ye?" she replied, coaxingly. "There's that X-ray invention, now. Why couldn't you show that at the World's Fair an' get a patent fer it?"

"I don't understand that business," he replied, sharply. "Besides I can't get one o' them X-ray machines – they cost a heap."

This was a blow to Phoebe's plan and she fell silent, thinking deeply. She had foreseen that Droop would take only a mercenary view of the matter and had relied upon the X-ray to provide him with a motive. But if he refused this, what was she to do?

Suddenly her face lighted up.

"I've got it!" she cried. "You know those movin' picture boxes ye see down to Keene, where ye turn a handle and a lot of photograph cards fly along like rufflin' the leaves of a book. Why, it just makes things look alive, Mr. Droop. I'm sure those weren't thought of six years ago. They're span spinter new. Why won't they do?"

"I ain't got one o' those either," Droop grumbled. "I've got a kodak an' a graphophone an' a lot o' Milliken's cough syrup with the recipe –"

"Why there!" cried Phoebe, exultantly. "Milliken's cough syrup is only four years old, ain't it?"

Droop did not reply, but his silence was a virtual assent.

"The's a mint o' money in that – you know there is, Mr. Droop," she urged. "Why, I guess Mr. Milliken must have two or three millions, hasn't he?"

Rebecca returned at this moment and seated herself on the haircloth settle, nodding silently to Droop.

"What's about Mr. Milliken's money, Phoebe?" she asked.

"Why Mr. Droop says the X-ray is no good because it costs a heap and he hasn't got a machine fer it – an' I was tellin' him that Milliken's cough syrup was just as good – for that wasn't invented six years ago, an' –"

"Phoebe Wise, what do you mean!" exclaimed Rebecca. "Why, it would be jest like robbery to take Mr. Milliken's syrup, an' palm it off as Mr. Droop's. I'm surprised at ye!"

This attack upon the ethical plane struck Phoebe speechless. She blushed and stammered, but had no reply to make. The seeming defeat really concealed a victory, however, for it instantly converted Copernicus into an ally.

"You don't understand the thing, Cousin Rebecca," he said, gently but firmly. "Ye see ef we go six years back, it'll be a time when Mr. Milliken hadn't ever thought of his cough syrup. How could we be robbin' him of somethin' he hasn't got?"

Rebecca looked confused for a moment, but was not to be so easily convinced.

"'Tain't somethin' he ain't thought of," she said, stoutly. "He's makin' money out of it, an' ef we get back before him, why, when time comes agin for him to invent it he won't have it to invent. I'm sure that's jest as bad as robbin' him, ain't it?"

Phoebe looked anxiously at Copernicus and was much pleased to find him apparently unmoved.

"Why, you certainly don't understand this yet," he insisted. "Milliken ain't agoin' back six years with us, is he? He'll jest go right along livin' as he's ben doin'."

"What!" Rebecca exclaimed. "Will he be livin' in one time an' we be livin' in another – both at the same –" She stopped. What *was* she saying!

"No – no!" replied Copernicus. "He'll go on livin'. That's what he *will* do. We'll go on havin' lived. Or to put it different – we *have* gone on livin' after we get back six years – to 1892. Ye see, we really have past all the six years – so the's no harm in it. Milliken won't be hurt."

Rebecca glanced at Phoebe, in whose face she found her own perplexity reflected. Then, throwing out her hands, as though pushing away her crowding mental obstructions, she cried:

"There – there! I can't get the hang of it. It's too much for me!"

"Oh, when you've done it once it'll be all easy and clear," said Droop, soothingly.

Phoebe looked hopefully into his face.

"Will you take us, Mr. Droop?" she asked.

"Oh, I s'pose I'll hev to."

"An' only unwind six years?"

"Yes – jest six years."

She jumped up excitedly.

"Then I'll be off to my packin'!"

She ran to the door and, pausing here, turned again to their visitor.

"Can we start tonight, Mr. Droop?"

"Yes, indeed!" he replied. "The sooner the better."

"That's splendid!" she cried, and ran quickly up the stairs.

The two older people sat for a while in melancholy silence, looking down. Each had hoped for more than this. Copernicus tried to convince himself that the profit from the cough syrup would comfort him for his disappointment. Rebecca dismissed with a sigh the dreams which she had allowed herself to entertain – those bright fictions centering on Joe Chandler – not the subdued old bachelor of 1898, but the jolly young fellow of the famous Centennial year.

At length Rebecca looked up and said:

"After all, Mr. Droop, come to think of it, you've no call to take us with ye. I can't do ye any good – goin' back only six years."

"Yes ye can," said Droop. "I'll need somebody to help me keep house in the Panchronicon. I ain't no hand at cookin' an' all, an' besides, it'll be mighty lonely without anybody in there."

"Well," she rejoined, rising, "I'll jest go up an' finish my packin'."

"An' I'll go tend to mine."

As they parted at the front door, it was arranged that Droop was to bring a wheelbarrow after supper and transport the sisters' belongings, preparatory to their departure.

The rest of the day was spent in preparation for the momentous voyage. Phoebe went to the little bank at Peltonville station and withdrew the entire savings of herself and sister, much to the astonishment and concern of the cashier. She walked all the way to the bank and back alone, for it was obviously necessary to avoid inconvenient questions.

When the two sisters stood in their little dining-room with the heap of greenbacks on the table before them, Rebecca was attacked by another conscientious scruple.

"I don't hardly know as we're doin' right, Phoebe," she said, shaking her head dubiously. "When we get back to 1892 we'd ought to find some money in the bank already. Ef we hev this with us, too, seems to me we'll hev more'n we're entitled to. Ain't it a good deal like cheatin' the bank?"

"Mercy, no!" Phoebe exclaimed, pettishly. "You're forever raisin' some trouble like that! Ain't this our money?"

"Yes – but –"

"Well, then, what's the use o' talkin' 'bout it? Just wait till we can mention your trouble to Mr. Droop. He'll have a good answer for you."

"But s'posin' he can't answer it?" Rebecca insisted.

"Well, if he can't we can give back the difference to the bank."

So saying, Phoebe took her share of the bills and quickly left the room.

"I've got lots of things to do before night," she remarked.

At promptly half-past nine all the lights in the house were extinguished, and the two sisters sat together in the dark parlor awaiting Copernicus. It was Rebecca who had insisted on putting out the lights.

"Ef folks was to see lights here so late in the night," she said, "they'd suspicion somethin' an' they might even call in."

Phoebe admitted the justness of this reasoning, and they had both directed every endeavour to completing all their arrangements before their accustomed bedtime.

It was not long after this that a stealthy step was heard on the gravel path and Phoebe hurried to the door. Copernicus came in with a low word of greeting and followed the ghostly shadow of his hostess into the parlor.

The three stood together in the dark and conversed in an undertone, like so many conspirators surrounded by spies.

"Hev ye got everythin' ready?" Droop asked.

"Yes," said Phoebe. "The's only two little trunks for you. Did you bring the wheelbarrow?"

"Yep – I left it outside the gate. 'Twould hev made a lot of noise on the gravel inside."

"That's right," said Phoebe. "I guess you'll not have any trouble to carry both o' those trunks at once. We haven't packed only a few things, 'cause I expect we'll find all our old duds ready for us in 1892, won't we?"

"Why, 'f course," said Droop.

"But how 'bout linen – sheets an' table-cloths an' all?" said Rebecca. "We'll need some o' them on the trip, won't we?"

"I've got a hull slew o' them things in the Panchronicon," said Copernicus. "Ye won't hev to bother a bit about sech things."

"How long do you s'pose it'll take to make the trip," asked Phoebe. "I mean by the clock? We won't have to do any washing on the way, will we?"

"I don't see how we can," Rebecca broke in. "The's not a blessed tub on the hull machine."

"No, no," said Droop, reassuringly. "We'll make a bee-line for the pole, an' we'll go 'bout three times as fast as a lightnin' express train. We'd ought to reach there in about twenty-four hours, I guess. Then we'll take it easy cuttin' meridians, so's not to suffer from side weight, an' –"

"Side weight!" exclaimed the two women together.

"Yes," said Droop. "That's a complaint ye get ef ye unwind the time too fast. Ye see, growin' young isn't a thing folks is used to, an' it disgrummages the hull constitution ef ye grow young too fast. Well, 's I was a-sayin', I guess it'll take 'bout eighteen hours by the clock to cut back six years. Thet's by the clock, ye understand. As a matter of fact, of course, we'll be just six years less'n no time in finishin' the trip."

"Well," said Phoebe, briskly, "that's no kind o' reason fer dawdlin' about it now. Let's be startin'."

"Where's the trunks?" said Droop.

The trunks were pointed out, and with very little trouble Copernicus put them onto the barrow. He then came to the door for his last instructions.

"'S anythin' more?" he asked.

"No," said Rebecca. "We'll bring on our special duds in our arms. We'll wait a spell an' come on separate."

The door was carefully closed and they soon heard the slight creak of the weighted wheel as Droop set off with the trunks for Burnham's swamp.

"Now, then," said Phoebe, bustling into the parlor, "let's get our things all together ready to start. Have ye got your satchel with the money in it?"

Rebecca gently slapped a black leather bag hanging at her side.

"Here 'tis," she said.

"Let's see," Phoebe went on. "Here's my box with the letters an' miniature, here's the box with the jewelry, an' here's that book Mrs. Bolton gave me about Bacon writin' Shakespeare."

"Whatever air ye takin' that old book fer, Phoebe?"

"Why, to read on the train – I mean on the way, ye know. We'll likely find it pretty pokey in that one room all day."

"I don't know what ye mean by 'all day,'" Rebecca exclaimed in a discouraged tone. "So far's I see, th'ain't goin' to be any days. What'll it feel like – livin' backward that way? D'ye guess it'll make us feel sick, like ridin' backward in the cars?"

"Don't ask me," Phoebe exclaimed, despairingly. "'F I knew what 'twas like, perhaps I wouldn't feel so like goin'."

She straightened herself suddenly and stood rigid.

"Hark!" she exclaimed. "Is that Mr. Droop comin' back, d'you s'pose?"

There were distinctly audible footsteps on the path.

Phoebe came out into the hall on tiptoe and stood beside her sister.

There was a knock on the door. The two sisters gripped each other's arms excitedly.

"'Taint Copernicus!" Rebecca whispered very low.

The knock was repeated; rather louder this time. Then –

"Miss Wise – Miss Wise – are ye to home?"

It was a woman's voice.

"Sarah Allen!" Phoebe exclaimed under her breath.

"Whatever shall we do?" Rebecca replied.

"Miss Wise," the voice repeated, and then their visitor knocked again, much more loudly.

"I'll go to the door," exclaimed Phoebe.

"But –"

"I must. She'll raise the whole town if I don't."

So saying, Phoebe walked noisily to the door and unlocked it.

"Is that you, Mis' Allen?" she asked.

The door was opened, and Phoebe found herself face to face with a short, light woman whose white garments shone gray in the night.

"Why, you're up'n dressed!" exclaimed Mrs. Allen. She did not offer to enter, but went on excitedly:

"Miss Phoebe," she said, "d'you know I b'lieve you've ben robbed."

"What!"

"Yes; on'y a minute ago I was a-comin' up the road from M'ria Payson's – you know she's right sick an' I've ben givin' her massidge – an' what sh'd I see but a man comin' out o' your gate with suthin' on his shoulder. I couldn't see who 'twas, an' he was so quiet an' sneaky without a light that I jest slipped behind a tree. You know I've ben dreadful skeery ever sence Tom was brought home with his arm broke after a fight with a strange man in the dark. Well, this man to-night he put the bundle or what not into a wheelbarrow an' set off quiet as a mouse. He went off down that way, an' says I to myself, 'It's a robber ben burglin' at the Wise's house,' says I, an' I come straight here to see ef ye was both murdered or what. Air ye all right? Hez he broken yer door? Hev ye missed anythin'?"

As the little woman paused for breath, Phoebe seized her opportunity.

"Did you say he went off to the north, Mis' Allen?" she said, with feigned excitement.

"Yes."

"Oh, dear – oh, dear!" cried Phoebe, wringing her hands. "Didn't I say I heard a noise – I told you I heard a burglar, Rebecca," she went on, hysterically, turning to her sister.

"Is Miss Rebecca there?" asked Mrs. Allen.

Rebecca came forward in silence. She was quite nonplussed. To tell the truth, Phoebe's sudden outburst was as great a tax upon her nerves as Mrs. Allen's unwelcome visit. Surely Phoebe had said nothing about a burglar! It was Droop that Mrs. Allen had seen – of course it was. She dared not say so in their visitor's presence, but she wondered mightily at Phoebe's apparent perturbation.

Phoebe guessed her sister's mental confusion, and she sought to draw Mrs. Allen's attention to herself to avoid the betrayal of their plans which would certainly follow Rebecca's joining the conversation.

"Mis' Allen," she exclaimed, excitedly, "the's just one thing to be done. Won't you run's quick's ever you can to Si Pray, an' ask him to bring his gun? You won't meet the burglar 'cause he's gone the other way. Rebecca 'nd I'll jest wait here for you an' Si. I'll get some hot water from the kitchen, in case the burglar should come back while you're gone. Oh, please will you do it?"

"Course I will," was the nervous reply. This hint of the possible return of the robbers made an immediate retreat seem very desirable. "I'll go right now. Won't be gone a minute. Lock your door now – quick!"

She turned and sped down the path. She had not reached the gate before Phoebe walked rapidly into the parlor.

"Quick – quick!" she panted, frantically gathering up her belongings. "Get your duds an' come along."

"But what d'you –"

"Come – come – come!" cried Phoebe. "Come quick or they'll all be here. Gun and all!"

With her arm full of bundles, Phoebe rushed back through the hall and out of the front door. Rebecca followed her, drawn along by the fiery momentum of her sister.

"Lock the front door, Rebecca," Phoebe cried. Then, as she reached the gate and found it fastened: "Here, I can't undo the gate. My hands are full. Oh, do hurry, Rebecca! We haven't a minute!"

The elder sister locked the front door and started down the path in such a nervous fever that she left the key in the lock. Half way to the gate she paused.

"Come on – come on!" Phoebe cried, stamping her foot.

"My land!" stammered Rebecca. "I've forgot everythin'!" She started back, running with short, unaccustomed steps.

"My umbrella!" she gasped. "My recipes – my slips!"

Phoebe was speechless with anger and apprehension at this delay, and Rebecca was therefore allowed to re-enter the house without objection.

In a short time she reappeared carrying an umbrella, two flower-pots, and a folded newspaper.

"There!" she panted, as she came up to her sister and opened the gate. "Now I guess I've got everythin'!"

Silently and swiftly the two women sped northward, following the imaginary burglar, while the devoted Mrs. Allen ran breathless in the opposite direction for Si Pray and his gun.

"We'll hev to go more careful here," said Rebecca as they turned into the lane leading down to the swamp.

With many a stumble and some scratches they moved more slowly down the rutted track until at length they reached the point where they were to turn into the swamp.

Here the sisters leaned against the wall to rest and recover breath.

"My goodness, but that was a narrow escape!" murmured Phoebe.

"Yes," said Rebecca, with reproachful sadness; "but I'm afraid you paid a heavy price fer it, Phoebe!"

"What do you mean?"

"Why, 's fur's I could make out, you told Mis' Allen a deliberate wrong story, Phoebe Wise."

"What did I say?" said Phoebe, in shocked surprise.

"You said you hed told me you'd heerd a burglar!"

"Did I say that? Those very words?"

"Why, you know you did."

"Wasn't it a question, Rebecca?" Phoebe insisted. "Didn't I *ask* you ef I hadn't told you I heard a burglar?"

"No, it was a plain downright wrong story, Phoebe, an' you needn't to try to sneak out of it."

Phoebe was silent for a few moments, and then Rebecca heard her laugh. It was a very little, rippling thing – but it was genuine – there was real light-heartedness behind it.

"Phoebe Wise!" exclaimed Rebecca, "how ken you laugh so? I wouldn't hev the weight of sech a thing on my mind fer a good deal."

"Well, Rebecca," tittered her sister, "I didn't have it on my mind yesterday, did I?"

"Course not – but –"

"An' won't it be yesterday for us mighty soon – yes, an' a heap longer ago than that?"

She laughed again merrily and began to climb over the wall, a proceeding not rendered easier by the various articles in her hands.

A few minutes later the two women had joined Copernicus within his mysterious machine and were standing in the brightly lighted antechamber at the head of the stairs.

"Well – well!" cried Droop, as he caught sight of the two women for the first time in the light. "Where ever did ye get them funny dresses? Why, your sleeves is all puffed out near the shoulders!"

"These are some of our old dresses," said Rebecca. "They was made in 1891, an' we thought they'd prob'bly be more in the fashion back in 1892 when we get there than our newer dresses."

"Never mind our dresses, Mr. Droop," said Phoebe. "Where can we put down all these things? My arms are breakin' off."

"Right here, Cousin Phoebe."

Droop bustled over to the state-rooms, opening both the doors at once.

"Here's a room apiece fer ye. Take yer choice."

"Oh, but where'll you sleep?" said Phoebe. "P'raps Rebecca and I'd better have one room together."

"Not a bit of it," said Droop. "I'll sleep on one o' them settles under the windows. They're real comfortable."

"Well – just as you say."

The sisters entered their rooms and deposited their bundles, but Phoebe returned at once and called to Droop, who had started down the stairs.

"Mr. Droop, you've got to start right straight off. Mrs. Allen knows 't you've carried off the trunk and she's comin' after us with Si Pray an' a gun."

Just then they heard the loud barking of a dog. He was apparently running rapidly down the lane.

"Sakes alive!" cried Phoebe, in alarm. "Slam to that door, Copernicus Droop! Si has let his dog loose an' he's on your tracks!"

The baying was repeated – now much nearer. Droop clattered frantically down the stairs, and shut the door with a bang. At the next moment a heavy body leaped against it, and a man's voice was heard close at hand.

"Sic um, Touser, sic um! Where is he, boy?"

Up the stairs went Copernicus two steps at a time. He dashed into the anteroom, pale and breathless.

"Lie down on the floor!" he shouted. "Lie down or ye'll get throwed down. I'm agoin' to start her!"

By this time he had opened the engine-room door.

The two women promptly lay flat on their backs on the carpet.

Droop braced himself firmly and had just grasped the starting lever when a cry from Rebecca arrested him.

"Copernicus Droop – hold on!" she cried.

He turned to her, his face full of anxious fear. Rebecca lay on her back with her hands at her sides, but her head was raised stiffly from the floor.

"Copernicus Droop," she said, solemnly, "hev ye brought any rum aboard with ye? 'Cause if ye have I won't –"

She never concluded, for at this moment her head was jerked back sharply against the floor by a tremendous upward leap of the machine.

There was a hissing roar as of a thousand rockets, and even as Rebecca was wondering, half stunned, why she saw so many jumping lights, Si Pray gazed open-mouthed at the ascension of a mysterious dark body apparently aimed at the sky.

The Panchronicon had started.

Chapter IV
A Change of Plan

IT WAS LONG AFTER their bed-time and the two sisters were utterly exhausted; but as the mysterious structure within which they lay glided northward between heaven and earth with the speed of a meteor, Rebecca and Phoebe long courted sleep in vain.

The excitement of their past adventures, the unreal wonder of their present situation, the bewildering possibilities and impossibilities of their future plans – all these conspired to banish sleep until long past midnight. It was not until, speeding due north with the unswerving obedience of a magnet, their vessel was sailing far above the waters of the upper Saguenay, that they at length sank to rest.

They were awakened next morning by a knocking upon Rebecca's door.

"It's pretty nigh eight-thirty," Droop cried. "I've got the kettle on the range, but I don't know what to do nex'."

"What! Why! Who! Where! Sakes! What's this?"

Rebecca sat up in bed, unable to place herself.

"It's pretty nigh half-past eight," Copernicus repeated. "Long after breakfast-time. I'm hungry!"

By this time Phoebe was wide awake.

"All right!" she cried. "We'll come in a minute."

Then Rebecca knew where she was – or rather realized that she did not know. But fortunately a duty was awaiting her in the kitchen and this steadied a mind which seemed to her to need some support in the midst of these unwonted happenings.

Phoebe was the first to leave her bedroom. She had dressed with frantic speed. In her haste to get to the windows and see the world from the sky, she had secured her hair very imperfectly, and Droop was favored with a charming display of bright locks, picturesquely disarranged.

"Good-mornin', Cousin Phoebe," he said, with his suavest manner.

"Good-morning, Mr. Droop," Phoebe replied. "Where are we? Is everything all right?"

She made straight for one of the windows the iron shutters of which were now open.

"I wish't you'd call me Cousin Copernicus," Droop remarked.

"Oh – oh! What a beautiful world!"

Phoebe leaned her face close to the glass and gazed spell-bound at the wonderful landscape spread before her.

The whole atmosphere seemed filled with a clear, cold sunlight whose brilliance irradiated the giant sphere of earth so far away.

Directly below and to the right of their course, as far as she could see, there was one vast expanse of dark blue sea, gilded dazzlingly over one portion where the sun's beams were reflected. Far ahead to the north and as far behind them the sea was bordered with the fantastic curves of a faint blue coast dotted and lined with the shadows of many a hill and mountain. It was a map on which she was gazing. Nature's own map – the only perfect chart in the world.

So new – so intensely, almost painfully, beautiful was this scene that Phoebe stood transfixed – fascinated. She did not even think of speaking.

The scene was not so new to Droop – and besides he was a prey to an insistent appetite. His mental energies, therefore, sought expression in speech.

Approaching Phoebe's side, he said:

"Mighty pretty, ain't it?"

She did not reply, so he continued:

"That water right under us is Hudson Strait. The ocean to the right is the Atlantic. Ye can see Hudson's Bay off to the left out o' one o' them windows. I've ben lookin' it up on the map."

He strolled toward the table, as if inviting Phoebe to see his chart which lay there unrolled. She did not follow him.

"Yes," he continued, "that's Hudson Strait, and we're four miles high, an' that's all I'll tell ye till I have my breakfast."

He gazed wistfully at Phoebe, who did not move or speak, but let her eyes wander in awed delight over the wonders thus brought before them.

Just then Rebecca emerged from her room.

"Good-mornin'," she said. "I guess I'm late."

"Good-mornin', Cousin Rebecca; I guess ye are a mite late. Cousin Phoebe won't move – so I'm sayin' we're four miles high an' right over Hudson Strait, an' that's all I'll tell ye till I get my breakfast."

"Goodness me!" exclaimed Rebecca. "Ain't that mos' too high, Mr. Droop?" She hurried to the window and looked out.

"Sakes alive!" she gasped.

She was silent for a moment, awed in her turn by the immensity of the prospect.

"Why – but – it's all water underneath!" she exclaimed at last. "Ef we was to fall now, we'd be drowned!"

"Now don't you be a mite skeert," said Droop, with reassuring politeness. "We've ben scootin' along like this all night an' – an' the fact is, I've got the kettle on – p'raps it's b'iled over."

Rebecca turned from the window at once and made for the kitchen.

"Phoebe," she said, briskly, "you set the table now an' I'll hev breakfast ready in a twinklin'."

Reluctantly Phoebe left the window and Droop soon had the satisfaction of sauntering back and forth between kitchen and dining-table in pleased supervision of the progress of both.

In due time a simple but substantial breakfast was in readiness, and the three travellers were seated around the table partaking of the meal each in his own way.

Droop was business-like, almost enthusiastic, in his voracious hunger. Rebecca ate moderately and without haste, precisely as though seated in the little Peltonville cottage. Phoebe ate but little. She was overcome by the wonders she had seen, realizing for the first time the marvellous situation in which she found herself.

It was not until the table was cleared and the two women were busy with the dishes that conversation was resumed. Droop sat with his chair tilted backward against the kitchen wall enjoying a quiet satisfaction with his lot and a kindly mental attitude toward all men.

He glanced through the kitchen door at the barometer on the wall in the outer room.

"We've climbed near a mile since before breakfast," he remarked.

Rebecca paused before hanging up the soap-shaker.

"Look here, Mr. Droop," she said, anxiously, "we are mos' too high a'ready, I think. S'posin' we was to fall down. Where do you s'pose we'd be?"

"Why, Rebecca," said Phoebe, laughing, "do you suppose five miles is any worse than four? I guess we'd be killed by falling one mile jest as quick as five."

"Quicker!" Droop exclaimed. "Considerable quicker, Cousin Rebecca, fer it would take us a good deal longer to fall five miles than it would one."

"But what ever's the use o' keepin' on a-climbin'?"

"Why, that's the nature of this machine," he replied. "Ye see, it runs on the rocket principle by spurtin' out gases. Ef we want to go up off the ground we squirt out under the machine an' that gives us a h'ist. Then, when we get 'way up high, we spread out a pair o' big wings like and start the propeller at the stern end o' the thing. Now them wings on'y holds us up by bein' inclined a mite in front, and consequence is we're mighty apt to climb a little right 'long."

"Well, but won't we get too high?" suggested Phoebe. "Ain't the air too thin up very high?"

"Of course, we mustn't go too high," Droop conceded, "an' I was just a-thinkin' it wouldn't go amiss to let down a spell."

He rose and started for the engine-room.

"How do you let down?" Phoebe asked, pausing in her work.

"Why, I jest turn the wings horizontal, ye know, an' then we sink very slow till I incline 'em up again."

He disappeared. Phoebe gave the last of the dishes a brief touch of the dish-towel and then ran into the main room to watch the barometer.

She was much interested to observe a gradual but continual decrease in their altitude. She walked to the window but could see no apparent change, save that they had now passed the sea and only the blue land with silver streaks of river and indigo hill shadows was beneath them.

"How fast do you s'pose we're flyin', Mr. Droop?" she asked.

"There's the speed indicator," he said, pointing to one of the dials on the wall. "Ye see it says we're a-hummin' along at about one hundred an' thirty miles an hour."

"My gracious!" cried Phoebe. "What if we was to hit something!"

"Nothin' to hit," said Droop, with a smile. "Ye see, the's no sort o' use goin' any slower, an' besides, this quick travellin' keeps us warm."

"Why, how's that?"

"The sides o' the machine rubbin' on the air," said Droop.

"That's so," Phoebe replied. "That's what heats up meteors so awful hot, ain't it?"

Rebecca came out of the kitchen at this moment.

"I must say ye wasn't particler about gettin' all the pans to rights 'fore ye left the kitchen, Phoebe. Ben makin' the beds?"

"Land, no, Rebecca!" said Phoebe, blushing guiltily.

"Well, there!"

Rebecca said no more, but her set lips and puckered forehead spoke much of displeasure as she stalked across to the state-rooms.

"Well, I declare to goodness!" she cried, as she opened her door. "Ye hevn't even opened the window to air the rooms!"

Phoebe looked quite miserable at thought of her remissness, but Copernicus came bravely to the rescue.

"The windows can't be opened, Cousin Rebecca," he said. "Ef ye was to open one, 'twould blow yer head's bald as an egg in a minute."

"What!"

"Yes," said Phoebe, briskly, "I couldn't air the beds an' make 'em because we're going one hundred and thirty odd miles an hour, Rebecca."

"D'you mean to tell me, Copernicus Droop," cried the outraged spinster, "that I've got to go 'thout airin' my bed?"

"No, no," Copernicus said, soothingly. "The's special arrangements to keep ventilation goin'. Jest leave the bed open half the day an' it'll be all aired."

Rebecca looked far from pleased at this.

"I declare, ef I'd known of all these doin's," she muttered.

Unable to remain idle, she set to work "putting things to rights," as she called it, while Phoebe took her book to the west window and was soon lost in certain modern theories concerning the Baconian authorship of Shakespeare's works.

"Is these duds yourn, Mr. Droop?" asked Rebecca, sharply, pointing to a motley collection of goods piled in one corner of the main room.

"Yes," Droop replied, coming quickly to her side. "Them's some of the inventions I'm carryin' along."

He stooped and gathered up a number of boxes and bundles in his arms. Then he stood up and looked about him as though seeking a safe place for their deposit.

"That's all right," said Rebecca. "Ye can put 'em right back, Mr. Droop. I jest wanted to see whether the' was much dust back in there."

Droop replaced his goods with a sigh of relief. One box he retained, however, and, placing it upon the table, proceeded to unpack it.

Rebecca now turned her attention to her own belongings. Lifting one of her precious flower-pots carefully, she looked all about for a more suitable location for her plants.

"Phoebe," she exclaimed at length, "where ever can I set my slips? They ought to be in the sun there by the east window, but it'll dirt up the coverin' of the settle."

Phoebe looked up from her book.

"Why don't ye spread out that newspaper you brought with you?" she said.

Rebecca shook her head.

"No," she replied, "I couldn't do thet. The's a lot o' fine recipes in there – I never could make my sweet pickle as good as thet recipe in the New York paper thet Molly sent me."

Phoebe laid down her book and walked over to her sister's side.

"Oh, the' must be some part of it you can use, Rebecca," she said. "Land sakes!" she continued, laughing. "Why, it's the whole of the *New York World* for a Sunday – pictures an' all! Here – take this advertisin' piece an' spread it out – so."

She tore off a portion of the voluminous paper and carefully spread it out on one of the eastern settles.

"Whatever did you bring those slips with you for?" she asked.

Rebecca deposited the flower-pots carefully in the sun and slapped her hands across each other to remove the dust on them.

"One o' them is off my best honeysuckle thet come from a slip thet Sam Mellick brought from Japan in 1894. This geranium come off a plant thet was given me by Arabella Slade, 'fore she died in 1896, an' she cut it off'n a geranium thet come from a lot thet Joe Chandler's father raised from slips cut off of some plants down to Boston in the ground that used to belong to our great-grandfather Wilkins 'fore the Revolution."

This train of reasoning seemed satisfactory, and Phoebe turned to resume her book.

Copernicus intercepted her as she passed the table.

"What d'ye think o' this little phonograph, Cousin Phoebe?" he said.

One of Droop's boxes stood open and beside it Phoebe saw a phonograph with the usual spring motor and brass megaphone.

"I paid twenty-five fer that, secon' hand, down to Keene," said the proud owner.

"There!" exclaimed Phoebe. "I've always wanted to know how those things worked. I've heard 'em, you know, but I've never worked one."

"It's real easy," said Droop, quite delighted to find Phoebe so interested. "Ye see, when it's wound up, all ye hev to do is to slip one o' these wax cylinders on here – so."

He adjusted the cylinder, dropped the stylus and pushed the starting lever.

Instantly the stentorian announcement rang out from the megaphone.

"The Last Rose of Summer – Sola – Sung by Signora Casta Diva – Edison Record!"

"Goodness gracious sakes alive!" cried Rebecca, turning in affright. "Who's that?"

Her two companions raised their right hands in a simultaneous appeal for silence. Then the song began.

With open eyes and mouth, the amazed Rebecca drew slowly nearer, and finally took her stand directly in front of the megaphone.

The song ended and Copernicus stopped the motor.

"Oh, ain't it lovely!" Phoebe cried.

"Well – I'll – be – switched!" Rebecca exclaimed, with slow emphasis. "Can it sing anythin' else?"

"Didn't you never hear one afore, Cousin Rebecca?" Droop asked.

"I never did," she replied. "What on the face of the green airth does it?"

"Have ye any funny ones?" Phoebe asked, quickly, fearful of receiving a long scientific lecture.

"Yes," said Droop. "Here's a nigger minstrels. The's some jokes in it."

The loud preliminary announcement made Rebecca jump again, but while the music and the songs and jokes were delivered, she stood earnestly attentive throughout, while her companions grinned and giggled alternately.

"Is thet all?" she asked at the conclusion.

"Thet's all," said Droop, as he removed the cylinder.

"Well, I don't see nothin' funny 'bout it," she said, plaintively.

Droop's pride was touched.

"Ah, but that ain't all it can do!" he cried. "Here's a blank cylinder. You jest talk at the machine while it's runnin', an' it'll talk back all you say."

This was too much for Rebecca's credulity, and Droop could not induce her to talk into the trumpet.

"You can't make a fool o' me, Copernicus Droop," she exclaimed.

"You try, Cousin Phoebe," he said at last.

Phoebe looked dubiously at her sister as though half of opinion that her shrewd example should be followed.

"You sure it'll do it?" she asked.

"Certain!" cried Copernicus, nodding his head with violence.

She stood a moment leaning over with her pretty lips close to the trumpet.

Then she straightened up with a face of comical despair.

"I don't know what to say," she exclaimed.

Droop stopped the motor and looked about the room. Suddenly his eyes brightened.

"There," he cried, pointing to the book Phoebe had been reading, "read suthin' out o' that into it."

Phoebe opened the book at random, and as Droop started the motor again she read the following lines slowly and distinctly into the trumpet:

"It is thus made clear from the indubitable evidence of the plays themselves that Francis Bacon wrote the immortal works falsely ascribed to William Shakespeare, and that the gigantic genius of this man was the result of the possession of royal blood. In this unacknowledged son of Elizabeth Tudor, Queen of England, was made manifest to all countries and for all centuries the glorious powers inherent in the regal blood of England."

"That'll do," said Droop. "Now jest hear it talk back."

He substituted the repeating stylus for the recording point and set the motor in motion once more. To the complete stupefaction of Rebecca, the repetition of Phoebe's words was perfect.

"Why! It's Phoebe's voice," she began, but Phoebe broke in upon her suddenly.

"Why, see the hills on each side of us, Mr. Droop," she cried.

Droop glanced out and leaped a foot from the ground.

"Goramighty!" he screamed, "She'll strike!" He dashed to the engine-room and threw up the forward edges of the aeroplanes. Instantly the vessel swooped upward and the hills Phoebe had seen appeared to drop into some great abyss.

The two women ran to a window and saw that they were over a bleak and rocky island covered with ice and snow.

Droop came to their side, quite pale with fright.

"Great Moses!" he exclaimed. "I warn't more'n jest in time, I tell ye! We was a-settlin' fast. A little more'n we'd ha' struck –" He snapped the fingers of both hands and made a gesture expressive of the complete destruction which would have resulted.

"I tell you what, Mr. Droop," said Rebecca, sternly, but with a little shake in her voice, "you've got to jest tend to business and navigate this thing we're a-ridin' on. You can't work and play too. Don't you say anythin' more to Phoebe or me till we get to the pole. What time'll that be?"

"About six or half-past, I expect," said Droop, humbly. "But I don't see how I can be workin' all the time. The machine don't need it, an', besides, I've got to eat, haven't I?"

"When it comes time fer your victuals, Phoebe'll watch the windows an' the little clocks on the wall while I feed ye. But don't open yer head agin now, only fer necessary talkin' an' eatin', till we get there. I don't want any smash-ups 'round here."

Copernicus found it expedient to obey these instructions, and under Rebecca's watchful generalship he was obliged to pace back and forth from engine-room to window while Phoebe read and her sister knitted. So passed the remainder of the day, save when at dinner-time the famished man was relieved by his young lieutenant.

Immediately after supper, however, they all three posted themselves at the windows, on the lookout for the North Pole. Droop slowed down the propeller, and the aeroplanes being thus rendered less effective they slowly descended.

They were passing over an endless plain of rough and ragged ice. In every direction all the way to the horizon nothing could be seen but the glare of white.

"How'll you know when we get there?" asked Phoebe.

Droop glanced apprehensively at Rebecca and replied in a whisper:

"We'll see the pole a-stickin' up. We can't go wrong, you know. The Panchronicon is fixed to guide itself allus due north."

"You don't need to whisper – speak right up, Mr. Droop," said Rebecca, sharply.

Copernicus started, looked nervously about and then stared out of the window northward with a very business-like frown.

"Is the' really an' truly a pole there?" Phoebe asked.

"Yes," said Droop, shortly.

"An' can ye see the meridians jammed together like in the geographies?" asked Rebecca.

"No," said Droop, "no, indeed – at least, I didn't see any."

"Why, Rebecca," said Phoebe, "the meridians are only conventional signs, you know. They don't –"

"Hallo!" Droop cried, suddenly, "What's that?" He raised a spyglass with which he had hitherto been playing and directed it northward for a few seconds. Then he turned with a look of relief on his face.

"It's the pole!" he exclaimed.

Phoebe snatched the spyglass and applied it to her eye.

Yes, on the horizon she could discern a thin black line, rising vertically from the plain of ice. Even as she looked it seemed to be nearer, so rapid was their progress.

Droop went to the engine-room, lessened speed and brought the aeroplanes to the horizontal. He could look directly forward through a thick glass port directly over the starting-handle. Gradually the great machine settled lower and lower. It was now running quite slowly and the aeroplanes acted only as parachutes as they glided still forward toward the black upright line.

In silence the three waited for the approaching end of this first stage of their journey. A few hundred yards south of their goal they seemed about to alight, but Droop slightly inclined the aeroplanes and speeded up the propeller a little. Their vessel swept gently upward and northward again, like a gull rising from the sea. Then Droop let it settle again. Just as they were about to fall rather violently upon the solid mass of ice below them, he projected a relatively small volume of gas from beneath the structure. Its reaction eased their descent, and they settled down without noise or shock.

They had arrived!

Copernicus came forward to the window and pointed to a tall, stout steel pole projecting from the ice a few yards to the right of the vessel.

"Thet, neighbors, is the North Pole!" he said, with a sweeping wave of the hand.

For some minutes the three voyagers stood in silence gazing through the window at the famous pole. This, then, was the goal of so much heroic endeavor! It was to reach this complete opposite of all that is ordinarily attractive that countless ambitious men had suffered – that so many had died!

"Well!" exclaimed Rebecca at length. "I be switched ef I see what there is fer so many folks to make sech a fuss about!"

Droop scratched his head thoughtfully and made no reply. Surely it would have been hard to point out any charms in the endless plain of opaque ice hummocks, unrelieved save by that gaunt steel pole.

"Where's the open sea?" Rebecca asked, after a few moments' pause. "Dr. Kane said the' was an open sea up here."

"Oh, Dr. Kane!" said Droop, contemptuously. "He's no 'count fer modern facts."

"What I can't understand," said Phoebe, "is how it comes that, if nobody's ever been up here, they all seem to know there's a North Pole here."

"That's a fact," Rebecca exclaimed. "How'd they know about it? The' ain't anythin' in the Bible 'bout it, is the'?"

Droop looked more cheerful at this and answered briskly:

"Oh, they don't know 'bout it. Ye see, that pole there ain't a nat'ral product of the soil at all. Et's the future man done that – the man who invented this Panchronicon and brought me up here before. He told me how that he stuck that post in there to help him run this machine 'round and 'round fer cuttin' meridians."

"Oh!" exclaimed both sisters together.

"Yes," Droop continued. "D'ye see thet big iron ring 'round the pole, lyin' on the ground?"

"I don't see any ground," said Rebecca, ruefully.

"Well, on the ice, then. Don't ye see it lyin' black there against the snow?"

"Yes – yes, I see it," said Phoebe.

"Well, that's what I'm goin' to hitch the holdin' rope on to. You'll see how it's done presently." He glanced at the clock.

"Seven o'clock," he said. "I guessed mighty close when I said 'twould take us twenty hours. We left Peltonville at ten-thirty last night."

"Seven o'clock!" cried Rebecca. "So 'tis. Why, what's the matter with the sun. Ain't it goin' to set at all?"

"Not much!" said Droop, chuckling. "Sun don't set up here, Cousin Rebecca. Not until winter-time, an' then et stays set till summer again."

"Well!" was the breathless reply. "An' where in creation does it go when it stays set?"

"Why, Rebecca," exclaimed Phoebe, "the sun is south of the equator in winter, you know."

"Shinin' on the South Pole then," Droop added, nodding.

For a moment Rebecca looked from one to the other of her companions, and then, realizing the necessity of keeping her mind within its accustomed sphere, she changed the subject.

"Come now – the' ain't any wind to blow us away now, I hope. Let's open our windows an' air out those state-rooms."

She started toward her door.

"Hold on!" cried Droop, extending his arm to stop her. "You don't want to fall down dead o' cold, do ye?"

"What!"

"Don't you know what a North Pole is like fer weather an' sich?" Droop continued. "Why, Cousin Rebecca, it's mos' any 'mount below zero outside. Don't you open a window – not a tiny crack – if ye don't want to freeze solid in a second."

"There!" Rebecca exclaimed. "You do provoke me beyond anythin', Copernicus Droop! Ef I'd a-knowed the kind o' way we'd had to live – why, there! It's wuss'n pigs!"

She marched indignantly into her room and closed the door. A moment later she put out her head.

"Phoebe Wise," she said, "if you take my advice, you'll make your bed an' tidy yer room at once. Ain't any use waitin' any longer fer a chance to air."

Phoebe smiled and moved toward her own door.

"Thet's a good idea," said Droop. "You fix yer rooms an' I'll do some figurin'. Ye see I've got to figure out how long it'll take us to get back six years. I've a notion it'll take about eighteen hours, but I ain't certain sure."

Poor Rebecca set to work in her rooms with far from enviable feelings. Her curiosity had been largely satisfied and the unwonted conditions were proving very trying indeed. Could she have set out with the prospect of returning to those magical days of youth and courtship, as Droop had originally proposed, the end would have justified the means. But they could not do this now if they would, for Phoebe had left her baby clothes behind. Thus her disappointment added to her burdens, and she found herself wishing that she had never left her comfortable home, however amazing had been her adventures.

"I could'v aired my bed at least," she muttered, as she turned the mattress of her couch in the solitude of her chamber.

She found the long-accustomed details of chamber work a comfort and solace, and, as she finally gazed about the tidy room at her completed work, she felt far more contented with her lot than she had felt before beginning.

"I guess I'll go help Phoebe," she thought. "The girl is that slow!"

As she came from her room she found Copernicus leaning over the table, one hand buried in his hair and the other wielding a pencil. He was absorbed in arithmetical calculations.

She did not disturb him, but turned and entered Phoebe's room without the formality of knocking. As she opened the door, there was a sharp clatter, as of a door or lid slamming.

"Who's there?" cried Phoebe, sharply.

She was seated on the floor in front of her trunk, and she looked up at her sister with a flushed and startled face.

"Oh, it's you!" she said, guiltily.

Rebecca glanced at the bed.

It had not been touched.

"Well, I declare!" Rebecca exclaimed. "Ain't you ever agoin' to fix up your room, Phoebe Wise?"

"Oh, in a minute, Rebecca. I was just agoin' over my trunk a minute."

She leaned back against the foot of the bed, and folding her hands gazed pensively into vacancy, while Rebecca stared at her in astonishment.

"Do you know," Phoebe went on, "I've ben thinkin' it's awful mean not to give you a chance to go back to 1876, Rebecca. Joe Chandler's a mighty fine man!"

Rebecca gave vent to an unintelligible murmur and turned to Phoebe's bed. She grasped the mattress and gave it a vicious shake as she turned it over. She was probably only transferring to this inoffensive article a process which she would gladly have applied elsewhere.

There was a long silence while Rebecca resentfully drew the sheets into proper position, smoothed them with swift pats and caressings, and tucked them neatly under at head and sides. Then came a soft, apologetic voice.

"Rebecca!"

The spinster made no reply but applied herself to a mathematically accurate adjustment of the top edge of the upper sheet.

"Rebecca!"

The second call was a little louder than the first, and there was a queer half-sobbing, half-laughing catch in the speaker's voice that commanded attention.

Rebecca looked up.

Phoebe was still sitting on the floor beside her trunk, but the trunk was open now and the young woman's rosy face was peering with a pathetic smile over a – what! – could it be!

Rebecca leaned forward in amazement.

Yes, it was! In Phoebe's outstretched hands was the dearest possible little baby's undergarment – all of cambric, with narrow ribbons at the neck.

For a few seconds the two sisters looked at each other over this unexpected barrier. Then Phoebe's lips quivered into a pathetic curve and she buried her face in the little garment, laughing and crying at once.

Rebecca dropped helplessly into a chair.

"Phoebe Martin Wise!" she exclaimed. "Do you mean – hev you brought –?"

She fell silent, and then, darting at her sister, she took her head in her hands and deposited a sudden kiss on the smooth bright gold-brown hair and whisked out of Phoebe's room and into her own.

In the meantime Copernicus was too deeply absorbed in his calculations to notice these comings and goings. Apparently he had been led into the most abstruse mathematical regions. Nothing short of the triple integration of transcendental functions should have been adequate to produce those lines of anxious care in his face as he slowly covered sheet after sheet with figures.

He was at length startled from his preoccupation by a gentle voice at his side.

"Can't I help, Mr. Droop?"

It was Phoebe, who, having made all right in her room and washed all traces of tears from her face, had come to note Droop's progress.

Dazed, he raised his head and looked unexpectedly into a lovely face made the more attractive by an expression only given by a sense of duty unselfishly done.

"I – I wish'd you'd call me Cousin Copernicus," he said for the fifth time.

She picked up one of the sheets on which he had been scribbling as though she had not heard him, and said:

"Why, dear me! How comes it you have so much figurin' to do?"

"Well," he began, in a querulous tone, "it beats all creation how many things a feller has to work out at once! Ye see, I've got a rope forty foot long that's got to tie the Panchronicon to the North Pole while we swing 'round to cut meridians. Now, then, the question is, How many times an hour shall we swing 'round to get to 1892, an' how long's it goin' to take an' how fast must I make the old thing hum along?"

"But you said eighteen hours by the clock would do it."

"Well, I jest guessed at that by the time the future man an' I took to go back five weeks, ye know. But I can't seem to figur it out right."

Phoebe seated herself at the table and took up a blank sheet of paper.

"Please lend me your pencil," she said. "Now, then, every time you whirl once 'round the pole to westward you lose one day, don't you?"

"That's it," said Droop, cheerfully. "Cuttin' twenty-four meridians –"

"And how many days in twenty-two years?" Phoebe broke in.

"You mean in six years."

"Why, no," she replied, glancing at Droop with a mischievous smile, "it's twenty-two years back to 1876, ain't it?"

"To '76 – why, but –"

He caught sight of her face and stopped short.

There came a pleased voice from one of the state-rooms.

"Yes, we've decided to go all the way back, Mr. Droop."

It was Rebecca.

She came forward and stood beside her sister, placing one hand affectionately upon her shoulder.

Droop leaned back in his chair with both hands on the edge of the table.

"Goin' all the way! Why, but then –"

He leaped to his feet with a radiant face.

"Great Jumpin' Jerusha!" he cried.

Slapping his thigh he began to pace excitedly up and down.

"Why, then, we'll get all the big inventions out – kodak an' phonograph and all. We'll marry Joe Chandler an' set things agoin' in two shakes fer millions."

"Eight thousand and thirty-five," said Phoebe in a quiet voice, putting her pencil to her lips. "We'll have to whirl round the pole eight thousand and thirty-five times."

"Whose goin' to keep count?" asked Rebecca, cheerfully. Ah, how different it all seemed now! Every dry detail was of interest.

Phoebe looked up at Droop, who now resumed his seat, somewhat sobered.

"Don't have to keep count," he replied. "See that indicator?" he continued, pointing to a dial in the ceiling which had not been noticed before. "That reads May 3, 1898, now, don't it? Well, it's fixed to keep always tellin' the right date. It counts the whirls we make an' keeps tabs on every day we go backward. Any time all ye hev to do is to read that thing an' it'll tell ye jest what day 'tis."

"Then what do you want to calculate how often to whirl round?" asked Phoebe, in disgusted tones.

"Well, ye see I want to plan out how long it'll take," Droop replied. "I want to go slow so as to avoid side weight – but I don't want to go too slow."

"I see," said Phoebe. "Well, then, how many times a minute did the future man take you when you whirled back five weeks?"

"'Bout two times a minute."

"That's one hundred and twenty times every hour. Did you feel much side weight then?"

"Scarcely any."

"Well, let's see. Divide eight thousand and thirty-five whirls by one hundred and twenty, an' you get sixty-seven hours. So that, ef we go at that rate it'll be two days and nineteen hours 'fore we get back to 1876."

"Don't talk about days," Droop objected. "It's sixty-seven hours by the clock – but it's twenty-two years less than no time in days, ye know."

"Sixty-seven hours," said Phoebe. "Well, that ain't so bad, is it? Why not go round twice a minute?"

"We can't air our beds fer three days, Phoebe," said Rebecca.

"But if we go much faster, we'll all be sick with this side weight trouble that Mr. Droop tells about."

"I vote fer twice a minute," said Droop. And so twice a minute was adopted.

"Air ye goin' to start to-night, Mr. Droop?" asked Rebecca.

"Well, no," he replied. "I think it's best to wait till tomorrow. Ye see, the power that runs the Panchronicon is got out o' the sunlight that falls on it. Of course, we're not all run out o' power by a good lot, but we've used considerable, an' I think it's a little mite safer to lie still fer a few hours here an' take in power from the sun. Ye see, it'll shine steady on us all night, an' we'll store up enough power to be sure o' reachin' 1876 in one clip."

"Well," said Rebecca, "ef thet's the plan, I'm goin' to bed right now. It's after eight o'clock, an' I didn't get to sleep las' night till goodness knows when. Goodnight! Hedn't you better go, too, Phoebe?"

"I guess I will," said Phoebe, turning to Copernicus. "Good-night, Mr. Droop."

"Good-night, Cousin Phoebe – good-night, Cousin Rebecca. I'll go to bed myself, I b'lieve."

The two doors were closed and Droop proceeded to draw the steel shutters in order to produce artificially the gloom not vouchsafed by a too-persistent sun.

In half an hour all were asleep within the now motionless conveyance.

Chapter V
Droop's Theory in Practice

ALL WERE UP betimes when the faithful clock announced that it ought to be morning. As for the sun, as though resenting the liberties about to be taken by these adventurers with its normal functions, it refused to set, and was found by the three travellers at the same altitude as the night before.

Promptly after breakfast Droop proceeded to don a suit of furs which he drew from a cupboard within the engine-room.

"Ye'd better hev suthin' hot ready when I come in again," he said. "I 'xpect I'll be nigh froze to death."

He drew on a huge cap of bear's fur which extended from his crown to his shoulders. There was a small hole in front which exposed only his nose and eyes.

"My, but you do look just like a pictur of Kris Kringle!" laughed Phoebe. "Don't he, Rebecca?"

Rebecca came to the kitchen door wiping a dish with slow circular movements of her towel.

"I don't guess you'll freeze very much with all that on," she remarked.

"Thet shows you don't know what seventy or eighty below zero means," said a muffled voice from within the fur cap. "You'll hev suthin' hot, won't ye?" Droop continued, looking appealingly at Phoebe.

"The'll be a pot o' good hot tea," she said. "That'll warm you all right."

Droop thought of something more stimulating and fragrant, but said nothing as he returned to the cupboard. Here he drew forth an apparently endless piece of stout rope. This he wound in a thick coil and hung over his head.

"Now, then," he said, "when I get down you shet the door at the top of the stairs tight, coz jest's soon's I open the outside door, thet hall's goin' to freeze up solid."

"All right!" said Phoebe. "I'll see to it."

Droop descended the stairs with a heavy tread, and as he reached the foot Phoebe closed the upper door, which she now noticed was provided with weather-strips.

Then the two women stood at the windows on the right-hand side of the vessel and watched Droop as he walked toward the pole. He raised the huge iron ring, snapping over it a special coupling hook fixed to the end of the rope.

Then he backed toward the vessel, unrolling the coil of rope as he moved away from the pole. Evidently they were within the forty-foot limit from the pole, for Droop had some rope to spare when he at length reached under the machine to attach the end to a ring which the sisters could not see.

He emerged from beneath the bulging side of the vessel swinging his arms and blowing a mighty volume of steam, which turned to snow as it left him. As he made directly for the entrance again, Phoebe ran to the kitchen.

"Poor man, he'll be perished!" she exclaimed.

As Droop entered the room, bringing with him a bitter atmosphere, Phoebe appeared with a large cup of hot tea.

"Here, Mr. Droop," she said, "drink this quick!"

Copernicus pulled off his cap and sat down to drink his tea without a word. When he had finished it, he pulled back his chair with a sigh.

"Whillikins! But 'twas cold!" he exclaimed. "Seems mos' like heaven to get into a nice warm room like this!"

"An' did ye get every thin' done right?" Rebecca asked.

"I guess I did," he said, emphatically. "I don't want to take no two bites out o' that kind o' cherry."

He rose and proceeded to remove his fur coverings.

"Goin' to start right now?" said Phoebe.

"Might's well, I guess."

He proceeded to the engine-room, followed by Phoebe, who watched his actions with the greatest interest.

"What you doin' with that handle?" she asked.

"That sets the airyplane on the uptilt. I'm only settin' it a mite – jest 'nough to keep the machine from sinkin' down when we get to movin'."

"How are you goin' to lift us up?"

"Just let out a mite o' gas below," said Droop. He suited the action to the word, and, with a tremendous hissing beneath it, the vessel rose slowly.

Droop pulled the starting lever and they moved forward with increasing speed. When they had gathered way, he shut off the gas escape and carefully readjusted the aeroplanes until the machine as a whole moved horizontally.

There was felt a slight jerk as they reached the end of the rope, and then they began to move in a circle from east to west.

Phoebe glanced at the clock.

"Just five minutes past eight," she said.

The sun was pouring its beams into the right-hand windows when they started, but the shafts of light now began to sweep circularly across the floor, and in a few moments, as they faced the sun, it ceased to shine in from the right. Immediately afterward it shone in at the left-hand windows and circled slowly around until again they were in shadow with the sun behind them.

Droop took out his watch and timed their revolutions by the sun's progress from window to window.

"'Bout one to the minute," he remarked. "Guess I'll speed her up a mite."

Carefully he regulated the speed, timing their revolutions accurately.

"There!" he said at length. "I guess that's pretty nigh two to the minute. D'ye feel any side weight?" he said, addressing his companions.

"No," said Rebecca.

Phoebe shook her head.

"You manage right well, Mr. Droop," she said. "You must have practised a good deal."

"Oh, not much," he replied, greatly pleased. "The future man showed me how to work it three – four times. It's simple 'nough when ye understand the principles."

These remarks brought a new idea to Rebecca's mind.

"Why, Mr. Droop," she exclaimed, "whatever's the use o' you goin' back to 1876! Why don't ye jest set up as the inventor o' this machine? I'm sure thet ought to make yer everlastin' fortune!"

"Oh, I thought o' that," he said. "But it's one thing to know how to work a thing an' it's a sight different to know how it's made an' all that. The future man tried to explain all the new scientific principles that was mixed into it – fer makin' power an' all – but I couldn't understand that part at all."

"An' besides," exclaimed Phoebe, "it's a heap more fun to be the only ones can use the thing, I think."

"Yes – seems like fun's all we're thinkin' of," said Rebecca, rising and moving toward the kitchen. "We're jest settin' round doin' nothin'. I'll finish with the breakfast things if you'll put to rights and dust, Phoebe. We can't make beds till night with the windows tight shut."

These suggestions were followed by the two women, while Droop, picking up the newspaper which Rebecca had brought, sat down to read.

After a long term of quiet reading, his attention was distracted by Rebecca's voice.

"I declare to goodness, Phoebe!" she was saying. "Seems's if every chance you get, you go to readin' those old letters."

"Well, the's one or two that's spelled so funny and written so badly that I haven't been able yet to read them," Phoebe replied.

Droop looked over his paper. Phoebe and her sister were seated near one of the windows on the opposite side.

"P'raps I could help ye, Cousin Phoebe," he said. "I've got mighty strong eyesight."

"Oh, 'tain't a question of eyesight," Phoebe replied, laughing.

"Oh, I see," said Droop, smiling slyly, "letters from some young feller, eh?"

He winked knowingly at Rebecca, who drew herself up indignantly and looked severely down at her knitting.

Phoebe blushed, but replied quite calmly:

"Yes – some of them from a young man, but they weren't any of them written to me."

"No?" said Droop. "Who was they to – 'f I may ask?"

"They were all written to this lady."

Phoebe held something out for Droop's inspection, and he walked over to take it.

He recognized at once the miniature on ivory which he had seen once before in Peltonville.

"Well," he said, taking the portrait from her and eying it with his head on one side, "if ye hadn't said 'twasn't you, I'd certainly a-thought 'twas. I'd mos' sworn 'twas your photygraph, Cousin Phoebe. Who is it, anyway?"

"It isn't anybody," she replied, "but it was Mistress Mary Burton of Burton Hall. I'm one of her descendants, an' these are some letters she had with her in this funny old carved box when she disappeared with her lover. They fled to Holland and were married there, the story goes, an' one o' their children came over in the early days o' New England. He brought the letters an' the picture with him."

"Well, now! I want to know!" exclaimed Droop, in great admiration. "'Twouldn't be perlite, I s'pose, to ask to hear some o' them letters?"

"Would you like to hear some of them?" Phoebe asked.

"I would fer a fact," he replied.

"Well, bring your chair over here and I'll read you one," she said.

Droop seated himself near the two sisters and Phoebe unfolded a large and rather rough sheet of paper, yellow with age, on which Droop perceived a bold scrawl in a faded ink.

"This seems to have been from Mary Burton's father," Phoebe said. "I don't think he can have been a very nice man. This is what he says:

"'Dear Poll' – horrid nickname, isn't it?"

"Seems so to me," said Droop.

"'Dear Poll – I'm starting behind the grays for London, on my way, as you know ere this, to be knighted by her Majesty. I send this ahead by Gregory on Bess – she being fast enow for my purpose – which is to get thee straight out of the grip of that' –"

Phoebe hesitated.

"He uses a bad word there," she said, in a low tone. "I'll go on and leave that out."

"Yes, do," said Droop.

"'That — aunt of thine,'" she continued, reading. "'I know her tricks and I learn how she hath suffered that' –"

"There's another," said Phoebe.

"Skip it," said Droop, gravely.

"'That — milk-and-water popinjay to come courting my Poll. So see you follow Gregory, mistress, and without wait or parley come with him to the Peacock Inn, where I lie tonight. The grays are in fine fettle and thy black mare grows too fat for want of exercise. Thy mother-in-law commands thy instant return with Gregory, having much business forward with preparing gowns and fallals against our presentation to her Majesty.'"

"It is signed 'Isaac Burton,'" said Phoebe, "and see, the paper was sealed with a steel gauntlet."

Droop examined the seal carefully and then returned it, saying:

"Looks to me like a bunch of 'sparagus tumbled over on one side."

Phoebe laughed.

"But what always interests me most in this letter is the postscript," she said. "It reads:

"Thy mother thinks thou wilt make better speed if I make thee to know that the players thou wottest of –"

"What's a 'wottest'?" said Droop, in puzzled tones.

"Wottest means knowest – haven't you read Shakespeare?"

"No," said Droop.

"'The players thou wottest of are to stop at the Peacock, and will be giving some sport there.'

"Now, those players always interest me," Phoebe continued. "Somehow I can't help but believe that William Shakespeare –"

"Fiddle ends!" Rebecca interrupted. "I've heard that talk fifty-leven times an' I'm pinin' fer relief. Mr. Droop, would you mind tellin' us what the time o' year is now. Seems to me that sun has whirled in an' out o' that window 'nough times to bring us back to the days o' creation."

Droop consulted the date indicator and announced that it was now September 5, 1897.

"Not a year yet!" cried the two women together.

"Why, no," said Copernicus. "Ye see, we are takin' about three hours to lose a year."

"Fer the lands sakes!" cried Rebecca. "Can't we go a little faster?"

"My gracious, yes!" said Droop. "But I'm 'fraid o' the side weight fer ye."

"I'd rather hev side weight than wait forever," said Rebecca, with a grim smile.

"D'ye think ye could stand a little more speed, Cousin Phoebe?" said Droop.

"We might try," she replied.

"Well, let's try, then," he said, and turned promptly to the engine-room.

Very soon the difference in speed was felt, and as they found themselves travelling more rapidly in a circle, the centrifugal force now became distinctly perceptible.

The two women found themselves obliged to lean somewhat toward the central pole to counteract this tendency, and as Copernicus emerged from the engine-room he came toward the others at a decided angle to the floor.

"There! Now ye feel the side weight," he exclaimed.

"My, ain't it funny!" exclaimed Rebecca. "Thet's the way I've felt afore now when the cars was goin' round a curve – kinder topplin' like."

"Why, that is the centrifugal force," Phoebe said, with dignity.

"It's the side weight – that's what I call it," Droop replied, obstinately, and for some time there was silence.

"How many years back are we makin' by the hour now, Mr. Droop?" Rebecca asked at length.

"Jest a little over two hours fer a year now," he replied.

"Well," said Rebecca, in a discontented tone, "I think the old Panchronicle is rayther a slow actin' concern, considerin' th' amount o' side weight it makes. I declare I'm mos' tired out leanin' over to one side, like old man Titus's paralytic cow."

Phoebe laughed and Droop replied:

"If ye can't stand it or set it, why lay, Cousin Rebecca. The's good settles all 'round."

With manifestly injured feelings Droop hunted up a book and sat down to read in silence. The Panchronicon was his pet and he did not relish its being thus contemned.

The remainder of the morning was spent in almost completely silent work or reading. Droop scarce took his eyes from his book. Phoebe spent part of the time deep in the Baconian work and part of the time contemplating the monotonous landscape. Rebecca was dreaming of her future past – or her past future, while her knitting grew steadily upon its needles.

The midday meal was duly prepared and disposed of, and, as the afternoon wore away, the three travellers began to examine the date indicator and to ask themselves surreptitiously whether or not they actually felt any younger. They took sly peeps at each other's faces to observe, if possible, any signs of returning youth.

By supper-time there was certainly a less aged air about each of the three and the elders inwardly congratulated themselves upon the unmistakable effects of another twelve hours.

Not long after the supper dishes had been washed, Rebecca took Phoebe aside and said:

"Phoebe, it seems to me you'd ought to be goin' to bed right soon, now. You're only 'bout eighteen years old at present, an' you'll certainly begin to grow smaller again very soon. It wouldn't hardly be respectable fer ye to do yer shrinkin' out here."

This view of the probabilities had not yet struck Phoebe.

"Why, no!" she exclaimed, rather startled. "I – I don't know's I thought about it. But I certainly don't want Mr. Droop to see me when my clothes begin to hang loose."

Then a new problem presented itself.

"Come to think of it, Rebecca," she said, dolefully, "what'll I do all the time between full-grown and baby size? I didn't bring anything but the littlest clothes, you know."

"Thet's so," said Rebecca, thoughtfully. Then, after a pause: "I don't see but ye'll hev to stay abed, Phoebe, till we get to th' end," she said, sympathetically.

"There it is," said Phoebe, crossly. "Gettin' sent to bed a'ready – even before I expected it."

"But 'tain't that, Phoebe," said Rebecca, with great concern. "I ain't sendin' ye to bed – but – but – whatever else *can* ye do with a *man* in the house!"

"Nothin'," Phoebe replied, with a toss of her chin.

She crossed the room and held out her hand to Droop.

"Good-night, Mr. Droop," she said.

Surprised at this sudden demonstration of friendship, he took her hand and tipped his head to one side as he looked into her face.

"Next time you see me, I don't suppose you'll know me, I'll be so little," she said, trying to laugh.

"I – I wish't you'd call me Cousin Copernicus," he said, coaxingly.

"Well, p'raps I will when I see ye again," she replied, freeing her hand with a slight effort.

Rebecca retired shortly after her sister and Copernicus was once more left alone. He rubbed his hands slowly, with a sense of satisfaction, and glanced at the date dial.

"July 2, 1892," he said to himself. "I'm only thirty-four years old. Don't feel any older than that, either."

He walked deliberately to the shutters, closed them and turned on the electric light. Surrounded thus by the wonted conditions of night, it was not long before he began to yawn. He removed his coat and shoes and lay back in an easy chair to meditate at ease. He faced toward the pole so that the 'side weight' would tend to press him gently backward into his chair and therefore not annoy him by calling for constant opposing effort.

He soon dozed off and was whisked through a quick succession of fantastic dreams. Then he awoke suddenly, and as though someone had spoken to him. Listening intently, he only heard the low murmur of the machinery below and the ticking of the many clocks and indicators all about him.

He closed his eyes, intending to take up that last dream where he had been interrupted. He recollected that he had been on the very point of some delightful consummation, but just what it was he could not recall.

Sleep evaded him, however. His mind reverted to the all-important question of the recovered years. He began to plan again.

This time he should not make his former mistakes. No – he would not only make immense wealth promptly with the great inventions, he would give up liquor forever. It would be so easy in 1876, for he had never taken up the unfortunate habit until 1888.

Then – rich, young, sober, he would seek out a charming, rosy, good-natured girl – something of the type of Phoebe, for instance. They would be married and –

He got up at this and looked at the clock. It was after midnight. He looked at the date indicator. It said October 9, 1890.

"Well, come!" he thought. "The old Panchronicon is a steady vessel. She's keepin' right on."

He put on his shoes again, for something made him nervous and he wished to walk up and down.

The first thing he did after his shoes were donned was to gaze at himself in the mirror.

"Don't look any younger," he thought, "but I feel so." He walked across the room once or twice.

"Shucks!" he exclaimed. "Couldn't expect to look younger in these old duds, an' at this time o' night, too – tired like I am."

For some time he walked up and down, keeping his eyes resolutely from the date indicator. Finally he threw himself down in the chair again and closed his eyes, nervous and exhausted. He did not feel sleepy, but he must have dozed, for the next time he looked at the clock it was half-past one.

He put out the light and crossed to a settle. Here he lay at full length courting sleep. When he awoke, he thought, refreshed and alert, he would show his youth unmistakably.

But sleep would not return. He tried every position, every trick for propitiating Morpheus. All in vain.

At length he rose again and turned on the light. It was two-fifteen. This time he could not resist looking at the date indicator.

It said September 30, 1889.

Again he looked into the glass.

"My, but I'm nervous!" he thought as he turned away, disappointed. "I look older than ever!"

As he paced the floor there all alone, he began to doubt for the first time the success of his plan.

"It must work right!" he said aloud. "Didn't I go back five weeks with that future man? Didn't he –"

A fearful thought struck him. Had he perhaps made a mistake? Had they been cutting meridians the wrong way?

But no; the indicator could not be wrong, and that registered a constantly earlier date.

"Ah, I know!" he suddenly exclaimed. "I'll ask Cousin Phoebe."

He reflected a moment. Yes – the idea was a good one. She would be only fifteen years old by this time, and must certainly have changed to an extent of which he was at his age incapable. Besides, she had been asleep, and nervous insomnia could not be responsible for retarding the evidences of youth in her case. His agony of dread lest this great experiment fail made him bold.

He walked directly to Phoebe's door and knocked – first softly, then more loudly.

"Cousin Phoebe – Cousin Phoebe," he said.

After a few calls and knockings, there came a sleepy reply from within.

"Well – what – who is it?"

"It's Cousin Copernicus," he said. "Please tell me. Hev ye shrunk any yet?"

"What – how?" The tones were very sleepy indeed.

"Hev ye shrunk any yet? Are ye growin' littler in there? Oh, please feel fer the footboard with yer toe!"

He waited and heard a rustling as of someone moving in bed.

"Did ye feel the footboard?" he asked.

"Yes – kicked it good – now let me sleep." She was ill-natured with much drowsiness.

Poor Droop staggered away from the door as though he had been struck.

All had failed, then. They were circling uselessly. Those inventions would never be his. The golden dreams he had been nursing – oh, impossible! It was unbearable!

He put both hands to his head and walked across the room. He paused half-consciously before a small closet partly hidden in the wall.

With an instinctive movement, he touched a spring and the door slid back. He drew from the cupboard thus revealed two bottles and a glass and returned to seat himself at the table.

A half an hour later the Panchronicon, circling in the outer brightness and silence, contained three unconscious travellers, and one of them sat with his arms flung across the table supporting his head, and beside him an empty bottle.

The complete and unabridged text is available online, from *flametreepublishing.com/extras*

Two Children Reported Missing

Scott Merrow

Fact #1: People don't vanish into thin air.
Fact #2: Almost anything you can imagine can be simulated on video.
Fact #3: You can imagine people vanishing into thin air.
Conclusion: This tape has been faked.

A NICE PIECE *of deductive reasoning,* Detective Stanchion thought, giving himself a mental pat on the back. Sherlock Holmes would've been proud.

Of course, Sherlock Holmes also said, "When you have eliminated the impossible, whatever remains, no matter how improbable, must be the truth." Hmm.

It was Henry P. Stanchion's first day on the job since his promotion to Detective, and his first day at the Columbia County Sheriff's Department, his new headquarters. He was a newbie on two counts. He was excited to be here, but his first day wasn't going quite as he'd expected.

After his initial sit-down with the Division Commander, he was handed off to Detective Sam Dunn to begin his orientation and for general introductions around the office. They never got that far because five minutes later, before any sort of orientation had even begun, Detective Dunn was called away on a matter of some urgency.

Before he left, though, he sat Detective Stanchion at an empty desk in a remote corner of the room. "Sorry, man," he said as he plunked a cardboard file box on the desk before him. "Honest to god, I remember what my first day as a detective was like. I was all set to go solve some crimes, and I know you are too. But don't worry, I won't be long," Dunn assured him.

He pushed the file box toward Stanchion. "While you're waiting, you might have a look through this stuff. It's paperwork and evidence from an old cold case. Two kids went missing about ten years ago. Never found 'em. We're getting ready to put this stuff in deep storage, but it can't hurt to take one last look. A fresh set of eyes and all that. Y'just never know what you might find."

After Dunn left, Stanchion began half-heartedly rummaging through the box. *Well, this is exciting,* he thought. Among all the folders and plastic baggies full of this-and-that, he came across a VHS tape in a worn cardboard sleeve. He slid the video tape out and read the label:

PROPERTY OF COLUMBIA COUNTY SHERIFF'S DEPARTMENT
* CONFIDENTIAL *
MISSING PERSONS CASE # 08-0033 (OPEN)
DIGITAL/VIDEO EVIDENCE, EXHIBIT 12
BENTLEY J. BARNES (AGE 11)
ANNA MARIA DE LA CRUZ (AGE 11)

Detective Stanchion brought the tape to a cop working at a desk across the room. "'Scuse me," he said, holding up the tape, "is there a VHS player around anywhere?"

The man looked up, thought about it a moment, then said, "I think there might be one in that storage area behind the briefing room," he said, pointing behind him with his thumb. "I have no idea if it works, though," he added. "I'm pretty sure nobody's used it in a while."

Detective Stanchion nodded and took the tape to the briefing room. Sure enough, under a dusty pile of old equipment and a tangle of wires, there was a VHS player. With a minimum of fuss he had it hooked up to an old TV. Surprisingly, it worked.

He slid the tape into the machine and pressed *PLAY*.

The tape began with a black screen and several seconds of silence. Then a young girl's voice said, "Hi. I'm Anna Maria De La Cruz, and this is my...oh. Oops."

A moment of silence followed, and then some scuffling noises and the black screen turned bright [as the lens cap came off the camera] to reveal a girl's face, up close, with a distorted, fish-eye appearance caused by her close proximity to the lens.

The girl was eleven-year-old Anna Maria De La Cruz, a pretty Hispanic girl and at the moment an amateur filmmaker. In the frame behind her was a massive gray stone Victorian-era building, obviously magnificent in its prime, but now slightly dingy and run-down.

It was immediately obvious to Detective Stanchion, and would have been to anyone watching, that this was amateur footage shot from a cheap video camera.

Onscreen, the girl backed up and resumed her position front and center before the camera. She smoothed her long, dark hair and resumed her narration.

"Hi," she began again, "I'm Anna Maria De La Cruz, but everyone calls me Annie. I'm a documentary filmmaker. And this...," she said making a sweeping motion with her arm, encompassing the large building looming behind her, "...is my documentary film. It's about life at the Saint Jerome Children's Institution."

She took a couple of steps toward the camera then turned and looked back over her shoulder at the old building. "Saint Jerome's is what many people call an orphanage. She turned toward the camera and grinned. "And I'm what many people might call...an orphan. Only, I don't call myself that. I call myself, I don't know, just a regular person."

She stepped forward and reached toward the camera, her hand becoming huge on the screen. Then the picture went black.

A second later it clicked back on, and the huge gray building of Saint Jerome's almost totally filled the screen. The picture was wobbly now; it appeared as if the camera was hand held. Annie was nowhere to be seen, but her voice continued the narration. "There are 223 'regular people' like me at Saint Jerome's, from age four to age eighteen. When you're eighteen, they kick you out," she said. "Good bye, adios, you're on your own. That'll be me in seven years, unless I get adopted, which I doubt, but you never know."

The picture on the screen zoomed further in on the building, specifically on a third-floor window. "That's my room," Annie's voice continued. "Along with five other 'regular people.'"

The picture zoomed out, and the building filled the screen again. "We eat here, we sleep here, go to school here, and every morning..."

Suddenly, the front door flew open and a young boy dashed out. He leapt down the front stairs three at a time, heading toward Annie. He was a small boy, disheveled, hair-too-long, wearing thick unfashionable glasses – in short, he was nerdy-looking.

"Annie!" he shouted, still sprinting toward her.

The picture on the screen zoomed in and followed him as he ran closer and closer.

Annie, still off screen, picked up her narration. "And here's another of Saint Jerry's *regular people*, Bentley Barnes. As you can see he's a little weird and nerdy," she explained. "That's because he's a mad scientist. *And* he's my best friend."

As he charged up, the camera followed his face until it completely filled the screen. "Annie, c'mon!" he demanded, gasping for breath.

"C'mon where?" she asked. "As you can plainly see, Bentley, I'm at work filming my documentary."

"Documentary? Forget that," he replied, the screen still full of his face. "I need you to film my test run. It's gonna be historic."

"What test run?" Annie asked. "What are you talking about?"

"Never mind," he replied brusquely. "C'mon. Hurry. I'll explain on the way."

The screen went black.

When the video returned the scene had changed.

The picture on the screen was still moving about, indicating a hand-held camera. It was indoors now, following close behind Bentley as he hurried down a dimly lit hallway. It appeared to be in a basement since the source of the grayish light was a window high in the wall at the far end of the hall. The walls were concrete and grimy.

The camera followed as Bentley turned into a doorway.

It was a dingy, rather rundown old basement storage room, poorly lit. It was filled with science apparatus and electronic gear; there were disassembled computer components and a multitude of odd-looking pieces and parts strewn everywhere.

Bentley's back was front and center on screen, entering the room. Annie was not in the frame. Obviously, she was the cameraperson. "Yikes!" she said, her voice over the picture. "What *is* this place?"

Bentley turned to face the camera. "It's an old storage room," he answered. "Sister Claude lets me use it for my science projects. And that..."

He pointed to a corner of the room, and the camera followed. There was a complex, but obviously homemade contraption in the corner. It was essentially a very large cardboard box covered with wires, gauges, computer parts, and various other gizmos.

"...is my time machine," he said proudly.

The odd-looking machine filled the screen as Annie's perplexed voice said, "So, explain this to me again, Bentley. You're going to travel through time...in a cardboard box?"

The camera moved to Bentley's face as he said, "The box doesn't matter. It's all about quantum physics. I'm gonna warp the space-time continuum..." He stopped and thought about it for a moment, then continued. "Look, I don't have time to explain it again right now. The window's gonna close."

"What window?" Annie asked.

Bentley flashed an exasperated look. "Not now." He glanced at his watch. "Timing is everything in time travel." He flipped a couple switches on the machine, and it came to life. Tiny colored lights winked on, some wheels began turning, and everything started vibrating. There was a low electronic hum.

He looked at the camera and said, "Set your tripod up over there," pointing to a spot off to the side. "Just start filming, and leave it running. I need a witness."

The view on the screen went black for a few moments. When it came back on the cardboard-box time machine filled the screen. The picture was noticeably steadier now with the camera mounted on a tripod.

The machine was vibrating wildly. There was a cacophony of humming and rattling sounds. Bentley stepped into the picture and walked up to the machine. He opened a cardboard hatch on the side and squirmed inside.

A whirring noise began, adding to the already considerable din. The whirring grew louder and louder, and a shower of sparks flew up from somewhere on the far side of the box. Then there was a loud *POP*, a bright flash of light, and a huge cloud of smoke billowed up and filled the screen.

"Holy moley!" Annie exclaimed, coughing.

When the smoke cleared, the machine was gone.

"Holy double moley!" she said, a tone of astonishment tingeing her voice.

On screen, nothing moved for a few seconds, then there was a loud crackling sound and bolts of static electricity filled the air. A whining buzz began, first very faint, then louder and louder, and…*WHUMP!*

The machine reappeared…out of thin air.

Thin wisps of steam emanated from the cardboard surfaces. After a few moments, the blinking lights winked out and all the whirling, spinning gizmos gradually slowed down and stopped.

Annie appeared on the screen as she rushed over to the machine. "Bentley?" she called out. "Bentley, are you all right?"

The hatch opened, and Bentley struggled to get out, stepping gingerly over the edge with one leg. He squeezed his body through the small opening, then followed with his other leg. He stood up and stretched.

As Annie watched, her mouth dropped open in astonishment.

Bentley was different. He was…taller. His clothes were nicer. The nerdy glasses were gone. And his features were strange somehow, more developed. More mature. He looked older. He looked like…a fifteen-year old.

As he stood there stretching the kinks out, Annie stammered, "Bentley? What…?" "Who are…?"

"It's me, Annie," he answered. "I went two hundred years into the future, to the year 2208. I stayed there for four years."

Annie's mouth dropped open even further. "But…" she continued stammering, "you were only gone for…"

"I know," Bentley said. "A few seconds. But for me it was four years. And do you know why I stayed there for so long?"

Annie was still in shock. "I can't…"

"Because the future is amazing, Annie," he said. "It's a utopia. The whole world. They've figured it all out. No wars, no crime, everybody's happy, nobody's hungry. It's amazing."

"But…"

"And do you know why I came back?"

"No," Annie replied.

"To get you."

"What?" she asked, stunned.

"C'mon, Annie, come back with me," Bentley pleaded. "You won't believe the world of the future. No disease, no suffering, no global warming. They've solved everything."

"For how long, though," she asked. "Go back for how long?"

"Forever, Annie," he answered. "What have we got here?" he asked, gesturing around with his arms outstretched. "We're orphans. Nobody cares about us. Not really."

"But I'm only eleven, Bentley," she said. "And you're only…whatever you are…"

"Fifteen," he interrupted.

"Yeah, fifteen," she repeated. "And what if I don't want to go to the future? What if I want to stay here and become a documentary filmmaker. It's my dream, y'know."

"Forget about it, Annie. At least for now." He pushed his shirt tail aside. "Look. I brought some stuff to show you." He was wearing a small pouch attached to his belt. He reached in and fished out a smooth translucent stone. "This is a healing stone," he said.

He grabbed a pair of scissors from a table, opened them, and ran the blade across his forearm drawing a thin line of blood.

"Bentley," Annie shrieked, "what are you doing?"

"Watch," he answered. He slowly ran the stone across the wound. It healed instantly.

"Oh my god," Annie exclaimed. She grabbed his forearm and examined it closely. "Oh my god," she repeated.

"That's nothing," he said. "Just the beginning." He reached into the pouch and took out a small jet-black cube, about the size of a dice. He held it up for her to see better. He twirled it slowly between his thumb and forefinger. "Are you hungry?" he asked. "Even a little bit?"

"I don't know," she replied. "A little, I guess."

"Here, then," he said handing it to her. "Put it in your mouth. Don't chew it or swallow it, just let it sit there." Then he added, "It's called a Borlaug cube."

She popped it into her mouth. "It's delicious," she said.

"Yes it is," he agreed, "and it tastes differently to everyone who uses it. But, more importantly, are you still hungry?"

She thought about it for a moment. "No," she said. "No, I'm not. Not a bit."

"That's because the cube detects your nutritional needs, and it fulfills them instantly. It pulls the nutrients out of the air, or in some cases it manufactures them from whatever molecules are available," he explained. "Two hundred years from now, everyone has one of these. There's no hunger. Anywhere."

"Wow," Annie said quietly, a note of awe in her voice. "What an amazing world." She looked thoughtfully at Bentley. "But, Bentley, I'm from *this* world. The world of today. And I don't really care about utopia. I just want to make documentaries."

Bentley reached into the pouch again. "Let me show you one more thing, Annie." He took a small silver sphere from the pouch and held it up in the palm of his hand. As Annie watched, he withdrew his hand, and the sphere remained in the same place, floating in mid-air.

"Whoa!" Annie exclaimed.

"This is a library orb," he told her. "Everyone has one. In its memory is every document ever created. Ever."

He touched it with a fingertip, and a hologram appeared, projected in mid-air in the room. It was small, the image of a document. Bentley touched the orb again, and the image grew much larger.

"Go ahead, read it," Bentley said to Annie.

She did. It was an old newspaper article, and it began with a black and white photo of an elderly woman receiving a framed certificate from a nun. The caption under the photo read:

Anna Maria De La Cruz (68) receives a lifetime appreciation award for her 50 years of service as Chief Cook at the St. Jerome's Children's Home.

Annie was stunned. "You mean…?"

"That's right, Annie," Bentley answered. "Apparently you're not gonna be a filmmaker after all." Then he added, "At least, not if you stay here."

Annie was crushed, her shoulders slumped with disappointment.

Then after a moment of reflection, she straightened up and said, "So, tell me Bentley, this time travel stuff. Does it hurt?"

Bentley grinned. "Not one bit." He opened the cardboard hatch on the machine. "It's kind of exhilarating, really."

They climbed in, and the hatch closed behind them.

The time machine filled the screen. It started vibrating, then a whirring sound began. Then a shower of sparks. A flash of light. And ...*POP*... a cloud of smoke filled the video screen.

Moments later, when it cleared, the time machine was gone.

* * *

In the Columbia County Sheriff's Department briefing room, Detective Henry P. Stanchion let the tape run, and he watched the video of an empty room for another five minutes, until the screen went black. He watched the black screen for a few more minutes, until he finally got up and rewound the tape.

He brought it back to his desk, and just as he got there Detective Dunn returned. "You ready to get rolling?" he asked.

"Yeah, I guess so," Stanchion replied, tentatively. He held up the tape. "Have you watched this?" he asked Dunn.

"What is it? The one with the time machine?"

"Yeah."

"Yeah, I watched it, years ago," Dunn replied. "Back when the case was open."

"Man, it's weird," Stanchion said. "They just disappeared."

Dunn chuckled. "You can fake anything on video these days."

"That's what I told myself, too, but what about those inventions the kid had? The healing stone, and the floating ball, and the newspaper article projected in mid-air?"

"Fake, fake, and fake," Dunn replied.

"Man, they didn't look fake," Stanchion said. "Plus, here we are, ten years later, and those kids are still gone. Where are they?"

"They probably ran away," Dunn conjectured. "Kids run away all the time. Plus these two were orphans. No family ties. Nothing much holding them back."

"Yeah, I guess not," Stanchion answered. He looked at the tape, then he tossed it into the cardboard file box with the rest of the evidence.

"You ready to start your orientation?" Dunn asked.

"Yeah, sure," Stanchion nodded, and the two detectives left the room.

As they walked down the hall they passed a technician, a young Hispanic woman, early twenties maybe, wearing a white lab coat. She entered the room they had just left and walked straight to Detective Stanchion's desk. She picked up the file box and left the room.

She carried the box to the basement and down a long, dark hallway to a small room with a sign on the door: *Evidence Locker: Cold Case Files*. The door was cracked open, a small wad of paper towels wedged between the door and the jamb. She brought the box into the room and locked the door behind her.

She set the box on a shelf. She fished through the contents, found the video tape, and slipped it into the pocket of her lab coat. She pushed the box to the back of the shelf and hid it among a group of similar evidence boxes.

Then she walked quickly between the rows of storage shelves to the farthest, darkest corner of the room. There on the floor was... the cardboard box time machine.

She opened the flap, and with a little effort she shoehorned herself inside.

After a few moments, the thing came to life, blinking lights, spinning wheels, vibrating, wild shaking, humming, whirring, the whole shebang. Then, a shower of sparks. A cloud of smoke.

POP!

A bright flash of light.

And the machine disappeared, departing the twenty-first century for the very last time.

The Clock that Went Backward

Edward Page Mitchell

I

A ROW of Lombardy poplars stood in front of my great-aunt Gertrude's house, on the bank of the Sheepscot River. In personal appearance my aunt was surprisingly like one of those trees. She had the look of hopeless anemia that distinguishes them from fuller blooded sorts. She was tall, severe in outline, and extremely thin. Her habiliments clung to her. I am sure that had the gods found occasion to impose upon her the fate of Daphne she would have taken her place easily and naturally in the dismal row, as melancholy a poplar as the rest.

Some of my earliest recollections are of this venerable relative. Alive and dead she bore an important part in the events I am about to recount: events which I believe to be without parallel in the experience of mankind.

During our periodical visits of duty to Aunt Gertrude in Maine, my cousin Harry and myself were accustomed to speculate much on her age. Was she sixty, or was she six score? We had no precise information; she might have been either. The old lady was surrounded by old-fashioned things. She seemed to live altogether in the past. In her short half-hours of communicativeness, over her second cup of tea, or on the piazza where the poplars sent slim shadows directly toward the east, she used to tell us stories of her alleged ancestors. I say alleged, because we never fully believed that she had ancestors.

A genealogy is a stupid thing. Here is Aunt Gertrude's, reduced to its simplest forms:

> *Her great-great-grandmother (1599–1642) was a woman of Holland who married a Puritan refugee, and sailed from Leyden to Plymouth in the ship Ann in the year of our Lord 1632. This Pilgrim mother had a daughter, Aunt Gertrude's great-grandmother (1640–1718). She came to the Eastern District of Massachusetts in the early part of the last century, and was carried off by the Indians in the Penobscot wars. Her daughter (1680–1776) lived to see these colonies free and independent, and contributed to the population of the coming republic not less than nineteen stalwart sons and comely daughters. One of the latter (1735–1802) married a Wiscasset skipper engaged in the West India trade, with whom she sailed. She was twice wrecked at sea – once on what is now Seguin Island and once on San Salvador. It was on San Salvador that Aunt Gertrude was born.*

We got to be very tired of hearing this family history. Perhaps it was the constant repetition and the merciless persistency with which the above dates were driven into our young ears that made us skeptics. As I have said, we took little stock in Aunt Gertrude's ancestors. They seemed highly improbable. In our private opinion the great-grandmothers and grandmothers and so forth were pure myths, and Aunt Gertrude herself was the principal in all the adventures attributed to them, having lasted from century to century while generations of contemporaries went the way of all flesh.

On the first landing of the square stairway of the mansion loomed a tall Dutch clock. The case was more than eight feet high, of a dark red wood, not mahogany, and it was curiously inlaid with silver. No common piece of furniture was this. About a hundred years ago there flourished in the town of Brunswick a horologist named Cary, an industrious and accomplished workman. Few well-to-do houses on that part of the coast lacked a Cary timepiece. But Aunt Gertrude's clock had marked the hours and minutes of two full centuries before the Brunswick artisan was born. It was running when William the Taciturn pierced the dikes to relieve Leyden. The name of the maker, Jan Lipperdam, and the date, 1572, were still legible in broad black letters and figures reaching quite across the dial. Cary's masterpieces were plebeian and recent beside this ancient aristocrat. The jolly Dutch moon, made to exhibit the phases over a landscape of windmills and polders, was cunningly painted. A skilled hand had carved the grim ornament at the top, a death's head transfixed by a two-edged sword. Like all timepieces of the sixteenth century, it had no pendulum. A simple Van Wyck escapement governed the descent of the weights to the bottom of the tall case.

But these weights never moved. Year after year, when Harry and I returned to Maine, we found the hands of the old clock pointing to the quarter past three, as they had pointed when we first saw them. The fat moon hung perpetually in the third quarter, as motionless as the death's head above. There was a mystery about the silenced movement and the paralyzed hands. Aunt Gertrude told us that the works had never performed their functions since a bolt of lightning entered the clock; and she showed us a black hole in the side of the case near the top, with a yawning rift that extended downward for several feet. This explanation failed to satisfy us. It did not account for the sharpness of her refusal when we proposed to bring over the watchmaker from the village, or for her singular agitation once when she found Harry on a stepladder, with a borrowed key in his hand, about to test for himself the clock's suspended vitality.

One August night, after we had grown out of boyhood, I was awakened by a noise in the hallway. I shook my cousin. "Somebody's in the house," I whispered.

We crept out of our room and on to the stairs. A dim light came from below. We held breath and noiselessly descended to the second landing. Harry clutched my arm. He pointed down over the banisters, at the same time drawing me back into the shadow.

We saw a strange thing.

Aunt Gertrude stood on a chair in front of the old clock, as spectral in her white nightgown and white nightcap as one of the poplars when covered with snow. It chanced that the floor creaked slightly under our feet. She turned with a sudden movement, peering intently into the darkness, and holding a candle high toward us, so that the light was full upon her pale face. She looked many years older than when I bade her good night. For a few minutes she was motionless, except in the trembling arm that held aloft the candle. Then, evidently reassured, she placed the light upon a shelf and turned again to the clock.

We now saw the old lady take a key from behind the face and proceed to wind up the weights. We could hear her breath, quick and short. She rested a band on either side of the case and held her face close to the dial, as if subjecting it to anxious scrutiny. In this attitude she remained for a long time. We heard her utter a sigh of relief, and she half turned toward us for a moment. I shall never forget the expression of wild joy that transfigured her features then.

The hands of the clock were moving; they were moving backward.

Aunt Gertrude put both arms around the clock and pressed her withered cheek against it. She kissed it repeatedly. She caressed it in a hundred ways, as if it had been a living and beloved thing. She fondled it and talked to it, using words which we could hear but could not understand. The hands continued to move backward.

Then she started back with a sudden cry. The clock had stopped. We saw her tall body swaying for an instant on the chair. She stretched out her arms in a convulsive gesture of terror and despair, wrenched the minute hand to its old place at a quarter past three, and fell heavily to the floor.

II

AUNT GERTRUDE'S WILL left me her bank and gas stocks, real estate, railroad bonds, and city sevens, and gave Harry the clock. We thought at the time that this was a very unequal division, the more surprising because my cousin had always seemed to be the favorite. Half in seriousness we made a thorough examination of the ancient timepiece, sounding its wooden case for secret drawers, and even probing the not complicated works with a knitting needle to ascertain if our whimsical relative had bestowed there some codicil or other document changing the aspect of affairs. We discovered nothing.

There was testamentary provision for our education at the University of Leyden. We left the military school in which we had learned a little of the theory of war, and a good deal of the art of standing with our noses over our heels, and took ship without delay. The clock went with us. Before many months it was established in a corner of a room in the Breede Straat.

The fabric of Jan Lipperdam's ingenuity, thus restored to its native air, continued to tell the hour of quarter past three with its old fidelity. The author of the clock had been under the sod for nearly three hundred years. The combined skill of his successors in the craft at Leyden could make it go neither forward nor backward.

We readily picked up enough Dutch to make ourselves understood by the townspeople, the professors, and such of our eight hundred and odd fellow students as came into intercourse. This language, which looks so hard at first, is only a sort of polarized English. Puzzle over it a little while and it jumps into your comprehension like one of those simple cryptograms made by running together all the words of a sentence and then dividing in the wrong places.

The language acquired and the newness of our surroundings worn off, we settled into tolerably regular pursuits. Harry devoted himself with some assiduity to the study of sociology, with especial reference to the round-faced and not unkind maidens of Leyden. I went in for the higher metaphysics.

Outside of our respective studies, we had a common ground of unfailing interest. To our astonishment, we found that not one in twenty of the faculty or students knew or cared a sliver about the glorious history of the town, or even about the circumstances under which the university itself was founded by the Prince of Orange. In marked contrast with the general indifference was the enthusiasm of Professor Van Stopp, my chosen guide through the cloudiness of speculative philosophy.

This distinguished Hegelian was a tobacco-dried little old man, with a skullcap over features that reminded me strangely of Aunt Gertrude's. Had he been her own brother the facial resemblance could not have been closer. I told him so once, when we were together in the Stadthuis looking at the portrait of the hero of the siege, the Burgomaster Van der Werf. The professor laughed. "I will show you what is even a more extraordinary coincidence," said he; and, leading the way across the hall to the great picture of the siege, by Warmers, he pointed out the figure of a burgher participating in the defense. It was true. Van Stopp might have been the burgher's son; the burgher might have been Aunt Gertrude's father.

The professor seemed to be fond of us. We often went to his rooms in an old house in the Rapenburg Straat, one of the few houses remaining that antedate 1574. He would walk with us through the beautiful suburbs of the city, over straight roads lined with poplars that carried us back to the bank of the Sheepscot in our minds. He took us to the top of the ruined Roman tower in the center of the town, and from the same battlements from which anxious eyes three centuries ago had watched the slow approach of Admiral Boisot's fleet over the submerged polders, he pointed out the great dike of the Landscheiding, which was cut that the oceans might bring Boisot's Zealanders to raise the leaguer and feed the starving. He showed us the headquarters of the Spaniard Valdez at Leyderdorp, and told us how heaven sent a violent northwest wind on the night of the first of October, piling up the water deep where it had been shallow and sweeping the fleet on between Zoeterwoude and Zwieten up to the very walls of the fort at Lammen, the last stronghold of the besiegers and the last obstacle in the way of succor to the famishing inhabitants. Then he showed us where, on the very night before the retreat of the besieging army, a huge breach was made in the wall of Leyden, near the Cow Gate, by the Walloons from Lammen.

"Why!" cried Harry, catching fire from the eloquence of the professor's narrative, "that was the decisive moment of the siege."

The professor said nothing. He stood with his arms folded, looking intently into my cousin's eyes.

"For," continued Harry, "had that point not been watched, or had defense failed and the breach been carried by the night assault from Lammen, the town would have been burned and the people massacred under the eyes of Admiral Boisot and the fleet of relief. Who defended the breach?"

Van Stopp replied very slowly, as if weighing every word:

"History records the explosion of the mine under the city wall on the last night of the siege; it does not tell the story of the defense or give the defender's name. Yet no man that ever lived had a more tremendous charge than fate entrusted to this unknown hero. Was it chance that sent him to meet that unexpected danger? Consider some of the consequences had he failed. The fall of Leyden would have destroyed the last hope of the Prince of Orange and of the free states. The tyranny of Philip would have been reestablished. The birth of religious liberty and of self-government by the people would have been postponed, who knows for how many centuries? Who knows that there would or could have been a republic of the United States of America had there been no United Netherlands? Our University, which has given to the world Grotius, Scaliger, Arminius, and Descartes, was founded upon this hero's successful defense of the breach. We owe to him our presence here today. Nay, you owe to him your very existence. Your ancestors were of Leyden; between their lives and the butchers outside the walls he stood that night."

The little professor towered before us, a giant of enthusiasm and patriotism. Harry's eyes glistened and his cheeks reddened.

"Go home, boys," said Van Stopp, "and thank God that while the burghers of Leyden were straining their gaze toward Zoeterwoude and the fleet, there was one pair of vigilant eyes and one stout heart at the town wall just beyond the Cow Gate!"

III

THE RAIN was splashing against the windows one evening in the autumn of our third year at Leyden, when Professor Van Stopp honored us with a visit in the Breede Straat. Never had I seen the old gentleman in such spirits. He talked incessantly. The gossip of the town, the news of Europe, science, poetry, philosophy, were in turn touched upon and treated with the same high and good humor. I sought to draw him out on Hegel, with whose chapter on the complexity and interdependency of things I was just then struggling.

"You do not grasp the return of the Itself into Itself through its Otherself?" he said smiling. "Well, you will, sometime."

Harry was silent and preoccupied. His taciturnity gradually affected even the professor. The conversation flagged, and we sat a long while without a word. Now and then there was a flash of lightning succeeded by distant thunder.

"Your clock does not go," suddenly remarked the professor. "Does it ever go?"

"Never since we can remember," I replied. "That is, only once, and then it went backward. It was when Aunt Gertrude –"

Here I caught a warning glance from Harry. I laughed and stammered, "The clock is old and useless. It cannot be made to go."

"Only backward?" said the professor, calmly, and not appearing to notice my embarrassment. "Well, and why should not a clock go backward? Why should not Time itself turn and retrace its course?"

He seemed to be waiting for an answer. I had none to give.

"I thought you Hegelian enough," he continued, "to admit that every condition includes its own contradiction. Time is a condition, not an essential. Viewed from the Absolute, the sequence by which future follows present and present follows past is purely arbitrary. Yesterday, today, tomorrow; there is no reason in the nature of things why the order should not be tomorrow, today, yesterday."

A sharper peal of thunder interrupted the professor's speculations.

"The day is made by the planet's revolution on its axis from west to east. I fancy you can conceive conditions under which it might turn from east to west, unwinding, as it were, the revolutions of past ages. Is it so much more difficult to imagine Time unwinding itself; Time on the ebb, instead of on the flow; the past unfolding as the future recedes; the centuries countermarching; the course of events proceeding toward the Beginning and not, as now, toward the End?"

"But," I interposed, "we know that as far as we are concerned the –"

"We know!" exclaimed Van Stopp, with growing scorn. "Your intelligence has no wings. You follow in the trail of Compte and his slimy brood of creepers and crawlers. You speak with amazing assurance of your position in the universe. You seem to think that your wretched little individuality has a firm foothold in the Absolute. Yet you go to bed tonight and dream into existence men, women, children, beasts of the past or of the future. How do you know that at this moment you yourself, with all your conceit of nineteenth-century thought, are anything more than a creature of a dream of the future, dreamed, let us say, by some philosopher of the sixteenth century? How do you know that you are anything more than a creature of a dream of the past, dreamed by some Hegelian of the twenty-sixth century? How do you know, boy, that you will not vanish into the sixteenth century or 2060 the moment the dreamer awakes?"

There was no replying to this, for it was sound metaphysics. Harry yawned. I got up and went to the window. Professor Van Stopp approached the clock.

"Ah, my children," said he, "there is no fixed progress of human events. Past, present, and future are woven together in one inextricable mesh. Who shall say that this old clock is not right to go backward?"

A crash of thunder shook the house. The storm was over our heads.

When the blinding glare had passed away, Professor Van Stopp was standing upon a chair before the tall timepiece. His face looked more than ever like Aunt Gertrude's. He stood as she had stood in that last quarter of an hour when we saw her wind the clock.

The same thought struck Harry and myself.

"Hold!" we cried, as he began to wind the works. "It may be death if you –"

The professor's sallow features shone with the strange enthusiasm that had transformed Aunt Gertrude's.

"True," he said, "it may be death; but it may be the awakening. Past, present, future; all woven together! The shuttle goes to and fro, forward and back –"

He had wound the clock. The hands were whirling around the dial from right to left with inconceivable rapidity. In this whirl we ourselves seemed to be borne along. Eternities seemed to contract into minutes while lifetimes were thrown off at every tick. Van Stopp, both arms outstretched, was reeling in his chair. The house shook again under a tremendous peal of thunder. At the same instant a ball of fire, leaving a wake of sulphurous vapor and filling the room with dazzling light, passed over our heads and smote the clock. Van Stopp was prostrated. The hands ceased to revolve.

IV

THE ROAR of the thunder sounded like heavy cannonading. The lightning's blaze appeared as the steady light of a conflagration. With our hands over our eyes, Harry and I rushed out into the night.

Under a red sky people were hurrying toward the Stadthuis. Flames in the direction of the Roman tower told us that the heart of the town was afire. The faces of those we saw were haggard and emaciated. From every side we caught disjointed phrases of complaint or despair. "Horseflesh at ten schillings the pound," said one, "and bread at sixteen schillings." "Bread indeed!" an old woman retorted: "It's eight weeks gone since I have seen a crumb." "My little grandchild, the lame one, went last night." "Do you know what Gekke Betje, the washerwoman, did? She was starving. Her babe died, and she and her man –"

A louder cannon burst cut short this revelation. We made our way on toward the citadel of the town, passing a few soldiers here and there and many burghers with grim faces under their broad-brimmed felt hats.

"There is bread plenty yonder where the gunpowder is, and full pardon, too. Valdez shot another amnesty over the walls this morning."

An excited crowd immediately surrounded the speaker. "But the fleet!" they cried.

"The fleet is grounded fast on the Greenway polder. Boisot may turn his one eye seaward for a wind till famine and pestilence have carried off every mother's son of ye, and his ark will not be a rope's length nearer. Death by plague, death by starvation, death by fire and musketry – that is what the burgomaster offers us in return for glory for himself and kingdom for Orange."

"He asks us," said a sturdy citizen, "to hold out only twenty-four hours longer, and to pray meanwhile for an ocean wind."

"Ah, yes!" sneered the first speaker. "Pray on. There is bread enough locked in Pieter Adriaanszoon van der Werf's cellar. I warrant you that is what gives him so wonderful a stomach for resisting the Most Catholic King."

A young girl, with braided yellow hair, pressed through the crowd and confronted the malcontent. "Good people," said the maiden, "do not listen to him. He is a traitor with a Spanish heart. I am Pieter's daughter. We have no bread. We ate malt cakes and rapeseed like the rest of you till that was gone. Then we stripped the green leaves from the lime trees and willows in our garden and ate them. We have eaten even the thistles and weeds that grew between the stones by the canal. The coward lies."

Nevertheless, the insinuation had its effect. The throng, now become a mob, surged off in the direction of the burgomaster's house. One ruffian raised his hand to strike the girl out of the way. In a wink the cur was under the feet of his fellows, and Harry, panting and glowing, stood at the maiden's side, shouting defiance in good English at the backs of the rapidly retreating crowd.

With the utmost frankness she put both her arms around Harry's neck and kissed him.

"Thank you," she said. "You are a hearty lad. My name is Gertruyd van der Wert."

Harry was fumbling in his vocabulary for the proper Dutch phrases, but the girl would not stay for compliments. "They mean mischief to my father"; and she hurried us through several exceedingly narrow streets into a three-cornered market place dominated by a church with two spires. "There he is," she exclaimed, "on the steps of St. Pancras."

There was a tumult in the market place. The conflagration raging beyond the church and the voices of the Spanish and Walloon cannon outside of the walls were less angry than the roar of this multitude of desperate men clamoring for the bread that a single word from their leader's lips would bring them. "Surrender to the King!" they cried, "Or we will send your dead body to Lammen as Leyden's token of submission."

One tall man, taller by half a head than any of the burghers confronting him, and so dark of complexion that we wondered how he could be the father of Gertruyd, heard the threat in silence. When the burgomaster spoke, the mob listened in spite of themselves.

"What is it you ask, my friends? That we break our vow and surrender Leyden to the Spaniards? That is to devote ourselves to a fate far more horrible than starvation. I have to keep the oath! Kill me, if you will have it so. I can die only once, whether by your hands, by the enemy's, or by the hand of God. Let us starve, if we must, welcoming starvation because it comes before dishonor. Your menaces do not move me; my life is at your disposal. Here, take my sword, thrust it into my breast, and divide my flesh among you to appease your hunger. So long as I remain alive expect no surrender."

There was silence again while the mob wavered. Then there were mutterings around us. Above these rang out the clear voice of the girl whose hand Harry still held-unnecessarily, it seemed to me.

"Do you not feel the sea wind? It has come at last. To the tower! And the first man there will see by moonlight the full white sails of the prince's ships."

For several hours I scoured the streets of the town, seeking in vain my cousin and his companion; the sudden movement of the crowd toward the Roman tower had separated us. On every side I saw evidences of the terrible chastisement that had brought this stout-hearted people to the verge of despair. A man with hungry eyes chased a lean rat along the bank of the canal. A young mother, with two dead babes in her arms, sat in a doorway to which they bore the bodies of her husband and father, just killed at the walls. In the middle of a deserted street I passed unburied corpses in a pile twice as high as my head. The pestilence had been there-kinder than the Spaniard, because it held out no treacherous promises while it dealt its blows.

Toward morning the wind increased to a gale. There was no sleep in Leyden, no more talk of surrender, no longer any thought or care about defense. These words were on the lips of everybody I met: "Daylight will bring the fleet!"

Did daylight bring the fleet? History says so, but I was not a witness. I know only that before dawn the gale culminated in a violent thunderstorm, and that at the same time a muffled explosion, heavier than the thunder, shook the town. I was in the crowd that watched from the Roman Mound for the first signs of the approaching relief. The concussion shook hope out of every face. "Their mine has reached the wall!" But where? I pressed forward until I found the burgomaster, who was standing among the rest. "Quick!" I whispered. "It is beyond the Cow Gate, and this side of the Tower of Burgundy." He gave me a searching glance, and then strode away, without making any attempt to quiet the general panic. I followed close at his heels.

It was a tight run of nearly half a mile to the rampart in question. When we reached the Cow Gate this is what we saw:

A great gap, where the wall had been, opening to the swampy fields beyond: in the moat, outside and below, a confusion of upturned faces, belonging to men who struggled like demons to achieve the breach, and who now gained a few feet and now were forced back; on the shattered rampart a handful of soldiers and burghers forming a living wall where masonry had failed; perhaps a double handful of women and girls, serving stones to the defenders and boiling water in buckets, besides pitch and oil and unslaked lime, and some of them quoiting tarred and burning hoops over the necks of the Spaniards in the moat; my cousin Harry leading and directing the men; the burgomaster's daughter Gertruyd encouraging and inspiring the women.

But what attracted my attention more than anything else was the frantic activity of a little figure in black, who, with a huge ladle, was showering molten lead on the heads of the assailing party. As he turned to the bonfire and kettle which supplied him with ammunition, his features came into the full light. I gave a cry of surprise: the ladler of molten lead was Professor Van Stopp.

The burgomaster Van der Werf turned at my sudden exclamation. "Who is that?" I said. "The man at the kettle?"

"That," replied Van der Werf, "is the brother of my wife, the clockmaker Jan Lipperdam."

The affair at the breach was over almost before we had had time to grasp the situation. The Spaniards, who had overthrown the wall of brick and stone, found the living wall impregnable. They could not even maintain their position in the moat; they were driven off into the darkness. Now I felt a sharp pain in my left arm. Some stray missile must have hit me while we watched the fight.

"Who has done this thing?" demanded the burgomaster. "Who is it that has kept watch on today while the rest of us were straining fools' eyes toward tomorrow?"

Gertruyd van der Werf came forward proudly, leading my cousin. "My father," said the girl, "he has saved my life."

"That is much to me," said the burgomaster, "but it is not all. He has saved Leyden and he has saved Holland."

I was becoming dizzy. The faces around me seemed unreal. Why were we here with these people? Why did the thunder and lightning forever continue? Why did the clockmaker, Jan Lipperdam, turn always toward me the face of Professor Van Stopp? "Harry!" I said, "Come back to our rooms."

But though he grasped my hand warmly his other hand still held that of the girl, and he did not move. Then nausea overcame me. My head swam, and the breach and its defenders faded from sight.

V

THREE DAYS LATER I sat with one arm bandaged in my accustomed seat in Van Stopp's lecture room. The place beside me was vacant.

"We hear much," said the Hegelian professor, reading from a notebook in his usual dry, hurried tone, "of the influence of the sixteenth century upon the nineteenth. No philosopher, as far as I am aware, has studied the influence of the nineteenth century upon the sixteenth. If cause produces effect, does effect never induce cause? Does the law of heredity, unlike all other laws of this universe of mind and matter, operate in one direction only? Does the descendant owe everything to the ancestor, and the ancestor nothing to the descendant? Does destiny, which may seize upon our existence, and for its own purposes bear us far into the future, never carry us back into the past?"

I went back to my rooms in the Breede Straat, where my only companion was the silent clock.

A Dream of John Ball
Chapters I–IV
William Morris

Chapter I
The Men of Kent

SOMETIMES I am rewarded for fretting myself so much about present matters by a quite unasked-for pleasant dream. I mean when I am asleep. This dream is as it were a present of an architectural peep-show. I see some beautiful and noble building new made, as it were for the occasion, as clearly as if I were awake; not vaguely or absurdly, as often happens in dreams, but with all the detail clear and reasonable. Some Elizabethan house with its scrap of earlier fourteenth-century building, and its later degradations of Queen Anne and Silly Billy and Victoria, marring but not destroying it, in an old village once a clearing amid the sandy woodlands of Sussex. Or an old and unusually curious church, much churchwardened, and beside it a fragment of fifteenth-century domestic architecture amongst the not unpicturesque lath and plaster of an Essex farm, and looking natural enough among the sleepy elms and the meditative hens scratching about in the litter of the farmyard, whose trodden yellow straw comes up to the very jambs of the richly carved Norman doorway of the church. Or sometimes 'tis a splendid collegiate church, untouched by restoring parson and architect, standing amid an island of shapely trees and flower-beset cottages of thatched grey stone and cob, amidst the narrow stretch of bright green water-meadows that wind between the sweeping Wiltshire downs, so well beloved of William Cobbett. Or some new-seen and yet familiar cluster of houses in a grey village of the upper Thames overtopped by the delicate tracery of a fourteenth-century church; or even sometimes the very buildings of the past untouched by the degradation of the sordid utilitarianism that cares not and knows not of beauty and history: as once, when I was journeying (in a dream of the night) down the well-remembered reaches of the Thames betwixt Streatley and Wallingford, where the foothills of the White Horse fall back from the broad stream, I came upon a clear-seen mediaeval town standing up with roof and tower and spire within its walls, grey and ancient, but untouched from the days of its builders of old. All this I have seen in the dreams of the night clearer than I can force myself to see them in dreams of the day. So that it would have been nothing new to me the other night to fall into an architectural dream if that were all, and yet I have to tell of things strange and new that befell me after I had fallen asleep. I had begun my sojourn in the Land of Nod by a very confused attempt to conclude that it was all right for me to have an engagement to lecture at Manchester and Mitcham Fair Green at half-past eleven at night on one and the same Sunday, and that I could manage pretty well. And then I had gone on to try to make the best of addressing a large open-air audience in the costume I was really then wearing – to wit, my night-shirt, reinforced for the dream occasion by a pair of braceless trousers. The consciousness of this fact so bothered me, that the earnest faces of my audience – who would *not* notice it, but were clearly preparing terrible anti-Socialist posers for me – began to fade away and my dream grew thin, and I awoke (as I thought) to find myself lying on a strip of wayside waste by an oak copse just outside a country village.

I got up and rubbed my eyes and looked about me, and the landscape seemed unfamiliar to me, though it was, as to the lie of the land, an ordinary English low-country, swelling into rising ground here and there. The road was narrow, and I was convinced that it was a piece of Roman road from its straightness. Copses were scattered over the country, and there were signs of two or three villages and hamlets in sight besides the one near me, between which and me there was some orchard-land, where the early apples were beginning to redden on the trees. Also, just on the other side of the road and the ditch which ran along it, was a small close of about a quarter of an acre, neatly hedged with quick, which was nearly full of white poppies, and, as far as I could see for the hedge, had also a good few rose-bushes of the bright-red nearly single kind, which I had heard are the ones from which rose-water used to be distilled. Otherwise the land was quite unhedged, but all under tillage of various kinds, mostly in small strips. From the other side of a copse not far off rose a tall spire white and brand-new, but at once bold in outline and unaffectedly graceful and also distinctly English in character. This, together with the unhedged tillage and a certain unwonted trimness and handiness about the enclosures of the garden and orchards, puzzled me for a minute or two, as I did not understand, new as the spire was, how it could have been designed by a modern architect; and I was of course used to the hedged tillage and tumbledown bankrupt-looking surroundings of our modern agriculture. So that the garden-like neatness and trimness of everything surprised me. But after a minute or two that surprise left me entirely; and if what I saw and heard afterwards seems strange to you, remember that it did not seem strange to me at the time, except where now and again I shall tell you of it. Also, once for all, if I were to give you the very words of those who spoke to me you would scarcely understand them, although their language was English too, and at the time I could understand them at once.

Well, as I stretched myself and turned my face toward the village, I heard horse-hoofs on the road, and presently a man and horse showed on the other end of the stretch of road and drew near at a swinging trot with plenty of clash of metal. The man soon came up to me, but paid me no more heed than throwing me a nod. He was clad in armour of mingled steel and leather, a sword girt to his side, and over his shoulder a long-handled bill-hook.

His armour was fantastic in form and well wrought; but by this time I was quite used to the strangeness of him, and merely muttered to myself, "He is coming to summon the squire to the leet;" so I turned toward the village in good earnest. Nor, again, was I surprised at my own garments, although I might well have been from their unwontedness. I was dressed in a black cloth gown reaching to my ankles, neatly embroidered about the collar and cuffs, with wide sleeves gathered in at the wrists; a hood with a sort of bag hanging down from it was on my head, a broad red leather girdle round my waist, on one side of which hung a pouch embroidered very prettily and a case made of hard leather chased with a hunting scene, which I knew to be a pen and ink case; on the other side a small sheath-knife, only an arm in case of dire necessity.

Well, I came into the village, where I did not see (nor by this time expected to see) a single modern building, although many of them were nearly new, notably the church, which was large, and quite ravished my heart with its extreme beauty, elegance, and fitness. The chancel of this was so new that the dust of the stone still lay white on the midsummer grass beneath the carvings of the windows. The houses were almost all built of oak frame-work filled with cob or plaster well whitewashed; though some had their lower stories of rubble-stone, with their windows and doors of well-moulded freestone. There was much curious and inventive carving about most of them; and though some were old and much worn, there was the same look of deftness and trimness, and even beauty, about every detail in them which I noticed before in the field-work. They were all roofed with oak shingles, mostly grown as grey as stone; but one was so newly built that its roof was yet pale and yellow. This was a corner house, and the corner post of it had a carved niche wherein stood a gaily painted figure holding an anchor – St. Clement to wit, as the dweller in the house was a blacksmith. Half a stone's throw from the east end of the churchyard wall was a tall cross of stone, new like the church, the head beautifully carved with a crucifix amidst leafage. It stood on a set of wide stone steps, octagonal in shape, where three roads from other villages met and formed a wide open space on which a thousand people or more could stand together with no great crowding.

All this I saw, and also that there was a goodish many people about, women and children, and a few old men at the doors, many of them somewhat gaily clad, and that men were coming into the village street by the other end to that by which I had entered, by twos and threes, most of them carrying what I could see were bows in cases of linen yellow with wax or oil; they had quivers at their backs, and most of them a short sword by their left side, and a pouch and knife on the right; they were mostly dressed in red or brightish green or blue cloth jerkins, with a hood on the head generally of another colour. As they came nearer I saw that the cloth of their garments was somewhat coarse, but stout and serviceable. I knew, somehow, that they had been shooting at the butts, and, indeed, I could still hear a noise of men thereabout, and even now and again when the wind set from that quarter the twang of the bowstring and the plump of the shaft in the target.

I leaned against the churchyard wall and watched these men, some of whom went straight into their houses and some loitered about still; they were rough-looking fellows, tall and stout, very black some of them, and some red-haired, but most had hair burnt by the sun into the colour of tow; and, indeed, they were all burned and tanned and freckled variously. Their arms and buckles and belts and the finishings and hems of their garments were all what we should now call beautiful, rough as the men were; nor in their speech was any of that drawling snarl or thick vulgarity which one is used to hear from labourers in civilisation; not that they talked like gentlemen either, but full and round and bold, and they were merry and good-tempered enough; I could see that, though I felt shy and timid amongst them.

One of them strode up to me across the road, a man some six feet high, with a short black beard and black eyes and berry-brown skin, with a huge bow in his hand bare of the case, a knife, a pouch, and a short hatchet, all clattering together at his girdle.

"Well, friend," said he, "thou lookest partly mazed; what tongue hast thou in thine head?"

"A tongue that can tell rhymes," said I.

"So I thought," said he. "Thirstest thou any?"

"Yea, and hunger," said I.

And therewith my hand went into my purse, and came out again with but a few small and thin silver coins with a cross stamped on each, and three pellets in each corner of the cross. The man grinned.

"Aha!" said he, "Is it so? Never heed it, mate. It shall be a song for a supper this fair Sunday evening. But first, whose man art thou?"

"No one's man," said I, reddening angrily; "I am my own master."

He grinned again.

"Nay, that's not the custom of England, as one time belike it will be. Methinks thou comest from heaven down, and hast had a high place there too."

He seemed to hesitate a moment, and then leant forward and whispered in my ear: "John the Miller, that ground small, small, small," and stopped and winked at me, and from between my lips without my mind forming any meaning came the words, "The king's son of heaven shall pay for all."

He let his bow fall on to his shoulder, caught my right hand in his and gave it a great grip, while his left hand fell among the gear at his belt, and I could see that he half drew his knife.

"Well, brother," said he, "stand not here hungry in the highway when there is flesh and bread in the Rose yonder. Come on."

And with that he drew me along toward what was clearly a tavern door, outside which men were sitting on a couple of benches and drinking meditatively from curiously shaped earthen pots glazed green and yellow, some with quaint devices on them.

Chapter II
The Man From Essex

I ENTERED THE DOOR and started at first with my old astonishment, with which I had woke up, so strange and beautiful did this interior seem to me, though it was but a pothouse parlour. A quaintly-carved side board held an array of bright pewter pots and dishes and wooden and earthen bowls; a stout oak table went up and down the room, and a carved oak chair stood by the chimney-corner, now filled by a very old man dim-eyed and white-bearded. That, except the rough stools and benches on which the company sat, was all the furniture. The walls were panelled roughly enough with oak boards to about six feet from the floor, and about three feet of plaster above that was wrought in a pattern of a rose stem running all round the room, freely and roughly done, but with (as it seemed to my unused eyes) wonderful skill and spirit. On the hood of the great chimney a huge rose was wrought in the plaster and brightly painted in its proper colours. There were a dozen or more of the men I had seen coming along the street sitting there, some eating and all drinking; their cased bows leaned against the wall, their quivers hung on pegs in the panelling, and in a corner of the room I saw half-a-dozen bill-hooks that looked made more for war than for hedge-shearing, with ashen handles some seven foot long. Three or four children were running about among the legs of the men, heeding them mighty little in their bold play, and the men seemed little troubled by it, although they were talking earnestly and seriously too. A well-made comely girl leaned up against the chimney close to the gaffer's chair, and seemed to be in waiting on the company: she was clad in a close-fitting gown of bright blue cloth, with a broad silver girdle daintily wrought, round her loins, a rose wreath was on her head and her hair hung down unbound; the gaffer grumbled a few words to her from time to time, so that I judged he was her grandfather.

The men all looked up as we came into the room, my mate leading me by the hand, and he called out in his rough, good-tempered voice, "Here, my masters, I bring you tidings and a tale; give it meat and drink that it may be strong and sweet."

"Whence are thy tidings, Will Green?" said one.

My mate grinned again with the pleasure of making his joke once more in a bigger company: "It seemeth from heaven, since this good old lad hath no master," said he.

"The more fool he to come here," said a thin man with a grizzled beard, amidst the laughter that followed, "unless he had the choice given him between hell and England."

"Nay," said I, "I come not from heaven, but from Essex."

As I said the word a great shout sprang from all mouths at once, as clear and sudden as a shot from a gun. For I must tell you that I knew somehow, but I know not how, that the men of Essex were gathering to rise against the poll-groat bailiffs and the lords that would turn them all into villeins again, as their grandfathers had been. And the people was weak and the lords were poor; for many a mother's son had fallen in the war in France in the old king's time, and the Black Death had slain a many; so that the lords had bethought them: "We are growing poorer, and these upland-bred villeins are growing richer, and the guilds of craft are waxing in the towns, and soon what will there be left for us who cannot weave and will not dig? Good it were if we fell on all who are not guildsmen or men of free land, if we fell on soccage tenants and others, and brought both the law and the strong hand on them, and made them all villeins in deed as they are now in name; for now these rascals make more than their bellies need of bread, and their backs of homespun, and the overplus they keep to themselves; and we are more worthy of it than they. So let us get the collar on their necks again, and make their day's work longer and their bever-time shorter, as the good statute of the old king bade. And good it were if the Holy Church were to look to it (and the Lollards might help herein) that all these naughty and wearisome holidays were done away with; or that it should be unlawful for any man below the degree of a squire to keep the holy days of the church, except in the heart and the spirit only, and let the body labour meanwhile; for does not the Apostle say, 'If a man work not, neither should he eat'? And if such things were done, and such an estate of noble rich men and worthy poor men upholden for ever, then would it be good times in England, and life were worth the living."

All this were the lords at work on, and such talk I knew was common not only among the lords themselves, but also among their sergeants and very serving-men. But the people would not abide it; therefore, as I said, in Essex they were on the point of rising, and word had gone how that at St. Albans they were wellnigh at blows with the Lord Abbot's soldiers; that north away at Norwich John Litster was wiping the woad from his arms, as who would have to stain them red again, but not with grain or madder; and that the valiant tiler of Dartford had smitten a poll-groat bailiff to death with his lath-rending axe for mishandling a young maid, his daughter; and that the men of Kent were on the move.

Now, knowing all this I was not astonished that they shouted at the thought of their fellows the men of Essex, but rather that they said little more about it; only Will Green saying quietly, "Well, the tidings shall be told when our fellowship is greater; fall-to now on the meat, brother, that we may the sooner have thy tale." As he spoke the blue-clad damsel bestirred herself and brought me a clean trencher – that is, a square piece of thin oak board scraped clean – and a pewter pot of liquor. So without more ado, and as one used to it, I drew my knife out of my girdle and cut myself what I would of the flesh and bread on the table. But Will Green mocked at me as I cut, and said, "Certes, brother, thou hast not been a lord's carver, though but for thy word thou mightest have been his reader. Hast thou seen Oxford, scholar?"

A vision of grey-roofed houses and a long winding street and the sound of many bells came over me at that word as I nodded 'Yes' to him, my mouth full of salt pork and rye-bread; and then I lifted my pot and we made the clattering mugs kiss and I drank, and the fire of the good Kentish mead ran through my veins and deepened my dream of things past, present, and to come, as I said: "Now hearken a tale, since ye will have it so. For last autumn I was in Suffolk at the good town of Dunwich, and thither came the keels from Iceland, and on them were some men of Iceland, and many a tale they had on their tongues; and with these men I foregathered, for I am in sooth a gatherer of tales, and this that is now at my tongue's end is one of them."

So such a tale I told them, long familiar to me; but as I told it the words seemed to quicken and grow, so that I knew not the sound of my own voice, and they ran almost into rhyme and measure as I told it; and when I had done there was silence awhile, till one man spake, but not loudly:

"Yea, in that land was the summer short and the winter long; but men lived both summer and winter; and if the trees grew ill and the corn throve not, yet did the plant called man thrive and do well. God send us such men even here."

"Nay," said another, "such men have been and will be, and belike are not far from this same door even now."

"Yea," said a third, "hearken a stave of Robin Hood; maybe that shall hasten the coming of one I wot of." And he fell to singing in a clear voice, for he was a young man, and to a sweet wild melody, one of those ballads which in an incomplete and degraded form you have read perhaps. My heart rose high as I heard him, for it was concerning the struggle against tyranny for the freedom of life, how that the wildwood and the heath, despite of wind and weather, were better for a free man than the court and the cheaping-town; of the taking from the rich to give to the poor; of the life of a man doing his own will and not the will of another man commanding him for the commandment's sake. The men all listened eagerly, and at whiles took up as a refrain a couplet at the end of a stanza with their strong and rough, but not unmusical voices. As they sang, a picture of the wild-woods passed by me, as they were indeed, no park-like dainty glades and lawns, but rough and tangled thicket and bare waste and heath, solemn under the morning sun, and dreary with the rising of the evening wind and the drift of the night-long rain.

When he had done, another began in something of the same strain, but singing more of a song than a story ballad; and thus much I remember of it:

> *The Sheriff is made a mighty lord,*
> *Of goodly gold he hath enow,*
> *And many a sergeant girt with sword;*
> *But forth will we and bend the bow.*
> *We shall bend the bow on the lily lea*
> *Betwixt the thorn and the oaken tree.*
>
> *With stone and lime is the burg wall built,*
> *And pit and prison are stark and strong,*
> *And many a true man there is spilt,*
> *And many a right man doomed by wrong.*
>
> *So forth shall we and bend the bow*
> *And the king's writ never the road shall know.*

Now yeomen walk ye warily,
And heed ye the houses where ye go,
For as fair and as fine as they may be,
Lest behind your heels the door clap to.
Fare forth with the bow to the lily lea
Betwixt the thorn and the oaken tree.

Now bills and bows I and out a-gate!
And turn about on the lily lea!
And though their company be great
The grey-goose wing shall set us free.
Now bent is the bow in the green abode
And the king's writ knoweth not the road.

So over the mead and over the hithe,
And away to the wild-wood wend we forth;
There dwell we yeomen bold and blithe
Where the Sheriff's word is nought of worth.

Bent is the bow on the lily lea
Betwixt the thorn and the oaken tree.

But here the song dropped suddenly, and one of the men held up his hand as who would say, Hist! Then through the open window came the sound of another song, gradually swelling as though sung by men on the march. This time the melody was a piece of the plain-song of the church, familiar enough to me to bring back to my mind the great arches of some cathedral in France and the canons singing in the choir.

All leapt up and hurried to take their bows from wall and corner; and some had bucklers withal, circles of leather, boiled and then moulded into shape and hardened: these were some two hand-breadths across, with iron or brass bosses in the centre. Will Green went to the corner where the bills leaned against the wall and handed them round to the first-comers as far as they would go, and out we all went gravely and quietly into the village street and the fair sunlight of the calm afternoon, now beginning to turn towards evening. None had said anything since we first heard the new-come singing, save that as we went out of the door the ballad-singer clapped me on the shoulder and said: "Was it not sooth that I said, brother, that Robin Hood should bring us John Ball?"

Chapter III
They Meet at the Cross

THE STREET was pretty full of men by then we were out in it, and all faces turned toward the cross. The song still grew nearer and louder, and even as we looked we saw it turning the corner through the hedges of the orchards and closes, a good clump of men, more armed, as it would seem, than our villagers, as the low sun flashed back from many points of bright iron and steel. The words of the song could now be heard, and amidst them I could pick out Will Green's late challenge to me and my answer; but as I was bending all my mind to disentangle more words from the music, suddenly from the new white tower behind us clashed out the church bells, harsh and hurried at first, but presently falling into measured chime; and at the first sound of them a great shout went up from us and was echoed by the new-comers, "John Ball hath rung our bell!" Then we pressed on, and presently we were all mingled together at the cross.

Will Green had good-naturedly thrust and pulled me forward, so that I found myself standing on the lowest step of the cross, his seventy-two inches of man on one side of me. He chuckled while I panted, and said:

"There's for thee a good hearing and seeing stead, old lad. Thou art tall across thy belly and not otherwise, and thy wind, belike, is none of the best, and but for me thou wouldst have been amidst the thickest of the throng, and have heard words muffled by Kentish bellies and seen little but swinky woollen elbows and greasy plates and jacks. Look no more on the ground, as though thou sawest a hare, but let thine eyes and thine ears be busy to gather tidings to bear back to Essex – or heaven!"

I grinned good-fellowship at him but said nothing, for in truth my eyes and ears were as busy as he would have them to be. A buzz of general talk went up from the throng amidst the regular cadence of the bells, which now seemed far away and as it were that they were not swayed by hands, but were living creatures making that noise of their own wills.

I looked around and saw that the newcomers mingled with us must have been a regular armed band; all had bucklers slung at their backs, few lacked a sword at the side. Some had bows, some 'staves' – that is, bills, pole-axes, or pikes. Moreover, unlike our villagers, they had defensive arms. Most had steel-caps on their heads, and some had body armour, generally a 'jack,' or coat into which pieces of iron or horn were quilted; some had also steel or steel-and-leather arm or thigh pieces. There were a few mounted men among them, their horses being big-boned hammer-headed beasts, that looked as if they had been taken from plough or waggon, but their riders were well armed with steel armour on their heads, legs, and arms. Amongst the horsemen I noted the man that had ridden past me when I first awoke; but he seemed to be a prisoner, as he had a woollen hood on his head instead of his helmet, and carried neither bill, sword, nor dagger. He seemed by no means ill-at-ease, however, but was laughing and talking with the men who stood near him.

Above the heads of the crowd, and now slowly working towards the cross, was a banner on a high-raised cross-pole, a picture of a man and woman half-clad in skins of beasts seen against a background of green trees, the man holding a spade and the woman a distaff and spindle rudely done enough, but yet with a certain spirit and much meaning; and underneath this symbol of the early world and man's first contest with nature were the written words:

> *When Adam delved and Eve span*
> *Who was then the gentleman?*

The banner came on and through the crowd, which at last opened where we stood for its passage, and the banner-bearer turned and faced the throng and stood on the first step of the cross beside me.

A man followed him, clad in a long dark-brown gown of coarse woollen, girt with a cord, to which hung a 'pair of beads' (or rosary, as we should call it today) and a book in a bag. The man was tall and big-boned, a ring of dark hair surrounded his priest's tonsure; his nose was big but clear cut and with wide nostrils; his shaven face showed a longish upper lip and a big but blunt chin; his mouth was big and the lips closed firmly; a face not very noteworthy but for his grey eyes well opened and wide apart, at whiles lighting up his whole face with a kindly smile, at whiles set and stern, at whiles resting in that look as if they were gazing at something a long way off, which is the wont of the eyes of the poet or enthusiast.

He went slowly up the steps of the cross and stood at the top with one hand laid on the shaft, and shout upon shout broke forth from the throng. When the shouting died away into a silence of the human voices, the bells were still quietly chiming with that far-away voice of theirs, and the long-winged dusky swifts, by no means scared by the concourse, swung round about the cross with their wild squeals; and the man stood still for a little, eyeing the throng, or rather looking first at one and then another man in it, as though he were trying to think what such an one was thinking of, or what he were fit for. Sometimes he caught the eye of one or other, and then that kindly smile spread over his face, but faded off it into the sternness and sadness of a man who has heavy and great thoughts hanging about him. But when John Ball first mounted the steps of the cross a lad at someone's bidding had run off to stop the ringers, and so presently the voice of the bells fell dead, leaving on men's minds that sense of blankness or even disappointment which is always caused by the sudden stopping of a sound one has got used to and found pleasant. But a great expectation had fallen by now on all that throng, and no word was spoken even in a whisper, and all men's hearts and eyes were fixed upon the dark figure standing straight up now by the tall white shaft of the cross, his hands stretched out before him, one palm laid upon the other.

And for me, as I made ready to hearken, I felt a joy in my soul that I had never yet felt.

Chapter IV
The Voice of John Ball

SO NOW I HEARD John Ball; how he lifted up his voice and said:

"Ho, all ye good people! I am a priest of God, and in my day's work it cometh that I should tell you what ye should do, and what ye should forbear doing, and to that end I am come hither: yet first, if I myself have wronged any man here, let him say wherein my wrongdoing lieth, that I may ask his pardon and his pity."

A great hum of good-will ran through the crowd as he spoke; then he smiled as in a kind of pride, and again he spoke:

"Wherefore did ye take me out of the archbishop's prison but three days agone, when ye lighted the archbishop's house for the candle of Canterbury, but that I might speak to you and pray you: therefore I will not keep silence, whether I have done ill, or whether I have done well. And herein, good fellows and my very brethren, I would have you to follow me; and if there be such here, as I know full well there be some, and may be a good many, who have been robbers of their neighbours ('And who is my neighbour?' quoth the rich man), or lechers, or despiteful haters, or talebearers, or fawners on rich men for the hurt of the poor (and that is the worst of all) – Ah, my poor brethren who have gone astray, I say not to you, go home and repent lest you mar our great deeds, but rather come afield and there repent. Many a day have ye been fools, but hearken unto me and I shall make you wise above the wisdom of the earth; and if ye die in your wisdom, as God wot ye well may, since the fields ye wend to bear swords for daisies, and spears for bents, then shall ye be, though men call you dead, a part and parcel of the living wisdom of all things, very stones of the pillars that uphold the joyful earth.

"Forsooth, ye have heard it said that ye shall do well in this world that in the world to come ye may live happily for ever; do ye well then, and have your reward both on earth and in heaven; for I say to you that earth and heaven are not two but one; and this one is that which ye know, and are each one of you a part of, to wit, the Holy Church, and in each one of you dwelleth the life of the Church, unless ye slay it. Forsooth, brethren, will ye murder the Church any one of you, and go forth a wandering man and lonely, even as Cain did who slew his brother? Ah, my brothers, what an evil doom is this, to be an outcast from the Church, to have none to love you and to speak with you, to be without fellowship! Forsooth, brothers, fellowship is heaven, and lack of fellowship is hell: fellowship is life, and lack of fellowship is death: and the deeds that ye do upon the earth, it is for fellowship's sake that ye do them, and the life that is in it, that shall live on and on for ever, and each one of you part of it, while many a man's life upon the earth from the earth shall wane.

"Therefore, I bid you not dwell in hell but in heaven, or while ye must, upon earth, which is a part of heaven, and forsooth no foul part.

"Forsooth, he that waketh in hell and feeleth his heart fail him, shall have memory of the merry days of earth, and how that when his heart failed him there, he cried on his fellow, were it his wife or his son or his brother or his gossip or his brother sworn in arms, and how that his fellow heard him and came and they mourned together under the sun, till again they laughed together and were but half sorry between them. This shall he think on in hell, and cry on his fellow to help him, and shall find that therein is no help because there is no fellowship, but every man for himself. Therefore, I tell you that the proud, despiteous rich man, though he knoweth it not, is in hell already, because he hath no fellow; and he that hath so hardy a heart that in sorrow he thinketh of fellowship, his sorrow is soon but a story of sorrow – a little change in the life that knows not ill."

He left off for a little; and indeed for some time his voice had fallen, but it was so clear and the summer evening so soft and still, and the silence of the folk so complete, that every word told. His eyes fell down to the crowd as he stopped speaking, since for some little while they had been looking far away into the blue distance of summer; and the kind eyes of the man had a curious sight before him in that crowd, for amongst them were many who by this time were not dry-eyed, and some wept outright in spite of their black beards, while all had that look as if they were ashamed of themselves, and did not want others to see how deeply they were moved, after the fashion of their race when they are strongly stirred. I looked at Will Green beside me: his right hand clutched his bow so tight, that the knuckles whitened; he was staring straight before him, and the tears were running out of his eyes and down his big nose as though without his will, for his face was stolid and unmoved all the time till he caught my eye, and then he screwed up the strangest face, of scowling brow, weeping eyes, and smiling mouth, while he dealt me a sounding thump in the ribs with his left elbow, which, though it would have knocked me down but for the crowd, I took as an esquire does the accolade which makes a knight of him.

But while I pondered all these things, and how men fight and lose the battle, and the thing that they fought for comes about in spite of their defeat, and when it comes turns out not to be what they meant, and other men have to fight for what they meant under another name – while I pondered all this, John Ball began to speak again in the same soft and dear voice with which he had left off.

"Good fellows, it was your fellowship and your kindness that took me out of the archbishop's prison three days agone, though God wot ye had nought to gain by it save outlawry and the gallows; yet lacked I not your fellowship before ye drew near me in the body, and when between me and Canterbury street was yet a strong wall, and the turnkeys and sergeants and bailiffs.

"For hearken, my friends and helpers; many days ago, when April was yet young, I lay there, and the heart that I had strung up to bear all things because of the fellowship of men and the blessed saints and the angels and those that are, and those that are to be, this heart, that I had strung up like a strong bow, fell into feebleness, so that I lay there a-longing for the green fields and the white-thorn bushes and the lark singing over the corn, and the talk of good fellows round the ale-house bench, and the babble of the little children, and the team on the road and the beasts afield, and all the life of earth; and I alone all the while, near my foes and afar from my friends, mocked and flouted and starved with cold and hunger; and so weak was my heart that though I longed for all these things yet I saw them not, nor knew them but as names; and I longed so sore to be gone that I chided myself that I had once done well; and I said to myself:

"Forsooth, hadst thou kept thy tongue between thy teeth thou mightest have been something, if it had been but a parson of a town, and comfortable to many a poor man; and then mightest thou have clad here and there the naked back, and filled the empty belly, and holpen many, and men would have spoken well of thee, and of thyself thou hadst thought well; and all this hast thou lost for lack of a word here and there to some great man, and a little winking of the eyes amidst murder and wrong and unruth; and now thou art nought and helpless, and the hemp for thee is sown and grown and heckled and spun, and lo there, the rope for thy gallows-tree! – all for nought, for nought.

"Forsooth, my friends, thus I thought and sorrowed in my feebleness that I had not been a traitor to the Fellowship of the Church, for e'en so evil was my foolish imagination.

"Yet, forsooth, as I fell a-pondering over all the comfort and help that I might have been and that I might have had, if I had been but a little of a trembling cur to creep and crawl before abbot and bishop and baron and bailiff, came the thought over me of the evil of the world wherewith I, John Ball, the rascal hedge-priest, had fought and striven in the Fellowship of the saints in heaven and poor men upon earth.

"Yea, forsooth, once again I saw as of old, the great treading down the little, and the strong beating down the weak, and cruel men fearing not, and kind men daring not, and wise men caring not; and the saints in heaven forbearing and yet bidding me not to forbear; forsooth, I knew once more that he who doeth well in fellowship, and because of fellowship, shall not fail though he seem to fail today, but in days hereafter shall he and his work yet be alive, and men be holpen by them to strive again and yet again; and yet indeed even that was little, since, forsooth, to strive was my pleasure and my life.

"So I became a man once more, and I rose up to my feet and went up and down my prison what I could for my hopples, and into my mouth came words of good cheer, even such as we today have sung, and stoutly I sang them, even as we now have sung them; and then did I rest me, and once more thought of those pleasant fields where I would be, and all the life of man and beast about them, and I said to myself that I should see them once more before I died, if but once it were.

"Forsooth, this was strange, that whereas before I longed for them and yet saw them not, now that my longing was slaked my vision was cleared, and I saw them as though the prison walls opened to me and I was out of Canterbury street and amidst the green meadows of April; and therewithal along with me folk that I have known and who are dead, and folk that are living; yea, and all those of the Fellowship on earth and in heaven; yea, and all that are here this day. Overlong were the tale to tell of them, and of the time that is gone.

"So thenceforward I wore through the days with no such faint heart, until one day the prison opened verily and in the daylight, and there were ye, my fellows, in the door – your faces glad, your hearts light with hope, and your hands heavy with wrath; then I saw and understood what was to do. Now, therefore, do ye understand it!"

His voice was changed, and grew louder than loud now, as he cast his hands abroad towards that company with those last words of his; and I could feel that all shame and fear was falling from those men, and that mere fiery manhood was shining through their wonted English shamefast stubbornness, and that they were moved indeed and saw the road before them. Yet no man spoke, rather the silence of the men-folk deepened, as the sun's rays grew more level and more golden, and the swifts wheeled about shriller and louder than before.

Then again John Ball spoke and said, "In good sooth, I deem ye wot no worse than I do what is to do – and first that somewhat we shall do – since it is for him that is lonely or in prison to dream of fellowship, but for him that is of a fellowship to do and not to dream.

"And next, ye know who is the foeman, and that is the proud man, the oppressor, who scorneth fellowship, and himself is a world to himself and needeth no helper nor helpeth any, but, heeding no law, layeth law on other men because he is rich; and surely everyone that is rich is such an one, nor may be other.

"Forsooth, in the belly of every rich man dwelleth a devil of hell, and when the man would give his goods to the poor, the devil within him gainsayeth it, and saith, 'Wilt thou then be of the poor, and suffer cold and hunger and mocking as they suffer, then give thou thy goods to them, and keep them not.' And when he would be compassionate, again saith the devil to him, 'If thou heed these losels and turn on them a face like to their faces, and deem of them as men, then shall they scorn thee, and evil shall come of it, and even one day they shall fall on thee to slay thee when they have learned that thou art but as they be.'

"Ah, woe worth the while! Too oft he sayeth sooth, as the wont of the devil is, that lies may be born of the barren truth; and sooth it is that the poor deemeth the rich to be other than he, and meet to be his master, as though, forsooth, the poor were come of Adam, and the rich of him that made Adam, that is God; and thus the poor man oppresseth the poor man, because he feareth the oppressor. Nought such are ye, my brethren; or else why are ye gathered here in harness to bid all bear witness of you that ye are the sons of one man and one mother, begotten of the earth?"

As he said the words there came a stir among the weapons of the throng, and they pressed closer round the cross, yet with held the shout as yet which seemed gathering in their bosoms.

And again he said:

"Forsooth, too many rich men there are in this realm; and yet if there were but one, there would be one too many, for all should be his thralls. Hearken, then, ye men of Kent. For overlong belike have I held you with words; but the love of you constrained me, and the joy that a man hath to babble to his friends and his fellows whom he hath not seen for a long season.

"Now, hearken, I bid you: To the rich men that eat up a realm there cometh a time when they whom they eat up, that is the poor, seem poorer than of wont, and their complaint goeth up louder to the heavens; yet it is no riddle to say that oft at such times the fellowship of the poor is waxing stronger, else would no man have heard his cry. Also at such times is the rich man become fearful, and so waxeth in cruelty, and of that cruelty do people misdeem that it is power and might waxing. Forsooth, ye are stronger than your fathers, because ye are more grieved than they, and ye should have been less grieved than they had ye been horses and swine; and then, forsooth, would ye have been stronger to bear; but ye, ye are not strong to bear, but to do.

"And wot ye why we are come to you this fair eve of holiday? And wot ye why I have been telling of fellowship to you? Yea, forsooth, I deem ye wot well, that it is for this cause, that ye might bethink you of your fellowship with the men of Essex."

His last word let loose the shout that had been long on all men's lips, and great and fierce it was as it rang shattering through the quiet upland village. But John Ball held up his hand, and the shout was one and no more.

Then he spoke again:

"Men of Kent, I wot well that ye are not so hard bested as those of other shires, by the token of the day when behind the screen of leafy boughs ye met Duke William with bill and bow as he wended Londonward from that woeful field of Senlac; but I have told of fellowship, and ye have hearkened and understood what the Holy Church is, whereby ye know that ye are fellows of the saints in heaven and the poor men of Essex; and as one day the saints shall call you to the heavenly feast, so now do the poor men call you to the battle.

"Men of Kent, ye dwell fairly here, and your houses are framed of stout oak beams, and your own lands ye till; unless some accursed lawyer with his false lying sheepskin and forged custom of the Devil's Manor hath stolen it from you; but in Essex slaves they be and villeins, and worse they shall be, and the lords swear that ere a year be over ox and horse shall go free in Essex, and man and woman shall draw the team and the plough; and north away in the east countries dwell men in poor halls of wattled reeds and mud, and the north-east wind from off the fen whistles through them; and poor they be to the letter; and there him whom the lord spareth, the bailiff squeezeth, and him whom the bailiff forgetteth, the Easterling Chapman sheareth; yet be these stout men and valiant, and your very brethren.

"And yet if there be any man here so base as to think that a small matter, let him look to it that if these necks abide under the yoke, Kent shall sweat for it ere it be long; and ye shall lose acre and close and woodland, and be servants in your own houses, and your sons shall be the lords' lads, and your daughters their lemans, and ye shall buy a bold word with many stripes, and an honest deed with a leap from the gallows-tree.

"Bethink ye, too, that ye have no longer to deal with Duke William, who, if he were a thief and a cruel lord, was yet a prudent man and a wise warrior; but cruel are these, and headstrong, yea, thieves and fools in one – and ye shall lay their heads in the dust."

A shout would have arisen again, but his eager voice rising higher yet, restrained it as he said:

"And how shall it be then when these are gone? What else shall ye lack when ye lack masters? Ye shall not lack for the fields ye have tilled, nor the houses ye have built, nor the cloth ye have woven; all these shall be yours, and whatso ye will of all that the earth beareth; then shall no man mow the deep grass for another, while his own kine lack cow-meat; and he that soweth shall reap, and the reaper shall eat in fellowship the harvest that in fellowship he hath won; and he that buildeth a house shall dwell in it with those that he biddeth of his free will; and the tithe barn shall garner the wheat for all men to eat of when the seasons are untoward, and the rain-drift hideth the sheaves in August; and all shall be without money and without price. Faithfully and merrily then shall all men keep the holidays of the Church in peace of body and joy of heart. And man shall help man, and the saints in heaven shall be glad, because men no more fear each other; and the churl shall be ashamed, and shall hide his churlishness till it be gone, and he be no more a churl; and fellowship shall be established in heaven and on the earth."

The complete and unabridged text is available online, from *flametreepublishing.com/extras*

Striking Light

Samantha Murray

AFTER HER SIXTH miscarriage Marlene cleaned the house.

She scrubbed at the blackened grout between the kitchen tiles with a hard-bristled brush, and sugar-soaped the skirting till the scuff-marks were vanquished. She sucked up the dust-bunnies that had a colony underneath the wide wooden-framed bed she shared with her husband, Reece. She knotted her hair behind her and went outside to clean the windows, until they sparkled and the sunlight streamed straight in, no longer muted.

She threw away old Christmas and birthday cards and she packed up the pretty shoes that always gave her blisters and dresses she hadn't worn for fifteen years and took the box down to the local op-shop.

"I don't know if that's a good idea," said Reece when she told him over dinner that she wanted to go to *Timely Voyages* – Temporal Adventure Clinic. Marlene looked away from him. He irritated her most of the time these days, with his sadness and his concern for her, with his hair that remained defiantly dark as he aged and his lashes that her mother had always said were longer than a man's should be, and with his fundamental *okayness*. "They sound so gimmicky, and who knows if they're even safe."

I don't care, Marlene said to herself. To Reece she said nothing at all.

* * *

A woman in Marlene's street had reportedly been time travelling with the clinic. Her name was Bellatrix but most of the neighbours called her Bella. Marlene knew her to say hello to, and her impression was of a middle-aged woman who was plump and pleasant, if a little vague. Bella's garden was always blooming with white camellias, one of the prettiest gardens on the street. After her adventure Bellatrix seemed to stay inside her house a lot. The one time Marlene had seen her at the shop she had looked oddly shrunken and furtive. Her garden, untended, was wilted and dying.

* * *

The outside of the Temporal Adventure Clinic was brightly colored and jumping with 3D advertisements. *See the Future, Touch the Past*, they proclaimed. It was too flashy and heavily marketed for Marlene's usual tastes, and she briefly paused, but the door slid open for her with a sound like a sigh, and she went in anyway, heels making small clicks against the polished floor.

Bevus McMann was the *stillest* man Marlene had ever encountered. He welcomed her to Timely Voyages, introduced himself, took her hand to shake, led her through the bundle of paperwork (disclaimers, waivers against all responsibility), with each action blending into the next in such a smooth, quiet, flowingly connected way that it felt somehow like he was not moving at all. He had white flowers in a vase on his desk, some species Marlene didn't know the name of. Not camellias.

"It's perfectly safe," he told her. "You stay here, safe and protected with us; and you get to see through someone else's eyes, in another time." And Marlene knew then that she absolutely was going to do this. She wanted to see through eyes that were not her own. To see through eyes that didn't feel like they had grit in them all the time.

"I'd like to see the past," she began, "I've always been fascinated by ancient Greece..."

"You don't get to choose, I'm afraid," Bevus said in his mild, even tones. "We can't tell you where you are going to end up before you go."

Marlene blinked, but the disappointment vanished even as it formed. Greece had been a quickly-concocted notion, perhaps even some kind of justification.

"We call it a Trace. We don't know where it is going to go. We just set up the potentials. It's a bit like lightening," he said, his eyes steady and holding hers. "The lightning decides where to go. It seems to follow the past of least resistance but at the same time it can be surprising. And it comes from both sides."

"Both sides?"

"The visible flash of lightning is usually from the ground upwards. It's called a 'return strike.' It's analogous to what happens with our technology. We create a bridge if you like, for the lightning, for the Trace, to come back to us."

There was something soothing about the very stillness of the man, Marlene decided. She transferred a large sum of money through to the clinic, signed all of the necessary waivers and legal documents and attempted a smile, although it wasn't as convincing as her usual, sinking down in the middle like a failed soufflé.

* * *

Floating in the Immersion tank Marlene thought of Reece, and just as quickly stopped thinking of Reece. He would brood like a thundercloud when he found out about this but he wouldn't be able to stop himself from forgiving her because that was just what he did. But at the moment he felt very far away and soon he would be even further, and the water was warm.

"Here we go. Are you ready?" Bevus's disconnected voice came piped into the tank, still retaining its calmness over the tinny intercom. Marlene would have preferred getting as far away as she could throw herself--going properly, physically and totally into another time rather than peeking at one as if it was a movie, but she supposed she would make do with this.

"Yes, I'm ready," she said, because she was.

* * *

The Trace felt like a tremendous pull at her core, and like she was falling rapidly, and floating upwards at the same time. Marlene went to take in a shocked, tight breath

– but she didn't because she was already breathing easily and steadily. Her heart was slow and relaxed.

It wasn't her heart. These weren't her hands she could see, tanned and strong, kneading and pulling at the dough on the bench top in practised rhythm. She swiped an errant hair out of her eyes and figured she'd left flour on her cheek. The bones in her face were vibrating a little, and she realized she was humming softly, a tune that grabbed at her with an almost-familiarity. Marlene didn't feel like she was doing these things but neither did she feel as if she wasn't. She felt *snug* somehow. Her dress sleeves were a blue so faded they were almost white, gathered at just above her elbows. She had an apron around her waist with a print of white flowers. The early morning light streamed through the wooden-framed window opposite, and when her gaze lifted she could see fields stretching out, shining in the sun.

And then a yank so abrupt Marlene felt like she had been turned inside out, and she was gaping like a fish back in her tank of water. *I want that back*, she thought, seized with a strange sharp sense of loss. The softness and stretchiness of the bread she was making, the resistance in her hands, the sunshine on her face.

"You've still got time left. I am going to set the potentials back up." She heard the voice but it took her a second to recognize it. Bevus.

"Okay," she said, or thought, but it didn't matter because she was gone, rushing towards something, or being rushed towards.

* * *

She stood in the sand. It was night time but the light from the half-moon in the sky was so bright it limned the rocks in silver. The rocks had a luminescence to them too, as did the schools of some kind of fish she could discern below the waves out beyond where they were crashing to the shore. Tiny life scuttled in the sand moving away from her, and she could hear the grim wild cries of thin pointed winged creatures that lunged and wheeled overhead.

She knelt down and removed her boots. The sand felt cool and moist and surprisingly scratchy. She walked a short distance leaving curved imprints of her feet which glistened. The second toe was longer than the first, and the little toe curved in too much. *They look like my toes* thought Marlene. Bleached white spurs of bone just taller than she was were jutting out of the sand further up the beach and she started towards them. Her hands came up to the clasp of her helmet. *Don't do that*, Marlene tried to put her hands back down, but her body didn't listen. Strangely, this served to relax instead of alarm her as she took the helmet off over her head. She breathed in deeply of air that felt cold and thick and tasted faintly of ozone.

Her ship was there, her *spaceship*, out hulking in the water, and she knew that would be in trouble with the others upon her return. Marlene did not know how she knew this, and she did not know if the exhilaration flooding through her was her own, but she was filled with the sharp, fierce cries of the creatures that arched and soared overhead, with the smell of the air and the light from the second moon that had started to rise from where the dark water met the horizon. It felt nothing at all like home.

* * *

When Marlene emerged, towelled and changed and feeling strangely light as a soap-bubble Bevus came to greet her. He was as composed, gentle and still as before, but something had changed. It's his eyes, Marlene realized. His eyes were excited.

"You went further ahead than anyone we've had before," he told her after she had finished the supplemental hypno-recording of her experience to add to their record-bank. "Much further."

"Okay," said Marlene.

"I didn't want to give you any preconceptions beforehand," Bevus said, even his voice now betraying his animation, "but there is a point in our future that the Traces don't go beyond. In fact I've only seen one go further, and that was yours."

"Why?" Marlene wasn't sure she understood, and she was not really concentrating. She wondered if she closed her eyes if she would feel the night wind of another planet on her face.

"It's been conjectured that it is a natural limit of the Trace, but I've disagreed and it seems I was right." Bevus startled her by grinning. "It's a product of history, and statistics. There is a point in our future that is a dark time. Our population is diminished greatly, massively. People who have had a Trace take them to this time come back disturbed and we haven't pieced together how it all starts, but it is catastrophic." Strangely enough Bevus's eyes were still dancing.

"Oh," Marlene said. Catastrophic? "You said it was safe."

"It is, it is," Bevus said. "Physically there is nothing that can harm you."

"Physically?" said Marlene, thinking of Bellatrix and her camellias. Marlene already knew that there were things that could harm you that were not physical. Poor Bella. Oh. Poor world.

"Emotional response, well, that's not something we have control over."

Of course not, thought Marlene, suddenly feeling cold, and wishing she had coarse sand under her toes.

"I've theorized personally that the reason we haven't had Traces go past that disaster period is because of our sample space--it's still quite small even with our marketing efforts, and the Trace depends on a direct genetic line, so Traces backward are always more likely than a Trace forwards. Everyone has ancestors of course."

"Ancestors?" Marlene said, suddenly feeling entirely in the present. "So that woman...?"

"Your first Trace was to an ancestor yes of course, it must be. But it is your second which is the interesting one. An unbroken line, all that way."

"It has to be, uh, direct?"

"Oh yes. And it often Traces to an ancestor or descendant of the same sex, although there are exceptions. There have been times I'll admit to you when I've wondered if the reason the Traces don't go further is because humanity doesn't go any further--but you've proven that wrong, and I am so glad you have."

"Oh," said Marlene.

* * *

When she got home Marlene took off her heels and tossed them by the door. She padded softly through the house and found Reece in the kitchen stirring a pan on the stovetop.

"Hi," he said, turning.

Marlene stood still and looked at him for a moment before hurtling into his arms and burying her face in his neck. She felt like she had been travelling down a dark tunnel and that at the end of it she would be coming out into joy.

A direct genetic line. Descendants. Catastrophic.

And she cried, finally, for all of the futures that weren't to be, and she cried as well for the one that was.

Armageddon – 2419 A.D.

Philip Francis Nowlan

Foreword

ELSEWHERE I have set down, for whatever interest they have in this, the 25th Century, my personal recollections of the 20th Century.

Now it occurs to me that my memoirs of the 25th Century may have an equal interest 500 years from now – particularly in view of that unique perspective from which I have seen the 25th Century, entering it as I did, in one leap across a gap of 492 years.

This statement requires elucidation. There are still many in the world who are not familiar with my unique experience. Five centuries from now there may be many more, especially if civilization is fated to endure any worse convulsions than those which have occurred between 1975 A.D. and the present time.

I should state therefore, that I, Anthony Rogers, am, so far as I know, the only man alive whose normal span of eighty-one years of life has been spread over a period of 573 years. To be precise, I lived the first twenty-nine years of my life between 1898 and 1927; the other fifty-two since 2419. The gap between these two, a period of nearly five hundred years, I spent in a state of suspended animation, free from the ravages of katabolic processes, and without any apparent effect on my physical or mental faculties.

When I began my long sleep, man had just begun his real conquest of the air in a sudden series of transoceanic flights in airplanes driven by internal combustion motors. He had barely begun to speculate on the possibilities of harnessing sub-atomic forces, and had made no further practical penetration into the field of ethereal pulsations than the primitive radio and television of that day. The United States of America was the most powerful nation in the world, its political, financial, industrial and scientific influence being supreme; and in the arts also it was rapidly climbing into leadership.

I awoke to find the America I knew a total wreck – to find Americans a hunted race in their own land, hiding in the dense forests that covered the shattered and leveled ruins of their once magnificent cities, desperately preserving, and struggling to develop in their secret retreats, the remnants of their culture and science – and the undying flame of their sturdy independence.

World domination was in the hands of Mongolians and the center of world power lay in inland China, with Americans one of the few races of mankind unsubdued – and it must be admitted in fairness to the truth, not worth the trouble of subduing in the eyes of the Han Airlords who ruled North America as titular tributaries of the Most Magnificent.

For they needed not the forests in which the Americans lived, nor the resources of the vast territories these forests covered. With the perfection to which they had reduced the synthetic production of necessities and luxuries, their remarkable development of scientific processes and mechanical accomplishment of work, they had no economic need for the forests, and no economic desire for the enslaved labor of an unruly race.

They had all they needed for their magnificently luxurious and degraded scheme of civilization, within the walls of the fifteen cities of sparkling glass they had flung skyward on the sites of ancient American centers, into the bowels of the earth underneath them, and with relatively small surrounding areas of agriculture.

Complete domination of the air rendered communication between these centers a matter of ease and safety. Occasional destructive raids on the waste lands were considered all that was necessary to keep the 'wild' Americans on the run within the shelter of their forests, and prevent their becoming a menace to the Han civilization.

But nearly three hundred years of easily maintained security, the last century of which had been nearly sterile in scientific, social and economic progress, had softened and devitalized the Hans.

It had likewise developed, beneath the protecting foliage of the forest, the growth of a vigorous new American civilization, remarkable in the mobility and flexibility of its organization, in its conquest of almost insuperable obstacles, in the development and guarding of its industrial and scientific resources, all in anticipation of that 'Day of Hope' to which it had been looking forward for generations, when it would be strong enough to burst from the green chrysalis of the forests, soar into the upper air lanes and destroy the yellow incubus.

At the time I awoke, the 'Day of Hope' was almost at hand. I shall not attempt to set forth a detailed history of the Second War of Independence, for that has been recorded already by better historians than I am. Instead I shall confine myself largely to the part I was fortunate enough to play in this struggle and in the events leading up to it.

It all resulted from my interest in radioactive gases. During the latter part of 1927 my company, the American Radioactive Gas Corporation, had been keeping me busy investigating reports of unusual phenomena observed in certain abandoned coal mines near the Wyoming Valley, in Pennsylvania.

With two assistants and a complete equipment of scientific instruments, I began the exploration of a deserted working in a mountainous district, where several weeks before, a number of mining engineers had reported traces of carnotite [1] and what they believed to be radioactive gases. Their report was not without foundation, it was apparent from the outset, for in our examination of the upper levels of the mine, our instruments indicated a vigorous radioactivity.

On the morning of December 15th, we descended to one of the lowest levels. To our surprise, we found no water there. Obviously it had drained off through some break in the strata. We noticed too that the rock in the side walls of the shaft was soft, evidently due to the radioactivity, and pieces crumbled under foot rather easily. We made our way cautiously down the shaft, when suddenly the rotted timbers above us gave way.

I jumped ahead, barely escaping the avalanche of coal and soft rock, but my companions, who were several paces behind me, were buried under it, and undoubtedly met instant death.

I was trapped. Return was impossible. With my electric torch I explored the shaft to its end, but could find no other way out. The air became increasingly difficult to breathe, probably from the rapid accumulation of the radioactive gas. In a little while my senses reeled and I lost consciousness.

When I awoke, there was a cool and refreshing circulation of air in the shaft. I had no thought that I had been unconscious more than a few hours, although it seems that the radioactive gas had kept me in a state of suspended animation for something like 500 years. My awakening, I figured out later, had been due to some shifting of the strata which reopened the shaft and cleared the atmosphere in the working. This must have been the case, for I was able to struggle back up the shaft over a pile of debris, and stagger up the long incline to the mouth of the mine, where an entirely different world, overgrown with a vast forest and no visible sign of human habitation, met my eyes.

I shall pass over the days of mental agony that followed in my attempt to grasp the meaning of it all. There were times when I felt that I was on the verge of insanity. I roamed the unfamiliar forest like a lost soul. Had it not been for the necessity of improvising traps and crude clubs with which to slay my food, I believe I should have gone mad.

Suffice it to say, however, that I survived this psychic crisis. I shall begin my narrative proper with my first contact with Americans of the year 2419 A.D.

Footnote 1. A hydrovanadate of uranium, and other metals; used as a source of radium compounds.

Chapter I
Floating Men

[Seen upon the ultroscope view plate, the battle looked as though it were being fought in daylight, perhaps on a cloudy day, while the explosions of the rockets appeared as flashes of extra brilliance.]

MY FIRST GLIMPSE of a human being of the 25th Century was obtained through a portion of woodland where the trees were thinly scattered, with a dense forest beyond.

I had been wandering along aimlessly, and hopelessly, musing over my strange fate, when I noticed a figure that cautiously backed out of the dense growth across the glade. I was about to call out joyfully, but there was something furtive about the figure that prevented me. The boy's attention (for it seemed to be a lad of fifteen or sixteen) was centered tensely on the heavy growth of trees from which he had just emerged.

He was clad in rather tight-fitting garments entirely of green, and wore a helmet-like cap of the same color. High around his waist he wore a broad, thick belt, which bulked up in the back across the shoulders, into something of the proportions of a knapsack.

As I was taking in these details, there came a vivid flash and heavy detonation, like that of a hand grenade, not far to the left of him. He threw up an arm and staggered a bit in a queer, gliding way; then he recovered himself and slipped cautiously away from the place of the explosion, crouching slightly, and still facing the denser part of the forest. Every few steps he would raise his arm, and point into the forest with something he held in his hand. Wherever he pointed there was a terrific explosion, deeper in among the trees. It came to me then that he was shooting with some form of pistol, though there was neither flash nor detonation from the muzzle of the weapon itself.

After firing several times, he seemed to come to a sudden resolution, and turning in my general direction, leaped – to my amazement sailing through the air between the sparsely scattered trees in such a jump as I had never in my life seen before. That leap must have carried him a full fifty feet, although at the height of his arc, he was not more than ten or twelve feet from the ground.

When he alighted, his foot caught in a projecting root, and he sprawled gently forward. I say 'gently' for he did not crash down as I expected him to do. The only thing I could compare it with was a slow-motion cinema, although I had never seen one in which horizontal motions were registered at normal speed and only the vertical movements were slowed down.

Due to my surprise, I suppose my brain did not function with its normal quickness, for I gazed at the prone figure for several seconds before I saw the blood that oozed out from under the tight green cap. Regaining my power of action, I dragged him out of sight back of the big tree. For a few moments I busied myself in an attempt to staunch the flow of blood. The wound was not a deep one. My companion was more dazed than hurt. But what of the pursuers?

I took the weapon from his grasp and examined it hurriedly. It was not unlike the automatic pistol to which I was accustomed, except that it apparently fired with a button instead of a trigger. I inserted several fresh rounds of ammunition into its magazine from my companion's belt, as rapidly as I could, for I soon heard, near us, the suppressed conversation of his pursuers.

There followed a series of explosions round about us, but none very close. They evidently had not spotted our hiding place, and were firing at random.

I waited tensely, balancing the gun in my hand, to accustom myself to its weight and probable throw.

Then I saw a movement in the green foliage of a tree not far away, and the head and face of a man appeared. Like my companion, he was clad entirely in green, which made his figure difficult to distinguish. But his face could be seen clearly. It was an evil face, and had murder in it.

That decided me. I raised the gun and fired. My aim was bad, for there was no kick in the gun, as I had expected, and I hit the trunk of the tree several feet below him. It blew him from his perch like a crumpled bit of paper, and he floated down to the ground, like some limp, dead thing, gently lowered by an invisible hand. The tree, its trunk blown apart by the explosion, crashed down.

There followed another series of explosions around us. These guns we were using made no sound in the firing, and my opponents were evidently as much at sea as to my position as I was to theirs. So I made no attempt to reply to their fire, contenting myself with keeping a sharp lookout in their general direction. And patience had its reward.

Very soon I saw a cautious movement in the top of another tree. Exposing myself as little as possible, I aimed carefully at the tree trunk and fired again. A shriek followed the explosion. I heard the tree crash down; then a groan.

There was silence for a while. Then I heard a faint sound of boughs swishing. I shot three times in its direction, pressing the button as rapidly as I could. Branches crashed down where my shells had exploded, but there was no body.

Then I saw one of them. He was starting one of those amazing leaps from the bough of one tree to another, about forty feet away.

I threw up my gun impulsively and fired. By now I had gotten the feel of the weapon, and my aim was good. I hit him. The 'bullet' must have penetrated his body and exploded. For one moment I saw him flying through the air. Then the explosion, and he had vanished. He never finished his leap. It was annihilation.

How many more of them there were I don't know. But this must have been too much for them. They used a final round of shells on us, all of which exploded harmlessly, and shortly after I heard them swishing and crashing away from us through the tree tops. Not one of them descended to earth.

Now I had time to give some attention to my companion. She was, I found, a girl, and not a boy. Despite her bulky appearance, due to the peculiar belt strapped around her body high up under the arms, she was very slender, and very pretty.

There was a stream not far away, from which I brought water and bathed her face and wound.

Apparently the mystery of these long leaps, the monkey-like ability to jump from bough to bough, and of the bodies that floated gently down instead of falling, lay in the belt. The thing was some sort of anti-gravity belt that almost balanced the weight of the wearer, thereby tremendously multiplying the propulsive power of the leg muscles, and the lifting power of the arms.

When the girl came to, she regarded me as curiously as I did her, and promptly began to quiz me. Her accent and intonation puzzled me a lot, but nevertheless we were able to understand each other fairly well, except for certain words and phrases. I explained what had happened while she lay unconscious, and she thanked me simply for saving her life.

"You are a strange exchange," she said, eying my clothing quizzically. Evidently she found it mirth provoking by contrast with her own neatly efficient garb. "Don't you understand what I mean by 'exchange?' I mean ah – let me see – a stranger, somebody from some other gang. What gang do you belong to?" (She pronounced it 'gan,' with only a suspicion of a nasal sound).

I laughed. "I'm not a gangster," I said. But she evidently did not understand this word. "I don't belong to any gang," I explained, "and never did. Does everybody belong to a gang nowadays?"

"Naturally," she said, frowning. "If you don't belong to a gang, where and how do you live? Why have you not found and joined a gang? How do you eat? Where do you get your clothing?"

"I've been eating wild game for the past two weeks," I explained, "and this clothing I – er – ah – ." I paused, wondering how I could explain that it must be many hundred years old.

In the end I saw I would have to tell my story as well as I could, piecing it together with my assumptions as to what had happened. She listened patiently; incredulously at first, but with more confidence as I went on. When I had finished, she sat thinking for a long time.

"That's hard to believe," she said, "but I believe it." She looked me over with frank interest.

"Were you married when you slipped into unconsciousness down in that mine?" she asked me suddenly. I assured her I had never married. "Well, that simplifies matters," she continued. "You see, if you were technically classed as a family man, I could take you back only as an invited exchange and I, being unmarried, and no relation of yours, couldn't do the inviting."

Chapter II
The Forest Gangs

SHE GAVE ME a brief outline of the very peculiar social and economic system under which her people lived. At least it seemed very peculiar from my 20th Century viewpoint.

I learned with amazement that exactly 492 years had passed over my head as I lay unconscious in the mine.

Wilma, for that was her name, did not profess to be a historian, and so could give me only a sketchy outline of the wars that had been fought, and the manner in which such radical changes had come about. It seemed that another war had followed the First World War, in which nearly all the European nations had banded together to break the financial and industrial power of America. They succeeded in their purpose, though they were beaten, for the war was a terrific one, and left America, like themselves, gasping, bleeding and disorganized, with only the hollow shell of a victory.

This opportunity had been seized by the Russian Soviets, who had made a coalition with the Chinese, to sweep over all Europe and reduce it to a state of chaos.

America, industrially geared to world production and the world trade, collapsed economically, and there ensued a long period of stagnation and desperate attempts at economic reconstruction. But it was impossible to stave off war with the Mongolians, who by now had subjugated the Russians, and were aiming at a world empire.

In about 2109, it seems, the conflict was finally precipitated. The Mongolians, with overwhelming fleets of great airships, and a science that far outstripped that of crippled America, swept in over the Pacific and Atlantic Coasts, and down from Canada, annihilating American aircraft, armies and cities with their terrific disintegrator rays. These rays were projected from a machine not unlike a searchlight in appearance, the reflector of which, however, was not material substance, but a complicated balance of interacting electronic forces. This resulted in a terribly destructive beam. Under its influence, material substance melted into "nothingness"; i.e., into electronic vibrations. It destroyed all then known substances, from air to the most dense metals and stone.

They settled down to the establishment of what became known as the Han dynasty in America, as a sort of province in their World Empire.

Those were terrible days for the Americans. They were hunted like wild beasts. Only those survived who finally found refuge in mountains, canyons and forests. Government was at an end among them. Anarchy prevailed for several generations. Most would have been eager to submit to the Hans, even if it meant slavery. But the Hans did not want them, for they themselves had marvelous machinery and scientific process by which all difficult labor was accomplished.

Ultimately they stopped their active search for, and annihilation of, the widely scattered groups of now savage Americans. So long as they remained hidden in their forests, and did not venture near the great cities the Hans had built, little attention was paid to them.

Then began the building of the new American civilization. Families and individuals gathered together in clans or 'gangs' for mutual protection. For nearly a century they lived a nomadic and primitive life, moving from place to place, in desperate fear of the casual and occasional Han air raids, and the terrible disintegrator ray. As the frequency of these raids decreased, they began to stay permanently in given localities, organizing upon lines which in many respects were similar to those of the military households of the Norman feudal barons, except that instead of gathering together in castles, their defense tactics necessitated a certain scattering of living quarters for families and individuals. They lived virtually in the open air, in the forests, in green tents, resorting to camouflage tactics that would conceal their presence from air observers. They dug underground factories and laboratories, that they might better be shielded from the electrical detectors of the Hans. They tapped the radio communication lines of the Hans, with crude instruments at first; better ones later on. They bent every effort toward the redevelopment of science. For many generations they labored as unseen, unknown scholars of the Hans, picking up their knowledge piecemeal, as fast as they were able to.

During the earlier part of this period, there were many deadly wars fought between the various gangs, and occasional courageous but childishly futile attacks upon the Hans, followed by terribly punitive raids.

But as knowledge progressed, the sense of American brotherhood redeveloped. Reciprocal arrangements were made among the gangs over constantly increasing areas. Trade developed to a certain extent, as between one gang and another. But the interchange of knowledge became more important than that of goods, as skill in the handling of synthetic processes developed.

Within the gang, an economy was developed that was a compromise between individual liberty and a military socialism. The right of private property was limited practically to personal possessions, but private privileges were many, and sacredly regarded. Stimulation to achievement lay chiefly in the winning of various kinds of leadership and prerogatives, and only in a very limited degree in the hope of owning anything that might be classified as 'wealth,' and nothing that might be classified as 'resources.' Resources of every description, for military safety and efficiency, belonged as a matter of public interest to the community as a whole.

In the meantime, through these many generations, the Hans had developed a luxury economy, and with it the perfection of gilded vice and degradation. The Americans were regarded as 'wild men of the woods.' And since they neither needed nor wanted the woods or the wild men, they treated them as beasts, and were conscious of no human brotherhood with them. As time went on, and synthetic processes of producing foods and materials were further developed, less and less ground was needed by the Hans for the purposes of agriculture, and finally, even the working of mines was abandoned when it became cheaper to build up metal from electronic vibrations than to dig them out of the ground.

The Han race, devitalized by its vices and luxuries, with machinery and scientific processes to satisfy its every want, with virtually no necessity of labor, began to assume a defensive attitude toward the Americans.

And quite naturally, the Americans regarded the Hans with a deep, grim hatred. Conscious of individual superiority as men, knowing that latterly they were outstripping the Hans in science and civilization, they longed desperately for the day when they should be powerful enough to rise and annihilate the Yellow Blight that lay over the continent.

At the time of my awakening, the gangs were rather loosely organized, but were considering the establishment of a special military force, whose special business it would be to harry the Hans and bring down their air ships whenever possible without causing general alarm among the Mongolians. This force was destined to become the nucleus of the national force, when the Day of Retribution arrived. But that, however, did not happen for ten years, and is another story.

Wilma told me she was a member of the Wyoming Gang, which claimed the entire Wyoming Valley as its territory, under the leadership of Boss Hart. Her mother and father were dead, and she was unmarried, so she was not a 'family member.' She lived in a little group of tents known as Camp 17, under a woman Camp Boss, with seven other girls.

Her duties alternated between military or police scouting and factory work. For the two-week period which would end the next day, she had been on 'air patrol.' This did not mean, as I first imagined, that she was flying, but rather that she was on the lookout for Han ships over this outlying section of the Wyoming territory, and had spent most of her time perched in the tree tops scanning the skies. Had she seen one she would have fired a "drop flare" several miles off to one side, which would ignite when it was floating vertically toward the earth, so that the direction or point from which if had been fired might not be guessed by the airship and bring a blasting play of the disintegrator ray in her vicinity. Other members of the air patrol would send up rockets on seeing hers, until finally a scout equipped with an ultrophone, which, unlike the ancient radio, operated on the ultronic ethereal vibrations, would pass the warning simultaneously to the headquarters of the Wyoming Gang and other communities within a radius of several hundred miles, not to mention the few American rocket ships that might be in the air, and which instantly would duck to cover either through forest clearings or by flattening down to earth in green fields where their coloring would probably protect them from observation. The favorite American method of propulsion was known as "rocketing." The rocket is what I would describe, from my 20th Century comprehension of the matter, as an extremely powerful gas blast, atomically produced through the stimulation of chemical action. Scientists of today regard it as a childishly simple reaction, but by that very virtue, most economical and efficient.

But tomorrow, she explained, she would go back to work in the cloth plant, where she would take charge of one of the synthetic processes by which those wonderful substitutes for woven fabrics of wool, cotton and silk are produced. At the end of another two weeks, she would be back on military duty again, perhaps at the same work, or maybe as a 'contact guard,' on duty where the territory of the Wyomings merged with that of the Delawares, or the 'Susquannas' (Susquehannas) or one of the half dozen other 'gangs' in that section of the country which I knew as Pennsylvania and New York States.

Wilma cleared up for me the mystery of those flying leaps which she and her assailants had made, and explained in the following manner, how the inertron belt balances weight:

'Jumpers' were in common use at the time I 'awoke,' though they were costly, for at that time inertron had not been produced in very great quantity. They were very useful in the forest. They were belts, strapped high under the arms, containing an amount of inertron adjusted to the wearer's weight and purposes. In effect they made a man weigh as little as he desired; two pounds if he liked.

'Floaters' are a later development of 'jumpers' – rocket motors encased in inertron blocks and strapped to the back in such a way that the wearer floats, when drifting, facing slightly downward. With his motor in operation, he moves like a diver, headforemost, controlling his direction by twisting his body and by movements of his outstretched arms and hands. Ballast weights locked in the front of the belt adjust weight and lift. Some men prefer a few ounces of weight in floating, using a slight motor thrust to overcome this. Others prefer a buoyance balance of a few ounces. The inadvertent dropping of weight is not a serious matter. The motor thrust always can be used to descend. But as an extra precaution, in case the motor should fail, for any reason, there are built into every belt a number of detachable sections, one or more of which can be discarded to balance off any loss in weight.

"But who were your assailants," I asked, "and why were you attacked?"

Her assailants, she told me, were members of an outlaw gang, referred to as 'Bad Bloods,' a group which for several generations had been under the domination of conscienceless leaders who tried to advance the interests of their clan by tactics which their neighbors had come to regard as unfair, and who in consequence had been virtually boycotted. Their purpose had been to slay her near the Delaware frontier, making it appear that the crime had been committed by Delaware scouts and thus embroil the Delawares and Wyomings in acts of reprisal against each other, or at least cause suspicions.

Fortunately they had not succeeded in surprising her, and she had been successful in dodging them for some two hours before the shooting began, at the moment when I arrived on the scene.

"But we must not stay here talking," Wilma concluded. "I have to take you in, and besides I must report this attack right away. I think we had better slip over to the other side of the mountain. Whoever is on that post will have a phone, and I can make a direct report. But you'll have to have a belt. Mine alone won't help much against our combined weights, and there's little to be gained by jumping heavy. It's almost as bad as walking."

After a little search, we found one of the men I had killed, who had floated down among the trees some distance away and whose belt was not badly damaged. In detaching it from his body, it nearly got away from me and shot up in the air. Wilma caught it, however, and though it reinforced the lift of her own belt so that she had to hook her knee around a branch to hold herself down, she saved it. I climbed the tree and, with my weight added to hers, we floated down easily.

Chapter III
Life in the 25th Century

WE WERE DELAYED in starting for quite a while since I had to acquire a few crude ideas about the technique of using these belts. I had been sitting down, for instance, with the belt strapped about me, enjoying an ease similar to that of a comfortable armchair; when I stood up with a natural exertion of muscular effort, I shot ten feet into the air, with a wild instinctive thrashing of arms and legs that amused Wilma greatly.

But after some practice, I began to get the trick of gauging muscular effort to a minimum of vertical and a maximum of horizontal. The correct form, I found, was in a measure comparable to that of skating. I found, also, that in forest work particularly the arms and hands could be used to great advantage in swinging along from branch to branch, so prolonging leaps almost indefinitely at times.

In going up the side of the mountain, I found that my 20th Century muscles did have an advantage, in spite of lack of skill with the belt, and since the slopes were very sharp, and most of our leaps were upward, I could have distanced Wilma easily. But when we crossed the ridge and descended, she outstripped me with her superior technique. Choosing the steepest slopes, she would crouch in the top of a tree, and propel herself outward, literally diving until, with the loss of horizontal momentum, she would assume a more upright position and float downward. In this manner she would sometimes cover as much as a quarter of a mile in a single leap, while I leaped and scrambled clumsily behind, thoroughly enjoying the novel sensation.

Half way down the mountain, we saw another green-clad figure leap out above the tree tops toward us. The three of us perched on an outcropping of rock from which a view for many miles around could be had, while Wilma hastily explained her adventure and my presence to her fellow guard; whose name was Alan. I learned later that this was the modern form of Helen.

"You want to report by phone then, don't you?" Alan took a compact packet about six inches square from a holster attached to her belt and handed it to Wilma.

So far as I could see, it had no special receiver for the ear. Wilma merely threw back a lid, as though she were opening a book, and began to talk. The voice that came back from the machine was as audible as her own.

She was queried closely as to the attack upon her, and at considerable length as to myself, and I could tell from the tone of that voice that its owner was not prepared to take me at my face value as readily as Wilma had. For that matter, neither was the other girl.

I could realize it from the suspicious glances she threw my way, when she thought my attention was elsewhere, and the manner in which her hand hovered constantly near her gun holster.

Wilma was ordered to bring me in at once, and informed that another scout would take her place on the other side of the mountain. So she closed down the lid of the phone and handed it back to Alan, who seemed relieved to see us departing over the tree tops in the direction of the camps.

We had covered perhaps ten miles, in what still seemed to me a surprisingly easy fashion, when Wilma explained, that from here on we would have to keep to the ground. We were nearing the camps, she said, and there was always the possibility that some small Han scoutship, invisible high in the sky, might catch sight of us through a projectoscope and thus find the general location of the camps.

Wilma took me to the Scout office, which proved to be a small building of irregular shape, conforming to the trees around it, and substantially constructed of green sheet-like material.

I was received by the assistant Scout Boss, who reported my arrival at once to the historical office, and to officials he called the Psycho Boss and the History Boss, who came in a few minutes later. The attitude of all three men was at first polite but skeptical, and Wilma's ardent advocacy seemed to amuse them secretly.

For the next two hours I talked, explained and answered questions. I had to explain, in detail, the manner of my life in the 20th Century and my understanding of customs, habits, business, science and the history of that period, and about developments in the centuries that had elapsed. Had I been in a classroom, I would have come through the examination with a very poor mark, for I was unable to give any answer to fully half of their questions. But before long I realized that the majority of these questions were designed as traps. Objects, of whose purpose I knew nothing, were casually handed to me, and I was watched keenly as I handled them.

In the end I could see both amazement and belief begin to show in the faces of my inquisitors, and at last the Historical and Psycho Bosses agreed openly that they could find no flaw in my story or reactions, and that unbelievable as it seemed, my story must be accepted as genuine.

They took me at once to Big Boss Hart. He was a portly man with a 'poker face.' He would probably have been the successful politician even in the 20th Century.

They gave him a brief outline of my story and a report of their examination of me. He made no comment other than to nod his acceptance of it. Then he turned to me.

"How does it feel?" he asked. "Do we look funny to you?"

"A bit strange," I admitted. "But I'm beginning to lose that dazed feeling, though I can see I have an awful lot to learn."

"Maybe we can learn some things from you, too," he said. "So you fought in the First World War. Do you know, we have very little left in the way of records of the details of that war, that is, the precise conditions under which it was fought, and the tactics employed. We forgot many things during the Han terror, and – well, I think you might have a lot of ideas worth thinking over for our raid masters. By the way, now that you're here, and can't go back to your own century, so to speak, what do you want to do? You're welcome to become one of us. Or perhaps you'd just like to visit with us for a while, and then look around among the other gangs. Maybe you'd like some of the others better. Don't make up your mind now. We'll put you down as an exchange for a while. Let's see. You and Bill

Hearn ought to get along well together. He's Camp Boss of Number 34 when he isn't acting as Raid Boss or Scout Boss. There's a vacancy in his camp. Stay with him and think things over as long as you want to. As soon as you make up your mind to anything, let me know."

We all shook hands, for that was one custom that had not died out in five hundred years, and I set out with Bill Hearn.

Bill, like all the others, was clad in green. He was a big man. That is, he was about my own height, five feet eleven. This was considerably above the average now, for the race had lost something in stature, it seemed, through the vicissitudes of five centuries. Most of the women were a bit below five feet, and the men only a trifle above this height.

For a period of two weeks Bill was to confine himself to camp duties, so I had a good chance to familiarize myself with the community life. It was not easy. There were so many marvels to absorb. I never ceased to wonder at the strange combination of rustic social life and feverish industrial activity. At least, it was strange to me. For in my experience, industrial development meant crowded cities, tenements, paved streets, profusion of vehicles, noise, hurrying men and women with strained or dull faces, vast structures and ornate public works.

Here, however, was rustic simplicity, apparently isolated families and groups, living in the heart of the forest, with a quarter of a mile or more between households, a total absence of crowds, no means of conveyance other than the belts called jumpers, almost constantly worn by everybody, and an occasional rocket ship, used only for longer journeys, and underground plants or factories that were to my mind more like laboratories and engine rooms; many of them were excavations as deep as mines, with well finished, lighted and comfortable interiors. These people were adepts at camouflage against air observation. Not only would their activity have been unsuspected by an airship passing over the center of the community, but even by an enemy who might happen to drop through the screen of the upper branches to the floor of the forest. The camps, or household structures, were all irregular in shape and of colors that blended with the great trees among which they were hidden.

There were 724 dwellings or 'camps' among the Wyomings, located within an area of about fifteen square miles. The total population was 8,688, every man, woman and child, whether member or 'exchange,' being listed.

The plants were widely scattered through the territory also. Nowhere was anything like congestion permitted. So far as possible, families and individuals were assigned to living quarters, not too far from the plants or offices in which their work lay.

All able-bodied men and women alternated in two-week periods between military and industrial service, except those who were needed for household work. Since working conditions in the plants and offices were ideal, and everybody thus had plenty of healthy outdoor activity in addition, the population was sturdy and active. Laziness was regarded as nearly the greatest of social offenses. Hard work and general merit were variously rewarded with extra privileges, advancement to positions of authority, and with various items of personal equipment for convenience and luxury.

In leisure moments, I got great enjoyment from sitting outside the dwelling in which I was quartered with Bill Hearn and ten other men, watching the occasional passers-by, as with leisurely, but swift movements, they swung up and down the forest trail, rising from the ground in long almost-horizontal leaps, occasionally swinging from one convenient branch overhead to another before 'sliding' back to the ground farther on. Normal traveling pace, where these trails were straight enough, was about twenty miles an hour.

Such things as automobiles and railroad trains (the memory of them not more than a month old in my mind) seemed inexpressibly silly and futile compared with such convenience as these belts or jumpers offered.

Bill suggested that I wander around for several days, from plant to plant, to observe and study what I could. The entire community had been apprised of my coming, my rating as an 'exchange' reaching every building and post in the community, by means of ultronic broadcast. Everywhere I was welcomed in an interested and helpful spirit.

I visited the plants where ultronic vibrations were isolated from the ether and through slow processes built up into sub-electronic, electronic and atomic forms into the two great synthetic elements, ultron and inertron. I learned something, superficially at least, of the processes of combined chemical and mechanical action through which were produced the various forms of synthetic cloth. I watched the manufacture of the machines which were used at locations of construction to produce the various forms of building materials. But I was particularly interested in the munitions plants and the rocket-ship shops.

Ultron is a solid of great molecular density and moderate elasticity, which has the property of being 100 per cent conductive to those pulsations known as light, electricity and heat. Since it is completely permeable to light vibrations, it is therefore absolutely invisible and non-reflective. Its magnetic response is almost, but not quite, 100 per cent also. It is therefore very heavy under normal conditions but extremely responsive to the repellor or anti-gravity rays, such as the Hans use as 'legs' for their airships.

Inertron is the second great triumph of American research and experimentation with ultronic forces. It was developed just a few years before my awakening in the abandoned mine. It is a synthetic element, built up, through a complicated heterodyning of ultronic pulsations, from 'infra-balanced' sub-ionic forms. It is completely inert to both electric and magnetic forces in all the orders above the ultronic; that is to say, the sub-electronic, the electronic, the atomic and the molecular. In consequence it has a number of amazing and valuable properties. One of these is the total lack of weight. Another is a total lack of heat. It has no molecular vibration whatever. It reflects 100 per cent of the heat and light impinging upon it. It does not feel cold to the touch, of course, since it will not absorb the heat of the hand. It is a solid, very dense in molecular structure despite its lack of weight, of great strength and considerable elasticity. It is a perfect shield against the disintegrator rays.

Rocket guns are very simple contrivances so far as the mechanism of launching the bullet is concerned. They are simple light tubes, closed at the rear end, with a trigger-actuated pin for piercing the thin skin at the base of the cartridge. This piercing of the skin starts the chemical and atomic reaction. The entire cartridge leaves the tube under its own power, at a very easy initial velocity, just enough to insure accuracy of aim; so the tube does not have to be of heavy construction. The bullet increases in velocity as it goes. It may be solid or explosive. It may explode on contact or on time, or a combination of these two.

Bill and I talked mostly of weapons, military tactics and strategy. Strangely enough he had no idea whatever of the possibilities of the barrage, though the tremendous effect of a 'curtain of fire' with such high-explosive projectiles as these modern rocket guns used was obvious to me. But the barrage idea, it seemed, has been lost track of completely in the air wars that followed the First World War, and in the peculiar guerilla tactics developed by Americans in the later period of operations from the ground against Han airships, and in the gang wars which, until a few generations ago I learned, had been almost continuous.

"I wonder," said Bill one day, "if we couldn't work up some form of barrage to spring on the Bad Bloods. The Big Boss told me today that he's been in communication with the other gangs, and all are agreed that the Bad Bloods might as well be wiped out for good. That attempt on Wilma Deering's life and their evident desire to make trouble among the gangs, has stirred up every community east of the Alleghenies. The Boss says that none of the others will object if we go after them. So I imagine that before long we will. Now show me again how you worked that business in the Argonne forest. The conditions ought to be pretty much the same."

I went over it with him in detail, and gradually we worked out a modified plan that would be better adapted to our more powerful weapons, and the use of jumpers.

"It will be easy," Bill exulted. "I'll slide down and talk it over with the Boss tomorrow."

During the first two weeks of my stay with the Wyomings, Wilma Deering and I saw a great deal of each other. I naturally felt a little closer friendship for her, in view of the fact that she was the first human being I saw after waking from my long sleep; her appreciation of my saving her life, though I could not have done otherwise than I did in that matter, and most of all my own appreciation of the fact that she had not found it as difficult as the others to believe my story, operated in the same direction. I could easily imagine my story must have sounded incredible.

It was natural enough too, that she should feel an unusual interest in me. In the first place, I was her personal discovery. In the second, she was a girl of studious and reflective turn of mind. She never got tired of my stories and descriptions of the 20th Century.

The others of the community, however, seemed to find our friendship a bit amusing. It seemed that Wilma had a reputation for being cold toward the opposite sex, and so others, not being able to appreciate some of her fine qualities as I did, misinterpreted her attitude, much to their own delight. Wilma and I, however, ignored this as much as we could.

Chapter IV
A Han Air Raid

THERE WAS A GIRL in Wilma's camp named Gerdi Mann, with whom Bill Hearn was desperately in love, and the four of us used to go around a lot together. Gerdi was a distinct type. Whereas Wilma had the usual dark brown hair and hazel eyes that marked nearly every member of the community, Gerdi had red hair, blue eyes and very fair skin. She has been dead many years now, but I remember her vividly because she was a throwback in physical appearance to a certain 20th Century type which I have found very rare among modern Americans; also because the four of us were engaged one day in a discussion of this very point, when I obtained my first experience of a Han air raid.

We were sitting high on the side of a hill overlooking the valley that teemed with human activity, invisible beneath its blanket of foliage.

The other three, who knew of the Irish but vaguely and indefinitely, as a race on the other side of the globe, which, like ourselves, had succeeded in maintaining a precarious and fugitive existence in rebellion against the Mongolian domination of the earth, were listening with interest to my theory that Gerdi's ancestors of several hundred years ago must have been Irish. I explained that Gerdi was an Irish type, evidently a throwback, and that her surname might well have been McMann, or McMahan, and still more anciently 'mac Mathghamhain.' They were interested too in my surmise that 'Gerdi' was the same name as that which had been 'Gerty' or 'Gertrude' in the 20th Century.

In the middle of our discussion, we were startled by an alarm rocket that burst high in the air, far to the north, spreading a pall of red smoke that drifted like a cloud. It was followed by others at scattered points in the northern sky.

"A Han raid!" Bill exclaimed in amazement. "The first in seven years!"

"Maybe it's just one of their ships off its course," I ventured.

"No," said Wilma in some agitation. "That would be green rockets. Red means only one thing, Tony. They're sweeping the countryside with their dis beams. Can you see anything, Bill?"

"We had better get under cover," Gerdi said nervously. "The four of us are bunched here in the open. For all we know they may be twelve miles up, out of sight, yet looking at us with a projecto'."

Bill had been sweeping the horizon hastily with his glass, but apparently saw nothing.

"We had better scatter, at that," he said finally. "It's orders, you know. See!" He pointed to the valley.

Here and there a tiny human figure shot for a moment above the foliage of the treetops.

"That's bad," Wilma commented, as she counted the jumpers. "No less than fifteen people visible, and all clearly radiating from a central point. Do they want to give away our location?"

The standard orders covering air raids were that the population was to scatter individually. There should be no grouping, or even pairing, in view of the destructiveness of the disintegrator rays. Experience of generations had proved that if this were done, and everybody remained hidden beneath the tree screens, the Hans would have to sweep mile after mile of territory, foot by foot, to catch more than a small percentage of the community.

Gerdi, however, refused to leave Bill, and Wilma developed an equal obstinacy against quitting my side. I was inexperienced at this sort of thing, she explained, quite ignoring the fact that she was too; she was only thirteen or fourteen years old at the time of the last air raid.

However, since I could not argue her out of it, we leaped together about a quarter of a mile to the right, while Bill and Gerdi disappeared down the hillside among the trees.

Wilma and I both wanted a point of vantage from which we might overlook the valley and the sky to the north, and we found it near the top of the ridge, where, protected from visibility by thick branches, we could look out between the tree trunks, and get a good view of the valley.

No more rockets went up. Except for a few of those warning red clouds, drifting lazily in a blue sky, there was no visible indication of man's past or present existence anywhere in the sky or on the ground.

Then Wilma gripped my arm and pointed. I saw it; away off in the distance; looking like a phantom dirigible airship, in its coat of low-visibility paint, a bare spectre.

"Seven thousand feet up," Wilma whispered, crouching close to me. "Watch."

The ship was about the same shape as the great dirigibles of the 20th Century that I had seen, but without the suspended control car, engines, propellors, rudders or elevating planes. As it loomed rapidly nearer, I saw that it was wider and somewhat flatter than I had supposed.

Now I could see the repellor rays that held the ship aloft, like searchlight beams faintly visible in the bright daylight (and still faintly visible to the human eye at night). Actually, I had been informed by my instructors, there were two rays; the visible one generated by the ship's apparatus, and directed toward the ground as a beam of 'carrier' impulses; and the true repellor ray, the complement of the other in one sense, induced by the action of the 'carrier' and reacting in a concentrating upward direction from the mass of the earth, becoming successively electronic, atomic and finally molecular, in its nature, according to various ratios of distance between earth mass and 'carrier' source, until, in the last analysis, the ship itself actually is supported on an upward rushing column of air, much like a ball continuously supported on a fountain jet.

The raider neared with incredible speed. Its rays were both slanted astern at a sharp angle, so that it slid forward with tremendous momentum.

The ship was operating two disintegrator rays, though only in a casual, intermittent fashion. But whenever they flashed downward with blinding brilliancy, forest, rocks and ground melted instantaneously into nothing, where they played upon them.

When later I inspected the scars left by these rays I found them some five feet deep and thirty feet wide, the exposed surfaces being lava-like in texture, but of a pale, iridescent, greenish hue.

No systematic use of the rays was made by the ship, however, until it reached a point over the center of the valley – the center of the community's activities. There it came to a sudden stop by shooting its repellor beams sharply forward and easing them back gradually to the vertical, holding the ship floating and motionless. Then the work of destruction began systematically.

Back and forth traveled the destroying rays, ploughing parallel furrows from hillside to hillside. We gasped in dismay, Wilma and I, as time after time we saw it plough through sections where we knew camps or plants were located.

"This is awful," she moaned, a terrified question in her eyes. "How could they know the location so exactly, Tony? Did you see? They were never in doubt. They stalled at a predetermined spot – and – and it was exactly the right spot."

We did not talk of what might happen if the rays were turned in our direction. We both knew. We would simply disintegrate in a split second into mere scattered electronic vibrations. Strangely enough, it was this self-reliant girl of the 25th Century, who clung to me, a relatively primitive man of the 20th, less familiar than she with the thought of this terrifying possibility, for moral support.

We knew that many of our companions must have been whisked into absolute non-existence before our eyes in these few moments. The whole thing paralyzed us into mental and physical immobility for I do not know how long.

It couldn't have been long, however, for the rays had not ploughed more than thirty of their twenty-foot furrows or so across the valley, when I regained control of myself, and brought Wilma to herself by shaking her roughly.

"How far will this rocket gun shoot, Wilma?" I demanded, drawing my pistol.

"It depends on your rocket, Tony. It will take even the longest range rocket, but you could shoot more accurately from a longer tube. But why? You couldn't penetrate the shell of that ship with rocket force, even if you could reach it."

I fumbled clumsily with my rocket pouch, for I was excited. I had an idea I wanted to try; a 'hunch' I called it, forgetting that Wilma could not understand my ancient slang. But finally, with her help, I selected the longest range explosive rocket in my pouch, and fitted it to my pistol.

"It won't carry seven thousand feet, Tony," Wilma objected. But I took aim carefully. It was another thought that I had in my mind. The supporting repellor ray, I had been told, became molecular in character at what was called a logarithmic level of five (below that it was a purely electronic 'flow' or pulsation between the source of the 'carrier' and the average mass of the earth). Below that level if I could project my explosive bullet into this stream where it began to carry material substance upward, might it not rise with the air column, gathering speed and hitting the ship with enough impact to carry it through the shell? It was worth trying anyhow. Wilma became greatly excited, too, when she grasped the nature of my inspiration.

Feverishly I looked around for some formation of branches against which I could rest the pistol, for I had to aim most carefully. At last I found one. Patiently I sighted on the hulk of the ship far above us, aiming at the far side of it, at such an angle as would, so far as I could estimate, bring my bullet path through the forward repellor beam. At last the sights wavered across the point I sought and I pressed the button gently.

For a moment we gazed breathlessly.

Suddenly the ship swung bow down, as on a pivot, and swayed like a pendulum. Wilma screamed in her excitement.

"Oh, Tony, you hit it! You hit it! Do it again; bring it down!"

We had only one more rocket of extreme range between us, and we dropped it three times in our excitement in inserting it in my gun. Then, forcing myself to be calm by sheer will power, while Wilma stuffed her little fist into her mouth to keep from shrieking, I sighted carefully again and fired. In a flash, Wilma had grasped the hope that this discovery of mine might lead to the end of the Han domination.

The elapsed time of the rocket's invisible flight seemed an age.

Then we saw the ship falling. It seemed to plunge lazily, but actually it fell with terrific acceleration, turning end over end, its disintegrator rays, out of control, describing vast, wild arcs, and once cutting a gash through the forest less than two hundred feet from where we stood.

The crash with which the heavy craft hit the ground reverberated from the hills – the momentum of eighteen or twenty thousand tons, in a sheer drop of seven thousand feet. A mangled mass of metal, it buried itself in the ground, with poetic justice, in the middle of the smoking, semi-molten field of destruction it had been so deliberately ploughing.

The silence, the vacuity of the landscape, was oppressive, as the last echoes died away.

Then far down the hillside, a single figure leaped exultantly above the foliage screen. And in the distance another, and another.

In a moment the sky was punctured by signal rockets. One after another the little red puffs became drifting clouds.

"Scatter! Scatter!" Wilma exclaimed. "In half an hour there'll be an entire Han fleet here from Nu-yok, and another from Bah-flo. They'll get this instantly on their recordographs and location finders. They'll blast the whole valley and the country for miles beyond. Come, Tony. There's no time for the gang to rally. See the signals. We've got to jump. Oh, I'm so proud of you!"

Over the ridge we went, in long leaps toward the east, the country of the Delawares.

From time to time signal rockets puffed in the sky. Most of them were the 'red warnings,' the 'scatter' signals. But from certain of the others, which Wilma identified as Wyoming rockets, she gathered that whoever was in command (we did not know whether the Boss was alive or not) was ordering an ultimate rally toward the south, and so we changed our course.

It was a great pity, I thought, that the clan had not been equipped throughout its membership with ultrophones, but Wilma explained to me, that not enough of these had been built for distribution as yet, although general distribution had been contemplated within a couple of months.

We traveled far before nightfall overtook us, trying only to put as much distance as possible between ourselves and the valley.

When gathering dusk made jumping too dangerous, we sought a comfortable spot beneath the trees, and consumed part of our emergency rations. It was the first time I had tasted the stuff – a highly nutritive synthetic substance called 'concentro,' which was, however, a bit bitter and unpalatable. But as only a mouthful or so was needed, it did not matter.

Neither of us had a cloak, but we were both thoroughly tired and happy, so we curled up together for warmth. I remember Wilma making some sleepy remark about our mating, as she cuddled up, as though the matter were all settled, and my surprise at my own instant acceptance of the idea, for I had not consciously thought of her that way before. But we both fell asleep at once.

In the morning we found little time for love making. The practical problem facing us was too great. Wilma felt that the Wyoming plan must be to rally in the Susquanna territory, but she had her doubts about the wisdom of this plan. In my elation at my success in bringing down the Han ship, and my newly found interest in my charming companion, who was, from my viewpoint of another century, at once more highly civilized and yet more primitive than myself, I had forgotten the ominous fact that the Han ship I had destroyed must have known the exact location of the Wyoming Works.

This meant, to Wilma's logical mind, either that the Hans had perfected new instruments as yet unknown to us, or that somewhere, among the Wyomings or some other nearby gang, there were traitors so degraded as to commit that unthinkable act of trafficking in information with the Hans. In either contingency, she argued, other Han raids would follow, and since the Susquannas had a highly developed organization and more than usually productive plants, the next raid might be expected to strike them.

But at any rate it was clearly our business to get in touch with the other fugitives as quickly as possible, so in spite of muscles that were sore from the excessive leaping of the day before, we continued on our way.

We traveled for only a couple of hours when we saw a multi-colored rocket in the sky, some ten miles ahead of us.

"Bear to the left, Tony," Wilma said, "and listen for the whistle."

"Why?" I asked.

"Haven't they given you the rocket code yet?" she replied. "That's what the green, followed by yellow and purple means; to concentrate five miles east of the rocket position. You know the rocket position itself might draw a play of disintegrator beams."

It did not take us long to reach the neighborhood of the indicated rallying, though we were now traveling beneath the trees, with but an occasional leap to a top branch to see if any more rocket smoke was floating above. And soon we heard a distant whistle.

We found about half the Gang already there, in a spot where the trees met high above a little stream. The Big Boss and Raid Bosses were busy reorganizing the remnants.

We reported to Boss Hart at once. He was silent, but interested, when he heard our story.

"You two stick close to me," he said, adding grimly, "I'm going back to the valley at once with a hundred picked men, and I'll need you."

Chapter V
Setting the Trap

INSIDE OF fifteen minutes we were on our way. A certain amount of caution was sacrificed for the sake of speed, and the men leaped away either across the forest top, or over open spaces of ground, but concentration was forbidden. The Big Boss named the spot on the hillside as the rallying point.

"We'll have to take a chance on being seen, so long as we don't group," he declared, "at least until within five miles of the rallying spot. From then on I want every man to disappear from sight and to travel under cover. And keep your ultrophones open, and tuned on ten-four-seven-six."

Wilma and I had received our battle equipment from the Gear boss. It consisted of a long-gun, a hand-gun, with a special case of ammunition constructed of inertron, which made the load weigh but a few ounces, and a short sword. This gear we strapped over each other's shoulders, on top of our jumping belts. In addition, we each received an ultrophone, and a light inertron blanket rolled into a cylinder about six inches long by two or three in diameter. This fabric was exceedingly thin and light, but it had considerable warmth, because of the mixture of inertron in its composition.

"This looks like business," Wilma remarked to me with sparkling eyes. (And I might mention a curious thing here. The word 'business' had survived from the 20th Century American vocabulary, but not with any meaning of 'industry' or 'trade,' for such things being purely community activities were spoken of as 'work' and 'clearing.' Business simply meant fighting, and that was all.)

"Did you bring all this equipment from the valley?" I asked the Gear Boss.

"No," he said. "There was no time to gather anything. All this stuff we cleared from the Susquannas a few hours ago. I was with the Boss on the way down, and he had me jump on ahead and arrange it. But you two had better be moving. He's beckoning you now."

Hart was about to call us on our phones when we looked up. As soon as we did so, he leaped away, waving us to follow closely.

He was a powerful man, and he darted ahead in long, swift, low leaps up the banks of the stream, which followed a fairly straight course at this point. By extending ourselves, however, Wilma and I were able to catch up to him.

As we gradually synchronized our leaps with his, he outlined to us, between the grunts that accompanied each leap, his plan of action.

"We have to start the big business – unh – sooner or later," he said. "And if – unh – the Hans have found any way of locating our positions – unh – it's time to start now, although the Council of Bosses – unh – had intended waiting a few years until enough rocket ships have been – unh – built. But no matter what the sacrifice – unh – we can't afford to let them get us on the run – unh –. We'll set a trap for the yellow devils in the – unh – valley if they come back for their wreckage – unh – and if they don't, we'll go rocketing for some of their liners – unh – on the Nu-yok, Clee-lan, Si-ka-ga course.

We can use – unh – that idea of yours of shooting up the repellor – unh – beams. Want you to give us a demonstration."

With further admonition to follow him closely, he increased his pace, and Wilma and I were taxed to our utmost to keep up with him. It was only in ascending the slopes that my tougher muscles overbalanced his greater skill, and I was able to set the pace for him, as I had for Wilma.

We slept in greater comfort that night, under our inertron blankets, and were off with the dawn, leaping cautiously to the top of the ridge overlooking the valley which Wilma and I had left.

The Boss scanned the sky with his ultroscope, patiently taking some fifteen minutes to the task, and then swung his phone into use, calling the roll and giving the men their instructions.

His first order was for us all to slip our ear and chest discs into permanent position.

These ultrophones were quite different from the one used by Wilma's companion scout the day I saved her from the vicious attack of the bandit Gang. That one was contained entirely in a small pocket case. These, with which we were now equipped, consisted of a pair of ear discs, each a separate and self-contained receiving set. They slipped into little pockets over our ears in the fabric helmets we wore, and shut out virtually all extraneous sounds. The chest discs were likewise self-contained sending sets, strapped to the chest a few inches below the neck and actuated by the vibrations from the vocal cords through the body tissues. The total range of these sets was about eighteen miles. Reception was remarkably clear, quite free from the static that so marked the 20th Century radios, and of a strength in direct proportion to the distance of the speaker.

The Boss's set was triple powered, so that his orders would cut in on any local conversations, which were indulged in, however, with great restraint, and only for the purpose of maintaining contacts.

I marveled at the efficiency of this modern method of battle communication in contrast to the clumsy signaling devices of more ancient times; and also at other military contrasts in which the 20th and 25th Century methods were the reverse of each other in efficiency. These modern Americans, for instance, knew little of hand to hand fighting, and nothing, naturally, of trench warfare. Of barrages they were quite ignorant, although they possessed weapons of terrific power. And until my recent flash of inspiration, no one among them, apparently, had ever thought of the scheme of shooting a rocket into a repellor beam and letting the beam itself hurl it upward into the most vital part of the Han ship.

Hart patiently placed his men, first giving his instructions to the campmasters, and then remaining silent, while they placed the individuals.

In the end, the hundred men were ringed about the valley, on the hillsides and tops, each in a position from which he had a good view of the wreckage of the Han ship. But not a man had come in view, so far as I could see, in the whole process.

The Boss explained to me that it was his idea that he, Wilma and I should investigate the wreck. If Han ships should appear in the sky, we would leap for the hillsides.

I suggested to him to have the men set up their long-guns trained on an imaginary circle surrounding the wreck. He busied himself with this after the three of us leaped down to the Han ship, serving as a target himself, while he called on the men individually to aim their pieces and lock them in position.

In the meantime Wilma and I climbed into the wreckage, but did not find much. Practically all of the instruments and machinery had been twisted out of all recognizable shape, or utterly destroyed by the ship's disintegrator rays which apparently had continued to operate in the midst of its warped remains for some moments after the crash.

It was unpleasant work searching the mangled bodies of the crew. But it had to be done. The Han clothing, I observed, was quite different from that of the Americans, and in many respects more like the garb to which I had been accustomed in the earlier part of my life. It was made of synthetic fabrics like silks, loose and comfortable trousers of knee length, and sleeveless shirts.

No protection, except that against drafts, was needed, Wilma explained to me, for the Han cities were entirely enclosed, with splendid arrangements for ventilation and heating. These arrangements of course were equally adequate in their airships. The Hans, indeed, had quite a distaste for unshaded daylight, since their lighting apparatus diffused a controlled amount of violet rays, making the unmodified sunlight unnecessary for health, and undesirable for comfort. Since the Hans did not have the secret of inertron, none of them wore anti-gravity belts. Yet in spite of the fact that they had to bear their own full weights at all times, they were physically far inferior to the Americans, for they lived lives of degenerative physical inertia, having machinery of every description for the performance of all labor, and convenient conveyances for any movement of more than a few steps.

Even from the twisted wreckage of this ship I could see that seats, chairs and couches played an extremely important part in their scheme of existence.

But none of the bodies were overweight. They seemed to have been the bodies of men in good health, but muscularly much underdeveloped. Wilma explained to me that they had mastered the science of gland control, and of course dietetics, to the point where men and women among them not uncommonly reached the age of a hundred years with arteries and general health in splendid condition.

I did not have time to study the ship and its contents as carefully as I would have liked, however. Time pressed, and it was our business to discover some clue to the deadly accuracy with which the ship had spotted the Wyoming Works.

The Boss had hardly finished his arrangements for the ring barrage, when one of the scouts on an eminence to the north, announced the approach of seven Han ships, spread out in a great semi-circle.

Hart leaped for the hillside, calling to us to do likewise, but Wilma and I had raised the flaps of our helmets and switched off our 'speakers' for conversation between ourselves, and by the time we discovered what had happened, the ships were clearly visible, so fast were they approaching.

"Jump!" we heard the Boss order, "Deering to the north. Rogers to the east."

But Wilma looked at me meaningly and pointed to where the twisted plates of the ship, projecting from the ground, offered a shelter.

"Too late, Boss," she said. "They'd see us. Besides I think there's something here we ought to look at. It's probably their magnetic graph."

"You're signing your death warrant," Hart warned.

"We'll risk it," said Wilma and I together.

"Good for you," replied the Boss. "Take command then, Rogers, for the present. Do you all know his voice, boys?"

A chorus of assent rang in our ears, and I began to do some fast thinking as the girl and I ducked into the twisted mass of metal.

"Wilma, hunt for that record," I said, knowing that by the simple process of talking I could keep the entire command continuously informed as to the situation. "On the hillsides, keep your guns trained on the circles and stand by. On the hilltops, how many of you are there? Speak in rotation from Bald Knob around to the east, north, west."

In turn the men called their names. There were twenty of them.

I assigned them by name to cover the various Han ships, numbering the latter from left to right.

"Train your rockets on their repellor rays about three-quarters of the way up, between ships and ground. Aim is more important than elevation. Follow those rays with your aim continuously. Shoot when I tell you, not before. Deering has the record. The Hans probably have not seen us, or at least think there are but two of us in the valley, since they're settling without opening up disintegrators. Any opinions?"

My ear discs remained silent.

"Deering and I remain here until they land and debark. Stand by and keep alert."

Rapidly and easily the largest of the Han ships settled to the earth. Three scouted sharply to the south, rising to a higher level. The others floated motionless about a thousand feet above.

Peeping through a small fissure between two plates, I saw the vast hulk of the ship come to rest full on the line of our prospective ring barrage. A door clanged open a couple of feet from the ground, and one by one the crew emerged.

Chapter VI
The 'Wyoming Massacre'

"THEY'RE COMING out of the ship." I spoke quietly, with my hand over my mouth, for fear they might hear me. "One – two – three – four, five – six – seven – eight – nine. That seems to be all. Who knows how many men a ship like that is likely to carry?"

"About ten, if there are no passengers," replied one of my men, probably one of those on the hillside.

"How are they armed?" I asked.

"Just knives," came the reply. "They never permit hand-rays on the ships. Afraid of accidents. Have a ruling against it."

"Leave them to us then," I said, for I had a hastily formed plan in my mind. "You, on the hillsides, take the ships above. Abandon the ring target. Divide up in training on those repellor rays. You, on the hilltops, all train on the repellors of the ships to the south. Shoot at the word, but not before.

"Wilma, crawl over to your left where you can make a straight leap for the door in that ship. These men are all walking around the wreck in a bunch. When they're on the far side, I'll give the word and you leap through that door in one bound. I'll follow. Maybe we won't be seen. We'll overpower the guard inside, but don't shoot. We may escape being seen by both this crew and ships above. They can't see over this wreck."

It was so easy that it seemed too good to be true. The Hans who had emerged from the ship walked round the wreckage lazily, talking in guttural tones, keenly interested in the wreck, but quite unsuspicious.

At last they were on the far side. In a moment they would be picking their way into the wreck.

"Wilma, leap!" I almost whispered the order.

The distance between Wilma's hiding place and the door in the side of the Han ship was not more than fifteen feet. She was already crouched with her feet braced against a metal beam. Taking the lift of that wonderful inertron belt into her calculation, she dove headforemost, like a green projectile, through the door. I followed in a split second, more clumsily, but no less speedily, bruising my shoulder painfully, as I ricocheted from the edge of the opening and brought up sliding against the unconscious girl; for she evidently had hit her head against the partition within the ship into which she had crashed.

We had made some noise within the ship. Shuffling footsteps were approaching down a well lit gangway.

"Any signs we have been observed?" I asked my men on the hillsides.

"Not yet," I heard the Boss reply. "Ships overhead still standing. No beams have been broken out. Men on ground absorbed in wreck. Most of them have crawled into it out of sight."

"Good," I said quickly. "Deering hit her head. Knocked out. One or more members of the crew approaching. We're not discovered yet. I'll take care of them. Stand a bit longer, but be ready."

I think my last words must have been heard by the man who was approaching, for he stopped suddenly.

I crouched at the far side of the compartment, motionless. I would not draw my sword if there were only one of them. He would be a weakling, I figured, and I should easily overcome him with my bare hands.

Apparently reassured at the absence of any further sound, a man came around a sort of bulkhead – and I leaped.

I swung my legs up in front of me as I did so, catching him full in the stomach and knocked him cold.

I ran forward along the keel gangway, searching for the control room. I found it well up in the nose of the ship. And it was deserted. What could I do to jam the controls of the ships that would not register on the recording instruments of the other ships? I gazed at the mass of controls. Levers and wheels galore. In the center of the compartment, on a massively braced universal joint mounting, was what I took for the repellor generator. A dial on it glowed and a faint hum came from within its shielding metallic case. But I had no time to study it.

Above all else, I was afraid that some automatic telephone apparatus existed in the room, through which I might be heard on the other ships. The risk of trying to jam the controls was too great. I abandoned the idea and withdrew softly. I would have to take a chance that there was no other member of the crew aboard.

I ran back to the entrance compartment. Wilma still lay where she had slumped down. I heard the voices of the Hans approaching. It was time to act. The next few seconds would tell whether the ships in the air would try or be able to melt us into nothingness. I spoke.

"Are you boys all ready?" I asked, creeping to a position opposite the door and drawing my hand-gun.

Again there was a chorus of assent.

"Then on the count of three, shoot up those repellor rays – all of them – and for God's sake, don't miss." And I counted.

I think my "three" was a bit weak. I know it took all the courage I had to utter it.

For an agonizing instant nothing happened, except that the landing party from the ship strolled into my range of vision.

Then startled, they turned their eyes upward. For an instant they stood frozen with horror at whatever they saw.

One hurled his knife at me. It grazed my cheek. Then a couple of them made a break for the doorway. The rest followed. But I fired pointblank with my hand-gun, pressing the button as fast as I could and aiming at their feet to make sure my explosive rockets would make contact and do their work.

The detonations of my rockets were deafening. The spot on which the Hans stood flashed into a blinding glare. Then there was nothing there except their torn and mutilated corpses. They had been fairly bunched, and I got them all.

I ran to the door, expecting any instant to be hurled into infinity by the sweep of a disintegrator ray.

Some eighth of a mile away I saw one of the ships crash to earth. A disintegrator ray came into my line of vision, wavered uncertainly for a moment and then began to sweep directly toward the ship in which I stood. But it never reached it. Suddenly, like a light switched off, it shot to one side, and a moment later another vast hulk crashed to earth. I looked out, then stepped out on the ground.

The only Han ships in the sky were two of the scouts to the south which were hanging perpendicularly, and sagging slowly down. The others must have crashed down while I was deafened by the sound of the explosion of my own rockets.

Somebody hit the other repellor ray of one of the two remaining ships and it fell out of sight beyond a hilltop. The other, farther away, drifted down diagonally, its disintegrator ray playing viciously over the ground below it.

I shouted with exultation and relief.

"Take back the command, Boss!" I yelled.

His commands, sending out jumpers in pursuit of the descending ship, rang in my ears, but I paid no attention to them. I leaped back into the compartment of the Han ship and knelt beside my Wilma. Her padded helmet had absorbed much of the blow, I thought; otherwise, her skull might have been fractured.

"Oh, my head!" she groaned, coming to as I lifted her gently in my arms and strode out in the open with her. "We must have won, dearest, did we?"

"We most certainly did," I reassured her. "All but one crashed and that one is drifting down toward the south; we've captured this one we're in intact. There was only one member of the crew aboard when we dove in."

Less than an hour afterward the Big Boss ordered the outfit to tune in ultrophones on three-twenty-three to pick up a translated broadcast of the Han intelligence office in Nu-yok from the Susquanna station. It was in the form of a public warning and news item, and read as follows:

This is Public Intelligence Office, Nu-yok, broadcasting warning to navigators of private ships, and news of public interest. The squadron of seven ships, which left Nu-yok this morning to investigate the recent destruction of the GK-984 in the Wyoming Valley, has been destroyed by a series of mysterious explosions similar to those which wrecked the GK-984.

The phones, viewplates, and all other signaling devices of five of the seven ships ceased operating suddenly at approximately the same moment, about seven-four-nine." (According to the Han system of reckoning time, seven and forty-nine one hundredths after midnight.) *"After violent disturbances the location finders went out of operation. Electroactivity registers applied to the territory of the Wyoming Valley remain dead.*

The Intelligence Office has no indication of the kind of disaster which overtook the squadron except certain evidences of explosive phenomena similar to those in the case of the GK-984, which recently went dead while beaming the valley in a systematic effort to wipe out the works and camps of the tribesmen. The Office considers, as obvious, the deduction that the tribesmen have developed a new, and as yet undetermined, technique of attack on airships, and has recommended to the Heaven-Born that immediate and unlimited authority be given the Navigation Intelligence Division to make an investigation of this technique and develop a defense against it.

In the meantime it urges that private navigators avoid this territory in particular, and in general hold as closely as possible to the official inter-city routes, which now are being patrolled by the entire force of the Military Office, which is beaming the routes generously to a width of ten miles. The Military Office reports that it is at present considering no retaliatory raids against the tribesmen. With the Navigation Intelligence Division, it holds that unless further evidence of the nature of the disaster is developed in the near future, the public interest will be better served, and at smaller cost of life, by a scientific research than by attempts at retaliation, which may bring destruction on all ships engaging therein. So unless further evidence actually is developed, or the Heaven-Born orders to the contrary, the Military will hold to a defensive policy.

Unofficial intimations from Lo-Tan are to the effect that the Heaven-Council has the matter under consideration.

The Navigation Intelligence Office permits the broadcast of the following condensation of its detailed observations:

The squadron proceeded to a position above the Wyoming Valley where the wreck of the GK-984 was known to be, from the record of its location finder before it went dead recently. There the bottom projectoscope relays of all ships registered the wreck of the GK-984. Teleprojectoscope views of the wreck and the bowl of the valley showed no evidence of the presence of tribesmen. Neither ship registers nor base registers showed any indication of electroactivity except from the squadron itself. On orders from the Base Squadron Commander, the LD-248, LK-745 and LG-25 scouted southward at 3,000 feet. The GK-43, GK-981 and GK-220 stood above at 2,500 feet, and the GK-18 landed to permit personal inspection of the wreck by the science committee. The party debarked, leaving one man on board in the control cabin. He set all projectoscopes at universal focus except RB-3, (this meant the third projectoscope from the bow of the ship, on the right-hand side of the lower deck) with which he followed the landing group as it walked around the wreck.

The first abnormal phenomenon recorded by any of the instruments at Base was that relayed automatically from projectoscope RB-4 of the GK-18, which as the party disappeared from view in back of the wreck, recorded two green missiles of roughly cylindrical shape, projected from the wreckage into the landing compartment of the ship. At such close range these were not clearly defined, owing to the universal focus at which the projectoscope was set. The Base Captain of GK-18 at once ordered the man in the control room to investigate, and saw him leave the control room in compliance with this order. An instant later confused sounds reached the control-room electrophone, such as might be made by a man falling heavily, and footsteps reapproached the control room, a figure entering and leaving the control room hurriedly. The Base Captain now believes, and the stills of the photorecord support his belief, that this was not the crew member who had been left in the control room.

Before the Base Captain could speak to him he left the room, nor was any response given to the attention signal the Captain flashed throughout the ship.

At this point projectoscope RB-3 of the ship now out of focus control, dimly showed the landing party walking back toward the ship. RB-4 showed it more clearly. Then on both these instruments, a number of blinding explosives in rapid succession were seen and the electrophone relays registered terrific concussions; the ship's electronic apparatus and projectoscopes apparatus went dead.

Reports of the other ships' Base Observers and Executives, backed by the photorecords, show the explosions as taking place in the midst of the landing party as it returned, evidently unsuspicious, to the ship. Then in rapid succession they indicate that terrific explosions occurred inside and outside the three ships standing above close to their rep ray generators, and all signals from these ships thereupon went dead.

Of the three ships scouting to the south, the LD-248 suffered an identical fate, at the same moment. Its records add little to the knowledge of the disaster. But with the LK-745 and the LG-25 it was different.

The relay instruments of the LK-745 indicated the destruction by an explosion of the rear rep ray generator, and that the ship hung stern down for a short space, swinging like a pendulum. The forward viewplates and indicators did not cease functioning, but their records are chaotic, except for one projectoscope still, which shows the bowl of the valley, and the GK-981 falling, but no visible evidence of tribesmen. The control-room viewplate is also a chaotic record of the ship's crew tumbling and falling to the rear wall. Then the forward rep ray generator exploded, and all signals went dead.

The fate of the LG-25 was somewhat similar, except that this ship hung nose down, and drifted on the wind southward as it slowly descended out of control.

As its control room was shattered, verbal report from its Action Captain was precluded. The record of the interior rear viewplate shows members of the crew climbing toward the rear rep ray generator in an attempt to establish manual control of it, and increase the lift. The projectoscope relays, swinging in wide arcs, recorded little of value except at the ends of their swings. One of these, from a machine which happened to be set in telescopic focus, shows several views of great value in picturing the falls of the other ships, and all of the rear projectoscope records enable the reconstruction in detail of the pendulum and torsional movements of the ship, and its sag toward the earth. But none of the views showing the forest below contain any indication of tribesmen's presence. A final explosion put this ship out of commission at a height of 1,000 feet, and at a point four miles S. by E. of the center of the valley.

The message ended with a repetition of the warning to other airmen to avoid the valley.

Chapter VII
Incredible Treason

AFTER RECEIVING this report, and reassurances of support from the Big Bosses of the neighboring Gangs, Hart determined to reestablish the Wyoming Valley community.

A careful survey of the territory showed that it was only the northern sections and slopes that had been 'beamed' by the first Han ship.

The synthetic-fabrics plant had been partially wiped out, though the lower levels underground had not been reached by the dis ray. The forest screen above it, however, had been annihilated, and it was determined to abandon it, after removing all usable machinery and evidences of the processes that might be of interest to the Han scientists, should they return to the valley in the future.

The ammunition plant, and the rocket-ship plant, which had just been about to start operation at the time of the raid, were intact, as were the other important plants.

Hart brought the Camboss up from the Susquanna Works, and laid out new camp locations, scattering them farther to the south, and avoiding ground which had been seared by the Han beams and the immediate locations of the Han wrecks.

During this period, a sharp check was kept upon Han messages, for the phone plant had been one of the first to be put in operation, and when it became evident that the Hans did not intend any immediate reprisals, the entire membership of the community was summoned back, and normal life was resumed.

Wilma and I had been married the day after the destruction of the ships, and spent this intervening period in a delightful honeymoon, camping high in the mountains. On our return, we had a camp of our own, of course. We were assigned to location 1017. And as might be expected, we had a great deal of banter over which one of us was Camp Boss. The title stood after my name on the Big Boss's records, and those of the Big Camboss, of course, but Wilma airily held that this meant nothing at all – and generally succeeded in making me admit it whenever she chose.

I found myself a full-fledged member of the Gang now, for I had elected to search no farther for a permanent alliance, much as I would have liked to familiarize myself with this 25th Century life in other sections of the country. The Wyomings had a high morale, and had prospered under the rule of Big Boss Hart for many years. But many of the gangs, I found, were badly organized, lacked strong hands in authority, and were rife with intrigue. On the whole, I thought I would be wise to stay with a group which had already proved its friendliness, and in which I seemed to have prospects of advancement. Under these modern social and economic conditions, the kind of individual freedom to which I had been accustomed in the 20th Century was impossible. I would have been as much of a nonentity in every phase of human relationship by attempting to avoid alliances, as any man of the 20th Century would have been politically, who aligned himself with no political party.

This entire modern life, it appeared to me, judging from my ancient viewpoint, was organized along what I called 'political' lines. And in this connection, it amused me to notice how universal had become the use of the word 'boss.' The leader, the person in charge or authority over anything, was a 'boss.' There was as little formality in his relations with his followers as there was in the case of the 20th Century political boss, and the same high respect paid him by his followers as well as the same high consideration by him of their interests. He was just as much of an autocrat, and just as much dependent upon the general popularity of his actions for the ability to maintain his autocracy.

The sub-boss who could not command the loyalty of his followers was as quickly deposed, either by them or by his superiors, as the ancient ward leader of the 20th Century who lost control of his votes.

As society was organized in the 20th Century, I do not believe the system could have worked in anything but politics. I tremble to think what would have happened, had the attempt been made to handle the A.E.F. this way during the First World War, instead of by that rigid military discipline and complete assumption of the individual as a mere standardized cog in the machine.

But owing to the centuries of desperate suffering the people had endured at the hands of the Hans, there developed a spirit of self-sacrifice and consideration for the common good that made the scheme applicable and efficient in all forms of human co-operation.

I have a little heresy about all this, however. My associates regard the thought with as much horror as many worthy people of the 20th Century felt in regard to any heretical suggestion that the original outline of government as laid down in the First Constitution did not apply as well to 20th Century conditions as to those of the early 19th.

In later years, I felt that there was a certain softening of moral fiber among the people, since the Hans had been finally destroyed with all their works; and Americans have developed a new luxury economy. I have seen signs of the reawakening of greed, of selfishness. The eternal cycle seems to be at work. I fear that slowly, though surely, private wealth is reappearing, codes of inflexibility are developing; they will be followed by corruption, degradation; and in the end some cataclysmic event will end this era and usher in a new one.

All this, however, is wandering afar from my story, which concerns our early battles against the Hans, and not our more modern problems of self-control.

Our victory over the seven Han ships had set the country ablaze. The secret had been carefully communicated to the other gangs, and the country was agog from one end to the other. There was feverish activity in the ammunition plants, and the hunting of stray Han ships became an enthusiastic sport. The results were disastrous to our hereditary enemies.

From the Pacific Coast came the report of a great transpacific liner of 75,000 tons 'lift' being brought to earth from a position of invisibility above the clouds. A dozen Sacramentos had caught the hazy outlines of its rep rays approaching them, head-on, in the twilight, like ghostly pillars reaching into the sky. They had fired rockets into it with ease, whereas they would have had difficulty in hitting it if it had been moving at right angles to their position. They got one rep ray. The other was not strong enough to hold it up. It floated to earth, nose down, and since it was unarmed and unarmored, they had no difficulty in shooting it to pieces and massacring its crew and passengers. It seemed barbarous to me. But then I did not have centuries of bitter persecution in my blood.

From the Jersey Beaches we received news of the destruction of a Nu-yok-a-lan-a liner. The Sand-snipers, practically invisible in their sand-colored clothing, and half buried along the beaches, lay in wait for days, risking the play of dis beams along the route, and finally registering four hits within a week. The Hans discontinued their service along this route, and as evidence that they were badly shaken by our success, sent no raiders down the Beaches.

It was a few weeks later that Big Boss Hart sent for me.

"Tony," he said, "There are two things I want to talk to you about. One of them will become public property in a few days, I think. We aren't going to get any more Han ships by shooting up their repellor rays unless we use much larger rockets. They are wise to us now. They're putting armor of great thickness in the hulls of their ships below the rep ray machines. Near Bah-flo this morning a party of Eries shot one without success. The explosions staggered her, but did not penetrate. As near as we can gather from their reports, their laboratories have developed a new alloy of great tensile strength and elasticity which nevertheless lets the rep rays through like a sieve. Our reports indicate that the Eries' rockets bounced off harmlessly. Most of the party was wiped out as the dis rays went into action on them.

"This is going to mean real business for all of the gangs before long. The Big Bosses have just held a national ultrophone council. It was decided that America must organize on a national basis. The first move is to develop sectional organization by Zones. I have been made Superboss of the Mid-Atlantic Zone.

"We're in for it now. The Hans are sure to launch reprisal expeditions. If we're to save the race we must keep them away from our camps and plants. I'm thinking of developing a permanent field force, along the lines of the regular armies of the 20th Century you told me about. Its business will be twofold: to carry the warfare as much as possible to the Hans, and to serve as a decoy, to beep their attention from our plants. I'm going to need your help in this.

"The other thing I wanted to talk to you about is this: Amazing and impossible as it seems, there is a group, or perhaps an entire gang, somewhere among us, that is betraying us to the Hans. It may be the Bad Bloods, or it may be one of those gangs who live near one of the Han cities. You know, a hundred and fifteen or twenty years ago there were certain of these people's ancestors who actually degraded themselves by mating with the Hans, sometimes even serving them as slaves, in the days before they brought all their service machinery to perfection.

"There is such a gang, called the Nagras, up near Bah-flo, and another in Mid-Jersey that men call the Pineys. But I hardly suspect the Pineys. There is little intelligence among them. They wouldn't have the information to give the Hans, nor would they be capable of imparting it. They're absolute savages."

"Just what evidence is there that anybody has been clearing information to the Hans?" I asked.

"Well," he replied, "first of all there was that raid upon us. That first Han ship knew the location of our plants exactly. You remember it floated directly into position above the valley and began a systematic beaming. Then, the Hans quite obviously have learned that we are picking up their electrophone waves, for they've gone back to their old, but extremely accurate, system of directional control. But we've been getting them for the past week by installing automatic re-broadcast units along the scar paths. This is what the Americans called those strips of country directly under the regular ship routes of the Hans, who as a matter of precaution frequently blasted them with their dis beams to prevent the growth of foliage which might give shelter to the Americans. But they've been beaming those paths so hard, it looks as though they even had information of this strategy. And in addition, they've been using code. Finally, we've picked up three of their messages in which they discuss, with some nervousness, the existence of our 'mysterious' ultrophone."

"But they still have no knowledge of the nature and control of ultronic activity?" I asked.

"No," said the Big Boss thoughtfully, "they don't seem to have a bit of information about it."

"Then it's quite clear," I ventured, "that whoever is 'clearing' us to them is doing it piecemeal. It sounds like a bit of occasional barter, rather than an out-and-out alliance. They're holding back as much information as possible for future bartering, perhaps."

"Yes," Hart said, "and it isn't information the Hans are giving in return, but some form of goods, or privilege. The trick would be to locate the goods. I guess I'll have to make a personal trip around among the Big Bosses."

Chapter VIII
The Han City

THIS CONVERSATION set me thinking. All of the Han electrophone inter-communication had been an open record to the Americans for a good many years, and the Hans were just finding it out. For centuries they had not regarded us as any sort of a menace. Unquestionably it had never occurred to them to secrete their own records. Somewhere in Nu-yok or Bah-flo, or possibly in Lo-Tan itself, the record of this traitorous transaction would be more or less openly filed. If we could only get at it! I wondered if a raid might not be possible.

Bill Hearn and I talked it over with our Han-affairs Boss and his experts. There ensued several days of research, in which the Han records of the entire decade were scanned and analyzed. In the end they picked out a mass of detail, and fitted it together into a very definite picture of the great central filing office of the Hans in Nu-yok, where the entire mass of official records was kept, constantly available for instant projectoscoping to any of the city's offices, and of the system by which the information was filed.

The attempt began to look feasible, though Hart instantly turned the idea down when I first presented it to him. It was unthinkable, he said. Sheer suicide. But in the end I persuaded him.

"I will need," I said, "Blash, who is thoroughly familiar with the Han library system; Bert Gaunt, who for years has specialized on their military offices; Bill Barker, the ray specialist, and the best swooper pilot we have." Swoopers are one-man and two-man ships, developed by the Americans, with skeleton backbones of inertron (during the war painted green for invisibility against the green forests below) and 'bellies' of clear ultron.

"That will be Mort Gibbons," said Hart. "We've only got three swoopers left, Tony, but I'll risk one of them if you and the others will voluntarily risk your existences. But mind, I won't urge or order one of you to go. I'll spread the word to every Plant Boss at once to give you anything and everything you need in the way of equipment."

When I told Wilma of the plan, I expected her to raise violent and tearful objections, but she didn't. She was made of far sterner stuff than the women of the 20th Century. Not that she couldn't weep as copiously or be just as whimsical on occasion; but she wouldn't weep for the same reasons.

She just gave me an unfathomable look, in which there seemed to be a bit of pride, and asked eagerly for the details. I confess I was somewhat disappointed that she could so courageously risk my loss, even though I was amazed at her fortitude. But later I was to learn how little I knew her then.

We were ready to slide off at dawn the next morning. I had kissed Wilma good-bye at our camp, and after a final conference over our plans, we boarded our craft and gently glided away over the tree tops on a course, which, after crossing three routes of the Han ships, would take us out over the Atlantic, off the Jersey coast, whence we would come up on Nu-yok from the ocean.

Twice we had to nose down and lie motionless on the ground near a route while Han ships passed. Those were tense moments. Had the green back of our ship been observed, we would have been disintegrated in a second. But it wasn't.

Once over the water, however, we climbed in a great spiral, ten miles in diameter, until our altimeter registered ten miles. Here Gibbons shut off his rocket motor, and we floated, far above the level of the Atlantic liners, whose course was well to the north of us anyhow, and waited for nightfall.

Then Gibbons turned from his control long enough to grin at me.

"I have a surprise for you, Tony," he said, throwing back the lid of what I had supposed was a big supply case. And with a sigh of relief, Wilma stepped out of the case.

"If you 'go into zero' (a common expression of the day for being annihilated by the disintegrator ray), you don't think I'm going to let you go alone, do you, Tony? I couldn't believe my ears last night when you spoke of going without me, until I realized that you are still five hundred years behind the times in lots of ways. Don't you know, dear heart, that you offered me the greatest insult a husband could give a wife? You didn't, of course."

The others, it seemed, had all been in on the secret, and now they would have kidded me unmercifully, except that Wilma's eyes blazed dangerously.

At nightfall, we maneuvered to a position directly above the city. This took some time and calculation on the part of Bill Barker, who explained to me that he had to determine our point by ultronic bearings. The slightest resort to an electronic instrument, he feared, might be detected by our enemies' locators. In fact, we did not dare bring our swooper any lower than five miles for fear that its capacity might be reflected in their instruments.

Finally, however, he succeeded in locating above the central tower of the city.

"If my calculations are as much as ten feet off," he remarked with confidence, "I'll eat the tower. Now the rest is up to you, Mort. See what you can do to hold her steady. No – here, watch this indicator – the red beam, not the green one. See – if you keep it exactly centered on the needle, you're OK. The width of the beam represents seventeen feet. The tower platform is fifty feet square, so we've got a good margin to work on."

For several moments we watched as Gibbons bent over his levers, constantly adjusting them with deft touches of his fingers. After a bit of wavering, the beam remained centered on the needle.

"Now," I said, "let's drop."

I opened the trap and looked down, but quickly shut it again when I felt the air rushing out of the ship into the rarefied atmosphere in a torrent. Gibbons literally yelled a protest from his instrument board.

"I forgot," I mumbled. "Silly of me. Of course, we'll have to drop out of compartment."

The compartment, to which I referred, was similar to those in some of the 20th Century submarines. We all entered it. There was barely room for us to stand, shoulder to shoulder. With some struggles, we got into our special air helmets and adjusted the pressure. At our signal, Gibbons exhausted the air in the compartment, pumping it into the body of the ship, and as the little signal light flashed, Wilma threw open the hatch.

Setting the ultron-wire reel, I climbed through, and began to slide down gently.

We all had our belts on, of course, adjusted to a weight balance of but a few ounces. And the five-mile reel of ultron wire that was to be our guide, was of gossamer fineness, though, anyway, I believe it would have lifted the full weight of the five of us, so strong and tough was this invisible metal. As an extra precaution, since the wire was of the purest metal, and therefore totally invisible, even in daylight, we all had our belts hooked on small rings that slid down the wire.

I went down with the end of the wire. Wilma followed a few feet above me, then Barker, Gaunt and Blash. Gibbons, of course, stayed behind to hold the ship in position and control the paying out of the line. We all had our ultrophones in place inside our air helmets, and so could converse with one another and with Gibbons. But at Wilma's suggestion, although we would have liked to let the Big Boss listen in, we kept them adjusted to short-range work, for fear that those who had been clearing with the Hans, and against whom we were on a raid for evidence, might also pick up our conversation. We had no fear that the Hans would hear us. In fact, we had the added advantage that, even after we landed, we could converse freely without danger of their hearing our voices through our air helmets.

For a while I could see nothing below but utter darkness. Then I realized, from the feel of the air as much as from anything, that we were sinking through a cloud layer. We passed through two more cloud layers before anything was visible to us.

Then there came under my gaze, about two miles below, one of the most beautiful sights I have ever seen; the soft, yet brilliant, radiance of the great Han city of Nu-yok. Every foot of its structural members seemed to glow with a wonderful incandescence, tower piled up on tower, and all built on the vast base-mass of the city, which, so I had been told, sheered upward from the surface of the rivers to a height of 728 levels.

The city, I noticed with some surprise, did not cover anything like the same area as the New York of the 20th Century. It occupied, as a matter of fact, only the lower half of Manhattan Island, with one section straddling the East River, and spreading out sufficiently over what once had been Brooklyn, to provide berths for the great liners and other air craft.

Straight beneath my feet was a tiny dark patch. It seemed the only spot in the entire city that was not aflame with radiance. This was the central tower, in the top floors of which were housed the vast library of record files and the main projectoscope plant.

"You can shoot the wire now," I ultrophoned Gibbons, and let go the little weighted knob. It dropped like a plummet, and we followed with considerable speed, but braking our descent with gloved hands sufficiently to see whether the knob, on which a faint light glowed as a signal for ourselves, might be observed by any Han guard or night prowler. Apparently it was not, and we again shot down with accelerated speed.

We landed on the roof of the tower without any mishap, and fortunately for our plan, in darkness. Since there was nothing above it on which it would have been worth while to shed illumination, or from which there was any need to observe it, the Hans had neglected to light the tower roof, or indeed to occupy it at all. This was the reason we had selected it as our landing place.

As soon as Gibbons had our word, he extinguished the knob light, and the knob, as well as the wire, became totally invisible. At our ultrophoned word, he would light it again.

"No gun play now," I warned. "Swords only, and then only if absolutely necessary."

Closely bunched, and treading as lightly as only inertron-belted people could, we made our way cautiously through a door and down an inclined plane to the floor below, where Gaunt and Blash assured us the military offices were located.

Twice Barker cautioned us to stop as we were about to pass in front of mirror-like 'windows' in the passage wall, and flattening ourselves to the floor, we crawled past them.

"Projectoscopes," he said. "Probably on automatic record only, at this time of night. Still, we don't want to leave any records for them to study after we're gone."

"Were you ever here before?" I asked.

"No," he replied, "but I haven't been studying their electrophone communications for seven years without being able to recognize these machines when I run across them."

Chapter IX
The Fight in the Tower

SO FAR we had not laid eyes on a Han. The tower seemed deserted. Blash and Gaunt, however, assured me that there would be at least one man on "duty" in the military offices, though he would probably be asleep, and two or three in the library proper and the projectoscope plant.

"We've got to put them out of commission," I said. "Did you bring the 'dope' cans, Wilma?"

"Yes," she said, "two for each. Here," and she distributed them.

We were now two levels below the roof, and at the point where we were to separate.

I did not want to let Wilma out of my sight, but it was necessary.

According to our plan, Barker was to make his way to the projectoscope plant, Blash and I to the library, and Wilma and Gaunt to the military office.

Blash and I traversed a long corridor, and paused at the great arched doorway of the library. Cautiously we peered in. Seated at three great switchboards were library operatives. Occasionally one of them would reach lazily for a lever, or sleepily push a button, as little numbered lights winked on and off. They were answering calls for electrograph and viewplate records on all sorts of subjects from all sections of the city.

I apprised my companions of the situation.

"Better wait a bit," Blash added. "The calls will lessen shortly."

Wilma reported an officer in the military office sound asleep.

"Give him the can, then," I said.

Barker was to do nothing more than keep watch in the projectoscope plant, and a few moments later he reported himself well concealed, with a splendid view of the floor.

"I think we can take a chance now," Blash said to me, and at my nod, he opened the lid of his dope can. Of course, the fumes did not affect us, through our helmets. They were absolutely without odor or visibility, and in a few seconds the librarians were unconscious. We stepped into the room.

There ensued considerable cautious observation and experiment on the part of Gaunt, working from the military office, and Blash in the library; while Wilma and I, with drawn swords and sharply attuned microphones, stood guard, and occasionally patrolled nearby corridors.

"I hear something approaching," Wilma said after a bit, with excitement in her voice. "It's a soft, gliding sound."

"That's an elevator somewhere," Barker cut in from the projectoscope floor. "Can you locate it? I can't hear it."

"It's to the east of me," she replied.

"And to my west," said I, faintly catching it. "It's between us, Wilma, and nearer you than me. Be careful. Have you got any information yet, Blash and Gaunt?"

"Getting it now," one of them replied. "Give us two minutes more."

"Keep at it then," I said. "We'll guard."

The soft, gliding sound ceased.

"I think it's very close to me," Wilma almost whispered. "Come closer, Tony. I have a feeling something is going to happen. I've never known my nerves to get taut like this without reason."

In some alarm, I launched myself down the corridor in a great leap toward the intersection whence I knew I could see her.

In the middle of my leap my ultrophone registered her gasp of alarm. The next instant I glided to a stop at the intersection to see Wilma backing toward the door of the military office, her sword red with blood, and an inert form on the corridor floor. Two other Hans were circling to either side of her with wicked-looking knives, while a third evidently a high officer, judging by the resplendence of his garb tugged desperately to get an electrophone instrument out of a bulky pocket. If he ever gave the alarm, there was no telling what might happen to us.

I was at least seventy feet away, but I crouched low and sprang with every bit of strength in my legs. It would be more correct to say that I dived, for I reached the fellow head on, with no attempt to draw my legs beneath me.

Some instinct must have warned him, for he turned suddenly as I hurtled close to him. But by this time I had sunk close to the floor, and had stiffened myself rigidly, lest a dragging knee or foot might just prevent my reaching him. I brought my blade upward and over. It was a vicious slash that laid him open, bisecting him from groin to chin, and his dead body toppled down on me, as I slid to a tangled stop.

The other two startled, turned. Wilma leaped at one and struck him down with a side slash. I looked up at this instant, and the dazed fear on his face at the length of her leap registered vividly. The Hans knew nothing of our inertron belts, it seemed, and these leaps and dives of ours filled them with terror.

As I rose to my feet, a gory mess, Wilma, with a poise and speed which I found time to admire even in this crisis, again leaped. This time she dove head first as I had done and, with a beautifully executed thrust, ran the last Han through the throat.

Uncertainly, she scrambled to her feet, staggered queerly, and then sank gently prone on the corridor. She had fainted.

At this juncture, Blash and Gaunt reported with elation that they had the record we wanted.

"Back to the roof, everybody!" I ordered, as I picked Wilma up in my arms. With her inertron belt, she felt as light as a feather.

Gaunt joined me at once from the military office, and at the intersection of the corridor, we came upon Blash waiting for us. Barker, however, was not in evidence.

"Where are you, Barker?" I called.

"Go ahead," he replied. "I'll be with you on the roof at once."

We came out in the open without any further mishap, and I instructed Gibbons in the ship to light the knob on the end of the ultron wire. It flashed dully a few feet away from us. Just how he had maneuvered the ship to keep our end of the line in position, without its swinging in a tremendous arc, I have never been able to understand. Had not the night been an unusually still one, he could not have checked the initial pendulum-like movements. As it was, there was considerable air current at certain of the levels, and in different directions too. But Gibbons was an expert of rare ability and sensitivity in the handling of a rocket ship, and he managed, with the aid of his delicate instruments, to sense the drifts almost before they affected the fine ultron wire, and to neutralize them with little shifts in the position of the ship.

Blash and Gaunt fastened their rings to the wire, and I hooked my own and Wilma's on, too. But on looking around, I found Barker was still missing.

"Barker, come!" I called. "We're waiting."

"Coming!" he replied, and indeed, at that instant, his figure appeared up the ramp. He chuckled as he fastened his ring to the wire, and said something about a little surprise he had left for the Hans.

"Don't reel in the wire more than a few hundred feet," I instructed Gibbons. "It will take too long to wind it in. We'll float up, and when we're aboard, we can drop it."

In order to float up, we had to dispense with a pound or two of weight apiece. We hurled our swords from us, and kicked off our shoes as Gibbons reeled up the line a bit, and then letting go of the wire, began to hum upward on our rings with increasing velocity.

The rush of air brought Wilma to, and I hastily explained to her that we had been successful. Receding far below us now, I could see our dully shining knob swinging to and fro in an ever widening arc, as it crossed and recrossed the black square of the tower roof. As an extra precaution, I ordered Gibbons to shut off the light, and to show one from the belly of the ship, for so great was our speed now, that I began to fear we would have difficulty in checking ourselves. We were literally falling upward, and with terrific acceleration.

Fortunately, we had several minutes in which to solve this difficulty, which none of us, strangely enough, had foreseen. It was Gibbons who found the answer.

"You'll be all right if all of you grab the wire tight when I give the word," he said. "First I'll start reeling it in at full speed. You won't get much of a jar, and then I'll decrease its speed again gradually, and its weight will hold you back. Are you ready? One – two – three!"

We all grabbed tightly with our gloved hands as he gave the word. We must have been rising a good bit faster than he figured, however, for it wrenched our arms considerably, and the maneuver set up a sickening pendulum motion.

For a while all we could do was swing there in an arc that may have been a quarter of a mile across, about three and a half miles above the city, and still more than a mile from our ship.

Gibbons skilfully took up the slack as our momentum pulled up the line. Then at last we had ourselves under control again, and continued our upward journey, checking our speed somewhat with our gloves.

There was not one of us who did not breathe a big sigh of relief when we scrambled through the hatch safely into the ship again, cast off the ultron line and slammed the trap shut.

Little realizing that we had a still more terrible experience to go through, we discussed the information Blash and Gaunt had between them extracted from the Han records, and the advisability of ultrophoning Hart at once.

Chapter X
The Walls of Hell

THE TRAITORS WERE, it seemed, a degenerate gang of Americans, located a few miles north of Nu-yok on the wooded banks of the Hudson, the Sinsings. They had exchanged scraps of information to the Hans in return for several old repellor-ray machines, and the privilege of tuning in on the Han electronic power broadcast for their operation, provided their ships agreed to subject themselves to the orders of the Han traffic office, while aloft.

The rest wanted to ultrophone their news at once, since there was always danger that we might never get back to the gang with it.

I objected, however. The Sinsings would be likely to pick up our message. Even if we used the directional projector, they might have scouts out to the west and south in the big inter-gang stretches of country. They would flee to Nu-yok and escape the punishment they merited. It seemed to be vitally important that they should not, for the sake of example to other weak groups among the American gangs, as well as to prevent a crisis in which they might clear more vital information to the enemy.

"Out to sea again," I ordered Gibbons. "They'll be less likely to look for us in that direction."

"Easy, Boss, easy," he replied. "Wait until we get up a mile or two more. They must have discovered evidences of our raid by now, and their dis-ray wall may go in operation any moment."

Even as he spoke, the ship lurched downward and to one side.

"There it is!" he shouted. "Hang on, everybody. We're going to nose straight up!" And he flipped the rocket-motor control wide open.

Looking through one of the rear ports, I could see a nebulous, luminous ring, and on all sides the atmosphere took on a faint iridescence.

We were almost over the destructive range of the disintegrator-ray wall, a hollow cylinder of annihilation shooting upward from a solid ring of generators surrounding the city. It was the main defense system of the Hans, which had never been used except in periodic tests. They may or may not have suspected that an American rocket ship was within the cylinder; probably they had turned on their generators more as a precaution to prevent any reaching a position above the city.

But even at our present great height, we were in great danger. It was a question how much we might have been harmed by the rays themselves, for their effective range was not much more than seven or eight miles. The greater danger lay in the terrific downward rush of air within the cylinder to replace that which was being burned into nothingness by the continual play of the disintegrators. The air fell into the cylinder with the force of a gale. It would be rushing toward the wall from the outside with terrific force also, but, naturally, the effect was intensified on the interior.

Our ship vibrated and trembled. We had only one chance of escape – to fight our way well above the current. To drift down with it meant ultimately, and inevitably, to be sucked into the destruction wall at some lower level.

But very gradually and jerkily our upward movement, as shown on the indicators, began to increase, and after an hour of desperate struggle we were free of the maelstrom and into the rarefied upper levels. The terror beneath us was now invisible through several layers of cloud formations.

Gibbons brought the ship back to an even keel, and drove her eastward into one of the most brilliantly gorgeous sunrises I have ever seen.

We described a great circle to the south and west, in a long easy dive, for he had cut out his rocket motors to save them as much as possible. We had drawn terrifically on their fuel reserves in our battle with the elements. For the moment, the atmosphere below cleared, and we could see the Jersey coast far beneath, like a great map.

"We're not through yet," remarked Gibbons suddenly, pointing at his periscope, and adjusting it to telescopic focus. "A Han ship, and a 'drop ship' at that – and he's seen us. If he whips that beam of his on us, we're done."

I gazed, fascinated, at the viewplate. What I saw was a cigar-shaped ship not dissimilar to our own in design, and from the proportional size of its ports, of about the same size as our swoopers. We learned later that they carried crews, for the most part of not more than three or four men. They had streamline hulls and tails that embodied universal-jointed double fish-tail rudders. In operation they rose to great heights on their powerful repellor rays, then gathered speed either by a straight nose dive, or an inclined dive in which they sometimes used the repellor ray slanted at a sharp angle. He was already above us, though several miles to the north. He could, of course, try to get on our tail and 'spear' us with his beam as he dropped at us from a great height.

Suddenly his beam blazed forth in a blinding flash, whipping downward slowly to our right. He went through a peculiar corkscrew-like evolution, evidently maneuvering to bring his beam to bear on us with a spiral motion.

Gibbons instantly sent our ship into a series of evolutions that must have looked like those of a frightened hen. Alternately, he used the forward and the reverse rocket blasts, and in varying degree. We fluttered, we shot suddenly to right and left, and dropped like a plummet in uncertain movements. But all the time the Han scout dropped toward us, determinedly whipping the air around us with his beam. Once it sliced across beneath us, not more than a hundred feet, and we dropped with a jar into the pocket formed by the destruction of the air.

He had dropped to within a mile of us, and was coming with the speed of a projectile, when the end came. Gibbons always swore it was sheer luck. Maybe it was, but I like pilots who are lucky that way.

In the midst of a dizzy, fluttering maneuver of our own, with the Han ship enlarging to our gaze with terrifying rapidity, and its beam slowly slicing toward us in what looked like certain destruction within the second, I saw Gibbons' fingers flick at the lever of his rocket gun and a split second later the Han ship flew apart like a clay pigeon.

We staggered, and fluttered crazily for several moments while Gibbons struggled to bring our ship into balance, and a section of about four square feet in the side of the ship near the stern slowly crumbled like rusted metal. His beam actually had touched us, but our explosive rocket had got him a thousandth of a second sooner.

Part of our rudder had been annihilated, and our motor damaged. But we were able to swoop gently back across Jersey, fortunately crossing the ship lanes without sighting any more Han craft, and finally settling to rest in the little glade beneath the trees, near Hart's camp.

Chapter XI
The New Boss

WE HAD ultrophoned our arrival and the Big Boss himself, surrounded by the Council, was on hand to welcome us and learn our news. In turn we were informed that during the night a band of raiding Bad Bloods, disguised under the insignia of the Altoonas, a gang some distance to the west of us, had destroyed several of our camps before our people had rallied and driven them off. Their purpose, evidently, had been to embroil us with the Altoonas, but fortunately, one of our exchanges recognized the Bad Blood leader, who had been slain.

The Big Boss had mobilized the full raiding force of the Gang, and was on the point of heading an expedition for the extermination of the Bad Bloods.

I looked around the grim circle of the sub-bosses, and realized the fate of America, at this moment, lay in their hands. Their temper demanded the immediate expenditure of our full effort in revenging ourselves for this raid. But the strategic exigencies, to my mind, quite clearly demanded the instant and absolute extermination of the Sinsings. It might be only a matter of hours, for all we knew, before these degraded people would barter clues to the American ultronic secrets to the Hans.

"How large a force have we?" I asked Hart.

"Every man and maid who can be spared," he replied. "That gives us seven hundred married and unmarried men, and three hundred girls, more than the entire Bad Blood Gang. Everyone is equipped with belts, ultrophones, rocket guns and swords, and all fighting mad."

I meditated how I might put the matter to these determined men, and was vaguely conscious that they were awaiting my words.

Finally I began to speak. I do not remember to this day just what I said. I talked calmly, with due regard for their passion, but with deep conviction. I went over the information we had collected, point by point, building my case logically, and painting a lurid picture of the danger impending in that half-alliance between the Sinsings and the Hans of Nu-yok.

I became impassioned, culminating, I believe, with a vow to proceed single-handed against the hereditary enemies of our race, "if the Wyomings were blindly set on placing a gang feud ahead of honor and duty and the hopes of all America."

As I concluded, a great calm came over me, as of one detached. I had felt much the same way during several crises in the First World War. I gazed from face to face, striving to read their expressions, and in a mood to make good my threat without any further heroics, if the decision was against me.

But it was Hart who sensed the temper of the Council more quickly than I did, and looked beyond it into the future.

He arose from the tree trunk on which he had been sitting.

"That settles it," he said, looking around the ring. "I have felt this thing coming on for some time now. I'm sure the Council agrees with me that there is among us a man more capable than I, to boss the Wyoming Gang, despite his handicap of having had all too short a time in which to familiarize himself with our modern ways and facilities. Whatever I can do to support his effective leadership, at any cost, I pledge myself to do."

As he concluded, he advanced to where I stood, and taking from his head the green-crested helmet that constituted his badge of office, to my surprise he placed it in my mechanically extended hand.

The roar of approval that went up from the Council members left me dazed. Somebody ultrophoned the news to the rest of the Gang, and even though the earflaps of my helmet were turned up, I could hear the cheers with which my invisible followers greeted me, from near and distant hillsides, camps and plants.

My first move was to make sure that the Phone Boss, in communicating this news to the members of the Gang, had not re-broadcast my talk nor mentioned my plan of shifting the attack from the Bad Bloods to the Sinsings. I was relieved by his assurance that he had not, for it would have wrecked the whole plan. Everything depended upon our ability to surprise the Sinsings.

So I pledged the Council and my companions to secrecy, and allowed it to be believed that we were about to take to the air and the trees against the Bad Bloods.

That outfit must have been badly scared, the way they were 'burning' the ether with ultrophone alibis and propaganda for the benefit of the more distant gangs. It was their old game, and the only method by which they had avoided extermination long ago from their immediate neighbors – these appeals to the spirit of American brotherhood, addressed to gangs too far away to have had the sort of experience with them that had fallen to our lot.

I chuckled. Here was another good reason for the shift in my plans. Were we actually to undertake the exterminations of the Bad Bloods at once, it would have been a hard job to convince some of the gangs that we had not been precipitate and unjustified. Jealousies and prejudices existed. There were gangs which would give the benefit of the doubt to the Bad Bloods, rather than to ourselves, and the issue was now hopelessly beclouded with the clever lies that were being broadcast in an unceasing stream.

But the extermination of the Sinsings would be another thing. In the first place, there would be no warning of our action until it was all over, I hoped. In the second place, we would have indisputable proof, in the form of their rep ray ships and other paraphernalia, of their traffic with the Hans; and the state of American prejudice, at the time of which I write held trafficking with the Hans a far more heinous thing than even a vicious gang feud.

I called an executive session of the Council at once. I wanted to inventory our military resources.

I created a new office on the spot, that of 'Control Boss,' and appointed Ned Garlin to the post, turning over his former responsibility as Plants Boss to his assistant. I needed someone, I felt, to tie in the records of the various functional activities of the campaign, and take over from me the task of keeping the records of them up to the minute.

I received reports from the bosses of the ultrophone unit, and those of food, transportation, fighting gear, chemistry, electronic activity and electrophone intelligence, ultroscopes, air patrol and contact guard.

My ideas for the campaign, of course, were somewhat tinged with my 20th Century experience, and I found myself faced with the task of working out a staff organization that was a composite of the best and most easily applied principles of business and military efficiency, as I knew them from the viewpoint of immediate practicality.

What I wanted was an organization that would be specialized, functionally, not as that indicated above, but from the angles of: intelligence as to the Sinsings' activities; intelligence as to Han activities; perfection of communication with my own units; co-operation of field command; and perfect mobilization of emergency supplies and resources.

It took several hours of hard work with the Council to map out the plan. First we assigned functional experts and equipment to each 'Division' in accordance with its needs. Then these in turn were reassigned by the new Division Bosses to the Field Commands as needed, or as Independent or Headquarters Units. The two intelligence divisions were named the White and the Yellow, indicating that one specialized on the American enemy and the other on the Mongolians.

The division in charge of our own communications, the assignment of ultrophone frequencies and strengths, and the maintenance of operators and equipment, I called 'Communications.'

I named Bill Hearn to the post of Field Boss, in charge of the main or undetached fighting units, and to the Resources Division, I assigned all responsibility for what few aircraft we had; and all transportation and supply problems, I assigned to 'Resources.' The functional bosses stayed with this division.

We finally completed our organization with the assignment of liaison representatives among the various divisions as needed.

Thus I had a 'Headquarters Staff' composed of the Division Bosses who reported directly to Ned Garlin as Control Boss, or to Wilma as my personal assistant. And each of the Division Bosses had a small staff of his own.

In the final summing up of our personnel and resources, I found we had roughly a thousand 'troops,' of whom some three hundred and fifty were, in what I called the Service Divisions, the rest being in Bill Hearn's Field Division. This latter number, however, was cut down somewhat by the assignment of numerous small units to detached service. Altogether, the actual available fighting force, I figured, would number about five hundred, by the time we actually went into action.

We had only six small swoopers, but I had an ingenious plan in my mind, as the result of our little raid on Nu-yok, that would make this sufficient, since the reserves of inertron blocks were larger than I expected to find them. The Resources Division, by packing its supply cases a bit tight, or by slipping in extra blocks of inertron, was able to reduce each to a weight of a few ounces. These easily could be floated and towed by the swoopers in any quantity. Hitched to ultron lines, it would be a virtual impossibility for them to break loose.

The entire personnel, of course, was supplied with jumpers, and if each man and girl was careful to adjust balances properly, the entire number could also be towed along through the air, grasping wires of ultron, swinging below the swoopers, or stringing out behind them.

There would be nothing tiring about this, because the strain would be no greater than that of carrying a one or two pound weight in the hand, except for air friction at high speeds. But to make doubly sure that we should lose none of our personnel, I gave strict orders that the belts and tow lines should be equipped with rings and hooks.

So great was the efficiency of the fundamental organization and discipline of the Gang, that we got under way at nightfall.

One by one the swoopers eased into the air, each followed by its long train or 'kite-tail' of humanity and supply cases hanging lightly from its tow line. For convenience, the tow lines were made of an alloy of ultron which, unlike the metal itself, is visible.

At first these 'tails' hung downward, but as the ships swung into formation and headed eastward toward the Bad Blood territory, gathering speed, they began to string out behind. And swinging low from each ship on heavily weighted lines, ultroscope, ultrophone, and straight-vision observers keenly scanned the countryside, while intelligence men in the swoopers above bent over their instrument boards and viewplates.

Leaving Control Boss Ned Garlin temporarily in charge of affairs, Wilma and I dropped a weighted line from our ship, and slid down about half way to the under lookouts, that is to say, about a thousand feet. The sensation of floating swiftly through the air like this, in the absolute security of one's confidence in the inertron belt, was one of never-ending delight to me.

We reascended into the swooper as the expedition approached the territory of the Bad Bloods, and directed the preparations for the bombardment. It was part of my plan to appear to carry out the attack as originally planned.

About fifteen miles from their camps our ships came to a halt and maintained their positions for a while with the idling blasts of their rocket motors, to give the ultroscope operators a chance to make a thorough examination of the territory below us, for it was very important that this next step in our program should be carried out with all secrecy.

At length they reported the ground below us entirely clear of any appearance of human occupation, and a gun unit of long-range specialists was lowered with a dozen rocket guns, equipped with special automatic devices that the Resources Division had developed at my request, a few hours before our departure. These were aiming and timing devices. After calculating the range, elevation and rocket charges carefully, the guns were left, concealed in a ravine, and the men were hauled up into the ship again. At the predetermined hour, those unmanned rocket guns would begin automatically to bombard the Bad Bloods' hillsides, shifting their aim and elevation slightly with each shot, as did many of our artillery pieces in the First World War.

In the meantime, we turned south about twenty miles, and grounded, waiting for the bombardment to begin before we attempted to sneak across the Han ship lane. I was relying for security on the distraction that the bombardment might furnish the Han observers.

It was tense work waiting, but the affair went through as planned, our squadron drifting across the route high enough to enable the ships' tails of troops and supply cases to clear the ground.

In crossing the second ship route, out along the Beaches of Jersey, we were not so successful in escaping observation. A Han ship came speeding along at a very low elevation. We caught it on our electronic location and direction finders, and also located it with our ultroscopes, but it came so fast and so low that I thought it best to remain where we had grounded the second time, and lie quiet, rather than get under way and cross in front of it.

The point was this. While the Hans had no such devices as our ultroscopes, with which we could see in the dark (within certain limitations of course), and their electronic instruments would be virtually useless in uncovering our presence, since all but natural electronic activities were carefully eliminated from our apparatus, except electrophone receivers (which are not easily spotted), the Hans did have some very highly sensitive sound devices which operated with great efficiency in calm weather, so far as sounds emanating from the air were concerned. But the "ground roar" greatly confused their use of these instruments in the location of specific sounds floating up from the surface of the earth.

This ship must have caught some slight noise of ours, however, in its sensitive instruments, for we heard its electronic devices go into play, and picked up the routine report of the noise to its Base Ship Commander. But from the nature of the conversation, I judged they had not identified it, and were, in fact, more curious about the detonations they were picking up now from the Bad Blood lands some sixty miles or so to the west.

Immediately after this ship had shot by, we took the air again, and following much the same route that I had taken the previous night, climbed in a long semi-circle out over the ocean, swung toward the north and finally the west. We set our course, however, for the Sinsings' land north of Nu-yok, instead of for the city itself.

Chapter XII
The Finger of Doom

AS WE CROSSED the Hudson River, a few miles north of the city, we dropped several units of the Yellow Intelligence Division, with full instrumental equipment. Their apparatus cases were nicely balanced at only a few ounces weight each, and the men used their chute capes to ease their drops.

We recrossed the river a little distance above and began dropping White Intelligence units and a few long and short range gun units. Then we held our position until we began to get reports. Gradually we ringed the territory of the Sinsings, our observation units working busily and patiently at their locators and scopes, both aloft and aground, until Garlin finally turned to me with the remark: "The map circle is complete now, Boss. We've got clear locations all the way around them."

"Let me see it," I replied, and studied the illuminated viewplate map, with its little overlapping circles of light that indicated spots proved clear of the enemy by ultroscopic observation.

I nodded to Bill Hearn. "Go ahead now, Hearn," I said, "and place your barrage men."

He spoke into his ultrophone, and three of the ships began to glide in a wide ring around the enemy territory. Every few seconds, at the word from his Unit Boss, a gunner would drop off the wire, and slipping the clasp of his chute cape, drift down into the darkness below.

Bill formed two lines, parallel to and facing the river, and enclosing the entire territory of the enemy between them. Above and below, straddling the river, were two defensive lines. These latter were merely to hold their positions. The others were to close in toward each other, pushing a high-explosive barrage five miles ahead of them. When the two barrages met, both lines were to switch to short-vision-range barrage and continue to close in on any of the enemy who might have drifted through the previous curtain of fire.

In the meantime Bill kept his reserves, a picked corps of a hundred men (the same that had accompanied Hart and myself in our fight with the Han squadron) in the air, divided about equally among the 'kite-tails' of four ships.

A final roll call, by units, companies, divisions and functions, established the fact that all our forces were in position. No Han activity was reported, and no Han broadcasts indicated any suspicion of our expedition. Nor was there any indication that the Sinsings had any knowledge of the fate in store for them. The idling of rep ray generators was reported from the center of their camp, obviously those of the ships the Hans had given them – the price of their treason to their race.

Again I gave the word, and Hearn passed on the order to his subordinates.

Far below us, and several miles to the right and left, the two barrage lines made their appearance. From the great height to which we had risen, they appeared like lines of brilliant, winking lights, and the detonations were muffled by the distances into a sort of rumbling, distant thunder. Hearn and his assistants were very busy: measuring, calculating, and snapping out ultrophone orders to unit commanders that resulted in the straightening of lines and the closing of gaps in the barrage.

The White Division Boss reported the utmost confusion in the Sinsing organization. They were, as might be expected, an inefficient, loosely disciplined gang, and repeated broadcasts for help to neighboring gangs. Ignoring the fact that the Mongolians had not used explosives for many generations, they nevertheless jumped at the conclusion that they were being raided by the Hans. Their frantic broadcasts persisted in this thought, despite the nervous electrophonic inquiries of the Hans themselves, to whom the sound of the battle was evidently audible, and who were trying to locate the trouble.

At this point, the swooper I had sent south toward the city went into action as a diversion, to keep the Hans at home. Its "kite-tail" loaded with long-range gunners, using the most highly explosive rockets we had, hung invisible in the darkness of the sky and bombarded the city from a distance of about five miles. With an entire city to shoot at, and the object of creating as much commotion therein as possible, regardless of actual damage, the gunners had no difficulty in hitting the mark. I could see the glow of the city and the stabbing flashes of exploding rockets. In the end, the Hans, uncertain as to what was going on, fell back on a defensive policy, and shot their 'hell cylinder,' or wall of upturned disintegrator rays into operation. That, of course, ended our bombardment of them. The rays were a perfect defense, disintegrating our rockets as they were reached.

If they had not sent out ships before turning on the rays, and if they had none within sufficient radius already in the air, all would be well.

I queried Garlin on this, but he assured me Yellow Intelligence reported no indications of Han ships nearer than 800 miles. This would probably give us a free hand for a while, since most of their instruments recorded only imperfectly or not at all, through the death wall.

Requisitioning one of the viewplates of the headquarters ship, and the services of an expert operator, I instructed him to focus on our lines below. I wanted a close-up of the men in action.

He began to manipulate his controls and chaotic shadows moved rapidly across the plate, fading in and out of focus, until he reached an adjustment that gave me a picture of the forest floor, apparently 100 feet wide, with the intervening branches and foliage of the trees appearing like shadows that melted into reality a few feet above the ground.

I watched one man setting up his long-gun with skillful speed. His lips pursed slightly as though he were whistling, as he adjusted the tall tripod on which the long tube was balanced. Swiftly he twirled the knobs controlling the aim and elevation of his piece. Then, lifting a belt of ammunition from the big box, which itself looked heavy enough to break down the spindly tripod, he inserted the end of it in the lock of his tube and touched the proper combination of buttons.

Then he stepped aside, and occupied himself with peering carefully through the trees ahead. Not even a tremor shook the tube, but I knew that at intervals of something less than a second, it was discharging small projectiles which, traveling under their own continuously reduced power, were arching into the air, to fall precisely five miles ahead and explode with the force of eight-inch shells, such as we used in the First World War.

Another gunner, fifty feet to the right of him, waved a hand and called out something to him. Then, picking up his own tube and tripod, he gauged the distance between the trees ahead of him, and the height of their lowest branches, and bending forward a bit, flexed his muscles and leaped lightly, some twenty-five feet. Another leap took him another twenty feet or so, where he began to set up his piece.

I ordered my observer then to switch to the barrage itself. He got a close focus on it, but this showed little except a continuous series of blinding flashes, which, from the viewplate, lit up the entire interior of the ship. An eight-hundred-foot focus proved better. I had thought that some of our French and American artillery of the 20th Century had achieved the ultimate in mathematical precision of fire, but I had never seen anything to equal the accuracy of that line of terrific explosions as it moved steadily forward, mowing down trees as a scythe cuts grass (or used to 500 years ago), literally churning up the earth and the splintered, blasted remains of the forest giants, to a depth of from ten to twenty feet.

By now the two curtains of fire were nearing each other, lines of vibrant, shimmering, continuous, brilliant destruction, inevitably squeezing the panic-stricken Sinsings between them.

Even as I watched, a group of them, who had been making a futile effort to get their three rep ray machines into the air, abandoned their efforts, and rushed forth into the milling mob.

I queried the Control Boss sharply on the futility of this attempt of theirs, and learned that the Hans, apparently in doubt as to what was going on, had continued to 'play safe,' and broken off their power broadcast, after ordering all their own ships east of the Alleghenies to the ground, for fear these ships they had traded to the Sinsings might be used against them.

Again I turned to my viewplate, which was still focussed on the central section of the Sinsing works. The confusion of the traitors was entirely that of fear, for our barrage had not yet reached them.

Some of them set up their long-guns and fired at random over the barrage line, then gave it up. They realized that they had no target to shoot at, no way of knowing whether our gunners were a few hundred feet or several miles beyond it.

Their ultrophone men, of whom they did not have many, stood around in tense attitudes, their helmet phones strapped around their ears, nervously fingering the tuning controls at their belts. Unquestionably they must have located some of our frequencies, and overheard many of our reports and orders. But they were confused and disorganized. If they had an Ultrophone Boss they evidently were not reporting to him in an organized way.

They were beginning to draw back now before our advancing fire. With intermittent desperation, they began to shoot over our barrage again, and the explosions of their rockets flashed at widely scattered points beyond. A few took distance 'pot shots.'

Oddly enough it was our own forces that suffered the first casualties in the battle. Some of these distance shots by chance registered hits, while our men were under strict orders not to exceed their barrage distances.

Seen upon the ultroscope viewplate, the battle looked as though it were being fought in daylight, perhaps on a cloudy day, while the explosions of the rockets appeared as flashes of extra brilliance.

The two barrage lines were not more than five hundred feet apart when the Sinsings resorted to tactics we had not foreseen. We noticed first that they began to lighten themselves by throwing away extra equipment. A few of them in their excitement threw away too much, and shot suddenly into the air. Then a scattering few floated up gently, followed by increasing numbers, while still others, preserving a weight balance, jumped toward the closing barrages and leaped high, hoping to clear them. Some succeeded. We saw others blown about like leaves in a windstorm, to crumple and drift slowly down, or else to fall into the barrage, their belts blown from their bodies.

However, it was not part of our plan to allow a single one of them to escape and find his way to the Hans. I quickly passed the word to Bill Hearn to have the alternate men in his line raise their barrages and heard him bark out a mathematical formula to the Unit Bosses.

We backed off our ships as the explosions climbed into the air in stagger formation until they reached a height of three miles. I don't believe any of the Sinsings who tried to float away to freedom succeeded.

But we did know later, that a few who leaped the barrage got away and ultimately reached Nu-yok.

It was those who managed to jump the barrage who gave us the most trouble. With half of our long-guns turned aloft, I foresaw we would not have enough to establish successive ground barrages and so ordered the barrage back two miles, from which positions our 'curtains' began to close in again, this time, however, gauged to explode, not on contact, but thirty feet in the air. This left little chance for the Sinsings to leap either over or under it.

Gradually, the two barrages approached each other until they finally met, and in the grey dawn the battle ended.

Our own casualties amounted to forty-seven men in the ground forces, eighteen of whom had been slain in hand to hand fighting with the few of the enemy who managed to reach our lines, and sixty-two in the crew and 'kite-tail' force of swooper No. 4, which had been located by one of the enemy's ultroscopes and brought down with long-gun fire.

Since nearly every member of the Sinsing Gang had, so far as we knew, been killed, we considered the raid a great success.

It had, however, a far greater significance than this. To all of us who took part in the expedition, the effectiveness of our barrage tactics definitely established a confidence in our ability to overcome the Hans.

As I pointed out to Wilma: "It has been my belief all along, dear, that the American explosive rocket is a far more efficient weapon than the disintegrator ray of the Hans, once we can train all our gangs to use it systematically and in co-ordinated fashion. As a weapon in the hands of a single individual, shooting at a mark in direct line of vision, the rocket-gun is inferior in destructive power to the dis ray, except as its range may be a little greater. The trouble is that to date it has been used only as we used our rifles and shot guns in the 20th Century.

The possibilities of its use as artillery, in laying barrages that advance along the ground, or climb into the air, are tremendous.

"The dis ray inevitably reveals its source of emanation. The rocket gun does not. The dis ray can reach its target only in a straight line. The rocket may be made to travel in an arc, over intervening obstacles, to an unseen target.

"Nor must we forget that our ultronists now are promising us a perfect shield against the dis ray in inertron."

"I tremble though, Tony dear, when I think of the horrors that are ahead of us. The Hans are clever. They will develop defenses against our new tactics. And they are sure to mass against us not only the full force of their power in America, but the united forces of the World Empire. They are a cowardly race in one sense, but clever as the very Devils in Hell, and inheritors of a calm, ruthless, vicious persistency."

"Nevertheless," I prophesied, "the Finger of Doom points squarely at them today, and unless you and I are killed in the struggle, we shall live to see America blast the Yellow Blight from the face of the Earth."

A Tale of the Ragged Mountains

Edgar Allan Poe

DURING the fall of the year 1827, while residing near Charlottesville, Virginia, I casually made the acquaintance of Mr. Augustus Bedloe. This young gentleman was remarkable in every respect, and excited in me a profound interest and curiosity. I found it impossible to comprehend him either in his moral or his physical relations. Of his family I could obtain no satisfactory account. Whence he came, I never ascertained. Even about his age – although I call him a young gentleman – there was something which perplexed me in no little degree. He certainly seemed young – and he made a point of speaking about his youth – yet there were moments when I should have had little trouble in imagining him a hundred years of age. But in no regard was he more peculiar than in his personal appearance. He was singularly tall and thin. He stooped much. His limbs were exceedingly long and emaciated. His forehead was broad and low. His complexion was absolutely bloodless. His mouth was large and flexible, and his teeth were more wildly uneven, although sound, than I had ever before seen teeth in a human head. The expression of his smile, however, was by no means unpleasing, as might be supposed; but it had no variation whatever. It was one of profound melancholy – of a phaseless and unceasing gloom. His eyes were abnormally large, and round like those of a cat. The pupils, too, upon any accession or diminution of light, underwent contraction or dilation, just such as is observed in the feline tribe. In moments of excitement the orbs grew bright to a degree almost inconceivable; seeming to emit luminous rays, not of a reflected but of an intrinsic lustre, as does a candle or the sun; yet their ordinary condition was so totally vapid, filmy, and dull as to convey the idea of the eyes of a long-interred corpse.

These peculiarities of person appeared to cause him much annoyance, and he was continually alluding to them in a sort of half explanatory, half apologetic strain, which, when I first heard it, impressed me very painfully. I soon, however, grew accustomed to it, and my uneasiness wore off. It seemed to be his design rather to insinuate than directly to assert that, physically, he had not always been what he was – that a long series of neuralgic attacks had reduced him from a condition of more than usual personal beauty, to that which I saw. For many years past he had been attended by a physician, named Templeton – an old gentleman, perhaps seventy years of age – whom he had first encountered at Saratoga, and from whose attention, while there, he either received, or fancied that he received, great benefit. The result was that Bedloe, who was wealthy, had made an arrangement with Dr. Templeton, by which the latter, in consideration of a liberal annual allowance, had consented to devote his time and medical experience exclusively to the care of the invalid.

Doctor Templeton had been a traveller in his younger days, and at Paris had become a convert, in great measure, to the doctrines of Mesmer. It was altogether by means of magnetic remedies that he had succeeded in alleviating the acute pains of his patient; and this success had very naturally inspired the latter with a certain degree of confidence in the opinions from which the remedies had been educed. The Doctor, however, like all enthusiasts, had struggled hard to make a thorough convert of his pupil, and finally so far gained his point as to induce the sufferer to submit to numerous experiments. By a frequent repetition of these, a result had arisen, which of late days has become so common as to attract little or no attention, but which, at the period of which I write, had very rarely been known in America. I mean to say, that between Doctor Templeton and Bedloe there had grown up, little by little, a very distinct and strongly marked rapport, or magnetic relation. I am not prepared to assert, however, that this rapport extended beyond the limits of the simple sleep-producing power, but this power itself had attained great intensity. At the first attempt to induce the magnetic somnolency, the mesmerist entirely failed. In the fifth or sixth he succeeded very partially, and after long continued effort. Only at the twelfth was the triumph complete. After this the will of the patient succumbed rapidly to that of the physician, so that, when I first became acquainted with the two, sleep was brought about almost instantaneously by the mere volition of the operator, even when the invalid was unaware of his presence. It is only now, in the year 1845, when similar miracles are witnessed daily by thousands, that I dare venture to record this apparent impossibility as a matter of serious fact.

The temperature of Bedloe was, in the highest degree sensitive, excitable, enthusiastic. His imagination was singularly vigorous and creative; and no doubt it derived additional force from the habitual use of morphine, which he swallowed in great quantity, and without which he would have found it impossible to exist. It was his practice to take a very large dose of it immediately after breakfast each morning – or, rather, immediately after a cup of strong coffee, for he ate nothing in the forenoon – and then set forth alone, or attended only by a dog, upon a long ramble among the chain of wild and dreary hills that lie westward and southward of Charlottesville, and are there dignified by the title of the Ragged Mountains.

Upon a dim, warm, misty day, toward the close of November, and during the strange interregnum of the seasons which in America is termed the Indian Summer, Mr. Bedloe departed as usual for the hills. The day passed, and still he did not return.

About eight o'clock at night, having become seriously alarmed at his protracted absence, we were about setting out in search of him, when he unexpectedly made his appearance, in health no worse than usual, and in rather more than ordinary spirits. The account which he gave of his expedition, and of the events which had detained him, was a singular one indeed.

"You will remember," said he, "that it was about nine in the morning when I left Charlottesville. I bent my steps immediately to the mountains, and, about ten, entered a gorge which was entirely new to me. I followed the windings of this pass with much interest. The scenery which presented itself on all sides, although scarcely entitled to be called grand, had about it an indescribable and to me a delicious aspect of dreary desolation. The solitude seemed absolutely virgin. I could not help believing that the green sods and the gray rocks upon which I trod had been trodden never before by the foot of a human being. So entirely secluded, and in fact inaccessible, except through a series of accidents, is the entrance of the ravine, that it is by no means impossible that I was indeed the first adventurer – the very first and sole adventurer who had ever penetrated its recesses.

"The thick and peculiar mist, or smoke, which distinguishes the Indian Summer, and which now hung heavily over all objects, served, no doubt, to deepen the vague impressions which these objects created. So dense was this pleasant fog that I could at no time see more than a dozen yards of the path before me. This path was excessively sinuous, and as the sun could not be seen, I soon lost all idea of the direction in which I journeyed. In the meantime the morphine had its customary effect – that of enduing all the external world with an intensity of interest. In the quivering of a leaf – in the hue of a blade of grass – in the shape of a trefoil – in the humming of a bee – in the gleaming of a dew-drop – in the breathing of the wind – in the faint odors that came from the forest – there came a whole universe of suggestion – a gay and motley train of rhapsodical and immethodical thought.

"Busied in this, I walked on for several hours, during which the mist deepened around me to so great an extent that at length I was reduced to an absolute groping of the way. And now an indescribable uneasiness possessed me – a species of nervous hesitation and tremor. I feared to tread, lest I should be precipitated into some abyss. I remembered, too, strange stories told about these Ragged Hills, and of the uncouth and fierce races of men who tenanted their groves and caverns. A thousand vague fancies oppressed and disconcerted me – fancies the more distressing because vague. Very suddenly my attention was arrested by the loud beating of a drum.

"My amazement was, of course, extreme. A drum in these hills was a thing unknown. I could not have been more surprised at the sound of the trump of the Archangel. But a new and still more astounding source of interest and perplexity arose. There came a wild rattling or jingling sound, as if of a bunch of large keys, and upon the instant a dusky-visaged and half-naked man rushed past me with a shriek. He came so close to my person that I felt his hot breath upon my face. He bore in one hand an instrument composed of an assemblage of steel rings, and shook them vigorously as he ran. Scarcely had he disappeared in the mist before, panting after him, with open mouth and glaring eyes, there darted a huge beast. I could not be mistaken in its character. It was a hyena.

"The sight of this monster rather relieved than heightened my terrors – for I now made sure that I dreamed, and endeavored to arouse myself to waking consciousness. I stepped boldly and briskly forward. I rubbed my eyes. I called aloud. I pinched my limbs. A small spring of water presented itself to my view, and here, stooping, I bathed my hands and my head and neck. This seemed to dissipate the equivocal sensations which had hitherto annoyed me. I arose, as I thought, a new man, and proceeded steadily and complacently on my unknown way.

"At length, quite overcome by exertion, and by a certain oppressive closeness of the atmosphere, I seated myself beneath a tree. Presently there came a feeble gleam of sunshine, and the shadow of the leaves of the tree fell faintly but definitely upon the grass. At this shadow I gazed wonderingly for many minutes. Its character stupefied me with astonishment. I looked upward. The tree was a palm.

"I now arose hurriedly, and in a state of fearful agitation – for the fancy that I dreamed would serve me no longer. I saw – I felt that I had perfect command of my senses – and these senses now brought to my soul a world of novel and singular sensation. The heat became all at once intolerable. A strange odor loaded the breeze. A low, continuous murmur, like that arising from a full, but gently flowing river, came to my ears, intermingled with the peculiar hum of multitudinous human voices.

"While I listened in an extremity of astonishment which I need not attempt to describe, a strong and brief gust of wind bore off the incumbent fog as if by the wand of an enchanter.

"I found myself at the foot of a high mountain, and looking down into a vast plain, through which wound a majestic river. On the margin of this river stood an Eastern-looking city, such as we read of in the Arabian Tales, but of a character even more singular than any there described. From my position, which was far above the level of the town, I could perceive its every nook and corner, as if delineated on a map. The streets seemed innumerable, and crossed each other irregularly in all directions, but were rather long winding alleys than streets, and absolutely swarmed with inhabitants. The houses were wildly picturesque. On every hand was a wilderness of balconies, of verandas, of minarets, of shrines, and fantastically carved oriels. Bazaars abounded; and in these were displayed rich wares in infinite variety and profusion – silks, muslins, the most dazzling cutlery, the most magnificent jewels and gems. Besides these things, were seen, on all sides, banners and palanquins, litters with stately dames close veiled, elephants gorgeously caparisoned, idols grotesquely hewn, drums, banners, and gongs, spears, silver and gilded maces. And amid the crowd, and the clamor, and the general intricacy and confusion – amid the million of black and yellow men, turbaned and robed, and of flowing beard, there roamed a countless multitude of holy filleted bulls, while vast legions of the filthy but sacred ape clambered, chattering and shrieking, about the cornices of the mosques, or clung to the minarets and oriels. From the swarming streets to the banks of the river, there descended innumerable flights of steps leading to bathing places, while the river itself seemed to force a passage with difficulty through the vast fleets of deeply – burthened ships that far and wide encountered its surface. Beyond the limits of the city arose, in frequent majestic groups, the palm and the cocoa, with other gigantic and weird trees of vast age, and here and there might be seen a field of rice, the thatched hut of a peasant, a tank, a stray temple, a gypsy camp, or a solitary graceful maiden taking her way, with a pitcher upon her head, to the banks of the magnificent river.

"You will say now, of course, that I dreamed; but not so. What I saw – what I heard – what I felt – what I thought – had about it nothing of the unmistakable idiosyncrasy of the dream. All was rigorously self-consistent. At first, doubting that I was really awake, I entered into a series of tests, which soon convinced me that I really was. Now, when one dreams, and, in the dream, suspects that he dreams, the suspicion never fails to confirm itself, and the sleeper is almost immediately aroused. Thus Novalis errs not in saying that 'we are near waking when we dream that we dream.' Had the vision occurred to me as I describe it, without my suspecting it as a dream, then a dream it might absolutely have been, but, occurring as it did, and suspected and tested as it was, I am forced to class it among other phenomena."

"In this I am not sure that you are wrong," observed Dr. Templeton, "but proceed. You arose and descended into the city."

"I arose," continued Bedloe, regarding the Doctor with an air of profound astonishment "I arose, as you say, and descended into the city. On my way I fell in with an immense populace, crowding through every avenue, all in the same direction, and exhibiting in every action the wildest excitement. Very suddenly, and by some inconceivable impulse, I became intensely imbued with personal interest in what was going on. I seemed to feel that I had an important part to play, without exactly understanding what it was. Against the crowd which environed me, however, I experienced a deep sentiment of animosity. I shrank from amid them, and, swiftly, by a circuitous path, reached and entered the city. Here all was the wildest tumult and contention. A small party of men, clad in garments half-Indian, half-European, and officered by gentlemen in a uniform partly British, were engaged, at great odds, with the swarming rabble of the alleys. I joined the weaker party, arming myself with the weapons of a fallen officer, and fighting I knew not whom with the nervous ferocity of despair. We were soon overpowered by numbers, and driven to seek refuge in a species of kiosk. Here we barricaded ourselves, and, for the present were secure. From a loop-hole near the summit of the kiosk, I perceived a vast crowd, in furious agitation, surrounding and assaulting a gay palace that overhung the river. Presently, from an upper window of this place, there descended an effeminate-looking person, by means of a string made of the turbans of his attendants. A boat was at hand, in which he escaped to the opposite bank of the river.

"And now a new object took possession of my soul. I spoke a few hurried but energetic words to my companions, and, having succeeded in gaining over a few of them to my purpose made a frantic sally from the kiosk. We rushed amid the crowd that surrounded it. They retreated, at first, before us. They rallied, fought madly, and retreated again. In the mean time we were borne far from the kiosk, and became bewildered and entangled among the narrow streets of tall, overhanging houses, into the recesses of which the sun had never been able to shine. The rabble pressed impetuously upon us, harrassing us with their spears, and overwhelming us with flights of arrows. These latter were very remarkable, and resembled in some respects the writhing creese of the Malay. They were made to imitate the body of a creeping serpent, and were long and black, with a poisoned barb. One of them struck me upon the right temple. I reeled and fell. An instantaneous and dreadful sickness seized me. I struggled – I gasped – I died." "You will hardly persist now," said I smiling, "that the whole of your adventure was not a dream. You are not prepared to maintain that you are dead?"

When I said these words, I of course expected some lively sally from Bedloe in reply, but, to my astonishment, he hesitated, trembled, became fearfully pallid, and remained silent. I looked toward Templeton. He sat erect and rigid in his chair – his teeth chattered, and his eyes were starting from their sockets. "Proceed!" he at length said hoarsely to Bedloe.

"For many minutes," continued the latter, "my sole sentiment – my sole feeling – was that of darkness and nonentity, with the consciousness of death. At length there seemed to pass a violent and sudden shock through my soul, as if of electricity. With it came the sense of elasticity and of light. This latter I felt – not saw. In an instant I seemed to rise from the ground. But I had no bodily, no visible, audible, or palpable presence. The crowd had departed. The tumult had ceased. The city was in comparative repose. Beneath me lay my corpse, with the arrow in my temple, the whole head greatly swollen and disfigured. But all these things I felt – not saw. I took interest in nothing. Even the corpse seemed a matter in which I had no concern. Volition I had none, but appeared to be impelled into motion, and flitted buoyantly out of the city, retracing the circuitous path by which I had entered it. When I had attained that point of the ravine in the mountains at which I had encountered the hyena, I again experienced a shock as of a galvanic battery, the sense of weight, of volition, of substance, returned. I became my original self, and bent my steps eagerly homeward – but the past had not lost the vividness of the real – and not now, even for an instant, can I compel my understanding to regard it as a dream."

"Nor was it," said Templeton, with an air of deep solemnity, "yet it would be difficult to say how otherwise it should be termed. Let us suppose only, that the soul of the man of today is upon the verge of some stupendous psychal discoveries. Let us content ourselves with this supposition. For the rest I have some explanation to make. Here is a watercolor drawing, which I should have shown you before, but which an unaccountable sentiment of horror has hitherto prevented me from showing."

We looked at the picture which he presented. I saw nothing in it of an extraordinary character, but its effect upon Bedloe was prodigious. He nearly fainted as he gazed. And yet it was but a miniature portrait – a miraculously accurate one, to be sure – of his own very remarkable features. At least this was my thought as I regarded it.

"You will perceive," said Templeton, "the date of this picture – it is here, scarcely visible, in this corner – 1780. In this year was the portrait taken. It is the likeness of a dead friend – a Mr. Oldeb – to whom I became much attached at Calcutta, during the administration of Warren Hastings. I was then only twenty years old. When I first saw you, Mr. Bedloe, at Saratoga, it was the miraculous similarity which existed between yourself and the painting which induced me to accost you, to seek your friendship, and to bring about those arrangements which resulted in my becoming your constant companion. In accomplishing this point, I was urged partly, and perhaps principally, by a regretful memory of the deceased, but also, in part, by an uneasy, and not altogether horrorless curiosity respecting yourself.

"In your detail of the vision which presented itself to you amid the hills, you have described, with the minutest accuracy, the Indian city of Benares, upon the Holy River. The riots, the combat, the massacre, were the actual events of the insurrection of Cheyte Sing, which took place in 1780, when Hastings was put in imminent peril of his life. The man escaping by the string of turbans was Cheyte Sing himself. The party in the kiosk were sepoys and British officers, headed by Hastings. Of this party I was one, and did all I could to prevent the rash and fatal sally of the officer who fell, in the crowded alleys, by the poisoned arrow of a Bengalee. That officer was my dearest friend. It was Oldeb. You will perceive by these manuscripts," (here the speaker produced a note-book in which several pages appeared to have been freshly written,) "that at the very period in which you fancied these things amid the hills, I was engaged in detailing them upon paper here at home."

In about a week after this conversation, the following paragraphs appeared in a Charlottesville paper:

"We have the painful duty of announcing the death of Mr. Augustus Bedlo, a gentleman whose amiable manners and many virtues have long endeared him to the citizens of Charlottesville.

"Mr. B., for some years past, has been subject to neuralgia, which has often threatened to terminate fatally; but this can be regarded only as the mediate cause of his decease. The proximate cause was one of especial singularity. In an excursion to the Ragged Mountains, a few days since, a slight cold and fever were contracted, attended with great determination of blood to the head. To relieve this, Dr. Templeton resorted to topical bleeding. Leeches were applied to the temples. In a fearfully brief period the patient died, when it appeared that in the jar containing the leeches, had been introduced, by accident, one of the venomous vermicular sangsues which are now and then found in the neighboring ponds. This creature fastened itself upon a small artery in the right temple. Its close resemblance to the medicinal leech caused the mistake to be overlooked until too late.

"N.B. The poisonous sangsue of Charlottesville may always be distinguished from the medicinal leech by its blackness, and especially by its writhing or vermicular motions, which very nearly resemble those of a snake."

I was speaking with the editor of the paper in question, upon the topic of this remarkable accident, when it occurred to me to ask how it happened that the name of the deceased had been given as Bedlo.

"I presume," I said, "you have authority for this spelling, but I have always supposed the name to be written with an e at the end."

"Authority? – No," he replied. "It is a mere typographical error. The name is Bedlo with an e, all the world over, and I never knew it to be spelt otherwise in my life."

"Then," said I mutteringly, as I turned upon my heel, "then indeed has it come to pass that one truth is stranger than any fiction – for Bedloe, without the e, what is it but Oldeb conversed! And this man tells me that it is a typographical error."

Ouroboros

Chris Reynolds

THE ROOM WAS QUIET. The soft murmur of the hospital corridors outside was muted as the door closed quietly behind Steve.

"You came."

Gloria's voice was deathly quiet, a mere whisper of the voice he had known for decades. Her skin, her beautiful porcelain skin, was grey and stretched tight over her frail body. Her dark wavy hair was gone with the treatments, and the sparkling emerald of her eyes was hidden behind the dark rims of her eye sockets. And yet, she still smiled.

He crossed the room quickly and gently took her hand. It felt like it was made of glass, or twigs, or something else that would break in a stiff breeze.

"As soon as I could, my love. I told the embassy that either they fire me or deport me, either way I wasn't going to miss seeing you before…before…"

She reached up, slowly, and ran a hand down his cheek. Steve lapsed into silence, tears rolling down both of their cheeks.

After a long time, he pulled up a chair and sat next to his wife. They talked, with Steve doing most of it. They reminisced, everything from their first meeting to their wedding to the birth of their children. They laughed, but the tears were never far.

It was well past midnight when Steve realised that he couldn't keep his eyes open any longer. He retrieved a couple of hospital blankets from the cupboard and covered himself in them on the chair. He looked her in the eye for a moment.

"I wish…I wish we had more time. I wish we could do it all again."

She smiled and he closed his eyes.

* * *

Steve felt warm, wet and comfortable. It was sort of like floating in a sleeping bag in the bath. He relaxed a little and tried to stretch, but felt confined by what he was sleeping in. The sensation wasn't unpleasant, and he vaguely realised that he must be in some sort of dream.

There was a gentle pressure on him, like a hand being laid on his back. He snuggled himself back into a ball and drifted back to sleep.

* * *

Steve felt like his head was being squeezed. He tried to open his eyes, but he was pinned in place. His whole body felt like it was being squeezed. He felt like he was being pushed through a hole in a blanket that was far too small for his body.

As severe as the sensation felt, there was no pain to accompany it. He drifted, lapsing in and out of sleep, each time returning to the squeezing feeling. He woke a final time to feel the squeezing sensation travel down his body.

He felt like he was falling, and it was freezing cold. He tried to hug his limbs around his chest, but they were strangely unresponsive. He opened his eyes but was blinded by the bright lights. He frowned and squinted, and heard muffled talking. It slowly resolved itself as his vision adjusted.

He looked up and saw a woman, vaguely familiar and yet not. She was sweating profusely, and her face was screwed up as she cried. Another face appeared next to hers, a man with a confused smile. Again, somehow familiar.

Steve tried to look around and see who else was there, but he wasn't able to move his head. He felt weak, as though he had no energy whatsoever. He flicked his eyes around the room and tried to take it all in, but the shapes were fuzzy.

"Congratulations, Mr. and Mrs. Whitely."

Steve felt a rough blanket wrap around him and he was lifted to the woman's face. She smiled and cried.

"Have you got a name for the certificate?"

Steve realised something. His head started spinning and his stomach tried to do a cartwheel.

"Steven Fitzgerald Whitely."

Oh God.

Steve realised the faces he was staring into. He screamed, and his newborn's voice wailed in his ears. He felt his mother's arms wrap around him, but it didn't help. He screamed to get out of here, to get out of this tiny, weak body, to get back to his Gloria. He screamed until he fell asleep from exhaustion.

* * *

When he awoke, the room was dim. He looked up at where the ceiling of the hospital room should be, and after a moment realised which hospital he was in. He tried to move his arms and legs, but they felt like leaden weights. He couldn't turn his head.

He wanted to scream again, to ask, no, to beg someone to help him get back to where he was supposed to be. But what good would it do? Even if someone were able to understand his baby wail, what could they do?

He closed his eyes slowly and thought of Gloria. He remembered her not as she was when he last saw her in the hospital, but how she was when they first met.

He remembered their eyes locking across the dance floor. He remembered her long dark and curly hair. He remembered her smooth white skin, her playful green eyes. He remembered her cheeky smile and the wave she gave him to come over.

He hadn't even remembered crossing the floor before he was holding her, picking her up in his arms and their lips locked.

Steve felt calmer and closed his eyes again.

* * *

He opened his eyes again to a brightly-lit room. He could hear his parents talking in murmuring voices, and he strained his ears to listen.

It was definitely them. He looked up and tried to discern some detail through his hazy vision. There was a calendar on the wall, and he forced his tiny eyes to focus on it…The date was correct. This was the day after his birthday. These people were his parents. He was the newborn first and only son that had just entered the world.

He cried a little, a sob coming out involuntarily. His father soon came into view and picked him up delicately, cradling him in the crook of his arm and making cooing noises. Steve watched his face carefully – he could barely remember how his dad looked at this age, so different from every other photograph he had seen.

The man was clean-shaven and had close-cropped hair. There were bags under his hazel eyes, but they sparkled at him nonetheless. He smiled constantly.

His father looked away for a moment, and then a bottle appeared in front of him. Steve realised how hungry he was and accepted the teat, sucking greedily at it. He looked along the bottle and at his father's face, and he tried to reach up to touch him. His fingers did find purchase, the tiny grasping movements catching his little finger as it held the bottle. He gripped it as tightly as he could.

Please don't go.

He felt full and released his grip on the bottle. His father took it away and held him close, patting his back to get the wind out.

Please don't leave me.

He felt himself being put down again, laying on his back in the crib. He suppressed the urge to cry. He thought instead of Gloria. His mind's eye lingered over her hair, her skin, her eyes, her smile. His belly felt full, and he was warm. He drifted off to sleep again.

* * *

When he woke again, Steve was cold. He shivered, but he could still feel the blanket wrapped around him. He looked around, but the room was dark.

He tried to remember the rest of his life before this rebirth happened to him. He recalled their house, with the broad steps out the back and the dogs playing under the fruit trees. He remembered the neighbours and their ready smiles. He thought about leaving to go to work each day and how much better he felt when he made it home again.

Wait a minute, he frowned, *where did I work again?*

The memory was misty, incomplete. He couldn't fathom where it was that he worked. He kept running back through his mind, but there was nothing there. He didn't even know what sort of industry he worked in, only that he went there like clockwork each day, dressed in some sort of office attire.

There was a loud knock at the door, causing him to recoil involuntarily. *Where's dad?*

The knock repeated itself, and he heard his mother get out of bed. She wrapped her dressing gown around herself and got up, pausing briefly to look in at him. He couldn't tell if she could see his eyes open in the dark, but she soon left to attend to the door.

There was a gasp from his mother and some muted voices. Steve couldn't make them out properly, but then he heard his mother crying. He tried to sit up, to see what was happening. He tried to speak, to ask for help, but he just made a mewling sound. His mother wailed, and Steve couldn't help himself from copying that same wail. It rose in his throat and echoed off the walls.

The lights came on then, brilliant and white. He was blinded and blinked rapidly. Into his vision came a face, completely unfamiliar to him this time, but she gave him a half-smile before picking him up. She was wearing a police hat, he realised, and looked down to see her blue uniform. She cradled him close and sang gently to him as tears started to run down her cheeks.

Steve saw his mother as they walked near the door, and she was curled up in the foetal position on the floor. A policeman was rubbing her back while she cried uncontrollably.

Where's dad?

"We're so sorry, Mrs. Whitely."

Where is he?

Steve knew, somewhere in his brain, about the car accident. He couldn't remember where he had heard about it, or when, but somehow he knew. He knew the date, so close to his birthday. He struggled to remember his father's name, but it wouldn't come. He cried.

* * *

Steve woke again, this time back in the cot. He tried to make sense of what was going on around him, but he couldn't. He remembered that something had happened to someone… someone he loved, but he couldn't remember who. He was having so much trouble keeping everything in place in his head.

His throat felt parched. He wanted something to drink, and tried to reach out for a bottle, or a cup, or…anything. He felt the tightly-wrapped blanket slowly give way under his pushing hands and feet, and it felt cold.

He couldn't help himself, he cried out. He wailed long and loud, but there was no response from anywhere. He tried to remember his past, his…future? He tried to grasp on to something new to remember, but there was nothing coming to mind.

He was nearly exhausted when he heard the door open and a shaft of light entered the room. There was a shout of surprise before the lights went on properly, the brightness stinging his eyes and making him cry even harder.

He heard multiple people run into the room and call to each other in excitement. It wasn't a good excitement, either. He kept crying.

At some point a woman picked him up and held him close, patting his back. He looked around and caught a glimpse of his mother, her eyes closed and doctors trying to perform CPR on her.

All that Steve could think about as he was walked out of the room and down the corridor was how much this seemed exactly like the stories he had been told…by someone…

He felt like he was slipping away into some sort of abyss. His memories were like smoke, and when he touched them they disappeared. He quickly sought the core of what he remembered…green eyes, long, dark hair, porcelain skin…and that smile.

He tried, but he couldn't remember the name.

* * *

Steven Fitzgerald Whitely pursed his lips and took another swig of his drink. He sat back on his stool and surveyed the heaving, flashing, thumping dance floor. He saw one young woman twirling with wild abandon and smiled almost involuntarily.

He'd always had a soft spot for her type…that long, dark, curly hair, green eyes. He was still looking when she came to a stop and looked back at him.

There was a long moment where Steve did his best impression of a deer in the headlights. She looked back at him with an open question on her face, but then gave him a playful smile. She pointed at him and gave the universal 'come here' signal.

Steve wasn't even aware of crossing the crowded dance floor, but soon he was holding her in his arms and lifting her up. Their lips locked and they both kissed passionately. They tumbled out of the throng and sat at a table.

"Hi…uh, I'm Steve."

She smiled in response.

"I'm Gloria."

He liked it. Right there and then, it was the best name he had ever heard. He gave a half-smile and cocked his head.

"Have we met before?"

The Berlin Doctrine

Anton Rose

September, 1916

SEVERAL HUNDRED MILES outside of the Earth's atmosphere, a man appeared in space. For a fleeting moment, he opened his eyes and looked down. The world glowed with a blue hue, illuminated by the brilliant light of the sun. From that distance, the man could not make out any features. No continents took shape before him, and no man-made structures rose up to his gaze. Instead he saw faint forms, patterns, slowly moving spectres across the surface of the globe. In the brief moments before his bodily functions ceased, before he began his final, silent drift through the blackness of space, the horror on his face turned into a smile. It was the most beautiful thing he had ever seen.

* * *

March, 1922

By the time Walter Schillerman arrived at the scene, a small crowd of locals had already gathered. When they saw him, they waved him over.

"Officer Schillerman, here!"

They stood in the middle of one of Mr. Schneider's fields. Mrs. Schneider had turned away, holding a handkerchief over her mouth. Her eyes met Walter's, and he saw that they were red and sore.

The scene in the field was unlike anything he had ever seen. The body – if it could still be called a body – had been shattered, splintered, ripped into a thousand different pieces. Blood and gore were strewn across a radius of about thirty feet. As Walter explored the area, straining to suppress the desire to vomit, he found bits and pieces he recognised. A shiny white canine here, a thin intestinal tube there.

There was clothing, too. Shreds of a white shirt, now crimson, and a brown jacket with matching trousers. Walter picked up a shoe, battered and ripped. With a cloth from his pocket, he wiped it clean.

He interviewed each person in turn. None of them had anything of significance to tell him, other than Mr. Schneider, who was the first on the scene.

"Did you see what happened?" he asked.

Mr. Schneider nodded.

Walter produced a notebook and pencil from his inside jacket pocket.

"Please explain to me what you saw. Be as detailed as possible."

Mr. Schneider paused, and looked away. After a few seconds, he spoke. "I'm not sure if I can."

"Why not?"

"You'll think I'm crazy."

"I'm not here to make judgments, Mr. Schneider. And I'm asking you as a witness, not as a suspect. Please, go on."

Mr. Schneider shifted back and forth, transferring his weight from one foot to the other, and back. He looked at his wife, who still held holding the handkerchief over her mouth. She nodded at him.

"I was a hundred yards away when it happened," he began, almost at a whisper. "I was walking through the field on my rounds when I heard a noise from above me, a kind of whistling. When I looked up, I saw –"

He paused, looked around in a circle, and then looked up.

"I saw a man. I think it was a man, anyway. I didn't see where he came from, but he was falling. And then he hit the ground. He made the most awful sound. I mean, he fell out of the sky. You think I'm crazy, don't you?"

Walter didn't answer. Instead, he gazed upwards. The sky was mostly covered in clouds, but every few seconds the sun broke through in slats of light. It was almost silent, apart from the gentle sound of the grass, rustling in the breeze. He opened the notebook, and began to write.

* * *

August, 1896

Surrounded and protected by dense shrubbery, a man watched the house. In one hand he held a small pair of binoculars, pressed up against his eyes. In the other, he held a knife.

The house sat at the top of a hillock, one of several perched in the undulating valley, lush green, spotted with patches of bright ferns and small yellow flowers, their petals like tiny dots of paint.

The man sat waiting at the point where the open meadows gave way to woodland, where sparser foliage became dense bunches of deciduous trees. He had been watching the house for six hours. Since dawn he had seen one man leave the building, only to return a quarter of an hour later.

At around eight o'clock – or so he estimated – a woman walked out of the house accompanied by a little boy. They were talking, but they were too far away for the man to hear their conversation. The woman patted the boy on the head, and he skipped away as she returned inside. The boy ran down the hillock, moving parallel with the line of the trees, and jogged across the grass until he reached a larger hill. His pace slowed as he climbed. The man watched him all the way.

The boy reached the top of the hill and dipped down over the other side, out of view of the house. The man stayed hidden for another few minutes, glancing back and forth between the boy and the house. There was no more movement.

Sliding the binoculars into his pocket, he tightened his grip on the knife, but held it behind his back. He swept back his hair and steadied his breathing. Finally, he left cover and approached the hill.

The boy sat on the grass. He held one of the yellow flowers in one hand, and with the other he plucked the petals, one by one, releasing them into the air and watching them flutter on the breeze.

The man walked as quietly as he could, but the boy heard him, and turned.

"Good morning," he said. The boy's German was soft and melodic.

"Hello," the man replied.

For months he had studied old tapes and recordings, memorising the lifts and the lulls, the cadences and rhythms, the regional variations and dialects. In a well-practiced lower Bavarian accent – with just a hint of Austrian – he spoke to the boy. "What is your name?" he asked.

"Ady," the boy said.

"Is that your full name, or your nickname?"

"My nickname."

Ady reached into his pocket and pulled out half a pretzel. It had a rich brown crust, with thick grains of salt embedded in the surface of the dough. He tore it in half again, and held one of the pieces out to the man. "Do you want some?" he said.

The man still held the knife behind his back, but now his grip was loosened, lubricated by sweat. He smiled at the boy, but his heart thumped in his chest. He eased the blade of the knife into the top of his trousers, and passed the bottom of his shirt over the handle. He wiped his hand against the fabric of his shirt, and took the pretzel. It was delicious, but chewing it was difficult; all the moisture had left his mouth.

"Thank you," he said.

"What's your name?" Ady asked.

The man stopped chewing. He clawed at his memory, trying to piece a sentence together. *Mein name ist….*

Ady continued to watch him.

The man stared at the boy's face. His cheeks were plump, with a red sheen like a freshly-picked apple. His eyes were blue and his hair was thick and dark, strands rising up when caught in the breeze.

He tried to think. Words came into his head, but they were the wrong ones. He tried to reassure himself, repeating the familiar phrases.

2: A person is at all times the totality of their past, present and future.

The boy continued to smile at him. The skin on his neck was pale and thin.

Mein name ist….

Open-mouthed, the man dropped the pretzel into the grass. He turned and ran, down the hill and into the trees, until the boy could no longer see him.

* * *

December, 1924

A man sat in the darkness of a prison cell. The cold was manageable, and the discomfort of solid, harsh corners was bearable. But the dampness of the cell crept inside him, worming through his clothes and into his skin, seeping into the marrow of his bones.

The plan had was risky, but it had worked. Right prison, right time. And if the operation up to this point had been about accuracy, he knew that the next stage would be about patience. So he waited.

After a couple of days of being alone, he was thrown into a larger cell, with more people. This exposed him to new dangers, but by keeping to himself he was able to avoid all but the most minor incidents.

In the first few weeks, he saw the mark a number of times. On each occasion, it was only in passing. A sight across the food hall, or walking past each other out in the yard. Always, the mark was accompanied by his loyal associates. He looked slightly different to most of the pictures, but he was still recognisable. The moustache was slightly longer, but it held the same rigid shape. His hair, too, was longer, less slick, but parted in the same way.

Preparation was important. He first procured some cigarettes, and with them he was able to get his hands on a razor blade. It was small, and not as sharp as the ones he had at home, but it would still slice through the skin of a man's neck if applied with the correct pressure.

He decided to do it in the evening, after dinner, when the other men would be lethargic. He wouldn't be able to escape, of course, but that was never an option. Even if he could escape, there was no way of getting home. The only thing that mattered was the job.

He loitered near the mark's cell. He saw him walking down the corridor, flanked by two of his minders. He held the blade concealed in his palm. He avoided eye contact, and when they passed him he took his chance. He leapt forward, aiming to grab him from behind, and to slice through his carotid artery. But as he pushed forward, his foot slipped in a moist spot on the floor; spilt water or drops of sweat. By slipping, he lost the small advantage he had, and seconds later he was being man-handled into one of the cells. They shut the door behind them.

After prying the blade from his fingers, they beat him. They demanded to know where he was from, who had sent him. He refused to answer them. The mark did not partake in the beating. Instead he sat watching, licking his dry lips.

The men stripped off his clothes and pushed him up against the wall.

"Look," said one of them, gesturing at his naked groin. "Jewish."

While they continued to beat him, the man with the moustache sat in the corner of the room, slowly shaking his head.

* * *

September, 1934

A man walked through the dark streets of Nuremberg. He had been there for a week. In that time he had led a kind of shadow existence, doing everything possible to avoid the attention of anyone who could cause a problem, anyone who might scupper his plans.

He had considered a number of different approaches. Of course, it would have been much easier if he had been able to bring equipment with him. A carbon rifle with a 32x magnifier would have made short work of the job. A remote-controlled drone would make it all but trivial. But he knew the doctrine as well as anyone. *6: No material anachronisms*

He considered using conventional weaponry, but there were a number of problems. First, he would have to procure the weapon without arousing suspicion. Second, he would have to find a suitable vantage point. Third, he would have to rely on the accuracy of an old-fashioned, unfamiliar weapon.

Instead, he had settled on explosives. The downside was that it would cause collateral damage, but this was deemed to be an acceptable cost.

1: The end will justify the means.

He knew how to make fourteen different types of improvised devices, all with materials he could expect to find on his arrival. During the week leading up to the rally, he gathered materials and scouted out the lay of the land, matching up the sights and smells of the city with the old maps and blueprints he memorised before the mission.

When the morning of the rally arrived, he woke early, feeling remarkably calm. He had set up his base of operations in an old gothic church, presently abandoned while repairs were done to the roof.

With plenty of time to spare, he went to the bakery for breakfast. Taking a bite of bread, it struck him that it was probably the last meal he would ever eat. He ate slowly. Walking back to the church, he saw signs of preparation for the rally. Flags hung in the windows of several houses. They were crimson red with white circles in the centre, finished with thick black angular lines. A girl skipped past him down the pavement, red and black ribbons flowing from her pigtails.

When he arrived back at the church, he walked around the outside of the building. The grass in the graveyard was overgrown, many of the gravestones covered with a thin layer of moss. A roofing tile, which had been getting increasingly loose over the past few weeks, finally dislodged. It dropped through the air and struck the man on the head, killing him instantly.

* * *

December, 2032

Dr. Phillips checked the readings from the blood test one last time. She turned to the man sitting across from her, who was watching her calmly.

"Everything okay?" he asked.

"Yes. Everything looks in order. You're ready. Put your uniform on and meet us by the chamber."

The man stood, saluted, and left the room. Dr. Phillips made her way to the chamber, where Dr. Stein greeted her.

A few minutes later, the man joined them. He wore rough brown trousers held up by braces over a thick blue shirt rolled up to the elbows. On his head he wore a flat cap.

"How do I look?" he asked.

Dr. Phillips smiled. "Positively Germanic," she said.

The man shook her hand, and then Dr. Stein's.

"How are you feeling?" Dr. Stein asked.

He paused for a moment. "I feel like I'm ready," he said.

A lab assistant led the man through a glass door, and then into what looked like an airlock chamber. The man went alone. Gas filtered into the chamber, almost invisible. After a few minutes, the door on the other side opened.

The man walked through the door and across a walkway, suspended in the middle of a huge room with curved walls, almost perfectly spherical. When he arrived in the centre he sat in a chair.

He closed his eyes. There was a faint whirring sound, and then he was gone.

Dr. Phillips returned to the main corridor. Dr. Stein followed her.

"Fancy a drink?" he asked.

They walked to Dr. Stein's office. He opened the door, and Dr. Phillips sat down. Dr. Stein pulled the stopper out of a carafe of brandy and filled two crystal glasses. He sat down and passed one of the glasses to his partner.

For a few minutes, they sat in silence, until Dr. Stein spoke. "Do you ever doubt what we're doing here?" he asked.

Dr. Phillips took a large gulp of her drink. It shot straight down her throat, burning pleasantly.

"No."

"What if we're just sending these boys to their deaths?"

"I know we're sending them to their deaths." She paused. "And I do regret that. Even with our most optimistic projections, fifty per cent of them won't make it there, or will arrive in the wrong place. We've probably sent some to the wrong continent, or materialised them under the earth's crust. Hell, we've probably sent some hurtling through space. But we're getting more accurate all the time. And they are all volunteers. They enter this program with their eyes wide open. You know that."

"I do. Number four, volunteers only; number five, complete operative transparency. But what if our calculations are wrong? What if none of them are successful?"

"They will be."

"How can you be so sure?"

"Because I must be."

"None of them have been successful so far."

"We don't know that."

Dr. Stein laughed. "Let's not go down that rabbit hole again."

There was a knock at the door. One of the lab assistants poked her head through.

"I'm clocking out," she said.

Dr. Stein nodded. When the lab assistant left, he topped up the glasses.

"Would you do it?" he asked, sitting down again.

"Do what?"

"Stick the knife in. Pull the trigger."

Dr. Phillips drained her glass and placed it firmly on her armrest. She looked at her partner, and he saw something in her eyes, flickering.

"I'd pull it twice," she said. "Just to be sure."

* * *

April, 1889

It was a light, airy evening. The man with the flat cap was walking down a dusty lane in Austria-Hungary. In his hands he held a long, thin piece of wire. As he walked, he wound the wire round his fingers and twirled it through the air.

He walked down the thin path, along the back of a row of houses. Half way along, he came across a wheelbarrow stuffed full with vegetables. He stopped for a moment and took in his surroundings, checking to see whether he was being watched. Confident he was in the clear, he reached into the wheelbarrow and took out a marrow. It was a few inches thick, with a firm skin, but when squeezed it, it felt soft inside. As he resumed his stroll down the lane, he put on a pair of gloves, and wrapped the wire round the middle of the marrow. He pulled both ends, and the vegetable was neatly sliced in two, sending the pieces tumbling through the air.

When he arrived at the town square, he looked at the clock, raised up on the side of the church. He had time. The thought made him chuckle to himself. With a few hours to spare, he entered into the first inn he came across, and sat at a table.

A woman approached him with a beaming smile. He asked her to bring him the best food she had, and a glass of beer to go along with it.

There were several other tables in the room, but only one of them was occupied. A couple of men sat nursing tall glasses of beer. As he waited, the man studied the paintings on the wall. There was a mixture of stoic portraits and pastoral scenes, green meadows and old trees. He thought of the smell of grass, and the feeling of sunshine on skin.

When the woman returned, she placed a plate in front of him. On it were three huge sausages, along with a pile of boiled potatoes, and a generous portion of sauerkraut. Next to the food she placed a large glass of beer with an inviting amber hue.

As he lifted the first forkful of food up to his mouth, the door opened, letting an extra shaft of light into the room. The woman, who had just walked away from the man's table, turned and moved towards the door, waving her hand and shaking her head.

"No, sorry," she said. "We're full."

She closed the door. As she turned, she saw the man, looking at her quizzically. She smiled at him.

"Jews," she said, and walked back into the kitchen.

For a second, the man considered standing up, but instead he gripped the table. He continued eating. The sausages were delicious, the sauerkraut heavenly.

His plate wiped clean, he put some money on the table and left. He asked a passerby for directions to the *Gasthof zum Pommer*, which, it turned out, was just nearby. He did a couple of sweeps around the area, and then waited.

In the middle of the night he picked the lock and entered. The building was quiet. A light rain tickled a gentle rhythm on the windows and the roof. He found the baby, sleeping, in a room adjacent to its parents.

Somewhere in the distance, there was a rumbling sound, like a peel of thunder. The man reached into his pocket and took out the wire. He pulled it taut, holding it between each gloved hand. As he prepared to reach forwards, the baby opened its eyes.

Omnipunks

Brian Trent

SHE HAD DOWNED three German planes and there was one remaining, somewhere, but her fuel tank was nearly dry and she needed to land. In the midst of the dogfight she had lost sight of the rest of her squadron. Three columns of black smoke were rising from the tiny Italian island below – wreckage from the ME-109s she'd disposed of in the mad, adrenaline-filled contest of life-and-death in the big blue sky. Now, she needed to put down, or her *Dueling Damsel* would create the next smoky column.

Dolores Vincent landed her P-40 Stormhawk in a field of wheat, the husks slapping at the hull as she taxied and stopped a dozen yards from a peculiar obelisk, milky jade in color and several meters tall. A sleepy village lay nearby, although the dogfight had brought out some of the inhabitants; farmers were gathering in a bewildered gaggle, gesticulating to the columns of smoke and her own landed plane.

Dolores hopped out of the cockpit and drew her pistol, wary that some German pilots might have survived their crash...and warier still that they might be robots.

The smoky tang of diesel burned in the back of her throat. Dolores undid her goggles and leather flying helmet. She squinted at the cloudy sky. There had been four *Luftwaffe* scouts; she'd downed three of them. She wondered if the survivor was the kind of man – or machine – who would circle back, guns chattering, to gun her down where she stood.

"Hello there!" she cried to the distant villagers. "I need fuel! Um, *benzina*!"

"*DOLORES!*"

She jumped at the thunderous voice. It had *not* come from the villagers, yet there was no one else nearby.

Dolores Vincent whirled about, scanning the rippling fields of wheat for signs of German automatons.

"Dolores!" the voice repeated, "I require your help."

"Yeah?" she snapped. "Who are you?"

"An entity from beyond time and space."

"Really?"

"Yes," the voice said. "Really."

The voice spoke perfect American English. Still, that flying robot she had battled with over Shanghai last April had bellowed at her in English that had been pretty jake, too.

Dolores instinctively fingered the locket she always wore around her neck. "Where are you? Who are you?" Dolores demanded.

"I am Overlord."

"Never heard of you." She regarded the nearby town, its ancient stone tower and seaside cottages. No way someone could be shouting at her from that distance. Her gaze gradually drew to the curious stone obelisk. It was oddly primitive in its lack of cultural motifs, like a javelin from a prehistoric era. The voice seemed to be resonating from it. But that was impossible, wasn't it?

"Please walk to the obelisk," the voice said, as if reading her thoughts. "You will not be harmed. In fact, we may be able to aid each other."

Dolores gazed at the jutting monument. It was just wide enough to display three sides. Was it a radio transmitter of some kind?

Scanning the skies once more for signs of the remaining German scout, Dolores edged closer to the obelisk. Play it safe, Dad always said, but that was one piece of advice she was never good at following. The thrill of the dogfight was still tapping in her wrists and heart. Her scarf wavered in the smoky breeze.

"Please cross into the circle," the voice instructed.

"Circle?" Dolores noticed that the ground beneath her feet was set with square bricks of the same greenish quality as the obelisk. She was no archaeologist or historian, but the whole thing seemed to exude an ancient presence that seemed out of place for such a rural, insignificant little isle. She wondered at the history of this place. Had some unknown stoneworker toiled here in the earliest days of Rome, carving this marker out of what appeared to be a single piece of stone? She ran a fingertip down its cool, smooth surface and her frown deepened. It felt like metal, but if so, it was unlike any metal she had ever seen.

"I wish to aid you in your war against the Germans," Overlord boomed, "but I have been trapped beneath this needle. Please step into the circle, and I will have others do the same."

"What others, pal?"

"This obelisk is a nexus point through which other people can lend their aid."

"Lend aid to do what?"

"To remove the source of my imprisonment, and release me back into the world. Your enemies, those, um, dastardly Germans, have trapped me on this island."

Dolores halted at the perimeter of the green circle. Still fingering her locket, she said, "I'm a capable dame, but I can't exactly uproot this needle-thing by myself."

"Two other people will assist you."

"I don't see anyone else here."

"They hail from different time periods. The three of you will collaborate across the centuries. In *this* century, I am asking you."

She waved her pistol towards the unoccupied sides of the obelisk. "So who exactly are these other people?"

* * *

Vin¢ awoke in the gloomy hospital room just in time to rip the IV line from his arm and throw himself through the window as the door burst open and two netrunner agents found him. The room was pulped by a storm of microflechettes as he plummeted nine stories through the humid night air.

There was barely time to select HEAL off his aug-menu. He struck the cobblestone hospital grounds and splattered on impact.

Vin¢'s bones were still knitting back together when the netrunners reached the hospital lobby. They spotted him easily enough. Not too many half-naked men wearing hospital gowns rising from puddles of their own blood.

He reached for his pistol. Remembered that he'd left it in Shimizu.

Damn.

Vin¢ somersaulted out of the way as the agents dashed outside and opened fire. Their microfleschettes stitched the ground where he'd been. He took cover behind the base of a weird greenish obelisk contained within a circle of equally green stones. Mind racing, trying to keep focus amid the sizzling pain of regeneration, he fingered open his thigh-panel, found the single steel *shuriken* he kept there.

"*Vin¢!*" an unseen voice thundered.

He almost leapt out of his skin. "Yeah?"

"I require your help."

"You require *my* help?" he cried.

One of the netrunners disappeared in a blur of optical camouflage. The man's invisible boots splashed through puddles of blood, so Vin¢ tracked the red prints until they stopped by a recycling bin on the perimeter of the hospital parking lot. Then he flung the *shuriken* into the goon's throat. The weapon's mini-EMP detonated in a brief flash of light, and the bastard dropped, any healing nanonics he might possess melted into slag.

One thug down. One left.

"I said," the mysterious voice repeated, "I require your help."

"Kinda busy. Who are you?"

"An entity from beyond time and space."

"Huh." Vin¢ scrambled to the dead netrunner, nabbed the man's flechette pistol, and fell back to the obelisk. A twig snapped; he twisted, narrowly avoided a stream of weaponsfire, and returned fire on the bodiless muzzle-flash only six yards away. The thug materialized as his camouflage fell away, the biocells on which they depended sinking into the big sleep.

Vin¢ sighed in relief. "Okay, bud. It's only a matter of time before more of these Yakuza netrunners come after me, so cut to it. Who are you and what do you want?"

"You can call me Overlord."

"IFF?"

"What?"

"You a friend or foe?"

"Friend. But there *is* a foe out there. An enemy threatening your world. It's those, um, Yakuza netrunners. They trapped me here. Only *you* can release me."

"Why's that?"

"This obelisk —"

"Is made from a material that's exhibiting unique tachyonic world-line properties," Vin¢ interrupted. "I'd even say it's multi-temporal. Am I right?"

"Yes," Overlord said, sounding surprised. "How did you —?"

Vin¢ rubbed his stubbly chin and winked his cybernetic eye. "Oh, I'm so crammed with tech I probably piss code."

"Nonetheless, you humans perceive time in very limited ways."

"Fuck you."

"Listen to me," Overlord said tersely. "Perhaps we can aid each other? I can only be released through coordinated assistance across history from three different time periods.

Three people, all operating in the same place, just from different eras. Will you help and, in doing so, let me help you?"

Vin¢ frowned. "You said three people. Who else –?"

* * *

Captain Silas Vincenzo stood among the steaming, twitching wreckage of the giant mecha-locust horde and wondered, not for the first time, if they represented a simple factory malfunction, or if this was the latest plot from the nefarious Professor Rogvold 'Crimson Khan' Filippovich.

"Can you hold right there?" the reporter for the *Global Gear & Gazette* asked, stooping behind the studio camera to photograph the famous airship captain. Silas' vessel floated overhead, its shadow immense darkening the fields of wheat and the cozy Italian village nearby. The airship was tethered by docking ropes to the crest of an ancient stone tower, its rope ladder twisting in the wind. It was all terribly out of place for such a remote little island, but then so was the mecha-locust horde that littered the field; Silas had bombed them to pieces before they could leap on their steam-powered serrated legs and do real damage to the innocent villagers.

"Perfect!" the reporter cried, ducking behind the camera's dark cloth. "Hold fast!"

Silas propped one leg upon the nearest steel monster – just one of hundreds which had hopped their way across western Europe on a path of destruction, their black eyes rimmed by rivets, steel mandibles chewing up every crop from Athens to Rome. The reporter emerged from the dark cloth and carried his camera to a new angle.

"*Captain Silas*!" said a mysterious voice.

"I am indeed," Silas said, looking around. Seeing no one, he wondered if this was a mecha-locust communication from the nefarious Crimson Khan. "Who addresses me?"

"I am Overlord. I require your help."

"Require?" Silas frowned and adjusted the feather on his iron airship helmet. "Seems you should make a *request*, rather than start this dialogue off with a demand, yes?"

"I *request*," gritted the voice, "That you lend aid to a battle across time and space. I have been imprisoned beneath the nearby obelisk by, um, the dastardly Crimson Khan!"

"I say! Today is looking rather thick!"

"If you aid me, I can in turn help you with –" But Silas was already striding towards the obelisk.

The reporter popped up from behind the camera. "Captain Vincenzo? I still need one more good shot…"

Silas drew his brass blunderbuss. To the invisible voice, he said, "What is the strategy, my good sir?"

"Oh," Overlord intoned, "just cross into the green circle and stand there for a bit."

* * *

When Dolores reached the circle she hesitated. Her boots stopped short of crossing its perimeter of greenish stone.

"That's right," prompted Overlord. "Step into the circle, please."

"Uh-huh." She felt a burn of anxiety in her chest, and it wasn't just from not knowing where the fourth German plane had gone to. "You know, I come from a long line of heroes. My great grandfather was one of the first airship pilots in history. He defended Europe from the mecha-locust plague and brought the Crimson Khan to justice –"

"Fascinating, but I do require you to enter the circle if I am to get out of here."

"Sorry. I blab when I'm nervous." Dolores lifted her boot to take another step, halted. "So who else is with us? These people from other times?"

"There's a netrunner aiding us."

"Netrunner? What's that, some kind of fisherman?"

"Please, I require you to –" "When's he from?"

"The year 2089, but that really doesn't matter. If you would please step into the circle and…wait, where are you going?"

Dolores hopped backwards from the obelisk. "Just a sec." She felt in her pocket for a pen, found only her lipstick, and began to write something on the inside of her aviator scarf.

Carefully, Dolores pried up one of the green cobblestones. She stuffed the scarf beneath it, and set the stone back into place.

Using her pistol's barrel – wincing as she did – she scraped the numerals 2089 onto the stone.

* * *

Vin¢ only noticed the faded etching on the cobblestone because his optical augs were in full spectrum mode, amassing and collating data across the entire wavelength of visible light.

2089.

That's what was carved into the brick. The current year of 2089, despite the obvious antiquity of the carving itself. What the hell was going on? Could this day get any stranger?

He pried the stone up from the ground. In the dry recesses beneath it, something was crumpled. Vin¢ retrieved an old scarf; it might have been white once, but now was faded to an aged, brittle brown. Words were written in some kind of red ink:

I'M DOLORES VINCENT. MY GREAT-GRANDFATHER WAS CAPTAIN SILAS VINCENZO, AND HISTORY RECORDS THAT HE DIED UNDER MYSTERIOUS CIRCUMSTANCES ON THIS VERY ISLAND.

Dolores Vincent? Vin¢ scratched his head.

He accessed the city's local web-brain. He ran a search on DOLORES VINCENT. The results spooled into his visual field:

Dolores Vincent, American flying ace and veteran of two world wars, pilot of the Dueling Damsel, was murdered by an unknown assailant on a small island off the Italian coast in 1938.

One-hundred-and-fifty-one years ago, he thought.

He prodded the web-brain for info on a Silas Vincenzo, and then once more for EARLY AVIATOR NONVERBAL COMMUNICATIONS. No sooner was that data unraveling in his head than he was neuro-texting a message via pulse beam into the obelisk itself, using the thing as a beacon, thumping its tachyonic resonance field in a deliberate pattern he hoped someone would understand.

* * *

Dolores noticed the needle pulsate suddenly with a dull, staccato glow and a pinging sound akin to metal reverberating off a sheet of ice.

"What the hell is this?" she asked aloud.

It *almost* seemed like Morse code; the short thumps peppering a sonic scale like electronic crickets to her ears. But it was older than Morse code, representing some style of communication that no one used anymore.

"What are you trying to say?" she asked the obelisk.

* * *

Captain Silas immediately recognized the thumping signals radiating from the needle as the Royal Airship Mecha-Locust Tracking Communication Code. He placed his pipe between his teeth and translated aloud from the pulses and clicks and trills.

> *"'I am Vin¢. It appears that you and your descendent Dolores were killed at the same stone obelisk that you're looking at now. Put simply, you were decapitated. Please take all necessary precautions to avoid this from happening.'"*

Silas chewed the end of his pipe. "I say, this is rather disconcerting! Surely no one can sneak up on *me*. My ears can detect a mecha-locust chirp from a good three miles..."

Nonetheless, he chanced to peek over his shoulder.

A hulking green pincer had risen, ghost-like, from the ground and was chopping for his head. Silas threw himself to the ground and the pincer closed on empty air.

He drew up his blunderbuss and opened fire on the pincer.

* * *

> *"Historical records indicate that a blunderbuss was discharged against whatever attacked you," Vin¢ continued texting. "However, as it's still recorded that you died, perhaps the blunderbuss isn't the most ideal weapon in this case –"*

* * *

Silas chanced to peek over his shoulder.

A hulking green pincer had risen, ghost-like, from the ground and was chopping for his head. Silas threw himself to the ground and the pincer closed on empty air.

He hurled his explosive pocketwatch up at the creature –

* * *

> *"Historical records indicate that an explosive pocketwatch was discharged against whatever attacked you. Unfortunately the resulting explosion killed you and injured a nearby reporter. Perhaps your famous blunderbuss is the better choice in battle –"*

* * *

"Humph!" Silas scoffed after translating the message. "I would never *open* a duel with my pocketwatch! I must have tried the blunderbuss during an earlier effort and, dear me, it failed!"

He spun around just in time to see the green pincer coming for him. It stretched wide, serrated edges glinting in the low light, coming for his neck.

Silas Vincenzo held his ground. He wound back his electric right fist and punched the pincer dead-center at the joint.

* * *

Dolores finished scribbling on her scarf:

> *I'M DOLORES VINCENT. MY GREAT-GRANDFATHER WAS CAPTAIN SILAS VINCENZO, AND HE WAS ATTACKED BY A MYSTERIOUS ASSAILANT ON THIS VERY ISLAND. HOWEVER, HE ENDED UP UTILIZING THE ELECTRICAL COIL IN HIS ARTIFICIAL RIGHT HAND TO DEBILITATE HIS ATTACKER AND ESCAPE THE CIRCLE.*

Dolores sensed movement. She leapt aside as pincers rose up behind her and slashed for her neck. She hit the ground, tucked into a roll, and was back on her feet as a forest of new claws sprang up from the earth, snipping, intent on separating her head from her neck.

"Why are you attacking us?" she demanded, retreating to the cover of the obelisk. "What exactly did we do to you?"

Overlord's voice seemed to come from everywhere at once:

"I arrived on this world when your people were only scavenging apes! *I was a god on a world of beasts!* You all groveled before me! You were mine to control and command!"

Three claws darted for her. Snip! Snip! Snip! Dolores bobbed and wove like a prized pugilist, and the breeze of their gyrations whipped over her head.

The ground erupted, disgorging a wild tangle of tendrils like thorny vines. Dolores had no time to react to this new threat; the tendrils entwined her legs, clashing and tearing through her pants. She was abruptly yanked against the obelisk, and she cried out as her back impacted the solid stone.

The eyestalk twisted around to glare into her face.

"I could have ruled this world!" the voice thundered at her, "Even with my vessel shattered around me from impact, I was unstoppable. Your spears and clubs could not harm me! *Nothing* on this world could have harmed me."

"Something did," Dolores taunted, thinking of the obelisk she was being strung up against. "Or was it some*one*?"

"One of you little apes trapped me! He used a shard of my own ship to stake me to this spot...he dared to grab it in his furry hand and run me through, burying me here for all time!"

Dolores couldn't move her legs, her body effectively pinned against the obelisk. But her arms were still free, and she suddenly knew what she needed to do. She snapped open her pistol and emptied out her bullets; they tinkled to the cobblestone at her feet. Grabbing the locket from around her neck, she snapped it from the necklace. She fingered open the case, and extracted a single bullet. A *special* bullet. A family heirloom that had passed to her from Silas Vincenzo himself.

"A caveman primitive defeated the great interstellar conqueror?!" Dolores taunted, trying to stall the decapitating claws.

"*He got lucky!*" the monster roared petulantly. "That one ape got *lucky –*"

* * *

Vin¢'s optical augs detected a frothing disruption in the temporal wavelength, like something bubbling up from the depths of the ocean. Claws! There were terrifying claws reaching for him across the gulf of time! And behind them was something else, a hideous eye-stalk like something off a mutant lobster.

He tucked and rolled aside as the monster erupted into his time period. He tried darting back to the safety of the hospital, or anywhere outside this strange circle of cobblestone, but a forest of alien appendages shot up from the ground, containing him within its deadly circle.

He was trapped.

And yet…so was the monster.

His augmented vision was reading more than just the creature itself. It was tallying data on the obelisk, and the mounting conclusion could not be denied: the obelisk was pinning straight through the center of the monster, staking it like a vampire to the earth. It was still dangerous, yet decidedly constrained. Someone, sometime, had succeeded in driving this multi-temporal material into the monster's body…

"I'll bet it was an ancestor of mine!" Vin¢ said aloud. "Isn't that right? Whoever trapped you here is someone from my own bloodline! It can't be a coincidence that the three people you lured here are all related! Someone from the ancient past – someone from my lineage – figured out that ordinary weapons were useless against you, so they grabbed a piece of this obelisk…a piece of your own starship and…"

* * *

"– and in touching that ship," Dolores said to the eyestalk, "something in the material seeped into his body, into his very blood…and therefore…"

Into me and my bloodline! My family and this devil united in eternal, cosmic enmity!

The veins on the eye bulged and twitched like snakes.

"Any hope I have to escape is thwarted by your bloodline!" Overlord hissed. "Every time a chance arrives, one of your blood defeats me! My only hope is to extinguish you from this wretched little planet! Then this world will be mine again!" The feelers tightened their grip. Dolores suppressed a scream as the thorns perforated her thighs. She almost dropped the special bullet.

But she didn't.

Her trembling fingers inserted it into her pistol's chamber with a neat, satisfying click. She raised the pistol and pointed it at the alien eye.

The eye swiveled to regard the weapon.

"Bullets?" Overlord taunted, and gave a scratchy sound that might have been laughter. "I am immune to your primitive steel and brass and copper and –"

"How about electricity?" Dolores snapped.

Before the beast could respond – before the horror of comprehension could fill its hateful, cyclopean stare – she squeezed the trigger.

The eyestalk instantly whipped backwards, flailing like an out-of-control firehose. The blinded creature screamed – a sound unlike anything she'd ever heard, like a chorus of separate agonies resonating across the ages. The thorny feelers shook her loose; she fell, collapsing into a bleeding heap at the base of the obelisk. The earth trembled beneath her.

She remembered Dad's advice, the day she entered the service: *My prayers and love go with you, Dolores, but they may not be enough. Take this bullet with you and keep it on your person at all times. Silas Vincenzo insisted that electricity had once saved his life. I had this bullet made special for you. Keep it in this locket, and look to it when all other options are exhausted.*

The monster continued shrieking and flailing around her. Dolores dragged herself out of the circle while the claws vanished back into the ether, abandoning this time period. She reached her Stormhawk, grunting as she pulled herself to her feet and bandaged her wounded legs. A moment later, a townsman arrived with a tank of diesel and helped her refuel the plane.

May the winds of Fortune stay with me and my bloodline, she thought proudly.

Above, the distinct droning of an ME-109 began to rise. Dolores squinted to the sky and spotted the last of the German squadron, circling high to the southwest.

"Oh yeah," she whispered. "You and I weren't finished yet."

She pulled herself into the *Dueling Damsel* cockpit and returned to the heavens.

* * *

Silas, sitting in his leather study at the age of eighty-two, used his quail feather-pen to scribble a set of instructions into his Last Will and Testament:

> *It must be told to every descendant of my bloodline that a terrible devil is on this world, and that electricity is the remedy. May the Lord's mercy protect us through the eons!*

* * *

Now it makes sense, Vin¢ thought as the blind eyestalk flailed around like a useless hydra neck in front of him, its claws snapping and grasping uselessly. *The tattoo on my arm, the one I had since childhood. The one showing a little electric volt. I never knew my parents or family lineage, but they clearly knew something about this strange fate we're all caught up in. An electric volt giving me a clue that just might save my life…*

Vin¢ called upon the last charge of his biocells, and selected BURN off his aug-menu. Then he aimed his fingers at the freakish monstrosity around him.

White electricity forked out from his nanonics and assailed the alien creature. Overlord shrieked wildly, an ululation that rippled along the frequencies and temporal corridors of the universe. Then the nightmarish apparition retreated, faded, sank away into whatever hellish Limbo it had been consigned to untold ages ago.

The cobblestone square was silent once again.

Vin¢ reached into the pocket of his hospital gown and retrieved a cigarette. Using the very last of his biocell's energy, he lit the butt and took a deep drag.

What a fucking day, he mused, retreating into the city. He blew smoke through his nostrils and, as uncharacteristic as it was, found himself grinning.

May vectors of quantum entanglement continue to preserve my family's *awesomeness*, he thought.

* * *

The night's rain had dressed the lemon trees and soft wheat in jewels of moisture as Caterina Vincentius glided down with her waxen Icarus wings from the stone tower. She landed, awkwardly but with a satisfied laugh, near a strange green obelisk that jutted up from a circle of green stone. Her mechanical wings squealed as she lowered her arms, its bronze underframe retracting like a fan.

From the tower, Master Leonardo squawked, "Caterina? Did it work? Return here at once and we can discuss! You cannot go up against our rivals unless you are fully equipped and trained with my inventions!"

Caterina playfully flapped her wings; the springs and cogs wheezing in their joints. She thought, too, of the vellum illustrations in her master's candle-lit workshop, of the strange potions and clockwork beasts, the incendiary bombs and spring-loaded grapples. Their enemies would never expect such ingenuities…or that an insignificant peasant girl would be wielding them! She twirled around in merriment.

"*Caterina*!" a mysterious unseen voice cried.

The woman gasped. Her and Master Leonardo were supposedly the only occupants of this island! Had the House of Salviati sent an assassin after her? Did they know of the Medici plot?

"Hello?" she replied awkwardly.

"I have come to you in a time of great need, mortal," the voice said. "Will you let me help you?"

She edged towards the odd needle in its prison of cobblestone. "Who are you?"

"An enemy to the, um, Salviati."

"Oh?"

"Come forward, and I shall tell you more!"

Caterina ignored Master Leonardo's shouts. So *this* was the day, she thought, feeling her heart pound with fierce purpose and resolve. The Vincentius clan had long told tales of an evil presence on this island. The legend had been circulating since before Rome sprouted upon her seven hills.

May the Fates guide and protect me, she prayed, and advanced to the obelisk.

A Connecticut Yankee in King Arthur's Court
Chapters I–IV
Mark Twain

Preface

THE UNGENTLE LAWS and customs touched upon in this tale are historical, and the episodes which are used to illustrate them are also historical. It is not pretended that these laws and customs existed in England in the sixth century; no, it is only pretended that inasmuch as they existed in the English and other civilizations of far later times, it is safe to consider that it is no libel upon the sixth century to suppose them to have been in practice in that day also. One is quite justified in inferring that whatever one of these laws or customs was lacking in that remote time, its place was competently filled by a worse one.

The question as to whether there is such a thing as divine right of kings is not settled in this book. It was found too difficult. That the executive head of a nation should be a person of lofty character and extraordinary ability, was manifest and indisputable; that none but the Deity could select that head unerringly, was also manifest and indisputable; that the Deity ought to make that selection, then, was likewise manifest and indisputable; consequently, that He does make it, as claimed, was an unavoidable deduction. I mean, until the author of this book encountered the Pompadour, and Lady Castlemaine, and some other executive heads of that kind; these were found so difficult to work into the scheme, that it was judged better to take the other tack in this book (which must be issued this fall), and then go into training and settle the question in another book. It is, of course, a thing which ought to be settled, and I am not going to have anything particular to do next winter anyway.

Mark Twain
Hartford, July 21, 1889

A Word of Explanation

IT WAS IN Warwick Castle that I came across the curious stranger whom I am going to talk about. He attracted me by three things: his candid simplicity, his marvelous familiarity with ancient armor, and the restfulness of his company – for he did all the talking. We fell together, as modest people will, in the tail of the herd that was being shown through, and he at once began to say things which interested me. As he talked along, softly, pleasantly, flowingly, he seemed to drift away imperceptibly out of this world and time, and into some remote era and old forgotten country; and so he gradually wove such a spell about me that I seemed to move among the specters and shadows and dust and mold of a gray antiquity, holding speech with a relic of it! Exactly as I would speak of my nearest personal friends or enemies, or my most familiar neighbors, he spoke of Sir Bedivere, Sir Bors de Ganis, Sir Launcelot of the Lake, Sir Galahad, and all the other great names of the Table Round – and how old, old, unspeakably old and faded and dry and musty and ancient he came to look as he went on! Presently he turned to me and said, just as one might speak of the weather, or any other common matter –

"You know about transmigration of souls; do you know about transposition of epochs – and bodies?"

I said I had not heard of it. He was so little interested – just as when people speak of the weather – that he did not notice whether I made him any answer or not. There was half a moment of silence, immediately interrupted by the droning voice of the salaried cicerone:

"Ancient hauberk, date of the sixth century, time of King Arthur and the Round Table; said to have belonged to the knight Sir Sagramor le Desirous; observe the round hole through the chain-mail in the left breast; can't be accounted for; supposed to have been done with a bullet since invention of firearms – perhaps maliciously by Cromwell's soldiers."

My acquaintance smiled – not a modern smile, but one that must have gone out of general use many, many centuries ago – and muttered apparently to himself:

"Wit ye well, *I saw it done*." Then, after a pause, added: "I did it myself."

By the time I had recovered from the electric surprise of this remark, he was gone.

All that evening I sat by my fire at the Warwick Arms, steeped in a dream of the olden time, while the rain beat upon the windows, and the wind roared about the eaves and corners. From time to time I dipped into old Sir Thomas Malory's enchanting book, and fed at its rich feast of prodigies and adventures, breathed in the fragrance of its obsolete names, and dreamed again. Midnight being come at length, I read another tale, for a nightcap – this which here follows, to wit:

How Sir Launcelot Slew Two Giants, and Made a Castle Free

ANON WITHAL came there upon him two great giants, well armed, all save the heads, with two horrible clubs in their hands. Sir Launcelot put his shield afore him, and put the stroke away of the one giant, and with his sword he clave his head asunder. When his fellow saw that, he ran away as he were wood [1], for fear of the horrible strokes, and Sir Launcelot after him with all his might, and smote him on the shoulder, and clave him to the middle. Then Sir Launcelot went into the hall, and there came afore him three score ladies and damsels, and all kneeled unto him, and thanked God and him of their deliverance. For, sir, said they, the most part of us have been here this seven year their prisoners, and we have worked all manner of silk works for our meat, and we are all great gentle-women born, and blessed be the time, knight, that ever thou wert born; for thou hast done the most worship that ever did knight in the world, that will we bear record, and we all pray you to tell us your name, that we may tell our friends who delivered us out of prison. Fair damsels, he said, my name is Sir Launcelot du Lake. And so he departed from them and betaught them unto God. And then he mounted upon his horse, and rode into many strange and wild countries, and through many waters and valleys, and evil was he lodged. And at the last by fortune him happened against a night to come to a fair courtilage, and therein he found an old gentle-woman that lodged him with a good-will, and there he had good cheer for him and his horse. And when time was, his host brought him into a fair garret over the gate to his bed. There Sir Launcelot unarmed him, and set his harness by him, and went to bed, and anon he fell on sleep. So, soon after there came one on horseback, and knocked at the gate in great haste. And when Sir Launcelot heard this he rose up, and looked out at the window, and saw by the moonlight three knights come riding after that one man, and all three lashed on him at once with swords, and that one knight turned on them knightly again and defended him. Truly, said Sir Launcelot, yonder one knight shall I help, for it were shame for me to see three knights on one, and if he be slain I am partner of his death. And therewith he took his harness and went out at a window by a sheet down to the four knights, and then Sir Launcelot said on high, Turn you knights unto me, and leave your fighting with that knight. And then they all three left Sir Kay, and turned unto Sir Launcelot, and there began great battle, for they alight all three, and strake many strokes at Sir Launcelot, and assailed him on every side. Then Sir Kay dressed him for to have holpen Sir Launcelot. Nay, sir, said he, I will none of your help, therefore as ye will have my help let me alone with them. Sir Kay for the pleasure of the knight suffered him for to do his will, and so stood aside. And then anon within six strokes Sir Launcelot had stricken them to the earth.

And then they all three cried, Sir Knight, we yield us unto you as man of might matchless. As to that, said Sir Launcelot, I will not take your yielding unto me, but so that ye yield you unto Sir Kay the seneschal, on that covenant I will save your lives and else not. Fair knight, said they, that were we loath to do; for as for Sir Kay we chased him hither, and had overcome him had ye not been; therefore, to yield us unto him it were no reason. Well, as to that, said Sir Launcelot, advise you well, for ye may choose whether ye will die or live, for an ye be yielden, it shall be unto Sir Kay. Fair knight, then they said, in saving our lives we will do as thou commandest us. Then shall ye, said Sir Launcelot, on Whitsunday next coming go unto the court of King Arthur, and there shall ye yield you unto Queen Guenever, and put you all three in her grace and mercy, and say that Sir Kay sent you thither to be her prisoners. On the morn Sir Launcelot arose early, and left Sir Kay sleeping; and Sir Launcelot took Sir Kay's armor and his shield and armed him, and so he went to the stable and took his horse, and took his leave of his host, and so he departed. Then soon after arose Sir Kay and missed Sir Launcelot; and then he espied that he had his armor and his horse. Now by my faith I know well that he will grieve some of the court of King Arthur; for on him knights will be bold, and deem that it is I, and that will beguile them; and because of his armor and shield I am sure I shall ride in peace. And then soon after departed Sir Kay, and thanked his host.

* * *

As I laid the book down there was a knock at the door, and my stranger came in. I gave him a pipe and a chair, and made him welcome. I also comforted him with a hot Scotch whisky; gave him another one; then still another – hoping always for his story. After a fourth persuader, he drifted into it himself, in a quite simple and natural way:

Footnote 1. Demented.

The Stranger's History

I AM AN AMERICAN. I was born and reared in Hartford, in the State of Connecticut – anyway, just over the river, in the country. So I am a Yankee of the Yankees – and practical; yes, and nearly barren of sentiment, I suppose – or poetry, in other words. My father was a blacksmith, my uncle was a horse doctor, and I was both, along at first.

Then I went over to the great arms factory and learned my real trade; learned all there was to it; learned to make everything: guns, revolvers, cannon, boilers, engines, all sorts of labor-saving machinery. Why, I could make anything a body wanted – anything in the world, it didn't make any difference what; and if there wasn't any quick new-fangled way to make a thing, I could invent one – and do it as easy as rolling off a log. I became head superintendent; had a couple of thousand men under me.

Well, a man like that is a man that is full of fight – that goes without saying. With a couple of thousand rough men under one, one has plenty of that sort of amusement. I had, anyway. At last I met my match, and I got my dose. It was during a misunderstanding conducted with crowbars with a fellow we used to call Hercules. He laid me out with a crusher alongside the head that made everything crack, and seemed to spring every joint in my skull and made it overlap its neighbor. Then the world went out in darkness, and I didn't feel anything more, and didn't know anything at all – at least for a while.

When I came to again, I was sitting under an oak tree, on the grass, with a whole beautiful and broad country landscape all to myself – nearly. Not entirely; for there was a fellow on a horse, looking down at me – a fellow fresh out of a picture book. He was in old-time iron armor from head to heel, with a helmet on his head the shape of a nail-keg with slits in it; and he had a shield, and a sword, and a prodigious spear; and his horse had armor on, too, and a steel horn projecting from his forehead, and gorgeous red and green silk trappings that hung down all around him like a bedquilt, nearly to the ground.

"Fair sir, will ye just?" said this fellow.

"Will I which?"

"Will ye try a passage of arms for land or lady or for –"

"What are you giving me?" I said. "Get along back to your circus, or I'll report you."

Now what does this man do but fall back a couple of hundred yards and then come rushing at me as hard as he could tear, with his nail-keg bent down nearly to his horse's neck and his long spear pointed straight ahead. I saw he meant business, so I was up the tree when he arrived.

He allowed that I was his property, the captive of his spear. There was argument on his side – and the bulk of the advantage – so I judged it best to humor him. We fixed up an agreement whereby I was to go with him and he was not to hurt me. I came down, and we started away, I walking by the side of his horse. We marched comfortably along, through glades and over brooks which I could not remember to have seen before – which puzzled me and made me wonder – and yet we did not come to any circus or sign of a circus. So I gave up the idea of a circus, and concluded he was from an asylum. But we never came to an asylum – so I was up a stump, as you may say. I asked him how far we were from Hartford. He said he had never heard of the place; which I took to be a lie, but allowed it to go at that. At the end of an hour we saw a far-away town sleeping in a valley by a winding river; and beyond it on a hill, a vast gray fortress, with towers and turrets, the first I had ever seen out of a picture.

"Bridgeport?" said I, pointing.

"Camelot," said he.

My stranger had been showing signs of sleepiness. He caught himself nodding, now, and smiled one of those pathetic, obsolete smiles of his, and said:

"I find I can't go on; but come with me, I've got it all written out, and you can read it if you like."

In his chamber, he said: "First, I kept a journal; then by and by, after years, I took the journal and turned it into a book. How long ago that was!"

He handed me his manuscript, and pointed out the place where I should begin:

"Begin here – I've already told you what goes before." He was steeped in drowsiness by this time. As I went out at his door I heard him murmur sleepily: "Give you good den, fair sir."

I sat down by my fire and examined my treasure. The first part of it – the great bulk of it – was parchment, and yellow with age. I scanned a leaf particularly and saw that it was a palimpsest. Under the old dim writing of the Yankee historian appeared traces of a penmanship which was older and dimmer still – Latin words and sentences: fragments from old monkish legends, evidently. I turned to the place indicated by my stranger and began to read – as follows.

The Tale of the Lost Land

Chapter I
Camelot

"CAMELOT – CAMELOT," said I to myself. "I don't seem to remember hearing of it before. Name of the asylum, likely."

It was a soft, reposeful summer landscape, as lovely as a dream, and as lonesome as Sunday. The air was full of the smell of flowers, and the buzzing of insects, and the twittering of birds, and there were no people, no wagons, there was no stir of life, nothing going on. The road was mainly a winding path with hoof-prints in it, and now and then a faint trace of wheels on either side in the grass – wheels that apparently had a tire as broad as one's hand.

Presently a fair slip of a girl, about ten years old, with a cataract of golden hair streaming down over her shoulders, came along. Around her head she wore a hoop of flame-red poppies. It was as sweet an outfit as ever I saw, what there was of it. She walked indolently along, with a mind at rest, its peace reflected in her innocent face. The circus man paid no attention to her; didn't even seem to see her. And she – she was no more startled at his fantastic make-up than if she was used to his like every day of her life. She was going by as indifferently as she might have gone by a couple of cows; but when she happened to notice me, then there was a change! Up went her hands, and she was turned to stone; her mouth dropped open, her eyes stared wide and timorously, she was the picture of astonished curiosity touched with fear. And there she stood gazing, in a sort of stupefied fascination, till we turned a corner of the wood and were lost to her view. That she should be startled at me instead of at the other man, was too many for me; I couldn't make head or tail of it. And that she should seem to consider me a spectacle, and totally overlook her own merits in that respect, was another puzzling thing, and a display of magnanimity, too, that was surprising in one so young. There was food for thought here. I moved along as one in a dream.

As we approached the town, signs of life began to appear. At intervals we passed a wretched cabin, with a thatched roof, and about it small fields and garden patches in an indifferent state of cultivation. There were people, too; brawny men, with long, coarse, uncombed hair that hung down over their faces and made them look like animals. They and the women, as a rule, wore a coarse tow-linen robe that came well below the knee, and a rude sort of sandal, and many wore an iron collar. The small boys and girls were always naked; but nobody seemed to know it. All of these people stared at me, talked about me, ran into the huts and fetched out their families to gape at me; but nobody ever noticed that other fellow, except to make him humble salutation and get no response for their pains.

In the town were some substantial windowless houses of stone scattered among a wilderness of thatched cabins; the streets were mere crooked alleys, and unpaved; troops of dogs and nude children played in the sun and made life and noise; hogs roamed and rooted contentedly about, and one of them lay in a reeking wallow in the middle of the main thoroughfare and suckled her family. Presently there was a distant blare of military music; it came nearer, still nearer, and soon a noble cavalcade wound into view, glorious with plumed helmets and flashing mail and flaunting banners and rich doublets and horse-cloths and gilded spearheads; and through the muck and swine, and naked brats, and joyous dogs, and shabby huts, it took its gallant way, and in its wake we followed.

Followed through one winding alley and then another, – and climbing, always climbing – till at last we gained the breezy height where the huge castle stood. There was an exchange of bugle blasts; then a parley from the walls, where men-at-arms, in hauberk and morion, marched back and forth with halberd at shoulder under flapping banners with the rude figure of a dragon displayed upon them; and then the great gates were flung open, the drawbridge was lowered, and the head of the cavalcade swept forward under the frowning arches; and we, following, soon found ourselves in a great paved court, with towers and turrets stretching up into the blue air on all the four sides; and all about us the dismount was going on, and much greeting and ceremony, and running to and fro, and a gay display of moving and intermingling colors, and an altogether pleasant stir and noise and confusion.

Chapter II
King Arthur's Court

THE MOMENT I got a chance I slipped aside privately and touched an ancient common looking man on the shoulder and said, in an insinuating, confidential way:

"Friend, do me a kindness. Do you belong to the asylum, or are you just on a visit or something like that?"

He looked me over stupidly, and said:

"Marry, fair sir, me seemeth –"

"That will do," I said; "I reckon you are a patient."

I moved away, cogitating, and at the same time keeping an eye out for any chance passenger in his right mind that might come along and give me some light. I judged I had found one, presently; so I drew him aside and said in his ear:

"If I could see the head keeper a minute – only just a minute –"

"Prithee do not let me."

"Let you *what*?"

"*Hinder* me, then, if the word please thee better. Then he went on to say he was an under-cook and could not stop to gossip, though he would like it another time;

for it would comfort his very liver to know where I got my clothes. As he started away he pointed and said yonder was one who was idle enough for my purpose, and was seeking me besides, no doubt. This was an airy slim boy in shrimp-colored tights that made him look like a forked carrot, the rest of his gear was blue silk and dainty laces and ruffles; and he had long yellow curls, and wore a plumed pink satin cap tilted complacently over his ear. By his look, he was good-natured; by his gait, he was satisfied with himself. He was pretty enough to frame. He arrived, looked me over with a smiling and impudent curiosity; said he had come for me, and informed me that he was a page.

"Go 'long," I said; "you ain't more than a paragraph."

It was pretty severe, but I was nettled. However, it never phased him; he didn't appear to know he was hurt. He began to talk and laugh, in happy, thoughtless, boyish fashion, as we walked along, and made himself old friends with me at once; asked me all sorts of questions about myself and about my clothes, but never waited for an answer – always chattered straight ahead, as if he didn't know he had asked a question and wasn't expecting any reply, until at last he happened to mention that he was born in the beginning of the year 513.

It made the cold chills creep over me! I stopped and said, a little faintly:

"Maybe I didn't hear you just right. Say it again – and say it slow. What year was it?"

"513."

"513! You don't look it! Come, my boy, I am a stranger and friendless; be honest and honorable with me. Are you in your right mind?"

He said he was.

"Are these other people in their right minds?"

He said they were.

"And this isn't an asylum? I mean, it isn't a place where they cure crazy people?"

He said it wasn't.

"Well, then," I said, "either I am a lunatic, or something just as awful has happened. Now tell me, honest and true, where am I?"

"*In King Arthur's Court.*"

I waited a minute, to let that idea shudder its way home, and then said:

"And according to your notions, what year is it now?"

"528 – nineteenth of June."

I felt a mournful sinking at the heart, and muttered: "I shall never see my friends again – never, never again. They will not be born for more than thirteen hundred years yet."

I seemed to believe the boy, I didn't know why. *Something* in me seemed to believe him – my consciousness, as you may say; but my reason didn't. My reason straightway began to clamor; that was natural. I didn't know how to go about satisfying it, because I knew that the testimony of men wouldn't serve – my reason would say they were lunatics, and throw out their evidence. But all of a sudden I stumbled on the very thing, just by luck. I knew that the only total eclipse of the sun in the first half of the sixth century occurred on the 21st of June, A.D. 528, O.S., and began at 3 minutes after 12 noon. I also knew that no total eclipse of the sun was due in what to *me* was the present year – i.e., 1879. So, if I could keep my anxiety and curiosity from eating the heart out of me for forty-eight hours, I should then find out for certain whether this boy was telling me the truth or not.

Wherefore, being a practical Connecticut man, I now shoved this whole problem clear out of my mind till its appointed day and hour should come, in order that I might turn all my attention to the circumstances of the present moment, and be alert and ready to make the most out of them that could be made. One thing at a time, is my motto – and just play that thing for all it is worth, even if it's only two pair and a jack. I made up my mind to two things: if it was still the nineteenth century and I was among lunatics and couldn't get away, I would presently boss that asylum or know the reason why; and if, on the other hand, it was really the sixth century, all right, I didn't want any softer thing: I would boss the whole country inside of three months; for I judged I would have the start of the best-educated man in the kingdom by a matter of thirteen hundred years and upward. I'm not a man to waste time after my mind's made up and there's work on hand; so I said to the page:

"Now, Clarence, my boy – if that might happen to be your name – I'll get you to post me up a little if you don't mind. What is the name of that apparition that brought me here?"

"My master and thine? That is the good knight and great lord Sir Kay the Seneschal, foster brother to our liege the king."

"Very good; go on, tell me everything."

He made a long story of it; but the part that had immediate interest for me was this: He said I was Sir Kay's prisoner, and that in the due course of custom I would be flung into a dungeon and left there on scant commons until my friends ransomed me – unless I chanced to rot, first. I saw that the last chance had the best show, but I didn't waste any bother about that; time was too precious. The page said, further, that dinner was about ended in the great hall by this time, and that as soon as the sociability and the heavy drinking should begin, Sir Kay would have me in and exhibit me before King Arthur and his illustrious knights seated at the Table Round, and would brag about his exploit in capturing me, and would probably exaggerate the facts a little, but it wouldn't be good form for me to correct him, and not over safe, either; and when I was done being exhibited, then ho for the dungeon; but he, Clarence, would find a way to come and see me every now and then, and cheer me up, and help me get word to my friends.

Get word to my friends! I thanked him; I couldn't do less; and about this time a lackey came to say I was wanted; so Clarence led me in and took me off to one side and sat down by me.

Well, it was a curious kind of spectacle, and interesting. It was an immense place, and rather naked – yes, and full of loud contrasts. It was very, very lofty; so lofty that the banners depending from the arched beams and girders away up there floated in a sort of twilight; there was a stone-railed gallery at each end, high up, with musicians in the one, and women, clothed in stunning colors, in the other. The floor was of big stone flags laid in black and white squares, rather battered by age and use, and needing repair. As to ornament, there wasn't any, strictly speaking; though on the walls hung some huge tapestries which were probably taxed as works of art; battle-pieces, they were, with horses shaped like those which children cut out of paper or create in gingerbread; with men on them in scale armor whose scales are represented by round holes – so that the man's coat looks as if it had been done with a biscuit-punch. There was a fireplace big enough to camp in; and its projecting sides and hood, of carved and pillared stonework, had the look of a cathedral door. Along the walls stood men-at-arms, in breastplate and morion, with halberds for their only weapon – rigid as statues; and that is what they looked like.

In the middle of this groined and vaulted public square was an oaken table which they called the Table Round. It was as large as a circus ring; and around it sat a great company of men dressed in such various and splendid colors that it hurt one's eyes to look at them. They wore their plumed hats, right along, except that whenever one addressed himself directly to the king, he lifted his hat a trifle just as he was beginning his remark.

Mainly they were drinking – from entire ox horns; but a few were still munching bread or gnawing beef bones. There was about an average of two dogs to one man; and these sat in expectant attitudes till a spent bone was flung to them, and then they went for it by brigades and divisions, with a rush, and there ensued a fight which filled the prospect with a tumultuous chaos of plunging heads and bodies and flashing tails, and the storm of howlings and barkings deafened all speech for the time; but that was no matter, for the dog-fight was always a bigger interest anyway; the men rose, sometimes, to observe it the better and bet on it, and the ladies and the musicians stretched themselves out over their balusters with the same object; and all broke into delighted ejaculations from time to time. In the end, the winning dog stretched himself out comfortably with his bone between his paws, and proceeded to growl over it, and gnaw it, and grease the floor with it, just as fifty others were already doing; and the rest of the court resumed their previous industries and entertainments.

As a rule, the speech and behavior of these people were gracious and courtly; and I noticed that they were good and serious listeners when anybody was telling anything – I mean in a dog-fightless interval. And plainly, too, they were a childlike and innocent lot; telling lies of the stateliest pattern with a most gentle and winning naivety, and ready and willing to listen to anybody else's lie, and believe it, too. It was hard to associate them with anything cruel or dreadful; and yet they dealt in tales of blood and suffering with a guileless relish that made me almost forget to shudder.

I was not the only prisoner present. There were twenty or more. Poor devils, many of them were maimed, hacked, carved, in a frightful way; and their hair, their faces, their clothing, were caked with black and stiffened drenchings of blood. They were suffering sharp physical pain, of course; and weariness, and hunger and thirst, no doubt; and at least none had given them the comfort of a wash, or even the poor charity of a lotion for their wounds; yet you never heard them utter a moan or a groan, or saw them show any sign of restlessness, or any disposition to complain. The thought was forced upon me: "The rascals – *they* have served other people so in their day; it being their own turn, now, they were not expecting any better treatment than this; so their philosophical bearing is not an outcome of mental training, intellectual fortitude, reasoning; it is mere animal training; they are white Indians."

Chapter III
Knights of the Table Round

MAINLY the Round Table talk was monologues – narrative accounts of the adventures in which these prisoners were captured and their friends and backers killed and stripped of their steeds and armor. As a general thing – as far as I could make out – these murderous adventures were not forays undertaken to avenge injuries, nor to settle old disputes or sudden fallings out; no, as a rule they were simply duels between strangers – duels between people who had never even been introduced to each other, and between whom existed no cause of offense whatever. Many a time I had seen a couple of boys, strangers, meet by chance, and say simultaneously, "I can lick you," and go at it on the spot; but I had always imagined until now that that sort of thing belonged to children only, and was a sign and mark of childhood; but here were these big boobies sticking to it and taking pride in it clear up into full age and beyond. Yet there was something very engaging about these great simple-hearted creatures, something attractive and lovable. There did not seem to be brains enough in the entire nursery, so to speak, to bait a fish-hook with; but you didn't seem to mind that, after a little, because you soon saw that brains were not needed in a society like that, and indeed would have marred it, hindered it, spoiled its symmetry – perhaps rendered its existence impossible.

There was a fine manliness observable in almost every face; and in some a certain loftiness and sweetness that rebuked your belittling criticisms and stilled them. A most noble benignity and purity reposed in the countenance of him they called Sir Galahad, and likewise in the king's also; and there was majesty and greatness in the giant frame and high bearing of Sir Launcelot of the Lake.

There was presently an incident which centered the general interest upon this Sir Launcelot. At a sign from a sort of master of ceremonies, six or eight of the prisoners rose and came forward in a body and knelt on the floor and lifted up their hands toward the ladies' gallery and begged the grace of a word with the queen. The most conspicuously situated lady in that massed flower-bed of feminine show and finery inclined her head by way of assent, and then the spokesman of the prisoners delivered himself and his fellows into her hands for free pardon, ransom, captivity, or death, as she in her good pleasure might elect; and this, as he said, he was doing by command of Sir Kay the Seneschal, whose prisoners they were, he having vanquished them by his single might and prowess in sturdy conflict in the field.

Surprise and astonishment flashed from face to face all over the house; the queen's gratified smile faded out at the name of Sir Kay, and she looked disappointed; and the page whispered in my ear with an accent and manner expressive of extravagant derision –

"Sir *Kay*, forsooth! Oh, call me pet names, dearest, call me a marine! In twice a thousand years shall the unholy invention of man labor at odds to beget the fellow to this majestic lie!"

Every eye was fastened with severe inquiry upon Sir Kay. But he was equal to the occasion. He got up and played his hand like a major – and took every trick. He said he would state the case exactly according to the facts; he would tell the simple straightforward tale, without comment of his own; "and then," said he, "if ye find glory and honor due, ye will give it unto him who is the mightiest man of his hands that ever bare shield or strake with sword in the ranks of Christian battle – even him that sitteth there!" and he pointed to Sir Launcelot. Ah, he fetched them; it was a rattling good stroke. Then he went on and told how Sir Launcelot, seeking adventures, some brief time gone by, killed seven giants at one sweep of his sword, and set a hundred and forty-two captive maidens free; and then went further, still seeking adventures, and found him (Sir Kay) fighting a desperate fight against nine foreign knights, and straightway took the battle solely into his own hands, and conquered the nine; and that night Sir Launcelot rose quietly, and dressed him in Sir Kay's armor and took Sir Kay's horse and gat him away into distant lands, and vanquished sixteen knights in one pitched battle and thirty-four in another; and all these and the former nine he made to swear that about Whitsuntide they would ride to Arthur's court and yield them to Queen Guenever's hands as captives of Sir Kay the Seneschal, spoil of his knightly prowess; and now here were these half dozen, and the rest would be along as soon as they might be healed of their desperate wounds.

Well, it was touching to see the queen blush and smile, and look embarrassed and happy, and fling furtive glances at Sir Launcelot that would have got him shot in Arkansas, to a dead certainty.

Everybody praised the valor and magnanimity of Sir Launcelot; and as for me, I was perfectly amazed, that one man, all by himself, should have been able to beat down and capture such battalions of practiced fighters. I said as much to Clarence; but this mocking featherhead only said:

"An Sir Kay had had time to get another skin of sour wine into him, ye had seen the accompt doubled."

I looked at the boy in sorrow; and as I looked I saw the cloud of a deep despondency settle upon his countenance. I followed the direction of his eye, and saw that a very old and white-bearded man, clothed in a flowing black gown, had risen and was standing at the table upon unsteady legs, and feebly swaying his ancient head and surveying the company with his watery and wandering eye. The same suffering look that was in the page's face was observable in all the faces around – the look of dumb creatures who know that they must endure and make no moan.

"Marry, we shall have it again," sighed the boy; "that same old weary tale that he hath told a thousand times in the same words, and that he *will* tell till he dieth, every time he hath gotten his barrel full and feeleth his exaggeration-mill a-working. Would God I had died or I saw this day!"

"Who is it?"

"Merlin, the mighty liar and magician, perdition singe him for the weariness he worketh with his one tale! But that men fear him for that he hath the storms and the lightnings and all the devils that be in hell at his beck and call, they would have dug his entrails out these many years ago to get at that tale and squelch it. He telleth it always in the third person, making believe he is too modest to glorify himself – maledictions light upon him, misfortune be his dole! Good friend, prithee call me for evensong."

The boy nestled himself upon my shoulder and pretended to go to sleep. The old man began his tale; and presently the lad was asleep in reality; so also were the dogs, and the court, the lackeys, and the files of men-at-arms. The droning voice droned on; a soft snoring arose on all sides and supported it like a deep and subdued accompaniment of wind instruments. Some heads were bowed upon folded arms, some lay back with open mouths that issued unconscious music; the flies buzzed and bit, unmolested, the rats swarmed softly out from a hundred holes, and pattered about, and made themselves at home everywhere; and one of them sat up like a squirrel on the king's head and held a bit of cheese in its hands and nibbled it, and dribbled the crumbs in the king's face with naive and impudent irreverence. It was a tranquil scene, and restful to the weary eye and the jaded spirit.

This was the old man's tale. He said:

"Right so the king and Merlin departed, and went until an hermit that was a good man and a great leech. So the hermit searched all his wounds and gave him good salves; so the king was there three days, and then were his wounds well amended that he might ride and go, and so departed. And as they rode, Arthur said, I have no sword. No force [2], said Merlin, hereby is a sword that shall be yours and I may. So they rode till they came to a lake, the which was a fair water and broad, and in the midst of the lake Arthur was ware of an arm clothed in white samite, that held a fair sword in that hand. Lo, said Merlin, yonder is that sword that I spake of. With that they saw a damsel going upon the lake. What damsel is that? said Arthur. That is the Lady of the lake, said Merlin; and within that lake is a rock, and therein is as fair a place as any on earth, and richly beseen, and this damsel will come to you anon, and then speak ye fair to her that she will give you that sword. Anon withal came the damsel unto Arthur and saluted him, and he her again. Damsel, said Arthur, what sword is that, that yonder the arm holdeth above the water?

I would it were mine, for I have no sword. Sir Arthur King, said the damsel, that sword is mine, and if ye will give me a gift when I ask it you, ye shall have it. By my faith, said Arthur, I will give you what gift ye will ask. Well, said the damsel, go ye into yonder barge and row yourself to the sword, and take it and the scabbard with you, and I will ask my gift when I see my time. So Sir Arthur and Merlin alight, and tied their horses to two trees, and so they went into the ship, and when they came to the sword that the hand held, Sir Arthur took it up by the handles, and took it with him.

And the arm and the hand went under the water; and so they came unto the land and rode forth. And then Sir Arthur saw a rich pavilion. What signifieth yonder pavilion? It is the knight's pavilion, said Merlin, that ye fought with last, Sir Pellinore, but he is out, he is not there; he hath ado with a knight of yours, that hight Egglame, and they have fought together, but at the last Egglame fled, and else he had been dead, and he hath chased him even to Carlion, and we shall meet with him anon in the highway. That is well said, said Arthur, now have I a sword, now will I wage battle with him, and be avenged on him. Sir, ye shall not so, said Merlin, for the knight is weary of fighting and chasing, so that ye shall have no worship to have ado with him; also, he will not lightly be matched of one knight living; and therefore it is my counsel, let him pass, for he shall do you good service in short time, and his sons, after his days. Also ye shall see that day in short space ye shall be right glad to give him your sister to wed. When I see him, I will do as ye advise me, said Arthur. Then Sir Arthur looked on the sword, and liked it passing well. Whether liketh you better, said Merlin, the sword or the scabbard? Me liketh better the sword, said Arthur. Ye are more unwise, said Merlin, for the scabbard is worth ten of the sword, for while ye have the scabbard upon you ye shall never lose no blood, be ye never so sore wounded; therefore, keep well the scabbard always with you. So they rode into Carlion, and by the way they met with Sir Pellinore; but Merlin had done such a craft that Pellinore saw not Arthur, and he passed by without any words. I marvel, said Arthur, that the knight would not speak. Sir, said Merlin, he saw you not; for and he had seen you ye had not lightly departed. So they came unto Carlion, whereof his knights were passing glad. And when they heard of his adventures they marveled that he would jeopard his person so alone. But all men of worship said it was merry to be under such a chieftain that would put his person in adventure as other poor knights did."

Footnote 2. From M.T.: No matter.

Chapter IV
Sir Dinadan the Humorist

IT SEEMED TO ME that this quaint lie was most simply and beautifully told; but then I had heard it only once, and that makes a difference; it was pleasant to the others when it was fresh, no doubt.

Sir Dinadan the Humorist was the first to awake, and he soon roused the rest with a practical joke of a sufficiently poor quality. He tied some metal mugs to a dog's tail and turned him loose, and he tore around and around the place in a frenzy of fright, with all the other dogs bellowing after him and battering and crashing against everything that came in their way and making altogether a chaos of confusion and a most deafening din and turmoil; at which every man and woman of the multitude laughed till the tears flowed, and some fell out of their chairs and wallowed on the floor in ecstasy. It was just like so many children. Sir Dinadan was so proud of his exploit that he could not keep from telling over and over again, to weariness, how the immortal idea happened to occur to him; and as is the way with humorists of his breed, he was still laughing at it after everybody else had got through.

He was so set up that he concluded to make a speech – of course a humorous speech. I think I never heard so many old played-out jokes strung together in my life. He was worse than the minstrels, worse than the clown in the circus. It seemed peculiarly sad to sit here, thirteen hundred years before I was born, and listen again to poor, flat, worm-eaten jokes that had given me the dry gripes when I was a boy thirteen hundred years afterwards. It about convinced me that there isn't any such thing as a new joke possible. Everybody laughed at these antiquities – but then they always do; I had noticed that, centuries later. However, of course the scoffer didn't laugh – I mean the boy. No, he scoffed; there wasn't anything he wouldn't scoff at. He said the most of Sir Dinadan's jokes were rotten and the rest were petrified. I said 'petrified' was good; as I believed, myself, that the only right way to classify the majestic ages of some of those jokes was by geologic periods. But that neat idea hit the boy in a blank place, for geology hadn't been invented yet. However, I made a note of the remark, and calculated to educate the commonwealth up to it if I pulled through. It is no use to throw a good thing away merely because the market isn't ripe yet.

Now Sir Kay arose and began to fire up on his history-mill with me for fuel. It was time for me to feel serious, and I did. Sir Kay told how he had encountered me in a far land of barbarians, who all wore the same ridiculous garb that I did – a garb that was a work of enchantment, and intended to make the wearer secure from hurt by human hands. However he had nullified the force of the enchantment by prayer, and had killed my thirteen knights in a three hours' battle, and taken me prisoner, sparing my life in order that so strange a curiosity as I was might be exhibited to the wonder and admiration of the king and the court. He spoke of me all the time, in the blandest way, as 'this prodigious giant,' and 'this horrible sky-towering monster,' and 'this tusked and taloned man-devouring ogre', and everybody took in all this bosh in the naivest way, and never smiled or seemed to notice that there was any discrepancy between these watered statistics and me. He said that in trying to escape from him I sprang into the top of a tree two hundred cubits high at a single bound, but he dislodged me with a stone the size of a cow, which 'all-to brast' the most of my bones, and then swore me to appear at Arthur's court for sentence. He ended by condemning me to die at noon on the 21st; and was so little concerned about it that he stopped to yawn before he named the date.

I was in a dismal state by this time; indeed, I was hardly enough in my right mind to keep the run of a dispute that sprung up as to how I had better be killed, the possibility of the killing being doubted by some, because of the enchantment in my clothes. And yet it was nothing but an ordinary suit of fifteen-dollar slop-shops. Still, I was sane enough to notice this detail, to wit: many of the terms used in the most matter-of-fact way by this great assemblage of the first ladies and gentlemen in the land would have made a Comanche blush.

Indelicacy is too mild a term to convey the idea. However, I had read *Tom Jones*, and *Roderick Random*, and other books of that kind, and knew that the highest and first ladies and gentlemen in England had remained little or no cleaner in their talk, and in the morals and conduct which such talk implies, clear up to a hundred years ago; in fact clear into our own nineteenth century – in which century, broadly speaking, the earliest samples of the real lady and real gentleman discoverable in English history – or in European history, for that matter – may be said to have made their appearance. Suppose Sir Walter, instead of putting the conversations into the mouths of his characters, had allowed the characters to speak for themselves? We should have had talk from Rebecca and Ivanhoe and the soft lady Rowena which would embarrass a tramp in our day. However, to the unconsciously indelicate all things are delicate. King Arthur's people were not aware that they were indecent and I had presence of mind enough not to mention it.

They were so troubled about my enchanted clothes that they were mightily relieved, at last, when old Merlin swept the difficulty away for them with a common-sense hint. He asked them why they were so dull – why didn't it occur to them to strip me. In half a minute I was as naked as a pair of tongs! And dear, dear, to think of it: I was the only embarrassed person there. Everybody discussed me; and did it as unconcernedly as if I had been a cabbage. Queen Guenever was as naively interested as the rest, and said she had never seen anybody with legs just like mine before. It was the only compliment I got – if it was a compliment.

Finally I was carried off in one direction, and my perilous clothes in another. I was shoved into a dark and narrow cell in a dungeon, with some scant remnants for dinner, some moldy straw for a bed, and no end of rats for company.

⚹

The complete and unabridged text is available online, from *flametreepublishing.com/extras*

A Brain, A Heart, A Home, The Nerve

Valerie Valdes

Subject: Cecilia Maria Alfonso Martinez.
Timeline Designation: 0000000000001.

"WHERE DO BRUISES come from?" Ceci whispered as Dr. Lila listened to her chest. Her question was almost smothered by screams from one of the many tiny rooms in the free shot clinic.

The doctor pulled off her stethoscope and leaned down to face the girl. "They come from getting hit, but instead of cutting yourself you bleed inside." She put the stethoscope back on and lifted Ceci's shirt, frowning. "Did you hit yourself?"

Ceci shook her head, kicking her legs so that her heels banged the side of the exam table. "Liam hit me at school, on my arm." *That means he likes you,* her mother had said. She didn't say anything now, but shot Ceci a look that made her stop kicking.

"Your arm, huh?" The doctor stood her up and pulled down her pants, turning her left and right before finally sliding her sleeves up to examine the purpling circle on her forearm. "Is everything okay at home?" Dr. Lila asked. "Anything you want to talk about?" Her blue eyes stared out the window behind Ceci's shoulder.

Ceci's mother mouthed "No" and Ceci shook her head again.

"You're sure?"

Ceci nodded.

"Let's do your shots, then." Dr. Lila's smile was too big to be real. "We've got four here, but we'll try to do them quickly."

The doctor stepped away to get the needles from the counter. Behind her was a picture on the wall: a scene from *The Wizard of Oz*, Dorothy and the rest on the yellow brick road staring at the Emerald City in the distance. Hidden throughout were images from Kansas: her aunt and uncle's faces nestled in a tree trunk, chickens made of leaves or rocks, even a bicycle with branches for spokes. Things where they didn't belong, but Dorothy couldn't see them. Only Ceci could.

She looked down at her forearm just in time to see the bruise vanish. Blink, gone. She'd wished for it so many times…Only she hadn't been wishing now, had she?

"Doctor," she said, raising her unblemished arm. "Where do bruises go?"

* * *

"Doctor Martinez? I'm Doctor Bachman."

"Call me Cecilia, please." She sat in the doctor's private office with her wrinkled hands folded in her lap. A holo of what she assumed was his family flickered on the side of his desk, which was obscenely tidy. *Empty desk, empty mind,* she thought.

He looked young, probably in his late thirties, and reminded her of someone she couldn't place. Big blue eyes.

He waved a hand and charts appeared on the wall next to him. Cecilia stared at them, watery vision barely making out letters and numbers, the orderly assemblage of medical data that formed a picture she had once been able to read. More understandable was the image of her lungs, ghostly, as if filled with cobwebs. A second image was colored, three-dimensional, and this one floated over to sit on that big, clean desk as he rotated it with a finger.

"At this point, the damage is extensive," he said. "We can attempt surgery, but at your age, anesthesia can be tricky. And temporal redistribution in this case is impossible, as you well know."

Cecilia thought of her husband Luis, his hand shivering on her face as the clot in his brain exploded.

"Would you like to go over the options?"

"No, thank you," she said. "I already have a plan in place."

* * *

Dr. Martinez rubbed her eyes with one hand, her lab briefly blurring into a morass of white, red and gray. She was sure the math checked out, that the simulation was running properly, but the damn machine still wasn't working. It sat in the middle of the room, taunting her like a sphinx that refused to speak its riddle. Her students would ask her about it in class, and she would have to tell them the same thing she kept telling the administration: not yet, but soon.

Except that wasn't good enough. This was her last chance. If she couldn't deliver, her funding was already earmarked for another department, whose chair Dr. Hunt had happened to stop by for a friendly chat that mostly involved him scoping out her lab so he'd know what he could poach. He'd also flirted with her, even though she was married and twenty years his junior, the vulture. Academia was such a pleasure.

One more try and she would call it a night. Morning. Whatever. The medical dummy lay on the machine's bed, its mouth half-open, its waxy chest gashed courtesy of a scalpel, a bottle of rum and a particularly frustrated lab assistant. Dr. Martinez turned on the machine, watched the calibrations run, then pressed 'Start.'

It went through all the right motions, and then, finally, not a damn thing happened. Again. She sighed and closed her eyes. It had to work eventually, if her theories were correct. It already had at least once, hadn't it? But that didn't mean she would be – had been? – the one to figure it out.

Dr. Martinez wandered over to the dummy and patted its cheek. No sense driving all the way home only to come back in a few hours. "Salpica," she muttered, shoving the plastic man off the bed and curling up on her side, arms over her chest.

* * *

"It's not okay," Marisol said, taking a deep drag from an e-cig. "This is an intervention. Your grades are crap, you've stopped talking to everyone, and now this? *Ponte pá tu número.*"

"You sound like my mother," Sissy said. A waiter appeared at her elbow to fill her water glass, and she flinched. Embarrassed, she turned the motion into a sunglasses adjustment, accidentally brushing the bruise next to her eye, which began to throb again. "I had that job interview, at least. They're supposed to call me back today."

"I hope your makeup didn't look this bad when you met them." Marisol leaned closer. "*Estas de pipi, mija.*"

Sissy felt hot, all right. The sun of a Miami summer scorched her legs through her pants, which weren't covered by the big umbrella over their table at the café.

"It was an accident," she said.

"You don't accidentally punch people in the face."

"It's not like that."

"It's totally like that." Marisol reached out to grab her shoulder, and Sissy jumped so hard she knocked over her water. She muttered curses in Spanish under her breath and mopped up the mess with her napkin. Overhead, the sky darkened as a storm rolled in from over the ocean.

"*De pipi,*" Marisol said, shaking her head. "We're going to get my cousin's truck right now and move you out. Don't even try to argue."

Thunder grumbled an answer, and Sissy thought of Gabriel. He would be furious.

"It's going to rain," she muttered.

"Then we'll get wet," Marisol replied.

* * *

Ceci twirled her umbrella in her small hands, watching drops of water fly all over the floor of the Metrorail car. "*Mami*, why didn't we tell the doctor about –"

"*Cállate.* It's none of her business." Ceci's mother got that look, where her eyes got all big and her lips went away, so Ceci stopped talking.

Instead, she watched a man sleep on the seats a few rows behind them. A teenager bobbed her head to music only she could hear. An old lady sat in the seat next to the door, gripping a tiny black dog by the throat. Ceci watched, and watched, and the world passed outside and inside.

* * *

Wiping tears from her cheeks, Cecilia stepped into the elevator of the office building that housed the temporal redistribution clinic. When she first fell ill, it had taken her some time to comb through the personnel files, to find a technician with the skill to accomplish what she needed, but she had known it would happen eventually. Time was a closed loop, after all, wasn't it? And besides, she had done this before herself.

The walls were a soothing teal, like the clear waters of the Caribbean she had cruised with Luis so many times. She was escorted to a private room and left to wait for the specialist.

The machine looked like one of the old open MRI contraptions phased out a few decades earlier, with a bed for her to lie on and an arced rotating arm that could be moved from head to toe. Cecilia's breath caught in her throat as she looked at it – her life's work – which started a coughing fit, her round back shaking as her lungs tried vainly to expel the bits of her that didn't belong.

"Can I offer you some water, Doctor Martinez?" Dr. Prudhomme crouched next to her, dark hands on his knees.

She shook her head. It would pass, as these things did. Eventually the coughs died down to throat clearing, and Dr. Prudhomme stood.

"I told you to call me Cecilia," she said.

"And I told you I could not do so, anymore than I could call the President by her first name. You are still certain of what you intend?"

She looked at the machine and nodded. "Yes. It's time."

"Then I will retrieve the consent forms." He helped her stand, and she leaned against his thick body for support.

* * *

Dr. Martinez couldn't sleep. The bed was uncomfortable, but failure was worse. She had been so sure…It should have worked as well on inanimate objects as it would on living ones. Theoretically. Maybe if she tried it on a small plant? There were no plants in the lab. The only organic thing around was her.

Cecilia Maria Alfonso Martinez, she told herself sternly, *you are not going to experiment on yourself.*

The thought gave her chills. It went against every shred of logic and reason and training. History was littered with the bones of scientists who had succumbed to the lure of their own vanity. And yet.

Maybe memory is the key, said a tiny voice in the back of her head. *Sentimental nonsense*, she replied. And yet.

If it worked, this could be it. The end. If it didn't, she might as well start packing.

* * *

Gabriel stood in the doorway with his hands clenched into fists, shoulders squared as if he could turn himself into a wall. "Where are you going?"

"Go fry ice," Marisol snapped. "*Esto no tiene nada que ver contigo.*"

"I wasn't talking to you."

Sissy trembled behind Marisol, holding the last box of her things. She had known this would happen.

"*No me importa un pito* who you're talking to." If Gabriel was a wall, Marisol was a jackhammer. "Move or I'm calling the cops."

Gabriel took a step toward Sissy. "*Mi amor, mi corazón*, please don't leave me. We'll figure this out. We always do. *Mi cielo, mi alma*…" He held out his hand.

Sissy wanted to take it. She felt cold and small, standing in their apartment, walls eerily bare where there had been pictures of her and Gabriel smiling and kissing until Marisol threw them into garbage bags. Everything was already in the van outside except for this one box, heavy as life, which she was so tired of carrying.

"Move already," Marisol said. "It's over."

Gabriel streaked toward Marisol with his fist half-cocked. Sissy knew that look, and recoiled even though he wasn't gunning for her.

Marisol was faster, her arm whipping up like she was born ready. The pepper spray hit him square in the face, some of it misting into the air so even Sissy's nose burned. Gabriel shrieked and clawed at his face as Marisol shook her head, lips curled in disgust.

"*Hijo de puta*," she said. Then she turned her back on him like he wasn't there and pushed Sissy out the door.

Her legs felt like they were made of brick. The sun had almost disappeared behind the endless rows of houses, but it still glinted off the wet sidewalks, and there was even a rainbow off to the west. She couldn't bear it. Everything was too bright.

* * *

Ceci hid under her blanket, examining her new bruises with a flashlight. One, two, three, four, five. Her teachers said she was good at counting, and adding, and even subtracting. But she wasn't always good at being quiet. She wasn't good at not being seen.

Her mother cried on the floor of the bathroom, wailed like the stray cats that sometimes sat in the alley outside their apartment. "Oh god," she sobbed. "Why does it have to be so hard?"

Shifting the flashlight to one hand, Ceci used the other to tuck the blanket under her toes. She didn't know why it had to be so hard. Maybe if she did, she could make it better.

* * *

A tiny green light blinked at Cecilia as she lay on the table, from the computer on the end of the mechanical arm that swept up and down the length of her body. Her bones ached, but she knew it would be over soon.

"It has almost finished calibrations," Dr. Prudhomme said.

"I know," Cecilia replied. She had invented the machine, after all.

He frowned. "Of course. Forgive me my nerves. The complexity of the modified procedure –"

"It's fine," she said. She thought again of her first experiments: scrawling formulas on a white board. Adjusting. Recalibrating. Then, the breakthrough. And since then, the waiting, for the inevitable day that had finally arrived.

"I am ready now," Dr. Prudhomme said.

"So am I," she said, her voice cracking. The green light overhead stopped blinking and stayed steady, bright and clear.

* * *

It took Dr. Martinez a few minutes to write a note to her husband. She wanted to call him, to hear the sound of his voice, but it would only weaken her resolve. She might let him talk her out of it. Especially if this was it.

As she lay in the bed, the machine whirring into action, she found her thoughts straying. Not to the day when everything changed, the one that had set her on this path, but earlier.

A doctor's office. A picture on the wall with faces that weren't really there. Flying monkeys. And that bruise on her arm, the one a boy at school had given her – what was his name? God, she hadn't thought of him in years.

The machine whirred, and whined, and dinged.

* * *

The lights were out again in the parking lot of Marisol's apartment building, but Sissy was so excited it barely registered. She had gotten the job at the college. It wasn't much – answering phones, forwarding emails, smiling – but it was steady money, and she could take classes for free at night. She had almost dropped out after losing her scholarship, and now she could stay. It would take a little longer, but someday, she would be Dr. Cecilia Alfonso.

Her mom had been ecstatic. Marisol had dragged her out to dinner to celebrate, and they'd laughed and drank and danced in their matching glittery red heels until they were sober enough to go home. Well, she was sober, anyway; Marisol was passed out in the passenger seat.

She unlocked the front door and threw it open, a voice in the back of her mind whispering that it hadn't actually been locked, and then the light clicked on. Living room, couch, motley collection of saint candles in their tall glass containers. Just like they'd left it. She picked up a candle with a picture of San Lazaro, mostly empty, with a few stray matches inside. Why did she feel like a ghost had stuck its hand up her skirt?

Behind her, a thundercrack, so loud it turned her hearing into a dull dial tone. She turned and crouched at the same time, eyes huge. In the dim light spilling out her front door, she saw a shape step away from her car. Gabriel.

"This is all her fault," he said. "You wouldn't have left if it weren't for her." His voice sounded hollow, far away, even though he was so close she could have spit on him.

Slowly, shaking, Sissy stood and looked at her car. Marisol was slumped sideways, oh god, they had just been dancing, Marisol had gotten some guy's number and she was asleep and now her head…

"Look at me," he said, and she did. His eyes were red, like he'd been crying or drinking or both. Sweat beaded on his forehead, rolled down his nose like an errant tear.

She wanted to be angry, to turn her fingers into claws and cut his face into pieces. Instead she trembled, frozen, still clutching the candle. He took one step forward, then another, deeper into the long shadow she cast standing there in her doorway, and she couldn't bring herself to back away. The gun in his hand seemed to suck up all the light as he leveled it at her chest.

"I'm sorry," Gabriel said. Like he always did.

Sissy closed her eyes as the gun went off again and again.

* * *

Ceci's mother watched her eat her cereal in silence, the bags under her eyes nearly the color of the five bruises on Ceci's arm.

"You'll have to wear a shirt with sleeves today," she said quietly.

Ceci kept chewing her chocolate puffs.

"Baby, you know I didn't mean to hurt you. You just make me so frustrated sometimes."

She knew. She knew it like she knew her favorite cereal tore up the roof of her mouth. She loved it anyway.

Ceci put her spoon down and got off her chair. She walked over to her mother and crawled into her lap, and let herself be held for a little while. In her bowl, her cereal softened and turned her milk to chocolate.

* * *

Cecilia gasped, eyes flying open as the pain hit. She had expected it, but she had thought death would be quick. Instead, she felt her heart stagger, struggle to keep pumping blood even though it was broken.

"Be at peace, Doctor," Dr. Prudhomme said gently, tapping something on his console. "It has been my honor to know you."

Drugs flooded her veins, burning cold. With a smile and a sigh, she laid a hand over the wounds in her chest.

* * *

Dr. Martinez looked down and smiled. "Suck it, Hunt. That funding is mine."

There on her arm, the size of a small boy's fist, was a perfect purple bruise.

* * *

Click. Click. Sissy opened her eyes.

Gabriel stared at his gun, turning it one way, then the other. "Que rayo –"

The confusion on his face broke something in her. She swung the San Lazaro candle at his face, where it shattered, shards of glass driving through his eyelids, his lips, his cheeks. He screamed, dropping the gun and clutching at his eyes. Blood fell in fat drops to the ground as he cursed at her, his words muddled.

It occurred to her that she should be dead, but the thought buzzed around her like a mosquito settling on a place to bite. Sirens wailed, drawing closer until they drowned out the sound of Gabriel's cries. One neighbor finally appeared, an old lady who took one look at the bullet casings on the asphalt before crossing herself and praying a fervent Hail Mary.

Sissy sat down at some point, on her doorstep, because her feet hurt. Someone stood in front of her and asked her a question in English, which she suddenly couldn't understand. The question was repeated in Spanish, and her eyes focused on a cop, huge and dark.

"Do you need medical attention?" he asked again. "Are you hurt?"

Sissy shook her head, then nodded, then burst into tears.

"Martinez, get over here," he said. One of the paramedics jogged over, kneeling next to her.

"Hey there, miracle," the man said softly. "Can you walk?"

She decided that she probably could. He offered her a hand but she waved it off and stood, hobbled to the ambulance by herself, kicking off her shiny red shoes as she went.

This Door is Locked

Adam Vine

THE CLIFFS stabbed like a crusted knife from dark sea to pale night. David pulled his step at the last second before he ran off the edge, barely avoiding a fall that would have smashed him to pieces on the jagged rocks lurking a thousand feet below. He stumbled backward and vomited on the snow.

Few things were more unpredictable, or harder on the stomach than traveling through the Doors. An air car dropping too fast off a high platform, maybe, or launching into space on the equatorial fast track for the first time.

The Escher Door had dropped him on top of a devil's tower, a five hundred foot-tall needle of black stone rising over a gnashing, alien sea. Beyond the salt water channel, at least ten miles away, a mainland of pale fjords marched away in every direction. There was nothing on top of David's tall, miserable little island but a single tree anchored bitterly beneath the permafrost.

Fragmented images rose through the murky penumbra of his memory: Rose's smile, an old man in a tower, a ship half-buried in snow.

I gotta keep moving, David told himself. *If I don't move I'm gonna die. The Last Door is out there. All I need to do is find it, and I'll be a fixture in the history books until the end of days. I'll finally be able make some real money, buy Rose that cottage on the bluffs of Bolinas. I must be getting close. Maybe this time I'll actually find it.*

Maybe this time.

Instinct drove his hands into his pockets, where he found his supplies were almost gone. He had a few vacuum-sealed bags of Earl Grey, enough water to last another day or two, three protein bars, and a picture of Rose smiling under an umbrella on a rainy Budapest riverside. Their second date, David remembered, back before they were both starving professors trying to eke out a living in the oversaturated, over-priced wasteland of New York.

An old, hollow pain in his heart made David think about taking a running leap off the cliff's edge, and suddenly he wanted nothing more than to splatter himself on those distant, glaive-like rocks, to feed whatever creatures lurked beneath the waves of this planet's briny, black ocean, wherever this planet was. But he knew it was just the pain of seeing her face again.

This world, the world of the fjords, is the best candidate we have for being their home world. If I'm going to do it, it's not going to be until after I find them.

There was no other way down from the devil's tower that David could see. Returning through the Door was never an option, either. Escher Doors were one-way.

Where the hell is my ship? He could remember landing it, but not where, which meant the memory wasn't very old or very recent, but somewhere in the middle.

The Escher Doors robbed you of your short-term memories. That was the price you paid to wander through them. But David had been wandering long enough that the oldest memories of his pilgrimage had started becoming fixed. It was only a matter of time until-

The wind howled, cold biting through David's jacket, making his knees buckle and collapse. He fell onto his knees and vomited again on the snow, the empty contents of his stomach an embarrassingly small offering to the gods of this stark, frozen world.

Gotta find shelter. Fast. Too weak to try climbing. Body temperature dropping. I need something to eat. I'm so hungry.

The thought of food was enough to motivate him to move. He found his feet, brushed the snow and loitering bits of vomit off his beard and clothes, and began frantically searching for something, anything, that would point the way to the next Door.

But there was nothing. Soon the gray, glass bottle bottom sun sank behind the fjords, and David was forced to make camp, digging a tiny shelter in the snowbank under the foot of the island's single tree that he hoped – no, prayed – would keep him alive until morning.

A green light caught his eye while he was digging, far off across the fjords and the bruised, purple sea, as the dusk finally deepened.

It was only a tiny, green glimmer, so miniscule that if David didn't know what it was, he might have mistaken it for some bioluminescent animal prowling the shoreline. He watched the soft, jade light flickering on and off, as regular as a heartbeat, until he was done digging, then as he laid shivering in his shelter, waiting for sleep to take him. He watched it when he woke up at night to urinate, and again when the wind howled like a blizzard of throwing knives over the mouth of his shelter.

David knew the light's source could only be one thing. It was one of the ten million-year lamps that guarded each Escher Door, the beacons set to guide the Wanderers on their long, endless pilgrimage.

He awoke to the grey light of dawn seeping over the fjords, and a soft, mechanical buzzing in his ear. David leapt up out of his snowy bed, and immediately kicked himself for being so easily startled. Each Escher Door was fitted with a resupply station to replenish those who traveled through it.

Rose would be laughing at me right now.

The pain of losing her was always the worst after waking up. Her voice echoed in his mind's ear: *I don't want you to go. What if something bad happens to you?*

He saw her wiping her eyes on the back of her wrists, took them, and kissed her on the eyelids.

Nothing bad is going to happen to me, babe.

What had the old man had said about redemption being the inversion of selfishness? David couldn't remember.

The whirring sound grew louder with each handful of snow. His fingers scraped metal less than a foot down, and the bare corner of the small, spherical delivery plate of a food printer peered up at him.

The machine had sensed him exit the Escher Door and cycled on sometime during the night. David couldn't blame a machine that was several million years old for taking a few hours to turn on. He only hoped that whatever it printed was still edible.

Thankfully, it was. The raw, dirty paste that fed from the printer's nozzle into an insta-fabbed leaf cup tasted disgusting, but it gave him enough strength to get up and move around.

He washed his face and hands with the snow, placed the leaf he'd eaten out of in the printer's recycling bay, and started looking for the path that would lead him to the next Door, which he now knew for certain was hidden on top of the devil's tower.

Within minutes, David found the hatch.

It was an old fashioned trapdoor built into the ground and hidden under several feet of snow, not five paces away from the nutrient station. The hatch hissed open as he muscled through the ages of rust and time that had sealed it.

David crouched and lowered himself into the dark dampness of the ancient stone stairwell. It was several degrees warmer here than up top, and grew even warmer as he descended. Automated lanterns in the ceiling and walls flickered on as he passed. The lanterns had been one of the first subjects of David's study when he began specializing in Wanderer culture back at the university in New York.

Feels like that life belonged to a different person, David reflected, as those old memories came back to him: of cramming to finish lesson plans, and braving hordes of students at office hours; of pinching every penny so he and Rose could make rent each month on that stupid, microscopic studio apartment that always stank of burning roaches; of practicing with the band, of missing practice; of the rare one or two days a year when they got a gig, and he could let it all go; of his fingers dancing up the worn neck of his Engelhart stand up double bass, the only item of any value he and Rose owned; of Rose's eyes glimmering, inches from the stage, as if they existed only for him.

At last, the stairwell opened to a wide tunnel hewn into the glistening rock of the channel floor. Huge dripstones hung from the ceiling like a theater of forgotten puppets, overgrowing the ancient pictograms the Wanderers had cut into the walls.

Those mood pictures were the only form of writing the Wanderers had left behind. David had once published a theory that the indecipherable, swirling doodles had held religious significance, that they didn't tell a story, but were more akin to visual hymns.

They are formless. Pure. Like jazz, they wander without knowing the road, only the destination.

But like all David's theories, that one would likely go unfulfilled unless David found what he was looking for. The Wanderers appeared to have destroyed all written records of their history once the Escher Doors were built, including any discernable map to where the Doors led, which was why David's mentor Dr. Liapis had informally given the long-since-vanished alien species their moniker. No physical remains of the Wanderers' bodies had ever been found.

They went through the Last Door, David thought, gazing at the swirling, mystic spirals that graced the cave walls. *And the Last Door is here. On this world. It has to be. All of my research pointed to the Fjord World being the end of the pilgrimage. It was some kind of last rite for their species, the last staging ground before moving on to their promised land.*

I'll never know until I find that Door. I'll never know until I walk through it.

The tunnel went on for so long that David lost all sense of time. He was hungry again when he finally saw the tunnel's endpoint, a filled-in halo of white light gleaming in the distance above him. The tunnel curved upward and David ascended into cold air.

The tunnel exited onto a snowbound isle in the middle of the fjord, a meter or so higher than sea level. The island's only feature was an ornate stone archway guarded by a blinking, floating buoy that spat bursts of brilliant green light every few seconds – the same light

David had seen from the top of the devil's tower. A few scaly birds resembling Terran sea gulls nested on the buoy.

The Escher Door was a little one, built for local on-world travel, not the slightly larger kind that could jump you across entire arms of the Milky Way in the blink of an eye. Wherever it led was somewhere relatively near, and paying for the ride would cost only a negligible amount of David's short-term memory. Any apprehension he might've felt was forgotten as soon as he stepped through, as was everything else he'd felt since waking up the previous afternoon: the cliffs, the tree, the shelter, the dirty paste, the tunnel and its incomprehensible wonders.

David forgot everything but jazz, and Rose.

* * *

A wall of cobwebs met him on the other side. He felt sick and tasted bile in his mouth. His memory came back much quicker this time, as did the pain of Rose's absence. Some old argument effervesced from the buried annals of his mind.

If you don't go, David, how will we ever have a future? How will we afford to have kids, a state-of-the-art home gym, to live in the Bay Area and buy a cottage on the bluffs of Bolinas, so you can busk with your band on Nob Hill?

I don't know, Rose. I don't know how we'll do those things. But this feels wrong. It feels like I'm about to make the worst mistake I've ever made.

Then don't go.

Don't say that. You know I won't.

I love you. And I'll support whatever decision you make.

His fingers instinctively found the worn, smooth corners of the amber bracelet she had given him to match the necklace he got for her their first Christmas together. They had chosen amber because it was the only precious stone either of them could afford. The sunburst stones still held their cool, dusky glow, but the silver setting was tarnished and ruined. Three of the amber leaves in its spiraling tree motif had fallen out. David couldn't remember when.

Still, it was the last piece of her David still had other than that old picture.

Rationally, he knew Rose might no longer be alive. Nobody knew how the Doors worked, if Door travel actually was as instantaneous as it seemed, or if there were relativistic effects like those that accompanied normal acceleration. Would he return to Earth to find that Rose had grown very old, like the twin who was left behind from Einstein's infamous paradox? Or worse, that she was several hundred, or several thousand years dead?

You made this choice for a reason, he reminded himself. *And now you're going to see it through.*

He exited onto a huge plaza at the heart of a vast stone city nestled between the walls of a great fjord. A hundred tawny torches blazed silently from the walls of the abandoned metropolis.

The plaza was made of many small islands floating upon an oblong lake, all connected by causeways that formed a shallow quincunx of canals. The horizontal pattern mirrored the vertical one the city itself carved from either side of the fjord. It was the most awesome architectural marvel David had ever seen.

Thousands, perhaps millions of stairways, tunnels, and arched doorways dotted the sheer cliff faces, weaving a singular, flowing mood picture a hundred times larger

TIME TRAVEL SHORT STORIES

than Manhattan. The telltale glimmers of uncountable lanterns sparkled in every groove and spiral.

At first glance, it looked like a giant, stone-wrought maze. But as David's eyes studied the rolling, fluid images cut into the escarpment, he began to see that none of it was supposed to be connected at all.

A city of neighbors who could never meet. A multitude of Doors leading to nowhere and everywhere at once. But that was the point, wasn't it?

As much as he wanted to stay and fall upward into the pale vertigo of that infinite city forever, David didn't have time to stand around gawking. The sun had set, the moons were rising, and despite the queer calm of the air, he didn't want to get stranded again without real shelter or food if the weather changed for the worse.

There was a small, minaret tower watching over the plaza of canals that looked different in style and structure than the surrounding buildings. Its light was yellow, not green, and it appeared to have been recently built.

David headed towards it, finding the most direct path he could across the interconnected islands of the plaza. When he was halfway across, he noticed that the yellow light wasn't a beacon, like those guarding the Doors, but an indoor light shining through an open window.

Someone still lives there, David thought. *Door Traffic Control, maybe? A caretaker? No. That's a human structure.*

Someone else is already here.

The possibility that he might not be the first to have discovered this world, that he wouldn't be the first to wander through the Last Door, filled David with deep, existential dread. His fear was tempered only by the thought of taking a long, deep drink of clean water and filling his belly with something hot.

Dr. Liapis and I were the only two people who were supposed to know about this Door-path. No one else so much as speculated about it, let alone that it could lead to the Last Door. It was a shot in the dark, which is why he sent me all the way out here instead of coming himself.

A dark shape blotted the light in the window. David's blood turned to cool sludge. *Who the hell is that?*

When David reached the foot of the tower, a distinctly human shape stuck his head out of the window and called down to him, in American English, "Look at you! You made it in one piece. Open the gate and come upstairs. There's hot food and tea. The door's automated. The password is Charles Mingus."

David tried, but the door of the tower wouldn't open. "Did you say Mingus? As in, the jazz bass player, Charles Mingus?"

"The legendary, the one and only. But just hold on. That old thing can be a real pain in the ass if you don't know how to jangle it right. I'll do it for you. Be right down," the man said.

An instant later the door to the tower slid open, and David was enveloped in a bubble of warmth and light.

An old man stood in front of him, silhouetted against the light spilling out from the interior, but David could see him clearly enough to know he was no one who had ever worked in the very small, very catty academic field of Xenoanthropology, at least while David was alive.

The man was short, much shorter than David, and completely bald save for two slender gray quasar jets of hair sprouting from either side of his head. He wore a water-reclaiming outskin that resembled a suit of tight, but comfortable pajamas, and his eyes held the two-tone look of someone who is used to having two conversations simultaneously – one with the person they are speaking to, and a separate one about that person inside their own head.

The old man extended his hand. "Pleasure to finally meet you, Doctor Tovakol. I've been waiting for you for a long time."

David shook the old man's hand and said, "Hi. Look, I don't mean to be blunt, but…"

The old man cut him off. "You thought you were the only one here. It appears you are not."

"All right," David said. "So, who are you?"

"I'm Nobody," the old man said.

Great, David thought. *This guy isn't just a lonely old nut living out here at the salty edge of bumfuck nowhere. He's a cracked lonely old nut living out here at the salty edge of bumfuck nowhere.*

"Is that your first name or surname?" David said.

The old man tilted his head, his tone losing its hint of jovial amusement. "Did I stutter, Doctor?"

"Look. I'm sorry. I'm really thirsty and I haven't eaten in…well, I can't remember how long, but it's been a while. Can I come in?" David said.

The old man shrugged. "I thought you'd never ask."

David followed the old man inside. "Wait," he said. "I have to know something. Were you really the first one? Or have there been others?"

The old man paused, setting one foot on the stairs. "I was, and remain, the first and only human being other than you to ever take a living breath on this world. Not that it matters. It was never ours to discover."

The old man's humility made David angry. "So I was right. This was their home world? Or at least, their capital?" David said.

"This entire galaxy was their home. But yes, this planet was where they first evolved from the primordial soup. It remained sentimental to them, until the very last shedding of their lower culture.

"Now, please, Doctor. I'd prefer if we had this conversation upstairs," the old man said.

They went up the tower, ascending a simple spiral stairwell lined with a hypnotizing array of stone panels floating in protective vacuum cases. At first David thought they were mood drawings, salvaged from some corner of the Wanderers' civilization he had yet to see, until he noticed they were laser-etched.

"You're mapping them," David said.

The old man turned and looked down at David over his shoulder, stopped and leaned on the handrail of the stairs. "I was, yes. Or rather, I was trying to, until I learned the Door-paths can't be mapped. Come along. These damned stairs get a little harder to climb each day, and soon I won't be able to ascend this phallic eyesore at all."

"But…" before David could speak, the old man cut him off.

"If you wanted to ask *why,* you should've majored in philosophy. Come along now. This way."

David kept his mouth shut, ascending the rest of the long, winding stairway in silence.

The tower's penthouse was a circular room with panoramic windows looking out over the dusk-lit fjords. The only furnishings were a twin bed and slapped-together kitchenette, and a crude worktable.

Instead of the expected, stereotypical piles of dusty vellum scrolls, glass beakers, and spider-infested grimoires, the old man's study was crowded with piles of curved, sanded wood in various stages of becoming large, stringed musical instruments.

David recognized the pieces instantly. *He's making standup double basses.*

Here was the scroll, half-finished. There, the neck and belly, missing only the final polish. The vices of the old man's workstation held the youngest iterations, naked in their raw hillocks of sawdust, while his completed works surrounded his bed like a guardianship of wooden soldiers.

"Curious, isn't it? That two musicians should find each other all the way out here, at the fuzzy edges of spacetime. Please, give one a try," the old man said.

David touched one of the finished basses, admiring the old man's handiwork, tilted the hollow body into his arms and plucked out a few notes, the opening riff of Mingus's *Hog Callin' Blues*. The instrument's sound was deep and elegant.

The old man beamed. It wasn't pride David saw gleaming in his eye, but the deep respect of process. "You haven't seen the trees of this world yet, but they are truly grand. The wood gives a different sound than what you get back on Earth. That's all it is. My skill as a luthier is still light years away from decent. But the wood compensates for my shoddy craftsmanship. I suppose in another fifty or a hundred years, I'll start to get the hang of it."

David gave a polite smile. "You've got one hell of a hobby," he said.

The old man went over to the kitchenette and put a pot of water on to boil. "Tea?"

David nodded.

"Earl Grey?"

David took a seat at the kitchen table. "Yes. Black."

"How would I get milk out here, young man, or sugar, for that matter? Even these tea bags are probably a few centuries old, taking Door travel into account. Thankfully, they're vacuum-sealed."

The old man handed him the steaming mug. David sipped it, letting the heat spill down through his body. When was the last time he'd had a cup of real tea? *Not since leaving the ship,* he thought. Days? Weeks? Or was it years ago?

"Now, let's get down to the nitty-gritty," the old man said, taking a seat at the table beside him. "I don't have all the answers, and the ones I have will not be satisfactory. You will just have to accept that you won't know everything, yet."

"I'm not sure I can do that," David said.

The old man cleared his throat and began: "The Doors have funny effects on time. You and I both have passed through probably one too many for our own good. Because of that, there are at least three of us who know about this place: you, your professor, and yours truly. I've dedicated my life to studying the Freeway, ever since I was your age, and I still haven't figured out exactly how it works, nor how I arrived before you did, you being the one who is actually credited with its discovery back on Earth."

"I am?" David said.

The old man nodded. "You are. I have scarce communication with them these days. The Freeway isn't as exotic a subject as it once was. Research into it barely receives any funding at all. The people's imagination has seemingly moved on."

David shook his head. "How? We barely know anything about the Wanderers back home. I've never even heard the Escher Doors referred to as the Freeway before you just said it. But, I admit, we know even less about the effects of traversing them, so, I'll concede that anything's possible," he said.

"Ha! Wanderers..." The old man cackled. "I remember when I used to call them that. Of course, it's been decades."

"What do you call them?" David said.

"Why, nothing. They were Nobodies. Like me."

"I don't understand," David said.

The old man gave him a sympathetic look. "The enigmatic ancients you have traveled so far and sacrificed so much to study were a self-annihilating culture. Not suicidal, mind you – they sought to eradicate the idea of personal importance, of being *someone*, from their cultural id. It's the entire reason they constructed the Freeway in the first place."

"That's a theory I haven't heard before," David said.

A fire lit in the old man's eyes. "It is only my professional opinion, but it's one I've formed over tens of thousands of hours of meticulous research, decades I spent here alone, freezing my bloody butt cheeks off and surviving off of protein paste so I could one day tell you about it. Do you think I would have chosen this path if I didn't have at least a solid inkling of what's going on?"

"I suppose not," David said.

"The Nobodies' civilization advanced to the point where they realized that rampant individualism was the driving force responsible for the worst evils of their world: greed, poverty, famine, war. Yet, it is in the nature of all intelligent beings to be self-interested, and technology only amplifies this primitive urge. Considering the level of technology they had, it was only a matter of time before they destroyed themselves, and the entire galaxy along with them.

"So the Nobodies started a gargantuan project, the largest in their history, to eradicate the ego from their species. They built the devices we call Escher Doors, a vast network of portals placed at seemingly random points throughout the Milky Way, which wipe the short-term memory of anyone who walks through them."

"I think I follow you, so far," David said.

"This network is what I have come to call the Freeway, because the Nobodies believed that traveling it was the only way for the individual, and thus society as a whole, to become totally free," the old man said.

"Free of what?" David said.

"Of the baggage of egoism," the old man said.

"And do you believe that?" David said.

A smirk curled up the side of the old man's lips. "Does it matter what I think? You're going to complete your journey regardless of what I tell you, even if I say with 100% certainty that doing so will mean not only erasing every last shred of your desire to become Someone of Importance...it will also mean you can never, ever return home."

"You found the Last Door," David said. It wasn't a question.

The old man's fingers tapped out a burning rhythm on the tabletop. "That is an interesting way to phrase it. The answer to your question is yes, but in my experience, that way of seeing things is not entirely accurate. The Doors work like jazz. You wander through them, experiencing riffs on a scale, but there is no definite structure, no pre-determined road to where you are going. The music can go on forever, or it can stop as soon as the musician – or the audience – grows tired."

"Did you find it or not?" David said.

"Calm down, Doctor. I already told you I found the Door you're looking for, and passed through it. But while it is true that all Doors lead to the same place, eventually, the Door you came here to find is certainly not the last."

David was about to open his mouth and demand that the old man take him, but the old man put a gentle hand on his, all blue veins and pale wrinkles, and said, "I know what it is you want. Why you came so far. Why you gave up what you did, even nearly losing your life. I have no quarrel with any of it, Doctor. I understand. I was young once, too. I simply want you to be ready before I take you there, to be prepared for what will happen to you. And it sure as hell isn't going to be before you finish your tea."

They set out into the eternal twilight, two lone pilgrims wandering through howling drifts of snow and shadow, their own shapes cast indecisively, growing long, then short, then long again as they passed under the periodic lights of the city.

"It took me almost a decade to realize they never lived here," the old man said as they walked.

"How?" David said.

"Tested the soil. No signs of carbon-based life ever having settled in these dwellings."

A sudden wind bit into them, driving the cold deep beneath his skin. It never seemed to end, that cold; hadn't, since he'd started wandering through the Doors; even the brief respite of warmth and light in the old man's study hadn't driven it away for long.

"Where are we going?" David said.

The old man pointed.

Far ahead of them, the ghostly tip of a high hill could be seen rising from the city's labyrinthine skyline, conjoining the massive canyon walls into a single line of impassable, craggy white.

They began to ascend, and soon David could see the city's shape falling away around them, a spiraling maze of concentric stone rings of which the hill they were now climbing was the center.

"So why'd they build a city they never intended to live in?" David said.

The old man shrugged. "Did you notice anything different about the doors of those houses we passed?"

David squinted to look at the distant, twisting avenues winding up the cliffs. All of the arched doorways had been intentionally sealed by piles of rubble.

"They're blocked," David said.

"Yes. They are," the old man said. "All of them, closed until the end of time. Except, those aren't houses. By the time this city was built, the Nobodies' society had already advanced past the point where they lived in houses at all. They carried everything they needed on their backs. Every door you see in this city is an Escher Door."

So they are, David realized. There were hundreds of them, thousands; uncountable portals leading to myriad worlds scattered further across space and time than the imagination could grasp.

This isn't a city. It's a transit hub. How did I miss it before? Or did I already know, and forgot?

The old man seemed to read David's mind. "Yes, this place was the great hub of the Nobodies' Freeway. And now every gate in the terminal is closed, every single Escher Door here, except the one you came through, is a collapsed, dead end."

"Why?" David said.

The old man's chest puffed. "Because I closed them. I was spending too much time wandering, and I had work to do. Funny, isn't it? Traveling through the Doors was the one thing that prevented me from crafting my theory about how they worked."

They reached the summit of the hill. A single, familiar light burned through the pirouetting snow devils, above an archway whose Escher Doorway was still open.

"I thought you said they were all closed," David said.

The old man cracked a smile. "Part of me wants to leave you to figure it out for yourself, but without knowing what I'm about to tell you, it will be impossible. Besides, I won't get another chance to say it. This is the last time we will see each other, Doctor Tavakol, for a very long time," the old man said.

"Tell me," David said.

"We were both mistaken about how the Doors worked when we first arrived at this place. The Doors are purposeful errors in the spacetime quantum structure, like playing a wrong note on purpose during a concert. Except, spacetime is a self-correcting architecture. It is always stable. The Nobodies found a way to exploit that stability, by hacking one of its fundamental rules, that forward motion through time is an inherently destabilizing motion. The universe balances itself by constantly replaying its own melodies and harmonies so there are no wrong notes.

"You aren't transmitted the way a photon is when you travel through the Doors. The act of the universe rebalancing itself is literally making you a false correction somewhere else, at some other time, to balance out the error you've made in the present by opening it.

"That is why Door travel costs memories, and why walking through *that*..." the old man pointed to the Last Door where it stood, now a mere fifty meters ahead of them across the hilltop's flat, snowy plateau, "...will not take you where you wish to go."

"Where does it go, then?" David said.

"Only where you need to," the old man said.

They were almost to the Door now, so close David could practically feel its shimmering veil washing the pain of regret from his mind.

The old man grabbed his arm as he was about to step through. "David, please. The Nobodies went through this Door for the exact opposite reason we did, that you still feel you must. But I promise you won't find them through this Door. I beg you to reconsider. This Door does not lead to Someone."

David looked down at the veiny, pale hand grasping his arm. The old man's sleeve had fallen back to reveal the ancient glimmer of a silver bracelet bearing the shape of a spiraling tree. Most of the tree's amber leaves were long since fallen, but the few that remained still held their dusky, sunburst glow.

The old man winced and withdrew his hand.

But David couldn't turn back, not after coming so far, after sacrificing so much. "If I don't, I'm nothing. We both know I have to do this," David said, and stepped through the Last Door.

The old man sighed. "I'll leave the light on for you."

* * *

The room was a tiny, hot mess high in the sky traffic zone of some ancient upper Manhattan smogscraper, the furniture all clinging to the corners between the poorly placed abutments and piles of discarded clothes, barely a hundred square feet if you included the bathroom and oven-less kitchen. The window was open, as always, an almost futile measure to beat the brutal heat of the New York autumn. Dusk had already settled, and far below, the slow, perpetual red storm of the city churned indifferently under sideways pillars of pollution. Somewhere in the apartment, a woman was crying.

David knocked on the bathroom door, wiggled the knob and found that it was locked. "Rose?" he said.

The sobbing ceased for a moment and resumed.

She's pretending not to hear me over the noise of the fan. He knocked again. "Hey baby? Are you all right?"

Another long pause, then a faint, whimpering, "No."

"Will you come out?"

A moment later the door opened. Rose stood in the doorway, her face framed by a halo of wild curls. She gave him a teary frown and hugged him like she'd never let go, said, "I don't want you to leave."

"I know, sweetheart. But we talked about this. This is what's best for both of us. You said that. Remember?"

Rose nodded.

"Do you know how much I love you?" David said.

Rose pulled back, wiping her eyes with the back of her wrist. She nodded. "Yeah."

He kissed her on the eyelid. "I'm sorry, baby. I wouldn't have taken this assignment if I knew it was going to hurt you. We both knew this was coming. We don't want to live like this forever, right? What about the cottage in Bolinas?"

A fresh wave of tears spouted. She buried her face in her hands, said, "I'm just going to miss you so much. What if something bad happens to you?"

"Nothing bad is going to happen. I'll be back. I promise," David said, feeling more false than he ever had in all his life.

She walked him out to the hall to pick up his bag, since there wasn't enough space for it on the floor of their former – now Rose's – apartment, then they stepped out onto the platform where the air taxi was waiting to take him to the university's orbital fast track. He kissed her deeply, gazing long into the eyes of the last woman he would ever love, whose heart he was again breaking in pursuit of a dream, as he had countless, unremembered times before, as he would countless, unremembered times again.

I'll fix this. I'll be back as soon as I find it, he convinced himself. But as the air car lurched and fell away from the platform and the waving, weeping figure it held, another, deeper part of him said, *No, David. You won't. The mistake has already been made. Every choice is a door, and this door is already locked.*

* * *

The cliffs stabbed like a crusted knife from dark sea to pale night. David pulled his step at the last second before he ran off the edge, barely avoiding a fall that would have smashed him to pieces on the jagged rocks lurking a thousand feet below. He stumbled backward and vomited on the snow.

The Escher Door had dropped him on top of a devil's tower, a five hundred foot-tall needle of black stone rising over a gnashing, alien sea. Beyond the salt water channel, at least ten miles away, a mainland of pale fjords marched away in every direction. There was nothing on top of David's tall, miserable little island but a single tree anchored bitterly beneath the permafrost.

Fragmented images rose through the murky penumbra of his memory: Rose's smile, an old man in a tower, a ship half-buried in snow.

I gotta keep moving, David told himself. *If I don't move I'm gonna die. The Last Door is out there. All I need to do is find it, and I'll be a fixture in the history books until the end of days. I'll finally be able make some real money, buy Rose that cottage on the bluffs of Bolinas. I must be getting close. Maybe this time I'll actually find it.*

Maybe this time.

The Time Machine
Chapters I–V

H.G. Wells

Chapter I

THE TIME TRAVELLER (for so it will be convenient to speak of him) was expounding a recondite matter to us. His grey eyes shone and twinkled, and his usually pale face was flushed and animated. The fire burned brightly, and the soft radiance of the incandescent lights in the lilies of silver caught the bubbles that flashed and passed in our glasses. Our chairs, being his patents, embraced and caressed us rather than submitted to be sat upon, and there was that luxurious after-dinner atmosphere when thought roams gracefully free of the trammels of precision. And he put it to us in this way – marking the points with a lean forefinger – as we sat and lazily admired his earnestness over this new paradox (as we thought it) and his fecundity.

"You must follow me carefully. I shall have to controvert one or two ideas that are almost universally accepted. The geometry, for instance, they taught you at school is founded on a misconception.'

"Is not that rather a large thing to expect us to begin upon?" said Filby, an argumentative person with red hair.

"I do not mean to ask you to accept anything without reasonable ground for it. You will soon admit as much as I need from you. You know of course that a mathematical line, a line of thickness nil, has no real existence. They taught you that? Neither has a mathematical plane. These things are mere abstractions.'

"That is all right," said the Psychologist.

"Nor, having only length, breadth, and thickness, can a cube have a real existence."

"There I object," said Filby. "Of course a solid body may exist. All real things –"

"So most people think. But wait a moment. Can an instantaneous cube exist?"

"Don't follow you," said Filby.

"Can a cube that does not last for any time at all, have a real existence?"

Filby became pensive. "Clearly," the Time Traveller proceeded, "any real body must have extension in four directions: it must have Length, Breadth, Thickness, and – Duration. But through a natural infirmity of the flesh, which I will explain to you in a moment, we incline to overlook this fact. There are really four dimensions, three which we call the three planes of Space, and a fourth, Time. There is, however, a tendency to draw an unreal distinction between the former three dimensions and the latter, because it happens that our consciousness moves intermittently in one direction along the latter from the beginning to the end of our lives.'

"That," said a very young man, making spasmodic efforts to relight his cigar over the lamp; "that ...very clear indeed.'

"Now, it is very remarkable that this is so extensively overlooked," continued the Time Traveller, with a slight accession of cheerfulness. "Really this is what is meant by the Fourth Dimension, though some people who talk about the Fourth Dimension do not know they mean it. It is only another way of looking at Time. There is no difference between Time and any of the three dimensions of Space except that our consciousness moves along it. But some foolish people have got hold of the wrong side of that idea. You have all heard what they have to say about this Fourth Dimension?'

"I have not," said the Provincial Mayor.

"It is simply this. That Space, as our mathematicians have it, is spoken of as having three dimensions, which one may call Length, Breadth, and Thickness, and is always definable by reference to three planes, each at right angles to the others. But some philosophical people have been asking why three dimensions particularly – why not another direction at right angles to the other three? – and have even tried to construct a Four-Dimension geometry. Professor Simon Newcomb was expounding this to the New York Mathematical Society only a month or so ago. You know how on a flat surface, which has only two dimensions, we can represent a figure of a three-dimensional solid, and similarly they think that by models of three dimensions they could represent one of four – if they could master the perspective of the thing. See?'

"I think so," murmured the Provincial Mayor; and, knitting his brows, he lapsed into an introspective state, his lips moving as one who repeats mystic words. "Yes, I think I see it now," he said after some time, brightening in a quite transitory manner.

"Well, I do not mind telling you I have been at work upon this geometry of Four Dimensions for some time. Some of my results are curious. For instance, here is a portrait of a man at eight years old, another at fifteen, another at seventeen, another at twenty-three, and so on. All these are evidently sections, as it were, Three-Dimensional representations of his Four-Dimensioned being, which is a fixed and unalterable thing.

"Scientific people," proceeded the Time Traveller, after the pause required for the proper assimilation of this, "know very well that Time is only a kind of Space. Here is a popular scientific diagram, a weather record. This line I trace with my finger shows the movement of the barometer. Yesterday it was so high, yesterday night it fell, then this morning it rose again, and so gently upward to here. Surely the mercury did not trace this line in any of the dimensions of Space generally recognized? But certainly it traced such a line, and that line, therefore, we must conclude was along the Time-Dimension." "But," said the Medical Man, staring hard at a coal in the fire, "if Time is really only a fourth dimension of Space, why is it, and why has it always been, regarded as something different? And why cannot we move in Time as we move about in the other dimensions of Space?"

The Time Traveller smiled. "Are you sure we can move freely in Space? Right and left we can go, backward and forward freely enough, and men always have done so. I admit we move freely in two dimensions. But how about up and down? Gravitation limits us there."

"Not exactly," said the Medical Man. "There are balloons."

"But before the balloons, save for spasmodic jumping and the inequalities of the surface, man had no freedom of vertical movement."

"Still they could move a little up and down," said the Medical Man.

"Easier, far easier down than up."

"And you cannot move at all in Time, you cannot get away from the present moment."

"My dear sir, that is just where you are wrong. That is just where the whole world has gone wrong. We are always getting away from the present moment. Our mental existences, which are immaterial and have no dimensions, are passing along the Time-Dimension with a uniform velocity from the cradle to the grave. Just as we should travel down if we began our existence fifty miles above the earth's surface."

"But the great difficulty is this," interrupted the Psychologist. "You can move about in all directions of Space, but you cannot move about in Time."

"That is the germ of my great discovery. But you are wrong to say that we cannot move about in Time. For instance, if I am recalling an incident very vividly I go back to the instant of its occurrence: I become absent-minded, as you say. I jump back for a moment. Of course we have no means of staying back for any length of Time, any more than a savage or an animal has of staying six feet above the ground. But a civilized man is better off than the savage in this respect. He can go up against gravitation in a balloon, and why should he not hope that ultimately he may be able to stop or accelerate his drift along the Time-Dimension, or even turn about and travel the other way?"

"Oh, this," began Filby, "is all –"

"Why not?" said the Time Traveller.

"It's against reason," said Filby.

"What reason?" said the Time Traveller.

"You can show black is white by argument," said Filby, "but you will never convince me.'

"Possibly not," said the Time Traveller. "But now you begin to see the object of my investigations into the geometry of Four Dimensions. Long ago I had a vague inkling of a machine –"

"To travel through Time!" exclaimed the Very Young Man.

"That shall travel indifferently in any direction of Space and Time, as the driver determines." Filby contented himself with laughter.

"But I have experimental verification," said the Time Traveller.

"It would be remarkably convenient for the historian," the Psychologist suggested. "One might travel back and verify the accepted account of the Battle of Hastings, for instance!"

"Don't you think you would attract attention?" said the Medical Man. "Our ancestors had no great tolerance for anachronisms."

"One might get one's Greek from the very lips of Homer and Plato," the Very Young Man thought.

"In which case they would certainly plough you for the Little-go. The German scholars have improved Greek so much."

"Then there is the future," said the Very Young Man. "Just think! One might invest all one's money, leave it to accumulate at interest, and hurry on ahead!"

"To discover a society," said I, "erected on a strictly communistic basis."

"Of all the wild extravagant theories!" began the Psychologist.

"Yes, so it seemed to me, and so I never talked of it until –"

"Experimental verification!" cried I. "You are going to verify that?"

"The experiment!" cried Filby, who was getting brain-weary.

"Let's see your experiment anyhow," said the Psychologist, "though it's all humbug, you know."

The Time Traveller smiled round at us. Then, still smiling faintly, and with his hands deep in his trousers pockets, he walked slowly out of the room, and we heard his slippers shuffling down the long passage to his laboratory.

The Psychologist looked at us. "I wonder what he's got?"

"Some sleight-of-hand trick or other," said the Medical Man, and Filby tried to tell us about a conjurer he had seen at Burslem; but before he had finished his preface the Time Traveller came back, and Filby's anecdote collapsed.

The thing the Time Traveller held in his hand was a glittering metallic framework, scarcely larger than a small clock, and very delicately made. There was ivory in it, and some transparent crystalline substance. And now I must be explicit, for this that follows – unless his explanation is to be accepted – is an absolutely unaccountable thing. He took one of the small octagonal tables that were scattered about the room, and set it in front of the fire, with two legs on the hearthrug. On this table he placed the mechanism. Then he drew up a chair, and sat down. The only other object on the table was a small shaded lamp, the bright light of which fell upon the model. There were also perhaps a dozen candles about, two in brass candlesticks upon the mantel and several in sconces, so that the room was brilliantly illuminated. I sat in a low arm-chair nearest the fire, and I drew this forward so as to be almost between the Time Traveller and the fireplace. Filby sat behind him, looking over his shoulder. The Medical Man and the Provincial Mayor watched him in profile from the right, the Psychologist from the left. The Very Young Man stood behind the Psychologist. We were all on the alert. It appears incredible to me that any kind of trick, however subtly conceived and however adroitly done, could have been played upon us under these conditions.

The Time Traveller looked at us, and then at the mechanism. "Well?" said the Psychologist.

"This little affair," said the Time Traveller, resting his elbows upon the table and pressing his hands together above the apparatus, "is only a model. It is my plan for a machine to travel through time. You will notice that it looks singularly askew, and that there is an odd twinkling appearance about this bar, as though it was in some way unreal." He pointed to the part with his finger. "Also, here is one little white lever, and here is another."

The Medical Man got up out of his chair and peered into the thing. "It's beautifully made," he said.

"It took two years to make," retorted the Time Traveller. Then, when we had all imitated the action of the Medical Man, he said: "Now I want you clearly to understand that this lever, being pressed over, sends the machine gliding into the future, and this other reverses the motion. This saddle represents the seat of a time traveller. Presently I am going to press the lever, and off the machine will go. It will vanish, pass into future Time, and disappear. Have a good look at the thing. Look at the table too, and satisfy yourselves there is no trickery. I don't want to waste this model, and then be told I'm a quack."

There was a minute's pause perhaps. The Psychologist seemed about to speak to me, but changed his mind. Then the Time Traveller put forth his finger towards the lever. "No," he said suddenly. "Lend me your hand." And turning to the Psychologist, he took that individual's hand in his own and told him to put out his forefinger. So that it was the Psychologist himself who sent forth the model Time Machine on its interminable voyage. We all saw the lever turn. I am absolutely certain there was no trickery. There was a breath of wind, and the lamp flame jumped. One of the candles on the mantel was blown out, and the little machine suddenly swung round, became indistinct, was seen as a ghost for a second perhaps, as an eddy of faintly glittering brass and ivory; and it was gone – vanished! Save for the lamp the table was bare.

Everyone was silent for a minute. Then Filby said he was damned.

The Psychologist recovered from his stupor, and suddenly looked under the table. At that the Time Traveller laughed cheerfully. "Well?" he said, with a reminiscence of the Psychologist.

Then, getting up, he went to the tobacco jar on the mantel, and with his back to us began to fill his pipe.

We stared at each other. "Look here," said the Medical Man, "are you in earnest about this? Do you seriously believe that that machine has travelled into time?'

"Certainly," said the Time Traveller, stooping to light a spill at the fire. Then he turned, lighting his pipe, to look at the Psychologist's face. (The Psychologist, to show that he was not unhinged, helped himself to a cigar and tried to light it uncut.) "What is more, I have a big machine nearly finished in there" – he indicated the laboratory – "and when that is put together I mean to have a journey on my own account."

"You mean to say that that machine has travelled into the future?" said Filby.

"Into the future or the past – I don't, for certain, know which."

After an interval the Psychologist had an inspiration. "It must have gone into the past if it has gone anywhere," he said.

"Why?" said the Time Traveller.

"Because I presume that it has not moved in space, and if it travelled into the future it would still be here all this time, since it must have travelled through this time."

"But," I said, "if it travelled into the past it would have been visible when we came first into this room; and last Thursday when we were here; and the Thursday before that; and so forth!'

"Serious objections," remarked the Provincial Mayor, with an air of impartiality, turning towards the Time Traveller.

"Not a bit," said the Time Traveller, and, to the Psychologist: "You think. You can explain that. It's presentation below the threshold, you know, diluted presentation."

"Of course," said the Psychologist, and reassured us. "That's a simple point of psychology. I should have thought of it. It's plain enough, and helps the paradox delightfully. We cannot see it, nor can we appreciate this machine, any more than we can the spoke of a wheel spinning, or a bullet flying through the air. If it is travelling through time fifty times or a hundred times faster than we are, if it gets through a minute while we get through a second, the impression it creates will of course be only one-fiftieth or one-hundredth of what it would make if it were not travelling in time. That's plain enough." He passed his hand through the space in which the machine had been. "You see?" he said, laughing.

We sat and stared at the vacant table for a minute or so. Then the Time Traveller asked us what we thought of it all.

"It sounds plausible enough tonight," said the Medical Man; "but wait until tomorrow. Wait for the common sense of the morning."

"Would you like to see the Time Machine itself?" asked the Time Traveller. And therewith, taking the lamp in his hand, he led the way down the long, draughty corridor to his laboratory. I remember vividly the flickering light, his queer, broad head in silhouette, the dance of the shadows, how we all followed him, puzzled but incredulous, and how there in the laboratory we beheld a larger edition of the little mechanism which we had seen vanish from before our eyes. Parts were of nickel, parts of ivory, parts had certainly been filed or sawn out of rock crystal. The thing was generally complete, but the twisted crystalline bars lay unfinished upon the bench beside some sheets of drawings, and I took one up for a better look at it. Quartz it seemed to be.

"Look here," said the Medical Man, "are you perfectly serious? Or is this a trick – like that ghost you showed us last Christmas?'

"Upon that machine," said the Time Traveller, holding the lamp aloft, "I intend to explore time. Is that plain? I was never more serious in my life.'

None of us quite knew how to take it.

I caught Filby's eye over the shoulder of the Medical Man, and he winked at me solemnly.

Chapter II

I THINK that at that time none of us quite believed in the Time Machine. The fact is, the Time Traveller was one of those men who are too clever to be believed: you never felt that you saw all round him; you always suspected some subtle reserve, some ingenuity in ambush, behind his lucid frankness. Had Filby shown the model and explained the matter in the Time Traveller's words, we should have shown him far less scepticism. For we should have perceived his motives; a pork butcher could understand Filby. But the Time Traveller had more than a touch of whim among his elements, and we distrusted him. Things that would have made the fame of a less clever man seemed tricks in his hands. It is a mistake to do things too easily. The serious people who took him seriously never felt quite sure of his deportment; they were somehow aware that trusting their reputations for judgment with him was like furnishing a nursery with egg-shell china. So I don't think any of us said very much about time travelling in the interval between that Thursday and the next, though its odd potentialities ran, no doubt, in most of our minds: its plausibility, that is, its practical incredibleness, the curious possibilities of anachronism and of utter confusion it suggested. For my own part, I was particularly preoccupied with the trick of the model. That I remember discussing with the Medical Man, whom I met on Friday at the Linnaean. He said he had seen a similar thing at Tubingen, and laid considerable stress on the blowing out of the candle. But how the trick was done he could not explain.

The next Thursday I went again to Richmond – I suppose I was one of the Time Traveller's most constant guests – and, arriving late, found four or five men already assembled in his drawing-room. The Medical Man was standing before the fire with a sheet of paper in one hand and his watch in the other. I looked round for the Time Traveller, and – "It's half-past seven now," said the Medical Man. "I suppose we'd better have dinner?'

"Where's –?" said I, naming our host.

"You've just come? It's rather odd. He's unavoidably detained. He asks me in this note to lead off with dinner at seven if he's not back. Says he'll explain when he comes.'

"It seems a pity to let the dinner spoil," said the Editor of a well-known daily paper; and thereupon the Doctor rang the bell.

The Psychologist was the only person besides the Doctor and myself who had attended the previous dinner. The other men were Blank, the Editor aforementioned, a certain journalist, and another – a quiet, shy man with a beard – whom I didn't know, and who, as far as my observation went, never opened his mouth all the evening. There was some speculation at the dinner-table about the Time Traveller's absence, and I suggested time travelling, in a half-jocular spirit. The Editor wanted that explained to him, and the Psychologist volunteered a wooden account of the 'ingenious paradox and trick' we had witnessed that day week. He was in the midst of his exposition when the door from the corridor opened slowly and without noise. I was facing the door, and saw it first. "Hallo!" I said. "At last!" And the door opened wider, and the Time Traveller stood before us. I gave a cry of surprise. "Good heavens! Man, what's the matter?" cried the Medical Man, who saw him next. And the whole tableful turned towards the door.

He was in an amazing plight. His coat was dusty and dirty, and smeared with green down the sleeves; his hair disordered, and as it seemed to me greyer – either with dust and dirt or because its colour had actually faded. His face was ghastly pale; his chin had a brown cut on it – a cut half healed; his expression was haggard and drawn, as by intense suffering. For a moment he hesitated in the doorway, as if he had been dazzled by the light. Then he came into the room. He walked with just such a limp as I have seen in footsore tramps. We stared at him in silence, expecting him to speak.

He said not a word, but came painfully to the table, and made a motion towards the wine. The Editor filled a glass of champagne, and pushed it towards him. He drained it, and it seemed to do him good: for he looked round the table, and the ghost of his old smile flickered across his face. "What on earth have you been up to, man?" said the Doctor. The Time Traveller did not seem to hear. "Don't let me disturb you," he said, with a certain faltering articulation. "I'm all right." He stopped, held out his glass for more, and took it off at a draught. "That's good," he said. His eyes grew brighter, and a faint colour came into his cheeks. His glance flickered over our faces with a certain dull approval, and then went round the warm and comfortable room. Then he spoke again, still as it were feeling his way among his words. "I'm going to wash and dress, and then I'll come down and explain things…Save me some of that mutton. I'm starving for a bit of meat."

He looked across at the Editor, who was a rare visitor, and hoped he was all right. The Editor began a question. "Tell you presently," said the Time Traveller. "I'm – funny! Be all right in a minute.'

He put down his glass, and walked towards the staircase door. Again I remarked his lameness and the soft padding sound of his footfall, and standing up in my place, I saw his feet as he went out. He had nothing on them but a pair of tattered, blood-stained socks. Then the door closed upon him. I had half a mind to follow, till I remembered how he detested any fuss about himself. For a minute, perhaps, my mind was wool-gathering. Then, "Remarkable Behaviour of an Eminent Scientist," I heard the Editor say, thinking (after his wont) in headlines. And this brought my attention back to the bright dinner-table.

"What's the game?" said the Journalist. "Has he been doing the Amateur Cadger? I don't follow." I met the eye of the Psychologist, and read my own interpretation in his face. I thought of the Time Traveller limping painfully upstairs. I don't think any one else had noticed his lameness.

The first to recover completely from this surprise was the Medical Man, who rang the bell – the Time Traveller hated to have servants waiting at dinner – for a hot plate. At that the Editor turned to his knife and fork with a grunt, and the Silent Man followed suit. The dinner was resumed. Conversation was exclamatory for a little while, with gaps of wonderment; and then the Editor got fervent in his curiosity. "Does our friend eke out his modest income with a crossing? Or has he his Nebuchadnezzar phases?" he inquired.

"I feel assured it's this business of the Time Machine," I said, and took up the Psychologist's account of our previous meeting. The new guests were frankly incredulous. The Editor raised objections. "What was this time travelling? A man couldn't cover himself with dust by rolling in a paradox, could he?" And then, as the idea came home to him, he resorted to caricature. Hadn't they any clothes-brushes in the Future? The Journalist too, would not believe at any price, and joined the Editor in the easy work of heaping ridicule on the whole thing. They were both the new kind of journalist – very joyous, irreverent young men.

"Our Special Correspondent in the Day after Tomorrow reports," the Journalist was saying – or rather shouting – when the Time Traveller came back. He was dressed in ordinary evening clothes, and nothing save his haggard look remained of the change that had startled me.

"I say," said the Editor hilariously, "these chaps here say you have been travelling into the middle of next week! Tell us all about little Rosebery, will you? What will you take for the lot?"

The Time Traveller came to the place reserved for him without a word. He smiled quietly, in his old way. "Where's my mutton?" he said. "What a treat it is to stick a fork into meat again!'

"Story!" cried the Editor.

"Story be damned!" said the Time Traveller. "I want something to eat. I won't say a word until I get some peptone into my arteries. Thanks. And the salt."

"One word," said I. "Have you been time travelling?'

"Yes," said the Time Traveller, with his mouth full, nodding his head.

"I'd give a shilling a line for a verbatim note," said the Editor. The Time Traveller pushed his glass towards the Silent Man and rang it with his fingernail; at which the Silent Man, who had been staring at his face, started convulsively, and poured him wine. The rest of the dinner was uncomfortable. For my own part, sudden questions kept on rising to my lips, and I dare say it was the same with the others. The Journalist tried to relieve the tension by telling anecdotes of Hettie Potter. The Time Traveller devoted his attention to his dinner, and displayed the appetite of a tramp. The Medical Man smoked a cigarette, and watched the Time Traveller through his eyelashes. The Silent Man seemed even more clumsy than usual, and drank champagne with regularity and determination out of sheer nervousness. At last the Time Traveller pushed his plate away, and looked round us. "I suppose I must apologize," he said. "I was simply starving. I've had a most amazing time." He reached out his hand for a cigar, and cut the end. "But come into the smoking-room. It's too long a story to tell over greasy plates." And ringing the bell in passing, he led the way into the adjoining room.

"You have told Blank, and Dash, and Chose about the machine?" he said to me, leaning back in his easy-chair and naming the three new guests.

"But the thing's a mere paradox," said the Editor.

"I can't argue tonight. I don't mind telling you the story, but I can't argue. I will," he went on, "tell you the story of what has happened to me, if you like, but you must refrain from interruptions. I want to tell it. Badly. Most of it will sound like lying. So be it! It's true – every word of it, all the same. I was in my laboratory at four o'clock, and since then…I've lived eight days…such days as no human being ever lived before! I'm nearly worn out, but I shan't sleep till I've told this thing over to you. Then I shall go to bed. But no interruptions! Is it agreed?'

"Agreed," said the Editor, and the rest of us echoed "Agreed." And with that the Time Traveller began his story as I have set it forth. He sat back in his chair at first, and spoke like a weary man. Afterwards he got more animated. In writing it down I feel with only too much keenness the inadequacy of pen and ink – and, above all, my own inadequacy – to express its quality. You read, I will suppose, attentively enough; but you cannot see the speaker's white, sincere face in the bright circle of the little lamp, nor hear the intonation of his voice. You cannot know how his expression followed the turns of his story! Most of us hearers were in shadow, for the candles in the smoking-room had not been lighted, and only the face of the Journalist and the legs of the Silent Man from the knees downward were illuminated. At first we glanced now and again at each other. After a time we ceased to do that, and looked only at the Time Traveller's face.

Chapter III

I TOLD some of you last Thursday of the principles of the Time Machine, and showed you the actual thing itself, incomplete in the workshop. There it is now, a little travel-worn, truly; and one of the ivory bars is cracked, and a brass rail bent; but the rest of it's sound enough.

I expected to finish it on Friday, but on Friday, when the putting together was nearly done, I found that one of the nickel bars was exactly one inch too short, and this I had to get remade; so that the thing was not complete until this morning. It was at ten o'clock today that the first of all Time Machines began its career. I gave it a last tap, tried all the screws again, put one more drop of oil on the quartz rod, and sat myself in the saddle. I suppose a suicide who holds a pistol to his skull feels much the same wonder at what will come next as I felt then. I took the starting lever in one hand and the stopping one in the other, pressed the first, and almost immediately the second. I seemed to reel; I felt a nightmare sensation of falling; and, looking round, I saw the laboratory exactly as before. Had anything happened? For a moment I suspected that my intellect had tricked me. Then I noted the clock. A moment before, as it seemed, it had stood at a minute or so past ten; now it was nearly half-past three!

"I drew a breath, set my teeth, gripped the starting lever with both hands, and went off with a thud. The laboratory got hazy and went dark. Mrs. Watchett came in and walked, apparently without seeing me, towards the garden door. I suppose it took her a minute or so to traverse the place, but to me she seemed to shoot across the room like a rocket. I pressed the lever over to its extreme position. The night came like the turning out of a lamp, and in another moment came tomorrow. The laboratory grew faint and hazy, then fainter and ever fainter. Tomorrow night came black, then day again, night again, day again, faster and faster still. An eddying murmur filled my ears, and a strange, dumb confusedness descended on my mind.

"I am afraid I cannot convey the peculiar sensations of time travelling. They are excessively unpleasant. There is a feeling exactly like that one has upon a switchback – of a helpless headlong motion! I felt the same horrible anticipation, too, of an imminent smash. As I put on pace, night followed day like the flapping of a black wing. The dim suggestion of the laboratory seemed presently to fall away from me, and I saw the sun hopping swiftly across the sky, leaping it every minute, and every minute marking a day. I supposed the laboratory had been destroyed and I had come into the open air. I had a dim impression of scaffolding, but I was already going too fast to be conscious of any moving things. The slowest snail that ever crawled dashed by too fast for me. The twinkling succession of darkness and light was excessively painful to the eye. Then, in the intermittent darknesses, I saw the moon spinning swiftly through her quarters from new to full, and had a faint glimpse of the circling stars. Presently, as I went on, still gaining velocity, the palpitation of night and day merged into one continuous greyness; the sky took on a wonderful deepness of blue, a splendid luminous colour like that of early twilight; the jerking sun became a streak of fire, a brilliant arch, in space; the moon a fainter fluctuating band; and I could see nothing of the stars, save now and then a brighter circle flickering in the blue.

"The landscape was misty and vague. I was still on the hill-side upon which this house now stands, and the shoulder rose above me grey and dim. I saw trees growing and changing like puffs of vapour, now brown, now green; they grew, spread, shivered, and passed away. I saw huge buildings rise up faint and fair, and pass like dreams. The whole surface of the earth seemed changed – melting and flowing under my eyes. The little hands upon the dials that registered my speed raced round faster and faster. Presently I noted that the sun belt swayed up and down, from solstice to solstice, in a minute or less, and that consequently my pace was over a year a minute; and minute by minute the white snow flashed across the world, and vanished, and was followed by the bright, brief green of spring.

"The unpleasant sensations of the start were less poignant now. They merged at last into a kind of hysterical exhilaration. I remarked indeed a clumsy swaying of the machine, for which I was unable to account. But my mind was too confused to attend to it, so with a kind of madness growing upon me, I flung myself into futurity. At first I scarce thought of stopping, scarce thought of anything but these new sensations. But presently a fresh series of impressions grew up in my mind – a certain curiosity and therewith a certain dread – until at last they took complete possession of me. What strange developments of humanity, what wonderful advances upon our rudimentary civilization, I thought, might not appear when I came to look nearly into the dim elusive world that raced and fluctuated before my eyes! I saw great and splendid architecture rising about me, more massive than any buildings of our own time, and yet, as it seemed, built of glimmer and mist. I saw a richer green flow up the hill-side, and remain there, without any wintry intermission. Even through the veil of my confusion the earth seemed very fair. And so my mind came round to the business of stopping.

"The peculiar risk lay in the possibility of my finding some substance in the space which I, or the machine, occupied. So long as I travelled at a high velocity through time, this scarcely mattered; I was, so to speak, attenuated – was slipping like a vapour through the interstices of intervening substances! But to come to a stop involved the jamming of myself, molecule by molecule, into whatever lay in my way; meant bringing my atoms into such intimate contact with those of the obstacle that a profound chemical reaction – possibly a far-reaching explosion – would result, and blow myself and my apparatus out of all possible dimensions – into the Unknown. This possibility had occurred to me again and again while I was making the machine; but then I had cheerfully accepted it as an unavoidable risk – one of the risks a man has got to take! Now the risk was inevitable, I no longer saw it in the same cheerful light. The fact is that, insensibly, the absolute strangeness of everything, the sickly jarring and swaying of the machine, above all, the feeling of prolonged falling, had absolutely upset my nerve. I told myself that I could never stop, and with a gust of petulance I resolved to stop forthwith. Like an impatient fool, I lugged over the lever, and incontinently the thing went reeling over, and I was flung headlong through the air.

"There was the sound of a clap of thunder in my ears. I may have been stunned for a moment. A pitiless hail was hissing round me, and I was sitting on soft turf in front of the overset machine. Everything still seemed grey, but presently I remarked that the confusion in my ears was gone. I looked round me. I was on what seemed to be a little lawn in a garden, surrounded by rhododendron bushes, and I noticed that their mauve and purple blossoms were dropping in a shower under the beating of the hail-stones. The rebounding, dancing hail hung in a cloud over the machine, and drove along the ground like smoke. In a moment I was wet to the skin. 'Fine hospitality,' said I, 'to a man who has travelled innumerable years to see you.'

"Presently I thought what a fool I was to get wet. I stood up and looked round me. A colossal figure, carved apparently in some white stone, loomed indistinctly beyond the rhododendrons through the hazy downpour. But all else of the world was invisible.

"My sensations would be hard to describe. As the columns of hail grew thinner, I saw the white figure more distinctly. It was very large, for a silver birch-tree touched its shoulder. It was of white marble, in shape something like a winged sphinx, but the wings, instead of being carried vertically at the sides, were spread so that it seemed to hover. The pedestal, it appeared to me, was of bronze, and was thick with verdigris. It chanced that the face was towards me; the sightless eyes seemed to watch me; there was the faint shadow of a smile on the lips. It was greatly weather-worn, and that imparted an unpleasant suggestion of disease. I stood looking at it for a little space – half a minute, perhaps, or half an hour. It seemed to advance and to recede as the hail drove before it denser or thinner. At last I tore my eyes from it for a moment and saw that the hail curtain had worn threadbare, and that the sky was lightening with the promise of the sun.

"I looked up again at the crouching white shape, and the full temerity of my voyage came suddenly upon me. What might appear when that hazy curtain was altogether withdrawn? What might not have happened to men? What if cruelty had grown into a common passion? What if in this interval the race had lost its manliness and had developed into something inhuman, unsympathetic, and overwhelmingly powerful? I might seem some old-world savage animal, only the more dreadful and disgusting for our common likeness – a foul creature to be incontinently slain.

"Already I saw other vast shapes – huge buildings with intricate parapets and tall columns, with a wooded hill-side dimly creeping in upon me through the lessening storm. I was seized with a panic fear. I turned frantically to the Time Machine, and strove hard to readjust it. As I did so the shafts of the sun smote through the thunderstorm. The grey downpour was swept aside and vanished like the trailing garments of a ghost. Above me, in the intense blue of the summer sky, some faint brown shreds of cloud whirled into nothingness. The great buildings about me stood out clear and distinct, shining with the wet of the thunderstorm, and picked out in white by the unmelted hailstones piled along their courses. I felt naked in a strange world. I felt as perhaps a bird may feel in the clear air, knowing the hawk wings above and will swoop. My fear grew to frenzy. I took a breathing space, set my teeth, and again grappled fiercely, wrist and knee, with the machine. It gave under my desperate onset and turned over. It struck my chin violently. One hand on the saddle, the other on the lever, I stood panting heavily in attitude to mount again.

"But with this recovery of a prompt retreat my courage recovered. I looked more curiously and less fearfully at this world of the remote future. In a circular opening, high up in the wall of the nearer house, I saw a group of figures clad in rich soft robes. They had seen me, and their faces were directed towards me.

"Then I heard voices approaching me. Coming through the bushes by the White Sphinx were the heads and shoulders of men running. One of these emerged in a pathway leading straight to the little lawn upon which I stood with my machine. He was a slight creature – perhaps four feet high – clad in a purple tunic, girdled at the waist with a leather belt. Sandals or buskins – I could not clearly distinguish which – were on his feet; his legs were bare to the knees, and his head was bare. Noticing that, I noticed for the first time how warm the air was.

"He struck me as being a very beautiful and graceful creature, but indescribably frail. His flushed face reminded me of the more beautiful kind of consumptive – that hectic beauty of which we used to hear so much. At the sight of him I suddenly regained confidence. I took my hands from the machine.

Chapter IV

"IN ANOTHER MOMENT we were standing face to face, I and this fragile thing out of futurity. He came straight up to me and laughed into my eyes. The absence from his bearing of any sign of fear struck me at once. Then he turned to the two others who were following him and spoke to them in a strange and very sweet and liquid tongue.

"There were others coming, and presently a little group of perhaps eight or ten of these exquisite creatures were about me. One of them addressed me. It came into my head, oddly enough, that my voice was too harsh and deep for them. So I shook my head, and, pointing to my ears, shook it again. He came a step forward, hesitated, and then touched my hand. Then I felt other soft little tentacles upon my back and shoulders. They wanted to make sure I was real. There was nothing in this at all alarming. Indeed, there was something in these pretty little people that inspired confidence – a graceful gentleness, a certain childlike ease. And besides, they looked so frail that I could fancy myself flinging the whole dozen of them about like nine-pins. But I made a sudden motion to warn them when I saw their little pink hands feeling at the Time Machine. Happily then, when it was not too late, I thought of a danger I had hitherto forgotten, and reaching over the bars of the machine I unscrewed the little levers that would set it in motion, and put these in my pocket. Then I turned again to see what I could do in the way of communication.

"And then, looking more nearly into their features, I saw some further peculiarities in their Dresden-china type of prettiness. Their hair, which was uniformly curly, came to a sharp end at the neck and cheek; there was not the faintest suggestion of it on the face, and their ears were singularly minute. The mouths were small, with bright red, rather thin lips, and the little chins ran to a point. The eyes were large and mild; and – this may seem egotism on my part – I fancied even that there was a certain lack of the interest I might have expected in them.

"As they made no effort to communicate with me, but simply stood round me smiling and speaking in soft cooing notes to each other, I began the conversation. I pointed to the Time Machine and to myself. Then hesitating for a moment how to express time, I pointed to the sun. At once a quaintly pretty little figure in chequered purple and white followed my gesture, and then astonished me by imitating the sound of thunder.

"For a moment I was staggered, though the import of his gesture was plain enough. The question had come into my mind abruptly: were these creatures fools? You may hardly understand how it took me. You see I had always anticipated that the people of the year Eight Hundred and Two Thousand odd would be incredibly in front of us in knowledge, art, everything. Then one of them suddenly asked me a question that showed him to be on the intellectual level of one of our five-year-old children – asked me, in fact, if I had come from the sun in a thunderstorm! It let loose the judgment I had suspended upon their clothes, their frail light limbs, and fragile features. A flow of disappointment rushed across my mind. For a moment I felt that I had built the Time Machine in vain.

"I nodded, pointed to the sun, and gave them such a vivid rendering of a thunderclap as startled them. They all withdrew a pace or so and bowed. Then came one laughing towards me, carrying a chain of beautiful flowers altogether new to me, and put it about my neck. The idea was received with melodious applause; and presently they were all running to and fro for flowers, and laughingly flinging them upon me until I was almost smothered with blossom. You who have never seen the like can scarcely imagine what delicate and wonderful flowers countless years of culture had created. Then someone suggested that their plaything should be exhibited in the nearest building, and so I was led past the sphinx of white marble, which had seemed to watch me all the while with a smile at my astonishment, towards a vast grey edifice of fretted stone. As I went with them the memory of my confident anticipations of a profoundly grave and intellectual posterity came, with irresistible merriment, to my mind.

"The building had a huge entry, and was altogether of colossal dimensions. I was naturally most occupied with the growing crowd of little people, and with the big open portals that yawned before me shadowy and mysterious. My general impression of the world I saw over their heads was a tangled waste of beautiful bushes and flowers, a long neglected and yet weedless garden. I saw a number of tall spikes of strange white flowers, measuring a foot perhaps across the spread of the waxen petals. They grew scattered, as if wild, among the variegated shrubs, but, as I say, I did not examine them closely at this time. The Time Machine was left deserted on the turf among the rhododendrons.

"The arch of the doorway was richly carved, but naturally I did not observe the carving very narrowly, though I fancied I saw suggestions of old Phoenician decorations as I passed through, and it struck me that they were very badly broken and weather-worn. Several more brightly clad people met me in the doorway, and so we entered, I, dressed in dingy nineteenth-century garments, looking grotesque enough, garlanded with flowers, and surrounded by an eddying mass of bright, soft-coloured robes and shining white limbs, in a melodious whirl of laughter and laughing speech.

"The big doorway opened into a proportionately great hall hung with brown. The roof was in shadow, and the windows, partially glazed with coloured glass and partially unglazed, admitted a tempered light. The floor was made up of huge blocks of some very hard white metal, not plates nor slabs – blocks, and it was so much worn, as I judged by the going to and fro of past generations, as to be deeply channelled along the more frequented ways. Transverse to the length were innumerable tables made of slabs of polished stone, raised perhaps a foot from the floor, and upon these were heaps of fruits. Some I recognized as a kind of hypertrophied raspberry and orange, but for the most part they were strange.

"Between the tables was scattered a great number of cushions. Upon these my conductors seated themselves, signing for me to do likewise. With a pretty absence of ceremony they began to eat the fruit with their hands, flinging peel and stalks, and so forth, into the round openings in the sides of the tables. I was not loath to follow their example, for I felt thirsty and hungry. As I did so I surveyed the hall at my leisure.

"And perhaps the thing that struck me most was its dilapidated look. The stained-glass windows, which displayed only a geometrical pattern, were broken in many places, and the curtains that hung across the lower end were thick with dust. And it caught my eye that the corner of the marble table near me was fractured. Nevertheless, the general effect was extremely rich and picturesque. There were, perhaps, a couple of hundred people dining in the hall, and most of them, seated as near to me as they could come, were watching me with interest, their little eyes shining over the fruit they were eating. All were clad in the same soft and yet strong, silky material.

"Fruit, by the by, was all their diet. These people of the remote future were strict vegetarians, and while I was with them, in spite of some carnal cravings, I had to be frugivorous also. Indeed, I found afterwards that horses, cattle, sheep, dogs, had followed the Ichthyosaurus into extinction. But the fruits were very delightful; one, in particular, that seemed to be in season all the time I was there – a floury thing in a three-sided husk – was especially good, and I made it my staple. At first I was puzzled by all these strange fruits, and by the strange flowers I saw, but later I began to perceive their import.

"However, I am telling you of my fruit dinner in the distant future now. So soon as my appetite was a little checked, I determined to make a resolute attempt to learn the speech of these new men of mine. Clearly that was the next thing to do. The fruits seemed a convenient thing to begin upon, and holding one of these up I began a series of interrogative sounds and gestures. I had some considerable difficulty in conveying my meaning. At first my efforts met with a stare of surprise or inextinguishable laughter, but presently a fair-haired little creature seemed to grasp my intention and repeated a name.

They had to chatter and explain the business at great length to each other, and my first attempts to make the exquisite little sounds of their language caused an immense amount of amusement. However, I felt like a schoolmaster amidst children, and persisted, and presently I had a score of noun substantives at least at my command; and then I got to demonstrative pronouns, and even the verb 'to eat.' But it was slow work, and the little people soon tired and wanted to get away from my interrogations, so I determined, rather of necessity, to let them give their lessons in little doses when they felt inclined. And very little doses I found they were before long, for I never met people more indolent or more easily fatigued.

"A queer thing I soon discovered about my little hosts, and that was their lack of interest. They would come to me with eager cries of astonishment, like children, but like children they would soon stop examining me and wander away after some other toy. The dinner and my conversational beginnings ended, I noted for the first time that almost all those who had surrounded me at first were gone. It is odd, too, how speedily I came to disregard these little people. I went out through the portal into the sunlit world again as soon as my hunger was satisfied. I was continually meeting more of these men of the future, who would follow me a little distance, chatter and laugh about me, and, having smiled and gesticulated in a friendly way, leave me again to my own devices.

"The calm of evening was upon the world as I emerged from the great hall, and the scene was lit by the warm glow of the setting sun. At first things were very confusing. Everything was so entirely different from the world I had known – even the flowers. The big building I had left was situated on the slope of a broad river valley, but the Thames had shifted perhaps a mile from its present position. I resolved to mount to the summit of a crest, perhaps a mile and a half away, from which I could get a wider view of this our planet in the year Eight Hundred and Two Thousand Seven Hundred and One A.D. For that, I should explain, was the date the little dials of my machine recorded.

"As I walked I was watching for every impression that could possibly help to explain the condition of ruinous splendour in which I found the world – for ruinous it was. A little way up the hill, for instance, was a great heap of granite, bound together by masses of aluminium, a vast labyrinth of precipitous walls and crumpled heaps, amidst which were thick heaps of very beautiful pagoda-like plants – nettles possibly – but wonderfully tinted with brown about the leaves, and incapable of stinging. It was evidently the derelict remains of some vast structure, to what end built I could not determine. It was here that I was destined, at a later date, to have a very strange experience – the first intimation of a still stranger discovery – but of that I will speak in its proper place.

"Looking round with a sudden thought, from a terrace on which I rested for a while, I realized that there were no small houses to be seen. Apparently the single house, and possibly even the household, had vanished. Here and there among the greenery were palace-like buildings, but the house and the cottage, which form such characteristic features of our own English landscape, had disappeared.

"'Communism,' said I to myself.

"And on the heels of that came another thought. I looked at the half-dozen little figures that were following me. Then, in a flash, I perceived that all had the same form of costume, the same soft hairless visage, and the same girlish rotundity of limb. It may seem strange, perhaps, that I had not noticed this before. But everything was so strange. Now, I saw the fact plainly enough. In costume, and in all the differences of texture and bearing that now mark off the sexes from each other, these people of the future were alike. And the children seemed to my eyes to be but the miniatures of their parents. I judged, then, that the children of that time were extremely precocious, physically at least, and I found afterwards abundant verification of my opinion.

"Seeing the ease and security in which these people were living, I felt that this close resemblance of the sexes was after all what one would expect; for the strength of a man and the softness of a woman, the institution of the family, and the differentiation of occupations are mere militant necessities of an age of physical force; where population is balanced and abundant, much childbearing becomes an evil rather than a blessing to the State; where violence comes but rarely and off-spring are secure, there is less necessity – indeed there is no necessity – for an efficient family, and the specialization of the sexes with reference to their children's needs disappears. We see some beginnings of this even in our own time, and in this future age it was complete. This, I must remind you, was my speculation at the time. Later, I was to appreciate how far it fell short of the reality.

"While I was musing upon these things, my attention was attracted by a pretty little structure, like a well under a cupola. I thought in a transitory way of the oddness of wells still existing, and then resumed the thread of my speculations. There were no large buildings towards the top of the hill, and as my walking powers were evidently miraculous, I was presently left alone for the first time. With a strange sense of freedom and adventure I pushed on up to the crest.

"There I found a seat of some yellow metal that I did not recognize, corroded in places with a kind of pinkish rust and half smothered in soft moss, the arm-rests cast and filed into the resemblance of griffins" heads. I sat down on it, and I surveyed the broad view of our old world under the sunset of that long day. It was as sweet and fair a view as I have ever seen. The sun had already gone below the horizon and the west was flaming gold, touched with some horizontal bars of purple and crimson. Below was the valley of the Thames, in which the river lay like a band of burnished steel. I have already spoken of the great palaces dotted about among the variegated greenery, some in ruins and some still occupied. Here and there rose a white or silvery figure in the waste garden of the earth, here and there came the sharp vertical line of some cupola or obelisk. There were no hedges, no signs of proprietary rights, no evidences of agriculture; the whole earth had become a garden.

"So watching, I began to put my interpretation upon the things I had seen, and as it shaped itself to me that evening, my interpretation was something in this way. (Afterwards I found I had got only a half-truth – or only a glimpse of one facet of the truth.)

"It seemed to me that I had happened upon humanity upon the wane. The ruddy sunset set me thinking of the sunset of mankind. For the first time I began to realize an odd consequence of the social effort in which we are at present engaged. And yet, come to think, it is a logical consequence enough. Strength is the outcome of need; security sets a premium on feebleness. The work of ameliorating the conditions of life – the true civilizing process that makes life more and more secure – had gone steadily on to a climax. One triumph of a united humanity over Nature had followed another. Things that are now mere dreams had become projects deliberately put in hand and carried forward. And the harvest was what I saw!

"After all, the sanitation and the agriculture of today are still in the rudimentary stage. The science of our time has attacked but a little department of the field of human disease, but even so, it spreads its operations very steadily and persistently. Our agriculture and horticulture destroy a weed just here and there and cultivate perhaps a score or so of wholesome plants, leaving the greater number to fight out a balance as they can. We improve our favourite plants and animals – and how few they are – gradually by selective breeding; now a new and better peach, now a seedless grape, now a sweeter and larger flower, now a more convenient breed of cattle. We improve them gradually, because our ideals are vague and tentative, and our knowledge is very limited; because Nature, too, is shy and slow in our clumsy hands. Some day all this will be better organized, and still better. That is the drift of the current in spite of the eddies. The whole world will be intelligent, educated, and co-operating; things will move faster and faster towards the subjugation of Nature. In the end, wisely and carefully we shall readjust the balance of animal and vegetable life to suit our human needs.

"This adjustment, I say, must have been done, and done well; done indeed for all Time, in the space of Time across which my machine had leaped. The air was free from gnats, the earth from weeds or fungi; everywhere were fruits and sweet and delightful flowers; brilliant butterflies flew hither and thither. The ideal of preventive medicine was attained. Diseases had been stamped out. I saw no evidence of any contagious diseases during all my stay. And I shall have to tell you later that even the processes of putrefaction and decay had been profoundly affected by these changes.

"Social triumphs, too, had been effected. I saw mankind housed in splendid shelters, gloriously clothed, and as yet I had found them engaged in no toil. There were no signs of struggle, neither social nor economical struggle. The shop, the advertisement, traffic, all that commerce which constitutes the body of our world, was gone. It was natural on that golden evening that I should jump at the idea of a social paradise. The difficulty of increasing population had been met, I guessed, and population had ceased to increase.

"But with this change in condition comes inevitably adaptations to the change. What, unless biological science is a mass of errors, is the cause of human intelligence and vigour? Hardship and freedom: conditions under which the active, strong, and subtle survive and the weaker go to the wall; conditions that put a premium upon the loyal alliance of capable men, upon self-restraint, patience, and decision. And the institution of the family, and the emotions that arise therein, the fierce jealousy, the tenderness for offspring, parental self-devotion, all found their justification and support in the imminent dangers of the young. Now, where are these imminent dangers? There is a sentiment arising, and it will grow, against connubial jealousy, against fierce maternity, against passion of all sorts; unnecessary things now, and things that make us uncomfortable, savage survivals, discords in a refined and pleasant life.

"I thought of the physical slightness of the people, their lack of intelligence, and those big abundant ruins, and it strengthened my belief in a perfect conquest of Nature. For after the battle comes Quiet. Humanity had been strong, energetic, and intelligent, and had used all its abundant vitality to alter the conditions under which it lived. And now came the reaction of the altered conditions.

"Under the new conditions of perfect comfort and security, that restless energy, that with us is strength, would become weakness. Even in our own time certain tendencies and desires, once necessary to survival, are a constant source of failure. Physical courage and the love of battle, for instance, are no great help – may even be hindrances – to a civilized man. And in a state of physical balance and security, power, intellectual as well as physical, would be out of place. For countless years I judged there had been no danger of war or solitary violence, no danger from wild beasts, no wasting disease to require strength of constitution, no need of toil. For such a life, what we should call the weak are as well equipped as the strong, are indeed no longer weak. Better equipped indeed they are, for the strong would be fretted by an energy for which there was no outlet. No doubt the exquisite beauty of the buildings I saw was the outcome of the last surgings of the now purposeless energy of mankind before it settled down into perfect harmony with the conditions under which it lived – the flourish of that triumph which began the last great peace. This has ever been the fate of energy in security; it takes to art and to eroticism, and then come languor and decay.

"Even this artistic impetus would at last die away – had almost died in the Time I saw. To adorn themselves with flowers, to dance, to sing in the sunlight: so much was left of the artistic spirit, and no more. Even that would fade in the end into a contented inactivity. We are kept keen on the grindstone of pain and necessity, and, it seemed to me, that here was that hateful grindstone broken at last!

"As I stood there in the gathering dark I thought that in this simple explanation I had mastered the problem of the world – mastered the whole secret of these delicious people. Possibly the checks they had devised for the increase of population had succeeded too well, and their numbers had rather diminished than kept stationary. That would account for the abandoned ruins. Very simple was my explanation, and plausible enough – as most wrong theories are!

Chapter V

"AS I STOOD" there musing over this too perfect triumph of man, the full moon, yellow and gibbous, came up out of an overflow of silver light in the north-east. The bright little figures ceased to move about below, a noiseless owl flitted by, and I shivered with the chill of the night. I determined to descend and find where I could sleep.

"I looked for the building I knew. Then my eye travelled along to the figure of the White Sphinx upon the pedestal of bronze, growing distinct as the light of the rising moon grew brighter. I could see the silver birch against it. There was the tangle of rhododendron bushes, black in the pale light, and there was the little lawn. I looked at the lawn again. A queer doubt chilled my complacency. 'No,' said I stoutly to myself, 'that was not the lawn.'

"But it was the lawn. For the white leprous face of the sphinx was towards it. Can you imagine what I felt as this conviction came home to me? But you cannot. The Time Machine was gone!

"At once, like a lash across the face, came the possibility of losing my own age, of being left helpless in this strange new world. The bare thought of it was an actual physical sensation. I could feel it grip me at the throat and stop my breathing. In another moment I was in a passion of fear and running with great leaping strides down the slope. Once I fell headlong and cut my face; I lost no time in stanching the blood, but jumped up and ran on, with a warm trickle down my cheek and chin. All the time I ran I was saying to myself: 'They have moved it a little, pushed it under the bushes out of the way.' Nevertheless, I ran with all my might. All the time, with the certainty that sometimes comes with excessive dread, I knew that such assurance was folly, knew instinctively that the machine was removed out of my reach. My breath came with pain. I suppose I covered the whole distance from the hill crest to the little lawn, two miles perhaps, in ten minutes. And I am not a young man. I cursed aloud, as I ran, at my confident folly in leaving the machine, wasting good breath thereby. I cried aloud, and none answered. Not a creature seemed to be stirring in that moonlit world.

"When I reached the lawn my worst fears were realized. Not a trace of the thing was to be seen. I felt faint and cold when I faced the empty space among the black tangle of bushes. I ran round it furiously, as if the thing might be hidden in a corner, and then stopped abruptly, with my hands clutching my hair. Above me towered the sphinx, upon the bronze pedestal, white, shining, leprous, in the light of the rising moon. It seemed to smile in mockery of my dismay.

"I might have consoled myself by imagining the little people had put the mechanism in some shelter for me, had I not felt assured of their physical and intellectual inadequacy. That is what dismayed me: the sense of some hitherto unsuspected power, through whose intervention my invention had vanished. Yet, for one thing I felt assured: unless some other age had produced its exact duplicate, the machine could not have moved in time. The attachment of the levers – I will show you the method later – prevented any one from tampering with it in that way when they were removed. It had moved, and was hid, only in space. But then, where could it be?

"I think I must have had a kind of frenzy. I remember running violently in and out among the moonlit bushes all round the sphinx, and startling some white animal that, in the dim light, I took for a small deer. I remember, too, late that night, beating the bushes with my clenched fist until my knuckles were gashed and bleeding from the broken twigs. Then, sobbing and raving in my anguish of mind, I went down to the great building of stone. The big hall was dark, silent, and deserted. I slipped on the uneven floor, and fell over one of the malachite tables, almost breaking my shin. I lit a match and went on past the dusty curtains, of which I have told you.

"There I found a second great hall covered with cushions, upon which, perhaps, a score or so of the little people were sleeping. I have no doubt they found my second appearance strange enough, coming suddenly out of the quiet darkness with inarticulate noises and the splutter and flare of a match. For they had forgotten about matches. 'Where is my Time Machine?' I began, bawling like an angry child, laying hands upon them and shaking them up together. It must have been very queer to them. Some laughed, most of them looked sorely frightened. When I saw them standing round me, it came into my head that I was doing as foolish a thing as it was possible for me to do under the circumstances, in trying to revive the sensation of fear. For, reasoning from their daylight behaviour, I thought that fear must be forgotten.

"Abruptly, I dashed down the match, and, knocking one of the people over in my course, went blundering across the big dining-hall again, out under the moonlight. I heard cries of terror and their little feet running and stumbling this way and that. I do not remember all I did as the moon crept up the sky. I suppose it was the unexpected nature of my loss that maddened me. I felt hopelessly cut off from my own kind – a strange animal in an unknown world. I must have raved to and fro, screaming and crying upon God and Fate. I have a memory of horrible fatigue, as the long night of despair wore away; of looking in this impossible place and that; of groping among moon-lit ruins and touching strange creatures in the black shadows; at last, of lying on the ground near the sphinx and weeping with absolute wretchedness. I had nothing left but misery. Then I slept, and when I woke again it was full day, and a couple of sparrows were hopping round me on the turf within reach of my arm.

"I sat up in the freshness of the morning, trying to remember how I had got there, and why I had such a profound sense of desertion and despair. Then things came clear in my mind. With the plain, reasonable daylight, I could look my circumstances fairly in the face. I saw the wild folly of my frenzy overnight, and I could reason with myself. 'Suppose the worst?' I said. 'Suppose the machine altogether lost – perhaps destroyed? It behoves me to be calm and patient, to learn the way of the people, to get a clear idea of the method of my loss, and the means of getting materials and tools; so that in the end, perhaps, I may make another.' That would be my only hope, perhaps, but better than despair. And, after all, it was a beautiful and curious world.

"But probably, the machine had only been taken away. Still, I must be calm and patient, find its hiding-place, and recover it by force or cunning. And with that I scrambled to my feet and looked about me, wondering where I could bathe. I felt weary, stiff, and travel-soiled. The freshness of the morning made me desire an equal freshness. I had exhausted my emotion. Indeed, as I went about my business, I found myself wondering at my intense excitement overnight. I made a careful examination of the ground about the little lawn. I wasted some time in futile questionings, conveyed, as well as I was able, to such of the little people as came by. They all failed to understand my gestures; some were simply stolid, some thought it was a jest and laughed at me. I had the hardest task in the world to keep my hands off their pretty laughing faces. It was a foolish impulse, but the devil begotten of fear and blind anger was ill curbed and still eager to take advantage of my perplexity. The turf gave better counsel. I found a groove ripped in it, about midway between the pedestal of the sphinx and the marks of my feet where, on arrival, I had struggled with the overturned machine. There were other signs of removal about, with queer narrow footprints like those I could imagine made by a sloth. This directed my closer attention to the pedestal. It was, as I think I have said, of bronze. It was not a mere block, but highly decorated with deep framed panels on either side. I went and rapped at these. The pedestal was hollow. Examining the panels with care I found them discontinuous with the frames. There were no handles or keyholes, but possibly the panels, if they were doors, as I supposed, opened from within. One thing was clear enough to my mind. It took no very great mental effort to infer that my Time Machine was inside that pedestal. But how it got there was a different problem.

"I saw the heads of two orange-clad people coming through the bushes and under some blossom-covered apple-trees towards me. I turned smiling to them and beckoned them to me. They came, and then, pointing to the bronze pedestal, I tried to intimate my wish to open it. But at my first gesture towards this they behaved very oddly. I don't know how to convey their expression to you. Suppose you were to use a grossly improper gesture to a delicate-minded woman – it is how she would look. They went off as if they had received the last possible insult. I tried a sweet-looking little chap in white next, with exactly the same result. Somehow, his manner made me feel ashamed of myself. But, as you know, I wanted the Time Machine, and I tried him once more. As he turned off, like the others, my temper got the better of me. In three strides I was after him, had him by the loose part of his robe round the neck, and began dragging him towards the sphinx. Then I saw the horror and repugnance of his face, and all of a sudden I let him go.

"But I was not beaten yet. I banged with my fist at the bronze panels. I thought I heard something stir inside – to be explicit, I thought I heard a sound like a chuckle – but I must have been mistaken. Then I got a big pebble from the river, and came and hammered till I had flattened a coil in the decorations, and the verdigris came off in powdery flakes. The delicate little people must have heard me hammering in gusty outbreaks a mile away on either hand, but nothing came of it. I saw a crowd of them upon the slopes, looking furtively at me. At last, hot and tired, I sat down to watch the place. But I was too restless to watch long; I am too Occidental for a long vigil. I could work at a problem for years, but to wait inactive for twenty-four hours – that is another matter.

"I got up after a time, and began walking aimlessly through the bushes towards the hill again. 'Patience,' said I to myself. 'If you want your machine again you must leave that sphinx alone. If they mean to take your machine away, it's little good your wrecking their bronze panels, and if they don't, you will get it back as soon as you can ask for it. To sit among all those unknown things before a puzzle like that is hopeless. That way lies monomania. Face this world. Learn its ways, watch it, be careful of too hasty guesses at its meaning. In the end you will find clues to it all.' Then suddenly the humour of the situation came into my mind: the thought of the years I had spent in study and toil to get into the future age, and now my passion of anxiety to get out of it. I had made myself the most complicated and the most hopeless trap that ever a man devised. Although it was at my own expense, I could not help myself. I laughed aloud.

"Going through the big palace, it seemed to me that the little people avoided me. It may have been my fancy, or it may have had something to do with my hammering at the gates of bronze. Yet I felt tolerably sure of the avoidance. I was careful, however, to show no concern and to abstain from any pursuit of them, and in the course of a day or two things got back to the old footing. I made what progress I could in the language, and in addition I pushed my explorations here and there. Either I missed some subtle point or their language was excessively simple – almost exclusively composed of concrete substantives and verbs. There seemed to be few, if any, abstract terms, or little use of figurative language. Their sentences were usually simple and of two words, and I failed to convey or understand any but the simplest propositions. I determined to put the thought of my Time Machine and the mystery of the bronze doors under the sphinx as much as possible in a corner of memory, until my growing knowledge would lead me back to them in a natural way. Yet a certain feeling, you may understand, tethered me in a circle of a few miles round the point of my arrival.

"So far as I could see, all the world displayed the same exuberant richness as the Thames valley. From every hill I climbed I saw the same abundance of splendid buildings, endlessly varied in material and style, the same clustering thickets of evergreens, the same blossom-laden trees and tree-ferns. Here and there water shone like silver, and beyond, the land rose into blue undulating hills, and so faded into the serenity of the sky. A peculiar feature, which presently attracted my attention, was the presence of certain circular wells, several, as it seemed to me, of a very great depth. One lay by the path up the hill, which I had followed during my first walk. Like the others, it was rimmed with bronze, curiously wrought, and protected by a little cupola from the rain. Sitting by the side of these wells, and peering down into the shafted darkness, I could see no gleam of water, nor could I start any reflection with a lighted match. But in all of them I heard a certain sound: a thud – thud – thud, like the beating of some big engine; and I discovered, from the flaring of my matches, that a steady current of air set down the shafts. Further, I threw a scrap of paper into the throat of one, and, instead of fluttering slowly down, it was at once sucked swiftly out of sight.

"After a time, too, I came to connect these wells with tall towers standing here and there upon the slopes; for above them there was often just such a flicker in the air as one sees on a hot day above a sun-scorched beach. Putting things together, I reached a strong suggestion of an extensive system of subterranean ventilation, whose true import it was difficult to imagine. I was at first inclined to associate it with the sanitary apparatus of these people. It was an obvious conclusion, but it was absolutely wrong.

"And here I must admit that I learned very little of drains and bells and modes of conveyance, and the like conveniences, during my time in this real future. In some of these visions of Utopias and coming times which I have read, there is a vast amount of detail about building, and social arrangements, and so forth. But while such details are easy enough to obtain when the whole world is contained in one's imagination, they are altogether inaccessible to a real traveller amid such realities as I found here. Conceive the tale of London which a negro, fresh from Central Africa, would take back to his tribe! What would he know of railway companies, of social movements, of telephone and telegraph wires, of the Parcels Delivery Company, and postal orders and the like? Yet we, at least, should be willing enough to explain these things to him! And even of what he knew, how much could he make his untravelled friend either apprehend or believe? Then, think how narrow the gap between a negro and a white man of our own times, and how wide the interval between myself and these of the Golden Age! I was sensible of much which was unseen, and which contributed to my comfort; but save for a general impression of automatic organization, I fear I can convey very little of the difference to your mind.

"In the matter of sepulture, for instance, I could see no signs of crematoria nor anything suggestive of tombs. But it occurred to me that, possibly, there might be cemeteries (or crematoria) somewhere beyond the range of my explorings. This, again, was a question I deliberately put to myself, and my curiosity was at first entirely defeated upon the point. The thing puzzled me, and I was led to make a further remark, which puzzled me still more: that aged and infirm among this people there were none.

"I must confess that my satisfaction with my first theories of an automatic civilization and a decadent humanity did not long endure. Yet I could think of no other. Let me put my difficulties. The several big palaces I had explored were mere living places, great dining-halls and sleeping apartments. I could find no machinery, no appliances of any kind. Yet these people were clothed in pleasant fabrics that must at times need renewal, and their sandals, though undecorated, were fairly complex specimens of metalwork. Somehow such things must be made. And the little people displayed no vestige of a creative tendency. There were no shops, no workshops, no sign of importations among them. They spent all their time in playing gently, in bathing in the river, in making love in a half-playful fashion, in eating fruit and sleeping. I could not see how things were kept going.

"Then, again, about the Time Machine: something, I knew not what, had taken it into the hollow pedestal of the White Sphinx. Why? For the life of me I could not imagine. Those waterless wells, too, those flickering pillars. I felt I lacked a clue. I felt – how shall I put it? Suppose you found an inscription, with sentences here and there in excellent plain English, and interpolated therewith, others made up of words, of letters even, absolutely unknown to you? Well, on the third day of my visit, that was how the world of Eight Hundred and Two Thousand Seven Hundred and One presented itself to me!

"That day, too, I made a friend – of a sort. It happened that, as I was watching some of the little people bathing in a shallow, one of them was seized with cramp and began drifting downstream. The main current ran rather swiftly, but not too strongly for even a moderate swimmer. It will give you an idea, therefore, of the strange deficiency in these creatures, when I tell you that none made the slightest attempt to rescue the weakly crying little thing which was drowning before their eyes. When I realized this, I hurriedly slipped off my clothes, and, wading in at a point lower down, I caught the poor mite and drew her safe to land. A little rubbing of the limbs soon brought her round, and I had the satisfaction of seeing she was all right before I left her. I had got to such a low estimate of her kind that I did not expect any gratitude from her. In that, however, I was wrong.

"This happened in the morning. In the afternoon I met my little woman, as I believe it was, as I was returning towards my centre from an exploration, and she received me with cries of delight and presented me with a big garland of flowers – evidently made for me and me alone. The thing took my imagination. Very possibly I had been feeling desolate. At any rate I did my best to display my appreciation of the gift. We were soon seated together in a little stone arbour, engaged in conversation, chiefly of smiles. The creature's friendliness affected me exactly as a child's might have done. We passed each other flowers, and she kissed my hands. I did the same to hers. Then I tried talk, and found that her name was Weena, which, though I don't know what it meant, somehow seemed appropriate enough. That was the beginning of a queer friendship which lasted a week, and ended – as I will tell you!

"She was exactly like a child. She wanted to be with me always. She tried to follow me everywhere, and on my next journey out and about it went to my heart to tire her down, and leave her at last, exhausted and calling after me rather plaintively. But the problems of the world had to be mastered. I had not, I said to myself, come into the future to carry on a miniature flirtation. Yet her distress when I left her was very great, her expostulations at the parting were sometimes frantic, and I think, altogether, I had as much trouble as comfort from her devotion. Nevertheless she was, somehow, a very great comfort. I thought it was mere childish affection that made her cling to me. Until it was too late, I did not clearly know what I had inflicted upon her when I left her. Nor until it was too late did I clearly understand what she was to me. For, by merely seeming fond of me, and showing in her weak, futile way that she cared for me, the little doll of a creature presently gave my return to the neighbourhood of the White Sphinx almost the feeling of coming home; and I would watch for her tiny figure of white and gold so soon as I came over the hill.

"It was from her, too, that I learned that fear had not yet left the world. She was fearless enough in the daylight, and she had the oddest confidence in me; for once, in a foolish moment, I made threatening grimaces at her, and she simply laughed at them. But she dreaded the dark, dreaded shadows, dreaded black things. Darkness to her was the one thing dreadful. It was a singularly passionate emotion, and it set me thinking and observing. I discovered then, among other things, that these little people gathered into the great houses after dark, and slept in droves. To enter upon them without a light was to put them into a tumult of apprehension. I never found one out of doors, or one sleeping alone within doors, after dark. Yet I was still such a blockhead that I missed the lesson of that fear, and in spite of Weena's distress I insisted upon sleeping away from these slumbering multitudes.

"It troubled her greatly, but in the end her odd affection for me triumphed, and for five of the nights of our acquaintance, including the last night of all, she slept with her head pillowed on my arm. But my story slips away from me as I speak of her. It must have been the night before her rescue that I was awakened about dawn. I had been restless, dreaming most disagreeably that I was drowned, and that sea anemones were feeling over my face with their soft palps. I woke with a start, and with an odd fancy that some greyish animal had just rushed out of the chamber. I tried to get to sleep again, but I felt restless and uncomfortable. It was that dim grey hour when things are just creeping out of darkness, when everything is colourless and clear cut, and yet unreal. I got up, and went down into the great hall, and so out upon the flagstones in front of the palace. I thought I would make a virtue of necessity, and see the sunrise.

"The moon was setting, and the dying moonlight and the first pallor of dawn were mingled in a ghastly half-light. The bushes were inky black, the ground a sombre grey, the sky colourless and cheerless. And up the hill I thought I could see ghosts. There several times, as I scanned the slope, I saw white figures. Twice I fancied I saw a solitary white, ape-like creature running rather quickly up the hill, and once near the ruins I saw a leash of them carrying some dark body. They moved hastily. I did not see what became of them. It seemed that they vanished among the bushes. The dawn was still indistinct, you must understand. I was feeling that chill, uncertain, early-morning feeling you may have known. I doubted my eyes.

"As the eastern sky grew brighter, and the light of the day came on and its vivid colouring returned upon the world once more, I scanned the view keenly. But I saw no vestige of my white figures. They were mere creatures of the half light. 'They must have been ghosts,' I said; 'I wonder whence they dated.' For a queer notion of Grant Allen's came into my head, and amused me. If each generation die and leave ghosts, he argued, the world at last will get overcrowded with them. On that theory they would have grown innumerable some Eight Hundred Thousand Years hence, and it was no great wonder to see four at once. But the jest was unsatisfying, and I was thinking of these figures all the morning, until Weena's rescue drove them out of my head. I associated them in some indefinite way with the white animal I had startled in my first passionate search for the Time Machine. But Weena was a pleasant substitute. Yet all the same, they were soon destined to take far deadlier possession of my mind.

"I think I have said how much hotter than our own was the weather of this Golden Age. I cannot account for it. It may be that the sun was hotter, or the earth nearer the sun. It is usual to assume that the sun will go on cooling steadily in the future. But people, unfamiliar with such speculations as those of the younger Darwin, forget that the planets must ultimately fall back one by one into the parent body. As these catastrophes occur, the sun will blaze with renewed energy; and it may be that some inner planet had suffered this fate. Whatever the reason, the fact remains that the sun was very much hotter than we know it.

"Well, one very hot morning – my fourth, I think – as I was seeking shelter from the heat and glare in a colossal ruin near the great house where I slept and fed, there happened this strange thing: Clambering among these heaps of masonry, I found a narrow gallery, whose end and side windows were blocked by fallen masses of stone. By contrast with the brilliancy outside, it seemed at first impenetrably dark to me. I entered it groping, for the change from light to blackness made spots of colour swim before me. Suddenly I halted spellbound. A pair of eyes, luminous by reflection against the daylight without, was watching me out of the darkness.

"The old instinctive dread of wild beasts came upon me. I clenched my hands and steadfastly looked into the glaring eyeballs. I was afraid to turn. Then the thought of the absolute security in which humanity appeared to be living came to my mind. And then I remembered that strange terror of the dark. Overcoming my fear to some extent, I advanced a step and spoke. I will admit that my voice was harsh and ill-controlled. I put out my hand and touched something soft. At once the eyes darted sideways, and something white ran past me. I turned with my heart in my mouth, and saw a queer little ape-like figure, its head held down in a peculiar manner, running across the sunlit space behind me. It blundered against a block of granite, staggered aside, and in a moment was hidden in a black shadow beneath another pile of ruined masonry.

"My impression of it is, of course, imperfect; but I know it was a dull white, and had strange large greyish-red eyes; also that there was flaxen hair on its head and down its back. But, as I say, it went too fast for me to see distinctly. I cannot even say whether it ran on all-fours, or only with its forearms held very low. After an instant's pause I followed it into the second heap of ruins. I could not find it at first; but, after a time in the profound obscurity, I came upon one of those round well-like openings of which I have told you, half closed by a fallen pillar. A sudden thought came to me. Could this Thing have vanished down the shaft? I lit a match, and, looking down, I saw a small, white, moving creature, with large bright eyes which regarded me steadfastly as it retreated. It made me shudder. It was so like a human spider! It was clambering down the wall, and now I saw for the first time a number of metal foot and hand rests forming a kind of ladder down the shaft. Then the light burned my fingers and fell out of my hand, going out as it dropped, and when I had lit another the little monster had disappeared.

"I do not know how long I sat peering down that well. It was not for some time that I could succeed in persuading myself that the thing I had seen was human. But, gradually, the truth dawned on me: that Man had not remained one species, but had differentiated into two distinct animals: that my graceful children of the Upper-world were not the sole descendants of our generation, but that this bleached, obscene, nocturnal Thing, which had flashed before me, was also heir to all the ages.

"I thought of the flickering pillars and of my theory of an underground ventilation. I began to suspect their true import. And what, I wondered, was this Lemur doing in my scheme of a perfectly balanced organization? How was it related to the indolent serenity of the beautiful Upper-worlders? And what was hidden down there, at the foot of that shaft? I sat upon the edge of the well telling myself that, at any rate, there was nothing to fear, and that there I must descend for the solution of my difficulties. And withal I was absolutely afraid to go! As I hesitated, two of the beautiful Upper-world people came running in their amorous sport across the daylight in the shadow. The male pursued the female, flinging flowers at her as he ran.

"They seemed distressed to find me, my arm against the overturned pillar, peering down the well. Apparently it was considered bad form to remark these apertures; for when I pointed to this one, and tried to frame a question about it in their tongue, they were still more visibly distressed and turned away. But they were interested by my matches, and I struck some to amuse them. I tried them again about the well, and again I failed. So presently I left them, meaning to go back to Weena, and see what I could get from her. But my mind was already in revolution; my guesses and impressions were slipping and sliding to a new adjustment. I had now a clue to the import of these wells, to the ventilating towers, to the mystery of the ghosts; to say nothing of a hint at the meaning of the bronze gates and the fate of the Time Machine! And very vaguely there came a suggestion towards the solution of the economic problem that had puzzled me.

"Here was the new view. Plainly, this second species of Man was subterranean. There were three circumstances in particular which made me think that its rare emergence above ground was the outcome of a long-continued underground habit. In the first place, there was the bleached look common in most animals that live largely in the dark – the white fish of the Kentucky caves, for instance. Then, those large eyes, with that capacity for reflecting light, are common features of nocturnal things – witness the owl and the cat. And last of all, that evident confusion in the sunshine, that hasty yet fumbling awkward flight towards dark shadow, and that peculiar carriage of the head while in the light – all reinforced the theory of an extreme sensitiveness of the retina.

"Beneath my feet, then, the earth must be tunnelled enormously, and these tunnellings were the habitat of the new race. The presence of ventilating shafts and wells along the hill slopes – everywhere, in fact, except along the river valley – showed how universal were its ramifications.

What so natural, then, as to assume that it was in this artificial Underworld that such work as was necessary to the comfort of the daylight race was done? The notion was so plausible that I at once accepted it, and went on to assume the how of this splitting of the human species. I dare say you will anticipate the shape of my theory; though, for myself, I very soon felt that it fell far short of the truth.

"At first, proceeding from the problems of our own age, it seemed clear as daylight to me that the gradual widening of the present merely temporary and social difference between the Capitalist and the Labourer, was the key to the whole position. No doubt it will seem grotesque enough to you – and wildly incredible! – and yet even now there are existing circumstances to point that way. There is a tendency to utilize underground space for the less ornamental purposes of civilization; there is the Metropolitan Railway in London, for instance, there are new electric railways, there are subways, there are underground workrooms and restaurants, and they increase and multiply. Evidently, I thought, this tendency had increased till Industry had gradually lost its birthright in the sky. I mean that it had gone deeper and deeper into larger and ever larger underground factories, spending a still-increasing amount of its time therein, till, in the end –! Even now, does not an East-end worker live in such artificial conditions as practically to be cut off from the natural surface of the earth?

"Again, the exclusive tendency of richer people – due, no doubt, to the increasing refinement of their education, and the widening gulf between them and the rude violence of the poor – is already leading to the closing, in their interest, of considerable portions of the surface of the land. About London, for instance, perhaps half the prettier country is shut in against intrusion. And this same widening gulf – which is due to the length and expense of the higher educational process and the increased facilities for and temptations towards refined habits on the part of the rich – will make that exchange between class and class, that promotion by intermarriage which at present retards the splitting of our species along lines of social stratification, less and less frequent. So, in the end, above ground you must have the Haves, pursuing pleasure and comfort and beauty, and below ground the Have-nots, the Workers getting continually adapted to the conditions of their labour. Once they were there, they would no doubt have to pay rent, and not a little of it, for the ventilation of their caverns; and if they refused, they would starve or be suffocated for arrears. Such of them as were so constituted as to be miserable and rebellious would die; and, in the end, the balance being permanent, the survivors would become as well adapted to the conditions of underground life, and as happy in their way, as the Upper-world people were to theirs. As it seemed to me, the refined beauty and the etiolated pallor followed naturally enough.

"The great triumph of Humanity I had dreamed of took a different shape in my mind. It had been no such triumph of moral education and general co-operation as I had imagined. Instead, I saw a real aristocracy, armed with a perfected science and working to a logical conclusion the industrial system of today. Its triumph had not been simply a triumph over Nature, but a triumph over Nature and the fellow-man. This, I must warn you, was my theory at the time. I had no convenient cicerone in the pattern of the Utopian books. My explanation may be absolutely wrong. I still think it is the most plausible one. But even on this supposition the balanced civilization that was at last attained must have long since passed its zenith, and was now far fallen into decay. The too-perfect security of the Upper-worlders had led them to a slow movement of degeneration, to a general dwindling in size, strength, and intelligence. That I could see clearly enough already. What had happened to the Under-grounders I did not yet suspect; but from what I had seen of the Morlocks – that, by the by, was the name by which these creatures were called – I could imagine that the modification of the human type was even far more profound than among the 'Eloi,' the beautiful race that I already knew.

"Then came troublesome doubts. Why had the Morlocks taken my Time Machine? For I felt sure it was they who had taken it. Why, too, if the Eloi were masters, could they not restore the machine to me? And why were they so terribly afraid of the dark? I proceeded, as I have said, to question Weena about this Under-world, but here again I was disappointed. At first she would not understand my questions, and presently she refused to answer them. She shivered as though the topic was unendurable. And when I pressed her, perhaps a little harshly, she burst into tears. They were the only tears, except my own, I ever saw in that Golden Age. When I saw them I ceased abruptly to trouble about the Morlocks, and was only concerned in banishing these signs of the human inheritance from Weena's eyes. And very soon she was smiling and clapping her hands, while I solemnly burned a match.

The complete and unabridged text is available online, from *flametreepublishing.com/extras*

The Sleeper Awakes
Chapters I–VIII
H.G. Wells

Preface to the New Edition

WHEN THE SLEEPER WAKES, whose title I have now altered to *The Sleeper Awakes*, was first published as a book in 1899 after a serial appearance in the *Graphic* and one or two American and colonial periodicals. It is one of the most ambitious and least satisfactory of my books, and I have taken the opportunity afforded by this reprinting to make a number of excisions and alterations. Like most of my earlier work, it was written under considerable pressure; there are marks of haste not only in the writing of the latter part, but in the very construction of the story. Except for certain streaks of a slovenliness which seems to be an almost unavoidable defect in me, there is little to be ashamed of in the writing of the opening portion; but it will be fairly manifest to the critic that instead of being put aside and thought over through a leisurely interlude, the ill-conceived latter part was pushed to its end. I was at that time overworked, and badly in need of a holiday. In addition to various necessary journalistic tasks, I had in hand another book, *Love and Mr. Lewisham*, which had taken a very much stronger hold upon my affections than this present story. My circumstances demanded that one or other should be finished before I took any rest, and so I wound up the Sleeper sufficiently to make it a marketable work, hoping to be able to revise it before the book printers at any rate got hold of it. But fortune was against me. I came back to England from Italy only to fall dangerously ill, and I still remember the impotent rage and strain of my attempt to put some sort of finish to my story of Mr. Lewisham, with my temperature at a hundred and two. I couldn't endure the thought of leaving that book a fragment. I did afterwards contrive to save it from the consequences of that febrile spurt – *Love and Mr. Lewisham* is indeed one of my most carefully balanced books – but the Sleeper escaped me.

It is twelve years now since the Sleeper was written, and that young man of thirty-one is already too remote for me to attempt any very drastic reconstruction of his work. I have played now merely the part of an editorial elder brother: cut out relentlessly a number of long tiresome passages that showed all too plainly the fagged, toiling brain, the heavy sluggish *driven* pen, and straightened out certain indecisions at the end. Except for that, I have done no more than hack here and there at clumsy phrases and repetitions. The worst thing in the earlier version, and the thing that rankled most in my mind, was the treatment of the relations of Helen Wotton and Graham. Haste in art is almost always vulgarisation, and I slipped into the obvious vulgarity of making what the newspaper syndicates call a 'love interest' out of Helen. There was even a clumsy intimation that instead of going up in the flying-machine to fight, Graham might have given in to Ostrog, and married Helen. I have now removed the suggestion of these uncanny connubialities. Not the slightest intimation of any sexual interest could in truth have arisen between these two. They loved and kissed one another, but as a girl and her heroic grandfather might love, and in a crisis kiss. I have found it possible, without any very serious disarrangement, to clear all that objectionable stuff out of the story, and so a little ease my conscience on the score of this ungainly lapse. I have also, with a few strokes of the pen, eliminated certain dishonest and regrettable suggestions that the People beat Ostrog. My Graham dies, as all his kind must die, with no certainty of either victory or defeat.

Who will win – Ostrog or the People? A thousand years hence that will still be just the open question we leave today.

H.G. Wells

Chapter I
Insomnia

ONE AFTERNOON, at low water, Mr. Isbister, a young artist lodging at Boscastle, walked from that place to the picturesque cove of Pentargen, desiring to examine the caves there. Halfway down the precipitous path to the Pentargen beach he came suddenly upon a man sitting in an attitude of profound distress beneath a projecting mass of rock. The hands of this man hung limply over his knees, his eyes were red and staring before him, and his face was wet with tears.

He glanced round at Isbister's footfall. Both men were disconcerted, Isbister the more so, and, to override the awkwardness of his involuntary pause, he remarked, with an air of mature conviction, that the weather was hot for the time of year.

"Very," answered the stranger shortly, hesitated a second, and added in a colourless tone, "I can't sleep."

Isbister stopped abruptly. "No?" was all he said, but his bearing conveyed his helpful impulse.

"It may sound incredible," said the stranger, turning weary eyes to Isbister's face and emphasizing his words with a languid hand, "but I have had no sleep – no sleep at all for six nights."

"Had advice?"

"Yes. Bad advice for the most part. Drugs. My nervous system….They are all very well for the run of people. It's hard to explain. I dare not take…sufficiently powerful drugs."

"That makes it difficult," said Isbister.

He stood helplessly in the narrow path, perplexed what to do. Clearly the man wanted to talk. An idea natural enough under the circumstances, prompted him to keep the conversation going. "I've never suffered from sleeplessness myself," he said in a tone of commonplace gossip, "but in those cases I have known, people have usually found something –"

"I dare make no experiments."

He spoke wearily. He gave a gesture of rejection, and for a space both men were silent.

"Exercise?" suggested Isbister diffidently, with a glance from his interlocutor's face to the touring costume he wore.

"That is what I have tried. Unwisely perhaps. I have followed the coast, day after day – from New Quay. It has only added muscular fatigue to the mental. The cause of this unrest was overwork – trouble. There was something –"

He stopped as if from sheer fatigue. He rubbed his forehead with a lean hand. He resumed speech like one who talks to himself.

"I am a lone wolf, a solitary man, wandering through a world in which I have no part. I am wifeless – childless – who is it speaks of the childless as the dead twigs on the tree of life? I am wifeless, childless – I could find no duty to do. No desire even in my heart. One thing at last I set myself to do.

"I said, I will do this, and to do it, to overcome the inertia of this dull body, I resorted to drugs. Great God, I've had enough of drugs! I don't know if *you* feel the heavy inconvenience of the body, its exasperating demand of time from the mind – time – life! Live! We only live in patches. We have to eat, and then comes the dull digestive complacencies – or irritations. We have to take the air or else our thoughts grow sluggish, stupid, run into gulfs and blind alleys. A thousand distractions arise from within and without, and then comes drowsiness and sleep. Men seem to live for sleep. How little of a man's day is his own – even at the best! And then come those false friends, those Thug helpers, the alkaloids that stifle natural fatigue and kill rest – black coffee, cocaine –"

"I see," said Isbister.

"I did my work," said the sleepless man with a querulous intonation.

"And this is the price?"

"Yes."

For a little while the two remained without speaking.

"You cannot imagine the craving for rest that I feel – a hunger and thirst. For six long days, since my work was done, my mind has been a whirlpool, swift, unprogressive and incessant, a torrent of thoughts leading nowhere, spinning round swift and steady –" He paused. "Towards the gulf."

"You must sleep," said Isbister decisively, and with an air of a remedy discovered. "Certainly you must sleep."

"My mind is perfectly lucid. It was never clearer. But I know I am drawing towards the vortex. Presently –"

"Yes?"

"You have seen things go down an eddy? Out of the light of the day, out of this sweet world of sanity – down –"

"But," expostulated Isbister.

The man threw out a hand towards him, and his eyes were wild, and his voice suddenly high. "I shall kill myself. If in no other way – at the foot of yonder dark precipice there, where the waves are green, and the white surge lifts and falls, and that little thread of water trembles down. There at any rate is...sleep."

"That's unreasonable," said Isbister, startled at the man's hysterical gust of emotion. "Drugs are better than that."

"There at any rate is sleep," repeated the stranger, not heeding him.

Isbister looked at him. "It's not a cert, you know," he remarked. "There's a cliff like that at Lulworth Cove – as high, anyhow – and a little girl fell from top to bottom. And lives today – sound and well."

"But those rocks there?"

"One might lie on them rather dismally through a cold night, broken bones grating as one shivered, chill water splashing over you. Eh?"

Their eyes met. "Sorry to upset your ideals," said Isbister with a sense of devil-may-careish brilliance. "But a suicide over that cliff (or any cliff for the matter of that), really, as an artist –" he laughed. "It's so damned amateurish."

"But the other thing," said the sleepless man irritably, "the other thing. No man can keep sane if night after night –"

"Have you been walking along this coast alone?"

"Yes."

"Silly sort of thing to do. If you'll excuse my saying so. Alone! As you say; body fag is no cure for brain fag. Who told you to? No wonder; walking! And the sun on your head, heat, fag, solitude, all the day long, and then, I suppose, you go to bed and try very hard – eh?"

Isbister stopped short and looked at the sufferer doubtfully.

"Look at these rocks!" cried the seated man with a sudden force of gesture. "Look at that sea that has shone and quivered there for ever! See the white spume rush into darkness under that great cliff. And this blue vault, with the blinding sun pouring from the dome of it. It is your world. You accept it, you rejoice in it. It warms and supports and delights you. And for me –"

He turned his head and showed a ghastly face, bloodshot pallid eyes and bloodless lips. He spoke almost in a whisper. "It is the garment of my misery. The whole world…is the garment of my misery."

Isbister looked at all the wild beauty of the sunlit cliffs about them and back to that face of despair. For a moment he was silent.

He started, and made a gesture of impatient rejection. "You get a night's sleep," he said, "and you won't see much misery out here. Take my word for it."

He was quite sure now that this was a providential encounter. Only half an hour ago he had been feeling horribly bored. Here was employment the bare thought of which, was righteous self-applause. He took possession forthwith. The first need of this exhausted being was companionship. He flung himself down on the steeply sloping turf beside the motionless seated figure, and threw out a skirmishing line of gossip.

His hearer lapsed into apathy; he stared dismally seaward, and spoke only in answer to Isbister's direct questions – and not to all of those. But he made no objection to this benevolent intrusion upon his despair.

He seemed even grateful, and when presently Isbister, feeling that his unsupported talk was losing vigour, suggested that they should reascend the steep and return towards Boscastle, alleging the view into Blackapit, he submitted quietly. Halfway up he began talking to himself, and abruptly turned a ghastly face on his helper. "What can be happening?" he asked with a gaunt illustrative hand. "What can be happening? Spin, spin, spin, spin. It goes round and round, round and round for evermore."

He stood with his hand circling.

"It's all right, old chap," said Isbister with the air of an old friend. "Don't worry yourself. Trust to me."

The man dropped his hand and turned again. They went over the brow and to the headland beyond Penally, with the sleepless man gesticulating ever and again, and speaking fragmentary things concerning his whirling brain. At the headland they stood by the seat that looks into the dark mysteries of Blackapit, and then he sat down. Isbister had resumed his talk whenever the path had widened sufficiently for them to walk abreast. He was enlarging upon the complex difficulty of making Boscastle Harbour in bad weather, when suddenly and quite irrelevantly his companion interrupted him again.

"My head is not like what it was," he said, gesticulating for want of expressive phrases. "It's not like what it was. There is a sort of oppression, a weight. No – not drowsiness, would God it were! It is like a shadow, a deep shadow falling suddenly and swiftly across something busy. Spin, spin into the darkness. The tumult of thought, the confusion, the eddy and eddy. I can't express it. I can hardly keep my mind on it – steadily enough to tell you."

He stopped feebly.

"Don't trouble, old chap," said Isbister. "I think I can understand. At any rate, it don't matter very much just at present about telling me, you know."

The sleepless man thrust his knuckles into his eyes and rubbed them. Isbister talked for awhile while this rubbing continued, and then he had a fresh idea. "Come down to my room," he said, "and try a pipe. I can show you some sketches of this Blackapit. If you'd care?"

The other rose obediently and followed him down the steep.

Several times Isbister heard him stumble as they came down, and his movements were slow and hesitating. "Come in with me," said Isbister, "and try some cigarettes and the blessed gift of alcohol. If you take alcohol?"

The stranger hesitated at the garden gate. He seemed no longer aware of his actions. "I don't drink," he said slowly, coming up the garden path, and after a moment's interval repeated absently, "No – I don't drink. It goes round. Spin, it goes – spin –"

He stumbled at the doorstep and entered the room with the bearing of one who sees nothing.

Then he sat down heavily in the easy chair, seemed almost to fall into it. He leant forward with his brows on his hands and became motionless. Presently he made a faint sound in his throat.

Isbister moved about the room with the nervousness of an inexperienced host, making little remarks that scarcely required answering. He crossed the room to his portfolio, placed it on the table and noticed the mantel clock.

"I don't know if you'd care to have supper with me," he said with an unlighted cigarette in his hand – his mind troubled with ideas of a furtive administration of chloral. "Only cold mutton, you know, but passing sweet. Welsh. And a tart, I believe." He repeated this after momentary silence.

The seated man made no answer. Isbister stopped, match in hand, regarding him.

The stillness lengthened. The match went out, the cigarette was put down unlit. The man was certainly very still. Isbister took up the portfolio, opened it, put it down, hesitated, seemed about to speak. "Perhaps," he whispered doubtfully. Presently he glanced at the door and back to the figure. Then he stole on tiptoe out of the room, glancing at his companion after each elaborate pace.

He closed the door noiselessly. The house door was standing open, and he went out beyond the porch, and stood where the monkshood rose at the corner of the garden bed. From this point he could see the stranger through the open window, still and dim, sitting head on hand. He had not moved.

A number of children going along the road stopped and regarded the artist curiously. A boatman exchanged civilities with him. He felt that possibly his circumspect attitude and position looked peculiar and unaccountable. Smoking, perhaps, might seem more natural. He drew pipe and pouch from his pocket, filled the pipe slowly.

"I wonder,"…he said, with a scarcely perceptible loss of complacency. "At any rate one must give him a chance." He struck a match in the virile way, and proceeded to light his pipe.

He heard his landlady behind him, coming with his lamp lit from the kitchen. He turned, gesticulating with his pipe, and stopped her at the door of his sitting-room. He had some difficulty in explaining the situation in whispers, for she did not know he had a visitor. She retreated again with the lamp, still a little mystified to judge from her manner, and he resumed his hovering at the corner of the porch, flushed and less at his ease.

Long after he had smoked out his pipe, and when the bats were abroad, curiosity dominated his complex hesitations, and he stole back into his darkling sitting-room. He paused in the doorway. The stranger was still in the same attitude, dark against the window. Save for the singing of some sailors aboard one of the little slate-carrying ships in the harbour the evening was very still. Outside, the spikes of monkshood and delphinium stood erect and motionless against the shadow of the hillside. Something flashed into Isbister's mind; he started, and leaning over the table, listened. An unpleasant suspicion grew stronger; became conviction. Astonishment seized him and became – dread!

No sound of breathing came from the seated figure!

He crept slowly and noiselessly round the table, pausing twice to listen. At last he could lay his hand on the back of the armchair. He bent down until the two heads were ear to ear.

Then he bent still lower to look up at his visitor's face. He started violently and uttered an exclamation. The eyes were void spaces of white.

He looked again and saw that they were open and with the pupils rolled under the lids. He was afraid. He took the man by the shoulder and shook him. "Are you asleep?" he said, with his voice jumping, and again, "Are you asleep?"

A conviction took possession of his mind that this man was dead. He became active and noisy, strode across the room, blundering against the table as he did so, and rang the bell.

"Please bring a light at once," he said in the passage. "There is something wrong with my friend."

He returned to the motionless seated figure, grasped the shoulder, shook it, shouted. The room was flooded with yellow glare as his landlady entered with the light. His face was white as he turned blinking towards her. "I must fetch a doctor," he said. "It is either death or a fit. Is there a doctor in the village? Where is a doctor to be found?"

Chapter II
The Trance

THE STATE OF cataleptic rigour into which this man had fallen, lasted for an unprecedented length of time, and then he passed slowly to the flaccid state, to a lax attitude suggestive of profound repose. Then it was his eyes could be closed.

He was removed from the hotel to the Boscastle surgery, and from the surgery, after some weeks, to London. But he still resisted every attempt at reanimation. After a time, for reasons that will appear later, these attempts were discontinued. For a great space he lay in that strange condition, inert and still – neither dead nor living but, as it were, suspended, hanging midway between nothingness and existence. His was a darkness unbroken by a ray of thought or sensation, a dreamless inanition, a vast space of peace. The tumult of his mind had swelled and risen to an abrupt climax of silence. Where was the man? Where is any man when insensibility takes hold of him?

"It seems only yesterday," said Isbister. "I remember it all as though it happened yesterday – clearer, perhaps, than if it had happened yesterday."

It was the Isbister of the last chapter, but he was no longer a young man. The hair that had been brown and a trifle in excess of the fashionable length, was iron grey and clipped close, and the face that had been pink and white was buff and ruddy. He had a pointed beard shot with grey. He talked to an elderly man who wore a summer suit of drill (the summer of that year was unusually hot). This was Warming, a London solicitor and next of kin to Graham, the man who had fallen into the trance. And the two men stood side by side in a room in a house in London regarding his recumbent figure.

It was a yellow figure lying lax upon a water-bed and clad in a flowing shirt, a figure with a shrunken face and a stubby beard, lean limbs and lank nails, and about it was a case of thin glass. This glass seemed to mark off the sleeper from the reality of life about him, he was a thing apart, a strange, isolated abnormality. The two men stood close to the glass, peering in.

"The thing gave me a shock," said Isbister. "I feel a queer sort of surprise even now when I think of his white eyes. They were white, you know, rolled up. Coming here again brings it all back to me."

"Have you never seen him since that time?" asked Warming.

"Often wanted to come," said Isbister; "but business nowadays is too serious a thing for much holiday keeping. I've been in America most of the time."

"If I remember rightly," said Warming, "you were an artist?"

"Was. And then I became a married man. I saw it was all up with black and white, very soon – at least for a mediocrity, and I jumped on to process. Those posters on the Cliffs at Dover are by my people."

"Good posters," admitted the solicitor, "though I was sorry to see them there."

"Last as long as the cliffs, if necessary," exclaimed Isbister with satisfaction. "The world changes. When he fell asleep, twenty years ago, I was down at Boscastle with a box of watercolours and a noble, old-fashioned ambition. I didn't expect that some day my pigments would glorify the whole blessed coast of England, from Land's End round again to the Lizard. Luck comes to a man very often when he's not looking."

Warming seemed to doubt the quality of the luck. "I just missed seeing you, if I recollect aright."

"You came back by the trap that took me to Camelford railway station. It was close on the Jubilee, Victoria's Jubilee, because I remember the seats and flags in Westminster, and the row with the cabman at Chelsea."

"The Diamond Jubilee, it was," said Warming; "the second one."

"Ah, yes! At the proper Jubilee – the Fifty Year affair – I was down at Wookey – a boy. I missed all that....What a fuss we had with him! My landlady wouldn't take him in, wouldn't let him stay – he looked so queer when he was rigid. We had to carry him in a chair up to the hotel. And the Boscastle doctor – it wasn't the present chap, but the G.P. before him – was at him until nearly two, with me and the landlord holding lights and so forth."

"Do you mean – he was stiff and hard?"

"Stiff! – wherever you bent him he stuck. You might have stood him on his head and he'd have stopped. I never saw such stiffness. Of course this" – he indicated the prostrate figure by a movement of his head – "is quite different. And the little doctor – what was his name?"

"Smithers?"

"Smithers it was – was quite wrong in trying to fetch him round too soon, according to all accounts. The things he did! Even now it makes me feel all – ugh! Mustard, snuff, pricking. And one of those beastly little things, not dynamos –"

"Coils."

"Yes. You could see his muscles throb and jump, and he twisted about. There were just two flaring yellow candles, and all the shadows were shivering, and the little doctor nervous and putting on side, and *him* – stark and squirming in the most unnatural ways. Well, it made me dream."

Pause.

"It's a strange state," said Warming.

"It's a sort of complete absence," said Isbister. "Here's the body, empty. Not dead a bit, and yet not alive. It's like a seat vacant and marked 'engaged.' No feeling, no digestion, no beating of the heart – not a flutter. *That* doesn't make me feel as if there was a man present. In a sense it's more dead than death, for these doctors tell me that even the hair has stopped growing. Now with the proper dead, the hair will go on growing –"

"I know," said Warming, with a flash of pain in his expression.

They peered through the glass again. Graham was indeed in a strange state, in the flaccid phase of a trance, but a trance unprecedented in medical history. Trances had lasted for as much as a year before – but at the end of that time it had ever been a waking or a death; sometimes first one and then the other. Isbister noted the marks the physicians had made in injecting nourishment, for that had been resorted to to postpone collapse; he pointed them out to Warming, who had been trying not to see them.

"And while he has been lying here," said Isbister, with the zest of a life freely spent, "I have changed my plans in life; married, raised a family, my eldest lad – I hadn't begun to think of sons then – is an American citizen, and looking forward to leaving Harvard. There's a touch of grey in my hair. And this man, not a day older nor wiser (practically) than I was in my downy days. It's curious to think of."

Warming turned. "And I have grown old too. I played cricket with him when I was still only a boy. And he looks a young man still. Yellow perhaps. But that is a young man nevertheless."

"And there's been the War," said Isbister.

"From beginning to end."

"And these Martians."

"I've understood," said Isbister after a pause, "that he had some moderate property of his own?"

"That is so," said Warming. He coughed primly. "As it happens – I have charge of it."

"Ah!" Isbister thought, hesitated and spoke: "No doubt – his keep here is not expensive – no doubt it will have improved – accumulated?"

"It has. He will wake up very much better off – if he wakes – than when he slept."

"As a business man," said Isbister, "that thought has naturally been in my mind. I have, indeed, sometimes thought that, speaking commercially, of course, this sleep may be a very good thing for him. That he knows what he is about, so to speak, in being insensible so long. If he had lived straight on –"

"I doubt if he would have premeditated as much," said Warming. "He was not a far-sighted man. In fact –"

"Yes?"

"We differed on that point. I stood to him somewhat in the relation of a guardian. You have probably seen enough of affairs to recognise that occasionally a certain friction – But even if that was the case, there is a doubt whether he will ever wake. This sleep exhausts slowly, but it exhausts. Apparently he is sliding slowly, very slowly and tediously, down a long slope, if you can understand me?"

"It will be a pity to lose his surprise. There's been a lot of change these twenty years. It's Rip Van Winkle come real."

"There has been a lot of change certainly," said Warming. "And, among other changes, I have changed. I am an old man."

Isbister hesitated, and then feigned a belated surprise. "I shouldn't have thought it."

"I was forty-three when his bankers – you remember you wired to his bankers – sent on to me."

"I got their address from the cheque book in his pocket," said Isbister.

"Well, the addition is not difficult," said Warming.

There was another pause, and then Isbister gave way to an unavoidable curiosity. "He may go on for years yet," he said, and had a moment of hesitation. "We have to consider that. His affairs, you know, may fall some day into the hands of – someone else, you know."

"That, if you will believe me, Mr. Isbister, is one of the problems most constantly before my mind. We happen to be – as a matter of fact, there are no very trustworthy connexions of ours. It is a grotesque and unprecedented position."

"Rather," said Isbister.

"It seems to me it's a case of some public body, some practically undying guardian. If he really is going on living – as the doctors, some of them, think. As a matter of fact, I have gone to one or two public men about it. But, so far, nothing has been done."

"It wouldn't be a bad idea to hand him over to some public body – the British Museum Trustees, or the Royal College of Physicians. Sounds a bit odd, of course, but the whole situation is odd."

"The difficulty is to induce them to take him."

"Red tape, I suppose?"

"Partly."

Pause. "It's a curious business, certainly," said Isbister. "And compound interest has a way of mounting up."

"It has," said Warming. "And now the gold supplies are running short there is a tendency towards…appreciation."

"I've felt that," said Isbister with a grimace. "But it makes it better for *him*."

"If he wakes."

"If he wakes," echoed Isbister. "Do you notice the pinched-in look of his nose, and the way in which his eyelids sink?"

Warming looked and thought for a space. "I doubt if he will wake," he said at last.

"I never properly understood," said Isbister, "what it was brought this on. He told me something about overstudy. I've often been curious."

"He was a man of considerable gifts, but spasmodic, emotional. He had grave domestic troubles, divorced his wife, in fact, and it was as a relief from that, I think, that he took up politics of the rabid sort. He was a fanatical Radical – a Socialist – or typical Liberal, as they used to call themselves, of the advanced school. Energetic – flighty – undisciplined. Overwork upon a controversy did this for him. I remember the pamphlet he wrote – a curious production. Wild, whirling stuff. There were one or two prophecies. Some of them are already exploded, some of them are established facts. But for the most part to read such a thesis is to realise how full the world is of unanticipated things. He will have much to learn, much to unlearn, when he wakes. If ever a waking comes."

"I'd give anything to be there," said Isbister, "just to hear what he would say to it all."

"So would I," said Warming. "Aye! so would I," with an old man's sudden turn to self pity. "But I shall never see him wake."

He stood looking thoughtfully at the waxen figure. "He will never awake," he said at last. He sighed. "He will never awake again."

Chapter III
The Awakening

BUT WARMING was wrong in that. An awakening came.

What a wonderfully complex thing! This simple seeming unity – the self! Who can trace its reintegration as morning after morning we awaken, the flux and confluence of its countless factors interweaving, rebuilding, the dim first stirrings of the soul, the growth and synthesis of the unconscious to the subconscious, the subconscious to dawning consciousness, until at last we recognise ourselves again. And as it happens to most of us after the night's sleep, so it was with Graham at the end of his vast slumber. A dim cloud of sensation taking shape, a cloudy dreariness, and he found himself vaguely somewhere, recumbent, faint, but alive.

The pilgrimage towards a personal being seemed to traverse vast gulfs, to occupy epochs. Gigantic dreams that were terrible realities at the time, left vague perplexing memories, strange creatures, strange scenery, as if from another planet. There was a distinct impression, too, of a momentous conversation, of a name – he could not tell what name – that was subsequently to recur, of some queer long-forgotten sensation of vein and muscle, of a feeling of vast hopeless effort, the effort of a man near drowning in darkness. Then came a panorama of dazzling unstable confluent scenes....

Graham became aware that his eyes were open and regarding some unfamiliar thing.

It was something white, the edge of something, a frame of wood. He moved his head slightly, following the contour of this shape. It went up beyond the top of his eyes. He tried to think where he might be. Did it matter, seeing he was so wretched? The colour of his thoughts was a dark depression. He felt the featureless misery of one who wakes towards the hour of dawn. He had an uncertain sense of whispers and footsteps hastily receding.

The movement of his head involved a perception of extreme physical weakness. He supposed he was in bed in the hotel at the place in the valley – but he could not recall that white edge. He must have slept. He remembered now that he had wanted to sleep. He recalled the cliff and Waterfall again, and then recollected something about talking to a passer-by....

How long had he slept? What was that sound of pattering feet? And that rise and fall, like the murmur of breakers on pebbles? He put out a languid hand to reach his watch from the chair whereon it was his habit to place it, and touched some smooth hard surface like glass. This was so unexpected that it startled him extremely. Quite suddenly he rolled over, stared for a moment, and struggled into a sitting position. The effort was unexpectedly difficult, and it left him giddy and weak – and amazed.

He rubbed his eyes. The riddle of his surroundings was confusing but his mind was quite clear – evidently his sleep had benefited him. He was not in a bed at all as he understood the word, but lying naked on a very soft and yielding mattress, in a trough of dark glass. The mattress was partly transparent, a fact he observed with a sense of insecurity, and below it was a mirror reflecting him greyly. About his arm – and he saw with a shock that his skin was strangely dry and yellow – was bound a curious apparatus of rubber, bound so cunningly that it seemed to pass into his skin above and below. And this bed was placed in a case of greenish coloured glass (as it seemed to him), a bar in the white framework of which had first arrested his attention. In the corner of the case was a stand of glittering and delicately made apparatus, for the most part quite strange appliances, though a maximum and minimum thermometer was recognisable.

The slightly greenish tint of the glass-like substance which surrounded him on every hand obscured what lay behind, but he perceived it was a vast apartment of splendid appearance, and with a very large and simple white archway facing him. Close to the walls of the cage were articles of furniture, a table covered with a silvery cloth, silvery like the side of a fish, a couple of graceful chairs, and on the table a number of dishes with substances piled on them, a bottle and two glasses. He realised that he was intensely hungry.

He could see no one, and after a period of hesitation scrambled off the translucent mattress and tried to stand on the clean white floor of his little apartment. He had miscalculated his strength, however, and staggered and put his hand against the glass like pane before him to steady himself. For a moment it resisted his hand, bending outward like a distended bladder, then it broke with a slight report and vanished – a pricked bubble. He reeled out into the general space of the hall, greatly astonished. He caught at the table to save himself, knocking one of the glasses to the floor – it rang but did not break – and sat down in one of the armchairs.

When he had a little recovered he filled the remaining glass from the bottle and drank – a colourless liquid it was, but not water, with a pleasing faint aroma and taste and a quality of immediate support and stimulus. He put down the vessel and looked about him.

The apartment lost none of its size and magnificence now that the greenish transparency that had intervened was removed. The archway he saw led to a flight of steps, going downward without the intermediation of a door, to a spacious transverse passage. This passage ran between polished pillars of some white-veined substance of deep ultramarine, and along it came the sound of human movements, and voices and a deep undeviating droning note. He sat, now fully awake, listening alertly, forgetting the viands in his attention.

Then with a shock he remembered that he was naked, and casting about him for covering, saw a long black robe thrown on one of the chairs beside him. This he wrapped about him and sat down again, trembling.

His mind was still a surging perplexity. Clearly he had slept, and had been removed in his sleep. But where? And who were those people, the distant crowd beyond the deep blue pillars? Boscastle? He poured out and partially drank another glass of the colourless fluid.

What was this place? – This place that to his senses seemed subtly quivering like a thing alive? He looked about him at the clean and beautiful form of the apartment, unstained by ornament, and saw that the roof was broken in one place by a circular shaft full of light, and, as he looked, a steady, sweeping shadow blotted it out and passed, and came again and passed. "Beat, beat," that sweeping shadow had a note of its own in the subdued tumult that filled the air.

He would have called out, but only a little sound came into his throat. Then he stood up, and, with the uncertain steps of a drunkard, made his way towards the archway. He staggered down the steps, tripped on the corner of the black cloak he had wrapped about himself, and saved himself by catching at one of the blue pillars.

The passage ran down a cool vista of blue and purple and ended remotely in a railed space like a balcony brightly lit and projecting into a space of haze, a space like the interior of some gigantic building. Beyond and remote were vast and vague architectural forms. The tumult of voices rose now loud and clear, and on the balcony and with their backs to him, gesticulating and apparently in animated conversation, were three figures, richly dressed in loose and easy garments of bright soft colourings. The noise of a great multitude of people poured up over the balcony, and once it seemed the top of a banner passed, and once some brightly coloured object, a pale blue cap or garment thrown up into the air perhaps, flashed athwart the space and fell. The shouts sounded like English, there was a reiteration of "Wake!" He heard some indistinct shrill cry, and abruptly these three men began laughing.

"Ha, ha, ha!" laughed one – a red-haired man in a short purple robe. "When the Sleeper wakes – *When*!"

He turned his eyes full of merriment along the passage. His face changed, the whole man changed, became rigid. The other two turned swiftly at his exclamation and stood motionless. Their faces assumed an expression of consternation, an expression that deepened into awe.

Suddenly Graham's knees bent beneath him, his arm against the pillar collapsed limply, he staggered forward and fell upon his face.

Chapter IV
The Sound of a Tumult

GRAHAM'S LAST IMPRESSION before he fainted was of the ringing of bells. He learnt afterwards that he was insensible, hanging between life and death, for the better part of an hour. When he recovered his senses, he was back on his translucent couch, and there was a stirring warmth at heart and throat. The dark apparatus, he perceived, had been removed from his arm, which was bandaged. The white framework was still about him, but the greenish transparent substance that had filled it was altogether gone. A man in a deep violet robe, one of those who had been on the balcony, was looking keenly into his face.

Remote but insistent was a clamour of bells and confused sounds, that suggested to his mind the picture of a great number of people shouting together. Something seemed to fall across this tumult, a door suddenly closed.

Graham moved his head. "What does this all mean?" he said slowly. "Where am I?"

He saw the red-haired man who had been first to discover him. A voice seemed to be asking what he had said, and was abruptly stilled.

The man in violet answered in a soft voice, speaking English with a slightly foreign accent, or so at least it seemed to the Sleeper's ears. "You are quite safe. You were brought hither from where you fell asleep. It is quite safe. You have been here some time – sleeping. In a trance."

He said, something further that Graham could not hear, and a little phial was handed across to him. Graham felt a cooling spray, a fragrant mist played over his forehead for a moment, and his sense of refreshment increased. He closed his eyes in satisfaction.

"Better?" asked the man in violet, as Graham's eyes reopened. He was a pleasant-faced man of thirty, perhaps, with a pointed flaxen beard, and a clasp of gold at the neck of his violet robe.

"Yes," said Graham.

"You have been asleep some time. In a cataleptic trance. You have heard? Catalepsy? It may seem strange to you at first, but I can assure you everything is well."

Graham did not answer, but these words served their reassuring purpose. His eyes went from face to face of the three people about him. They were regarding him strangely. He knew he ought to be somewhere in Cornwall, but he could not square these things with that impression.

A matter that had been in his mind during his last waking moments at Boscastle recurred, a thing resolved upon and somehow neglected. He cleared his throat.

"Have you wired my cousin?" he asked. "E. Warming, 27, Chancery Lane?"

They were all assiduous to hear. But he had to repeat it. "What an odd *blurr* in his accent!" whispered the red-haired man. "Wire, sir?" said the young man with the flaxen beard, evidently puzzled.

"He means send an electric telegram," volunteered the third, a pleasant-faced youth of nineteen or twenty. The flaxen-bearded man gave a cry of comprehension. "How stupid of me! You may be sure everything shall be done, sir," he said to Graham. "I am afraid it would be difficult to – *wire* to your cousin. He is not in London now. But don't trouble about arrangements yet; you have been asleep a very long time and the important thing is to get over that, sir." (Graham concluded the word was sir, but this man pronounced it '*Sire*.')

"Oh!" said Graham, and became quiet.

It was all very puzzling, but apparently these people in unfamiliar dress knew what they were about. Yet they were odd and the room was odd. It seemed he was in some newly established place. He had a sudden flash of suspicion! Surely this wasn't some hall of public exhibition! If it was he would give Warming a piece of his mind. But it scarcely had that character. And in a place of public exhibition he would not have discovered himself naked.

Then suddenly, quite abruptly, he realised what had happened. There was no perceptible interval of suspicion, no dawn to his knowledge. Abruptly he knew that his trance had lasted for a vast interval; as if by some processes of thought-reading he interpreted the awe in the faces that peered into his. He looked at them strangely, full of intense emotion. It seemed they read his eyes. He framed his lips to speak and could not. A queer impulse to hide his knowledge came into his mind almost at the moment of his discovery. He looked at his bare feet, regarding them silently. His impulse to speak passed. He was trembling exceedingly.

They gave him some pink fluid with a greenish fluorescence and a meaty taste, and the assurance of returning strength grew.

"That – that makes me feel better," he said hoarsely, and there were murmurs of respectful approval. He knew now quite clearly. He made to speak again, and again he could not.

He pressed his throat and tried a third time. "How long?" he asked in a level voice. "How long have I been asleep?"

"Some considerable time," said the flaxen-bearded man, glancing quickly at the others.

"How long?"

"A very long time."

"Yes – yes," said Graham, suddenly testy. "But I want – Is it – it is – some years? Many years? There was something – I forget what. I feel – confused. But you –" he sobbed. "You need not fence with me. How long –?"

He stopped, breathing irregularly. He squeezed his eyes with his knuckles and sat waiting for an answer.

They spoke in undertones.

"Five or six?" he asked faintly. "More?"

"Very much more than that."

"More!"

"More."

He looked at them and it seemed as though imps were twitching the muscles of his face. He looked his question.

"Many years," said the man with the red beard.

Graham struggled into a sitting position. He wiped a rheumy tear from his face with a lean hand. "Many years!" he repeated. He shut his eyes tight, opened them, and sat looking about him from one unfamiliar thing to another.

"How many years?" he asked.

"You must be prepared to be surprised."

"Well?"

"More than a gross of years."

He was irritated at the strange word. "More than a *what*?"

Two of them spoke together. Some quick remarks that were made about 'decimal' he did not catch.

"How long did you say?" asked Graham. "How long? Don't look like that. Tell me."

Among the remarks in an undertone, his ear caught six words: "More than a couple of centuries."

"*What?*" he cried, turning on the youth who he thought had spoken. "Who says –? What was that? A couple of *centuries*!"

"Yes," said the man with the red beard. "Two hundred years."

Graham repeated the words. He had been prepared to hear of a vast repose, and yet these concrete centuries defeated him.

"Two hundred years," he said again, with the figure of a great gulf opening very slowly in his mind; and then, "Oh, but –!"

They said nothing.

"You – did you say –?"

"Two hundred years. Two centuries of years," said the man with the red beard.

There was a pause. Graham looked at their faces and saw that what he had heard was indeed true.

"But it can't be," he said querulously. "I am dreaming. Trances – trances don't last. That is not right – this is a joke you have played upon me! Tell me – some days ago, perhaps, I was walking along the coast of Cornwall –?"

His voice failed him.

The man with the flaxen beard hesitated. "I'm not very strong in history, sir," he said weakly, and glanced at the others.

"That was it, sir," said the youngster. "Boscastle, in the old Duchy of Cornwall – it's in the south-west country beyond the dairy meadows. There is a house there still. I have been there."

"Boscastle!" Graham turned his eyes to the youngster. "That was it – Boscastle. Little Boscastle. I fell asleep – somewhere there. I don't exactly remember. I don't exactly remember."

He pressed his brows and whispered, "More than *two hundred years*!"

He began to speak quickly with a twitching face, but his heart was cold within him. "But if it *is* two hundred years, every soul I know, every human being that ever I saw or spoke to before I went to sleep, must be dead."

They did not answer him.

"The Queen and the Royal Family, her Ministers, Church and State. High and low, rich and poor, one with another … Is there England still?"

"That's a comfort! Is there London?"

"This *is* London, eh? And you are my assistant-custodian; assistant-custodian. And these –? Eh? Assistant-custodians too!"

He sat with a gaunt stare on his face. "But why am I here? No! Don't talk. Be quiet. Let me –"

He sat silent, rubbed his eyes, and, uncovering them, found another little glass of pinkish fluid held towards him. He took the dose. Directly he had taken it he began to weep naturally and refreshingly.

Presently he looked at their faces, suddenly laughed through his tears, a little foolishly. "But – two – hun – dred – years!" he said. He grimaced hysterically and covered his face again.

After a space he grew calm. He sat up, his hands hanging over his knees in almost precisely the same attitude in which Isbister had found him on the cliff at Pentargen. His attention was attracted by a thick domineering voice, the footsteps of an advancing personage. "What are you doing? Why was I not warned? Surely you could tell? Someone will suffer for this. The man must be kept quiet. Are the doorways closed? All the doorways? He must be kept perfectly quiet. He must not be told. Has he been told anything?"

The man with the fair beard made some inaudible remark, and Graham looking over his shoulder saw approaching a short, fat, and thickset beardless man, with aquiline nose and heavy neck and chin. Very thick black and slightly sloping eyebrows that almost met over his nose and overhung deep grey eyes, gave his face an oddly formidable expression. He scowled momentarily at Graham and then his regard returned to the man with the flaxen beard. "These others," he said in a voice of extreme irritation. "You had better go."

"Go?" said the red-bearded man.

"Certainly – go now. But see the doorways are closed as you go."

The two men addressed turned obediently, after one reluctant glance at Graham, and instead of going through the archway as he expected, walked straight to the dead wall of the apartment opposite the archway. A long strip of this apparently solid wall rolled up with a snap, hung over the two retreating men and fell again, and immediately Graham was alone with the newcomer and the purple-robed man with the flaxen beard.

For a space the thickset man took not the slightest notice of Graham, but proceeded to interrogate the other – obviously his subordinate – upon the treatment of their charge. He spoke clearly, but in phrases only partially intelligible to Graham. The awakening seemed not only a matter of surprise but of consternation and annoyance to him. He was evidently profoundly excited.

"You must not confuse his mind by telling him things," he repeated again and again. "You must not confuse his mind."

His questions answered, he turned quickly and eyed the awakened sleeper with an ambiguous expression.

"Feel queer?" he asked.

"Very."

"The world, what you see of it, seems strange to you?"

"I suppose I have to live in it, strange as it seems."

"I suppose so, now."

"In the first place, hadn't I better have some clothes?"

"They –" said the thickset man and stopped, and the flaxen-bearded man met his eye and went away. "You will very speedily have clothes," said the thickset man.

"Is it true indeed, that I have been asleep two hundred –?" asked Graham.

"They have told you that, have they? Two hundred and three, as a matter of fact."

Graham accepted the indisputable now with raised eyebrows and depressed mouth. He sat silent for a moment, and then asked a question, "Is there a mill or dynamo near here?" He did not wait for an answer. "Things have changed tremendously, I suppose?" he said.

"What is that shouting?" he asked abruptly.

"Nothing," said the thickset man impatiently. "It's people. You'll understand better later – perhaps. As you say, things have changed." He spoke shortly, his brows were knit, and he glanced about him like a man trying to decide in an emergency. "We must get you clothes and so forth, at any rate. Better wait here until they can be procured. No one will come near you. You want shaving."

Graham rubbed his chin.

The man with the flaxen beard came back towards them, turned suddenly, listened for a moment, lifted his eyebrows at the older man, and hurried off through the archway towards the balcony. The tumult of shouting grew louder, and the thickset man turned and listened also. He cursed suddenly under his breath, and turned his eyes upon Graham with an unfriendly expression. It was a surge of many voices, rising and falling, shouting and screaming, and once came a sound like blows and sharp cries, and then a snapping like the crackling of dry sticks. Graham strained his ears to draw some single thread of sound from the woven tumult.

Then he perceived, repeated again and again, a certain formula. For a time he doubted his ears. But surely these were the words: "Show us the Sleeper! Show us the Sleeper!"

The thickset man rushed suddenly to the archway.

"Wild!" he cried. "How do they know? Do they know? Or is it guessing?"

There was perhaps an answer.

"I can't come," said the thickset man; "I have *him* to see to. But shout from the balcony."

There was an inaudible reply.

"Say he is not awake. Anything! I leave it to you."

He came hurrying back to Graham. "You must have clothes at once," he said. "You cannot stop here – and it will be impossible to –"

He rushed away, Graham shouting unanswered questions after him. In a moment he was back.

"I can't tell you what is happening. It is too complex to explain. In a moment you shall have your clothes made. Yes – in a moment. And then I can take you away from here. You will find out our troubles soon enough."

"But those voices. They were shouting –?"

"Something about the Sleeper – that's you. They have some twisted idea. I don't know what it is. I know nothing."

A shrill bell jetted acutely across the indistinct mingling of remote noises, and this brusque person sprang to a little group of appliances in the corner of the room. He listened for a moment, regarding a ball of crystal, nodded, and said a few indistinct words; then he walked to the wall through which the two men had vanished. It rolled up again like a curtain, and he stood waiting.

Graham lifted his arm and was astonished to find what strength the restoratives had given him. He thrust one leg over the side of the couch and then the other. His head no longer swam. He could scarcely credit his rapid recovery. He sat feeling his limbs.

The man with the flaxen beard re-entered from the archway, and as he did so the cage of a lift came sliding down in front of the thickset man, and a lean, grey-bearded man, carrying a roll, and wearing a tightly-fitting costume of dark green, appeared therein.

"This is the tailor," said the thickset man with an introductory gesture. "It will never do for you to wear that black. I cannot understand how it got here. But I shall. I shall. You will be as rapid as possible?" he said to the tailor.

The man in green bowed, and, advancing, seated himself by Graham on the bed. His manner was calm, but his eyes were full of curiosity. "You will find the fashions altered, Sire," he said. He glanced from under his brows at the thickset man.

He opened the roller with a quick movement, and a confusion of brilliant fabrics poured out over his knees. "You lived, Sire, in a period essentially cylindrical – the Victorian. With a tendency to the hemisphere in hats. Circular curves always. Now –" he flicked out a little appliance the size and appearance of a keyless watch, whirled the knob, and behold – a little figure in white appeared kinetoscope fashion on the dial, walking and turning. The tailor caught up a pattern of bluish white satin. "That is my conception of your immediate treatment," he said.

The thickset man came and stood by the shoulder of Graham.

"We have very little time," he said.

"Trust me," said the tailor. "My machine follows. What do you think of this?"

"What is that?" asked the man from the nineteenth century.

"In your days they showed you a fashion-plate," said the tailor, "but this is our modern development. See here." The little figure repeated its evolutions, but in a different costume. "Or this," and with a click another small figure in a more voluminous type of robe marched on to the dial. The tailor was very quick in his movements, and glanced twice towards the lift as he did these things.

It rumbled again, and a crop-haired anemic lad with features of the Chinese type, clad in coarse pale blue canvas, appeared together with a complicated machine, which he pushed noiselessly on little castors into the room. Incontinently the little kinetoscope was dropped, Graham was invited to stand in front of the machine and the tailor muttered some instructions to the crop-haired lad, who answered in guttural tones and with words Graham did not recognise. The boy then went to conduct an incomprehensible monologue in the corner, and the tailor pulled out a number of slotted arms terminating in little discs, pulling them out until the discs were flat against the body of Graham, one at each shoulder blade, one at the elbows, one at the neck and so forth, so that at last there were, perhaps, two score of them upon his body and limbs. At the same time, some other person entered the room by the lift, behind Graham. The tailor set moving a mechanism that initiated a faint-sounding rhythmic movement of parts in the machine, and in another moment he was knocking up the levers and Graham was released. The tailor replaced his cloak of black, and the man with the flaxen beard proffered him a little glass of some refreshing fluid. Graham saw over the rim of the glass a pale-faced young man regarding him with a singular fixity.

The thickset man had been pacing the room fretfully, and now turned and went through the archway towards the balcony, from which the noise of a distant crowd still came in gusts and cadences. The crop-headed lad handed the tailor a roll of the bluish satin and the two began fixing this in the mechanism in a manner reminiscent of a roll of paper in a nineteenth century printing machine. Then they ran the entire thing on its easy, noiseless bearings across the room to a remote corner where a twisted cable looped rather gracefully from the wall. They made some connexion and the machine became energetic and swift.

"What is that doing?" asked Graham, pointing with the empty glass to the busy figures and trying to ignore the scrutiny of the new comer. "Is that – some sort of force – laid on?"

"Yes," said the man with the flaxen beard.

"Who is *that*?" He indicated the archway behind him.

The man in purple stroked his little beard, hesitated, and answered in an undertone, "He is Howard, your chief guardian. You see, Sire – it's a little difficult to explain. The Council appoints a guardian and assistants. This hall has under certain restrictions been public. In order that people might satisfy themselves. We have barred the doorways for the first time. But I think – if you don't mind, I will leave him to explain."

"Odd!" said Graham. "Guardian? Council?" Then turning his back on the new comer, he asked in an undertone, "Why is this man *glaring* at me? Is he a mesmerist?"

"Mesmerist! He is a capillotomist."

"Capillotomist!"

"Yes – one of the chief. His yearly fee is sixdoz lions."

It sounded sheer nonsense. Graham snatched at the last phrase with an unsteady mind. "Sixdoz lions?" he said.

"Didn't you have lions? I suppose not. You had the old pounds? They are our monetary units."

"But what was that you said – sixdoz?"

"Yes. Six dozen, Sire. Of course things, even these little things, have altered. You lived in the days of the decimal system, the Arab system – tens, and little hundreds and thousands. We have eleven numerals now. We have single figures for both ten and eleven, two figures for a dozen, and a dozen dozen makes a gross, a great hundred, you know, a dozen gross a dozand, and a dozand dozand a myriad. Very simple?"

"I suppose so," said Graham. "But about this cap – what was it?"

The man with the flaxen beard glanced over his shoulder.

"Here are your clothes!" he said. Graham turned round sharply and saw the tailor standing at his elbow smiling, and holding some palpably new garments over his arm. The crop-headed boy, by means of one ringer, was impelling the complicated machine towards the lift by which he had arrived. Graham stared at the completed suit. "You don't mean to say –!"

"Just made," said the tailor. He dropped the garments at the feet of Graham, walked to the bed, on which Graham had so recently been lying, flung out the translucent mattress, and turned up the looking-glass. As he did so a furious bell summoned the thickset man to the corner. The man with the flaxen beard rushed across to him and then hurried out by the archway.

The tailor was assisting Graham into a dark purple combination garment, stockings, vest, and pants in one, as the thickset man came back from the corner to meet the man with the flaxen beard returning from the balcony. They began speaking quickly in an undertone, their bearing had an unmistakable quality of anxiety. Over the purple under-garment came a complex garment of bluish white, and Graham, was clothed in the fashion once more and saw himself, sallow-faced, unshaven and shaggy still, but at least naked no longer, and in some indefinable unprecedented way graceful.

"I must shave," he said regarding himself in the glass.

"In a moment," said Howard.

The persistent stare ceased. The young man closed his eyes, reopened them, and with a lean hand extended, advanced on Graham. Then he stopped, with his hand slowly gesticulating, and looked about him.

"A seat," said Howard impatiently, and in a moment the flaxen-bearded man had a chair behind Graham. "Sit down, please," said Howard.

Graham hesitated, and in the other hand of the wild-eyed man he saw the glint of steel.

"Don't you understand, Sire?" cried the flaxen-bearded man with hurried politeness. "He is going to cut your hair."

"Oh!" cried Graham enlightened. "But you called him –"

"A capillotomist – precisely! He is one of the finest artists in the world."

Graham sat down abruptly. The flaxen-bearded man disappeared. The capillotomist came forward, examined Graham's ears and surveyed him, felt the back of his head, and would have sat down again to regard him but for Howard's audible impatience. Forthwith with rapid movements and a succession of deftly handled implements he shaved Graham's chin, clipped his moustache, and cut and arranged his hair. All this he did without a word, with something of the rapt air of a poet inspired. And as soon as he had finished Graham was handed a pair of shoes.

Suddenly a loud voice shouted – it seemed from a piece of machinery in the corner – "At once – at once. The people know all over the city. Work is being stopped. Work is being stopped. Wait for nothing, but come."

This shout appeared to perturb Howard exceedingly. By his gestures it seemed to Graham that he hesitated between two directions. Abruptly he went towards the corner where the apparatus stood about the little crystal ball. As he did so the undertone of tumultuous shouting from the archway that had continued during all these occurrences rose to a mighty sound, roared as if it were sweeping past, and fell again as if receding swiftly. It drew Graham after it with an irresistible attraction. He glanced at the thickset man, and then obeyed his impulse. In two strides he was down the steps and in the passage, and in a score he was out upon the balcony upon which the three men had been standing.

Chapter V
The Moving Ways

HE WENT TO THE railings of the balcony and stared upward. An exclamation of surprise at his appearance, and the movements of a number of people came from the great area below.

His first impression was of overwhelming architecture. The place into which he looked was an aisle of Titanic buildings, curving spaciously in either direction. Overhead mighty cantilevers sprang together across the huge width of the place, and a tracery of translucent material shut out the sky. Gigantic globes of cool white light shamed the pale sunbeams that filtered down through the girders and wires. Here and there a gossamer suspension bridge dotted with foot passengers flung across the chasm and the air was webbed with slender cables. A cliff of edifice hung above him, he perceived as he glanced upward, and the opposite façade was grey and dim and broken by great archings, circular perforations, balconies, buttresses, turret projections, myriads of vast windows, and an intricate scheme of architectural relief. Athwart these ran inscriptions horizontally and obliquely in an unfamiliar lettering. Here and there close to the roof cables of a peculiar stoutness were fastened, and drooped in a steep curve to circular openings on the opposite side of the space, and even as Graham noted these a remote and tiny figure of a man clad in pale blue arrested his attention. This little figure was far overhead across the space beside the higher fastening of one of these festoons, hanging forward from a little ledge of masonry and handling some well-nigh invisible strings dependent from the line. Then suddenly, with a swoop that sent Graham's heart into his mouth, this man had rushed down the curve and vanished through a round opening on the hither side of the way. Graham had been looking up as he came out upon the balcony, and the things he saw above and opposed to him had at first seized his attention to the exclusion of anything else. Then suddenly he discovered the roadway! It was not a roadway at all, as Graham understood such things, for in the nineteenth century the only roads and streets were beaten tracks of motionless earth, jostling rivulets of vehicles between narrow footways. But this roadway was three hundred feet across, and it moved; it moved, all save the middle, the lowest part. For a moment, the motion dazzled his mind. Then he understood. Under the balcony this extraordinary roadway ran swiftly to Graham's right, an endless flow rushing along as fast as a nineteenth century express train, an endless platform of narrow transverse overlapping slats with little interspaces that permitted it to follow the curvatures of the street. Upon it were seats, and here and there little kiosks, but they swept by too swiftly for him to see what might be therein. From this nearest and swiftest platform a series of others descended to the centre of the space. Each moved to the right, each perceptibly slower than the one above it, but the difference in pace was small enough to permit anyone to step from any platform to the one adjacent, and so walk uninterruptedly from the swiftest to the motionless middle way. Beyond this middle way was another series of endless platforms rushing with varying pace to Graham's left. And seated in crowds upon the two widest and swiftest platforms, or stepping from one to another down the steps, or swarming over the central space, was an innumerable and wonderfully diversified multitude of people.

"You must not stop here," shouted Howard suddenly at his side. "You must come away at once."

Graham made no answer. He heard without hearing. The platforms ran with a roar and the people were shouting. He perceived women and girls with flowing hair, beautifully robed, with bands crossing between the breasts. These first came out of the confusion. Then he perceived that the dominant note in that kaleidoscope of costume was the pale blue that the tailor's boy had worn. He became aware of cries of "The Sleeper. What has happened to the Sleeper?" and it seemed as though the rushing platforms before him were suddenly spattered with the pale buff of human faces, and then still more thickly. He saw pointing fingers. He perceived that the motionless central area of this huge arcade just opposite to the balcony was densely crowded with blue-clad people. Some sort of struggle had sprung into life. People seemed to be pushed up the running platforms on either side, and carried away against their will. They would spring off so soon as they were beyond the thick of the confusion, and run back towards the conflict.

"It is the Sleeper. Verily it is the Sleeper," shouted voices. "That is never the Sleeper," shouted others. More and more faces were turned to him. At the intervals along this central area Graham noted openings, pits, apparently the heads of staircases going down with people ascending out of them and descending into them. The struggle it seemed centred about the one of these nearest to him. People were running down the moving platforms to this, leaping dexterously from platform to platform. The clustering people on the higher platforms seemed to divide their interest between this point and the balcony. A number of sturdy little figures clad in a uniform of bright red, and working methodically together, were employed it seemed in preventing access to this descending staircase. About them a crowd was rapidly accumulating. Their brilliant colour contrasted vividly with the whitish-blue of their antagonists, for the struggle was indisputable.

He saw these things with Howard shouting in his ear and shaking his arm. And then suddenly Howard was gone and he stood alone.

He perceived that the cries of "The Sleeper!" grew in volume, and that the people on the nearer platform were standing up. The nearer platform he perceived was empty to the right of him, and far across the space the platform running in the opposite direction was coming crowded and passing away bare. With incredible swiftness a vast crowd had gathered in the central space before his eyes; a dense swaying mass of people, and the shouts grew from a fitful crying to a voluminous incessant clamour: "The Sleeper! The Sleeper!" and yells and cheers, a waving of garments and cries of "Stop the Ways!" They were also crying another name strange to Graham. It sounded like "Ostrog." The slower platforms were soon thick with active people, running against the movement so as to keep themselves opposite to him.

"Stop the Ways," they cried. Agile figures ran up from the centre to the swift road nearest to him, were borne rapidly past him, shouting strange, unintelligible things, and ran back obliquely to the central way. One thing he distinguished: "It is indeed the Sleeper. It is indeed the Sleeper," they testified.

For a space Graham stood motionless. Then he became vividly aware that all this concerned him. He was pleased at his wonderful popularity, he bowed, and, seeking a gesture of longer range, waved his arm. He was astonished at the violence of uproar that this provoked. The tumult about the descending stairway rose to furious violence. He became aware of crowded balconies, of men sliding along ropes, of men in trapeze-like seats hurling athwart the space. He heard voices behind him, a number of people descending the steps through the archway; he suddenly perceived that his guardian Howard was back again and gripping his arm painfully, and shouting inaudibly in his ear.

He turned, and Howard's face was white. "Come back," he heard. "They will stop the ways. The whole city will be in confusion."

He perceived a number of men hurrying along the passage of blue pillars behind Howard, the red-haired man, the man with the flaxen beard, a tall man in vivid vermilion, a crowd of others in red carrying staves, and all these people had anxious eager faces.

"Get him away," cried Howard.

"But why?" said Graham. "I don't see –"

"You must come away!" said the man in red in a resolute voice. His face and eyes were resolute, too. Graham's glances went from face to face, and he was suddenly aware of that most disagreeable flavour in life, compulsion. Someone gripped his arm....

He was being dragged away. It seemed as though the tumult suddenly became two, as if half the shouts that had come in from this wonderful roadway had sprung into the passages of the great building behind him. Marvelling and confused, feeling an impotent desire to resist, Graham was half led, half thrust, along the passage of blue pillars, and suddenly he found himself alone with Howard in a lift and moving swiftly upward.

Chapter VI
The Hall of the Atlas

FROM THE MOMENT when the tailor had bowed his farewell to the moment when Graham found himself in the lift, was altogether barely five minutes. As yet the haze of his vast interval of sleep hung about him, as yet the initial strangeness of his being alive at all in this remote age touched everything with wonder, with a sense of the irrational, with something of the quality of a realistic dream. He was still detached, an astonished spectator, still but half involved in life. What he had seen, and especially the last crowded tumult, framed in the setting of the balcony, had a spectacular turn, like a thing witnessed from the box of a theatre. "I don't understand," he said. "What was the trouble? My mind is in a whirl. Why were they shouting? What is the danger?"

"We have our troubles," said Howard. His eyes avoided Graham's enquiry. "This is a time of unrest. And, in fact, your appearance, your waking just now, has a sort of connexion –"

He spoke jerkily, like a man not quite sure of his breathing. He stopped abruptly.

"I don't understand," said Graham.

"It will be clearer later," said Howard.

He glanced uneasily upward, as though he found the progress of the lift slow.

"I shall understand better, no doubt, when I have seen my way about a little," said Graham puzzled. "It will be – it is bound to be perplexing. At present it is all so strange. Anything seems possible. Anything. In the details even. Your counting, I understand, is different."

The lift stopped, and they stepped out into a narrow but very long passage between high walls, along which ran an extraordinary number of tubes and big cables.

"What a huge place this is!" said Graham. "Is it all one building? What place is it?"

"This is one of the city ways for various public services. Light and so forth."

"Was it a social trouble – that – in the great roadway place? How are you governed? Have you still a police?"

"Several," said Howard.

"Several?"

"About fourteen."

"I don't understand."

"Very probably not. Our social order will probably seem very complex to you. To tell you the truth, I don't understand it myself very clearly. Nobody does. You will, perhaps – bye and bye. We have to go to the Council."

Graham's attention was divided between the urgent necessity of his inquiries and the people in the passages and halls they were traversing. For a moment his mind would be concentrated upon Howard and the halting answers he made, and then he would lose the thread in response to some vivid unexpected impression. Along the passages, in the halls, half the people seemed to be men in the red uniform. The pale blue canvas that had been so abundant in the aisle of moving ways did not appear. Invariably these men looked at him, and saluted him and Howard as they passed.

He had a clear vision of entering a long corridor, and there were a number of girls sitting on low seats, as though in a class. He saw no teacher, but only a novel apparatus from which he fancied a voice proceeded. The girls regarded him and his conductor, he thought, with curiosity and astonishment. But he was hurried on before he could form a clear idea of the gathering. He judged they knew Howard and not himself, and that they wondered who he was. This Howard, it seemed, was a person of importance. But then he was also merely Graham's guardian. That was odd.

There came a passage in twilight, and into this passage a footway hung so that he could see the feet and ankles of people going to and fro thereon, but no more of them. Then vague impressions of galleries and of casual astonished passers-by turning round to stare after the two of them with their red-clad guard.

The stimulus of the restoratives he had taken was only temporary. He was speedily fatigued by this excessive haste. He asked Howard to slacken his speed. Presently he was in a lift that had a window upon the great street space, but this was glazed and did not open, and they were too high for him to see the moving platforms below. But he saw people going to and fro along cables and along strange, frail-looking bridges.

Thence they passed across the street and at a vast height above it. They crossed by means of a narrow bridge closed in with glass, so clear that it made him giddy even to remember it. The floor of it also was of glass. From his memory of the cliffs between New Quay and Boscastle, so remote in time, and so recent in his experience, it seemed to him that they must be near four hundred feet above the moving ways. He stopped, looked down between his legs upon the swarming blue and red multitudes, minute and foreshortened, struggling and gesticulating still towards the little balcony far below, a little toy balcony, it seemed, where he had so recently been standing. A thin haze and the glare of the mighty globes of light obscured everything. A man seated in a little openwork cradle shot by from some point still higher than the little narrow bridge, rushing down a cable as swiftly almost as if he were falling. Graham stopped involuntarily to watch this strange passenger vanish below, and then his eyes went back to the tumultuous struggle.

Along one of the faster ways rushed a thick crowd of red spots. This broke up into individuals as it approached the balcony, and went pouring down the slower ways towards the dense struggling crowd on the central area. These men in red appeared to be armed with sticks or truncheons; they seemed to be striking and thrusting. A great shouting, cries of wrath, screaming, burst out and came up to Graham, faint and thin. "Go on," cried Howard, laying hands on him.

Another man rushed down a cable. Graham suddenly glanced up to see whence he came, and beheld through the glassy roof and the network of cables and girders, dim rhythmically passing forms like the vanes of windmills, and between them glimpses of a remote and pallid sky. Then Howard had thrust him forward across the bridge, and he was in a little narrow passage decorated with geometrical patterns.

"I want to see more of that," cried Graham, resisting.

"No, no," cried Howard, still gripping his arm. "This way. You must go this way." And the men in red following them seemed ready to enforce his orders.

Some negroes in a curious wasp-like uniform of black and yellow appeared down the passage, and one hastened to throw up a sliding shutter that had seemed a door to Graham, and led the way through it. Graham found himself in a gallery overhanging the end of a great chamber. The attendant in black and yellow crossed this, thrust up a second shutter and stood waiting.

This place had the appearance of an ante-room. He saw a number of people in the central space, and at the opposite end a large and imposing doorway at the top of a flight of steps, heavily curtained but giving a glimpse of some still larger hall beyond. He perceived white men in red and other negroes in black and yellow standing stiffly about those portals.

As they crossed the gallery he heard a whisper from below, "The Sleeper," and was aware of a turning of heads, a hum of observation. They entered another little passage in the wall of this ante-chamber, and then he found himself on an iron-railed gallery of metal that passed round the side of the great hall he had already seen through the curtains. He entered the place at the corner, so that he received the fullest impression of its huge proportions. The black in the wasp uniform stood aside like a well-trained servant, and closed the valve behind him.

Compared with any of the places Graham had seen thus far, this second hall appeared to be decorated with extreme richness. On a pedestal at the remoter end, and more brilliantly lit than any other object, was a gigantic white figure of Atlas, strong and strenuous, the globe upon his bowed shoulders. It was the first thing to strike his attention, it was so vast, so patiently and painfully real, so white and simple. Save for this figure and for a dais in the centre, the wide floor of the place was a shining vacancy. The dais was remote in the greatness of the area; it would have looked a mere slab of metal had it not been for the group of seven men who stood about a table on it, and gave an inkling of its proportions. They were all dressed in white robes, they seemed to have arisen that moment from their seats, and they were regarding Graham steadfastly. At the end of the table he perceived the glitter of some mechanical appliances.

Howard led him along the end gallery until they were opposite this mighty labouring figure. Then he stopped. The two men in red who had followed them into the gallery came and stood on either hand of Graham.

"You must remain here," murmured Howard, "for a few moments," and, without waiting for a reply, hurried away along the gallery.

"But, *why* –?" began Graham.

He moved as if to follow Howard, and found his path obstructed by one of the men in red. "You have to wait here, Sire," said the man in red.

"*Why?*"

"Orders, Sire."

"Whose orders?"

"Our orders, Sire."

Graham looked his exasperation.

"What place is this?" he said presently. "Who are those men?"

"They are the lords of the Council, Sire."

"What Council?"

"*The* Council."

"Oh!" said Graham, and after an equally ineffectual attempt at the other man, went to the railing and stared at the distant men in white, who stood watching him and whispering together.

The Council? He perceived there were now eight, though how the newcomer had arrived he had not observed. They made no gestures of greeting; they stood regarding him as in the nineteenth century a group of men might have stood in the street regarding a distant balloon that had suddenly floated into view. What council could it be that gathered there, that little body of men beneath the significant white Atlas, secluded from every eavesdropper in this impressive spaciousness? And why should he be brought to them, and be looked at strangely and spoken of inaudibly? Howard appeared beneath, walking quickly across the polished floor towards them. As he drew near he bowed and performed certain peculiar movements, apparently of a ceremonious nature. Then he ascended the steps of the dais, and stood by the apparatus at the end of the table.

Graham watched that visible inaudible conversation. Occasionally, one of the white-robed men would glance towards him. He strained his ears in vain. The gesticulation of two of the speakers became animated. He glanced from them to the passive faces of his attendants....When he looked again Howard was extending his hands and moving his head like a man who protests. He was interrupted, it seemed, by one of the white-robed men rapping the table.

The conversation lasted an interminable time to Graham's sense. His eyes rose to the still giant at whose feet the Council sat. Thence they wandered to the walls of the hall. It was decorated in long painted panels of a quasi-Japanese type, many of them very beautiful. These panels were grouped in a great and elaborate framing of dark metal, which passed into the metallic caryatidae of the galleries, and the great structural lines of the interior. The facile grace of these panels enhanced the mighty white effort that laboured in the centre of the scheme. Graham's eyes came back to the Council, and Howard was descending the steps. As he drew nearer his features could be distinguished, and Graham saw that he was flushed and blowing out his cheeks. His countenance was still disturbed when presently he reappeared along the gallery.

"This way," he said concisely, and they went on in silence to a little door that opened at their approach. The two men in red stopped on either side of this door. Howard and Graham passed in, and Graham, glancing back, saw the white-robed Council still standing in a close group and looking at him. Then the door closed behind him with a heavy thud, and for the first time since his awakening he was in silence. The floor, even, was noiseless to his feet.

Howard opened another door, and they were in the first of two contiguous chambers furnished in white and green. "What Council was that?" began Graham. "What were they discussing? What have they to do with me?" Howard closed the door carefully, heaved a huge sigh, and said something in an undertone. He walked slantingways across the room and turned, blowing out his cheeks again. "Ugh!" he grunted, a man relieved.

Graham stood regarding him.

"You must understand," began Howard abruptly, avoiding Graham's eyes, "that our social order is very complex. A half explanation, a bare unqualified statement would give you false impressions. As a matter of fact – it is a case of compound interest partly – your small fortune, and the fortune of your cousin Warming which was left to you – and certain other beginnings – have become very considerable. And in other ways that will be hard for you to understand, you have become a person of significance – of very considerable significance – involved in the world's affairs."

He stopped.

"Yes?" said Graham.

"We have grave social troubles."

"Yes?"

"Things have come to such a pass that, in fact, it is advisable to seclude you here."

"Keep me prisoner!" exclaimed Graham.

"Well – to ask you to keep in seclusion."

Graham turned on him. "This is strange!" he said.

"No harm will be done you."

"No harm!"

"But you must be kept here –"

"While I learn my position, I presume."

"Precisely."

"Very well then. Begin. Why *harm*?"

"Not now."

"Why not?"

"It is too long a story, Sire."

"All the more reason I should begin at once. You say I am a person of importance. What was that shouting I heard? Why is a great multitude shouting and excited because my trance is over, and who are the men in white in that huge council chamber?"

"All in good time, Sire," said Howard. "But not crudely, not crudely. This is one of those flimsy times when no man has a settled mind. Your awakening – no one expected your awakening. The Council is consulting."

"What council?"

"The Council you saw."

Graham made a petulant movement. "This is not right," he said. "I should be told what is happening."

"You must wait. Really you must wait."

Graham sat down abruptly. "I suppose since I have waited so long to resume life," he said, "that I must wait a little longer."

"That is better," said Howard. "Yes, that is much better. And I must leave you alone. For a space. While I attend the discussion in the Council…. I am sorry."

He went towards the noiseless door, hesitated and vanished.

Graham walked to the door, tried it, found it securely fastened in some way he never came to understand, turned about, paced the room restlessly, made the circuit of the room, and sat down. He remained sitting for some time with folded arms and knitted brow, biting his finger nails and trying to piece together the kaleidoscopic impressions of this first hour of awakened life; the vast mechanical spaces, the endless series of chambers and passages, the great struggle that roared and splashed through these strange ways, the little group of remote unsympathetic men beneath the colossal Atlas, Howard's mysterious behaviour. There was an inkling of some vast inheritance already in his mind – a vast inheritance perhaps misapplied – of some unprecedented importance and opportunity. What had he to do? And this room's secluded silence was eloquent of imprisonment!

It came into Graham's mind with irresistible conviction that this series of magnificent impressions was a dream. He tried to shut his eyes and succeeded, but that time-honoured device led to no awakening.

Presently he began to touch and examine all the unfamiliar appointments of the two small rooms in which he found himself.

In a long oval panel of mirror he saw himself and stopped astonished. He was clad in a graceful costume of purple and bluish white, with a little greyshot beard trimmed to a point, and his hair, its blackness streaked now with bands of grey, arranged over his forehead in an unfamiliar but pleasing manner. He seemed a man of five-and-forty perhaps. For a moment he did not perceive this was himself.

A flash of laughter came with the recognition. "To call on old Warming like this!" he exclaimed, "and make him take me out to lunch!"

Then he thought of meeting first one and then another of the few familiar acquaintances of his early manhood, and in the midst of his amusement realised that every soul with whom he might jest had died many score of years ago. The thought smote him abruptly and keenly; he stopped short, the expression of his face changed to a white consternation.

The tumultuous memory of the moving platforms and the huge façade of that wonderful street reasserted itself. The shouting multitudes came back clear and vivid, and those remote, inaudible, unfriendly councillors in white. He felt himself a little figure, very small and ineffectual, pitifully conspicuous. And all about him, the world was – *strange*.

Chapter VII
In the Silent Rooms

PRESENTLY GRAHAM RESUMED his examination of his apartments. Curiosity kept him moving in spite of his fatigue. The inner room, he perceived, was high, and its ceiling dome shaped, with an oblong aperture in the centre, opening into a funnel in which a wheel of broad vanes seemed to be rotating, apparently driving the air up the shaft. The faint humming note of its easy motion was the only clear sound in that quiet place. As these vanes sprang up one after the other, Graham could get transient glimpses of the sky. He was surprised to see a star.

This drew his attention to the fact that the bright lighting of these rooms was due to a multitude of very faint glow lamps set about the cornices. There were no windows. And he began to recall that along all the vast chambers and passages he had traversed with Howard he had observed no windows at all. Had there been windows? There were windows on the street indeed, but were they for light? Or was the whole city lit day and night for evermore, so that there was no night there?

And another thing dawned upon him. There was no fireplace in either room. Was the season summer, and were these merely summer apartments, or was the whole city uniformly heated or cooled? He became interested in these questions, began examining the smooth texture of the walls, the simply constructed bed, the ingenious arrangements by which the labour of bedroom service was practically abolished. And over everything was a curious absence of deliberate ornament, a bare grace of form and colour, that he found very pleasing to the eye. There were several very comfortable chairs, a light table on silent runners carrying several bottles of fluids and glasses, and two plates bearing a clear substance like jelly. Then he noticed there were no books, no newspapers, no writing materials. "The world has changed indeed," he said.

He observed one entire side of the outer room was set with rows of peculiar double cylinders inscribed with green lettering on white that harmonized with the decorative scheme of the room, and in the centre of this side projected a little apparatus about a yard square and having a white smooth face to the room. A chair faced this. He had a transitory idea that these cylinders might be books, or a modern substitute for books, but at first it did not seem so.

The lettering on the cylinders puzzled him. At first sight it seemed like Russian. Then he noticed a suggestion of mutilated English about certain of the words.

'Thi Man huwdbi Kin' forced itself on him as 'The Man who would be King.'

"Phonetic spelling," he said. He remembered reading a story with that title, then he recalled the story vividly, one of the best stories in the world. But this thing before him was not a book as he understood it. He puzzled out the titles of two adjacent cylinders. 'The Heart of Darkness' he had never heard of before nor 'The Madonna of the Future' – no doubt if they were indeed stories, they were by post-Victorian authors.

He puzzled over this peculiar cylinder for some time and replaced it. Then he turned to the square apparatus and examined that. He opened a sort of lid and found one of the double cylinders within, and on the upper edge a little stud like the stud of an electric bell. He pressed this and a rapid clicking began and ceased. He became aware of voices and music, and noticed a play of colour on the smooth front face. He suddenly realised what this might be, and stepped back to regard it.

On the flat surface was now a little picture, very vividly coloured, and in this picture were figures that moved. Not only did they move, but they were conversing in clear small voices. It was exactly like reality viewed through an inverted opera glass and heard through a long tube. His interest was seized at once by the situation, which presented a man pacing up and down and vociferating angry things to a pretty but petulant woman. Both were in the picturesque costume that seemed so strange to Graham. "I have worked," said the man, "but what have you been doing?"

"Ah!" said Graham. He forgot everything else, and sat down in the chair. Within five minutes he heard himself, named, heard "when the Sleeper wakes," used jestingly as a proverb for remote postponement, and passed himself by, a thing remote and incredible. But in a little while he knew those two people like intimate friends.

At last the miniature drama came to an end, and the square face of the apparatus was blank again.

It was a strange world into which he had been permitted to see, unscrupulous, pleasure seeking, energetic, subtle, a world too of dire economic struggle; there were allusions he did not understand, incidents that conveyed strange suggestions of altered moral ideals, flashes of dubious enlightenment. The blue canvas that bulked so largely in his first impression of the city ways appeared again and again as the costume of the common people. He had no doubt the story was contemporary, and its intense realism was undeniable. And the end had been a tragedy that oppressed him. He sat staring at the blankness.

He started and rubbed his eyes. He had been so absorbed in the latter-day substitute for a novel, that he awoke to the little green and white room with more than a touch of the surprise of his first awakening.

He stood up, and abruptly he was back in his own wonderland. The clearness of the kinetoscope drama passed, and the struggle in the vast place of streets, the ambiguous Council, the swift phases of his waking hour, came back. These people had spoken of the Council with suggestions of a vague universality of power. And they had spoken of the Sleeper; it had not really struck him vividly at the time that he was the Sleeper. He had to recall precisely what they had said....

He walked into the bedroom and peered up through the quick intervals of the revolving fan. As the fan swept round, a dim turmoil like the noise of machinery came in rhythmic eddies. All else was silence. Though the perpetual day still irradiated his apartments, he perceived the little intermittent strip of sky was now deep blue – black almost, with a dust of little stars....

He resumed his examination of the rooms. He could find no way of opening the padded door, no bell nor other means of calling for attendance. His feeling of wonder was in abeyance; but he was curious, anxious for information. He wanted to know exactly how he stood to these new things. He tried to compose himself to wait until someone came to him. Presently he became restless and eager for information, for distraction, for fresh sensations.

He went back to the apparatus in the other room, and had soon puzzled out the method of replacing the cylinders by others. As he did so, it came into his mind that it must be these little appliances had fixed the language so that it was still clear and understandable after two hundred years. The haphazard cylinders he substituted displayed a musical fantasia. At first it was beautiful, and then it was sensuous. He presently recognised what appeared to him to be an altered version of the story of Tannhauser. The music was unfamiliar. But the rendering was realistic, and with a contemporary unfamiliarity. Tannhauser did not go to a Venusberg, but to a Pleasure City. What was a Pleasure City? A dream, surely, the fancy of a fantastic, voluptuous writer.

He became interested, curious. The story developed with a flavour of strangely twisted sentimentality. Suddenly he did not like it. He liked it less as it proceeded.

He had a revulsion of feeling. These were no pictures, no idealisations, but photographed realities. He wanted no more of the twenty-second century Venusberg. He forgot the part played by the model in nineteenth century art, and gave way to an archaic indignation. He rose, angry and half ashamed at himself for witnessing this thing even in solitude. He pulled forward the apparatus, and with some violence sought for a means of stopping its action. Something snapped. A violet spark stung and convulsed his arm and the thing was still. When he attempted next day to replace these Tannhauser cylinders by another pair, he found the apparatus broken....

He struck out a path oblique to the room and paced to and fro, struggling with intolerable vast impressions. The things he had derived from the cylinders and the things he had seen, conflicted, confused him. It seemed to him the most amazing thing of all that in his thirty years of life he had never tried to shape a picture of these coming times. "We were making the future," he said, "and hardly any of us troubled to think what future we were making. And here it is!"

"What have they got to, what has been done? How do I come into the midst of it all?" The vastness of street and house he was prepared for, the multitudes of people. But conflicts in the city ways! And the systematised sensuality of a class of rich men!

He thought of Bellamy, the hero of whose Socialistic Utopia had so oddly anticipated this actual experience. But here was no Utopia, no Socialistic state. He had already seen enough to realise that the ancient antithesis of luxury, waste and sensuality on the one hand and abject poverty on the other, still prevailed. He knew enough of the essential factors of life to understand that correlation. And not only were the buildings of the city gigantic and the crowds in the street gigantic, but the voices he had heard in the ways, the uneasiness of Howard, the very atmosphere spoke of gigantic discontent. What country was he in? Still England it seemed, and yet strangely 'un-English.' His mind glanced at the rest of the world, and saw only an enigmatical veil.

He prowled about his apartment, examining everything as a caged animal might do. He was very tired, with that feverish exhaustion that does not admit of rest. He listened for long spaces under the ventilator to catch some distant echo of the tumults he felt must be proceeding in the city.

He began to talk to himself. "Two hundred and three years!" he said to himself over and over again, laughing stupidly. "Then I am two hundred and thirty-three years old! The oldest inhabitant. Surely they haven't reversed the tendency of our time and gone back to the rule of the oldest. My claims are indisputable. Mumble, mumble. I remember the Bulgarian atrocities as though it was yesterday. 'Tis a great age! Ha ha!" He was surprised at first to hear himself laughing, and then laughed again deliberately and louder. Then he realised that he was behaving foolishly. "Steady," he said. "Steady!"

His pacing became more regular. "This new world," he said. "I don't understand it. *Why?*...But it is all *why*!"

"I suppose they can fly and do all sorts of things. Let me try and remember just how it began."

He was surprised at first to find how vague the memories of his first thirty years had become. He remembered fragments, for the most part trivial moments, things of no great importance that he had observed. His boyhood seemed the most accessible at first, he recalled school books and certain lessons in mensuration. Then he revived the more salient features of his life, memories of the wife long since dead, her magic influence now gone beyond corruption, of his rivals and friends and betrayers, of the decision of this issue and that, and then of his last years of misery, of fluctuating resolves, and at last of his strenuous studies. In a little while he perceived he had it all again; dim perhaps, like metal long laid aside, but in no way defective or injured, capable of re-polishing. And the hue of it was a deepening misery. Was it worth re-polishing? By a miracle he had been lifted out of a life that had become intolerable....

He reverted to his present condition. He wrestled with the facts in vain. It became an inextricable tangle. He saw the sky through the ventilator pink with dawn. An old persuasion came out of the dark recesses of his memory. "I must sleep," he said. It appeared as a delightful relief from this mental distress and from the growing pain and heaviness of his limbs. He went to the strange little bed, lay down and was presently asleep....

He was destined to become very familiar indeed with these apartments before he left them, for he remained imprisoned for three days. During that time no one, except Howard, entered the rooms. The marvel of his fate mingled with and in some way minimised the marvel of his survival. He had awakened to mankind it seemed only to be snatched away into this unaccountable solitude. Howard came regularly with subtly sustaining and nutritive fluids, and light and pleasant foods, quite strange to Graham. He always closed the door carefully as he entered. On matters of detail he was increasingly obliging, but the bearing of Graham on the great issues that were evidently being contested so closely beyond the sound-proof walls that enclosed him, he would not elucidate. He evaded, as politely as possible, every question on the position of affairs in the outer world.

And in those three days Graham's incessant thoughts went far and wide. All that he had seen, all this elaborate contrivance to prevent him seeing, worked together in his mind. Almost every possible interpretation of his position he debated – even as it chanced, the right interpretation. Things that presently happened to him, came to him at last credible, by virtue of this seclusion. When at length the moment of his release arrived, it found him prepared....

Howard's bearing went far to deepen Graham's impression of his own strange importance; the door between its opening and closing seemed to admit with him a breath of momentous happening. His enquiries became more definite and searching. Howard retreated through protests and difficulties. The awakening was unforeseen, he repeated; it happened to have fallen in with the trend of a social convulsion. "To explain it I must tell you the history of a gross and a half of years," protested Howard.

"The thing is this," said Graham. "You are afraid of something I shall do. In some way I am arbitrator – I might be arbitrator."

"It is not that. But you have – I may tell you this much – the automatic increase of your property puts great possibilities of interference in your hands. And in certain other ways you have influence, with your eighteenth century notions."

"Nineteenth century," corrected Graham.

"With your old world notions, anyhow, ignorant as you are of every feature of our State."

"Am I a fool?"

"Certainly not."

"Do I seem to be the sort of man who would act rashly?"

"You were never expected to act at all. No one counted on your awakening. No one dreamt you would ever awake. The Council had surrounded you with antiseptic conditions. As a matter of fact, we thought that you were dead – a mere arrest of decay. And – but it is too complex. We dare not suddenly – -while you are still half awake."

"It won't do," said Graham. "Suppose it is as you say – why am I not being crammed night and day with facts and warnings and all the wisdom of the time to fit me for my responsibilities? Am I any wiser now than two days ago, if it is two days, when I awoke?"

Howard pulled his lip.

"I am beginning to feel – every hour I feel more clearly – a system of concealment of which you are the face. Is this Council, or committee, or whatever they are, cooking the accounts of my estate? Is that it?"

"That note of suspicion –" said Howard.

"Ugh!" said Graham. "Now, mark my words, it will be ill for those who have put me here. It will be ill. I am alive. Make no doubt of it, I am alive. Every day my pulse is stronger and my mind clearer and more vigorous. No more quiescence. I am a man come back to life. And I want to *live* –"

"*Live*!"

Howard's face lit with an idea. He came towards Graham and spoke in an easy confidential tone.

"The Council secludes you here for your good. You are restless. Naturally – an energetic man! You find it dull here. But we are anxious that everything you may desire – every desire – every sort of desire…There may be something. Is there any sort of company?"

He paused meaningly.

"Yes," said Graham thoughtfully. "There is."

"Ah! *Now*! We have treated you neglectfully."

"The crowds in yonder streets of yours."

"That," said Howard, "I am afraid – But –"

Graham began pacing the room. Howard stood near the door watching him. The implication of Howard's suggestion was only half evident to Graham. Company? Suppose he were to accept the proposal, demand some sort of *company*? Would there be any possibilities of gathering from the conversation of this additional person some vague inkling of the struggle that had broken out so vividly at his waking moment? He meditated again, and the suggestion took colour. He turned on Howard abruptly.

"What do you mean by company?"

Howard raised his eyes and shrugged his shoulders. "Human beings," he said, with a curious smile on his heavy face. "Our social ideas," he said, "have a certain increased liberality, perhaps, in comparison with your times. If a man wishes to relieve such a tedium as this – by feminine society, for instance. We think it no scandal. We have cleared our minds of formulae. There is in our city a class, a necessary class, no longer despised – discreet –"

Graham stopped dead.

"It would pass the time," said Howard. "It is a thing I should perhaps have thought of before, but, as a matter of fact, so much is happening –"

He indicated the exterior world.

Graham hesitated. For a moment the figure of a possible woman dominated his mind with an intense attraction. Then he flashed into anger.

"*No!*" he shouted.

He began striding rapidly up and down the room. "Everything you say, everything you do, convinces me – of some great issue in which I am concerned. I do not want to pass the time, as you call it. Yes, I know. Desire and indulgence are life in a sense – and Death! Extinction! In my life before I slept I had worked out that pitiful question. I will not begin again. There is a city, a multitude – . And meanwhile I am here like a rabbit in a bag."

His rage surged high. He choked for a moment and began to wave his clenched fists. He gave way to an anger fit, he swore archaic curses. His gestures had the quality of physical threats.

"I do not know who your party may be. I am in the dark, and you keep me in the dark. But I know this, that I am secluded here for no good purpose. For no good purpose. I warn you, I warn you of the consequences. Once I come at my power –"

He realised that to threaten thus might be a danger to himself. He stopped. Howard stood regarding him with a curious expression.

"I take it this is a message to the Council," said Howard.

Graham had a momentary impulse to leap upon the man, fell or stun him. It must have shown upon his face; at any rate Howard's movement was quick. In a second the noiseless door had closed again, and the man from the nineteenth century was alone.

For a moment he stood rigid, with clenched hands half raised. Then he flung them down. "What a fool I have been!" he said, and gave way to his anger again, stamping about the room and shouting curses.... For a long time he kept himself in a sort of frenzy, raging at his position, at his own folly, at the knaves who had imprisoned him. He did this because he did not want to look calmly at his position. He clung to his anger – because he was afraid of fear.

Presently he found himself reasoning with himself. This imprisonment was unaccountable, but no doubt the legal forms – new legal forms – of the time permitted it. It must, of course, be legal. These people were two hundred years further on in the march of civilisation than the Victorian generation. It was not likely they would be less – humane. Yet they had cleared their minds of formulae! Was humanity a formula as well as chastity?

His imagination set to work to suggest things that might be done to him. The attempts of his reason to dispose of these suggestions, though for the most part logically valid, were quite unavailing. "Why should anything be done to me?"

"If the worst comes to the worst," he found himself saying at last, "I can give up what they want. But what do they want? And why don't they ask me for it instead of cooping me up?"

He returned to his former preoccupation with the Council's possible intentions. He began to reconsider the details of Howard's behaviour, sinister glances, inexplicable hesitations. Then, for a time, his mind circled about the idea of escaping from these rooms; but whither could he escape into this vast, crowded world? He would be worse off than a Saxon yeoman suddenly dropped into nineteenth century London. And besides, how could anyone escape from these rooms?

"How can it benefit anyone if harm should happen to me?"

He thought of the tumult, the great social trouble of which he was so unaccountably the axis. A text, irrelevant enough, and yet curiously insistent, came floating up out of the darkness of his memory. This also a Council had said:

"It is expedient for us that one man should die for the people."

Chapter VIII
The Roof Spaces

AS THE FANS in the circular aperture of the inner room rotated and permitted glimpses of the night, dim sounds drifted in thereby. And Graham, standing underneath, was startled by the sound of a voice.

He peered up and saw in the intervals of the rotation, dark and dim, the face and shoulders of a man regarding him. Then a dark hand was extended, the swift vane struck it, swung round and beat on with a little brownish patch on the edge of its thin blade, and something began to fall therefrom upon the floor, dripping silently.

Graham looked down, and there were spots of blood at his feet. He looked up again in a strange excitement. The figure had gone.

He remained motionless – his every sense intent upon the flickering patch of darkness. He became aware of some faint, remote, dark specks floating lightly through the outer air. They came down towards him, fitfully, eddyingly, and passed aside out of the uprush from the fan. A gleam of light flickered, the specks flashed white, and then the darkness came again. Warmed and lit as he was, he perceived that it was snowing within a few feet of him.

Graham walked across the room and came back to the ventilator again. He saw the head of a man pass near. There was a sound of whispering. Then a smart blow on some metallic substance, effort, voices, and the vanes stopped. A gust of snowflakes whirled into the room, and vanished before they touched the floor. "Don't be afraid," said a voice.

Graham stood under the vane. "Who are you?" he whispered.

For a moment there was nothing but a swaying of the fan, and then the head of a man was thrust cautiously into the opening. His face appeared nearly inverted to Graham; his dark hair was wet with dissolving flakes of snow upon it. His arm went up into the darkness holding something unseen. He had a youthful face and bright eyes, and the veins of his forehead were swollen. He seemed to be exerting himself to maintain his position.

For several seconds neither he nor Graham spoke.

"You were the Sleeper?" said the stranger at last.

"Yes," said Graham. "What do you want with me?"

"I come from Ostrog, Sire."

"Ostrog?"

The man in the ventilator twisted his head round so that his profile was towards Graham. He appeared to be listening. Suddenly there was a hasty exclamation, and the intruder sprang back just in time to escape the sweep of the released fan. And when Graham peered up there was nothing visible but the slowly falling snow.

It was perhaps a quarter of an hour before anything returned to the ventilator. But at last came the same metallic interference again; the fans stopped and the face reappeared. Graham had remained all this time in the same place, alert and tremulously excited.

"Who are you? What do you want?" he said.

"We want to speak to you, Sire," said the intruder. "We want – I can't hold the thing. We have been trying to find a way to you – these three days."

"Is it rescue?" whispered Graham. "Escape?"

"Yes, Sire. If you will."

"You are my party – the party of the Sleeper?"

"Yes, Sire."

"What am I to do?" said Graham.

There was a struggle. The stranger's arm appeared, and his hand was bleeding. His knees came into view over the edge of the funnel. "Stand away from me," he said, and he dropped rather heavily on his hands and one shoulder at Graham's feet. The released ventilator whirled noisily. The stranger rolled over, sprang up nimbly and stood panting, hand to a bruised shoulder, and with his bright eyes on Graham.

"You are indeed the Sleeper," he said. "I saw you asleep. When it was the law that anyone might see you."

"I am the man who was in the trance," said Graham. "They have imprisoned me here. I have been here since I awoke – at least three days."

The intruder seemed about to speak, heard something, glanced swiftly at the door, and suddenly left Graham and ran towards it, shouting quick incoherent words. A bright wedge of steel flashed in his hand, and he began tap, tap, a quick succession of blows upon the hinges. "Mind!" cried a voice. "Oh!" The voice came from above.

Graham glanced up, saw the soles of two feet, ducked, was struck on the shoulder by one of them, and a heavy weight bore him to the earth. He fell on his knees and forward, and the weight went over his head. He knelt up and saw a second man from above seated before him.

"I did not see you, Sire," panted the man. He rose and assisted Graham to rise. "Are you hurt, Sire?" he panted. A succession of heavy blows on the ventilator began, something fell close to Graham's face, and a shivering edge of white metal danced, fell over, and lay flat upon the floor.

"What is this?" cried Graham, confused and looking at the ventilator. "Who are you? What are you going to do? Remember, I understand nothing."

"Stand back," said the stranger, and drew him from under the ventilator as another fragment of metal fell heavily.

"We want you to come, Sire," panted the newcomer, and Graham glancing at his face again, saw a new cut had changed from white to red on his forehead, and a couple of little trickles of blood starting therefrom. "Your people call for you."

"Come where? My people?"

"To the hall about the markets. Your life is in danger here. We have spies. We learned but just in time. The Council has decided – this very day – either to drug or kill you. And everything is ready. The people are drilled, the Wind-Vane police, the engineers, and half the way-gearers are with us. We have the halls crowded – shouting. The whole city shouts against the Council. We have arms." He wiped the blood with his hand. "Your life here is not worth –"

"But why arms?"

"The people have risen to protect you, Sire. What?"

He turned quickly as the man who had first come down made a hissing with his teeth. Graham saw the latter start back, gesticulate to them to conceal themselves, and move as if to hide behind the opening door.

As he did so Howard appeared, a little tray in one hand and his heavy face downcast. He started, looked up, the door slammed behind him, the tray tilted side-ways, and the steel wedge struck him behind the ear. He went down like a felled tree, and lay as he fell athwart the floor of the outer room. The man who had struck him bent hastily, studied his face for a moment, rose, and returned to his work at the door.

"Your poison!" said a voice in Graham's ear.

Then abruptly they were in darkness. The innumerable cornice lights had been extinguished. Graham saw the aperture of the ventilator with ghostly snow whirling above it and dark figures moving hastily. Three knelt on the vane. Some dim thing – a ladder – was being lowered through the opening, and a hand appeared holding a fitful yellow light.

He had a moment of hesitation. But the manner of these men, their swift alacrity, their words, marched so completely with his own fears of the Council, with his idea and hope of a rescue, that it lasted not a moment. And his people awaited him!

"I do not understand," he said. "I trust. Tell me what to do."

The man with the cut brow gripped Graham's arm. "Clamber up the ladder," he whispered. "Quick. They will have heard –"

Graham felt for the ladder with extended hands, put his foot on the lower rung, and, turning his head, saw over the shoulder of the nearest man, in the yellow flicker of the light, the first-comer astride over Howard and still working at the door. Graham turned to the ladder again, and was thrust by his conductor and helped up by those above, and then he was standing on something hard and cold and slippery outside the ventilating funnel.

He shivered. He was aware of a great difference in the temperature. Half a dozen men stood about him, and light flakes of snow touched hands and face and melted. For a moment it was dark, then for a flash a ghastly violet white, and then everything was dark again.

He saw he had come out upon the roof of the vast city structure which had replaced the miscellaneous houses, streets and open spaces of Victorian London. The place upon which he stood was level, with huge serpentine cables lying athwart it in every direction. The circular wheels of a number of windmills loomed indistinct and gigantic through the darkness and snowfall, and roared with a varying loudness as the fitful wind rose and fell. Some way off an intermittent white light smote up from below, touched the snow eddies with a transient glitter, and made an evanescent spectre in the night; and here and there, low down, some vaguely outlined wind-driven mechanism flickered with livid sparks.

All this he appreciated in a fragmentary manner as his rescuers stood about him. Someone threw a thick soft cloak of fur-like texture about him, and fastened it by buckled straps at waist and shoulders. Things were said briefly, decisively. Someone thrust him forward.

Before his mind was yet clear a dark shape gripped his arm. "This way," said this shape, urging him along, and pointed Graham across the flat roof in the direction of a dim semicircular haze of light. Graham obeyed.

"Mind!" said a voice, as Graham stumbled against a cable. "Between them and not across them," said the voice. And, "We must hurry."

"Where are the people?" said Graham. "The people you said awaited me?"

The stranger did not answer. He left Graham's arm as the path grew narrower, and led the way with rapid strides. Graham followed blindly. In a minute he found himself running. "Are the others coming?" he panted, but received no reply. His companion glanced back and ran on. They came to a sort of pathway of open metal-work, transverse to the direction they had come, and they turned aside to follow this. Graham looked back, but the snowstorm had hidden the others.

"Come on!" said his guide. Running now, they drew near a little windmill spinning high in the air. "Stoop," said Graham's guide, and they avoided an endless band running roaring up to the shaft of the vane. "This way!" and they were ankle deep in a gutter full of drifted thawing snow, between two low walls of metal that presently rose waist high. "I will go first," said the guide. Graham drew his cloak about him and followed. Then suddenly came a narrow abyss across which the gutter leapt to the snowy darkness of the further side. Graham peeped over the side once and the gulf was black. For a moment he regretted his flight. He dared not look again, and his brain spun as he waded through the half liquid snow.

Then out of the gutter they clambered and hurried across a wide flat space damp with thawing snow, and for half its extent dimly translucent to lights that went to and fro underneath. He hesitated at this unstable looking substance, but his guide ran on unheeding, and so they came to and clambered up slippery steps to the rim of a great dome of glass. Round this they went. Far below a number of people seemed to be dancing, and music filtered through the dome….Graham fancied he heard a shouting through the snowstorm, and his guide hurried him on with a new spurt of haste. They clambered panting to a space of huge windmills, one so vast that only the lower edge of its vanes came rushing into sight and rushed up again and was lost in the night and the snow. They hurried for a time through the colossal metallic tracery of its supports, and came at last above a place of moving platforms like the place into which Graham had looked from the balcony. They crawled across the sloping transparency that covered this street of platforms, crawling on hands and knees because of the slipperiness of the snowfall.

For the most part the glass was bedewed, and Graham saw only hazy suggestions of the forms below, but near the pitch of the transparent roof the glass was clear, and he found himself looking sheerly down upon it all. For awhile, in spite of the urgency of his guide, he gave way to vertigo and lay spread-eagled on the glass, sick and paralysed. Far below, mere stirring specks and dots, went the people of the unsleeping city in their perpetual daylight, and the moving platforms ran on their incessant journey. Messengers and men on unknown businesses shot along the drooping cables and the frail bridges were crowded with men. It was like peering into a gigantic glass hive, and it lay vertically below him with only a tough glass of unknown thickness to save him from a fall. The street showed warm and lit, and Graham was wet now to the skin with thawing snow, and his feet were numbed with cold. For a space he could not move. "Come on!" cried his guide, with terror in his voice. "Come on!"

Graham reached the pitch of the roof by an effort.

Over the ridge, following his guide's example, he turned about and slid backward down the opposite slope very swiftly, amid a little avalanche of snow. While he was sliding he thought of what would happen if some broken gap should come in his way. At the edge he stumbled to his feet ankle deep in slush, thanking heaven for an opaque footing again. His guide was already clambering up a metal screen to a level expanse.

Through the spare snowflakes above this loomed another line of vast windmills, and then suddenly the amorphous tumult of the rotating wheels was pierced with a deafening sound. It was a mechanical shrilling of extraordinary intensity that seemed to come simultaneously from every point of the compass.

"They have missed us already!" cried Graham's guide in an accent of terror, and suddenly, with a blinding flash, the night became day.

Above the driving snow, from the summits of the wind-wheels, appeared vast masts carrying globes of livid light. They receded in illimitable vistas in every direction. As far as his eye could penetrate the snowfall they glared.

"Get on this," cried Graham's conductor, and thrust him forward to a long grating of snowless metal that ran like a band between two slightly sloping expanses of snow. It felt warm to Graham's benumbed feet, and a faint eddy of steam rose from it.

"Come on!" shouted his guide ten yards off, and, without waiting, ran swiftly through the incandescent glare towards the iron supports of the next range of wind-wheels. Graham, recovering from his astonishment, followed as fast, convinced of his imminent capture....

In a score of seconds they were within a tracery of glare and black shadows shot with moving bars beneath the monstrous wheels. Graham's conductor ran on for some time, and suddenly darted sideways and vanished into a black shadow in the corner of the foot of a huge support. In another moment Graham was beside him.

They cowered panting and stared out.

The scene upon which Graham looked was very wild and strange. The snow had now almost ceased; only a belated flake passed now and again across the picture. But the broad stretch of level before them was a ghastly white, broken only by gigantic masses and moving shapes and lengthy strips of impenetrable darkness, vast ungainly Titans of shadow. All about them, huge metallic structures, iron girders, inhumanly vast as it seemed to him, interlaced, and the edges of wind-wheels, scarcely moving in the lull, passed in great shining curves steeper and steeper up into a luminous haze. Wherever the snow-spangled light struck down, beams and girders, and incessant bands running with a halting, indomitable resolution, passed upward and downward into the black. And with all that mighty activity, with an omnipresent sense of motive and design, this snow-clad desolation of mechanism seemed void of all human presence save themselves, seemed as trackless and deserted and unfrequented by men as some inaccessible Alpine snowfield.

"They will be chasing us," cried the leader. "We are scarcely halfway there yet. Cold as it is we must hide here for a space – at least until it snows more thickly again."

His teeth chattered in his head.

"Where are the markets?" asked Graham staring out. "Where are all the people?"

The other made no answer.

"*Look*!" whispered Graham, crouched close, and became very still.

The snow had suddenly become thick again, and sliding with the whirling eddies out of the black pit of the sky came something, vague and large and very swift. It came down in a steep curve and swept round, wide wings extended and a trail of white condensing steam behind it, rose with an easy swiftness and went gliding up the air, swept horizontally forward in a wide curve, and vanished again in the steaming specks of snow. And, through the ribs of its body, Graham saw two little men, very minute and active, searching the snowy areas about him, as it seemed to him, with field glasses. For a second they were clear, then hazy through a thick whirl of snow, then small and distant, and in a minute they were gone.

"*Now*!" cried his companion. "Come!"

He pulled Graham's sleeve, and incontinently the two were running headlong down the arcade of iron-work beneath the wind-wheels. Graham, running blindly, collided with his leader, who had turned back on him suddenly. He found himself within a dozen yards of a black chasm. It extended as far as he could see right and left. It seemed to cut off their progress in either direction.

"Do as I do," whispered his guide. He lay down and crawled to the edge, thrust his head over and twisted until one leg hung. He seemed to feel for something with his foot, found it, and went sliding over the edge into the gulf. His head reappeared. "It is a ledge," he whispered. "In the dark all the way along. Do as I did."

Graham hesitated, went down upon all fours, crawled to the edge, and peered into a velvety blackness. For a sickly moment he had courage neither to go on nor retreat, then he sat and hung his leg down, felt his guide's hands pulling at him, had a horrible sensation of sliding over the edge into the unfathomable, splashed, and felt himself in a slushy gutter, impenetrably dark.

"This way," whispered the voice, and he began crawling along the gutter through the trickling thaw, pressing himself against the wall. They continued along it for some minutes. He seemed to pass through a hundred stages of misery, to pass minute after minute through a hundred degrees of cold, damp, and exhaustion. In a little while he ceased to feel his hands and feet.

The gutter sloped downwards. He observed that they were now many feet below the edge of the buildings. Rows of spectral white shapes like the ghosts of blind-drawn windows rose above them. They came to the end of a cable fastened above one of these white windows, dimly visible and dropping into impenetrable shadows. Suddenly his hand came against his guide's. "*Still*!" whispered the latter very softly.

He looked up with a start and saw the huge wings of the flying machine gliding slowly and noiselessly overhead athwart the broad band of snow-flecked grey-blue sky. In a moment it was hidden again.

"Keep still; they were just turning."

For awhile both were motionless, then Graham's companion stood up, and reaching towards the fastenings of the cable fumbled with some indistinct tackle.

"What is that?" asked Graham.

The only answer was a faint cry. The man crouched motionless. Graham peered and saw his face dimly. He was staring down the long ribbon of sky, and Graham, following his eyes, saw the flying machine small and faint and remote. Then he saw that the wings spread on either side, that it headed towards them, that every moment it grew larger. It was following the edge of the chasm towards them.

The man's movements became convulsive. He thrust two cross bars into Graham's hand. Graham could not see them, he ascertained their form by feeling. They were slung by thin cords to the cable. On the cord were hand grips of some soft elastic substance. "Put the cross between your legs," whispered the guide hysterically, "and grip the holdfasts. Grip tightly, grip!"

Graham did as he was told.

"Jump," said the voice. "In heaven's name, jump!"

For one momentous second Graham could not speak. He was glad afterwards that darkness hid his face. He said nothing. He began to tremble violently. He looked sideways at the swift shadow that swallowed up the sky as it rushed upon him.

"Jump! Jump – in God's name! Or they will have us," cried Graham's guide, and in the violence of his passion thrust him forward.

Graham tottered convulsively, gave a sobbing cry, a cry in spite of himself, and then, as the flying machine swept over them, fell forward into the pit of that darkness, seated on the cross wood and holding the ropes with the clutch of death. Something cracked, something rapped smartly against a wall. He heard the pulley of the cradle hum on its rope. He heard the aeronauts shout. He felt a pair of knees digging into his back….He was sweeping headlong through the air, falling through the air. All his strength was in his hands. He would have screamed but he had no breath.

He shot into a blinding light that made him grip the tighter. He recognised the great passage with the running ways, the hanging lights and interlacing girders. They rushed upward and by him. He had a momentary impression of a great round mouth yawning to swallow him up.

He was in the dark again, falling, falling, gripping with aching hands, and behold! a clap of sound, a burst of light, and he was in a brightly lit hall with a roaring multitude of people beneath his feet. The people! His people! A proscenium, a stage rushed up towards him, and his cable swept down to a circular aperture to the right of this. He felt he was travelling slower, and suddenly very much slower. He distinguished shouts of "Saved! The Master. He is safe!" The stage rushed up towards him with rapidly diminishing swiftness. Then –

He heard the man clinging behind him shout as if suddenly terrified, and this shout was echoed by a shout from below. He felt that he was no longer gliding along the cable but falling with it. There was a tumult of yells, screams, and cries. He felt something soft against his extended hand, and the impact of a broken fall quivering through his arm….

He wanted to be still and the people were lifting him. He believed afterwards he was carried to the platform and given some drink, but he was never sure. He did not notice what became of his guide. When his mind was clear again he was on his feet; eager hands were assisting him to stand. He was in a big alcove, occupying the position that in his previous experience had been devoted to the lower boxes. If this was indeed a theatre.

A mighty tumult was in his ears, a thunderous roar, the shouting of a countless multitude. "It is the Sleeper! The Sleeper is with us!"

"The Sleeper is with us! The Master – the Owner! The Master is with us. He is safe."

Graham had a surging vision of a great hall crowded with people. He saw no individuals, he was conscious of a froth of pink faces, of waving arms and garments, he felt the occult influence of a vast crowd pouring over him, buoying him up. There were balconies, galleries, great archways giving remoter perspectives, and everywhere people, a vast arena of people, densely packed and cheering. Across the nearer space lay the collapsed cable like a huge snake. It had been cut by the men of the flying machine at its upper end, and had crumpled down into the hall. Men seemed to be hauling this out of the way. But the whole effect was vague, the very buildings throbbed and leapt with the roar of the voices.

He stood unsteadily and looked at those about him. Someone supported him by one arm. "Let me go into a little room," he said, weeping; "a little room," and could say no more. A man in black stepped forward, took his disengaged arm. He was aware of officious men opening a door before him. Someone guided him to a seat. He staggered. He sat down heavily and covered his face with his hands; he was trembling violently, his nervous control was at an end. He was relieved of his cloak, he could not remember how; his purple hose he saw were black with wet. People were running about him, things were happening, but for some time he gave no heed to them.

He had escaped. A myriad of cries told him that. He was safe. These were the people who were on his side. For a space he sobbed for breath, and then he sat still with his face covered. The air was full of the shouting of innumerable men.

⁂

The complete and unabridged text is available online, from *flametreepublishing.com/extras*

Biographies & Sources

F. Anstey

Tourmalin's Time Cheques

(Originally Published by J.W. Arrowsmith, 1891)

F. Anstey, real name Thomas Anstey Guthrie (1856–1934), was born in London, England. The son of a tailor, he studied law at Trinity Hall, Cambridge, but decided to start writing and publishing stories in the 1870s. Going by the pseudonym F. Anstey (possibly a play on the word 'fantasy'), he gained recognition after publishing the novel *Vice Versa* in 1882. Following this success, he contributed to the magazine *Punch* and continued to write several comedic novels, including *A Fallen Idol* and *The Brass Bottle*. Anstey later participated in both the dramatization and film adaption of several of his works, until his death in 1934 after suffering from pneumonia.

Bo Balder

The Meaning that You Choose

(Originally Published in *Crossed Genres #35*, 2015)

Bo Balder lives and works near Amsterdam. She is the first Dutch author to have been published in *F&SF* and *Clarkesworld*, after winning the prestigious Dutch Paul Harland Award twice. Her short fiction has also appeared in *Nature Futures, Futuristica Vol. I* and more. Her SF novel *The Wan*, by Pink Narcissus Press, was published in 2016. She works freelance as a futurist writer for SciFutures, California, and guest-lectures at Erasmus University on science fiction. Visit her website at boukjebalder.nl.

Edward Bellamy

Looking Backward (chapters I–III)

(Originally Published by Ticknor & Company, 1888)

Edward Bellamy (1850–98) was born in Chicopee, Massachusetts. He initially studied law in Germany, exposing him to the issues of the impoverished in the city. He eventually turned to journalism, working as an editor for the *Springfield Union* and the *New York Evening Post*. Though he did not have much success with his early novels, he achieved immense fame with his utopian novel *Looking Backward*, in which a man travels over a century into the future, which promoted a socialist ideology that encouraged a harmonious world through cooperation and brotherhood.

John Buchan

The Gap in the Curtain (part I)

(Originally Published by Hodder & Stoughton, 1932)

John Buchan (1875–1940) was born in Perth, Scotland. He trained as a barrister, though his working life went on to span several sectors, including publishing, politics and war correspondence. He wrote solidly during this time, producing a number of short stories and novels, as well as historical and biographical works. He is perhaps best known for his thriller *The Thirty-Nine Steps*. Most of his horror stories are influenced by the wild and strange places he experienced during his time as a government administrator in South Africa. In 1935, Buchan was made Governor-General of Canada, and lived there until his death.

Dominick Cancilla
Shaping Things to Come
(First Publication)
Currently living in Santa Monica, California, Dominick Cancilla has been writing both fiction and non-fiction on and off for many years. His previous works include dozens of short stories, one book of philosophy, and one novel, *Revenant Savior*. He's also a rather extreme fan of Disney parks and his most recent works – a pair of travel guides for vampires and other unusual creatures planning Disney vacations – include advice for theme-park-visiting time travelers.

L. Maria Child
Hilda Silfverling
(Originally Published in *The Columbian Magazine*, 1845)
Lydia Maria Child (1802–80) was born in Medford, Massachusetts. She received her education first at home, then a local dame school and later a women's seminary. She established herself as a social reformer – advocating abolition, women's rights and Native American rights. These themes were explored through much of her writing as she published novels, journals and domestic advice books. She spent the 1840s and 1850s writing for numerous periodicals and newspapers as well as producing a variety of short stories addressing the issues of slavery and promoting the emancipation of slaves and their incorporation into American society.

Nino Cipri
The Shape of My Name
(Originally Published on Tor.com, 2015)
Nino Cipri is a queer, non-binary transgender writer, and a fiction MFA candidate at the University of Kansas. A multidisciplinary artist, Nino has also written plays, essays, and radio features; performed as a dancer, actor, and puppeteer; and worked as a backstage theater tech. They also invest large portions of their time to thinking about food, organizing around labor issues, and sitting on porches. One time, an angry person called Nino a verbal terrorist, which was pretty cool.

Charles Dickens
A Christmas Carol (chapter IV)
(Originally Published by Chapman & Hall, 1843)
The iconic and much-loved Charles Dickens (1812–70) was born in Portsmouth, England, though he spent much of his life in Kent and London. At the age of 12 Charles was forced into working in a factory for a couple of months to support his family. He never forgot his harrowing experience there, and his novels always reflected the plight of the working class. A prolific writer, Dickens kept up a career in journalism as well as writing short stories and novels, with much of his work being serialized before being published as books. He gave a view of contemporary England with a strong sense of realism, yet incorporated the occasional ghost and horror elements.

Kate Estabrooks
Hostage
(First Publication)
Kate Estabrooks enjoys the speculative side of science almost as much as the real thing. She has studied Mechanical Engineering and Geology, and was at one time not so long ago

an aerospace engineer (translation: middle manager) in the Royal Canadian Air Force. She has also spent enough time on boats over the years to know she'd rather sleep on dry land, preferably with a comfortable mattress and two pillows. Her writing has appeared in *Mad Scientist Journal* and *JukePop Serials*. She lives in Kingston, Ontario. Learn more about Kate and her writing at writingbykesta.com.

K.L. Evangelista

Try, Try Again

(First Publication)

K.L. Evangelista lives in Canberra, Australia. Her time travel piece 'Try, Try Again' features a protagonist determined to become the first female President. She has two other published pieces of fiction: a post-apoc rom-com, which can be found in the *Defying Doomsday* anthology; and a space-jelly sci-fi, which will be published in the 2018 *Young Explorer's Adventure Guide*. If K.L. Evangelista could go back in time, she would visit Jane Austen and thank her for that lake scene. Find her on Twitter @GelistarK.

Tony Genova

All for Bellkins

(First Publication)

Tony Genova lives in Connecticut, where he was born and raised. He spends his days crunching numbers, though he doesn't expect to solve time travel anytime soon. After half a lifetime spent reading fiction, he knew he needed to begin writing fiction. He counts Stephen King, Dean Koontz, Duane Swierczynski, Steve Hamilton, Richard Russo, and Paul Auster among his strongest writing influences. He also considers himself heavily influenced by thousands of hours well spent with movies, TV, and comic books over the years. He can be found at authortonygenova.com and on Twitter @TonyGenova.

Beth Goder

Murder or a Duck

(Originally Published in *Escape Pod*, 2016)

Beth Goder is an archivist living in California. By day, she processes the historical papers of economists, scientists, and other interesting folks. It's great fun to read the diaries and letters deposited in the archives, which Beth does whenever she gets the chance. In the past, Beth has played percussion in a community band and been a member of a Renaissance Faire dance troupe, but now she spends most of her free time writing. Her fiction has appeared in *Escape Pod* and *Mothership Zeta*. You can find her online at bethgoder.com and on Twitter @Beth_Goder.

Kate Heartfield

Cattail Heart

(Originally Published in *Daily Science Fiction*, 2014)

Kate Heartfield grew up in Manitoba and lives now in Ottawa, Canada. Her story 'Six Aspects of Cath Baduma' appeared in Flame Tree's *Murder Mayhem* anthology. Her fiction has also appeared recently in *Liminal Stories*, *Strange Horizons*, *Podcastle* and *Lackington's*, and the anthologies *Clockwork Canada* and *Monstrous Little Voices: New Tales from Shakespeare's Fantasy World*. She's currently writing a historical fantasy novel, and a game based on *The Canterbury Tales* for Choice of Games.

Larry Hodges

Eternity and the Devil

(Originally Published in *Dark Portals*, 2009)

Larry Hodges's third SF novel *Campaign 2100: Game of Scorpions* was published by World Weaver Press in 2016, covering the election for President of Earth in the year 2100. His fourth, *When Parallel Lines Meet*, co-written with Mike Resnick and Lezli Robyn, comes out Summer 2017. A resident of Germantown, MD, USA, he's a member of SFWA with over 80 short story sales, plus 14 books and over 1700 published articles in over 150 different publications. He's a graduate of the Odyssey Writing Workshop. He's also a member of the USA Table Tennis Hall of Fame. Visit him at larryhodges.org.

Rudyard Kipling

Wireless

(Originally Published in *Scribner's Magazine,* 1902)

English writer and poet Rudyard Kipling (1865–1936) was born in Bombay, India. He was educated in England but returned to India in his youth which would inspire many of his later writings, most famously seen in *The Jungle Book*. He would later return to England and after travelling across the United States settled in Vermont, America. He was awarded the Nobel Prize for Literature in 1907, which made him the first English-language writer to receive the accolade. His narrative style is inventive and engaging, making it no surprise that his works of fiction and poetry have become classics.

Jack London

Before Adam (chapters I–V)

(Originally Published by The Macmillan Company, 1906)

Jack London (1876–1916) was born as John Griffith Chaney in San Francisco, California. As a young man he went to work in the Klondike during the Gold Rush, which became the setting for two of his best-known novels: *White Fang* and *The Call of the Wild*. Coming from a working-class background, London was a keen social activist and wrote several stories and articles from a socialist standpoint. His novel *Before Adam* explores how a man's consciousness might time travel, as the main character is haunted by dreams of living as a prehistoric man.

Harold Steele MacKaye

The Panchronicon (chapters I–V)

(Originally Published by Charles Scribner's Sons, 1904)

Harold Steele MacKaye (1866–1928) was born in France, but lived primarily in New York, after his family moved there in his infancy. He was the son of actor and dramatist James Steele MacKaye (1842–94) and one of six children. *The Panchronicon* tells the story of a time traveler who travels back from the year 2582 to the 19th century. When he dies, his machine ends up in the hands of a town drunk. The novel presents the idea of time travel in a rather comedic light, seeming to parody the idea quite heavily. It remains the work for which MacKaye is best-known.

Scott Merrow

Two Children Reported Missing

(First Publication)

Scott Merrow has been writing short fiction for 12 years. He's had several stories published recently, both online and in print, with a few more forthcoming soon. Publications include

Mystery Weekly Magazine, The Literary Hatchet, and *Fabula Argentea*, among others. He and his wife Paula Merrow also co-write short screenplays. To date, 10 of them have been produced, with another currently in pre-production. Scott and Paula live in Colorado, USA.

Edward Page Mitchell
The Clock that Went Backward
(Originally Published in *The New York Sun*, 1881)
Pioneer of the science fiction genre, American author Edward Page Mitchell (1852–1927) was a short story writer and editor for *The Sun* newspaper in New York. His work featured predominantly in *The Sun*, and most of his stories were published anonymously. His story 'The Clock That Went Backward', which is a contender for the first time-travel story and predates H.G. Wells's *The Time Machine*, was also published anonymously in *The Sun* and Mitchell wasn't revealed as the author until 40 years after his death.

William Morris
A Dream of John Ball (chapters I–IV)
(Originally Published in *The Commonweal*, 1886–87)
William Morris (1834–96) was born in Essex, England. He was a writer, textile designer, socialist activist and artist. He wrote a large collection of fiction, poetry and essays and his most famous written works include *The Defence of Guenevere and Other Poems, The Earthly Paradise, News from Nowhere* and *A Dream of John Ball*, which uses time travel as a plot device to compare and contrast medieval and modern ethics. Novels such as *A Dream of John Ball* and *News from Nowhere* feature Morris's common theme of praising the medieval period. He is credited with helping develop the model for modern fantasy and promoting early socialism in Britain.

Samantha Murray
Striking Light
(First Publication)
Samantha Murray is a writer, mathematician, and mother. Not particularly in that order. Her fiction has appeared in places such as *Clarkesworld, Lightspeed, Escape Pod, Writers of the Future Vol. 31, Flash Fiction Online, Nature Magazine, Daily Science Fiction*, and *Beneath Ceaseless Skies*. She is the winner of the 2016 Aurealis Award for best SF short story. You can find her at mailbysea.wordpress.com or on Twitter as @SamanthaNMurray. Samantha lives in Western Australia in a household of unruly boys.

Philip Francis Nowlan
Armageddon – 2419 A.D.
(Originally Published in *Amazing Stories*, 1928)
Born in Philadelphia, Pennsylvania, science fiction author Philip Francis Nowlan (1888–1940) originally worked as a newspaper columnist. He wrote the novella *Armageddon – 2419 A.D.*, which involved the first appearance of the fictional character 'Anthony Rogers', a space explorer who became known as 'Buck Rogers' in the hugely popular comic strip that followed. The character made a lasting imprint on American popular culture, with the comic strip running for over forty years. As a result, Nowlan is most famously associated with Buck Rogers, although he is also remembered for writing fiction that consistently featured strong female characters.

Edgar Allan Poe

A Tale of the Ragged Mountains

(Originally Published by Louis Antoine Godey, 1844)

The versatile writer Edgar Allan Poe (1809–49) was born in Boston, Massachusetts. He is extremely well known as an influential author, poet, editor and literary critic that wrote during the American Romantic Movement. Poe is generally considered the inventor of the detective fiction genre, and his works are famously filled with terror, mystery, death and hauntings. Some of his better-known works include his poems 'The Raven' and 'Annabel Lee', and the short stories 'The Tell Tale Heart' and 'The Fall of the House of Usher'. The dark, mystifying characters of his tales have captured the public's imagination.

Chris Reynolds

Ouroboros

(First Publication)

Chris Reynolds is an author from Canberra, Australia. He has previously published several short stories, including the *Chinatown* series with Monolith and works in various anthologies. He writes in a range of genres, including paranormal, military thrillers, sci-fi and fantasy. If you're interested in reading more of his work, please find him on Facebook at facebook.com/Chrisreynoldsauthor. He's always up for a chat, but just remember that he lives in the future (+10/11 hours from GMT), so he may start frantically giving you a dire warning of things to come. Heed those warnings.

Anton Rose

The Berlin Doctrine

(Originally Published in *Sci Phi Journal*, 2016)

A native of the Northeast of England, Anton Rose now lives in London. His work has appeared in a number of print and online journals including *Apex*, *Flash Fiction Online*, and *Terraform*, and he is a 2017 Writers of the Future winner. As well as writing fiction and poetry, he reads submissions for *Firewords Quarterly* and co-edits *Unlost*, an online journal for found poetry. He spends much of his time dreaming of the ocean. Find him at antonrose.com or @antonjrose.

Brian Trent

Omnipunks

(Originally Published in *Time Travel Tales*, 2016)

Brian Trent's speculative fiction appears regularly in the industry's top magazines including *Analog*, *Fantasy & Science Fiction*, *Orson Scott Card's Intergalactic Medicine Show*, *Daily Science Fiction*, *Escape Pod*, *Cosmos*, *Galaxy's Edge*, *Nature*, and more. He is a winner in the Writers of the Future contest and Baen Fantasy Adventure Award finalist. His literary influences are varied, and his interests include technology, classical history, and sociology – particularly the interplay between all three. Brian lives in New England, where he is a novelist, poet, and screenwriter. His website and blog can be found at briantrent.com.

Mark Twain

A Connecticut Yankee in King Arthur's Court (chapters I–IV)

(Originally Published by Charles L. Webster and Co., 1889)

Mark Twain (1835–1910) was born Samuel Langhorne Clemens in Florida, Missouri. Twain's name is synonymous with his American classics *The Adventures of Tom Sawyer* and its sequel,

Adventures of Huckleberry Finn. Twain was born shortly after an appearance by Halley's Comet, and he predicted that he would 'go out with it', too. As chance would have it, he died the day after the comet returned in 1910. Twain was a very influential author whose works are timeless pieces that are still being taught today in classrooms to students of all ages.

Valerie Valdes

A Brain, A Heart, A Home, The Nerve
(First Publication)
Valerie Valdes lives in Miami, Florida, where she writes, copy edits, moonlights as a muse and occasionally plays video games if her son and husband are distracted by Transformers. Once upon a time, she attended the University of Miami, where she majored in English literature with minors in creative writing and motion pictures. She is a graduate of Viable Paradise and her latest work is published in *Nightmare Magazine*. Join her in opining about books, BioWare games and robots in disguise on Twitter @valerievaldes.

Adam Vine

This Door is Locked
(First Publication)
Adam Vine was born in Northern California. By day, he is a game writer and designer. He has lived in four countries and visited thirty. He is the author of two novels and many short stories. When he is not writing, he is traveling, reading something icky, or teaching himself to play his mandolin. He currently lives in Germany. His latest novel, *Corruption: Book One of the Corruption Cycle*, is out now from Lilydog Books.

H.G. Wells

The Time Machine (chapters I–V)
(First serialized in its present form in *The New Review*, 1895)
The Sleeper Awakes (chapters I–VIII)
(Originally Published in *Graphic*, 1899 as 'When the Sleeper Wakes'; renamed in 1910)
Herbert George Wells (1866–1946) was born in Kent, England. Novelist, journalist, social reformer and historian, Wells is one of the greatest ever science fiction writers and along with Jules Verne is sometimes referred to as a 'founding father' of the genre. With Aldous Huxley and, later, George Orwell he defined the adventurous, social concern of early speculative fiction where the human condition was played out on a greater stage. Wells wrote over 50 novels, including his famous works *The Time Machine, The Invisible Man, The Island of Doctor Moreau* and *The War of the Worlds*, as well as a fantastic array of short stories.

David Wittenberg

Foreword: Time Travel Short Stories
David Wittenberg teaches in English, Comparative Literature, and Cinematic Arts at the University of Iowa. He is the author of two books, *Time Travel: The Popular Philosophy of Narrative* (Fordham University Press, 2013) and *Philosophy, Revision, Critique: Rereading Practices in Heidegger, Nietzsche, and Emerson* (Stanford University Press, 2001), and the co-editor of a forthcoming critical anthology, *Scale in Literature and Culture* (Palgrave Macmillan). Currently he is completing several other research projects including a book about very large objects and images, tentatively titled *Big Culture: Toward an Aesthetics of Magnitude*.

FLAME TREE PUBLISHING
Short Story Series
New & Classic Writing

Flame Tree's Gothic Fantasy books offer a carefully curated series of new titles, each with combinations of original and classic writing:

Chilling Horror Short Stories
Chilling Ghost Short Stories
Science Fiction Short Stories
Murder Mayhem Short Stories
Crime & Mystery Short Stories
Swords & Steam Short Stories
Dystopia Utopia Short Stories
Supernatural Horror Short Stories
Lost Worlds Short Stories
Time Travel Short Stories
Heroic Fantasy Short Stories

as well as new companion titles which offer rich collections of classic fiction from masters of the gothic fantasy genres:

H.G. Wells Short Stories
Lovecraft Short Stories
Sherlock Holmes Short Stories
Edgar Allan Poe Short Stories

Available from all good bookstores, worldwide, and online at
flametreepublishing.com